the Last open road

by B.S. Levy

THINK FAST INK
Oak Park, Illinois
1994

published by
THINK FAST INK
1010 Lake Street
Oak Park, Illinois
60301

written and manufactured in the United States of America

First printing July, 1994
Second printing, October 1995

Library of Congress Cataloging in Publication Data

Levy, Burt S., 1945-

The Last Open Road

1. American sportscar racing in the 1950s. 2. Automobile mechanics. I. Title

LIBRARY OF CONGRESS CATALOG CARD NUMBER: 94-60833

SPECIAL THANKS GO OUT TO BILL SIEGFRIEDT, JOHN GARDNER, BROOKS STEVENS, JIM SITZ, BILL GREEN,
MY BROTHER MAURICE, AND MY DEAR FRIEND AND RACING TEAMMATE DAVID WHITESIDE FOR THEIR INVALUABLE
ASSISTANCE WITH RESEARCH MATERIALS AND INFORMATION FOR THIS BOOK, AND ALSO TO THE NAVISTAR CORPORATE
ARCHIVES FOR THEIR KIND PERMISSION TO USE THE WONDERFUL OLD PHOTOGRAPHS ON THE DUST JACKET.
THANK YOU ALL!

ISBN: 0-6642107-0-3

for Carol and Adam, my wonderful family

Introduction: Buddy's Place

Sure, I can fix your MG. No problem. Hell, I've forgotten more about MGs than most guys will ever know. Jaguars, too. Fact is, I'm known as sort of an expert --a real *maestro*-- when it comes to Jags. Not that I'm bragging or anything. It's just I been around those cars since the very beginning. All the way back to 1952. Why, we used to *race* a couple of 'em right outta this shop. Honest to God we did.

Things were lots different back then. It's hard to imagine these days, but television was just catching on --heck, *no*body wanted to be last jerk on the block with a TeeVee antenna stuck on his chimney-- and radio was still real popular. And not just when you were driving someplace in your car, either. We listened to the Yankee games and "Amos 'n Andy" and hummed along with dimbulb songs like "Shrimp Boats," "The Tennessee Waltz," and Johnny Raye sobbing his way through "The Little White Cloud That Cried." You have to understand that there was no such thing as rock 'n roll back in 1952. Not hardly.

General Eisenhower was about to get himself elected president --hey, *everybody* liked Ike-- and we were all messed up with the Chinese Reds over in Korea. That was a really big deal in the early fifties, and people like Tailgunner Joe McCarthy told us they were planning to atom bomb everybody and take over the whole damn world. Folks believed him, too. In fact, rich people built bomb shelters under their back yards and stocked 'em up with canned goods, bottled water, old copies of *National Geographic,* and plenty of toilet paper. Just in case, you know? Of course, nobody in our neighborhood could afford a bomb shelter, so we had to settle for Civil Defense air raid drills in highschool. We'd curl up under our desks, right, as if *that* was gonna protect us from a goddam A-bomb!

The only reason I didn't go to Korea with the rest of my graduating class is on account of I got a bad right eye. Had it since I was born, you know, so I don't even notice it. But it kept me out of the Army, and that's how I wound up back here in Passaic, messing around with all sorts of Jaguars and MGs while the rest of my buddies were getting their asses shot off in Korea.

It was a pretty sweet deal, no lie, working on all these fancy imported sportscars and going to the races with Big Ed Baumstein and Cal Carrington and hanging around with all these rich Black Sheep-types like you read about in the tabloid newspapers.

Boy, we had us some *real* road races back then, running on closed-off country backroads around Watkins Glen and Bridge-hampton and Elkhart Lake, Wisconsin. Sure, it was *dangerous*, what with all those trees and signposts and mailboxes and other relatively solid objects right there next to the roadway, not to mention blind corners, bad pavement, and nothing much at all in the way of crowd control. People got hurt now and then. Dead, even. But, once you got bit by the bug, it was just too much fun and excitement to stay away from.

We did the 12 hours of Sebring one year, all the way down in Florida. And a speed record run on the Bonneville salt flats, too. Plus the *Carrera Panamericana* in Mexico, which, believe me, was one God Damn *hell* of an automobile race! It went from the bottom end of Mexico clear to the top --two *thousand* miles!-- going as fast as you dared around cliffs with sheer dropoffs and racing like hell through these little Mexican towns, scattering roosters and chickens while the people jumped up and down and cheered like crazy. And it was all on ordinary 2-lane blacktop highway with no guardrails or catch fences and nothing much in the way of runoff area. It was just an open road, you know? And, like I said, it was dangerous. But I guess we just didn't know any better back then....

Sure, I can tell you about it. Happy to oblige. It's damn near closing anyway, and the parts never showed up for that Healey I got up on the lift. Needs a new exhaust system, of course. Hell, you run one a'them Healeys over a railroad crossing at anything much faster than a slow walk and you'll rip the muffler right off the bottom. Every damn time. Sometimes I wonder what kind of roads they have around that Austin Healey factory over in England. Gotta be smooth as a baby's ass, no lie.

Anyhow, c'mon inside while I put my tools away and wash up. There's some cold Knickerbockers over there in the fridge. Right next to the tire balancer. And pop one for me while you're at it. By the way, my name's Buddy Palumbo, and I sorta run this place.

Chapter 1: The Old Man's Sinclair

I guess it all started while I was working as head mechanic at Old Man Finzio's Sinclair station, not a year out of high school. Actually, I was more or less the *only* mechanic working at the Sinclair back then, on account of Old Man Finzio wasn't what you would exactly call a whiz around a set of tools. Which made you wonder why in hell he picked the garage business in the first place. But of course you couldn't just flat-out ask him, "Hey, whyd'ja go inta the garage business, jackass?" because he'd spit right in your eye. Old Man Finzio was one of those mean, scrawny old farts who walk like there's no oil in their joints and kick stray dogs just for the fun of it. And you could no way miss how the Old Man always managed to have a three- or four-day growth of stubble on his chin. All the time. Which made you wonder sometimes how he did it. I mean, you either shave every couple days or eventually it grows out into a beard, right? But not Old Man Finzio. No sir. Four days of stubble, all the time. It was one of those Eternal Mysteries, you know, like they tell you about in church.

I remember the Old Man smoked a lot, too --two, maybe three packs of Camels a day-- and he was forever weaseling his last scraggly, bent-up cigarette out of a pack that always looked like it'd been run over by a farm tractor. That's on account of he carried his smokes in the hip pocket of his coveralls, seeing as how the chest pocket was ripped clear off and the Old Man was too damn cheap to buy himself a new pair. Every night he'd take off those same raggedy coveralls, carefully remove the crumpled remains of his latest pack of smokes, and hang 'em up on that nail over there, right next to the space heater. He wore those same damn coveralls every single day, and they were about the same color and texture as the inside walls of a trash incinerator. Smelled like it, too. Truth is, I don't believe they ever got washed. Not unless it rained, anyway.

Now don't get me wrong, the Old Man was pretty sharp about running a gas station, and no question he knew a thing or two about automobiles. He just wasn't much good at *fixing* 'em. Just didn't have the hands for it. Or the patience. Oh, he could

change a tire or swap sparkplugs or maybe flush out a radiator
without too much trouble, but he'd get stuck, and I mean *stuck*,
on jobs a real honest-to-goodness professional mechanic could
breeze through without even thinking about it. Especially if he hit
a frozen-up bolt or a rounded-off nut or maybe something hidden
away under an exhaust manifold or water pump pulley where you
couldn't hardly get at it. And the Old Man was a certified *disaster* when it came to electrical work of any description. Or take a
simple brake job. Most times, he'd get one of the drums wedged
all catty-wumpus trying to pull it off the axle, and naturally the
harder he tugged, beat, and levered on it, the worse it got. He'd
squint and stare and sneer at that brake drum, cussing a blue
streak through the few teeth he had left, and pretty soon he'd be
reaching for the cutting torch and the biggest damn sledgehammer he could lay his hands on. Within fifteen minutes, he'd have
the whole rear end glowing cherry red and be wailing away with
the sledge like a country blacksmith. By the time you pulled him
off, the brake drum, wheel studs, and mounting flange'd usually
be nothing but junk. Sometimes he'd even get the wheel cylinders, too. And every now and again he'd set a whole damn car
on fire. So you can see how important it was for Old Man Finzio
to have a decent mechanic working for him at the Sinclair.

The Old Man's gas station was right down the street from my
folks' house in Passaic, and I'd pass it every day on my way
home from school. Starting in about eighth grade, I'd kind of
stop by after classes were over and hang around for a few hours.
Maybe even help out here and there. For some reason, I really
liked being around automobiles and watching them get fixed. It
fascinated me how cars were put together out of all these odd-
looking chunks of metal and snaky rubber hoses and endless
spaghetti strands of copper wire, all of it fitted and pieced together like some enormous three-dimensional jigsaw puzzle. And if
you got all those bits and pieces bolted together just right, you
could twist a key or punch a starter button and the whole thing
would Come Alive, as if it was some kind of living, breathing,
ready-for-street-prowling steel animal. But the best part was
when a car stopped working properly --when it *died*-- a sharp
mechanic could do a little head-scratching and wrench-twisting
and bring it back to life again. Good as new. Maybe even better.
A guy could feel pretty damn swell about something like that.

This tough, crewcut ex-Marine named Butch Bohunk was chief mechanic at the Sinclair when I started hanging around there after school, and for my money, Butch was sharp as they come. Especially when it came to Fords. Butch had a beatup old Ford coupe himself (I think it was a '40, but you couldn't hardly tell from all the rust) and I swear he kept that heap running by just *thinking* about fixing it. Honest to God he did. I don't know if you've noticed or not, but automobile mechanics generally drive the sickest, sorriest-looking cars on the highway --like the old story about the shoemaker's kids, you know? I guess that's because a good mechanic understands precisely what's going wrong with his automobile and considers it a matter of highest professional pride and sensitivity to see just how long he can keep the old heap running on mechanical sympathy alone.

Fact is, Butch's old Ford was so raggedy-looking that Old Man Finzio made him park it out back behind the building where the paying customers couldn't see it. I remember one Saturday afternoon Butch took me for a ride across town to pick up some parts or something, and I swear the steering wheel was shaking so bad he could hardly hang on to the rim. "Gee whiz, Butch," I asked him, "what the hell's wrong with the steering?"

"Aw, I got me a busted shock and a bent wheel on the left front, see, and it's just about finished off the damn bearings and tie-rod ends." Then he calmly fished a cigarette out of his pocket and lit up --just to show me it was nothing to worry about, you know? Come to think of it, that cigarette lighter was about the only electrical component on the whole damn dashboard that worked.

So we're flying down this side street in Newark at better than 50, the whole car shaking and wobbling so bad you couldn't hardly focus, and I had to swallow hard a couple times before I finally got up the nerve to say, "Jeez, Butch, isn't this sorta, you know, *dangerous?*"

"Naw," he grinned, taking himself a long, deep draw through a fresh Pall Mall, "not unless the whole damn wheel falls off."

General opinion around Passaic held that Butch Bohunk was a pretty mean article, mostly on account of he'd get into bar fights and scrapes with the law every now and then when he drank, and recreational bar-room drinking was something he did on a pretty regular basis. In fact, he used to brag that he could drink up a whole damn case of beer in one sitting (not counting getting up to pee, of course) although that one sitting usually lasted the better part of an entire evening. And sometimes on into the wee hours when the bars shut down.

But Butch always treated me right, no matter what everybody else thought or said about him. He was a lumpy, burly, beatup fireplug sort of guy, with tattoos all up and down his arms and a nasty scar down his forehead from the edge of his Marine crew-cut clear through the arch of his left eyebrow. Damn near took his eye out, whatever it was. Sometimes, when he was working on a bolt he couldn't see or pouring oil in a crankcase, Butch'd get this faraway look in his eye and tell me the story of how he got that scar. It was always a totally different yarn (so I knew it was all bullshit, right?) but they were some pretty great stories anyway, each one uglier and gorier than the last. Old Man Finzio told me the *real* scoop was that Butch's wife came after him with a meat cleaver early one ayem when he staggered in around sunup with his shirt buttoned wrong.

Butch's wife was a dumpy little white-trash girl from Tennessee with stringy red-orange hair, a beer belly that made her look pregnant all the time, and one hell of a nasty temper. Her name was Marlene, and Butch always referred to her as "my mean Marlene." And was she *ever*. In fact, I could never figure out what on earth possessed Butch to make him marry her in the first place. Or want to stay married to her afterwards, for that matter. I mean, they didn't seem to *like* each other very much, you know? But then I guess there's just no figuring guys when it comes to women. No sir. Not to mention that Butch wasn't any damn Prince Charming himself. Not hardly. He drank and he brawled, and when you get right down to it, most women don't want anything to do with garage mechanics in general. Especially after they've taken a good look at your hands.

Married or not, Butch was pretty much what you could call a loner, and that made perfect sense because there were all sorts of people that Butch just flat didn't like. He didn't like rich people because they were rich, and he didn't like poor people because they were poor. Nor did he much appreciate bosses, toadies, middle-managers, noncoms, lawyers, insurance salesmen, tax accountants, niggers, kikes, krauts, polaks, wops, American indians, Indian indians, japs, chinks, a-rabs, mexicans, or college-professor types. And I'm sure I've missed a few. In fact, about the only people Butch could tolerate at all were tough, independent, grunt-level working stiffs like himself. Unless they were union men, that is. Butch didn't have much use for trade unions, either.

So old Butch could be a pretty hard guy to get along with. Especially after he had a few beers under his belt. And even more especially if you didn't appreciate that, more than anything else, Butch Bohunk just wanted to be left alone. Although you couldn't ever have called him a particularly religious type --not hardly!-- Butch firmly and steadfastly adhered to a sort of blue-collar, redneck code of ethics that strictly divided "what a man did" from "what a man didn't do." Not that it was written down anyplace or anything like that. It was just something a guy like Butch *knew*, without even thinking about it. Which was probably why he got in so damn many bar fights, because one of the most important things "a man didn't do" was to back down when somebody yanked his chain --even if that somebody was six inches taller and 60 pounds heavier. Or smaller, but packing a serious meat cleaver.

Truth is, I learned most of what I know about fixing cars from Butch Bohunk. He didn't so much sit me down and *teach* it to me as let me watch and maybe help out every now and then --you know, grab him a wrench or clean off a grungy engine block or maybe hold the back end of a bolt while he ratcheted the nut off on the other side. Butch had been a hardhat diver in the Marines --the guys with the rubberized-canvas diving suits and the big brass helmets, right?-- and he liked to brag about how the U.S. Marines sent him all over the whole blessed world just because he could weld a perfect bead underwater. Believe me, that's not an easy thing to do. And even though he bitched about it constantly, you could tell Butch really loved his life in the Marines. After all, that's where he learned how to duck a sucker punch, throw a knife so it'd stick in a wooden door, find the back way out of any harbor bar, and cuss a blue streak in five or six different languages.

That's also where he learned how to be a mechanic, and believe me, Butch was one of the best. He had a special knack for understanding what was wrong with sick machines, and then he could go in and fix whatever it was without thinking about it twice. To Butch, broken mufflers, burned-out clutches, and even seized engines were simply mounds of dirt that had to be moved, and *he* was the bulldozer. It made quite a contrast to Old Man Finzio, who most often made things worse instead of better when he went in for any kind of heavy repairs. Sometimes the Old Man'd get himself stuck on something --like fr'instance that brake job I told you about-- and after he'd worked himself into a foamy-mouthed frenzy cursing at it and beating on it and heating it up cherry red with the torch, he'd eventually have no choice but to shuffle over and ask Butch to bail him out. "Hey Butch," he'd mutter through tightly clenched teeth, "cud'ja maybe cm' overhere an' take a'lookathis?"

Butch always pretended like he didn't quite hear him the first time, so the Old Man'd have to ask him again, only louder. He'd keep it up until the Old Man was beet red and hollering right in his ear, and then Butch'd turn around real slow and calm and say, "Gee whiz, old man, you ain't gotta *yell.*" Of course, he was careful not to get real obvious about it, on account of he didn't want to get fired (not that I think he really cared too much one way or the other) and then he'd get this mean little smirk flickering up in the corners of his eyes while he quietly walked over and put things right.

It drove the Old Man *nuts*.

Let me take a moment to explain to you how it is with automobile mechanics. Personally, I divvy them up into three basic categories. First off, you've got your Shadetree Butchers. Old Man Finzio was pretty much a Butcher, even though he ran a gas station for a living, but most of your rank-and-file Butchers are amateur, home-garage operators who only bring their cars to a professional shop after they've already made a total godawful mess out of whatever it was they were trying to fix in the first place. Butchers can be counted on to snap studs, shear bolts, strip threads by forcing fine-thread nuts onto coarse-thread fasteners (or vice-versa) and usually employ vise grips (or a *very* large pair of channel locks) to get the necessary leverage. And that's not even mentioning how they leave cotter pins and washers off entirely when putting stuff back together, wedge bearing races in cockeyed, and turn every electrical problem they encounter into a stinking, steaming, smoldering glob of molten plastic and charred wire insulation. No self-respecting mechanic likes working around a Butcher, and cleaning up after one is even worse.

One giant step up from the Butcher is the Parts Replacer. Parts Replacers know their way around a toolbox and an automobile all right, but they don't understand *at all* how car stuff operates. To them, every mechanical component on an automobile is like a sealed vault filled with some kind of rare, magical pudding that makes it work. When one of these types runs into a difficult problem, he invariably starts yanking off old parts and throwing new ones at it until either the problem goes away or the car's owner declares bankruptcy. Whichever comes first. God certainly must have loved Parts Replacers, because he made so damn many of them.

And then you've got The Fixers. The *maestros*. The Real McCoy. Fixers can diagnose a hiccup in your carburetor or a death rattle down in the bottom of your crankcase --just like a medical doctor-- and then go in so slick and clean that when they're done, you can't even tell the car's been worked on. Except that it runs better than ever. A good fixer can even *make* parts. "It's all done, Mr. Jones. The choke was sticking because the linkage was going over-center, so I made a new bracket to bring the cable in at a better angle." Things like that may not impress you, but they impress the living hell out of me. Of course, most average citizens don't really want to know what's going on inside their automobiles. Like it's some kind of disgusting internal medical stuff or something.

Anyhow, I wound up working part-time at Old Man Finzio's Sinclair during my senior year, pumping gas and changing tires and helping out here and there, and even though it wasn't what you could honestly call a steady job, Butch'd always slip me a couple bucks or make Old Man Finzio slip me a couple bucks for my trouble. By the time graduation rolled around, they'd let me fix some cars all by myself. Hard stuff, too, like clutch jobs and cylinder heads, not just oil changes and tire swaps. I'd clear twenty or thirty bucks on a good week. Honest I would. And I was learning one hell of a lot about auto mechanicing. Watching Butch taught me how to figure things out and make proper repairs, and watching Old Man Finzio taught me, well, what *not* to do. Which is just as important, believe me. The better I got at fixing automobiles, the more I liked it working around Old Man Finzio's gas station, on account of it made me feel like I could, you know, *do* something.

And there was something else that kept me coming around the Sinclair. Her name was Julie Finzio, and she was the Old Man's niece. Julie dropped by every day or so to straighten up around the office and help the Old Man out with his books, mostly on account of she had real nice handwriting. Julie was just out of highschool herself, but I never knew her then because I went to public school and she went to Immaculate Conception with the rest of the good Catholic girls in Passaic. Sure, I'd seen her around town here and there, but I never paid too much attention because she was kinda plain-looking and maybe a little on the chunky side. But Julie really filled out during her sophomore year --I mean *really* filled out-- and all of a sudden she was OK to look at. Better than OK, even. In fact, you could say she was sort of pretty (in a baby-fat kind of way) what with her curly black hair, dark, happy eyes, and this wicked red-lipstick smile she picked up off the cover of a movie magazine someplace. Not that I spent all that much time looking at her face, you understand, since I was eighteen myself and naturally kept getting distracted by the mysterious new bulges squirming around inside her sweaters like a pair of frisky otters. And of course Julie always knew *exactly* what I was looking at, and had the kind of mouth to let me know about it, too. "Hey, put your eyeballs back in your head, willya?" she'd snort, "yer startin' to *drool.*" But then she'd smile and maybe even lean over the counter on tiptoes a little so's I could get an even better look.

That drove me crazy.

So did the way she'd wink at me out of the corner of her eye or roll the eraser end of her pencil around with the tip of her tongue while she worked on the Old Man's books. And it sure got my attention the way her butt blossomed up like a huge, heart-shaped valentine everytime she bent down to pick up something I'd, uh, *accidentally* dropped on the floor. Not that she was a slut or anything. Not hardly. Julie Finzio was just a nice, respectable Immaculate Conception girl from Passaic who liked to flirt and tease around with you until it drove you right up a goddam wall. In fact, you could say that was kind of a favorite sport among the Italian Catholic girls around Passaic. So I could never really tell if Julie meant anything by it, seeing as how I was the only guy anywheres close to her age working at the Sinclair, and sometimes even Nice Girls do stuff like that, just to make sure the old equipment is working. No question Julie's did, because she never failed to turn me all steamy-queasy inside every time I saw her. I even had this inkling, you know, that maybe she really sort of *liked* me. But I couldn't be sure. You know how it is with girls. And of course Old Man Finzio was always skulking around in the background, giving me the hairy eyeball any time I started getting a little too chummy with Julie. The thing I could never understand was how a mean, ornery old fart like him rated a hot, bubbly, hormone-pie of a niece like Julie. It just didn't seem natural, you know?

Julie had her heart set on being a Fashion Illustrator and drawing those high-fashion women with long gowns and flowing hair and swan-like necks you see every weekend in the Sunday newspaper supplements. I always thought those women looked sort of dumb, you know, the way they were always arched waaaay over backwards so any kind of decent breeze would topple 'em right over. But Julie thought they were real *artistic* and *dramatic*, and spent an awful lot of time doodling artistic, high-fashion women in dramatic, topple-over poses inside the big, spiral-bound sketchbooks she carried with her almost everywhere she went. Julie kept talking about going to art school, too, but there was no way on account of her dad got killed in the Philippines during the Big One and her mom couldn't do much better than a job as a hairdresser and a cheap little apartment on the second floor of somebody else's house. So instead of going to art school, Julie was stuck helping out in her uncle's gas station three days a week and working part-time at the Doggie Shake up on Fremont Avenue evenings and weekends. It was a damn shame, too, because Julie could draw really good --honest to God she could-- and not just those arched-over fashion models, either. Her sketchbooks were filled with prancing horses and creaky old houses and ducks on a pond, not to mention flowerpots on windowsills, driftwood on the beach, and even some of the niftier cars she saw around the Sinclair. Those were my favorites, as you can imagine, and as far as I was concerned they were one hell of a lot more interesting than any of those topple-over women in the Sunday newspaper supplements.

Needless to say, my folks weren't too keen on having their one and only son turn into a gas station grease monkey. Especially my dad. Heck, I had four older sisters, and he never complained too much when one of them took a job as a waitress at the short-order grill over on Camden Street. Or when the youngest one, Mary Frances, decided she wanted to cut hair and paint nails for a living someplace across the bridge in downtown Manhattan. I remember my mom wasn't too happy about that at all. In particular, she didn't approve of the apartment Mary Frances shared with three other girls near Greenwich Village. But they let her do it, you know? The way my dad saw it, girls were supposed to spend their formative years mostly just waiting around to get married so they could raise families themselves and have kids of their own to worry over and yell at. That's just the way life went around Passaic back in the 1950s. My two oldest sisters were already married, and the third one, Sarah Jean, was getting pretty close with this guy who said he ran a trucking company over in Jersey City. The word around town was that his dad and uncle actually did most of the important lifting, driving, hollering, and decision-making around that trucking company, and that this guy was just another one of those overpaid son-in-the-business bozos who amount to a kind of permanent skin disease on the face of American commerce. But my dad was pretty high on him because of the way he flashed money around, even though I figured him right away for a scumbag jerk who was just stringing Sarah Jean along for what he could get out of it (and of course I was right, not that anybody will admit it today or even talk about it much any more).

But I was a son, and somehow that was *different*. Especially considering my dad was some kind of bigtime union shop steward (at least to hear him tell it) at this huge chemical plant over in Newark. He had this crazy notion I ought to save up a bunch of money and maybe go off to college someplace, even though I personally thought I was pretty damn lucky just to make it out of highschool. There may be duller, more confusing things in life than algebra or geometry classes, but I sure as hell don't know what they could be. After all, I was eighteen, and all I really wanted from life was to get out of school, fix cars at the Sinclair, and goof around with Julie whenever I got the chance. But my old man wasn't having any part of it. Not hardly. "You're gonna work down at the chemical plant," he'd tell me, eyes hard as a tombstone, "and *that's the way it's going to be!*" That approach was kind of an Old Standard around our house, and I wouldn't be surprised if you've heard something like it once or twice while you were growing up yourself.

To tell the truth, my old man could be a real jerk when he put his mind to it. And he put his mind to it a lot. After bossing people around all day at work, 6:30 ayem to 4:30 pm, five days a week, he'd most usually come home and do a little light evening bullying on my mom and me. Just to keep in practice. My poor mom. She always wound up getting the brunt of it whenever my dad and I had a fight, and we had fights on an increasingly regular basis once I started hanging around and fixing cars at Old Man Finzio's Sinclair. The screwy part was, it never seemed to bother her too much. Not at all. In fact, it made you wonder sometimes if maybe she just didn't *get* it, you know? My dad and me could be screaming at each other at the top of our lungs and she would just *sit* there, looking out the back window or thumbing through one of her pocket-sized birdspotter guides like nothing was happening at all.

See, my mom was a birdwatcher. No kidding. She used to keep this old pair of Army surplus fieldglasses over by her kitchen window, and I swear she'd just about wet her pants any time one of her favorite sapsuckers flew through our yard. She'd stand at our kitchen window for hours at a stretch, up on tiptoes with those damn binoculars jammed into her eye sockets, making these goofy birdcalls through her teeth like she was holding a real-life *conversation* with those damn birds. She'd coo at pigeons and twitter at chickadees and warble at warblers until it got to where I just couldn't bring anybody *over,* you know, because my mom would get so blessed weird about those stupid idiot birds of hers.

Truth is, an awful lot of stuff seemed to sneak right past my mom. Or maybe she was just smart enough to understand that it was better to stay stupid about things she couldn't do much of anything about. Like my old man and his temper, for example. She was a tiny little thing with a laugh that reminded you of chickens in a henhouse and eyes always lit up dumb and sparkly like a kid on Christmas morning. Everybody in the neighborhood thought she was the nicest, sweetest person they ever met, on account of she was always volunteering for the newspaper drive at the highschool or selling tickets to the church variety show or baking a triple chocolate cake for a neighbor who was laid up with stomach flu --that kind of thing. You have anybody like that in your family? Sometimes they get so stinking nice and sweet that you just can't *stand* it anymore.

But she was a dish of ice cream with a cherry on top compared to my old man. What with three of my sisters moved out already and Sarah Jean being one of those sweet, quiet, cooking-and-sewing types herself, it didn't leave much for my dad to do except concentrate all his considerable talent and energy on bossing *me* around. On weekends, he'd make me mow the lawn or wash his two-year-old Mercury while he laid in the hammock out back and listened to the ball game. He'd down himself a fresh beer every inning, and then afterwards, regular as clockwork, he'd call me over to tell me what a lousy job I'd done on the lawn edging or how I'd left a Criminally Negligent number of waterspots on the hood and/or windshield of his car. Then he'd invariably launch into one of these long, rambling, parent-type lectures about *ambition* and *direction* and *career opportunities,* none of which had anything to do with Old Man Finzio's Sinclair station as far as he could see. Of course, he didn't know how much *ambition* and *direction* I had focused on getting into Miss Julie Finzio's underpants. But I had to admit it wasn't what you or anybody else would really call a *career opportunity.*

Anyhow, this chemical plant job paid union scale (which was one *hell* of a lot of money for a kid just out of highschool) but I flat couldn't stand it. The place was hot and dark and smelled something awful, and every day was the same stupid grind, over and over and over and over again. I never understood how those union guys could keep on coming back --day after day, week after week, year after year-- without going stark raving batty one morning and blowing their brains out with a .45 pistol. I swear, every goddam day they'd swap the same wisecracking hellos in the morning when they got to the plant, put on the same baggy coveralls, work gloves, hardhats, and safety goggles, drink the same thermos of coffee from the same plastic cup, eat the same tin-box lunches with the sandwiches wrapped in waxed paper bags, and spend eight solid hours loading and unloading the same stinking 55-gallon drums full of chemical shit that made your eyes burn and your nose run like a damn faucet. You'd work as slow as you could (which is always a matter of fierce professional pride in any union shop) and every night you'd hear the same stale dick jokes in the shower, blow the same globs of weird, yellow-green snot out your nostrils, and head home for a few beers and dinner before going to bed --just so's you could get up in the morning and do it all over again....

You call that a life?

Plus it was no barrel of laughs working for my old man. Some guys'd try to take it a little easy on their own kid, right? But not *my* dad. No sir. He didn't want anybody to think I got this job just because he was my father or abything (which, of course, is exactly why I did) so he made sure I worked twice as hard as anybody else. Honest to God he did.

It got to where I hated waking up in the morning.

Chapter 2: On My Own

Even though I was working full-time at my old man's stupid chemical plant job that summer of 1951, I'd make sure to drop by the Sinclair every now and again on evenings and weekends, just to have a cup of coffee and shoot the breeze with Butch. Or maybe to see Julie and goof around with her a little. Then I showed up this one cold Saturday morning when the leaves were starting to turn and noticed that Butch's old Ford wasn't parked out back where it belonged. For a crazy second, I thought maybe he had it inside on the lift, finally fixing that bad wheel and tie-rod end on the left front. But Old Man Finzio was all alone inside the shop, cutting torch ablaze and sledgehammer in hand, trying to beat a helpless Buick into submission. "Where's Butch?" I hollered over the banging.

The Old Man stopped his hammering and looked at me with the queerest expression on his face. Then he laid down the hammer and slowly turned the gas down on the cutting torch until it shut off with a hollow *pop*. "Ya don't know, d'ya?" the Old Man said softly, wiping his hands on a greasy shop rag.

"Know what?"

"Butch got hisself inna car accident with that Ford of his. A real bad one. He's in the hospital down by Elizabeth. Intensive care, the way I hear it."

"He *what??*"

And that's about when the towtruck pulled in, dragging what was left of Butch's battered old Ford. Jee-zus, that thing was so smashed up you could hardly even recognize it was a car. Looking at it turned me all icy-white inside, and I ran out to see if maybe that left front had finally sheared itself off and caused the crash. But everything was so torn up there was no way to tell, what with the front end pushed clear back to the firewall, the roof buckled in, and the transmission tailshaft sticking right up through the front seat like one of those compound fractures where the bone comes through the skin. What a mess. You could see where Butch's hands busted two solid chunks clear out of the steering wheel, and there was shattered glass and these rusty paintbrush streaks of dried blood all over the place. It made you sick just looking at it, honest it did, and you knew right away that whoever was behind the wheel of that car ought to be dead.

I must've walked around that twisted hulk two dozen times, as though if I looked at it long enough and hard enough, it would somehow straighten itself out or maybe even disappear. But of course it didn't. It just hung there off the back of that towtruck like a slaughtered side of beef, swaying ever so slightly to and fro and leaking little dribbles of blackened oil and slippery green anti-freeze into the asphalt. I just flat couldn't believe something like that had happened to Butch, an ex-Marine hardhat diver who could drink a case of beer in one sitting, weld a perfect bead underwater, cuss fluently in six different languages, and bring dead cars back to life.

The story going around town was that Butch and Marlene got into a big godawful argument after work one day and she wound up packing her things and heading off home to Tennessee. And it was Good Riddance, far as I was concerned. But a few nights later --right after the bars closed down-- Butch took himself a notion to chase after her. The poor bastard didn't even make it to Perth Amboy before he flattened that old Ford against a concrete bridge abutment and damn near killed himself.

Naturally I went to visit Butch in the hospital, and believe me, it was a real, honest-to-God horror show. I hate hospitals anyway. I hate the smell of disinfectant and the fluorescent lights that don't cast any shadows and the way the nurses' shoes squeak on the linoleum floors. And I most especially hate how everybody talks in these hushed whispers out in the hall, like it's a damn funeral parlor or something. It gives me the creeps, you know? Anyhow, they had Butch laid out in a long, narrow room with just some pull-drapes to separate him from a dozen or so other desperate cases, and the poor guy was all covered up in plaster and gauze from head to toe like one of those ancient Egyptian mummies. They had his arms and legs dangling on pulleys and wires and there were all kinds of needles and tubes running in and out of him, and you could tell right away that he was never going to be the same again. It was tough understanding how a car accident could change your whole entire life in a single instant --just like *that*-- as if some giant hand reached down out of the sky and flicked you off like a damn lightswitch. The thought of it made you go all dry and hollow inside, you know?

But I knew I was there to visit Butch and let him know at least one person in New Jersey gave a shit about him, so I swallowed hard a couple of times, walked over by the bed, and tried my best to make a little small talk. To tell the truth, it was like talking into an empty closet. But I gave it my best shot anyway, rambling on and on about Old Man Finzio and the helpless Buick he had up on the lift and what a jerk my dad was and how much I hated his stupid chemical plant job over in Newark. It didn't seem to have much effect on Butch, and about all he could do was just lay there, arms and legs dangling, staring up at the ceiling like he couldn't really see it. It made me feel all dumb and clumsy trying to carry on a conversation by myself, but every time I stopped talking, Butch'd give off a coarse little grunt --like the sound a car with a flat battery makes when you try to turn it over-- just to let me know he was listening. Then I more or less ran out of stuff to say and just stood there for awhile, watching what looked like bloody pee drain out of Butch through a clear plastic tube. But when I finally turned to leave, Butch gathered up every bit of strength he had and called me back over by his bed to tell me something. It was real hard to understand, on account of his voice came out so faint and hoarse and whispery that I had to lean my ear right up next to the gauze to make it out at all. "The Plymouth...," he rasped, fighting his way through every word, "bad water pump....parts under my bench....toolbox key....under trash drum....don't let the Old Man....get *near* that car....." It took a moment to sink in, but then I nodded to let Butch know I understood. "An' lissen," Butch choked, his whole body straining upwards, "*you take carra my fuckin' tools or I'll break yer goddam arms, y'hear?*"

So I stopped by the Sinclair early the next morning, and just like Butch said, I found his toolbox key hidden under the trash drum, Mr. Altobelli's Plymouth in the service bay, and a rebuilt water pump on the shelf under his workbench, all neatly wrapped in oiled paper. Now you have to understand that Butch never let *any*body mess with his tools. Oh, he'd let me borrow a socket or a special wrench or something when I needed it, but just one tool at a time on a strictly ask-and-return basis. Most often I worked with Old Man Finzio's tools, which were inevitably scattered around the shop like the remnants of a recently exploded fragmentation bomb. Hell, you could never find *any*thing. But Butch always kept his tools neat, clean, and perfectly organized, and was careful to wipe them off and pack them away at the end of the day or whenever he finished up a job. Or even part of a job. Every topflight mechanic I ever met was the exact same way. So it was really quite an honor that an accomplished wrench like Butch Bohunk would trust me with his toolbox.

Old Man Finzio never actually offered me a job that day. Not in so many words, anyway. But he allowed as how I could maybe help out here and there around the Sinclair while Butch was laid up --*if* I thought I could spare the time, of course. So I played hooky from the chemical plant job (what else?) and spent the day replacing the water pump on Mr. Altobelli's Plymouth. Then I repaired some church organist lady's Ford with a bum u-joint, and it sure as hell felt good to work on cars again. I decided right then and there I was going to stay on at the Sinclair. Hell, I'd had it up to *here* with that dumbass union job at the chemical plant. Sure, fixing cars didn't pay as good (in fact, it didn't pay anywhere *near* as good) but as a car mechanic you at least got to work on your own, at your own pace, and every single job was its own special kind of problem and challenge. Best of all, there was a golden little Appreciation Moment at the end when you finally got a car all buttoned back together and running smooth and steady as a fine Swiss watch.

As you can imagine, my old man was pretty burned up about my plan to stiff his stupid chemical plant job and go to work at Old Man Finzio's Sinclair. He thought I was absolutely *nuts* to roll over a secure, high-paying union job just to become a lousy streetcorner gas station grease monkey. Not to mention that it made him look pretty damn lame in front of all his union buddies back at the chemical plant. So of course we had a big enormous fight about it. I bet you've had fights like that in your own family. You know, the kind where you end up storming out of the house and slam the front door so hard behind you it shatters all the little glass windows on top.

I wandered the streets for hours that night, feeling pissed off at my old man, sorry for my mom, worrying about Butch, and wondering just what the hell I was going to do next. I wanted to call Julie, you know, but it was awful late and I was afraid her mom might answer, and the last thing in the world I wanted or needed about then was another angry parent. Besides, I didn't especially want Julie to hear my voice right then, on account of I was pretty choked up and maybe even a little scared. Who knows, I might've even cried once or twice. Not a *real* cry, of course, but one of those Restricted Male versions where your face goes all taut and flushed and you can feel the old eye juice backing up in the ducts. But you don't let it leak out. Not hardly. After all, that's for girls and sissies and little crybaby boys who've fallen down and skinned their knees. At the very least, you don't let anybody see you do it.

I remember it was real chilly that night, and of course I was in such a mad stinking rush to get out of my dad's house that I forgot to grab my jacket out of the front hall closet. So now I was getting pretty cold and even shivering a little and hadn't the foggiest idea where I could go or what to do next. I counted up the money in my jeans pockets to see if it was maybe enough to take me anywhere --anywhere at all-- but it was just a bunch of loose change, and mostly pennies at that. I thought about walking the mile and a half to the bus station and spending the night there or maybe trying to break into the Sinclair so I could sleep in the office next to the space heater, but neither of those sounded like permanent solutions at all, on account of I'd just have to limp home the next day with my tail between my legs and take another heaping dose of bullshit from my father. A giant, economy-sized dose, for sure. And breaking into Old Man Finzio's gas station would undoubtedly get me fired by the time Old Man Finzio rolled in, and the whole idea here was that I wanted to work as a car mechanic at the Sinclair instead of wasting my time at that piece-of-shit chemical plant job in Newark.

And then I had a brilliant idea. My maiden aunt Rosamarina lived a couple blocks away on Buchanan Street, and she had this empty sort-of apartment over her garage that would be absolutely *perfect* for a young working guy just out of highschool. Poor old Aunt Rosamarina was a retired librarian, and I guess you could say she was more or less the black sheep of the family (until I came along, anyway) because she lived alone with about three dozen cats, never answered her door, and spent most of her time reading thick old poetry books with very small type and no pictures in them at all. My aunt was one of those thin, sad-eyed, ashen-cheeked old maids who get nervous around other human beings the way some people get palsy or throw epileptic fits. Even the simplest everyday encounters with mailmen or milkmen or the kid who delivered newspapers could get her to trembling and stuttering and wobbling at the knees. Which is why you could usually find her holed up there in her house with her poetry books and her legion of cats and multiple chain locks on all the doors. I remember she'd come over by our house for Christmas dinner every year while I was growing up, and sometimes the relatives would arrange to have some Eligible Male Of Appropriate Age on hand to talk to her a little or maybe even ask her out. But every single time she'd just park herself in the corner by the front window --all by her lonesome-- and not say a word. My mom would keep pouring her these longstemmed glasses full of Asti Spumante to get her loosened up, but my Aunt Rosamarina could suck up eight, ten, even a full baker's dozen of them without so much as cracking a Christmas smile or even tittering now and then like most of your elderly retired ladies do when they've gotten a bit too chummy with the punchbowl. To tell the truth, we all suspected my aunt might be putting in a little solo practice with the old liquor bottle back home.

But now, all of a sudden, the fact that my Aunt Rosamarina was never especially comfortable or chatty around other people was transformed into a fabulous social asset. It meant I could count on her to leave me totally and completely alone if I moved into the one-room apartment over her garage. Why, it was *perfect!* Sure, I knew she'd watch my every move through her little crack in the draperies, but that didn't matter because she'd never actually *say* anything to anybody. Except maybe her cats.

To tell the truth, the "apartment" over my Aunt Rosamarina's garage wasn't really an apartment at all, but more like some pygmy-sized storage space under the rafters. A couple summers before, my dad and me put in a space heater and a couple rolls of tarpaper insulation and even a john and an 18x18 shower stall (which is the smallest size Sears sells, and has barely enough room inside for both a live human being and a decent-sized bar of bath soap). The idea was that my aunt could maybe rent it out to somebody (like perhaps a convenient recent widower or a quiet young divinity student) and have herself a little extra income. I mean, they don't pay too awful much to retired librarians. Not hardly. But poor old Aunt Rosamarina never got up the nerve to rent it. My dad even put an ad in the newspaper himself one time, just a few months after we finished fixing the place up for her. Seems like whenever people showed up at the front door to take a look at it, she'd check them out through the side window --peering out through her little crack in the draperies-- and I don't believe she ever got up the nerve to answer the door. Not once. So that apartment over my Aunt Rosamarina's garage was just sitting there --*waiting* for me, you know?-- like somehow it had all been planned out in advance.

So I went over and sneaked in about three ayem that night, shinnying up the cherry tree next to the garage and going in through the window, and the next morning I knocked on my Aunt Rosamarina's front door and made a deal on the spot to move in immediately and pay her at the end of the month. Twenty bucks sounded a little steep to me, but, what the heck, I could afford it. After all, I had a job that paid, well, to tell the truth, I wasn't sure exactly how much it paid at all. But I figured it'd probably be more than enough. Or at least I hoped it would, anyway. As I remember, my aunt made the whole transaction without ever taking the chain lock off the door. Not once.

That apartment over Aunt Rosamarina's garage was everything a young guy on his own could ask for. Oh, maybe it was a little weird that the john, shower, and sink were right in the middle of the floor on the far end, but that's because the space over my aunt's garage was shaped like the inside of a pup tent and the only place you could stand up straight to shave or brush your teeth was right in the middle. Well, almost straight, anyway. And I had to remember not to wake up real quick in the middle of the night (like if I had a nightmare about the chemical plant job or something) because the bed was over to the side where the ceiling was only a foot or so off the floor, and you could split your forehead wide open on the rafters if you sat up in anything like a hurry.

But it was *mine,* and I couldn't believe how great it felt to be out there in the Real World, enjoying the *dignity* and *privacy* of living on my own. Like I could drink a beer after work anytime I wanted (if I could just get one of the local rumpots who hung around the liquor store to buy it for me, anyway) or even invite Julie over to share one with me if I had the notion. Not that I ever got up the nerve to actually *ask* her, you understand. But you need the privacy of your own place to even think about doing that kind of thing. And speaking of that, I could, uhh, *think* about being with Julie as much as I wanted, without worrying about somebody hearing me in the next room or maybe waltzing in unexpectedly (if you know what I mean). You worry about that sort of thing a lot when you grow up in a house with four older sisters. But now I was finally on my own and totally, completely independent. By God, in *my* apartment, I could do *whatever* I wanted, with *whoever* I wanted, whenever the hell *I* wanted to do it.

After the first couple weeks, I was bored a lot.

Chapter 3: Big Ed's Jaguar

Big Ed Baumstein owned the first Jaguar sportscar I ever saw. It was an XK120 Super Sport roadster --creamy white with rich red leather upholstery-- and my whole world stopped cold the day he wheeled it into the Sinclair for the very first time. It was the early spring of 1952, and I'd been working at Old Man Finzio's Sinclair all through the winter and living in that little wooden pup-tent of an apartment over my Aunt Rosamarina's garage. I about froze my ass off, too, on account of all I had between me and the snow on the roof was a couple thin sheets of tarpaper insulation, and if I stoked the space heater up enough to take the frost off my shaving mirror, the snow would start melting in through the ceiling and I'd get leaks. *Big* leaks. Somehow they always seemed to be right over the bed, no matter where the hell I moved it (not that you could move *anything* very far in the space over my Aunt Rosamarina's garage) and it didn't help my personal ambient temperature any that I worked all day long at a gas station. You just ask anybody how cold it gets in a concrete-and-brick garage during the wintertime (and especially when you're raising and lowering the damn overhead door every half hour or so to let one car out and bring in another that's been sitting outside for three days with snow up to the hubcaps and icicles hanging off the grille). I swear, some of my body parts never thawed out until spring that year.

At least things had smoothed out a little with my folks, and my dad would even pass the meat or vegetables over for a second helping when my mom had me over to dinner every Sunday evening. Of course he wouldn't say much --just sort of grunt now and then and mutter under his breath-- but I had to figure that represented a major improvement in our relationship. My mom wanted me to move back home (what else?) but of course I'd counter with the old "how important it was for a young man to assume responsibility for his own life" gambit (one of my old man's very favorite lines, but I wasn't above borrowing it on occasions when the situation demanded). Besides, I was only a couple blocks away on Buchanan Street if the worst happened and the Commies launched a nuclear missile attack on New York.

And it seemed like old Butch was doing a little better. Or at least that's what the doctors said, anyway. They'd moved him over to the veterans hospital near Iselin, and I even took the bus all the way down there to visit him a couple times. It was a long, hard trip for a guy who didn't own a car (and no way was my old man gonna lend me his Mercury to go see another gas station grease monkey --not even in the hospital) so I didn't make it very often. But I'd call him every week or so, and he'd always tell me how the doctors and nurses were saying he was making great progress, but that they were really all full of shit and didn't know what the fuck they were talking about. And I personally had to agree, since I honestly couldn't see much change when I came to visit except that he could sit up and talk a little better and he was maybe wearing a few less pounds of plaster than the last time I saw him. Then again, I guess that *is* progress when you start out like a busted-up bag of stew meat. By degrees, anyway. Natural-ly Butch always wanted to know what was going on around the Sinclair, and I made sure to keep him up-to-date on all the latest poop. Especially after Big Ed started showing up every couple days with that brand new Jaguar roadster of his.

Big Ed Baumstein was a rich Jewish guy from Teaneck who'd had about three or four divorces and dealt in scrap industrial machinery for a living. Actually he was only half-Jewish, seeing as how his mother's side of the family were mostly all Italian. Calabraese, I think. Anyhow, Big Ed and his cousin Vincenzo (on his mother's side, natch) had this huge wrecking yard over by the Jersey shore, and although neither of them wore suits or ties except on special family occasions like weddings and funerals and stuff, they both had plenty of money to throw around. Any damn way they wanted. Not that they made a big show of it or put on any of those snooty, rich-guy airs like the highly manicured jerks you see cluttering up the society pages.

Big Ed had been a regular around the Old Man's gas station for years because he liked the way Butch took care of his cars, and as far back as anybody could remember, Big Ed Baumstein always drove Cadillacs. In fact, he had *two* of them when I start-ed in working at the Sinclair: an enormous black Sixty Special sedan for the fall and winter months and the occasional important business meeting downtown, plus an absolutely *gorgeous* white-on-white convertible that he only drove during the spring and summer and never took out of his garage if it was raining. Not even a drop. They were hardly a year old, either one of them, but Big Ed was forever dropping one or the other off for an oil change or a lube job or a full Simonize wax or maybe to fix a little squeak or rattle he thought he heard. Big Ed didn't trust the mechanics at the Caddy dealership at all, and he took a real shine to me one day when I tracked down a nasty grating noise that had started up behind the dashboard of the white convert. It was just the speedo cable, for gosh sakes. Needed a little grease. But he was thrilled as all getout when the noise was gone and I only let Old Man Finzio charge him a dollar. I mean, it was *nothing,* you know? Afterwards, Big Ed flashed me a wink and a smile (he even took out his cigar for the occasion!) and palmed me a five buck tip. That was one hell of a big tip in 1952.

Big Ed could afford it. Sure, I'd heard all the whispering about how Big Ed's scrapyard business was somehow, you know, *connected.* Like how maybe a few ex-business associates of certain Influential People might have occasionally wound up inside the crushed-up blocks of scrap steel his workers sent back to the smelters for reprocessing. Perhaps even a key prosecution witness or two. But I never asked Big Ed how he made the fivers he started slipping me every time I passed a wrench over one of his Caddies. After all, I figured that kind of curiosity was for the people who work downtown in the Federal Building. I mean, that's what taxes are for, right? Besides, I *liked* Big Ed, because Big Ed loved his cars and wanted them to be perfect. You had to respect a guy who felt that way about automobiles.

As you probably figured, Big Ed Baumstein was a genuinely massive edition of a human being. He stood six-four and a yard wide, and could pretty much fill up your average side doorway in both directions. The funny part was you'd never figure Big Ed to be that tall if you saw him standing out in the open someplace, on account of he was shaped sort of like an Anjou pear and favored bright, clashy clothes that more or less broke up the landscape of his body. But if you stood right next to him, you'd all of a sudden realize that you were barely eye-level with his neck (or where his neck would've been if Big Ed had such a thing) and talking more or less directly into his chest hairs. Not that you ever got to do that much talking when you were around Big Ed

Baumstein. No, sir. *Listening* was more like it. Sure, he could be loud and pushy and irritating and always wanted things his own way, but I've got to admit that Big Ed Baumstein brought more thrills, fun, heartache, and excitement into my life than anybody I ever met. No two ways about it.

I'll always remember Big Ed the way he looked the Sunday afternoon of that last race weekend at Road America. They'd just finished building the track that year --guess that'd make it some-time around early September of 1955-- and if I close my eyes, I can almost see him now, wearing those huge, baggy, bright yellow golf pants of his, a shirt with w-i-d-e red and white stripes, and the stupid straw hat he picked up from a pushcart vendor at Sebring the time we ran the 12 hours in 1954. It looked like the roof of a native hut, honest it did, but Big Ed needed it pretty bad because he was bald as an egg on top and quickly turned the color of a redskin potato in direct sunlight. He had on a pair of those goofy Mexican sandals, too. You know, the kind with tire-tread soles? I remember Big Ed bought them in Ciudad Juarez at the end of the Mexican Road Race when we were down there, just a few hours after that crazy sonofabitch Javier Premal tried to kill me with Big Ed's brand new Ferrari. Or what *would* have been Big Ed's brand new Ferrari if Javier Premal hadn't driven it over a God-damn cliff. With me in it, too....

But I was telling you about Big Ed and his stupid tire-tread sandals, wasn't I? He had to walk along on little bitty steps whenever he wore those things, on account of otherwise they'd flop right off his feet. So Big Ed looked like a damn circus tent on casters as he rolled and shuffled and bumped his way down the freshly poured asphalt pitlane at Road America. As always, Big Ed had the chewed-off end of a fat Cuban cigar clenched between his teeth. You weren't supposed to smoke in the pits --not *ever*-- but Big Ed invariably kept a cigar stuck in his face even when he couldn't light up. He'd wave it around like a soggy baton while he was telling you what to do, and you always knew Big Ed was hatching a wild idea whenever that stogie started rolling from one side of his mouth to the other. Big Ed was World Class when it came to hatching wild ideas.

Anyhow, I'll never forget the bright spring morning Big Ed wheeled his shiny new Jaguar roadster up to the pumps for the very first time. Jee-*zus*, I'd never seen a car like that in my entire life. The bodywork arched and slinked and curled from one end to the other like some huge steel jungle cat, all coiled up and ready to pounce. And the sound was perfect, too: a rich, deep, buttery six-cylinder growl that just seemed to purr its way out the tailpipes. *JAGUARRRRRR!!!* Boy, they sure picked the right name for *that* automobile. "Whaddaya think?" Big Ed crowed, his cigar sticking straight up like an exclamation point.

"Boy, it sure is *something!*" I said, running my eyes up and down the bodywork, trying to take in all the curves at once.

"Wanna go for a l'il ride?"

"Jeez, I dunno," I told him. "Old Man Finzio'll have a conniption fit if I just take off...."

"Ahh, screw him," Big Ed snorted, "c'mon, climb aboard."

Needless to say, I decided to chance it. Only the big ace Fulltime Professional Automobile Mechanic couldn't find the damn door handle! Big Ed let out a huge laugh --*HawwHawHa-HawHawHawww*-- and reached over to open it from the inside. Believe it or not, that's how you open the door on an XK120 roadster. From the *in*side. Right away I could see this car was put together a little bit different from the Fords and Chevys and Plymouths and even Cadillacs I was accustomed to. I also noticed that reaching across the interior was quite a stretch for Big Ed, on account of he was wedged in just about rock solid between the seatback and the steering wheel. To tell the truth, Big Ed didn't fit the Jag too good. Big as it was (and it was goddam *big* for a two-seater automobile) the XK120 didn't really have enough gut, chest, or shoulder room for a guy the size of Big Ed Baumstein.

To this day, I remember climbing into the passenger side of Big Ed's brand new XK120 and leaning myself back in that rich red leather upholstery for the very first time. It smelled like fine kid gloves, honest it did, and felt just as soft against my skin. Warm, too, as if perhaps some elegant lady's hands were still inside them. Then Big Ed revved her up and dumped the clutch (he was never what you could call real arty with a stickshift) and we squealed away from the pumps in a haze of burning rubber. That certainly got Old Man Finzio's attention, and I caught a glimpse of him out the corner of my eye as we rocketed out onto

Pine Street. He just stood there and stared --dumbstruck, you know?-- as if Big Ed's Jaguar was a naked Girl Scout on roller-skates. XK120s did that to *everybody* back in 1952. They were so damn gorgeous it made your eyes ache just to look at them.

Big Ed drove us out past the edge of town and gave it a quick blast in second and third gear. Jee-*zus*, was that car ever FAST! *"That's eighty!"* Big Ed hollered over the wind noise, *"and we're not even outta third yet!"* Right at that exact moment, with hair whipping in my eyes and the yowl of that big twincam six filling my ears and the ·white lines on the highway coming at me like tracer bullets, right *then* I fell in love with Jaguars.

Old Man Finzio didn't say a single word when we tooled back into the station a good half-hour later. Not one. He just sort of waltzed his way over by the pumps --real nonchalant, you know?-- to get himself a little closer look at Big Ed's new toy. I swear he must've walked his way around that car six or seven times, and I can't recall as I'd ever seen so much white around the Old Man's eyeballs.

"Say," I asked Big Ed, "d'ya think we could maybe take a look under the hood?"

"Suuure," Big Ed grinned. But then of course we couldn't find the damn hood release. Heck, we crawled all *over* that car before I finally located a suspicious-looking knob that the Jaguar factory had thoughtfully hidden way up under the dashboard on the passenger side, clear back against the firewall. I popped it and walked around front, pausing to wipe my hands ever-so-carefully on my dirty coveralls before lifting that long, crocodile-snout XK120 hood. And then I damn near fell right in! Why, neither me or Old Man Finzio had ever seen *any*thing like the engine compartment of Big Ed's new Jaguar. The motor was lean and long and incredibly handsome, what with these two gleaming aluminum valvecovers fastened down with neat little rows of chrome-plated acorn nuts and twin S.U. carburetors sprouting off the righthand side like a pair of English guard towers. The exhaust manifolds on the opposite side were elegant, too, all smooth and graceful as a seagull in flight, and right away I knew that Jaguar engine was the single most beautiful automotive powerplant I had ever laid eyes on. It was like a piece of fine sculptured jewelry, honest to God it was.

"Y'know," Big Ed mused while the Old Man and I drooled our way around the Jag's engine compartment, "I wonder if youse guys could make it so's the seat moves back a little more. It's kinda *snug* in there, y'know? And maybe fix the turn signals, too. I can't get the damn things to work at all."

"I don't know...," Old Man Finzio started in, kind of shaking his head, but I broke in right away:

"Sure I can, Mr. Baumstein. I can fix it. No problem."

Big Ed smiled and gave me one of his patented five-dollar winks. "I bet you can, Buddy. I bet you can."

And sure enough I could.

After a couple false starts, anyway.

Chapter 4: The Jaguar's Lair

Big Ed became a frequent visitor at the Old Man's Sinclair that spring and summer of 1952. Actually, it was Big Ed's Jag that became sort of a regular. I got to know that XK120 pretty well, on account of it always seemed to be needing a little attention here and there. The Jag was *fussy,* you know, like some rich, highclass woman who's used to nice clothes and servants and stuff. I even had to buy myself a special set of sockets and open-end combination wrenches to work on it because nothing in Butch's toolbox fit anything on Big Ed's Jag except the sparkplug wrench. That's on account of the English used something called British Standard nuts and bolts, and they're unlike anything else in the whole world. Probably on purpose. See, you measure a normal bolt --no matter if it's coarse thread, fine thread, or even that strange metric stuff they have over in Europe-- by the diameter of the shaft. And that makes sense. But the Brits decided (for some reason that absolutely eludes me) to measure *their* bolts by the length of one flat up on the head. So, while a seven-sixteenths American-style bolt would be considered pretty damn dinky, a seven-sixteenths British Standard bolt is a rather hefty item. Not to mention that they're sized in such a way that no regulation American wrench will fit snugly on a British Standard nut or bolt. Oh, you can try, but you'll inevitably wind up with the wrench slipping off at an inopportune moment (like when you're trying to torque that last little quarter-twist into a nut or bolt head that's hidden way down in the bottom of the engine compartment) and that's how you wind up leaving half the skin off your knuckles embedded in the radiator core like a smear of the suet my mom leaves out for her stupid damn birds in the wintertime.

Those British Standard wrenches were expensive, too, and it took our regular tool guy more than a whole damn week to come up with them. And no way would Old Man Finzio lay out *his* money just so's I could work on Big Ed's Jag. But I didn't mind. Hell no. In fact, I was real glad to have Big Ed's XK120 dropping by for service and routine maintenance every few days, because working on it made me feel pretty darn special compared to the Chevys, Fords, Nash Ambassadors, Henry Js, and even

Cadillacs, Packards, and Lincolns I was used to. Plus that Jag was nothing short of a Certified Goldmine for a decent automobile mechanic. And that's not even counting Big Ed's five-buck tips! Best of all, that XK120 intimidated the living shit out of Old Man Finzio. Why, he couldn't even look in the engine bay without his eyelids starting to twitch and his jaw tightening up like a damn vise grip. Truth is, Old Man Finzio didn't understand or appreciate Jaguars one bit, and I did what I could to encourage the situation by sort of *talking* to the car whenever I had it in for service. Like my mom talks to her stupid damn birds, you know? I came up with this phony baloney Lord-Earl-of-the-Sinclair British accent, see, and every now and then I'd hold a dashpot dampener or voltage regulator or something up to my ear and pretend like it was answering me back. I guess it must've looked and sounded pretty loony, because soon I had Old Man Finzio creeping around the back of the shop on tiptoes every time I worked on Big Ed's XK120. In fact, sometimes he'd just give up and go hide in the can or hang around out by the gas pumps until he heard it fire up and roll back out of the service bay. That sure beat hell out of putting brake shoes on some rinky-dink tax accountant's Plymouth.

Of course there were a lot of little mechanical secrets to learn about Jaguars, and right there at the beginning, I didn't know *any* of 'em. Like I'll never forget the day Big Ed's Jag staggered into the station with the engine popping and banging something awful and these enormous sooty-black clouds blowing out the tailpipe. He'd only owned the Jag five or six weeks then, and boy oh boy, did he ever look *pissed*. In fact, I recall his face was about the color of a fresh radish, and you could tell by the droop of his cigar that Big Ed was someplace well west of merely disappointed. "This goddam Limey piece of shit," he snarled, reaching over and yanking the hood cable so hard it damn near came off in his hand, "take a look at it, willya?"

To tell the truth, I hadn't the foggiest notion what was wrong. But I pulled the sparkplugs (always a good place to start) and it didn't take a Nuclear Physicist to see that they were all gas fouled pretty bad. So I sandblasted the plugs and screwed 'em back in, and then just kind of leaned into the engine bay and stared at those weird S.U. carburetors for twenty minutes or so, trying to figure out how the hell they worked. Can't say as I'd ever seen anything remotely like S.U.s before. They had these elegant-looking aluminum towers on top --standing up there at attention like the Queen's Royal Guard or something-- and I had no idea on earth what they had to do with mixing air and gasoline together into something an internal combustion engine might want to swallow. Finally I gave up and punched the starter button --just to see what would happen you know?-- and of course the Jag fired up instantly and settled down to an absolutely *perfect* 550 rpm idle. It was like a miracle!

Needless to say, my stock soared with Big Ed Baumstein, and this time he slipped me a tenner. Honest to God he did. But my newfound stardom as a British car mechanic fizzled out less than twenty minutes later, when Big Ed's Jag stumbled back into the station with its engine halting and bucking on maybe two live cylinders and even bigger, blacker-looking clouds belching out the back end. There was a purple cast to Big Ed's face this time, and his cigar was dangling straight down his chin on account of he'd bitten clear through it. *"Wh-what the hell's wrong with this G-Goddam thing!"* Big Ed sputtered, really on a boil.

So I checked it over again --same thing exactly-- and to say I was mystified just about covers it. So I reached in my back pocket and fished around for Big Ed's sawbuck. "I'm sorry, Mr. Baumstein," I told him, sounding extraordinarily lame, "but your Jaguar is really, aah, *different* from all the other stuff I've worked on. It's gonna take me a little time to figure it out," and I handed him back his tenspot.

To my everlasting surprise, Big Ed's face came down three or four shades until it wasn't much more than a warm pink. Then he reached out and pushed the tenner back into my shirt pocket. "You'll figger it out though, won'cha Buddy?" he said, staring me right in the eyes.

"S-sure, Mr. Baumstein," I nodded.

"Good fer you!" he nodded, and slapped me on the back hard enough so there was maybe a little hint of a warning in it. Like maybe I sure as hell *better* figure it out.

So I looked into the Jag's engine compartment again, and all those strange, shiny, foreign-looking pieces stared right back at me. "Y'know, Mr. Baumstein," I told him, "at the very least I'm gonna need me a shop manual. You got any idea where I might find one?"

"Well," he said, "the Jaguar dealership's way the hell over in Manhattan. Tellya what, Buddy, I'll borrow ya the black Caddy tomorrow so's ya can drive over an' buy us one." It was springtime, so Big Ed wasn't using his Sixty Special for much of anything. "And one more thing...," he continued, resting a hand the size of a calf's head on my shoulder.

"What's that, Mr. Baumstein?"

"Call me Big Ed, willya?"

And that's how I wound up driving into Manhattan in Big Ed's black Caddy sedan (which, by the way, had *real* thick glass in all the windows) for my first-ever look at a foreign sportscar dealership. Naturally I'd asked Julie if she wanted to come along, since it was always kind of exciting going into Manhattan. Especially in Big Ed's Cadillac Sixty Special with by far the biggest, widest, softest, most sumptuous front seat you ever saw (I don't even need to mention what the back seat was like). In fact, just thinking about Julie and all that soft, cushy real estate was enough to get my hormones working overtime (if you catch my drift) but she couldn't make it on account of she had a date to go over to the beauty parlor with one of her girlfriends so they could get their damn hair done and nails painted. How *that* ever compared to visiting a Jaguar dealership in Manhattan was beyond me, but I guess that's just one of the many important differences between women and normal people.

Anyhow, the very next day I found myself crossing the George Washington Bridge into New York City all by my lonesome (with that magnificent expanse of Cadillac front seat going totally and completely to waste) and followed the directions Big Ed had scribbled on the back of an envelope down towards the southern tip of Manhattan and Battery Park. The Jaguar agency was on a little sidestreet near the river, mixed in with a bunch of factory buildings and warehouses and stuff, and it was really just an ordinary cinderblock garage that somebody'd dressed up with a fresh coat of whitewash and some brown 2x4 trim to make it look like one of those two-door English houses. There was a small wooden sign hanging out over the door, and it was done up in the kind of fancy Olde English script that you commonly see on Scotch labels and eye doctor diplomas. It read:

Westbridge Motor Car Company, Ltd.

thoroughbred motorcars for discriminating drivers

Colin St. John, proprietor

Two MG TDs and a bright red Jag XK120 were parked out front, and gee whiz, did that Jag ever look sharp in red! The MGs were sorta nifty, too, come to think of it. I'd seen a few TCs and TDs around on the street, but I never paid too much attention on account of I always thought they looked kind of rickety and spindly --like old baby buggies or something-- and I knew they weren't especially fast since I'd gotten into a sort of stoplight drag race with one when I was out, uhh, *"test driving"* Mr. Altobelli's Plymouth sedan. It came out pretty much a dead heat as I recall, and that should tell you a little something about how screamingly fast T-series MGs are. But they looked snappy as hell parked by the curbside, no two ways about it.

Just as I pulled up in front of the Westbridge Motor Car Company (Ltd.), this tall, natty-looking guy with a tweed cap, leather elbow patches, and a gold-topped cane stepped out through the front door, took a long, down-the-nose gander at me, and limped briskly over to one of the MGs. He tossed his cane behind the seat, folded himself neatly inside, pulled the choke knob full out, yanked smartly on the starter, and listened with his head cocked to one side as the engine ground a few times and clattered to life. While it warmed up, he gave himself a thorough once-over in the little pocket-sized mirror you find perched on the dash cowling of all T-series MGs. He straightened his tie, tweaked the ends of his mustache, realigned his cap, then wet the tip of his finger and ran it delicately over both eyebrows. "Right-o," he nodded at last, giving himself an appreciative wink in the mirror. Then he reached in the MG's door pocket and pulled out the most enormous curlycue smoking pipe you have ever seen in your life. I swear, that thing was big as a damn French Horn, and the guy spent the better part of five whole minutes getting it packed, tamped, leveled off, and fired up just exactly the way he wanted. Made a regular Church Ritual out of it, you know? Once the pipe was puffing away to his complete and utter satisfaction, the tweedy guy folded his tobacco pouch neatly away, pushed the choke knob all the way in, blipped the throttle once or twice, selected first gear, and tootled off down the street, looking jaunty as all getout and trailing an aromatic cloud of burnt Cavendish in his wake. He ripped off a crisp shift into second and yanked the wheel hard left at the next intersection --without even *touching* the brakes!-- and I watched in awe as that MG skittered around the corner like a beagle puppy on a freshly-waxed linoleum floor. Right *then* I came to a new appreciation of what MGs were all about. So what if they weren't particularly fast in a straight line? Those things could scoot around tight corners like nothing you ever saw. Plus they had a certain *style* and *spirit* that was almost as good as sheer, pavement-scorching acceleration. Maybe even better, since a really *fast* car could land you in a heap of serious trouble if you didn't know what you were doing.

Or sometimes even if you did.

Inside the Westbridge shop were more damn British automobiles than I'd ever seen in my life. There must've been five or six XK120s and near a dozen MG TCs and TDs, and almost every one of them had its hood wide open or was perched up on a set of jackstands with the wheels off. Or both. There were some other cars, too. Cars I'd never seen or even heard of before. Up against the side wall was this magnificent Jaguar Mk. VII sedan that looked like the damn Lincoln Monument on wheels, and right next to it was a pudgy little Morris Minor coupe that could have easily belonged to Elmer Fudd. A few TDs and XK120s down from the Morris was this *incredible* torpedo-shaped Frazer-Nash racing car with cycle fenders and numbers painted on the sides. It was done up in a deep stringbean green, and it sure as hell didn't look like any Nash automobile *I'd* ever seen before. Of course, I didn't know at the time that Frazer-Nash was just one of several dozen pint-sized English sportscar companies that nobody on this side of the planet ever heard of, and it didn't have one single thing do with Nash automobiles here in the states. Over in England, it seems like anybody with a gas welder, a pile of scrap steel, and a roof over his head can set himself up in business as an automobile manufacturer. I think all you gotta do is hang out a shingle.

Anyhow, I'd have to say that particular Frazer-Nash was the first actual, honest-to-gosh *racing* sportscar I ever saw close up or stood right next to. And gee whiz, did it ever give me goosebumps. Oh, it was a little beat up and scruffy-looking, what with a bunch of scrapes and dings here and there and all these dried insect splatters and genuine, hundred-mile-an-hour stone chips on the nose and fenders. But you couldn't miss the nifty little half-moon racing windscreen or the serious-looking leather strap they had buckled across the hood to keep it from flying open at high speed, or how the exhaust pipe ran right down the side of the car, just below the driver's elbow. *Wow!* No question about it, that Frazer-Nash was a real War Machine.

I didn't see much of anybody hanging around inside the Westbridge shop, and I started thinking about maybe unbuckling that leather strap and taking a peek at whatever might be lurking under the hood of that Frazer-Nash. That's when an unknown finger extended itself out of nowhere and tapped me on the right shoulder. "Need any 'elp there, guv'nor?" said a voice right out of Piccadilly Circus.

I wheeled around to find this short, hollow-faced guy in a blue shop coat staring up at me through a pair of sad, watery-grey eyes. "Mister St. John?" I asked, real formal-like. A name like Colin St. John does that to you.

"Naw, Barry Spline's the naime," he wheezed through a nose pointy enough to open oil cans, "glad t'meetcher." Barry Spline had one of those rare British accents that never once made you think about royalty. "Yer missed 'is bleedin' 'ighness. That was 'im sportin' off in the TD just now. Bloody supercharged, that one is. Quick as a blink."

"I saw."

"But not near s'quick as *this* little beauty," he grinned, patting the Frazer-Nash on its nose emblem. "She's just got back from Sebring. Florida, y'know. Won the big bloody twelve hour there. Yer probably read about it in the bleedin' papers."

"S-sure," I lied, wondering just what in the hell he was talking about.

"Any'ow," he continued, extending a hand that obviously worked on cars for a living, "I'm the bloke gets most things done 'ere around the Westbridge shop. 'Ow can we be of service, eh?"

I explained as how I was looking for a Jaguar XK120 shop manual, and right away the grin melted off his face and Barry Spline's eyes narrowed down to suspicious catlike slits. "And just why would yer want a Jagyewahr shop manual for, eh?" So I told him about Old Man Finzio's Sinclair and Big Ed's Jag and the fouled plugs and clouds of black smoke belching out the back, and as I did, Barry Spline's lips spread out in a mean little sliver of a smile. "Starting carburetor," he snickered.

"What?"

"The thermostatic actuator fr'the bloody starting carburetor. You'll find out."

"I will?"

Barry Spline nodded. "As a general practice, we don't h'encourage the h'untrained to h'attempt maintenance or repairs on Jag-ye-wahr automobiles. Company policy, you know. But seeing as 'ow you're way over in Jersey, and seeing as 'ow it's only one bloody car...," his eyes swept around the shop, "and seeing as 'ow I've got more flippin' work than I know what to do with, I suppose we might be able to make an h'exception. Just don't let 'is bloody 'ighness know about it, eh?"

I nodded. "Mum's the word."

"Right. Just step over t'the parts counter and ring the bell. Our Spares Consultant will be only too 'appy to 'elp yer out."

So I went over to the parts counter and rang the little bell and who pops up on the other side of the parts counter but Barry Spline. Only now he's wearing a *white* shop coat. "'Ow can I 'elp yer, sir?" he says with a perfectly straight face.

"I want a shop manual for an XK120," I tell him again, "You know that."

"Shop manual for an hex-kay-one-twenty," he says real slow, rubbing his chin like he's mulling it over. "I'm h'afraid we're fresh h'out of stock at the moment."

"All right," I said, measuring my words carefully, "when do you expect you might have one?"

Barry Spline the Spares Consultant rubbed his chin some more. "Most normally, we don't sell Jag-ye-wahr shop manuals to the public at large. Matter of general company policy." Then he leaned over the counter and added in a near whisper, "You h'understand, of course...."

"Oh, of course," I nodded, not exactly sure that I did. "But you said yourself it was just one car, and that it's way over in Jersey...." I was starting to get a little annoyed, you know?

"Ah, well," he said with an elaborate sigh, "I suppose we *could* put one on order for yer, seeing as 'ow its just one bloody car, and 'ow it's way over in Jersey...."

"Gee," I told him, trying not to grind my teeth, "that'd be *real* swell of you."

"Takes h'about six weeks...h'unless yer wanter pay Air Freight, that is."

"Air Freight is fine."

"Payment in h'advance, of course."

"Oh, naturally."

So I handed over a large wad of Big Ed's folding money and, after making a few quick mental calculations, Barry Spline returned to me a quarter, a nickel, and a few pennies in change. Judging from the price, they must write those Jaguar shop manuals on parchment from the Dead Sea Scrolls. Then I asked for a receipt so I could prove to Big Ed that I hadn't bought myself a gold watch or maybe booked a private railcar to Atlantic City. Barry Spline acted sort of offended that I'd ask for such a thing, but then he shrugged one of those home town New Yorker shrugs --what can you do?-- and dashed one off longhand on a piece of ordinary plain white notepad paper he had sitting on the counter. "There you are, guv'nor," he cooed through the self-satisfied grin of a man who has really put the screws to a fellow human being, "that oughter do yer up right and proper. And willyer be needin' anything else terday?"

"Yeah," I growled, doing a slow burn right in front of him, "can anybody here tell me how to keep one of these damn Jaguar shitcans *running?*"

Barry Spline stiffened up a couple notches. "If yer 'ave a *specific* sort of a problem, yer might be able t'take it up with the Shop Foreman."

"And just where do I find the Shop Foreman?"

"One moment, eh," and Barry Spline the Spares Consultant (white coat) vanished, only to reappear a few seconds later as Barry Spline, Shop Foreman (blue coat). "What seems ter be the trouble, guv'nor?"

It took me awhile to get the gist of things, but the basic deal around Westbridge was that Barry Spline/Spares Consultant and Barry Spline/Shop Foreman had to be *paid* separately. See, you could buy any sort of Jaguar part you wanted from Barry-in-white (as long as you were willing to pay a left nut for it --in advance, of course-- and then wait around until the Twelfth Of Never to get it) but then you still had to pay Barry-in-the-blue-coat for whatever information, advice, and/or encouragement it took to get the damn thing properly installed. And we're not talking about offhand tips like the fivers Big Ed palmed off, either. Barry-in-blue charged "consultation fees" whenever he could get away with it, and he'd even write you up one of his plain white paper notepad "receipts" if you wanted one. At least if Colin St. John wasn't around to see him do it, anyway.

But once he'd relieved me of all the loose cash I had on my person, Barry Spline lightened up considerably and actually took me on a tour of the Westbridge shop --one mechanic to another, you know. "Yer've gotter h'understand about sportscars," he explained, waving his hand through the air. "The people who buy them could all drive bleedin' Cadillacs if they wanted. Cars like that great bloody black sedan yer rolled up in." His eyes glazed over just thinking about Big Ed's Sixty Special. "Oh, those are some marvelous smooth cars, Cadillacs are..." --you could tell Barry Spline really admired Caddies-- "but that's not what these flippin' sportycar people want. Oh, no! They claim t'*like* the 'ard ride and the 'eavy steering and enough bloody 'eat through the floorboards to roast bleedin' chestnuts. These people *h'enjoy* the engine racket and picking insects out of their 'air after every bleedin' run t'market. And believe me," he said, raising an important finger towards the rafters, "they absolutely *live* for the roadside breakdowns and h'expensive repairs...," Barry Spline looked me squarely in the eye, "...and do you know *why?*"

I shook my head.

"Because they're all bloody *masochists!*"

"They're *what?!*"

"Masochists."

"What the hell are masochists?"

Barry Spline licked his lips and thought for a moment. "Before intercourse, 'ave yer ever been tied down to a bed with red silk ropes and 'ad some fine young thing go over yer private parts with an eggbeater?"

I couldn't say as I had.

"Neither 'ave I," he said wistfully, "but the point is that a masochist is someone who *h'enjoys* things like pain, suffering, and humiliation."

I looked it up in my aunt's dictionary when I got home, and Barry Spline was telling the truth.

Honest he was.

Chapter 5: Invasion of the Colonies

Colin St. John first came to these United States of America in early 1946, carrying a slight limp that was a souvenir of The Big One and deep, empty pockets he intended to fill with Yankee greenbacks. He was a tall, elegant-looking English gent with a gold-topped cane, leather patches at his elbows, and the aristocratic bearing of a stiff buggy whip. Colin always wore one of those snappy English tweed caps "whilst motoring in an open car," and was forever puffing away on this big curlycue Swiss pipe with little silver dangle-chains and perforated tin breeze lids. I thought it was the coolest thing I'd ever seen. And the way he talked! Like a blessed Duke or Prime Minister or something. Why, it made you feel like some kind of crude New Jersey Neanderthal slob just listening to him.

Turns out the disappearing act Colin pulled that very first time I drove up in front of the Westbridge shop was part of a carefully orchestrated scheme he worked on every new customer. By vanishing the moment a virgin prospect appeared, he set the idea in motion that he was a *very* busy guy who really didn't *need* any more damn business --thank you very much-- but, if you wanted, you could wait around for a chance opening to appear in his *frightfully* busy schedule (pronounced shedge-yewel). You did have an appointment, didn't you?

I witnessed that performance many times over the next several months, on account of I got to be something of a regular at the Westbridge Motor Car Company, Ltd. Seems like I was forever dropping by for a few parts or some of Barry Spline's "consultation" to keep Big Ed's Jag running right. Or just running, if you want to get really technical about it. Not that the XK120 was a *bad* car. Hell, no. Why, that Jaguar was the most magnificent automobile I'd ever worked on in my entire life. But it was kind of *fussy,* you know, and needed to be stroked and petted every now and then to keep it in perfect condition. And perfect was the only way Big Ed wanted *any* of his cars. It got to where Old Man Finzio didn't mind too much, either, since Big Ed was paying him a small fortune for my time (including those frequent trips across the George Washington bridge into Manhattan) and that's not even counting the fivers Big Ed was palming me on the side every time I passed a wrench over his Jag. Which was often.

So I got to know Barry Spline and Colin St. John pretty well, and spent an awful lot of time listening to Colin tell exciting sportscar stories and stirring World War II adventures in that fancy British accent of his. Once Colin saw you were spending some serious cash in the Westbridge parts department, he'd flash you a sneaky behind-the-hand wink and draw you off to the side for a semi-private snort of scotch. Especially if it was around lunchtime or towards the end of the day. Colin kept a couple small souvenir glasses from Niagara Falls and a dark green bottle of Glen-something-or-other single malt scotch hidden behind the service counter (where everybody and his brother knew exactly where it was) and it was a sign that you had indeed joined the Inner Circle at Westbridge when Colin St. John asked you to "share a swifty" with him. "Care for a swifty, Sport?" he'd say, pouring a couple quick shots down Niagara Falls. Personally, I thought Colin's fancy single malt scotch tasted an awful lot like mineral spirits, and suspected he might be topping up the bottle from time to time with whatever was on sale at the liquor store down the street. So I put a little pencil mark on the label one day when Colin wasn't looking, and would bet you a double sawbuck he's got that same damn bottle today, still precisely two-thirds full of the cheapest rotgut Scotch, Irish, Rye, Canadian, or Old Kentucky Sour Mash whiskey he can lay his hands on. He doesn't believe Americans can tell the difference....

Like everyone else in England, Colin St. John had a rough time of it during World War Two. That's where he got the stiff-legged limp he carried around all the time (and which sometimes --I swear!-- seemed to move from one leg to the other) along with the most vivid and astounding collection of personal, first-hand, eyewitness combat war stories you ever heard in your life. A couple snorts would get him rolling anytime: Up against Rommel in North Africa! Barely scraping out at Dunkirk! Taking on Goering's Finest in a shot-up Spitfire! Cheating death with the Bomb Disposal lads! They were all *true,* too. Every single one of them. That's because Colin heard them all with his own two ears in the hospital ward where he spent the great majority of 1942 and 1943 after falling off the liftgate of a truck in a dark London alley one night while unloading a shipment of black market creamed chipped beef. I guess it was touch and go for awhile, and there was some question as to whether Colin would ever walk again (before the war ended, anyway) but a Luftwaffe bombardier brought about a miracle recovery late one evening when he accidentally dropped a 1000-pound incendiary smack on top of their hospital wing. Colin amazed the entire staff by being first man to the far side of the lawn, handily beating out an army surgeon who'd been something of a track star at Cambridge.

After the war, Colin St. John journeyed to America to seek his fortune (or anybody else's fortune that might be available --he wasn't real particular in that respect) and opened up his first little back-alley foreign car agency on the west side of Manhattan. It was just off the George Washington bridge, and for that reason Colin decided to name it Westbridge (get it?) and the moniker was just *perfect* for a lah-de-dah British sportscar shop, on account of it sounded properly Upper Crust, blue-blooded, and snooty. Jaguar customers expected that sort of thing.

Colin's business at Westbridge grew and prospered over the years in spite of high prices, shoddy service, and the business ethics of an Armenian rug merchant. That was mostly because every single playboy, sugar daddy, and black sheep heir in the greater metropolitan New York area just *had* to have himself one of those sexy new Jaguar sportscars. Or at the very least an MG. As Colin made sure to explain repeatedly to every new sales prospect: "A true *sport* requires a true *sportscar*," and the rich, trendy, fashionable types around the greater metropolitan New York area were all ears.

The Westbridge agency sold just about everything that crossed the Atlantic at one time or another (including such gems of European automotive artistry as the Renault Dauphine, BMW Isetta, Hillman Husky, Borgward Isabella, Singer Gazelle, Simca Aronde, Citroen Traction Avant, Humber Super Snipe, and the usual assortment of Fiats) but Colin's main stock in trade was always Jaguars and MGs. Business was better than good, and Westbridge moved to larger quarters in 1951 and again in '57. Colin St. John made himself a *lot* of money during the 1950s.

But success in the car business came naturally to Colin, on account of he grew up "in the motor trade" (as he called it) and knew all the ropes to pull, fancies to tickle, and angles to shoot.

His father had owned a garage near London that sold rough, high-mileage Rolls Royces and Bentleys to people who probably should've bought a new Ford instead, and Colin learned at his father's knee that the only important thing in *any* automotive transaction was the split between how cheap you could buy and how high you could sell (after bumping out a few dents, patching over the rust, and covering it all with a quick-and-dirty respray, anyway). Barry Spline told me a great story about a particular gentleman (or would-be gentleman) who bought a well-abused Bentley from Colin's dad, then tried to return it the same afternoon after hitting a pothole at speed and knocking a chunk the size of a league football out of the rocker panel. Underneath was nothing but a gigantic rust crater filled with chicken wire and wadded-up newspaper. As you can imagine, the guy was pretty upset. *"Look at THIS!!"* he screamed, waving his fists under Colin's father's nose. *"You told me this car was in absolutely PERFECT and PRISTINE condition!"*

"Oh, and I truly thought it *was*," Colin's dad told him, real sincere and disappointed-like. "The agent I bought it through has always been *total*ly reliable in the past." He wrung his hands as though his entire faith in human honor and decency had been savagely trampled to the earth. "Just *imag*ine," he continued soft-ly, shaking his head, "the scoundrel swore up and down it came from an estate sale in the North. Told me this motorcar belonged to a third cousin of Duke of Windsor himself! Why, to think *any*one would have the brass to patch up a *Bentley* with putty and old newspapers...."

"OLD??" the guy bellowed, grabbing Colin's dad by the necktie and yanking it towards him. *"Why, this is YESTERDAY MORNING'S BLOODY FIRST EDITION!!"*

Of course, Colin's dealership in Manhattan was entirely dif-ferent from his father's used car garage in England, on account of the new car and used car businesses were, to use Colin's own words, "as different as chalk and cheese." After a few shots of scotch, he'd explain at length how "every *used* car is unique --has its own character, its own perfume, its own *romance*-- while every *new* automobile is essentially i-*dent*-i-cal to every other blasted one they push off the bloody assembly line. The only real differences are color and trim."

"So?"

"So, indeed!" Colin would snort, tamping a fresh wad of Cavendish into his pipe. "The price of a *used* car is governed only by the glimmer in a chap's eye or the faintly detectable quickening of his pulse, whilst the profit on any *new* car is sadly subject to the eternal, inevitable, and wholly inescapable laws of supply and demand."

Colin St. John understood the laws of supply and demand, and that's why he kept every shipment of new Jaguars stashed quietly away in a windowless meat truck garage on the other side of town. All except one, that is, which he would place on the little 12x16 oriental carpet in front of the fake maple partition that more or less separated Colin's "showroom" from the rest of the Westbridge shop. You had to be impressed with the way every single XK120 Colin St. John sold was "absolutely the last one in the country." And he wasn't above taking multiple deposits on that one new car in his possession (or even futures on "the next one coming in") and using the money for general operating expenses. Plus there was *always* a story. A little romance. Like fr'instance: "This par*ti*cular example was ordered for the Earl of Buxton. He summers in the Hamptons, don't you know. But the poor chap was killed in a hunting accident before he could take delivery. Happened just a fortnight ago. *Most* unfortunate business. On safari in Africa with his new bride, as I understand it (don't think she was a day over eighteen --it was *quite* the scandal in the House of Lords) and the poor devil got himself trampled to death by a bull elephant. Bloody gun jammed. A shame, really. And the lads in Coventry worked *so* hard to match that precise shade of royal blue from the family crest."

Colin's trendy, upscale New York customers ate it up.

But the *real* money at Westbridge didn't come from selling cars. No sir. It was in the maintenance and repair business they generated once those Jags and MGs were out the door and prowling the streets. Because if there was one thing a Jaguar or MG needed with great regularity, it was to be fixed. Especially if it belonged to some lah-de-dah country club rube who grew up on a diet of substantial American cars like Caddies and Packards and Lincolns and such, and even more especially if it spent a lot of time scuffling around in bumper-to-bumper Manhattan traffic.

Inevitably the more cars Colin sold, the more sick ones came stumbling and coughing and wobbling their way through the Westbridge service entrance, desperately in need of attention. Tuneups, lube jobs, carburetor balancing, valve adjustments, timing chains, clutches, brakes, wheel bearings, tires, generators, starters, wiper motors, heater blowers, replacing gearbox syn-chros, decarbonizing cylinder heads --it was all money in the bank to Colin St. John. Easy money, too, since Colin wasn't above cutting a few corners, and fully appreciated the incredible ignorance of stylish, high-line New Yorkers when it came to any sort of actual nuts-and-bolts mechanical stuff. For example, fastening up a simple loose wire could be good for the price of a brand new starter, so long as you kept yourself a can of shiny black spray paint stashed behind the service counter.

The hard part --*always*-- was finding decent, competent, reliable mechanics who could actually fix the damn cars. In fact, the most amazing single thing about Colin's shop was the stagger-ing turnover of wrenching personnel I witnessed as the weeks and months passed by. Barry Spline was always there and seemed to be sort of a partner in the business (or maybe "accomplice" would be more like it), but the two or three bodies shuffling and clanking their way around in the back of the Westbridge shop changed names and faces faster than a movie-house marquee. Then again, I suppose it was difficult to find topnotch foreign car mechanics who could meet the many stringent employment re-quirements of the Westbridge Motor Car Company, Ltd. To begin with, you had to be foreign. It didn't matter exactly what *kind* of foreign (except for maybe Eskimo) but it was absolutely essential to have an exotic look about you and some sort of impossible-to-understand offshore accent. Part of the Westbridge image, don't you know? Plus not just anybody could learn how to fix cars The Westbridge Way. For example, not many mechanics know how to repair a car so it runs absolutely *perfect* when it leaves the shop, yet assure that something totally unrelated will break, fail, burn out, or fall off within a maximum of two weeks time. And a Westbridge employee had to uphold the time-hon-ored Westbridge tradition of returning every single car with at least two greasy handprints on the leather upholstery and a minimum of one gooey smear of non-hardening Permatex matted into the wool carpeting. Most important of all, a job could never

--*ever*-- be finished on time. Colin was a real stickler about that, since it was the very cornerstone of the carefully nurtured relationship between the Westbridge Motor Car Company, Ltd., and its trendy, upscale, New York clientele. Due to these rigorous standards (not to mention low pay and lousy working conditions) the Westbridge technical staff amounted to an endlessly rotating parade of thickly accented grease monkeys that included, at one time or another, a Graham, a Raoul, a Miles, a Vito, an Ian, a Hans, one each Martine and Bjorn, two Hugos, a Philippe, and even a Juan. All in less than a single year.

And then there was Sylvester. Sylvester Jones. He was a colored guy from the edge of Harlem who worked at Westbridge on-and-off from the very beginning. Sylvester didn't have much in the way of formal automotive training, but he was a natural-born handyman who'd lived out of a toolbox most all his life, and hard experience had left him with a real keen practical sympathy for machinery. Even Uncle Sam's Army recognized Sylvester was awful good, and they had him wrenching away on everything from Jeeps to tanks to night fighters to the broken jukebox in the officers' club bar during World War II. Honest to God they did. Why, Sylvester Jones could fix damn near *any*-thing. But then the war ended and he got his discharge, and it didn't take long before Sylvester Jones discovered that he was shit out of luck as far as finding any kind of civilian job with a title, a future, or even a decent take-home wage was concerned. Sure, a lot of it was on account of he was colored, but part of it was also due to the fact that Sylvester was a mean, surly, argumentative son-of-a-bitch with a bad attitude and a little bit of a drinking problem. Not that Sylvester Jones ever saw drinking as a problem. No sir. He considered it more of a hobby.

Then again, Sylvester Jones had a lot of things to drink about. His wife was already on the chubby side when they got married a few years before the war, and she'd put on another two or three pounds every single month while he was away in the service (and Sylvester was gone more than two whole years). So she was not exactly the kind of woman you daydream about coming home to (unless your tastes run to the fat lady at the Barnum and Bailey circus, that is). And the cute little twin babies Sylvester left behind had likewise turned into a sticky, bawling, foul-smelling pair of toddlers. Plus it wasn't long before his big fat wife had herself another set of twins on the way. "Sheee-it," Sylvester'd shrug with a bewildered sense of pride, "Ah jus' shoots doubles ever' damn time. It mus' be in the genes here, see," and he'd nod towards the bulge under his zipper like it was a prize bowling trophy or something.

But there wasn't much legitimate mechanical work around town for a handy colored guy with special jeans like Sylvester Jones --just cruddy factory jobs and stuff-- so he kind of split up his time between drinking half-pints of sweet wine and fixing broken-down cars to sell on the cheap in Harlem. Sylvester made pretty good money doing that, but it wasn't steady and every now and then his lardass wife would get after him to pound the pavements and find himself a job with a regular weekly paycheck attached. In fact, it was on exactly such an expedition that Sylvester happened to be wandering past the old, back-alley West-bridge garage one early Tuesday afternoon in 1949, just about the time Barry Spline was attempting to yank a stubborn transmission out the bottom side of a Jaguar Mk. V sedan. Barry worked pretty much alone in those early days, and just between you and me, he was never real good at grunt jobs. Oh, he could tune an engine up sharp as a razor or true a wire wheel until it'd spin like a damn electric motor, but when it came to the heavy, knuckle-busting ins-and-outs of mechanicing, Barry Spline was better off letting somebody else do it. Which is exactly what must've run through his mind when that Jag tranny unexpectedly popped loose and landed right on top of him, pinning him underneath the car. *"HELP!HELP!HELP!HELP!"* he screamed into the cast iron driveshaft flange that had come to rest directly across the bridge of his nose. Sylvester heard the commotion and wandered in to see what all the fuss was about, and in two shakes he had that car jacked up a foot higher, freed up the shifter where it was snagged on the carpeting, unscrewed the speedometer cable, and dragged both Barry and that Jaguar transmission out by the heels.

He was hired on the spot.

Of course, Barry could only offer Sylvester Jones a position as a car porter at Westbridge, on account of he was colored. That went without saying. Now car porters are the guys you see knocking around the backside of all car dealerships, washing cars and cleaning floormats and changing license plates --you know,

nigger work-- but it wasn't long before Barry Spline and even
Colin St. John realized what a highly talented guy Sylvester Jones
was when it came to tools and automobiles. He *understood* sick
machinery, and could usually see right through the blackened oil
and busted metal to the root cause of every breakdown and failure. And *nothing* intimidated him. Not Jaguar valve adjustments
or Bentley bottom ends or anything else on earth that had anything whatsoever to do with four wheels and an internal combustion engine. "They's alla same upside down," he'd explain with a
wolfish smile, "jes' like wimmen."

And, although Sylvester Jones' official title remained "car
porter" for all the many years he worked at Westbridge, he was
the best damn all-around sportscar mechanic they ever had. And
everybody who worked there knew it.

"I say, Sylvester, could you pop over and 'ave a look at the
voltage regulator on the One-Twenty in my stall?"

Sylvester'd be lying on a creeper under some Jag or MG, and
he'd always kind of sputter when he talked on account of he
inevitably had the butt end of a Lucky poking up out of the
corner of his mouth, dribbling ashes into his eyes. "Aw shit,
man, jus' push the damn blade down. Same as on m'old Plymouth parked in the lot out there. Sheee-*it!*"

And Graham or Raoul or Vito or Martine or whoever would
wander back to the car they were working on and know what to
do next --even if they hadn't the slightest notion why.

To be perfectly honest, Sylvester Jones wasn't a particularly
nice edition of a human being. He had a mean streak a mile wide
and didn't like anybody 'messing with him'. "Don't mess with
me," he'd tell Graham or Raoul or Vito or Martine or Barry
Spline or even Colin St. John himself. And, if they knew what
was good for them, they wouldn't. In that respect he was a lot
like Butch (although Butch would've given anybody a solid punch
in the nose for suggesting he had anything at all in common with
any sort of colored person).

Sylvester's dark moods came and went like the weather, and
probably had something to do with his shitty job, his 360-pound
wife, his four kids, his occasional side girlfriends, a mean dice
habit, and most especially drinking the old sauce. Every so often,
Sylvester'd get himself a king-sized thirst worked up and decide

to more or less disappear for a few hours. Or days. Sometimes a week, even. But he always came back. And each time he came back --regular as clockwork-- Colin St. John would fire him. I swear, Colin must've fired Sylvester Jones an average of once or twice a month. "You're bloody *FIRED!!*" he'd holler at Sylvester, his cheeks going all ruddy pink. "Do you *understand??!!*"

"Fine wit' me, man," Sylvester'd sneer back. "Dat's jes' *fine* wit' me. Sheeeee-*it!*" and he'd shuffle off down the sidewalk, mumbling and grumbling to himself. Then Colin would look around at all the sick automobiles cluttering up his shop and wonder how the hell he was going to get the damn things fixed without the advice and assistance of Sylvester Jones. So when Sylvester stumbled in a few days later to pick up his tools and his last paycheck --eyes all yellow and bloodshot, hands shaking just a little, Lucky Strike dangling from his lower lip-- Colin would inevitably be prepared to grant him "one last chance. Just *one more.*" Sylvester'd nod and grunt and blow his nose in his hand while Colin rambled on (like it made a damn difference, you know?) and then they'd shake on it and Colin'd head for the can to wash the snot off his hand while Sylvester went back to fixing whatever needed to be fixed so he could earn enough money to take care of his family, his girlfriends, his dice game, and maybe disappear with a bottle again the next time he felt like it.

I learned most of what I know about fixing fancy European sportscars from Sylvester Jones. Oh, he'd never really sit me down and *tell* me stuff, you know, but if I didn't get in his way and asked the right questions --like fr'instance why Big Ed's Jag was fouling all its plugs and blowing sooty black clouds out the tailpipe-- he'd first off snarl and growl and shake his head like I was some kind of prize-winning moron, but then he'd take the time to show me what was wrong and explain how to fix it. Barry Spline couldn't always do that. Not even for money. When Barry talked, he wrapped everything up in that snooty brand of English they use in the British shop manuals, and sometimes I got the impression he didn't really know what the hell he was talking about. But Sylvester could pick up something --like the S.U. carburetor body that was sitting on his workbench the very first day I met him-- and explain how it worked in language an ordinary knucklehead wrench-twister from New Jersey could understand. I remember he stuck one lumpy, calloused finger into the throat of that S.U. and worked the piston up and down in the vacuum chamber so I could see how the tapered needle moved up and down in the jet seat, giving more fuel as the engine inhaled more air. It was simple, really. Then Sylvester showed me the starting carburetor, which was nothing but a little electric solenoid doohickey on the rear float bowl that let extra fuel directly into the intake manifold to richen up the mixture when the engine was cold. *That's* what was making Big Ed's Jag run rat and foul its sparkplugs all the time. The damn solenoid wasn't shutting off like it was supposed to when the engine warmed up.

Like I said, it was *simple*.

Really it was.

Chapter 6: Julie

Big Ed was pretty thrilled when I finally got the starting carburetor problem sorted out on his Jag, and he decided to give me a little reward. Believe it or not, he lent me the white Caddy convert one Saturday night so I could take Julie out on the town. Honest to God he did. Like I explained, Julie and me had gotten kind of chummy with each other around the station, but we'd never had what you could actually call a date. One reason is I never got up the nerve to ask her, but a lot of that was simply on account of I didn't have a car to pick her up and take her anyplace. Needless to say, my old man wasn't about to lend me his Mercury after I ditched his dumbass union job and went to work at the gas station, and you'd have to be a real doofus to ask a girl to *walk* to the movies. Especially at the drive-in. Then this one Saturday afternoon --right out of the blue-- Big Ed handed me the keys to the white Caddy and said, "Why doncha take that Julie out someplace nice, huh?" and slipped me a couple sawbucks to take care of expenses, too. You don't find many guys who'd do a thing like that for their garage mechanic. "Have a swell time, kid," Big Ed grinned as he climbed into the Jag (which was purring like a well-fed tomcat, if I do say so myself) but before he pulled out the overhead door, Big Ed grabbed himself a fistful of my shirtsleeve and gently added: "You put so much as one tiny *scratch* on that Cadillac of mine and I'll cut yer goddam head off at the neck an' use it for a bowling ball."

He would, too.

I watched Big Ed's Jag squeal away up Pine Street, leaving a hot streak of rubber and a good six months' worth of clutch lining behind it, and then I was standing there all alone with two crisp, neatly folded tenspots in the palm of my hand and Big Ed's Cadillac keys dangling from my fingertips like a live baby water moccasin. Truth is, I think I might have been just a little nervous. After all, inviting Julie out on a real, live date was a lot different than just goofing around with her at the gas station. I mean, what if she turned me down? So I bought myself a soda out of the cooler and drank it real slow while I worked on getting up the courage to call her, and I must've dialed her number and hung up two or three dozen times before I finally got up the nerve to let the call ring through. And once I got her on the line, I spent an awful long time hemming and hawing and beating around the bullshit before I gathered up the gonads to take a deep breath and ask her point-blank if she perhaps might sorta possibly be interested in a real sit-down dinner --with waiters and cloth napkins and everything-- and then maybe a show or even a cruise along the shoreline over to Palisades amusement park in Big Ed's Cadillac convertible. I made sure to mention that shiny white Caddy twenty or thirty times, and to my everlasting surprise, Julie said *yes*. In fact, she sounded real eager to go (although there was really no way of telling if it was because of me or because of Big Ed's Cadillac). "Oh, yeah, that sounds *great*, Buddy," she just about gushed, "pick me up around seven."

Oh *boy!*

"And Buddy..."

"Yeah?"

"Wash your hands real good, okay?"

So I hustled like mad to finish the Olds muffler job I had up on the lift (wouldn't you know it, muffler jobs are the *dirtiest*) and then took a good half inch off the bar of Lava soap in the john trying to get all that rusty, gritty, exhaust-pipe grunge off my hands. After that I spread a bunch of old newspapers across the front seat of Big Ed's Caddy so's I could drive over to my folks' house without my head winding up as Big Ed's bowling ball. No question a date with Julie required a real Major League bathroom with shampoo, scented soap, clean towels, Brylcreem, and underarm deodorant (not to mention freshly washed socks and undershorts and a neatly ironed shirt) and the sad fact is not *one* of those items was regularly on tap in the apartment over my Aunt Rosamarina's garage. Not hardly.

Truth is, I felt pretty damn smug as I wheeled Big Ed's shiny white Caddy into the driveway by my old man's house, and I was even a little disappointed that I didn't see his car in the garage. I was kind of hoping the rat bastard would be home, you know, just to see the expression on his face. So I left Big Ed's Caddy parked right smack dead-center in the middle of the drive, where my dad would have to drive clear *through* it if he wanted to get that precious piece-of-shit Mercury of his into the garage.

Nobody answered when I knocked on the front door, so I circled around back and found my mom in her usual position, standing on tiptoes at the kitchen window with her field glasses pressed up against the glass. She was watching a squadron of her dirty brown twitterbirds flitting around the garbage cans (real exciting, huh?) but stuff like that got my mom so wrapped up she wouldn't hear the phone ring or even somebody knocking at the front door. No question she was in another world when it came to those stupid birds of hers. That's why I decided to sneak along the outside wall (like Jimmy Cagney in one of those old black-and-white gangster movies) and crouch myself down beneath the kitchen windowsill. When the timing seemed about right, I just sort of *popped up* in front of her binoculars and went into a little bird dance of my own, flapping my arms and scratching for worms and making noises like a duck caught in a hydraulic press.

It got a pretty good rise out of her, no lie.

Like always, my mom seemed real happy to see me (once she got her breath back, anyways) and of course nothing would do but that I try some of her famous Dutch Apple pie --a la mode, natch-- while she told me all about the nice young couple of Baltimore Orioles who were building a nest *right in our back yard!* To hear my mom tell it, this was the biggest news to hit our neighborhood since the old widower Pasquinelli had a heart attack and died right there in his living room window. I think Mr. Pasquinelli was about eighty-five or ninety at the time, and the poor guy had been living all alone in this big stucco house on the other side of Monroe Street ever since his wife passed on. You'd see him there all the time, sitting in a big overstuffed chair with a blanket over his lap and a glass of iced tea at his side, looking out his living room window at the trees and the kids on their bicycles and the neighborhood dogs peeing on the local fire hydrants. That's why a whole week went by before anybody much noticed how he just *sat* there in the same exact position --morning, noon, and night-- without changing his pajamas or getting up to take a leak or *anything*. Finally the postman started wondering why Mr. Pasquinelli's mail was backing up in the chute, so he tiptoed around the bushes and took a good look through the window, and he couldn't help noticing how old Mr. Pasquinelli was all sort of puffy and purplish and didn't even blink when he tapped real hard on the window glass.

So the mailman called the cops, and next thing you know a bunch of Medical Emergency-types in white uniforms showed up and carted poor old Mr. Pasquinelli away in an ambulance. Naturally they had the lights flashing and siren wailing (not that there was any particular hurry any more) and since it happened on a Saturday afternoon in the middle of August, all the neighborhood kids swarmed around that ambulance like it was a Good Humor ice cream truck or something. Only the smell was more like bad hamburger meat than any kind of strawberry milk shakes or toasted almond bars.

But we were talking about my mom's Dutch Apple pie a la mode, weren't we? Well, it was better than scrumptious --as usual-- and I swear my mom would've kept feeding me fresh slices and telling me all the latest hot bird gossip until my gut burst and my ears fell off, but of course I was in something of a hurry (to say the least) on account of my big date with Julie. So I excused myself somewhere in the middle of a story about three sweet little wrens and a cantankerous bluejay and went upstairs to shower, shave, put a few dabs of Brylcreem on my hair, and sneak some of my dad's Old Spice after shave out of the medicine cabinet. He never used the stuff anyway. Besides, *I'm* the one who gave it to him every year for Christmas.

Speaking of my old man, I heard him pulling into the drive just as I was buttoning the shirt my mom ironed for me, and I couldn't wait to see the look on his face when he got a load of Big Ed's Caddy parked in the driveway. But the weasel didn't so much as lift an eyebrow. Typical. "Who left that kikey road barge in front of my garage?" was all he wanted to know, looking around the kitchen like there was maybe somebody else in the room besides my mom and me. What a jerk. But I guess he was still pretty burned up about how I blew off his wonderful chemical plant job and moved into that apartment over my Aunt Rosamarina's garage. You know how parents can nurse a grudge.

I left my folks' house in plenty of time to cruise over by the liquor store on Fremont and wait around for one of the many wobbly regulars who'd pick you up an extra pint or sixpack in return for a small monetary consideration. Being Saturday night, it didn't take long at all, and pretty soon I was tooling my way over to Julie's mom's place with a smile on my face and a fresh pint of Bacardi dark in the glove compartment. Along the way, I kept thinking about what it would be like to kiss Julie Finzio --right on the lips, you know?-- and one time this lady in a blue DeSoto looked over at a stoplight and caught me with my eyes half-closed and my lips all puckered up. I had no choice but to pretend I was whistling along with Bing Crosby singing "Count Your Blessings" on the radio.

Julie and her mom lived in an apartment on the second floor of an old frame house over on Fourteenth, and if you ask me, the place really could've used a little fixing up. Or at the very least a fresh coat of paint. But the guy they rented from was one of those two-bit, broken-English real estate tycoons who are mort-gaged up to the asshole in one or two shitty buildings and claw-ing for every last nickel so they can someday get it up to three or four. Naturally I felt like some kind of uptown Knight In Shining Armor pulling up to the curb in front of that dump in Big Ed's freshly waxed Cadillac. I beeped the horn, of course, just so's everybody on the block would be sure to take a gander out their windows, but then I walked up the steps and rang the bell, too. I mean, I didn't want Julie's mom to think I was one of those greaseball hoods who waits for a girl out in the car.

Luckily it was Julie who answered the door (thank goodness) and boy oh boy, did she ever look *great!* Her face was so fresh and bright it almost seemed to glow, and she was wearing this sleeveless yellow Angora sweater that really, you know, *clung.* And believe me, Miss Julie Finzio had some really interesting stuff for a tight sweater to cling to. I saw her mom kind of hover-ing around in the background (you know how girls' moms do), giving me the old hairy eyeball like I'd just finished biting the head off a live chicken. Julie's mom was a short, wiry, tough-looking Italian woman with penciled-in eyebrows and a big, stiff hairdo that was too black and shiny to believe. "Yooda boy from my brudderenlaw's gas station?" she wanted to know.

"Yes, I..."

"What kinna future you ever gonna have inna lousy job like dat, hey? Workin' in alladat grease and filt'?"

"Oh, *mom!*" Julie groaned, grabbing me by the elbow and hustling us out to the car.

"You take carra my girl Joolie, you hear?" Mrs. Finzio holl-ered after us. "She gotta be home by eleven."

Jee-*zus!* She sounded just like my old man, you know?

"Sorry about my mom," Julie said once we were in the car and safely on our way.

"Aw, that's okay," I told her. "My folks are the same exact way. Sometimes I think parents must have these secret meetings where they do nothing at all but swap ideas for new and better ways to embarrass their kids."

Julie laughed at that and squeezed me on the arm. Boy, it sent a charge through my system like I'd stuck a couple straight pins in a wall socket. Honest to God it did.

Thanks to Big Ed, I had enough ready cash to take Julie just about anyplace at all in New Jersey. New York, even. But all she wanted to do was to cruise over by the Doggie Shake and show off a little in front of the other girls. And I had to admit, Julie and me looked pretty damn sharp in Big Ed's white-on-white Caddy convert, sitting there on all those yards and yards of creamy-soft leather with the top down and the wind rustling through our hair and the radio bringing in Nat "King" Cole so loud and clear you would've sworn he was crouched in the back seat. *When I fall in lovvveee, it will be for eveerrrrr....*

About two blocks from the Doggie Shake, Julie out-of-the-blue did something that nearly caused us to have a serious accident. Without saying a single word, she suddenly slid herself across that huge front seat so she was sitting right next to me. I mean *right* next to me. I felt the soft heat and weight of her all up and down my body and my nostrils filled with the smell of her perfume, and of course that's precisely when I damn near drove us squarely into the rear end of a city bus that was stopped to pick up passengers. *"Hey!"* Julie yelped, "be careful, willya?"

"S-sure, Julie. You know me...."

"Yeah," she snickered. "*Suuure* I do. My uncle says Big Ed's gonna use your head for a bowling ball if you hurt this car."

"Aw, that's just what he *said* he'd do."

"You think he really would?" Julie giggled.

"Well," I told her, "Big Ed's never given me a reason not to believe he wouldn't do something he said he was gonna do...."

"Huh?"

"Let's just say I'd rather not find out."

"Sounds like a wise plan to me."

"Besides, I don't think my head would make too good of a bowling ball. Too lumpy."

"Yeah, you'd probably hook to the right. And your holes look a little too small for Big Ed's fingers."

"We could always use a reamer."

"A *what?*"

"You know, a reamer. Like you use on valve guides. To open up the holes a little."

"That's disgusting."

"And we could maybe try an orbital sander to take down some of the high spots."

"Like your nose, for example?"

"Yeah, like my nose."

"No, I think I like that head better the way it is," Julie said through her best movie magazine smile, "it's such a *nice* head."

"It is?"

"Yes, it is," she whispered in my ear, and gave my thigh a little squeeze for emphasis. All by itself, Big Ed's Caddy picked up five or six miles-per-hour, and I knew right then there was no way on earth I could climb out of that car and walk into a damn restaurant. Not for awhile, anyway. But we were in luck and found ourselves a curb-service slot right smack in front of the Doggie Shake, and you should've seen all the pointing and tittering going on inside when the other girls got a load of Julie and me in Big Ed's Cadillac. Sure, I was in love with his Jaguar, but there's still an awful lot to be said for a shiny white-on-white Caddy convert parked stage-center at the local burger shop on a warm summer Saturday night. Especially with somebody as hot and pretty as Miss Julie Finzio sitting right there beside you --smiling like a prom queen-- holding an oliveburger with all the trimmings in one hand and a root beer with a quarter-pint of rum in it in the other. Everything seemed so damned *perfect,* you know? Which, as I have come to learn from countless bitter personal experiences, is almost always the way things feel just before they go straight to hell....

After we left the Doggy Shake, Julie and me cruised up the parkway towards Palisades amusement park, polishing off the last of the rum-laced root beer along the way. I had my arm around her shoulder and she sort of let her head lean over so I could feel her hair brushing against my cheek, and even though I'd filled

Big Ed's Caddy clear up to the top (with Ethyl, no less) I would've gladly kept driving around like that until the very last drop drained through the fuel line. But all too soon we arrived at the amusement park and had to get out. That was a hard thing to do, if you catch my drift.

With Julie Finzio by my side and a wad of Big Ed's greenbacks burning a hole in my pocket, naturally nothing would do but that we rode all four roller coasters --one right after the other-- not to mention the Flying Turns and the Flash Gordon Sky Scooters and visited every single concession stand along the midway for caramel corn and peanut pralines and chocolate fudge and even a butterscotch ice cream sundae shoveled in on top of the oliveburgers, onion rings, and spiked root beer we'd already packed away. We were having a swell time --no lie!-- and I kept asking Julie if she wanted to go on the Tunnel of Love boatride with me. I figured I might maybe get a kiss off her back there in the darkness where nobody could see us. But Julie wasn't having any part of it, on account of one of her girlfriends told her she'd seen a rat in there once. Heck, it was probably just a mouse, you know? But there was no talking her into it, so I switched tactics and steered us over towards the ferris wheel. If I couldn't get her into the Tunnel of Love, I thought perhaps I could do some good when the ferris wheel stopped way up there at the very top, high over the midway in the nighttime summer sky. Just the two of us. All by our lonesome.

It didn't quite work out that way.

Now, you've probably been to an amusement park once or twice and noticed how slow and stately and graceful a ferris wheel looks from the far end of the midway. In fact, you'd swear they were powered by the world's smoothest-ever fluid drive. But climb aboard one of those suckers and you quickly discover that they clank and creak and scrape and shudder something awful whenever they start and stop. And the damn things have to start and stop every twenty seconds or so to load and unload passengers. So it takes absolutely for*ever* for your average, large-scale amusement park ferris wheel to go all the way around. Which, as far as I'm concerned, leaves a person entirely too much time to look down at the ground --*waaaay* down at the ground!-- and likewise glance around at all the corroded, rust-infected rivets, guywires, clevis pins, and turnbuckles that are *supposed* to hold a ferris wheel together. Confidence inspiring they are not. In fact, if you have any sort of mechanical aptitude whatsoever, those things can get you very nervous indeed. To make matters worse, there was a pretty stiff breeze blowing in off the Hudson that particular night, so all the gondolas were swaying back and forth, baack and forth, baaack and forth....

Which is probably why Julie's face suddenly turned the same shade of green the East River gets in the middle of summers. Just as we were closing in on the very top. "Hey, Julie" I asked her, "you feelin' okay?"

She opened her mouth to answer, but all that came out was this sickly sort-of groan, followed shortly thereafter by approximately five whole dollars worth of oliveburgers, onion rings, root beer, rum, and assorted candy snacks. Fortunately she managed to blow most of it over the rail, but unfortunately it landed directly on the gondola car just below us. Jee-*zus*, you should've heard all the yelling and screaming. Those people were *very* unhappy. Pretty vocal about it, too.

After she was finished up-chucking, Julie sagged back into the seat, not looking especially well at all. I noticed her face had changed color again (this time to a sort of chalky off-white) and she was gulping for air like one of those freshly caught flounders you see on the Jersey pier. "Hey, Julie?" I whispered gently (while still making sure her head stayed pointed in the opposite direction), "you feelin' allright?"

She half-nodded, wiping off her chin.

"Do you think you can walk?"

She looked at me with this blank expression.

"How 'bout *run?* Huh? Julie?? Do you think you can *run?*"

Julie didn't understand what I was driving at, but the instant we hit bottom, I grabbed her hand and took off down the midway as fast as I could go, dragging her behind me like a coaster wagon with a busted wheel. We sure as hell didn't want to be around when that next gondola car hit ground level. Not hardly.

Poor Julie got sick once more out in the parking lot (before we sat down in Big Ed's Caddy, thank goodness!) and, needless to say, that first date with Miss Julie Finzio didn't quite turn out the way I'd hoped and planned. In fact, I even took a pass on our first good-night kiss.

You would have, too.

I remember Julie made herself pretty scarce around the Sinclair for a few weeks after that. Embarrassed, you know? And I can't say as I blamed her. For sure it was a long, long time before I could kid her about that night on the ferris wheel at Palisades park and get a laugh out of her instead of dagger-eyes. That didn't stop me from doing it, though. But Julie was a good sport --she could *take* it-- and that's one of the reasons I got so excited when she said she'd think about going out with me again. Even if I didn't have Big Ed's Caddy to tool around in! *Wow!* Of course, I never knew if it was because Julie really *liked* me or just because there wasn't much of anybody else her age around the station for her to hang around with or date. But, whatever the reason, Julie and me started going out to the movies and stuff pretty regular on Friday and Saturday nights.

As you can imagine, Old Man Finzio wasn't real keen about me dating his niece, and he made it clear he'd knock one of Big Ed's Caddies off the jackstands while I was working underneath it if "anything happened." And for a long time nothing did. But that wasn't for lack of trying on my part. On the other hand, the Old Man *would* let us borrow his scruffy old Dodge towtruck every now and again when I couldn't get my hands on one of Big Ed's off-season Caddies. But I had to beg and plead and crawl on my belly like a damn reptile any time we wanted to use it, and the Old Man made me fill the damn thing up with gas, too --out of my own pocket, natch-- and you can bet your ass the needle was stuck on dead empty any time he felt like letting us use it.

Saturday-night dates with Julie usually started off with a movie show or maybe a round or two of miniature golf, and afterwards we'd head over to Weedermen's for cokes or malteds and a couple orders of french fries. Julie didn't especially want the girls from the Doggie Shake to see us in her uncle's beat-up old towtruck. But every now and then, when I'd fixed up his Jag extra nice, Big Ed would borrow me one of the Caddies, and then Julie and me would hit the Doggie Shake in *style*. Maybe even take in a movie at the drive-in. No way would she do anything like that in Old Man Finzio's towtruck.

In fact, that's where we kissed for the very first time. At the drive-in. I remember we were in Big Ed's black Sixty Special sedan (the one with the extra-thick windows) watching some dimbulb bible movie with Victor Mature in it. I couldn't follow the story too good, on account of I had my arm around Julie and she was sort of nuzzling her forehead into my neck, and that of course made the action in the front seat of Big Ed's Cadillac *lots* more entertaining than watching Victor Mature parade his biceps around in what looked like a used beach towel. During one real boring scene, I kind of leaned over into Julie's hair and my lips sort of grazed her left eyebrow --hell, I wasn't really aiming or anything-- and all of a sudden her face rolled up into mine and we were *kissing!* Boy, she was one hell of a good kisser (in fact, I kind of wondered where she picked it up) and that's about all we did for the next two hours. Of course she wouldn't open up her mouth to french kiss or anything on account of she was a good Immaculate Conception girl, but to tell the truth I wasn't sure I knew exactly how to do that anyway. Then we came up for air this one time and there were headlights flashing and horns honking all around us. The damn picture had been over for ten minutes! It was kind of embarrassing, you know?

After that night, making out in a parked car became sort of a regular part of our dates (and, not too surprisingly, it was the part I looked forward to the most). In fact, it got to where I was thinking and daydreaming about making out with Julie all the time. And I mean *all* the time. It never failed to get me all hot and bothered --just *thinking* about her, you know-- but I'd also get this strange, dry-mouth queasy feeling at the same time. And every time I dreamed up something really vivid and sexy about Julie, I'd always feel sort of ashamed and guilty about it after- wards. It's a sure sign your brain is suffering from some kind of major pulp disorder when you start feeling guilty about your blessed daydreams....

Anyhow, most Saturday night dates would usually wind up with Julie and me parked out back behind the Sinclair after the show was over, kissing and groping and wrestling around in the two-by-four cab of Old Man Finzio's towtruck. It wasn't the most accommodating place you could imagine for that kind of thing --not hardly!-- what with the floor shift sticking up in the middle and the steering wheel so close you couldn't really get two normal size human torsos wedged in behind it (and no way would Julie ever let us get much more than 15% off vertical plumb). But it was dark and quiet back there behind the Sinclair, and at least nobody could see us from the highway. That was real important, on account of Julie didn't want any flack from her mom or uncle about being, you know, one of those *easy* girls. Plus I sure as hell didn't fancy the thought of one of Big Ed's Caddies falling on my skull. Or his Jaguar, for that matter.

A couple times I asked Julie if she wanted to maybe come over to the apartment above my Aunt Rosamarina's garage, but no way would she even consider it. Personally, I couldn't see the difference between making out in the Old Man's towtruck and making out in my apartment (except that my apartment would've been a *lot* more comfortable) but Julie had some kind of Major Distinction about it. Girls *always* have Major Distinctions when it comes to making out. For example, they all seem to have these Invisible Boundaries laid out across their bodies --like the Great Wall of China, you know?-- so that touching one spot can pass for Acceptable Behavior, while a half-inch further south amounts to Criminal Trespass. You figure it out. But I had to admit Julie's makeout boundaries were a lot closer to pay dirt than any of the other girls I'd known. Then again, the girls I'd known before didn't exactly represent a true cross-section of national public opinion. Either one of them.

Anyhow, Julie and me would park there out back behind the Sinclair and start kissing and stuff --boy, could she ever *kiss!*-- and pretty soon she'd have me worked up into a genuine, grade-A hormone frenzy. It took all of about thirty seconds on your average Saturday night. Then Julie would just sort of *hold* me there --right on the brink of explosion-- for as much as forty or fifty minutes at a stretch. I guess she was going for some kind of new world record. But whenever I'd get really, *really* desperate (like when I started peeling the chrome moldings off the dashboard with my fingernails) she'd all of a sudden back off and make that whimpering little "please stop" noise all the girls knew how to make back in the fifties.

You remember.

And that's when she'd sit up, straighten her skirt, brush out her hair, and say something like "Gee, Buddy, it's getting *awfully* late...," as if nothing was going on at all! Can you believe it? I'd plead and beg and grovel and drool all over my shirt, but once Julie decided it was time to go home, there was no changing her mind. So I'd wind up driving her back to her mom's apartment, grinding my teeth into powder the whole seven blocks, and when we pulled up in front she'd always give me one last, long, wet, deep, lingering, Hollywood-style kiss, after which she'd lean up and whisper "I had a *wonderful* time, Buddy" directly into my ear and maybe even run her tongue lightly down the lobe after it. Just to drive me nuts, you know? I don't know where the hell she learned that trick, but the effect was about equal to pouring a bucket of molten-hot lava in my lap! By the time I got back to the apartment over my Aunt Rosamarina's garage, I damn near needed a cold chisel to get my shorts off.

Julie sure knew how to get me *hot,* no two ways about it.

Chapter 7: Manual Labor

Fortunately, I found something besides Julie Finzio to keep my mind occupied during that spring and summer of 1952 (which was a good thing, since otherwise I might've worn out some of my more precious and vital body parts). But everything changed the day Big Ed's copy of the official Jaguar Factory Service Manual arrived --airmail, no less-- all the way from Coventry, England. It was bound in dark maroon leather (or maybe it was leatherette, but so good you couldn't tell the difference) with an embossed Jaguar logo on the front and fancy gold lettering like an Encyclopedia Britannica. It was thick as a damn encyclopedia, too (and not one of those skinny little volumes like "I" or "V" either). I started taking it home after work every night and reading it before I went to sleep like it was a detective story or something. Then I'd bring it back to the Sinclair each morning and leave it in the john, so I could thumb through it a little more whenever I had some time to myself (if you know what I mean).

To tell the truth, that Jaguar Service Manual was harder to figure than any highschool textbook I'd ever come across, on account of the English speak a somewhat different brand of English than we use here in Jersey. Like fr'instance, a *"hood"* in Passaic, New Jersey, is a *"bonnet"* over in England. And a *"hood"* over there is what we call a *"convertible top"* here in the States. And that's just the tip of the damn iceberg, as they say both places. I learned that an open-end wrench was really "a *spanner,"* and that a Jaguar XK120's "petrol gauge," "screen-wiper switch," and "revolution counter" were mounted on a *"centre facia"* rather than an ordinary Jersey-style dashboard. A muffler was "a silencer" (at least that one made sense) while a trunk was "a boot," a fender was "a wing" (go figure) and a piston fastened to its connecting rod with "a gudgeon pin." What we call a generator in American English was "a *dynamo"* in English English, and on top of that English cars were "positive earthed" instead of negative ground like normal automobiles. Sometimes it seemed like the Brits did stuff just to be *different,* you know? As if hanging around Jaguars made you part of some kind of private social club with special, split-finger handshakes and secret insider passwords....

But the biggest kick of all was the way that Jaguar Shop Manual described routine repair procedures. Such as:

Fit a new felt washer into each recess in the striking rod holes at the rear of the cover. Thread the plate over one or other of the outside rods and slide the rod into the cover, not forgetting to fit the change-speed fork before the rod enters the front hole in the cover, until it occupies the neutral position. This can be checked by looking through the grub screw hole on top of the cover and aligning the neutral groove in the rod under the hole. Enter the other outside rod in a like manner through the plate in the change-speed fork, into the neutral position. Place an interlock ball in the groove in each rod using the centre hole to gain access to the rods which are already in position. Fit the interlock plunger in the hole of the centre rod and pass the rod, through the plate and the change-speed fork, into position. Fit lock bolts to the three change-speed forks and lock with new wire. Fit stop pins to first/second and third/fourth top striking rods and lock with new wire.

Whaaa? Or try this one:

The torsion bars, which are 52" (127cm.) long, are positioned along the inner vertical faces of the chassis frame side members. Both ends of the torsion bar have raised splines, a reaction lever with companion splines and clamp bolt being attached to the rear end while a splined muff is fitted to the front end. The reaction lever is forked and the forks are supported on a trunion positioned by an adjusting barrel nut and bolt, the bolt being attached to the chassis frame. The splined muff at the front end is spigoted and bolted to the inner end of the lower wishbone lever.

Sure thing. But even if some of it read like Sanskrit, other passages in that Jaguar Service Manual were downright elegant. For instance:

Attention to the following points of maintenance will be amply repaid by satisfactory operation of the engine and will materially add to the life of the unit.

Pure poetry, right? Made you feel like putting on a jacket and tie before you ever touched a wrench to one. Or maybe a judge's robe and a powdered wig might've been more appropriate, since a Jaguar mechanic had to:

Check the top face of the cylinder block for truth.

But my overall personal favorite was:
Offer up the camshaft sprocket to the flange....
It sounded like some kind of pagan sacrifice, you know?

Of course, Big Ed's Jag didn't really need any heavy-duty fixing down in its iron and alloy guts (it was damn near brand new, for gosh sakes!) but I enjoyed reading all that stuff anyway, and figured the information might come in handy some day. Anytime I got stuck on an unfamiliar word or a strange, weird-ass explanation, I'd dream up an excuse to cruise over by Westbridge and have a talk with Sylvester. I'd usually come by around noon, so I could treat him to lunch (which was a half-pint of sweet wine every day but Friday, when he switched to rock n' rye to sort of kick off his weekend) and it never failed to amaze me how Sylvester could listen to my questions, take a pull off his bottle, and turn all those highbrow Limey paragraphs into a couple simple grunts, shrugs, and finger-circles in the air that an ordinary knuckle-buster from Passaic could understand. Sylvester was really special that way.

The Westbridge shop always got super busy in the springtime, on account of that's when all the Jaguars and MGs came out of hibernation and started running around New York, New Jersey, and all up and down the New England seaboard with their tops down and gas pedals mashed clear to the floorboards. That inevitably resulted in a whole shitload of burnt-up clutches, shredded gearbox synchros, broken engines, pretzelized suspension pieces, and assorted electrical malfunctions requiring immediate --and expensive-- service attention. As you can imagine, that made springtime Colin St. John's absolute favorite time of year. In fact, his repair shop got so swamped that Barry Spline even offered *me* a job. Honest to God he did. I was real flattered, you know, seeing as how I didn't have much in the way of a foreign accent. But I had to turn him down. I mean, who wanted to fight traffic in and out of Manhattan every morning and night (especially considering I didn't own a car, which makes fighting traffic more difficult under any circumstances). Besides, there were some undeniable advantages to my situation at Old Man Finzio's Sinclair. Like fr'instance I was pretty much my own boss at the gas station (as long as I got the work done, anyway) but I could see how the deal at Westbridge was more like my old man's chemical plant job. You had to punch a damn time clock at Westbridge --even to go out for lunch!-- and take a lot of guff off Barry Spline and Colin St. John whenever they felt like dishing it out (which looked to be a pretty regular occurrence, best as I could figure). Plus I was still doing my wrenching out of Butch Bohunk's toolbox, and it just didn't seem right to pack up all his gear and haul it off to another garage in another state, even if it *was* just across the bridge into Manhattan. But I'd have to admit the most important thing was that they didn't have anybody like Miss Julie Finzio hanging around the Westbridge Motor Car Company, Ltd., and no question that was a major consideration as far as I was concerned.

So I begged off. But I did it in a thoughtful, proper, forthright, and gentlemanly fashion. In other words, I lied right through my teeth, telling Barry some bullshit story about how I was taking care of my poor old sickly maiden aunt Rosamarina back in Passaic and how it just wouldn't *do* for me to be way over in Manhattan every day in case she needed me for anything. It was a total load of crap, of course, since about all I did around my Aunt Rosamarina's house was haul the garbage cans out to the curb whenever the smell of used kitty litter back behind the garage got strong enough to make your eyes water and ears ring. But I knew it was important to decline Barry's offer in such a way that he'd keep me in mind in case things ever, you know, *changed*. After all, you never want to burn your Westbridges....

Turns out I made the right move, because who should roll into the Sinclair a few days later but my old pal and mechanical mentor Butch Bohunk. And I do mean rolls. The poor bastard was still laid up in a wheelchair, and none other than Mean Marlene herself was doing the pushing, wearing her usual, grumpy, "I'd rather be *any*place else" scowl and a pair of bright turquoise slacks about four sizes too small for her. Gee whiz, they made her butt look like a pair of bright blue party balloons filled with butterscotch pudding. Honest they did. And Lord only knows how she ever got them on and off. But fat and nasty as she was, Marlene still looked one hell of a lot better than Butch. One of his legs was still in plaster clear up to the hip --sticking straight out in front of him like a damn concrete post-- and he had big, dark sunglasses over his eyes to cover up some of the purplish-red scar tissue that spiderwebbed all over his face. I guess that's what happens when your head goes through a windshield. "Hey, Butch," I hollered through a pasted-on grin, "long time no see. How'ya doin'?" Not that I really meant it, you know, since even a moron could tell that old Butch wasn't doing very good at all. Not hardly.

"Aw, I'm doin' real fuckin' great," he grunted, extending a hand with most of the fingers missing. It was nothing more than a thumb and a bunch of blunt, crooked little stumps, and felt like a big lump of Easter ham when I shook it.

"So," I said, still staring at his hand, "Howz things?"

"Couldn't be better, Buddy, couldn't be better," he told me, working up half a smile. "But I don't guess I'll be playing no concert piano anymore."

"I guess not."

"Hey, what the hell. I can still pick my nose, wipe my ass, and beat my meat. What more could a guy ask?"

"Not a thing, Butch. Not a thing."

"You got that right."

"And how're *you* doin'?" I said to Marlene, trying my best to be polite.

"Somethin' wrong with yer eyes, honey?" she answered in her high, hillbilly twang. "Anybody kin see I'm havin' me the time of my en-tire life here, wheelin' *this* fat asshole around town like a blessed shopping cart." I guess Marlene wore out her welcome back home in Tennessee (not hard to imagine at all) and decided to come back once she found out Butch was laid up in a wheelchair and couldn't go traipsing off to the bars anymore (which also meant he also couldn't stay out all night with his tavern buddies or come home drunk and give her a hard time, either). Fact is, the poor guy couldn't even fight back if she took a notion to pop him one. Which I'm sure she did from time to time. Not to mention that Butch was getting some pretty decent disability benefits every month off an insurance plan he had through the Veteran's Administration, and no question that made him a lot more desirable as far as Mean Marlene was concerned.

We shot the shit for awhile --just small talk about car stuff and old times, you know-- and behind the dark glasses I could see Butch's eyes sweeping around the shop like a prison searchlight, checking out the tools and workbenches and car projects in progress. Since he showed up right out of the blue, I didn't have a chance to tidy the place up or put his tools away or anything (which is probably just exactly what he had in mind, you know?) but I'd been doing things the way Butch taught me, and the service bays didn't look too bad at all. At least if you didn't count the big new charcoal smudge on the ceiling directly above where Old Man Finzio tried to braze the filler neck on a Buick radiator without taking it out of the car and managed to set the carburetor and engine wiring on fire. Outside of that, the shop was pretty well squared away (if I do say so myself) with all of Butch's tools packed neatly away except for the 3/8ths-drive ratchet and a few specific sockets, extensions, and box-end wrenches I needed for the Pontiac head gasket job I was working on. After Butch'd checked it all out, he allowed me a nice little half-nod of approval. "So," he wanted to know, "how're things goin' fer you?"

"Real good, Butch. Real good."

"I hear you been workin' on a coupla those Jag-warz."

"Just one, Butch. Big Ed Baumstein bought himself one of those XK120 Super Sports roadsters. White with red leather. Wait'll you see it."

"That fat hebe. You an' the Old Man'll rake in a pisspot fulla money off of him. Them fuckin' Jag-warz needs work alla damn time from what I hear."

"They sure do," I nodded. "But gee whiz, Butch, when you get everything just right and they're *runnin'....*"

"Yeah," he sighed, "I 'spect they're pretty slick, all right."

"'Course, Old Man Finzio can't *stand* 'em."

"Figures."

"Yeah."

"Hey, that reminds me. I heard you been dickin' his niece." Boy, I turned bright red. I mean *bright* red. Hell, Marlene was standing *right there*, you know? But she didn't so much as bat an eyelash. In fact, she hardly even seemed to notice. "So," Butch repeated, "you been puttin' the old pork t'Julie or not?"

"Jeez, Butch," I gulped, "it's not like *that....*"

"Oh, *sure*, honey," Marlene snorted, giving off a dirty little knife-blade of a laugh. I guess she was listening, after all.

Butch and me shot the breeze some more after that, just stuff about the car jobs passing through the shop and all the latest mechanical disasters Old Man Finzio had gotten himself into around the station. That was always good for a couple laughs. But then we sorta ran out of things to say and it suddenly got real quiet --like it always does whenever you're around sick friends who aren't likely to get much better-- and for the longest time the only sound was a soft hiss off some leaky air compressor line someplace in the back of the shop and the rumble of the cars and trucks rolling past out on the highway. I got to wishing one of them would pull in for gas or directions or something, you know?

"Say," Butch said at last, "where the hell is that old fart Finzio, anyway?"

"Aw, he's out chasin' parts or something."

"Good. I can't stand that sonofabitch."

"Aw, he ain't so bad."

"Sure he is," Butch grinned. "That old bastard's gotta be the worst God Damn tight-ass, mean-streaked, camel-faced, angry-at-the-whole-damn-world son-of-a-bitch you ever met!"

"You know," I said, mulling it over real slow like I was giving it careful consideration, "you're probably right!"

We both got a hellacious good laugh off that one.

"Well," Butch said, wiping a tear out of the corner of his eye with the back of his bum hand, "you be sure and tell the old prick I stopped by."

"Sure will, Butch."

But as he started to turn his wheelchair around and head out the overhead door, Mean Marlene stopped him with a hard cuff to the back of the head. "*Ask* him," she hissed none-too-silently in his ear, "like yew promised yew would...."

"Aw, Marlene, he don't know...."

"I SAID *ASK* HIM!"

Butch squirmed around in that wheelchair like he wanted to crawl off under a car someplace and die, but old Marlene had her mind made up and jammed him another good shot in the ear to get him going. You could see it made all the air drain out of Butch, sort of like an innertube with a bad leak, and he had to clear his throat a couple or three times before he got around to actually speaking. "Uh, lissen, Buddy," he finally mumbled, staring down into his lap, "would'ja maybe do me a little favor when the Old Man comes back?"

"Sure, Butch. Anything you want. Just name it."

Then his voice went down so quiet I had to bend over right next to him to make it out. "Would'ja mind askin' the Old Man if he can maybe use a lil' help around the station here? Part time, even. I can still do lotsa stuff...."

"Sure you can," I told him.

"Yeah," he sighed in barely a whisper, "sure I can."

There wasn't much of anything to say after that, and I caught myself listening to the cars out on the highway again. Like you listen to the sound of the ocean in a seashell, you know? But then Butch shook it off and flashed me a grim shadow of the nasty, rugged old smile he used to whip out all the time around the Sinclair. "Well," he said, "me an' Marlene here gotta be gettin' along. We got stuff t'do...."

"A'course you do, Butch."

"You takin' good care a'my tools, boy?"

"Sure am, Butch. You know that."

"You damn well better had."

Then Marlene started rolling him off towards the street, but all of a sudden I got a bright idea. "Say, Butch," I yelled after him, "maybe I oughta be *paying* you something for those tools."

Butch grabbed the wheels with both hands and spun that wheelchair around, angry as all getout. *"What th'FUCK makes you think I'd wanna sell you my God Damn tools?"*

"N-nothing, Butch," I stammered. "I mean, that's not what I meant. Not at all, Butch. No sir."

"Well, that's sure what th'fuck it *sounded* like."

"Geez, Butch, I just thought, you know, like maybe I oughta be *payin'* you, I dunno, some kinda *rent* or something."

"Rent?"

"S-sure," I said. "After all, I been using your tools for quite awhile now. Maybe I oughta be payin' rent fer 'em, doncha think? I mean, it's only fair...."

Butch thought it over, rubbing his chin with his bad hand. "Naw," he said finally, shaking his head, "I don't think I'd feel real happy about that. You just take care a'them tools until I'm ready t'use 'em again."

"Honest, Butch," I told him, "I can afford it. I'm doin' *real* good here at the station these days."

"I 'spect you are, Buddy. I 'spect you are. But I'm doin' okay, too. I got some money comin' in from the V.A. disability insurance and stuff. Fact is, I got more now than I ever had when I was workin'. Can't get out t'the damn tavern anymore an' spend it. Ask Marlene."

"Sure thing, honey," she cooed, real sarcastic, "Ol' Butch here is one *hell* of a provider these days...."

"Ah, button yer lip, y'old bag."

"Or else *what*, jerkoff? Yew planning t'button it *for* me?"

Butch arched up like he was gonna take a swipe at her, but Marlene simply stepped back out of range and there was nothing Butch could do but paw a few times at the air in front of him. Finally he slumped back in his wheelchair, slowly shook his head, and for the first time lifted those armor-plate sunglasses over his forehead. "Lissen, Buddy," he said, staring me right square in the eyes, "it ain't just about money, see."

"It isn't?"

"Hell no, it ain't. A man's gotta *work,* Buddy. He's gotta get out of th' damn house an' *do* something. Life ain't worth two shits just sittin' around with yer dick in yer lap." And with that, Butch turned the wheelchair around so Marlene could grab the handles and wheel him off down the street.

In a heartbeat they were gone.

I told Old Man Finzio about Butch's visit when he got back from his parts run, but decided that I had to be sort of honest about the shape Butch was in. I mean, there was no point lying about it, right? So naturally the Old Man wasn't real keen on hiring him back. And, to tell the truth, I couldn't really blame him. Sure, I felt bad about it, but it was just one more lousy deal in life that I couldn't do a single God Damn thing about. It seems like the older you get, the more of that shit you run into.

Chapter 8: The King Kong of Sportscars

We had sort of a warm spell towards the middle of May where the temperature soared up to damn near eighty for a couple days, and right on cue, Big Ed's XK120 started overheating anytime it got stuck in traffic for more than a few minutes at a stretch. It wasn't one of your steaming, gurgling, car-disabling boil-overs, but rather one of those edgy, irritating deals where the needle on the temp gauge creeps up into the Worry Zone and the engine starts skipping and stuttering at idle on account of fuel is percolating someplace in the fuel pump, gas lines, or float bowls. As you can imagine, that aggravated the living hell out of Big Ed --hey, he wanted his cars *perfect*-- so he brought the Jag over early one Tuesday evening for me to check it out. But of course it was cooler then and naturally Big Ed's 120 ran like an absolute charm and never missed a beat. Happens every time.

"Aw, this G-goddam thing," Big Ed sputtered. "If Cadillac built cars like this, they'd be outta God Damn business."

"I'm sorry," I shrugged, "but I can't find anything wrong at all, Mr. Baumstein. She seems t'be runnin' fine."

"Oh, suuurre," he grumbled. *"Now* th' damn thing runs fine. Purrs like a God Damn kitten. Lissen, Buddy, *you* drive the sonofabitch over t'Westbridge tomorrow. Across the damn George Washington bridge during rush hour. *You'll* see," and Big Ed handed over the keys to his brand new Jaguar XK120 Super Sports roadster. Just like that. Can you believe it?

But of course that meant Big Ed needed a lift home to Teaneck, and believe it or not, he let *me* drive that Jaguar the whole blessed way. Probably wanted to see if I could handle it, you know? As you can imagine, I took it *very* easy, squeezing on the gas like there was an egg under the pedal and getting on the brakes so gently you could've set a line of beer steins on the hood and not lost a drop. But even creeping along like a little old lady, I could tell Big Ed's XK120 was the most exciting piece of machinery I'd ever had my hands on. As you can imagine, I couldn't *wait* to drop Big Ed off so's I could maybe find a nice piece of road and stretch its legs a little.

Big Ed's house in Teaneck was set back at the end of a long, woodsy drive that just about deserved its own street sign, and I swear I'd never seen a place like that in all my life. At least not in person, anyways. It looked more like a country club or a small municipal library than the private residence of an ordinary two-armed, two-legged, shot-and-a-beer human being. Why, it was two stories high and a half-a-block long! And everything on it was all brick and stone --all different kinds of brick and stone, in fact-- and there were big marble columns in front and one of those rounded turret deals right in the middle with one of those strange pin cushion tops like you see on Russian Orthodox churches. In fact, there were fancy architectural doodads *all over* Big Ed's place, including a bunch of carved stone gargoyles staring down from the corners of the roof and a pair of mean-looking concrete lions flanking the main entrance on either side. Across the driveway from the lions was this big oval fountain with green ceramic carp spouting water at one end and a little bronze boy pissing off a rock at the other. Wow! To be perfectly honest, I thought Big Ed's house was just a tad, you know, *overdone* for a private home. But it was sure as hell impressive, no two ways about it.

And of course Big Ed had a special sort of place for all his automobiles. Around the side of his house was an *attached* five-car garage --all brick, natch-- with Big Ed's two Caddies off to one side, an empty slot for his Jag right in the middle, one of the maroon-and-gold GMC half-ton pickups from Big Ed's scrapyard up against the wall, and the current Mrs. Baumstein's butter-scotch-yellow Chrysler convertible in the remaining stall beside it. The Chrysler was one of those handsome "Town and Country" jobs with the real honest-to-goodness wood trim, and even though it was two years old (same as Big Ed's marriage to this particular Mrs. Baumstein) you couldn't tell it from brand-spanking new. Big Ed allowed as how he wanted to buy her one of the brand new '52 Packard converts, but the reigning Mrs. Big Ed wouldn't hear of it because she was so fond of the snazzy solid maple trim on her Chrysler. I kind of liked it myself, and could never figure why Chrysler decided to shitcan the Town and Country wood-work for the '51 model year. When you get right down to it, Chryslers were big, fat, lardy-looking cars that needed all the dress-up help they could get.

Nobody around the Sinclair had ever met Big Ed's wife (I mean, Big Ed never brought her around when he dropped any of his cars off for service or anything) and I have to admit I was more than casually curious as to just what kind of woman a guy like Big Ed Baumstein might marry. Not to mention vise-versa. But I begged off when Big Ed invited me in for a bite to eat, seeing as how I was still wearing my greasy mechanic's coveralls and Big Ed's house did not exactly look like the kind of place where a guy with a full day's garage work spread all over him could plop down in an old swivel-backed chair, prop his feet up on a soda case, and scarf himself down a bottle of Coke and a hamburger sandwich. Not hardly. Besides, I had *better* things to do. After all, it was fine spring evening and I had the keys to Big Ed's XK120 Super Sports roadster burning a hole in my pocket...

Who needed to eat?

I took it real easy on the way back to my apartment --just getting the feel of things, you know-- and spent a few seconds in my aunt's driveway to disconnect the Jag's speedo cable (it's easy on an XK120, you just reach behind the dash and unscrew the fitting) so I could maybe go for a little midnight spin without anybody being the wiser. Then I went inside to shower, shave, and put on the freshest shirt and pair of pants I could find. I mean, you don't want to go cruising in a gleaming ivory-white Jaguar roadster while looking and smelling like some sort of blue-collar working stiff who changes oil, adjusts valves, and greases kingpins for a living, now do you? Even if that's exactly what you are. Anyhow, I walked down to the corner grocery store after I got myself all spiffed up and gave Julie a ring from the pay phone to see if maybe she'd like to join me for a late-night Jaguar prowl down the parkway. But her mom answered (what else?) and no way would she even consider it. In fact, she flat refused to put Julie on the line at all and proceeded to give me a real major league earful on account of I called so late. You know how that goes with girls' moms.

So there was nothing to do but take Big Ed's Jaguar for a spin all by my lonesome. Which was okay too, but not near as nice as sharing it with someone like Julie. Especially considering it was such a perfect spring night, what with the smell of new green things in the air and just enough chill so's a person could really appreciate the soft waves of heat rolling up off the Jag's firewall and transmission tunnel. I remember the Manhattan skyline was shimmering over the Hudson like the string of lights on a cruise ship, and I just drove up and down the Jersey shore for hours, enjoying the gutty purr out the Jag's tailpipe, the rich scent of that English leather upholstery, and the taut, *right there* feel through the steering and suspension. Every once in a while I'd double-clutch her down into second and lay into the gas for a quarter mile or so, just to feel that big twincam six uncoil. Boy, it had a *lot* of urge. More than any car I'd ever driven in my life. Fact is, I didn't make it back to my apartment until the sky was already turning light. But who cared? Jaguar XK120 roadsters were just *made* for nights like that.

As you can imagine, I was groggy as hell when my alarm went off at six-twenty-five the next morning, and I had half a mind to shut it off, roll over, pull the covers up over my head, and go right back to sleep. But I'd promised Big Ed that I was gonna drive his Jaguar into Manhattan during rush hour, and by God, that's exactly what I planned to do. Just as soon as I could find the damn keys, that is. And my socks. And my toothbrush. And my cleanest remaining pair of undershorts. Truth is, I was stumbling and bumbling around my apartment like some kind of broken-down Bowery wino that particular ayem, and probably set a new world's record for bumping my head on the rafter beams where the roof is real low over by the bed. But an ice-cold shower and a couple cups of reheated, day-old coffee (*ugh!*) blew out enough cobwebs so's I could climb down the stairs, hop into Big Ed's Jaguar, and take off for the City.

Traffic was packed like a tin of sardines across the George Washington Bridge that morning, and it didn't take but fifteen minutes of bumper-to-bumper, stop-and-go creeping before the needle on the Jag's temp gauge started climbing towards the peg. Yep, overheating all right. No two ways about it. By the time I pulled up in front of Westbridge, Big Ed's Jag was gurgling like a turkey with its throat cut and little wisps of steam were curling out from under the hood on both sides. Barry Spline heard all the hissing and spitting going on out in his driveway and wandered out to see what was up. "Yer drove the bloody thing over 'ere during *rush hour?*" he gasped, watching Big Ed's Jag pee hot coolant all over the sidewalk.

"She's been overheating," I told him, "and Big Ed wanted me t'check her out."

Barry Spline slowly, sadly shook his head, the way mechanics do when you've proved beyond doubt that you have no inherent mechanical sympathy whatsoever. Then he put his arm gently around my shoulder and explained as how there wasn't one God Damn thing wrong with Big Ed's Jaguar. Not one. "Jagyewahr one-twenties over'eat in traffic as a matter of routine bloody operation," Barry said, waving his free hand in the air for emphasis. "Think of it as a Jagyewahr's way of telling yer it rather prefers the open road...."

"But that's *crazy!*"

"Maybe so, mate," Barry sighed, looking me squarely in the eye, "but a bloke's gotter be *sensitive* t'such things if 'e ever expects ter get along with a bleedin' Jagyewahr."

Well, I personally figured there ought to be some way to keep a damn Jaguar from overheating in traffic --like maybe a thicker radiator core or a smaller fan pulley or a different thermostat or *something*-- but Barry Spline refused to even discuss the possibility. Instead, Barry told me to have Big Ed run with the heater on full blast --in the goddam *summertime!*-- anytime he got himself stuck in stop-and-go traffic on a hot day. Better yet was to simply avoid summer commuting in a Jaguar entirely. Boy, Big Ed's face was going to turn the color of a beefsteak tomato when he heard *that* little tidbit of professional Jaguar service advice. So I asked Barry Spline again if we couldn't maybe try this or that with the cooling system to fix the problem, but he wasn't the least bit interested in any mechanical improvements that didn't come directly from the Jaguar factory in Coventry, England. "If there was a better bloody way ter do it," he sniffed, "I'm certain the lads at Jagyewahr would've sussed it out by now themselves." Over the years, I've noticed an awful lot of that head-in-the-sand crap in new car dealership service departments. In fact, it's more or less universal.

While I waited for Big Ed's Jag to cool down, I noticed a real flurry of activity going on in the back of the Westbridge shop. There were more than two dozen cars packed cheek-by-jowl into the service department and no less than five (or maybe even *six*) coverall-clad mechanics climbing all over them. And they were *hustling,* too, which seemed more or less completely out of character considering Colin St. John's normal mode of operation. MGs were getting oil changes, sparkplugs, fresh tires, grease jobs, and what-have-you every place you looked, while Sylvester and Barry were handling the complicated and expensive stuff like valve lash adjustments on a couple Jag 120 roadsters. I noticed Westbridge's latest foreign mechanic (the second of the two Hugos) was bent over that torpedo-shaped Frazer-Nash, trying his best to balance the carburetors. That was no easy task, on account of the Frazer-Nash had a six-cylinder Bristol engine with no less than *three* Solex carburetors, and I remember Sylvester had already advised me that even a single downdraft Solex could give a decent mechanic fits. To make matters worse, the Frazer-Nash didn't have much in the way of mufflers --not hardly-- so Hugo II had his ear jammed right down into the carburetor throats in order to hear them hiss, and listening to the exact pitch and volume of that hiss is the most important part of accurate carburetor balancing. Now Sylvester had showed me my very first day at Westbridge how a wise mechanic could use a length of 3/8ths-inch rubber hose to keep his head a meaningful distance away from an engine while attempting to balance carburetors, but I guess Hugo The Second made a big point of never asking Sylvester for *anything,* and for sure Sylvester Jones wasn't about to offer up advice where it wasn't wanted. Anyhow, it seems the engine in that Frazer-Nash was maybe still a little cold (or per- haps running a trifle rich?) because it backfired something awful --KA-_BANG!_-- and damn near blew Hugo Two's right-side ear- drum clear out his left-side ear. The blast sent him reeling backwards like he'd taken a solid right from Rocky Marciano.

"Oh, this one's a real bleedin' *genius,"* Barry muttered as we observed Hugo the Deuce staggering blindly around the shop, bouncing off cars, lifts, workbenches, floor jacks, and several of the other foreign-accented Westbridge mechanics. "Why, the idiot damn near *killed* Sylvester Jones yesterday. Backed a bloody great Mark Seven inter the TC Sylvester was working under. Almost dumped h'it right off the bleedin' jackstands!" He shook his head disgustedly from side to side. "Took out *both* bloody 'eadlamps on the TC and put a Godawful deep crease in the Jagyewahr's fender. 'E won't be here past week's end, that one won't. Mark my words."

As we watched Hugo 2 trip over a creeper and perform a final, near-perfect chin-first swan dive into a pile of used oil-dry, I had to agree that he was hardly the image of a keen, competent automotive technician --foreign or otherwise. "Why don'cha just *fire* him?" I wondered out loud.

"Bloody can't," Barry shrugged. "Too much flippin' work t'finish by Friday afternoon."

That sounded a little odd, you know, since getting cars back to customers on time had never been much of a priority around Westbridge Motor Car Company, Ltd. Not hardly. "What's the big rush?" I wanted to know.

Barry looked at me like I'd just arrived from outer space. "Bridgehampton," he said simply, like that one word should mean something to me.

"Bridgehampton?"

"Why, the S.C.M.A. races at Bridgehampton," Colin St. John chimed in from somewhere behind my back.

"The *what?*"

"The S.C.M.A.," Colin explained while oh-so-casually filling his curlycue pipe, "puts on a bit of a speed event at Bridgehampton every spring. Real wheel-to-wheel stuff, you know. Many of our best customers compete. It's *quite* the place to be."

"You mean actual *racing?!*"

"Right-o, sport."

Boy, I could feel the old pulse picking up. "Jeez, that sounds *neat!* Say, where the heck is Bridgehampton, anyway?"

Colin pulled a wooden stick match out of his tweed jacket and struck it off the edge of the service counter with a flourish. "Out on Long Island," he said thoughtfully, sucking through his pipe, "near the very tip."

"They got some kind of racetrack out there?"

"We race on the country roads around town, actually. You know, uphill, downhill, left, right, sweeping bends, hairpins...."

"Jeez, don't the locals get kind of, you know, *upset?*"

"Certainly not. In fact, it's something of a major occasion every year at Bridgehampton." Colin leaned back against the doorway and folded his arms across his chest like some kind of high-toned college professor so he could properly elaborate. "The S.C.M.A. chaps have a sort of, um, *arrangement* with the local Lion's Club organization. Charity and all that. Here," he said, pointing to a poster tacked to the back of the fake maple partition between the Westbridge showroom and service department, "see for yourself." Sure enough, right in the middle were two screaming, wheel-to-wheel Jaguar 120s --charging right at you!-- with hundred-mile-an-hour speed lines streaking off the fenders and huge hundred-mile-an-hour dust clouds trailing off behind. Wow! In large type up at the top it said:

ROAD RACES
*** BRIDGEHAMPTON, LONG ISLAND ***
SATURDAY, MAY 24

And underneath the drawing, in much smaller type, it read: *Presented by the S.C.M.A. and the Bridgehampton Lions Club.* And at the very bottom, in the smallest type of all: *by invitation.*

"Say," I wondered out loud, "what the heck does S.C.M.A. stand for, anyway?"

"Why, *Sports Car Motoring Association*, of course." Colin said it like you had to be from under a rock someplace not to know. But I didn't care. I was too busy thinking what a whole herd of Jaguars might look like, barreling flat-out towards a tight hairpin at a hundred-plus miles an hour. Just thinking about it sent a shiver up my spine.

Barry Spline nudged me in the elbow. "Wanter get a look at the winning car?"

"The winning car?"

"Right-o," Colin nodded.

"Hey, wait a minute," I protested, "how can you possibly know it's the winning car if the race doesn't even happen till this coming weekend?"

"I'll lay yer a bloody fiver on it, mate," Barry grinned. "C'mon back and 'ave a bleedin' look fer yerself," and with that, Barry led me back into the rearmost corner of the Westbridge shop. There, hunkered down in the shadows, was the biggest, meanest, *toughest*-looking sportscar I had ever seen in my life. It was slippery jet black with red wire wheels and roughly about the same size and shape as the atom bomb they dropped on Nagasaki.

It looked just as dangerous, too.

"Jee-*zus*, Barry," I gasped, "what the hell *is* it?"

"An Allard J2X, Buddy. Brand new model. Fresh in from England just last week." My God, what a *beast* that car was! The grille was nothing but a huge chromium sneer and there were scoops and vents and louvers chopped all over the place to let the heat breathe out (or cool air in, I could never figure out which) and you couldn't miss how they had the hood buttoned down with no less than five separate butterfly-fasteners and two great wide leather straps, each one hefty enough to harness a prize bull. Whatever monstrous kind of motor was in there, they weren't taking any chances on it breaking out.

"Gee whiz, Barry," I asked in a dry-mouthed whisper, "what the heck kind of motor's *in* that thing?"

"See fer yerself, mate," Barry said with a twinkle in his eye, and set about unbuckling the straps. When he finally lifted the hood, my eyeballs damn near popped out of my skull and rolled clear across the floor. Stuffed inside that black monster was a great, enormous, hulking, three-hundred-thirty-one cubic inch and made-right-here-in-America Cadillac V8. Just like the one in Big Ed's Sixty Special sedan. I flat couldn't believe it!

"B-b-but you said this was an *English* car...," I stammered.

"English as the Queen, it 'tis."

"But this is a goddam *Cadillac* engine."

"Sure as bloody hell is," Barry grinned. "Sylvester and I just finished buttoning 'er in this morning."

"Sylvester and you?"

"Right," Barry nodded. "See, most often the chaps at Allard ship their cars across without engines. That way owners can put in whatever bloody pleases them. Some use Fords and some use Mercurys, but they're all great cracking American V8s. Lots of bloody displacement. Bags of torque. Cheap as hell to run. And reliable as a bloody ten-pound sledge."

I let out a low whistle.

"The owner wanted one of those new Cadillac 331s shoved in this one. Bloody good choice, too." You could see this wasn't any garden-variety Caddy V8, either, what with a twin-carburetor Detroit Speed Equipment intake manifold bolted on top and a bright blue Scintilla Vertex racing magneto sticking up off the back of the engine block.

"What kind of horsepower d'ya think it makes?"

"Well," Barry whispered, looking over his shoulder like somebody might be eavesdropping on us, "we've gotter bored and stroked to damn near six litres, so I'd reckon somewheres around *two-hundred-sixty* at the bloody flywheel," he shot me a wink, "give or take a few."

No question that was one *hell* of a big motor for a 2-seater sportscar. Even a hulking King Kong monster like that Allard.

"Jeez, Barry," I wondered, "is it faster than a 120 Jaguar?"

"Bloody hell *yes!!*" he grinned, elbowing me in the ribs. "Why, just *look* at the bloody thing. There's not an ounce of fat on it! Not one. And do the bleedin' math, mate. Six thumping litres to a tiddly three-point-four? No bloody contest."

Somehow, the idea of anything as tall, blunt, and ugly as an Allard outrunning Big Ed's sleek, sexy, double-overhead-cam-shaft Jaguar didn't sound right at all. Especially with some kind of homegrown Detroit sedan engine under the hood.

Just then Sylvester shuffled over from his workbench carrying a short length of throttle linkage with little ball-end swivel-couplers at both ends. "This been one hell of a fuckin' deal," he growled, shaking his head from side to side. He laid the rod between the carburetors and eyeballed it carefully from several different directions. "Sheee-it," he groaned, "I ain't got this fucker right *yet!*" And with that he headed back to his workbench to shorten it up some more.

Barry pulled me gently over to the side. "We've been working on this bleedin' job three days solid," he told me softly, "and it's been some bloody rough going for old Sylvester there. Why, yer should've *seen* the bloody thing when it rolled through the bleedin' door. Nothing but a chassis and body with a great huge empty hole in the middle."

You had to be impressed with something like that. I mean, I'd never had the nerve (or the opportunity) to tackle anything *near* that ambitious with an automobile. Not hanging around the Old Man's Sinclair in Passaic. See, it's one thing to take a little test drive or listen to the duff sound an engine makes and diagnose what's wrong with a car, then tear it apart, replace the bad pieces, and screw it all back together so it works properly again. No sweat. But building from scratch is something else entirely. You have to be a real *maestro* to get away with that sort of thing.

Every single part has to be measured and figured and cussed at and worried over and adjusted ten kazillion different times before you get it right. If you ever do. And most guys don't....

Anyhow, you could see there was still a bunch of plumbing and wiring and stuff to do on that Allard, and I wondered out loud if they'd ever get the thing buttoned up and running in time for the race at Bridgehampton that weekend. "Yer can bloody bank money on it, mate," Barry assured me, patting one of the Caddy's valve covers. "Why, old Sylvester's near got it licked already, and we've two bloody days in hand. Mark my words, Buddy, yer lookin' at this year's overall winner at the bleedin' Bridgehampton sportscar races." I have to admit, he sounded pretty damn definite about it.

I walked around to the driver's side and stared into the cockpit. "Say, Barry, d'you think I could maybe *sit* in it? Huh? Just for a minute?"

"Sure thing, mate. Climb aboard."

So I opened the flimsy little aluminum door (which was about the size of a cigar-box lid) and eased myself inside. Gee whiz, what a view! The dash cowling was curved in two separate humps like the top of Jane Russell's swimsuit, and there was a little half-moon plexiglass windscreen mounted on top of each one. Speedboat-fashion, you know? Underneath, the instrument panel was all done up in shiny, engine-turned aluminum, and you couldn't miss how they had the tachometer right smack in front of the driver and the speedo way over on the other side where it couldn't do much except scare the living bejeesus out of passengers. What a swell idea! I couldn't find much legroom down in the driver's-side footwell --not hardly!-- but the gas pedal had this nifty little roller-deal on the end so it'd more or less *glide* your foot all the way to the firewall. *Neat!* The steering wheel and shifter were big and heavy (like they came off a damn school bus or a farm tractor or something) and no question it took a lot of muscle and moxie to wheel a brute like this Allard around. Which naturally got me wondering as to exactly what sort of human being was planning to set himself down behind that little plexiglass windscreen come Saturday morning and mash that rollerized gas pedal all the way to the throttle stops. "Say," I asked Barry, "who's gonna be driving this monster, anyway?"

"Tommy Edwards."

"Who's he?" I wanted to know. Hell, I'd never even heard of the guy before.

Colin St. John looked at me like I was a bad smell. "Tommy Edwards," he answered down his nose, "is *only* the premiere Allard driver in the entire United States of America. Perhaps even the world. He's won Bridgehampton two years on the trot now. And the race at Watkins Glen as well."

I nodded like I knew what the hell Colin was talking about. "So," I said, "where'd this Tommy Edwards guy come from?"

"Well, he's English --*nat*urally-- but I believe he makes his home in White Plains these days. Don't know exactly what the fellow does for a living --if anything-- but no question he's one *hell* of a decent racing driver. In fact, he drives for the *fact*ory Allard team at Le Mans every year."

"Le Mans?"

"Over in France, don't you know. Biggest bloody motor race in the entire world. No question about it"

"It *is?*"

"Without a doubt, young man. Without a doubt. Why, it's a full bloody twenty-four hours long --night and day, day and night, you understand-- *flat out* and balls-to-the-wall against the greatest teams, fastest cars, and most daring, skillful, and courageous drivers in the world."

"Wow!" I said, my mouth hanging wide open. "And this Tommy Edwards guy has raced there?"

"Indeed he has, indeed he has. In fact, Tommy most usually shares the ride with none other than Sydney Allard himself. Why, they damn near won the bloody thing outright two years ago. Would've, too, but the transmission gave trouble and the poor devils had to run the last eleven hours with naught but top gear. Rotten luck, that. But they came through to finish second in spite of it. Bloody gallant effort."

"That's *always* the bleedin' problem with Allards," Barry grumbled, "can't find a bloody gearbox stout enough ter 'andle the bleedin' torque. The monsters tend t'tear up whatever sort of cog box yer put in 'em."

"True enough," Colin agreed.

"They're bloody 'ard on brakes, too," Barry added. "An Allard driver either learns to baby his brakes or he bloody well learns t'do without!"

Colin nodded solemnly and I swallowed hard, mulling over the possible consequences of two-hundred-sixty thundering V8 horsepower and no brakes. "Jeez," I mumbled, "this Tommy Edwards guy must be pretty good."

"Oh, he's quite a bit better than *pretty* good," Colin sniffed, looking at his nails.

I laid awake that whole night back in Passaic, just trying to imagine what that twenty-four hour sportscar race over in France might be like. It was pitch-black nighttime, see, with an evil spit of rain in the air, but the racecars were hammering flat-out down the front straight at top speed anyway --the fast ones doing well over one-fifty!-- their headlamps burning furious holes into the night. Then the brake lights would flicker desperately for an instant and you could hear the sound of crisp, gurgling down-shifts as one car after another slowed for the upcoming corner. And there *I* was, standing on the pit wall with stopwatch in hand, keeping track of the opposition. Then suddenly this Allard came thundering out of the night and slithered to a tire-smoking halt right in front of me. Tommy Edwards (who, by the way, looked *exactly* like Errol Flynn in the movie *Dawn Patrol*) jumped out, swiped a blackened hand across his brow, and in desperate tones informed me that first and second gears were gone. *Gone!* So I leaped underneath to check it out while the rest of the lads gassed her up and hurriedly changed tires. But the trouble was obviously *inside* the box --not the linkage!-- so there really wasn't much of anything I could do. Not in the middle of the bloody race, anyway. But maybe, if we babied it, she'd hold together long enough to make the finish? Maybe....

I watched my crew as they finished up the pitstop (they were good lads, every last one of them) and then my second driver (who was a dead ringer for the David Niven part in the same movie) scrambled himself behind the wheel. "Take care," I told him solemnly, "you've got nothing left but top."

"Well then, we'll just have to make do, won't we?" he grinned through one of those devil-may-care David Niven smiles.

"Right then. Off you go."

"Cheerio," David Niven shouted over the engine noise as he gingerly pulled away, slipping the clutch something awful. Why, you could actually hear the busted gearteeth gnashing around inside that poor old transmission.

After our Allard disappeared into the night, I climbed up on the pit counter next to Errol Flynn and put my arm gently around his shoulders. "It's a bit dodgy at the moment," I told him in my best Earl-of-Passaic accent, "but I built that gearbox myself, and I reckon she might just hold herself together long enough to win this bloody race."

He smiled and thanked me, the hint of a single tear glistening in the corner of his eye.

And of course that gearbox held together (what else?) and afterwards everything went into one of those swirling Hollywood Special Effects dissolves to a madhouse victory celebration on the flag- and bunting-draped podium at the start/finish line. I was standing right at the very top (natch!) with a grimy Errol Flynn and an even grimier David Niven flanked to either side, and the three of us were smiling and waving and laughing like madmen while a tumultuous crowd of wildly cheering Frenchmen seethed all around us. In fact, it took an entire regiment of uniformed gendarmes with gold braid on their caps and short, velvet-lined capes across their shoulders to hold the people back. Corks popped off twenty-four hundred bottles of the finest champagne in all of France, and silver serving trays came around loaded with longstemmed crystal glasses, each one filled to overflowing. Errol, David, and I toasted one another repeatedly while beautiful young French girls in rakishly cocked berets and slit leather skirts swarmed around us on all sides, begging for even the slightest little scrap of attention. They were all virgins (of course!) but even so, the more adventurous ones would look us right in the eye, wink, and smile....

You gotta admit, I have a pretty darn good imagination when it comes to that sort of thing!

Chapter 9: Beaten With A Club

Next day when Big Ed came in to pick up his Jaguar, I made sure to tell him about those races out at Bridgehampton, and right away his eyes glassed over and that big Cuban stogie started rolling from one side of his mouth to the other. Clear out of the blue, he asked if I'd maybe like to join him on a little Jaguar excursion across Long Island for a personal looksee come next Saturday morning. *Would I!* He even said I could ask Julie along, which sounded even better yet. Especially considering the amount of room you had left in an XK120 cockpit once you had somebody the size of Big Ed Baumstein wedged in behind the wheel (not much at all) and the notion of me and Julie riding all the way out to the tip of Long Island and back with our laps mashed together had a certain undeniable appeal.

But, wouldn't you know it, one of Julie's cousins or nieces or neighbors or something was getting married that day, so no way could she go. In fact, Julie wanted *me* to dress up in a dumb suit and tie and tag along with *her*. Can you believe it? I mean, who the hell cared about some stupid old wedding over in Jersey City --two people you don't even *know*, for Chrissakes!-- when an actual highspeed, wheel-to-wheel sportscar race was happening out on Long Island the very same day. Get serious! But Julie had her heart set on that damn church ceremony (you know how women are when it comes to weddings) and she got pretty bent out of shape when I told her I wasn't about to go with her and miss that race. In fact, she even cried a little. But it wasn't a *real* cry, you know, just one of those sad, pouty whimpers girls pull out of their bag of tricks once they realize you're not gonna do whatever it is they want you to do. The whole idea is to make you feel guilty (with a capital "G") so that *next* time you'll cave in and take 'em wherever the hell it is they want to go.

It's like an investment.

Anyhow, Big Ed wanted me ready outside my aunt's house by 5:30 ayem on Saturday morning, but the truth is I was up much earlier on account of I couldn't sleep too well. Excited, I guess. And maybe even feeling a little guilty about Julie and her stupid damn church wedding in Jersey City. You ever notice how women can eat and eat and eat and *eat* at you --even when you *know* deep down inside that you're doing just exactly what it is you want to do? It's the damndest thing....

Anyhow, it was still pitch dark outside when I woke up, and there was just no way I could persuade my body to fall back to sleep. And believe me, I tried everything. So I just laid there in bed for the longest time, staring at the eerie glow-in-the-dark green numerals on my alarm clock and wondering why the hell the hands weren't moving at all. It reminded me of waking up early on Christmas morning back when I was a kid, lying there perfectly still with my eyes slammed shut --*pretending* to sleep, right?-- while all my nerve endings clanged and jangled like a chorus of alarm bells and ah-ooo-gah horns. That's when time barely seems to ooze (imagine 90-weight drooling down off a transmission casing in subzero weather) from one second to the next. I finally gave up and rolled out of the sack about quarter past four, made a pot of coffee, and sat myself down on the can for twenty minutes or so, just sort of casually leafing my way through the Jaguar shop manual. But my butt went numb about halfway through the part about cylinder head decarbonizing and I had to get up again. So I poured myself another slug of java and decided to put in a little housekeeping time, picking up the odd shirts, socks, and undershorts that were forever scattering themselves every which way around my apartment. Sometimes I wondered where the hell they came from, you know? Especially all those orphan half-pairs of socks.

Needless to say, I was out front a good half hour before Big Ed was due to arrive, and gee whiz, was it ever *quiet* out there at five o'clock in the morning. The sky was just turning that serious purplish-grey color it gets right before sunup, and the only sounds were a few early trucks rumbling along the highway a mile or so away and some·of my mom's stupid insomniac birds chirping and fluttering their way around in the treetops, way up high where you couldn't actually see them. It made me think about her, you know? And then it was like I could almost *see* her, standing there on tiptoes at her favorite kitchen window with those dumbass military surplus binoculars pressed against the glass, making her goofy dove coos and chickadee twitters with her lips all pursed together like she'd been sucking on a damn lemon. And for a crazy second it was like I was really *there*, you know, because I thought I smelled bacon frying and waffle batter rising up golden-brown in the griddle and even a pot of real fresh-roast percolated coffee. Boy, did that ever smell *good!* I reckon you move away from home for the Friday and Saturday nights, but you can sure miss your mom's kitchen early on a Saturday or Sunday morning.

It seemed I was out there an awful long time before I heard the unmistakable growl of Big Ed's Jaguar tooling down the main highway, and I could follow it with my ears as he turned off on Taft, cruised up the hill to Cherry --left on Cherry-- and followed it all the way down to Buchanan, where my aunt lives. Boy, it really got my blood pumping when I saw that XK120 wheel around our corner, all freshly waxed and glowing in the early light like polished ivory. Big Ed glided her up to the curb, flashed me two halves of a smile with his fat Cuban stogie stuck in the middle, handed over a thermos of hot coffee, and off we went --without a word!-- like we were on some sort of deadly serious Secret Mission that both of us understood.

We headed east out of Passaic under a mother-of-pearl sky, drinking coffee against the chill and watching the sun come up clear and fine behind the Manhattan skyline. It was a perfect late-May kind of morning, but I was glad I brought my jacket on account of Big Ed had the top down (natch!) and there was plenty of cold, damp wind spilling over and around the XK120's fighter-style split windshield. On the other hand, the crisp early air and light traffic sure agreed with Big Ed's Jaguar, and she was running cool, sweet, and strong. Which of course meant Big Ed had a huge smile plastered across his kisser --stogie angled up at about 45 degrees-- and I remember he was wearing this bright yellow cheese-cutter cap with a shiny gold Jaguar emblem embroidered on top. He said he got it out of some foreign car mail-order catalog from California. Believe me, you can get any kind of car shit you could possibly imagine out in California.

As we continued eastward out of the city, we saw more and more Jaguars and MGs and such heading our way, most all of them piled high with picnic baskets and folded-up lawn chairs and other assorted bits and pieces of vital racing paraphernalia. It was like there was some enormous magnet out there somewhere on the tip of Long Island, pulling every damn low-slung, two-seater European sportscar on the Eastern seaboard towards Bridgehampton. Why, if you closed your eyes, you could almost feel the suction....

But the coolest thing of all was how those other sportycar people would wave and smile and flash their lights and tootle their horns at us --like we were dear old close personal chums or something!-- just because we were driving a damn Jaguar. That's all it took --we *belonged!* Naturally we waved and smiled and tootled our horn right back at them, and if it happened to be another XK120 (or if there was an especially pretty girl in the passenger seat) Big Ed'd give a blast off the Maserati air horns he had me install behind the Jaguar's radiator. They came from that same mail-order outfit in California, and I'm not exaggerating one bit when I tell you they made the sort of noise usually associated with the crash dive alarm on a submarine. Hell, that sound would lift you right off the damn upholstery if it caught you by surprise. Honest to God it would....

Personally, I thought all this arm waving and horn honking and headlight flashing was really *neat*. I mean, Buick and Oldsmobile owners didn't do that sort of thing. Not hardly. And if (God forbid) your Jag was pulled over to the side of the road with a flat tire or a duff fuel pump or a cloud of stinky steam rising from the hood, another Jaguar driver would stop to help you out --even if he was on his way to his own damn kidney operation! Hell, a Buick owner could be lying in the middle of the road with his large intestine wrapped around his earlobes and nobody'd give the poor jerk so much as a courtesy head-swivel.

Big Ed and me made it out to the village of Bridgehampton a little before ten, and you would simply not believe what was going on there. The whole damn town was up for grabs like there was a street carnival or something going on, what with banners flying and people milling around all over the place --thousands of them!-- and cars creeping along in search of parking places everywhere you looked. And not all of them sportscars, either. Truth is, most of the cars clogging the streets and byways of Bridgehampton, Long Island, that particular Saturday morning were just ordinary, everyday American sedans that the rank-and-file rubberneckers drove out from the city to watch the races. Regular old Fords and Dodges and Mercurys and Chevrolets lined the pavements of Bridgehampton bumper-to-bumper on both sides, overflowing into private driveways and onto front lawns where the local fast-buck artists were charging a quarter or more for the privilege.

Of course Big Ed figured our XK120 entitled us to something a bit better than Ordinary Drool Spectator status, so he gunned right past the guys with the S.C.M.A. armbands who were sort of halfheartedly directing traffic towards some empty fields that had been pressed into duty as parking lots about a mile outside of town. The armband people would take a gander at Big Ed's Jaguar, see him smiling and waving his cigar through the air like we were somebody important, and finally leap aside at the last possible instant once they realized he was not about to stop. Not hardly. Truth is, I think a few of them were a tiny bit upset with us (at least judging by some of the unkind names they shouted or the way they shook their fists in the air) but luckily none of them chased after us, since there was no way in hell we could've gotten away with all those people around. At least not without mowing down a thousand or two.

But it was slow going --barely a walking pace, actually-- and therefore I had to keep one eye constantly glued to the Jag's temperature gauge. Whenever it started to climb much past 200 (like every time we got bogged down in a particularly dense herd of meandering pedestrians) I'd nudge Big Ed and he'd reach under the dash and push the button that controlled those Maserati air horns once or twice. I swear, those things made people scatter like we'd opened fire with a damn machine gun!

Fortunately we arrived at this big roped-off parking area just about the time our Jag hit full broil, and you could see right away that it had to be Race Central on account of it was filled from one side to the other with more damn foreign sportscars than you ever saw in your life. At the entrance to the lot was this huge, yellow-and-white circus tent filled to overflowing with laughing, jabbering, coffee-drinking, story-telling, cigarette-smoking, glad-t'see-you/how've-you-been S.C.M.A. sportycar people, all busy getting themselves signed up and organized for the day's activities. So naturally Big Ed pulled up and parked us right smack-dab in front of that tent, between a coral-red XK120 drophead and this big, pea-soup-green Mk. VII Jaguar sedan. But we weren't there two seconds before this skinny little twerp with thinning hair and basset-hound eyes came barreling out of the tent full tilt, flapping his arms like he was trying to take off. "Wait! *Wait!! WAIT!!!*" he wailed excitedly, "these spaces are re*served!*"

"Who sez?" Big Ed wanted to know.

"*I* do," the skinny guy shot back, leaning over our windshield jaw first so he was staring Big Ed squarely in the kisser. "You simply *cannot* park here. It's im*poss*ible!"

"Oh, yeah? Why not?" You could see Big Ed didn't like this guy's tone one bit. Neither did I, come to think of it.

"Because these spaces are *reserved*. For *official* cars. *Only!*" The guy had one of those nasally, upper-crust New England voices with sort of a permanent sniff to it. It was the kind of voice you'd just as soon have shut up, if you know what I mean.

Big Ed peeled his eyes around at the other two Jags, then glared back at the skinny guy. "Saaay, how d'ya know *this* ain't an official car?"

"Nice try," the guy sneered, "but I know *all* the officials and *all* the official cars. Besides, you haven't got a sticker!"

"A sticker?"

"Yes, a sticker. An *official* sticker." He pointed a lump-jointed finger at the red Jag's windshield. Sure enough, down there in the lower lefthand corner was a little silver and red wire wheel decal with "Sports Car Motoring Association" written across it in dark blue letters.

"Oh, really?" Big Ed snorted, not sounding particularly convinced. Then he opened his door and started to climb out.

"*WAIT!*" the skinny guy shrieked, his voice going up five or six octaves, "WHERE DO YOU THINK YOU'RE *GOING?!*"

"Me?" Big Ed said calmly, closing the Jag's door deliberately behind him, "I'm goin' inta this tent here and see about gettin' me one a'those parking stickers." And with that, Big Ed walked right past the skinny guy like he was a fencepost or something.

As you can imagine, this left me in a pretty damn awkward position, sitting there all by my lonesome on the passenger side of Big Ed's Jaguar while this enraged S.C.M.A. parking-lot monitor glared at me full blast through his saggy little basset-hound eyes, his arms folded so tightly across his chest that it must've damn near cut off the circulation. It didn't look like he was planning to stop any time soon, so I decided that maybe the best course of action was to simply ease myself out the other side of Big Ed's XK120 and more or less melt off into the crowd, eyeballing the scuffmarks on my shoes along the way.

Things didn't look too awfully interesting inside the big yellow-and-white tent --just a bunch of rich, highclass sportycar types standing around drinking coffee and shooting the breeze while they waited their turn at the registration tables-- so I waltzed off to reconnoiter the area and maybe snoop around the cars a little. And believe me, there was plenty to look at. Why, there were low-slung, foreign-built 2-seater sportscars of every possible color and description scattered in haphazard rows and bunched-up clusters all over the roped-off area behind the big yellow-and-white S.C.M.A. circus tent. I overheard some of the armband types calling it a "racing paddock" (like it was a big deal or something) but it looked just like an ordinary, everyday gravel parking lot to me. Except for the cars, that is....

The vast majority were the MGs and Jag 120s I'd come to know at Westbridge, but there were other cars, too. Like that Frazer-Nash thing that won the big 12-hour endurance race down in Florida. And maybe four or five of those burly, brutal-looking Allards from over in England that carried big old All-American Ford, Mercury, and Cadillac V8s under their bulging hoods. I recognized the shiny new black one with the red wire wheels that Sylvester and Barry Spline had just finished buttoning together for that Englishman from White Plains, and I sort of wondered how they were doing with it. You know how it goes whenever you try to throw something together in a last-minute panic. Right next to the Cad-Allard (more or less in its shadow, actually) were these two slender, delicate-looking French Bugattis, wearing elegant little horseshoe-shaped radiators and nifty machined-alloy wheels and bodywork as sleek as sailboat hulls. I heard somebody say they were built way back in the thirties, but they still looked pretty damn racey to me. And parked across from them was this incredible deep-red Alfa Romeo 2900 from Italy, which was also from before the war but still looked a hell of a lot faster and more flamboyant than anything you saw rolling off the assembly lines in Detroit. They had the hood up, and underneath was the most magnificent supercharged straight 8 automobile engine I had ever seen, all done up with machined brass fittings

and finned aluminum castings that looked like things you might
see in a sculpture exhibition. Wow! Further on I stumbled upon a
whole damn litter of these runty-looking German Porsches, all
squatted down over their tires like puppydogs taking a dump.
They didn't look like much compared to the Jags and Allards (or
even that old Alfa) but their owners seemed awful damn proud of
them anyway. No kidding. And you simply would not believe the
marvelous sounds when all those different kinds of cars with all
their different types of engines fired up and drove around the
paddock from one spot to another. Each one had its own special
voice and its own private song --it was like *music,* you know?
For a guy who truly loved automobiles, that S.C.M.A. paddock
at Bridgehampton was like a forty acre dessert cart. The only
hard part was figuring out where to look next.

What made it even tougher was that you could easily get
distracted by all the Real Live Big Screen Celebrities meandering
all over the place. Like who should I see standing next to this
shiny white SS100 Jaguar --not two feet away!-- but that Dave
Garroway guy from "The Today Show" on television! No lie!
And I saw Jackie Cooper (I'm *sure* it was him!) yakking with one
of the armband people outside the tent. And Robert Montgomery
--you know, the movie actor?-- was on hand to drive the pace car
for all the races. It was a brand new Nash Healey convertible
--the very first one in the country! Why, I'd never been around
so many rich, famous, lah-de-dah people or snazzy, exotic
automobiles in my entire life. Not hardly! You could damn near
smell the money. In fact, to tell the honest truth, it made me feel
just a little out of place. But all those celebrity-types blended
right in with the S.C.M.A. club regulars. It was like they were
all poured from the same mold, all tanned and groomed and
dressed in the kind of perfectly pressed, oh-so-casual casual
clothes you see in glossy magazine ads featuring yacht parties and
country club golf outings and that sort of thing.

Poor Julie would've gone absolutely *nuts,* you know?

On the other hand, you could see that not too many of these
fashionable, upscale sportycar types were particularly, aah,
mechanically inclined. But I reckon if you got the bucks, you can
always hire some poor working stiff to handle the dirty part for
you. Lord knows I'd do it in a heartbeat. For *nothing.* Just so's
they'd let me hang around.

Everywhere I wandered around the Bridgehampton paddock that morning, I saw people hustling like mad to get their stuff unloaded and their cars ready for the races. They were rummaging in toolboxes and stacking cases of oil and pulling off spare tires and folding down windshields (or undoing a few bolts and taking them right off!) and laying out racing numbers on their hoods and doors with liquid shoe polish or rolls of white tape. You couldn't miss the buzz of real urgency crackling in the air.

I noticed this short, intense-looking older guy squatted down in front of a white XK120 like Big Ed's, putting layer after layer of adhesive tape over the headlamp lenses. I kind of wondered what on earth it was for, so I walked over, cleared my throat a couple times, and asked: "Hey, uh, 'scuse me, mister, but what the heck's all that tape for, huh?"

The guy wheeled around and looked me up and down with flinty little eyes that had maybe a small hint of mental disturbance in them. "It's for a *shunt,*" he snapped --like it was obvious, you know?-- and went right back to his taping.

"A *what?*"

But it was like he didn't hear me, on account of he was too damn busy layering on more and more tape until both of the Jag's headlights looked like lead characters in one of those creepy old black-and-white Mummy movies. And you could see the guy wasn't particularly handy, either, on account of not one single strip of that tape went down straight or laid the least bit flat. But he compensated with sheer volume, using damn near a half-roll of tape to cover the two Lucas headlamps. When he finished (in other words, when he had tape globbed on a good half-inch thick over both lenses) the little guy stepped back and eyeballed his handiwork like it was the roof of the damn Sistine Chapel. *"Purrrrr-*fect!" he purred, rolling his rr's like a tomcat, "just *purrrr*-fect." Then he swiveled around and flashed me this strange, misshapen smile with a gold tooth glittering in the middle of it. "It's for a shunt," he said proudly.

"A what?"

"A shunt. A spin. An off. A big one. A quick trip through the tulies. A --heh heh-- *misadventure* amongst the haybales."

"You mean an accident?"

The guy nodded gravely, eyebrows pumping up and down. "It can happen, young man. Believe me it can. Should the worst occur --heh heh-- we *must* keep shattered glass off the racing line. It could --heh-- puncture a tire and cause *untold* mayhem." He waved his hand desperately through the air so I might understand just exactly how untold the mayhem might get. Then he leaned in real close, snaked his arm around my shoulder, and whispered, "This your first time, sonny?" like we were parachuting behind enemy lines or something.

"Uh, yeah," I nodded, "I came up with Bi--, I mean, Ed Baumstein. He's got a white XK120 just like yours."

The guy's eyebrows just about popped off his forehead. *"Just like mine, you say? JUST LIKE MINE?!"* he wailed, his face jumping and twitching like a freshly squashed bug. "Do you realize what you're *saying,* young man?!"

I allowed as how I didn't, and without warning the guy launched into a fifteen-minute dissertation on the many important differences between an *ordinary* Jaguar XK120 roadster and an XK120*M* Special Equipment edition. Then we got to Phase Two: the many important differences between an *ordinary* XK120*M* Special Equipment Super Sports roadster and his *particular* XK120*M* Special Equipment Super Sports roadster, which was a certified *ex-works* racing car. The very one, in fact, that Creighton Pendleton the Third drove to six S.C.M.A. production-class victories in 1951! I made a point of looking real impressed, you know, even though I hadn't a clue what *M* stood for or what was so damn "special" about Special Equipment or who the hell Creighton Pendleton the Third was. Or what in the world "ex-works" or "production-class" meant, for that matter. Far as I could see, the only difference between this guy's Jag and Big Ed's was it had knockoff wire wheels and no fender skirts in back. Personally, I thought his XK120 looked kind of naked without the skirt panels over the rear wheels. They really *make* the car, you know? But I didn't say anything. I mean, who wanted to encourage this guy?

Turns out I'd chanced upon the infamous Skippy Welcher, sole heir to the Welcher Waxout ear swab fortune. His real name was Reginald, but he got the nickname "Skippy" from the way his conversation regularly skipped from one topic to another (often in mid-sentence). Skippy's family had piles and piles and *piles* of money, and The Skipper was justly proud of the fact that he'd never worked a single day in his life to earn any of it. Skippy Welcher was known as an "investment principal" in Manhattan, a "sportsman" in Connecticut, a "yachtsman" in Palm Beach, and a "pigeon" in Atlantic City, but the truth is he was nothing but a stinking-rich, ne'er-do-well nutcase who'd been born into more goddam money than he knew what to do with.

It made you want to puke, honest to God it did.

Especially considering Skippy Welcher was one of the original founding members of the S.C.M.A., and made a big point of attending every race, club meeting, and social event on the S.C.M.A. calendar. Then again, he didn't have much else to do, did he? This made him something of a key fixture around the sport, even if not one single person on the S.C.M.A. membership roster could stand to listen to him for more than two minutes at a stretch, or look him in the eye while they were doing it. Believe me, people did a lot of staring off in the opposite direction whenever they found themselves around Skippy Welcher. Turns out he wasn't much of a race driver, either, in spite of being ignorantly confident behind the wheel and brave to the point of foolhardiness. That's because The Skipper drove his racecars with all the finesse, style, and sensitivity of an ax murderer on a rampage, and most always found a way to break them, blow them up, or run them into the local scenery. Which is precisely why The Skipper loved the S.C.M.A. so much, on account of nobody could deny him his inalienable right to be there, no matter how brutal or ham-fisted a driver he was. After all, he had all the necessary S.C.M.A. credentials: he was rich, he owned a bunch of neat cars, he showed up for all the club events, and he hadn't killed anybody yet.

While I was standing there next to Skippy's ultra-special XK120*M*, a chipmunk-faced little geek with coke-bottle-bottom glasses, orthopedic shoes, and baggy olive-green coveralls with "M.F." embroidered above the pocket wandered over carrying a small grey toolbox and a little piece of sisal floormat rolled up under his arm. And of course it was none other than Milton Fitting, The Skipper's own *personal* race mechanic. Milton looked a lot like a grownup edition of Howdy Doody (honest he did!) and he moved like it, too --as though his arms and legs were dangling from a set of invisible guywires. Skippy regularly referred to

Milton Fitting as "my attendant" and "my squire" all the time (like The Skipper was Sir Lancelot of the Round Table or something, you know?) and I didn't much care for that at all. Not one bit. But it didn't seem to bother Milton Fitting. Not hardly. In fact, not much of *anything* seemed to upset that character, and you had to figure it was on account of he was off in his own little world most of the time (somewheres slightly north-northeast of Neptune, if you catch my drift).

It didn't take long to come to the conclusion that Milton Fitting and Skippy Welcher were both nuttier than fruitcakes. But looking back, I guess that's exactly what made them such a perfect pair. They *needed* each other. Old Skippy desperately needed himself a fulltime wrench on account of he was forever bending, breaking, or blowing up his ex-works, ex-Creighton Pendleton XK120*M*, and likewise not too many car shops would keep a creepy drool like Milton Fitting on the payroll. Oh, he could fix stuff all right --no two ways about it-- but he was, without a doubt, the absolute *slowest* mechanic I have ever seen in my life. Bar none. Even the smallest, simplest sort of mechanical jobs took him for*ever*. I swear, he worked slower than the night shift union stiffs at my dad's chemical plant job in Newark, and those guys hardly move at all.

Anyhow, I tried striking up a conversation with Milton there in the Bridgehampton paddock --you know, one mechanic to another-- but I swear it was like talking to a bowl of raspberry jello. Fr'instance, I asked him what carb needles he was using (just to show him I knew all there was to know about S.U. carburetors --even though I didn't) but all he did was gurgle and wheeze and stare back at me through a pair of glasses that made his eyeballs look like fried eggs. Never said a single God Damn word. The Skipper made up for it, though. In fact, once you got him started, you couldn't shut the bastard up. Why, Skippy Welcher could peel off into brand new topics --one right after the other-- without so much as pausing to take a breath.

Which is precisely why I was still standing there a half-hour later, listening to a rambling, highly convoluted dissertation on the relative merits of castor bean-based versus mineral-based lubricating oils for dual-overhead-cam British racing engines (like the one in his Jaguar, for example) and I might as well have been a cardboard cutout propped up with a stick.

And you couldn't miss how Skippy got himself worked into a real lather whenever he got rolling on one of his many favorite subjects, what with every muscle on his face popping and twitching like pea soup coming to a boil and sweat beads snapping off in all directions. Plus there was just no stopping the sonofabitch once he got a head of steam up. I was starting to get worried that maybe Big Ed might be missing me, you know? But there was no polite, proper, dignified way on earth to disengage yourself from Skippy Welcher. It was like having your bumpers locked with a shit wagon. So, someplace about halfway through The Skipper's *personal* recommendations concerning proper washing, waxing, and polishing techniques for authentic English paint finishes, I just said, "Well, nice t'meetcha. Seeya. Bye." and simply walked away. When I looked back from a safe distance, I could see The Skipper was still hard at it, yakking away into the empty atmosphere as fast as he could make the words come out....

I found Big Ed back in the registration tent, huddled over a card table with none other than the same skinny twerp who tried to shoo us off the Official Parking Spaces. His name was Charlie Priddle, and sure enough, *he* turned out to be the S.C.M.A.'s one-and-only Membership Chairman. Oh, swell. In fact, Charlie Priddle was on every damn committee the S.C.M.A. had. And believe me, they had *plenty*. Now, you have to understand that Charlie Priddle never once drove in a car race --not *ever*-- but for some inexplicable reason, he considered S.C.M.A. club activities the single most important thing in his life.

No, I didn't understand it either.

Seems Charles Winthrop Martingale Priddle came from some old, old, *old* Old Money up in Connecticut somewheres, and he owned maybe five or six of the latest, snazziest, most expensive imported sportscars you could buy. Not one of which he could drive worth a lick. But Charlie bragged about his fancy European sportscars all the time, not to mention about how much better the *racing* was "on The Continent" and how much better the *food* was "on The Continent" and how his family originally came *over* "from The Continent" on the damn Mayflower.

First Class, too, to hear him tell it.

Anyhow, Big Ed was trying to find out how he could join the S.C.M.A., and, without actually saying it in so many words, Charlie Priddle was making it perfectly clear that he didn't care much for families who arrived in this country by way of Ellis Island. Or folks who believed in any sort of off-brand, oddball, non-Protestant religions. Or people who had actually had to *work* for a living. Which was three quick strikes against Big Ed right off the bat. Not to mention that, in the short period of time they'd known one another, Charlie Priddle had developed a very deep and personal dislike for Big Ed Baumstein that had nothing whatsoever to do with his occupation, religion, or family background. So Charlie Priddle was giving Big Ed the runaround. And he was pretty damn good at it, too.

"Say, whazzit take to join this Goddamn club, anyway?" Big Ed was asking for maybe the fifteenth or sixteenth time, leaning forward so the business end of his cigar was maybe half an inch from Charlie Priddle's eyelid.

"Well, let's see," Charlie sniffed, looking Big Ed up and down like he was 300 pounds of fresh horse manure. "First, you of course must own one of the *recognized* marques...."

"Whatsa *mark?*" Big Ed wanted to know.

"A marque is --what would *you* call it?--" Charlie Priddle rolled his eyeballs up into his forehead, pretending to fish for a word somebody as dumb and coarse and crude and uncultured as Big Ed Baumstein might understand. "A marque," he said at last, "is what a person such as yourself might refer to as the *brand name* of an automobile."

"Oh, yeah?" Big Ed nodded. "Well, y'saw my Jag 120 parked out front."

"Ah, yes. Indeed I did. But you *also* have to be ap*proved* by the S.C.M.A. *mem*bership committee."

"So tell me," Big Ed asked without so much as skipping a beat, "just how does a guy get himself approved by this here membership committee?"

"Oooh, they have to *vote* on it, of course."

"So how do I get voted on?"

"Oooh, I'm afraid they won't vote on *you.* "

"Why not?"

"Because I'm quite *cer*tain your name won't come up."

"Whyzzat?"

"Because your name won't be sub*mit*ted."

"Submitted?"

"Of course. Every single *new* club member must be *spon*-sored by an ex*ist*ing member. Can't you see? That's the only way *any* name can come before our membership committee."

"Lookee here," Big Ed growled, biting into his cigar. "Why don'cha just do us both a favor and put my name up t'yer damn committee, huh? C'mon, whaddaya say?"

"Oooh, I couldn't do *that.*"

"Why not?"

"Because I don't *know* you. And, more importantly, Mister Bommb-Steeen, I'm not quite sure I *like* you. Besides," Charlie Priddle continued, delicately stroking his chin, "shouldn't you be off in one of your, aah, *sin*-a-gogs today?"

Boy, you could really feel the heat start to rise off Big Ed, even from two or three feet away.

But Charlie Priddle wasn't finished with Big Ed. Not quite yet. He rolled his face upwards with all the heartfelt sincerity and righteousness he could muster in those sorry-looking basset-hound eyes of his and asked, "Don't you *prac*tice your faith, Mister Bommb-Steeeen?"

Big Ed's nostrils flared like a bull getting ready to charge, but somehow he held himself in check. Lord only knows how. And when he finally spoke, the words came out so soft and keen and carefully measured it was downright scary. "I don't *need* t'prac-tice, see," he growled in a steel-edged whisper, "I do it just fine already." Then he leaned in so close you about needed a feeler gauge to check the distance between Big Ed's nose and what little remained of Charlie Priddle's hairline. "Now I'm gonna ask you one more time, Bub: *will you put my friggin' name up t'yer frig-gin' membership committee or not?!*"

Charlie Priddle took a deep breath and eased his chair gently back out of Big Ed's shadow. "I'm afraid that's im*pos*sible," he sighed. "You see, I'm *on* the committee. In fact, I'm *chair*man of the committee. It wouldn't work out, don't you see?"

"No, I don't," Big Ed snarled.

"Good. I'm glad you understand."

"But I DON'T understand!" Big Ed bellowed, slamming his fist down so hard it made the legs on Charlie Priddle's little folding card table buckle.

As you can imagine, that startled the living hell out of Charlie Priddle --not to mention everybody else in the tent-- but I gotta hand it to the little pipsqueak. He sure didn't spook easy. In fact, he rose right up out of his chair, squared his skinny little shoulders, leaned right into the glow of Big Ed's cigar, and started explaining the way things worked in the S.C.M.A. Real loud and slow, too, like you do when somebody doesn't understand the English language very well. "Look here, Mr. Bommb-Steeen," he said with a threatening hint of a tremble to his voice, "I have a lot of *very* important things to do today, and I'm afraid talking to you definitely *isn't* one of them. So let me give you a little bit of advice. There will be a towtruck outside this tent within the next two minutes, and I suggest you either move your automobile *now,* or perhaps you'd prefer to make arrangements with the local Bridgehampton police department later on this afternoon. It's entirely *your* choice, Mr. Bommb-steeen. And now, if you will ex*cuse* me...," and with that, Charlie Priddle sat back down in his chair, buried his skinny Anglican nose in a stack of entry forms, and started ignoring Big Ed. He was true World Class when it came to ignoring people.

Chapter 10: Paddock Playthings

Even our run-in with that asshole Charlie Priddle couldn't put a damper on the swell time Big Ed and me had out at Bridgehampton. Sure, he was plenty pissed off about having to move his car from its cozy spot in front of the S.C.M.A. tent to a stinking little weedpatch next to some old geezer's garden shed, damn near a mile away. Especially when the guy charged us fifty whole cents to park there, just on account of we were driving a Jaguar. So there was still quite a bit of steam rising off Big Ed as we made our way back towards the paddock, and his big Cuban stogie was about making figure-eights from one side of his mouth to the other. He sure as hell didn't appreciate the way that scrawny, nose-in-the-air Charlie Priddle jerk shut him off like a damn lightswitch, and you could almost hear wheels turning and gears grinding underneath Big Ed's yellow cheese-cutter cap. It was a question of *class* --yeah, *that* was it! Big Ed understood all about class, and was smart and savvy enough to know he really didn't have any. At least not the kind those tightass S.C.M.A. bastards cared about. So what! He was *proud* of his family and religion (even if he didn't pay much attention to either one on a regular, day-to-day basis) and most especially of the way he and his cousin Vito built up that scrap machinery business --from *nothing!*-- so that now he could afford any God Damn kind of car he wanted. Or any car *club,* for that matter. Which meant he sure didn't enjoy getting the high-hat routine from a rich, snotty WASP creep like Charlie Priddle. Not one bit. And Big Ed wasn't the kind of guy to take it lying down, either.

I tried to get Big Ed's mind off the situation by telling him about spotting Dave Garroway and Jackie Cooper and Robert Montgomery around the Bridgehampton paddock (not to mention all the cool cars I'd seen) but you could tell he wasn't really listening. So I decided to steer us over by Skippy Welcher and his ex-everything XK120*M*, just so Big Ed could get himself a closeup personal glimpse at the kind of rigorous, highclass, top-quality membership standards they had in the S.C.M.A.

As you can imagine, Big Ed's eyes lit up like a pair of Marchal driving lamps the instant he got a look at The Skipper's Jag. "Say," he grinned, "I gotta XK120 just like this one."

Naturally that bit of news got The Skipper's face popping and twitching like weevils were swarming under the skin, and in less than a heartbeat he was off into that same rambling, incoherent speech I got earlier --you know, about the many important differences between an *ordinary* XK120 Super Sports roadster and *his* goddam car-- blah, blah, blah, blah. I'd estimate it didn't take old Skippy more than thirty seconds to start getting on Big Ed's nerves, especially since he had this habit of putting his face right up into yours when he talked and then yelled loud enough so's you could hear the sonofabitch two blocks away. You'd get wet, too, on account of The Skipper always blew a little spit once he got up a head of steam. Not to mention that there wasn't a way in hell of shutting the bastard up once he got rolling on a topic (or a rapid-fire *series* of topics, to be more accurately precise). Besides which every discussion with Skippy Welcher was bound to be full of strange tangents, hairpin turns, mental bank shots, and twirling about-faces. For example, Skippy was smack dab in the middle of explaining to Big Ed why you should never, *ever,* use anything but genuine, high-altitude mountain air to fill racing tires ("Air's thinner and cooler up there --*heh*-- with fewer impurities. That's why I have my squire Milton --that's him over there with the tire gauge-- haul our compressor and air tanks up to Bear Mountain every couple weeks to get some for us. Y'gotta be over three thousand feet to get the really *good* stuff, of course. Makes an *enormous* difference on the track...") when, without warning, he made one of his trademark conversational U-turns and gently laid both of his hands up on Big Ed's shoulders --like they were old long-lost army buddies or something, you know?-- while his face blossomed out into his absolute best and sincerest misshapen gold-tooth smile. "You know, Mr. Blackstone..." he began.

"Ah, that's *Baumstein,*" Big Ed corrected him.

But it was like The Skipper didn't hear him at all. "Yes sir, Mr. Bockstein, I can't tell you how *thrilled* and *deee-lighted* I always am to meet another Jaguar *aficionado.*" Whatever the hell that meant. Then again, I bet Skippy was always "thrilled" and "deee-lighted" whenever he got a run at a fresh pair of ears. By that juncture Big Ed had gotten himself a good, deep gander into

The Skipper's eyes and realized that you could no way see bottom, so he and I made screwy finger-and-eyeball signals back and forth while The Skipper rambled on and on about all the races his car had won (none with him at the wheel, far as I could tell), how to clean wire wheels with your toothbrush, and the size of the larger and more interesting bug splats he'd picked off his Jag's windshield after a high-speed run.

And twenty minutes later The Skipper was still hard at it, expounding on the science and technique of proper braking point selection ("y'gotta find yourself a trackside shutoff marker of some kind, see. Preferably in a --heh heh-- *tight* sweater") when this enormous black-over-silver Rolls Royce Phantom IV limousine slinked into the paddock with a mysterious, tarp-covered racecar strapped to a trailer behind it. Believe it or not, the sight was enough to stop Skippy Welcher dead in mid-sentence. Honest it was. And he wasn't the only one, either. In fact, you could see heads swiveling around like gun turrets and hear tools thudding to the ground all over the place as that Rolls/trailer combination paraded itself leisurely around the paddock. I looked at Big Ed and he looked back at me, and the both of us craned our necks forward as that Rolls limo glided past, ghostly silent except for the soft crunch of gravel under its tires and a faint, mouselike squeak off the trailer springs....

Sitting behind the wheel was an honest-to-gosh Park Avenue edition of a chauffeur, all done up in brass buttons and a peaked cap, but you couldn't make out who was in back on account of they had pleated wool curtains drawn over the rear windows and a venetian-blind sort of windowshade in the backlight. I noticed the Massachusetts license plate on the decklid read "CP3," and it was mounted right above the one and only trailer hitch I have *ever* seen fastened to a Rolls Royce automobile.

But the racecar strapped down on the trailer was even more intriguing. You couldn't really tell what it was, on account of they had it all covered up with this fancy tan chamois tarp (which was even *tailored,* you know, with special seams and pleats and darts and stuff to show off the car's shape) but you could see it had a lean, wide, *muscular* sort of build to it, causing the fabric to stretch up over the fender arches like those tight cashmere sweaters the Hollywood starlets wear. Even lashed up on a trailer and covered with a tarp, you knew right away this was no ordinary sportscar. Not hardly. I sized it up as a good bit shorter, sleeker, and lower to the ground than any Jag or Allard in the paddock, yet at the same time it was unmistakably broader and more curvaceous in the chest, hips, and shoulders. I'd never seen anything like it before, and the only clues peeking out below the tarp's elastic bottom were four shiny crescents of wire wheel. Whatever it was, that tarp-covered racecar was gathering itself one hellacious crowd as it toured its way slowly around the Bridgehampton paddock. "Jeez, what the hell is *that?*" Big Ed wanted to know.

"Oh," The Skipper said grandly, "that must be Creighton Pendleton's new four-point-one Ferrari. Used to drive a two-point-six, you know, but she didn't --heh heh-- have enough of the old *steam* down the old straightaways. See, y'gotta have that *BIG* horsepower under the old hood for those long straightaways --heh-- *always* gotta have the ponies." Then Skippy leaned in real close, like he was letting us in on a big atomic secret or something. "You watch. Creighton'll knock everybody in the weeds with that baby. Suck their headlights out. Blow their doors off. Feed 'em fumes. Make 'em eat dust. Run away and hide...."

But Big Ed and me were *gone,* off to join the crowd following that Rolls Royce Phantom around the Bridgehampton paddock like it was some important rich stiff's funeral procession, what with everybody shuffling along behind that mysterious shroud-covered racecar on careful, quiet little Funeral Procession steps and talking in those hushed, behind-the-hand Funeral Parlor whispers where your lips hardly move....

The Rolls/trailer rig made two complete parade laps around the paddock before it finally pulled up next to a brand new, spanking white International Travelall with "Carlo Sebastian Import Specialties" and a little Italian tricolor painted on the side. Instantly the doors on the Travelall flew open and two stocky, swarthy, tough-looking southern Italian (or maybe Sicilian) types in matching white shortsleeve coveralls leaped out and sprinted towards the trailer. They were a perfectly matched pair, with barrel chests and huge, hairy forearms, and I swear they pounced on that mystery racecar like hyenas on a fresh kill, shouting and arguing and cussing the living hell out of each other:

"*Ey, Stugatz, at's notta way!*"

"*Waddaya mean, at's notta way?*"

"You gonna droppada whole fuckin' ting onna groun'!"

"Ba fangu, Stroontz! You tinkin' widdayou dick again!"

"Oh yeah? I'm-a bedder tink widda my fuckin' dick den talk outta my fuckin' assa-hole!"

"Yeah? Well why donnayou gedda you ear down a liddle close, ey? I'm-a no tink you can hear me so good...."

It kept up like that virtually non-stop, and a couple times I thought it was actually going to break out into a fistfight. But it never did. And did those two guys ever know what they were doing! In less time than it takes to tell, they had that trailer chocked, angled, ramps down, tiedowns pulled, and everything ready to unload. Only then did a third crewman climb out of the Travelall, wearing the same kind of crisp white coveralls and carrying a special flannel-lined canvas bag for the car cover. But unlike the other two, this guy was tall, thin, pale, and gangly, with thick wire-rim glasses and the remnants of what must have once been a really nice carpet of reddish-brown hair thatched around a set of enormous, flamingo-pink ears. He had a real whopper of a nose, too, but it was more one of your vulture-beak Hebraic models than the rounded, Roman Empire variety sported by the other two mechanics.

By this time, a twelve- or fourteen-deep crowd had gathered in all directions, and for exactly that reason the two tough-looking dago mechanics elected to change tempo (just to get the proper dramatic effect, you know?) and very slowly --almost painfully-- one of them lifted the rear corner of that chamois tarp and gingerly began rolling it back. You could almost feel a breeze off the mass intake of breath as the fabric gently peeled away: underneath was the leanest, meanest, reddest, and most dangerous-looking chunk of metal I had ever seen in my life. It was the color of arterial bleeding and taut and sleek as a young woman's body, what with smooth, graceful fenderlines arching up over the wheelwells and finned alloy brake drums --big as ashcan lids!-- peering out from behind the knockoff wire wheels. Then the tarp came off the front, and I found myself staring into the wide-open jaws of a hungry killer shark! Jee-*zus*, what a vicious-looking automobile! I tried elbowing my way around to get a better angle, and I swear the headlights on that car seemed to follow me like eyes. Why, you could damn near feel a *pulse* off that thing if you leaned in close to the fenders....

Above the grille I noticed a small enameled badge --fine as a piece of jewelry!-- featuring the silhouette of a wild black stallion reared up against a brilliant bright yellow background and the word "F-E-R-R-A-R-I" spelled out below in serious block letters.

FERRARI!

The name was like fire on your tongue.

With help from the other two, the mechanic with the big ears folded up the special chamois car cover (doing it four times lengthwise and then in neat little triangles, like a blessed troop flag or something) before stuffing it away in its special flannel-lined bag. That done, he more or less stepped off to the side while the two burly-looking crewmen eased the Ferrari gently down off its trailer. They acted like it was a damn concert grand piano or something, working the winch no more than one or two clicks at a time and checking underneath every six inches or so to make sure the tires were still perfectly aligned on the ramps. The pale guy with the big ears just stood over by the Travelall, shifting his weight from one foot to the other and chewing nervously on his fingernails. My guess was they didn't trust him with much except tarp-folding duty, and it was easy to see why. He was obviously one of those tight, jittery types, and no way had sure hands or quick feet like the other two. Not hardly. In fact, you couldn't miss how he seemed to drop or trip over things at every opportunity and stumble over his own feet a lot.

After they got the Ferrari safely to the ground, one of the Sicilian mechanics popped the hood --just for an instant!-- to give everybody in the peanut gallery a quick two-second glimpse of the magnificent single-overhead-camshaft, all-alloy Ferrari Vee-12 nestled underneath. What a motor! It had three two-barrel Weber carburetors lined up right down the center of the vee --each with its own little louvered air cleaner-- and the valve covers were done up in that crinkly-smooth black satin finish you usually see on telescopes and binoculars and stuff. I was hoping they'd leave it open so I could shoulder my way around to get a closer look (or better yet, that they'd fire it up!) but it turned out to be nothing but a tease for the crowd, and the other mechanic closed the lid as soon as he'd checked the oil and water and brake fluid. After that they checked the tire pressures in perfect unison, each doing one side of the car, and when they were done, one of them motioned for the vulture-beak to bring them over a couple cold soda pops out of a cooler in the back of the white Travelall. Then the three of them kind of leaned back against the fenders (but *carefully,* since it was all desperately-thin aluminum alloy!) and lit themselves up a round of cigarettes. Real nonchalant, you know, as if nobody was watching them at all....

You could tell they really enjoyed the limelight.

A half-hour later Big Ed and me were still standing around, gawking at that Ferrari, when all of a sudden we heard a whole slew of tiny 4-cylinder engines firing up someplace on the other side of the paddock. Boy, there's nothing on this earth like the chorus scream of a hundred or so teacup-sized pistons pounding up and down their cylinder bores at a hellish rate. Imagine an angry swarm of six-pound bumblebees! The noise made me tingle all over, and I sure as hell wanted to get over by the racetrack and see what was up. Big Ed had the fever, too, and in a heartbeat he was elbowing his way through the crowd, heading for the noise, plowing us a path that would've done credit to the Notre Dame offensive line.

We finally broke through up against a wobbly stretch of snow fencing, no more than fifty feet or so downstream from the start/finish line. To tell the truth, it was really nothing more than an ordinary smalltown village street, but the S.C.M.A. and the local charity-types had dressed it up for the occasion with a couple K.L.G. sparkplug signs, some Shell Oil pennants, and a big banner strung across between a tree and a light pole that read:

S.C.M.A. BRIDGEHAMPTON SPORTS CAR RACES
sponsored by the Lions Club of Bridgehampton

Pretty soon we heard the swarm of angry bumblebees again, and then a whole shoving, jostling freight train of MGs and Porsches and stuff I couldn't recognize came roaring out of the last corner, blew past us at a giddy 65 or 70 miles per hour --engines twisted clear to the redline!-- and in a flash they were gone and everything went quiet again. Big Ed looked at me and I looked back at him, and I swear both of us were blinking like we had short circuits in our eyelids or something. Next time around the cars were more strung out, and to tell the truth, it wasn't too many more laps before I started wondering what all the fuss was about. I mean, I'd been to the big oval racetrack at Langhorne once, and there you could see the whole damn layout from any seat in the grandstands. Not to mention that those oval-track racers always came blasting around in mad, scrambling bunches --sometimes three abreast!-- snaking and sliding and banging off each other and showering up great monster roostertails of dirt. Far as I could tell, this sportycar racing looked pretty damn tame by comparison. A car or two would zip past, and then another, and another, and then they'd disappear again and you wouldn't see them again for almost four whole minutes! Why, it was like standing beside a damn county highway, for gosh sakes, watching a bunch of fancy-ass imported European sportscars whiz past. Exactly where was the big enormous thrill in that?

Then Big Ed bought us a souvenir program (which was all of four pages long and cost him a whole half a buck!) and inside I found a crude little map of the so-called "Bridgehampton Grand Prix Road Racing Circuit." Why, it was nothing more than four ordinary blacktop country roads stitched together in a big, squiggly sort of rectangle, damn near four miles around. It didn't take long to figure that the *real* action had to be out on the corners --not here on this dumbass front straightaway-- so I had Big Ed bull us a path down towards the first turn, and that's where everything finally started making sense.

Turn One at Bridgehampton was just a regular, everyday 4-way crossroad intersection where the S.C.M.A.'s "Grand Prix Road Racing Circuit" made a sharp, 90-degree right off Ocean Road and onto Sagaponack. They'd sort of fixed things up for the occasion by installing two or three Armband People with a bunch of colored flags and a few stacks of haybales to keep overeager drivers out of the local scenery, but it was still just an ordinary right-angle chunk of country road. Which was the point, actually, since the whole idea in sportycar racing is to see what cars and which drivers can make the best job of tearing their way around the kind of two-lane, through-the-countryside open roads that normally take you from one small town to another. And it didn't take Big Ed and me but a few minutes on that corner to realize what all the excitement was about! Cars came barreling towards us --the fastest ones doing better than 80!-- and somewheres along the line, each driver had to make a Big Personal Decision about removing his foot from the gas and laying into the brakes. As you can imagine, the general idea was to stay in the loud pedal until the Last Possible Instant, but you could see there were a *lot* of different opinions as to exactly where and when that might be. Plus you had to drop down a gear or two for the corner, and it obviously took a bit of skill and coordination to get that handled while you were simultaneously pushing down for all you were worth on the binders. Why, some of those guys were bobbing and lurching and weaving and slithering all over the place as they desperately attempted to operate three pedals with two feet. But the really, truly slick ones had mastered how to "heel-and-toe," sort of rolling their right foot so they could goose the throttle for each double-clutch downshift while simultaneously keeping hard, steady pressure on the brakes. Which naturally left the other foot free to work the clutch. And it was sheer magic when a guy got it just exactly right, hauling his car down hard, straight, and true while blipping the motor and matching the revs perfectly for each lower gear. I swear, you could sort out the legit hotshoes from the rank-and-file clods just from the sound!

But the fun was just beginning, on account of those cars still had to negotiate their way through the corner itself. And believe me, we observed a whole *bunch* of different driving styles! Some guys steered gingerly around on tiptoes, like they were afraid it was gonna jump up and bite them. Some fidgeted their way around in a jagged, sawtooth fashion, darting and feinting every which way. A few others would just grit their teeth, yank the wheel, and hang on for dear life. But you could pick out the fast guys real easy. They skated through that turn in one single, graceful swoop, sliding like they were driving on ice.

Wow!

And it got even more exciting when two cars charged towards that corner side-by-side, battling for position. See, while the roadway was a generous two lanes wide heading down the front straightaway, the racing line turned pretty much single-file through the corner. At least if you didn't want to ricochet off somebody's fender or go plowing off into the haybales, anyways. So a sort-of *funneling* process had to take place. Very simply, it boiled down to who was gonna be last guy on the brakes. Period. Like a big game of "chicken," you know?

Only better....

Turns out that first session was for the S.C.M.A.'s "small-bore" class, which was limited to cars under 1500cc. That works out to about ninety Cubes American, if you want to do the math. The great majority were MG TCs and TDs, but they were in against those tubby little Porsche cars from Germany, and far as I could tell, the Porsches had them pretty much *covered*. Sure, they looked like ripe tin fruit and sounded worse than a fart in a bathtub, but those Porsches were *fast*. In fact, this one guy in a bare-aluminum colored Porsche convertible appeared to have the legs on everybody. Or maybe you couldn't really call it a con-vertible, since it didn't have a top on board at all. Or even a proper windshield. The owner was a guy named Hoffman, and I overheard as to how he was some kind of major bigwig European sportscar importer. No question he'd imported himself one hell of a fast automobile with that tin-silver Porsche. The thing I didn't understand (at the time, anyways) was how one Porsche or MG or whatever could be so much *quicker* than another Porsche or MG or whatever. I mean, they were basically the same, right?

In a pig's eye....

Why, a sharp mechanic could even *hear* the difference! Some of those Porsches and MGs sounded a whole lot healthier than their brothers and sisters. All lean meat, you know? And that intrigued me, the idea that you could maybe *build* yourself a little faster Porsche or MG or whatever than the next guy. Take that tin-silver Porsche, for example. You could see it was stripped to the bare bones (they didn't even *paint* it, for gosh sakes, which I suppose makes perfect sense if you've ever hefted a gallon can of paint) and the engine note was a whole lot crisper than any of the other German piglets. That Hoffman guy looked to be a pretty decent driver, too (although maybe a bit rough around the edges, since he'd lock up the brakes now and then or maybe nick a haybale or drop a wheel in the dirt every couple laps --then again, he was pushing it pretty hard....)

After smallbore practice ended, the Armband People strolled out to perform their justly famous Inspection Of The Pavement ritual (like what they were doing was real scientific and impor-tant, you know?) and then it was time for the *big* cars to come out and play. Jee-*zus,* what a spectacle! Why, we heard them thundering out of the paddock a full half-mile away, and it was the kind of sound that echoes in your head forever after, what with the twincam Jaguar sixes blaring like a brass section from hell and the throaty gut-rumble of the Caddy, Ford, and Mercury V8s in the Allards throbbing right up through the ground you're standing on! And then came a voice above all the others: a wild, perfectly meshed howl that was more teeth and claws than steel and iron. Of course it was Creighton Pendleton's new 4.1-liter Ferrari Vee-12, snarling its way up through the gears like something escaped from a cage. I swear, it made the hair stand up on the back of your neck. Honest to God it did.

That Creighton Pendleton character could *drive,* too. He started at the very back of the pack (on purpose, most likely) and carved his way up through the field like there was nothing to it at all, passing car after car until he'd gotten around damn near everybody by the time the practice session was over. Looked smooth as silk doing it, too, leaned back all calm and relaxed behind the wheel with his head cocked ever so slightly to one side. Why, the sonofabitch made it look *easy.*

Far as I could tell, the only car anywheres near as quick as Creighton Pendleton's 4.1 Ferrari was that new Cad-Allard from Westbridge with Tommy Edwards at the wheel. But he didn't look smooth or silky at all. Not hardly. In fact, you didn't have to be much of a racing expert to see that Tommy Edwards was fighting that monster every damn inch of the way. He'd haul it down for our corner with the brakes snatching and grabbing and little plumes of rubbersmoke chirping off the tires, and then he'd grab himself a godawful huge handful of steering lock and heel that Allard *hard* into the turn. And that beast of a car would fight him *back,* bucking and snorting and yanking its inside-front wheel clear off the asphalt, pawing the air like a caged lion. *Wow!* But once Tommy got that monster gathered up and pointed straight again, he'd put the spurs to the twin-carburetor, 331 cubic inch Caddy V8 under the hood and that Allard would just about *take off,* snaking side-to-side from the wheelspin and bellowing like a bull elephant in heat. Why, he'd be gone over the next rise before you could so much as blink!

To tell the truth, trying to drive the absolute 10/10ths limit in a Cad-Allard didn't exactly look like ha-ha fun. But it was sure as hell spectacular to watch, no two ways about it.

Chapter 11: The Bug Bites

There was a lunch break after the big car practice, so Big Ed bought us each a couple hot dogs and a soda pop and we wandered our way back into the paddock, just feeding our faces and nosing around all the racecars. Everywhere you looked, people were crammed under fenderwells or buried armpit-deep in engine compartments, hustling like crazy to get things ready --or just back together!-- in time for the afternoon races. Like I told you before, a lot of these so-called "pit crews" were nothing but drivers' wives and brothers and cousins and girlfriends and next-door neighbors and old school chums, so not too many of them were particularly, ahh, *keen* when it came to actual hands-on, nuts-and-bolts mechanical stuff. Not hardly! In fact, it was difficult for a legitimate *professional* grease monkey to keep a straight face. Sure wish I'd had the bandaid, iodine, and burn ointment concession at Bridgehampton that day!

I noticed Barry Spline and some guy in a tan army jacket crouched down around the front of that black Cad-Allard from Westbridge, thrashing away like madmen, so naturally I waltzed over to see what was up. They were in dead trouble all right, what with the brakes torn apart on all four corners and pieces scattered around everywhere on the ground. Looked to me like the linings had more or less disintegrated themselves right off the shoes (lousy riveting job was my guess) and Barry and the army jacket guy were humping like crazy to get new ones installed and everything buttoned back together in time for the afternoon race. Boy, you could sure feel the urgency of *A Big Job* and *No Time Left* sizzling in the air.

I asked the guy in the army jacket if I could maybe help out a little (I mean, you could tell right off he wasn't much with a set of tools) but he just sort of snarled at me like a chained German Shepherd and waved me off. Real nasty, too, on account of he was having one devil of a bad time with the brake shoe return springs. So I stuck my hands in anyway and showed him how a smart, experienced sort of foreign car mechanic could hook them up in a jiffy (*without* putting holes in both thumbs!) and in two

shakes he was out of my way so I could get the job done properly. "How yer doin', Mate?" Barry Spline called over from the
other side of the car.

"Real good," I grunted as I slapped one of the Allard's
huge, finned aluminum brake drums into place.

"Bloody glad yer could make it, Palumbo. Right on time,
too. Think yer can get that side screwed down by yerself?"

"Piece of cake, Barry. Piece of cake."

"There's a good lad."

So Barry and I got the front brakes buttoned up, set the
click-adjusters, went through the whole drill again on the rears,
and finished up with plenty of time to spare. Why, we even had a
few minutes so the army jacket guy could sit behind the wheel
while we bled a couple quick squirts through the hydraulics.
Barry got down by the left-rear and I got down by the right, and
we had the guy in the car pump up the brake pedal a couple
dozen times to build up pressure and then lean on it hard while
we opened up the bleed screws (in perfect unison, of course) with
our thumbs pressed over the bleed holes so no air could leak back
into the system. It's a messy way to do the job (and no good at
all if you've got to live with the floor where you're working!) but
it sure as hell is quick. Then we scooted up to the fronts and did
the same, gave the knockoffs one final slap each with the brass-
head hammer, topped off the oil, water, and brake fluid levels,
re-checked tire pressures, and we were *done* (in, I might add,
what most certainly amounted to an Alltime World's Record for
an Allard J2X brake job --if only somebody'd had a watch on it).

Hey, what do you expect from a couple *professionals?*

While we were busy slaving away on the Allard's brakes, I
had a chance to check out the army jacket guy sitting in the
driver's seat. The first thing I noticed was that his army jacket
was British --R.A.F., actually-- and that the fellow wearing it
was a large, broad-shouldered, thickly set Englishman with ruddy
cheeks, a pencil-thin mustache, and eyes like a fighter pilot.
Which, it turned out, is exactly what Tommy Edwards did during
the war years, personally shooting down no less than eight
German planes (and going down twice himself "the bloody *'ard*
way" according to Barry Spline). Oh, he didn't look much like
Errol Flynn or David Niven in *Dawn Patrol* --not hardly!-- what
with thinning salt-and-pepper hair slicked back across the top of

his head and the beginnings of a middle-aged beer paunch rolling over the top of his trouser belt. But even so, you could tell from the moment you looked into his eyes that Tommy Edwards had whatever kind of moxie it took to drive a racing car. Even a musclebound brute like that Allard.

As soon as we were done with the brakes and the final flight-check, Tommy clambered out from behind the wheel and walked right up to me. "Hey, thanks an awful bunch, sport," he said with a smart British clip to his voice, "I'm afraid I might have been a bit rude to you when you first popped over...."

"Aw, that's okay," I told him.

"No, really. No bloody excuse for that type of behavior."

"'Ee's useter much worse, Tommy," Barry tossed in, "yer can bank on it."

"Well, we couldn't have bloody well done it without you," the guy in the Royal Air Force jacket continued, extending a large, freshly manicured hand with little halos of grease under all the fingernails. "Can't tell you how much we appreciate it." Boy, that Tommy Edwards had a grip like a damn bench vise!

"Aw," I said, toeing the gravel, "it wuz nothin'."

"For *you*, perhaps," Tommy Edwards laughed, "but I'm all bloody thumbs when it comes to mechanical things. Ask Barry."

"It's God's own truth," Barry sighed, wiping his brow with the back of his hand and leaving an absolutely spectacular grease smear all the way across his forehead.

Tommy looked at the large, black smudge over Barry's eyebrows and shot me a wink so quick I wasn't sure I saw it. "Well," he sighed, tossing a weatherbeaten green racing helmet into the passenger seat, "I'd best be getting off. Want to be on grid when Mr. Pendleton arrives so I can put the needle in a bit."

"Think yer can put him off his game?" Barry asked from beneath his magnificent new grease smear.

"Oh, I doubt it, actually. He's a pretty cool customer, you know. Then again, it's always fun trying...."

"Well, 'ave yerself a good run. And try ter bring the bloody car back in one piece, eh?"

"That is *always* my intention, Mr. Spline," Tommy answered with a smart little two-finger salute. Then he turned to me again. "Thanks again for lending a hand, sport. Ever so much. Never could have done it without you. No bloody way a'tall."

"Hey, no problem," I told him again, feeling the color coming up in my cheeks.

"You be sure and pop by for a cold one after the shooting stops, aah...bloody hell, I don't even know your name."

"'Is name's Buddy Palumbo."

"Well, Buddy Palumbo, thanks again for saving the day. As I said, I'm not very much good at mechanics...."

"Yer can bloody well say that again!" Barry snickered.

"Very well, Mr. Spline, I believe I shall." And with that, Tommy Edwards took a deep breath, raised his jaw skyward, and bellowed, *"I'M NOT MUCH BLOODY GOOD AT AUTO MECHANICS. NOT MUCH BLOODY GOOD AT ALL!"* at the very top of his lungs. Jeez, it made all the people around us drop what they were doing and stare. "There," Tommy said with a sharp military heel-click, *"that* ought to put a proper cap on it, I should think. I trust you're satisfied, Mr. Spline?"

"Suits me," Barry grinned, "'owbout you, Buddy?"

"Well," I said, trying to get just the right hint of swagger in my voice, "I *guess* so."

"Very well, then," Tommy nodded, "that should do it. Oh, and Mr. Palumbo?"

"Yes?"

"Do see if you can find Mr. Spline here a bloody mirror and a bit of handkerchief, won't you?"

As you can tell, we were getting a pretty good charge off the sensation of a job well done and finished in the very nick of time. Believe me, there's no feeling like it. Not in the whole blessed world. In fact, as I watched Tommy climb behind the wheel, fire up that big hotrod Caddy --Jee-*zus*, it made the damn *ground* shake!-- and roar away in a shower of gravel, I realized that my hands were trembling just a little and my mouth tasted like I'd been chewing on a roll of medical gauze. That's how *pumped* you can get when a race is on the line and you've only got thirty minutes to finish a job that books two-hours-plus in the flat rate manual. I mean, you could never get that excited replacing the damn starter motor or heater core in some old lady's Chevy wagon just so's she can pick her brat kids up after school....

With Tommy off to join the cars gridding up for the big car feature race, Barry and me headed over by trackside to watch what was left of the smallbore contest. Along the way, I asked him why he didn't bring Sylvester Jones to help out with the wrenching duties. "Oh, we couldn't do *that*," Barry said, raising his eyebrows like it should have been obvious. "Why, Sylvester'd be a bit of a bloody, er, *problem* 'ere at Bridgehampton, mate. After all, we don't exactly wanter *advertise* that we've got a bleedin' Jungle Bunny workin' on people's Jagyewhars, now do we?" Looking around, I could sort of understand what Barry was talking about. I mean, you didn't see much of anybody like Sylvester Jones in the paddock at Bridgehampton. Not hardly. Or many like Big Ed Baumstein either, come to think of it.

Anyhow, we muscled our way down to the first corner, and just like I figured, that Hoffman guy in the tin-silver Porsche roadster was way, *way* out front. Second place --damn near forty seconds back-- was a nifty little Italian job called an Osca. It was bright red (what else?) and quite a bit sleeker and prettier to look at than the Porsche. Made a nicer noise, too. But it wasn't anywheres near as quick (at least not with that particular driver at the wheel, anyways) and so that hopped-up, stripped-down Porsche roadster was simply running away with the race. Not much of a contest, if you want to know the truth of it.

But things were hardly dull, since we had a whole passle of TCs and TDs scrapping for the MG-class trophy further back in the pack, and a few of those guys were really going at it. In fact, there was one certified lunatic in an old dingy-green righthand-drive '47 TC who kept the crowd on its feet by braking so late and hauling into the corners so incredibly, impossibly deep that everybody figured he was going to fly right into the haybales. But he never did. And was he ever exciting to watch! Lap after lap, he'd wait until he was almost *in* the damn corner before laying into the brakes, and then he'd snatch her down a gear, toss the car ass-out sideways, and *drift* his way through in a wild, tire-shuddering slide, barely kissing the dirt at the exit every single time. Not that it did him much good, since the motor was loading up something awful through the middle of the corner (float level or a duff needle-and-seat, most likely) which caused it to stumble and stutter and run rat for the next couple hundred yards down the straightaway. What can you do?

Big Ed's program said the driver of that old TC was a guy named Calvin Carrington from Palm Beach, Florida, and believe me, he was braver than Dick Tracy. But, like I said, his car wasn't much good (in fact, it was what those of us in the professional auto mechanicing trade would refer to as "a roach" or "a "rat") and no question he was driving maybe just a little bit *past* the ragged edge of control in a desperate effort to make it up. Which is undoubtedly why he went missing about halfway through the event. "Yer can't carry a bloody car on yer back, mate," Barry sighed. "No driver on earth's so bleedin' great 'e can make the bloody metal do more than it's willing...."

There was an important lesson in that.

And speaking of lessons, the guy in the tin-silver Porsche had the race all sewed up, but the idiot just didn't have the brains to back off and cruise his way to an easy win. No sir. Why, he was pushing and *pushing* that little aluminum bucket, shifting at the redline, braking at the Last Possible Instant, dropping a wheel off the pavement here and there.... And then he simply didn't come around. There was just this big, empty silence where the Porsche should have been, followed about forty seconds back by that pretty red Italian Osca, tooling along all by its lonesome, leading the damn race! The Porsche was nowhere to be seen. Behind the Osca came another long silence and then the quickest of the MGs zipped past, still battling each other tooth and nail, and behind them (at long last) the tin-silver Porsche reappeared with its left-front fender all crumpled to shit. I couldn't believe it! Seemed like it was still running okay, because it did manage to pick off the MGs before the checker fell, but that slick little Osca was long gone. Boy, I bet that Porsche driver felt stupid. I mean, he had the race in the bag, you know? And so I learned yet another invaluable motorsports lesson: *it's not who goes fastest at first, but who FINISHES first at the end.*

There was quite a bit of cleanup work to be done between races, including deceased-car removal for Calvin Carrington's ratty-but-spectacular '47 TC, which had apparently lost itself a front wheel and clobbered the haybales somewheres on the backside of the course. Big Ed bought Barry and me a couple sodas (at a whole damn quarter *each!*) from some privateer pop vendor who was apparently working on his early retirement plan at

Bridgehampton that particular Saturday afternoon, and then we strolled over by the start/finish line to check out the grid for the big-car feature. I was proud to see Tommy Edwards' black Cad-Allard on the very first row (I mean, he was *my* driver now, right?) but lined up next to him --on the *in*side-- was that Creighton Pendleton character in his blood-red 4.1 Ferrari. My God, was that car ever *beautiful.* And just a little bit *evil,* too. "That's sure one hell of an automobile," I observed with a low whistle.

"Yer bloody well right about that, mate," Barry nodded. "All-alloy Vee-twelve. Over'ead cams. Triple Weber carburetors right down the middle. The 'ole bleedin' lot. She'll be a man-sized load for our boy Tommy t'manage. No bloody doubt about it." Then Barry leaned in a little closer and whispered, "'Ee's a stuckup bastard, that Creighton Pendleton is, but the bloke can bloody well *drive....* "

"Saaay," Big Ed wanted to know, "how much does one a'them Ferrari things *cost,* anyway?"

Barry Spline rolled his eyes. "Damn near three times a Jagyewahr one-twenty. *Three times!* And that's *if* yer can get yer bloody 'ands on one."

Even Big Ed had to be impressed with that.

On the grid behind Creighton Pendleton's 4.1 Ferrari and "our" Cad-Allard were a few more Allards powered by assorted Cadillac, Ford, and Mercury V8s, followed by a whole damn flight squadron of Jaguar XK120s. Here and there I noticed a couple of those cycle-fendered Frazer-Nash things and some other oddball stuff I couldn't quite recognize. Our friend Skippy Welcher and his ex-everything XK120*M* were situated well back towards the tail-end of the grid (occupying the outside slot on the second-to-last row, in fact) and I must admit it did my heart good to see the old asshole doing so poorly.

I'd never been around the start of a big-bore sportscar race before, and let me tell you, it was pretty God Damn exciting. First off things were strangely quiet, with the cars lined up in two silent rows and just a few last-minute *whaps* of brass-head hammers on knockoff ears to punctuate the hushed chatter of the S.C.M.A. officials and some off-the-cuff wisecracking between drivers who found themselves gridded side-by-side. Then one of the armband people circled his arm in the air and all those big, powerful, highly tuned internal combustion engines exploded to life --Jee-*zus*, it sounded like a damn artillery barrage!-- and then that Robert Montgomery guy from Hollywood led the pack around on a parade lap behind that brand new Nash-Healey convertible I told you about. It seemed to take an awful long time (you know how actor-types can get when they have a crowd to play to) and you could feel the tension building as we waited for the cars to reappear at the other end of the straightaway. You could tell that Robert Montgomery character had a thing or two to learn about highly tweaked racing engines, because he took it so ridiculously slow on the pace lap (waving to the fans, no doubt) that a lot of those motors were steaming and snorting and popping impatiently back through the carburetors by the time they crept up to their grid positions on the start/finish straight-away. And there they sat, glistening in the sun, twenty-six of the newest, fastest, most exciting, most powerful racing sportscars in the entire world. Waiting....

As if on cue, this important-looking stiff in a Great White Hunter outfit (I kid you not) marched up between the rows of cars, carrying a large green flag rolled up under his arm like a drill sergeant's favorite baton. When he reached the front of the pack, he turned smartly about-face and faced the drivers, hiding the flag behind his back. Engines revved like crazy as twenty-six left feet poised hair-trigger on their clutch pedals, ready to side-step out of the way at a split-second's notice. But the Great White Hunter guy just stood there like a statue, glaring back at them, waiting to see if anybody was going to flinch. Engines raced even higher, and just as I was preparing myself for a meteor shower of molten piston bits and connecting-rod fragments, the Great White Hunter guy whipped out the green and waved it like his arm was on fire. Clutches popped, engines screamed, and tires shrieked in protest as the field exploded away towards corner one, leaving a pungent haze of burning rubber and castor oil fumes in its wake. It looked to me like Tommy's Allard got just a hair of a jump off the line, but then I saw Creighton Pendleton's Ferrari nip smartly to the inside as the pack disappeared from sight.

"Hey!" I hollered to Big Ed, "let's go watch down by the corner." Big Ed nodded and began bulling us a path towards turn one, and we were about halfway there by the time the cars blast-ed by to complete the first lap, with Creighton Pendleton's Fer-rari on the point and "our" Allard right on his decklid. Jeez, you wouldn't *believe* the blessed noise, what with the angry gut-rumble of that twin-carb Caddy all twisted up around the incredible, wild-animal howl of that twelve-cylinder Ferrari, the both of them W.F.O. (*Wide Fucking Open!*) and straining for more. Why, it was enough to crust your jeans. Honest it was!

Next lap the Allard was back in front *--just--* with Creighton Pendleton's Ferrari right up his tailpipes and crowding him something awful. And you could see Tommy was having to battle that brute of an automobile every damn step of the way, pulling back hard on the reins every time it reared up and tried to get away from him. No question the Ferrari looked every bit as fast (or maybe even *faster*) and a *lot* less work to drive. It braked without slewing this way and that all over the road and went through the corners in neat, smooth, nicely balanced drifts instead of bucking and leaping and snaking every which way like a damn rodeo bull. In fact, you got the notion that Creighton Pendleton was maybe just playing cat-and-mouse with Tommy Edwards. But every time he sneaked past into the lead, Tommy'd put on a wild-ass charge and somehow, somewhere, manage to get him back again. I swear, those two must've swapped positions a dozen times --maybe more!-- until the crowd was whooping and hollering every lap like it was the final minute of the damn Army-Navy football game.

What a *race!*

But a hundred miles at Bridgehampton is a long, *long* way --well over an hour-- and by two-thirds distance Tommy was having trouble with the brakes again. You could see he was backing off earlier and earlier for the corners, and it was only a matter of time before Creighton Pendleton pulled neatly alongside, gave him a little "I told you so" finger wave, and motored off into the distance. There wasn't a damn thing Tommy could do about it. But he hung on and finished second (*with no brakes at all!*) and you had to give him credit for that. Not many drivers know how to ease off and keep their cool when things get really desperate and First Place is on the line....

Why, some guys can't even keep their heads when they're muddling along all by their lonesome at the back of the pack! Take our friend Skippy Welcher, for example. He was soldiering on in his customary position (near the tail of the field, natch) when Creighton Pendleton came up to lap him for maybe the fifth or sixth time towards the end of the race. I guess the sight of that red Ferrari looming up in his mirrors got The Skipper a little over-stimulated. Or perhaps Skippy decided it was time to show the world that *he* could go through a corner just as fast as the race leader. Which, of course, he couldn't. Or maybe Skippy simply forgot where one of his precious braking markers was. Or where his brake *pedal* was, even. Whatever the reason, The Skipper came charging into our corner *waaay* too hot, realized he was in over his head, and slammed down for all he was worth on the brake pedal (instantly locking up all four wheels, so now he couldn't steer, either). The Jag slewed left-right-left and quickly snap-spun into the haybales *--KA-WHUMPHFF!--* showering straw and dust all over the place. Creighton Pendleton had to make a Phenomenal Avoidance so as not to collect The Skipper broadside, and then we had S.C.M.A. Armband People chasing around in all directions, blowing whistles and waving yellow flags and tossing chunks of busted haybale off the racing line. To tell the truth, there wasn't much in the way of serious damage --just a big, ugly ding in the Jag's rear fender and a busted tail-light lens-- but the crowd went absolutely nuts, cheering and hooting and clapping their hands in the air as Skippy reversed out of the hay, flashed that misshapen gold-tooth smile of his, waved a two-finger salute to his many legions of fans, and fishtailed away, scattering straw and terrified S.C.M.A. corner workers in his wake. What a moron.

That final drama over, Creighton Pendleton went on to win the race by a revoltingly comfortable margin with Tommy's brakeless Allard a distant second, and afterwards he paraded his Ferrari around on a victory lap accompanied by, without question, *the single most gorgeous female creature I had ever seen in my life!* In person or otherwise. Her hair was the iridescent chestnut color of a Kentucky Derby winner, and I swear you could catch the sparkle off her smile from the far side of the fences. The two of them made quite a pair, laughing and smiling and waving to the crowd as that Ferrari snarled past --checkered flag snapping in the breeze-- looking like some sort of billboard advertisement for a life the rest of us poor slobs can only dream about. When they disappeared over the next rise, everything went deadly quiet. Like after the circus closes down....

Neither Big Ed or me felt much like leaving, so we decided to head over by the trophy presentation at the start/finish line and see what was up. To tell the truth, it was a pretty dull affair, since the S.C.M.A. had scads of trophies to hand out (all the way down through sixth place in a truly bewildering assortment of classes!) not to mention a bunch of "special" awards for Sportsmanship and Hard Luck and Best Looking Car and Furthest Distance Traveled (which went to some masochist who drove a TD all the way from Nebraska!) and Lord Only Knows what else. I guess the important thing was for every single S.C.M.A. driver to get *some* sort of pewter cup or dangly trinket to hang on the old mantelpiece back home. And if you somehow didn't manage to actually *win* anything, a bent or broken racecar was almost as good. Just so long as you had something --*anything*-- to brag on in the bar after the racing was over.

Unless you were Cal Carrington, that is. Why, that poor kid looked absolutely shell-shocked, walking around and around his bent-up, dust-covered TC with his head in his hands, trying like hell to figure out what he was going to tell his father. You could tell from his clothes that Cal Carrington came from some pretty serious money somewheres along the line, but it didn't take Sherlock Holmes and Dr. Watson to figure he'd put that ragtag TC together out of embezzled college money or something and gone racing on the sly. And now that car was in very sad shape indeed, what with both front fenders bashed in and the steering gear skewed hard left on the right side and hard right on the left (pigeon toed, you know?) not to mention that the brake drum was ground clear through to the shoes on the side where the wheel came off. Oh, and the headlamp buckets were now resting on the lefthand (passenger) side floorboards like a pair of crumpled-up tin cans. No question that TC looked pretty damn grim.

And so did Cal Carrington, come to think of it. He was a lanky, good-looking rich kid with wavy sun-blond hair, Bass Weejun loafers, and eyes as blue as the ocean on a picture postcard from Hawaii. He didn't look a single day older than me (if that!) so I knew he must've had himself a truly topnotch line of bullshit --not to mention a set of excellent phony IDs-- in order to convince the S.C.M.A. club regulars to let him race. Of course, Cal *was* from a good family, and that always counted for an awful lot with the S.C.M.A.

I walked around that poor old TC myself a couple times, and it didn't take more than one tour to reach the conclusion that Cal Carrington didn't know Jack Shit about automobile mechanics. Why, he was even worse than Old Man Finzio! But it wasn't because he was a Butcher or a Hasher or anything like that. No sir. The problem here was simply that Cal Carrington didn't know one damn thing about what makes pistons go up and down or wheels go around. Like fr'instance the reason that tire parted company with his car and put him into the haybales was on account of the rim came more or less completely unlaced from the hub. That has a habit of happening with wire wheels when you don't bother to check the spoke tension every now and again. But you could tell this was Front Page News to Cal Carrington when I explained it to him. "Gee whiz," he said, "I sure wish I'd known about that. Why, my old man's gonna absolutely *kill* me when he sees this." Truth is, there wasn't much you could do to that ratty old MG and have it look like fresh damage, but Cal had sure managed it (and apparently his dad had a keen enough eye to tell the difference, too).

Considering the way Cal drove that heap before the wheel came off, I felt like maybe doing a little something to help him out. He was one of those helplessly handsome All-American Boy types you just can't help liking, even though it'd drive you nuts how Cal never seemed to have any cash money in his pockets --not *ever!*-- even though he came from a very wealthy family. It'd also make you crazy how he never seemed to get dirty when he worked on cars. Even scruffy old shitboxes like that TC. I swear, it was like grease just flat wouldn't *stick* to him! Plus Cal was one of those disgustingly athletic gazelle hybrids who can leap over any obstacle on a dead run or one-hand a set of car keys anytime you toss them over. Some guys are just born real quick and graceful and coordinated that way. Why, it makes you want to tie their shoelaces together (or better yet lop off a couple of their toes with a meat cleaver, you know?).

Anyhow, I was surprised to see a New Jersey tag on the back of Cal's busted TC (after all, the race program said he came from Florida) and suddenly a little light popped on in my head. "Say," I asked him, "you come up here from Jersey?"

Cal nodded.

"But the program says you're from Palm Beach."

"Aw, that's just my uncle's winter place. I put it down on the entry form so they won't send any newsletters or race results or anything to my folks' house. Why, they'd ground me for*ever* if they ever got wind I was racing."

"Don't you worry your uncle might say something?"

"Nah, not really. He's dead."

"Then who lives there?"

"Oh, just the servants, mostly. I guess we go down now and then in the wintertime, and so does my mom's sister."

"And they never see the mail?"

"Nah. I got a deal with the gardener. He burns everything addressed to me."

"You have to pay him off?"

"Not necessary. I saw him with my older sister once. He's happy to help out. Besides, he likes me."

I'd only known Cal Carrington for five minutes, but I could easily see why. He was just that kind of guy. "So," I asked him, "whereabouts you live back in Jersey?"

"Cedar Grove. Why?"

"Why, that's *perfect!*"

"It is?"

"*Sure* it is!" I said, clapping my hand on his shoulder. "I work at a Sinclair station over in Passaic. I'm a mechanic, see. In fact, I'm the *head* mechanic around our place...."

"You *are?*"

"Sure am," I nodded, showing off my knuckles as proof, "and if you can get this heap towed over there, I'll be glad to help you fix it up to go racing again." You say stupid stuff like that when you've just gotten your first taste of the sport and it's still buzzing around inside your head like a hornet in a glass jar. You'll notice I didn't stop for one single, solitary second to consider what Old Man Finzio might think of the idea.

"Gee, that'd be *great!*" Cal whooped. But then his eyes narrowed down and he looked at me kind of sideways. "Now, you gotta understand, I don't have a lot of ready cash on hand for parts or labor or anything...."

Big Ed cleared his throat. "Well, I could maybe see my way clear to lending ya a few dibs. Just t'help out, see. Yer *good* fer it, aint'cha."

Cal looked down at his shiny Bass Weejun loafers, "Yeah. Sure I am...*eventually*, anyways."

Big Ed pulled out a wad thick as a ham sandwich and peeled a couple crisp greenbacks off the top. "You be sure I get this back, Bub, or else--"

"--or else he'll use your head for a bowling ball!"

"That's *right!*" Big Ed growled, slipping me a wink.

"Wow! Thanks a *lot,*" Cal gushed, folding the bills and stuffing them in his hip pocket. "Now all I gotta figure is what the heck I'm gonna tell my father. Geez, if he ever finds out I been *racing....*"

Fortunately for Cal Carrington, he was pitching directly to my greatest strength: making up believable bullshit stories about broken automobiles. "Oh, just tell him, umm, tell him the car, umm, tell him the car broke down near Passaic and, umm, and you hadda leave it off to be fixed. Tell him, umm, tell him the *clutch* went out."

"But I just had a new clutch put in. Just last month."

"Okay, no problem. How 'bout a starter motor."

"Just had one of those, too."

"Saaay," I wondered out loud, "you don't get your work done at Westbridge, do you?"

"How'd you know?"

"Just a lucky guess."

So Cal Carrington went off to hunt up a towtruck and me and Big Ed wandered over by Tommy Edwards' Allard to congratulate him on a really super race, even if it only got him a second place finish at the checker. I mean, he still beat all the other Allards, and that had to be worth something. Tommy was sitting on the ground beside his racecar with his shoulders propped up against a front tire, drinking beer out of his shiny new second-place mug and looking pretty well exhausted. You could see the race with that Ferrari had taken a lot of the starch out of him. But he brightened up the moment he saw us. "Hey, sport," he called out to me, waving his free hand weakly through the air, "how about a short cool one."

As you can imagine, Big Ed and me were happy to oblige.

"Thanks again for all the help," Tommy said, "that was one hell of a decent job you did on the brakes."

"But they went out again," I reminded him.

"Of *course* they went out again," Tommy grinned. "Allards always run a bit shy of brakes towards the end of a race. Especially on a circuit with fiddly tight little corners like this one. Bloody characteristic of the breed, don't you know. But they lasted a bit longer than usual today, so nicely done."

While we were standing there shooting the breeze, this short, dimply brunette wandered up carrying a wrinkled stub roll of toilet paper in her hand and a distinctly unpleasant look on her face. It was Tommy Edwards' wife, Ronnie, and you could see she was less than impressed with the powder room facilities at the Bridgehampton Grand Prix Road Races. "This is undoubtedly the last roll of toilet tissue on Long Island," she growled without the least hint of a smile, "and by God, I'm hanging on to it." I noticed Tommy's wife had a pair of big front teeth and a pushed-up little pug nose that made her look kind of cute (if you like mice, anyway) but she seemed a tad edgy and impatient for my tastes. I mean, racetrack sanitary facilities have always been a little, er, *basic,* and it's one of those things you just have to get used to if you're planning to hang around the sport. Anyhow, Tommy introduced us all around and asked Ronnie to rustle us up a couple cold beers. She said "sure," but it came out in such a way that it easily could've been mistaken for "drop dead, asshole."

Turns out that Ronnie Edwards came from some well-to-do banking family in upper Westchester County, and I guess she met Tommy while she was working as a U.S.O. volunteer in England during the war. It must have been very romantic, what with him as a devil-may-care fighter pilot who might not survive his next mission and her working day and night with all the famous bandleaders and movie celebrities and such who came over on tour. My guess is they only got to see each other once or twice a week, and probably most of that was spent in the sack. But then the war ended and they came back stateside to join her family (not to mention her family's money) and that's when things started going straight to hell. Without the R.A.F. and the U.S.O. and the dramas and uncertainties of war to keep it interesting, their marriage quickly disintegrated into an uneasy truce between two people who didn't so much *hate* each other as have nothing much in common. Not at all. Ronnie liked charity balls and garden parties and theater openings and such, while Tommy Edwards liked Ronnie's family's money and the fact that it allowed him the wherewithal and free time to go racing. She struck me as one of those well-bred Finishing School types who work real hard at being gracious and pleasant and correct all the time, but even so, you couldn't miss that there were maybe eight or nine thousand other places she would've rather been that particular Saturday afternoon. And you'd be amazed at the high percentage of racers' wives who feel the same exact way.

Anyhow, Ronnie brought Big Ed and me a couple beers and afterwards we helped them load up, and I reckon we must've congratulated Tommy a dozen times apiece for the swell job he did in the race. "Oh," he said with a shrug, "it wasn't much of anything. After all, we didn't manage a win, now did we?"

"Maybe not," I argued, "but gee whiz, you ran outta brakes. Besides, this thing looks like a real God Damn *handful* compared to that Ferrari you were up against."

"Oh, it's not so bad as it looks," Tommy grinned, patting the Allard gently on its nose emblem. "These old girls are just a mite *stubborn* about slowing down and turning every now and again. One gets used to it. And the buggers *do* go like bloody stink down the straightaways, don't they?"

"Yeah, they do," I agreed, "but they're sure all over the place in the corners."

"You know, a chap once said if I ever saw what it looks like from the outside, I'd never get *in* the bloody thing again."

We had a good laugh over that, and I must admit I felt pretty damn special, hanging around and shooting the breeze with an ex-fighter-pilot automobile racer like Tommy Edwards.

Right out of the blue, Big Ed asked if he could maybe sit in Tommy's Allard. "Sure. By all means," Tommy told him. So Big Ed lifted and scrunched and wiggled and folded himself inside. *Uugh. Scrape. Grunt.* In spite of how huge it was on the outside, there wasn't much room in the cockpit of that Allard at all, and I swear Big Ed couldn't do much more than *breathe* once he got himself crammed behind the wheel. And shallow, at that. But you should've seen the look flickering up in his eyes as Big Ed glared out at the world through that little speedboat-style racing windscreen. Why, you could hear the old gears meshing and wheels turning again under Big Ed's Jaguar cap, and his fat Cuban stogie was damn near *twirling* between his teeth.

After Tommy and Ronnie took off for home, me and Big Ed made our way across the paddock and joined the big victory celebration around Creighton Pendleton's first-place Ferrari. It looked just magnificent, you know, glistening there in the late afternoon sunlight with a few heat waves still shimmering off it and the smell of crisp metal and roasted brake linings hanging in the air. As you can imagine, people were milling around it on all sides, talking and laughing and smoking cigarettes and guzzling beers, and right in the middle of everything was Creighton Pendleton himself: a tall, dark, cologne-ad type wearing powder blue racing coveralls with "Creighton Pendleton III" embroidered above the breast pocket in bright silvery thread. Boy, did he ever look the part! He had a deep Bermuda tan and perfect teeth and a thick wave of jet-black hair slicked back from his forehead like Rudy Valentino. A gaggle of well-wishers were taking turns pumping his hand and slapping him on the back and congratulating him --one right after the other-- but through it all he just stood there, nonchalant as can be, leaning back ever-so-casually against a blood-red fender while nodding and shrugging and every now and again flashing this Knowing Smile he kept on tap for special occasions. You could tell Creighton Pendleton got a *lot* of mileage out of that smile.

Then the girl who rode with him on the victory lap --without a doubt the smoothest, sleekest, most thoroughbred specimen of a young woman I had *ever* seen-- stepped out of the crowd, draped her arms around his neck, closed her eyes, and drew him down into a long, lingering kiss with a whole lot of tongue in it.

Wow!

Chapter 12: Aunt Rosamarina's Race Shop

Imagine my surprise when I showed up at the Sinclair Monday morning and found Old Man Finzio in the process of throwing the remains of Cal Carrington's raggedy old TC off the property. I guess Cal managed to get it hauled into the station late Sunday evening, then just sort of *left* it there --right smack in front of the overhead door!-- without so much as a note or a phone number or *any*thing. Naturally the bent-up heap wouldn't roll, what with the steering gear all twisted to shit and the right front brake drum scraping on the pavement, so the Old Man was busily hitching it up behind the towtruck so's he could drag it off to a back alley someplace and ditch it. I have to admit, Cal's TC looked about hopeless enough for that type of disposal. "Hey, Mr. Finzio," I yelled over, "where ya goin' with that *customer's automobile?*" See, the Old Man was real particular that we never worked on "people's cars" at the Sinclair. Oh, no. They were always *"customers' automobiles."*

"This trash heap?" the Old Man grunted, digging yet another mashed-up Camel out of his back pocket. "I thought mebbe I'd haul it over by the boneyard and see if they'd gimme ennything good fer it."

"You can't do *that,*" I told him. "Why, that's a *race* car."

"A racecar? This piece of shit? *Haw!* You gotta be joking."

"No, honest. It just had a little, er, a little *racing accident,* that's all."

Old Man Finzio gave the MG a thorough eyeballing. "Looks t'me like it's had itself a whole major-league *assortment* of racing accidents. And none of 'em was particular little, either.... Say, who owns this shitbox, anyways?"

"It belongs to, aah, *Mister* Carrington," I told him, "from over in Cedar Grove. Big Ed and me met him at the races in Bridgehampton this last weekend. Gee whiz, you shoulda seen him *drive* this thing. Until the wheel came off, anyhow."

"Hmm. I s'pect that slowed him down a tad, didn't it?"

"Yeah. That and the haybales. Anyhow, I told him to haul it over here so's we could maybe fix it up for him."

"*Fix* it?!" the Old Man snorted, "and just where in the hell didja plan t'*start?*" He took a short, hard drag on his cigarette. "Lissen t'me, sonny, the only thing *this* car needs is a few words from a preacher and a decent burial." The Old Man decided that was real damn funny and started to laugh, but just like always it started him hacking and choking and coughing something awful. Imagine a truckload of wet coal rattling down a rusty tin chute. Sometimes it got so bad he'd double over and gasp for air like he was about to grab his chest and flop over dead right in front of you. Which is probably the reason Old Man Finzio worked so damn hard at not being amused.

Anyhow, there was no question we had to do something with Cal's MG (I mean, we couldn't very well leave it blocking the entrance to the service bay, could we?) so the Old Man and me finished hitching it up to the towtruck and dragged it out back behind the building. There wasn't enough room between the garage and the fence to simply haul it all the way to the spot next to the rusty steel oil tank where Old Man Finzio wanted it, so we had to do the last part by hand with a floor jack run up under the corner where the wheel was missing. As you can imagine, the Old Man and me had to wrestle and fight and heave and lever that heap around like a pair of dock workers in order to get it into that particular slot, and it didn't help matters any that the concrete turned to gravel right there so the damn thing kept trying to slip off the jack and fall on Old Man Finzio's toes. Needless to say, we were both worked into a pretty good lather by the time we finally got Cal's ratty TC snug up against the outside wall, and it didn't take any special genius to see the Old Man was developing a very deep and personal dislike for this particular example of British automotive artistry. Not only had he found it abandoned and immobilized directly in front of his place of business, but it had since managed to scrape all his knuckles, bang both his knees, repeatedly attempted to crush his toes, and in the bargain got him to wheezing and coughing so bad he was making the sort of weird gurgling and strangling noises you most often associate with a Jaycees spook house on Halloween.

Just like always, the Old Man grabbed the rumpled-up pack out of his back pocket and lit himself up another fresh Camel to take care of it.

Three whole days passed before Cal Carrington bothered to show up and talk to Old Man Finzio about his car. He just tooled in out of the blue late one afternoon at the wheel of his mom's new two-tone Packard, and immediately set some kind of first-time-rookie World Record for pissing off Old Man Finzio. I didn't have a watch on it or anything, but I reckon Cal got the job handled in less than thirty seconds flat. The problem was he just didn't see anything particularly *wrong* with dumping his busted MG smack-dab in front of the Old Man's service door, not calling for three days, and then expecting Old Man Finzio to drop whatever the hell he was doing the instant Cal rolled in and devote his full and undivided attention to Cal's broken-down MG. I guess you could say Cal Carrington was maybe a little bit spoiled. Maybe more than a little, even.

"Now see here, sonnyboy," the Old Man hissed, running his eyes over Cal's mom's new Packard, "we *work* fer a living around this here service station. We got things t'*do*, unnerstand?"

"Yeah, sure," Cal said, not understanding one little bit. "All I wanna know is when my MG'll be ready."

"Ready fer *what?* A decent burial?" The Old Man started to snigger, and I was worried he might be about to go off on one of his disgusting laughing/hacking/coughing/choking/gasping-for-air jags, but I guess the joke wasn't so funny the second time around and he decided he'd rather light himself up another wrinkled Camel instead. "Now lissen here, sonnyboy," he said, taking a long, thoughtful drag on his cigarette, "if you really want, I can have my *associate* here," the Old Man nodded in my direction, "write'cha up a *estimate* on that automobile of yers."

"An *estimate?*" Cal gulped, flashing me one of those wide-eyed Judas looks.

"That's right, sonnyboy, a *estimate,*" the Old Man nodded, blowing a cloud of smoke into Cal's face for emphasis, "an' I want you should check it over *reeeal* careful. Make sure it looks *right* t'ya, see. Sure wouldn't want fer there t'be no *misunderstandings* later...."

"Oh, of course not," Cal mumbled, kind of swaying back and forth on his heels.

"An' then y'could mebbe give us, oh, say, a little *deposit* on the parts?"

"A d-deposit?" Cal stammered.

"That's right, a deposit. You just check over that estimate real careful, then fork us over a little earnest-money deposit t'cover the cost of parts. *That's* when we'll get started fixing yer car." The Old Man took a long, deep drag off his cigarette, savored it, and slowly exhaled. "You unnerstand?"

"Uh, well, er, exactly how *much* of a deposit are you thinking about?" Cal wanted to know.

Old Man Finzio looked Cal up and down, checking out his neatly pressed ivy league clothes and Bass Weejun loafers. Then his eyes shifted out to the brand new, two-tone blue Packard Patrician parked out by the pumps. "Oh, I dunno," the Old Man mused, rubbing the four-day growth of stubble on his chin, "how does, oh, say, a hunnert dollars sound."

"*A hundred dollars!*" Cal yelped. "Gee whiz, mister, I, uh, never, um, never carry that much cash *on* me."

"But you could *git* it, right?" the Old Man snapped.

"Oh, uh, s-sure. Sure I could. No problem. It's just that, well..." Cal's eyes slipped down to the cuffs of the Old Man's coveralls, "my, uh, *assets* aren't real, aah, *liquid* right now...."

Well, Old Man Finzio may have been just a grizzled old gas station grease monkey from Passaic, but he sure as hell understood flat broke when he heard it. In *any* language. The Old Man raised up a bony, tobacco-stained finger and waggled it back and forth directly under Cal's nose. "Now lissen here, sonnyboy, we ain't runnin' no charity benefit fer runnynose rich kids around *my* service station. No siree. Way I figger it, y'owe me a dollar fifty fer storage already. An' that's not even *countin'* haulin' that damn wreck of yers around back with the towtruck an' stickin' it inna slot. Normally, I charge folks two bucks just t'hitch up."

Now you could tell Cal Carrington wasn't used to getting pushed around like that --especially by dirty-fingernail types like Old Man Finzio-- and no question he was starting to get a little hot under the collar. Which of course was the worst thing he could possibly do. "Now look here, mister," Cal growled with a steely new edge to his voice, "I don't think you *understand....*"

"*Like HELL I don't!*" the Old Man snarled, jumping out from behind the counter and jamming his pointy, stubble-covered chin squarely up into Cal's face, "It's *you* who don't unnerstand things, sonnyboy. Y'got till noon Sattiday t'come up with *at least* fifty bucks, or I'm draggin' that so-called 'automobile' of yers off t'the junkyard an' sellin' it fer scrap t'cover the storage an' towing charges an' all."

Cal's eyes flew open. "B-but you can't *do* that."

"You just *watch* me, sonnyboy," the Old Man sneered, calmly putting a fresh match to the remaining half-inch stub of his latest Camel.

And that, in a roundabout way, is how Cal Carrington's beatup TC wound up downstairs from my apartment in my Aunt Rosamarina's garage (at least *after* I lent Cal one of Big Ed's five-buck tips so's he could pay off Old Man Finzio's hitchup, storage, and towing ransom, that is). Now don't get me wrong, Calvin Wescott Carrington was an awfully nice guy in a lot of ways, and I'd have to say we got to be really good friends over the next couple racing seasons. But to *know* Cal was to be *owed* by Cal, even though he came from more damn money than people like you and me ever see in a lifetime. Like he told Old Man Finzio, his "assets" weren't always "liquid," and believe me, that's the way they stayed for as long as I knew him. And on those rare occasions when Cal *did* happen to be carrying a little folding money (which happened every now and again on a more or less totally irregular, flash-flood kind of basis) he'd invariably blow it on anything and everything that struck his fancy until it was all used up again. Like he was in some sort of frantic, desperate, balls-out *race* to see just how quickly he could get himself flat broke, you know? And then he'd turn back into his usual old "not liquid" self for as long as it took him to glom onto another pocketload of the old Carrington family cash. But there was one huge fundamental difference between Cal and all the other deadbeats I knew, in that Cal Carrington always *felt* rich and *thought* rich, even when he had nothing but lint in his pockets. Maybe that's on account of it was 100 percent Cashmere lint.

Anyhow, I wound up arranging bail for Cal's MG with Old Man Finzio, and even managed to borrow the Old Man's Dodge towtruck for my date with Julie that Friday evening. Only first I planned to make a quick little side trip to haul Cal's three-legged MG over to the garage by my aunt's house. I was supposed to pick Julie up at 7:30, and naturally I had it all timed right down to the last split-second. I'd figured myself fifteen minutes to hitch up, ten minutes (tops!) for the tow, and a generous twenty-five minutes to get that old crate stuffed inside my aunt's garage, all of which (according to my calculations, anyways) would have got me up the steps to Julie's front door with an easy 45 or 50 seconds to spare. Except that I ran into a few little, aah, Unforeseen Obstacles along the way (which, to tell the honest truth, is *always* what seems to happen whenever you're doing anything even remotely connected with race cars and garages). Like fr'instance Old Man Finzio had shoved Mr. Beadle's Oldsmobile 66 into the slot beside Cal's TC, and wouldn't you know it had a busted rear spring on account of old Grandma Beadle (who had to be at least 100 years old and couldn't see as far as the damn hood ornament from behind the wheel) ran over a set of railroad tracks where there wasn't what you or I would recognize as an actual crossing. So now I had *two* three-legged, tire-rubbing, ground-gouging automobiles to shift and shove around before I could even hitch up the TC. Plus Cal came along to help, and that meant I was spending an awful lot of time getting cars back in the air after he'd put his shoulder into it and popped them clear off the jack. He was only trying to help, of course, but brute muscle just doesn't account for much around automotive projects unless you know exactly where and how to apply it, and my buddy Cal was a textbook example of how an inexperienced person --no matter how strong, eager, or willing-- could be counted on to get it all wrong. As Butch himself often told me, the mark of a True Mechanic was knowing just exactly how much of a hell of a hit you could give something without breaking it. And my new friend Cal simply had no idea....

Then we got to my aunt's house (I was barely a half-hour late by that point) only to find there wasn't enough room for Cal's three-wheeled MG in my aunt's garage. In fact, there wasn't room for much of *any*thing in there, on account of she had it piled wall-to-wall and floor-to-ceiling with rusty old garden tools and even older wooden yard furniture and sections of picket fencing that were apparently too beatup to use yet somehow too good to throw away, plus at least fifty or sixty cardboard boxes full of moldy, musty, cat-turd decorated books and magazines. I swear, my Aunt Rosamarina had every blessed issue of *Life*, *Look*, *Collier's*, and *National Geographic* ever published. Not to mention every single coloring book, study text, project folio, and class notebook she'd ever laid a finger on from kindergarten clear through grad school, all of it covered with a thick, gritty layer of dust and these sad little brown spitballs of spider eggs. I glanced through some of it, and to tell the truth, it felt kind of spooky, what with the pages all damp and yellow-orange around the edges and smelling like last year's leaves after the snow melts. But the weirdest part was seeing how they didn't have cars or airplanes or anything back when my Aunt Rosamarina went to school. Why, I would've been flat out of a job (along with most everybody else I knew) just fifty-odd years before! It made me feel real strange inside, you know?

What with nosing around my aunt's old magazines and one thing and another, it was damn near ten o'clock by the time Cal and me got everything moved around enough so's we could sneak his crippled-up MG into my aunt's garage. But we did it, and when we were done that old TC was resting peacefully (if a bit off-plumb) on its three flat-spotted tires and the edge of a wooden pop crate, surrounded on all sides by rickety, teetering stacks of furniture, garden tools, picket fencing, and book boxes, with just enough space remaining for a reasonably slender human being to walk all the way around that MG without banging his shins more than once or twice.

"Mission Accomplished!" Cal grinned, and we shook on it.

"How 'bout a beer?"

"You got any?"

"Does a chicken have lips?"

"Absolutely!" Cal grinned even broader.

So we headed up to my apartment for the ritual celebratory beer that absolutely *must* accompany the completion of every major racecar project, regardless of how late you may be for any other real-life appointment, engagement, or commitment. Like a date with Julie, for example. As we climbed the stairs, I noticed my Aunt Rosamarina peering out like a cornered ferret (albeit wearing bifocals) from behind her flower-print kitchen curtains, and I wondered if she was planning to say or do anything about the large new chunk of badly abused English iron in her garage. But she never came out her door (not even after Cal left) so I figured we were home free. That was a good thing, on account of it looked like Cal's TC might be convalescing for quite a spell.

I was cleaned up and on my way over to Julie's mom's house by about 10:25, and, as you can imagine, I couldn't *wait* to pick her up so I could tell her about Cal Carrington and the MG in my aunt's garage and especially about the races I'd seen out at Bridgehampton. But for some inexplicable reason, Julie seemed more interested in precisely why I was three hours late for our date. Of course, she would soon discover that was about spot-on average for a racing-type Garage Evening, but I recall she was plenty pissed off at the time (not to mention still a little miffed about that stupid wedding I missed over in Jersey City). In fact, I remember doing the whole drive over to Weedermen's with my head ducked down inside my collar (tortoise-fashion, you know?) so as not to get frostbite of the ears.

But after I bought us a couple double-scoop hot fudge sundaes (her favorite, natch) and casually mentioned Robert Montgomery and Jackie Cooper and Dave Garroway a couple dozen times, Julie started to come around in a hurry. You know how women are about movie stars --like maybe some of the glitter rubs off when you actually get to see one in person. Why, you'd think they were baseball players or something, you know?

Anyhow, Julie's eyes got bright and sparkly as Christmas Tree lights when I told her about all the fancy-pants rich people and in-the-flesh celebrities I'd seen hanging around the Bridge-hampton paddock. And right away I started thinking what a swell deal it would be if Julie could come to the races with me some-time. I mean, it's always nicer when you have somebody, you know, *special* to share the fun and excitement with. Especially somebody as easy on the eyes and soft to the touch as Julie. Besides, according to the schedule Cal had tacked to the wall of my aunt's garage, a lot of those S.C.M.A. races were two-day weekend extravaganzas, and the idea of getting Julie away someplace where she didn't have to be home by eleven o'clock (or home at all, come to think of it!) had a magical appeal all its own. In fact, the possibilities that started running through my head were enough to put my entire glandular system on Red Alert. The problem was Julie's mom (what else?), who'd been around the block a time or two herself and didn't much fancy any long road trips or overnight lodging arrangements that included her daughter and any male person over the age of six. But every

once in awhile I'd allow myself a little daydream about it anyways, and they inevitably ended with Julie and me waking up
together. In the same room. In the same bed. With nothing on
but the sheets. Then I'd generally go lock myself in the john and
think about it some more (if you know what I mean).

So I kept hammering the old hard-sell line at Julie every
chance I got, talking sportycar racing pretty much non-stop every
time she dropped by the station to tidy up the office or help Old
Man Finzio with the books. I talked about it on our way to the
movies on Friday nights, too, and usually picked up wherever I'd
left off as soon as the show was over. And I'd keep it up afterwards at Weederman's or the Doggie Shake over a couple cokes
and orders of fries. Truth is, I was yakking about road racing all
the time. Except when we were parked out behind the Sinclair,
that is. I mean, a guy's gotta keep his priorities straight.

I knew I was making progress one day when Julie casually
allowed as how the races might be a good place to do some
pencil sketching. *"Yeah!"* I told her, "they got some *great* subject
matter at those races." That's what artistic types look for, see, is
"subject matter" (which is just a fancyass way of saying "something to draw," when you get right down to it). "In fact," I told
her, "there's no question that sportscar racing is absolutely *lousy*
with prime, Grade-A subject matter."

"It is?"

"Absolutely!"

Julie didn't look entirely convinced, and that was easy to
understand if you ever leafed through one of her sketchpads.
Truth is, I didn't think too much of the stuff Julie picked to
draw, on account of it was mostly horses and flowerpots and
driftwood and whole production-number garden parties of these
slender, arched-over-backwards young women in flowing satin
gowns and enormous piled-up hairdos that just about required
external scaffolding to keep them from falling over. Dullsville,
you know? In my opinion, a couple MG TDs and Jaguar 120s (or
maybe even Tommy Edwards' Allard mixing it up with Creighton Pendleton's 4.1 Ferrari!) would really put some *zing* in Julie's artwork. Besides, I was tongue-hanging-out *dying* to have
Julie Finzio come to the races with me sometime, and if "subject
matter" would get the job done, hell, I was all for it.

Meanwhile I had Cal Carrington dropping by the garage behind my aunt's house every couple days to help out with his beatup MG (or maybe leave off a couple fresh parts from West-bridge if he was in one of his flash-flood "liquid" stages) but it was slow going on account of every time I took another gander at that rattletrap TC, I saw more and more stuff that needed to be fixed. Why, every single wheelspoke on that entire car was either bent, busted, or in serious need of tightening. And the tires were just plain shot --even the spare!-- what with the rubber worn clear down to the cords and the canvas showing through on all the outside edges (not hard to understand at all if you'd ever watched Cal drive). No question we needed *at least* two complete wheel rims, four decent tires, a fistful of inner and outer spokes, a new hub, a new brake drum, and a set of tie-rod ends. I thought I could *maybe* straighten out the tie-rods themselves with a little judicious heating and beating. And when I finally managed to worry that ground-up brake drum off the right front (following two solid hours of tugging, hammering, prying, spitting, lever-ing, and cursing in the best Old Man Finzio tradition) I discov-ered the linings were worn clear down to the rivets, brake fluid weeping all over the place, and wheel bearings dry as burnt toast (and damn near the same color and smell, come to think of it). The control-arm bushings were shot, the shocks all needed re-building, there was play in the steering --and we hadn't even *started* with the stupid engine or driveline yet (not that you could really miss how both S.U.s leaked like lawn sprinklers and that either the gauge was busted or that poor old motor didn't have much to speak of in the way of oil pressure). To put it bluntly, it was impossible to find *anything* on Cal's MG that wasn't in desperate need of repair, with possible exceptions awarded to the gas tank, shift knob, hood latches, horn button, and rear-view mirror. And I wasn't real sure about the hood latches.

To make matters worse, my Aunt Rosamarina's garage was a godawful shitass *lousy* place to work on any sort of automobile project, be it foreign, domestic, sports, racing, or otherwise. There was hardly any room, the lighting stunk (as did the used kitty litter in the garbage cans just outside) and I had no lift, engine hoist, compressor, acetylene torch, hydraulic press, bench vise, or even a decent floorjack to work with. In fact, the only tools I had were the crude assortment of stone-age implements

that come in what the MG factory laughingly refers to as a tool
kit, along with the ones I carefully selected out of Butch's toolbox late each afternoon and sneaked home from the Sinclair in a
folded-up grocery bag. And that's not even mentioning the teetering piles of books, magazines, picket fencing, yard tools, and old
furniture that came crashing down on my head once or twice a
night --regular as clockwork-- as if the place had been booby-
trapped by the North Korean army.

But I kept after it, five or six nights a week, all afternoon
and evening on Saturday, and of course all day Sunday, too,
doing my level best with the cave-man equipment and facilities I
had on hand and the piece-at-a-time hardware Cal brought me
every few days from Westbridge. I was even sneaking stuff into
the Sinclair early in the morning so's I could work on Cal's TC
while Old Man Finzio was out chasing parts or picking up dead
cars. Of course Cal would help out wherever he could around my
aunt's place --he wasn't exactly welcome around the Old Man's
gas station-- and I must admit, he turned out to be reasonably
handy with a set of tools once he had some shop time in. Like I
explained before, Cal's main problem was he just didn't *know*
anything. But that could change.

And it did.

For example, I remember Cal dropped by on Memorial Day,
and the two of us sort of "borrowed" my aunt's big old upright
radio and dragged it out to the garage so's we could listen to The
Indy 500 while we worked on Cal's MG and swilled down an
occasional cold beer from the icebox upstairs. Troy Ruttman won
the 500 that year in 3 hours, 52 minutes, and 41.88 seconds, and
I swear it took that entire time for Cal to do the front brake shoes
and wheel bearings on one blessed side of the car. But then he
turned around and got the other side handled in less than a half-
hour. As I said, all he needed was *experience*. Like anybody else
who's ever dug his mitts into a toolbox, Cal had to pay his rightful dues in ruined parts, torn shirts, blood blisters, split fingernails, busted knuckles, and localized second-degree burns before
he could call himself any kind of automobile mechanic.

But he'd come right. I'd see to it. Or at least I'd try. Once
he got the hang of all the basic toolbox stuff (like not using pliers
on bolt heads and never grabbing for the nearest screwdriver
when what you really want is a chisel, punch, or prybar) Cal's

biggest problem was that he was so damned *impatient*. He wanted
that TC *done*, and he wanted it done *right now* (if not sooner!)
so's he could throw his helmet in the back and go off racing
again. And that made him a little bit of a short-cutter and angle-
shooter when it came to getting jobs done in a hurry. Like I said,
he'd tacked a dogeared copy of the S.C.M.A. schedule to the
wall of my aunt's garage, and all he could *think* about was the
damn Giant's Despair Hillclimb and Brynfan Tyddyn Road Races
(whatever the hell *they* were) coming up July 25th and 26th in
Wilkes-Barre, Pennsylvania. As far as Cal was concerned, the
whole blessed world would absolutely come to an end if he didn't
make that event. Why, it was bigger than Judgment Day!

Now and then, I'd accidentally let Cal's crazy enthusiasm
get the better of me (which was easy to do, on account of I had a
pretty serious touch of the old racing bug myself) and I'd start
ignoring everything else in my life except that God Damn, piece-
of-shit MG and the stupid hillclimb and race we were trying to
make somewheres in Pennsylvania. In fact, the only thing that
saved me from a terminal case of total, falling-down, foaming-at-
the-mouth Racing Mania was that I worked on cars all day long
at the Sinclair, and that tends to give you a little sense of True
Perspective. Believe me, after eight or nine solid hours fixing
Hudsons and Henry Js for Old Man Finzio, the last thing in the
world I wanted to see was another sick automobile. Especially a
desperate case like Cal's old TC. Plus every now and then I'd get
this crazy notion that I was maybe entitled to a life of my own,
you know? Heck, I wanted time to go out with Julie on the
weekends. Take in a show. Share a couple cheeseburgers and
cokes at Weederman's or the Doggie Shake. Park in back of the
Sinclair and neck for an hour or so in the Old Man's towtruck.
But that kind of stuff gets damn near impossible when you've
been thrashing away on busted automobiles from 7 ayem to 3 the
next morning, six, sometimes even seven days a week. And on
those rare occasions when you *do* manage to steal a few hours to
try and act like a normal human being again, you inevitably find
yourself stumbling around in a sort of shell-shocked, grease-
tinged stupor, looking and behaving a lot like one of those
creepy, dead-eyed zombie characters you remember from old
black-and-white Bela Lugosi movies.

Needless to say, Julie Finzio was not real pleased with the situation (to say the least!) and it all came to a head one night when I did the totally unthinkable and actually *dozed off* while we were parked out back behind the Sinclair in the Old Man's tow-truck. *"Hey!"* Julie hollered, giving me a solid shot to the ear, "sorry I'm keepin' you *up*, Palumbo!"

"Huh...oh...uh, sorry, Julie, I was just, uhh...."

"Lissen, Bozo," she growled, jumping over to the far side of the seat, "you ain't gotta feel sorry about *me*, Palumbo. Not in this lifetime. I mean, if it's I *bore* you...."

"Aw, Jul--"

"I mean, if I'm keepin you *awake*.... "

"Aw, Julie, you know...."

"Yeah? *What* do I know? *Huh?* You *tell* me!"

"Aw, you know I...."

"Lissen here, Mister Buddy Palumbo, if you really *want*, I can fix it so I stay home and do my frickin' nails on Friday and Saturday nights. Makes no difference to me...."

From there it only got worse.

But back at my Aunt Rosamarina's garage, Cal Carrington was after me like a hound on the scent, pushing for us to work *quicker*, work *later*, work *longer*, work *more nights a week*, even though we didn't have near all the hardware we needed to finish his damn car. No question Cal had gone absolutely blind *crazy* with the idea of making that stupid race and hillclimb event the fourth weekend in July, and there was just no reasoning with him at all. And to tell the honest truth, I didn't think we had much of a chance. Time was running short and there was still a tremendous amount of stuff to do (I mean, we hadn't even pulled the valve cover off the engine yet!) not to mention that my buddy Cal kept running out of money every other week like he was a damn state legislature or something. But Cal's heart was set and his mind was made up, so naturally he kept prodding me and pushing me and scrounging for parts wherever and however he could. And he got pretty good at it, too (although I suspected he was busily rifling through every stray purse, pocketbook, jacket, and pair of pants back home at Castle Carrington in order to feed his dirty little habit). This was really my first close personal look at the racing disease, and I can't honestly say I appreciated its seriousness at the time. But I learned....

Chapter 13: A Fifth, a Fourth, and a Forgery

Who should tool into the Old Man's gas station the first day of July but Butch Bohunk and Mean Marlene. They were in a ratty old prewar Ford sedan done up in four shades of primer grey (where it wasn't solid rust, anyways) and you couldn't help but notice how that car listed down and to the rear like a garbage scow with a serious leak. It was hardly one of your more elegant or refined modes of transportation, what with a weathered slab of plywood over the back window and a web of plumber's strap holding up the lefthand headlamp, but Butch was proud as hell of that old heap. That was on account of he had less than a tenspot in it and said he'd done every bit of the mechanical work himself. "Take a look at this little beauty," he beamed, unhooking the strand of fence wire that held the passenger-side door shut. "I got her down in Tennessee fer five bucks. *Five bucks!* The engine was froze up s'bad she wouldn't turn a lick. Not even with a three-foot plumber's wrench on the pulley! Some jackass musta run her bone friggin' dry on oil. *Haw!* Picked up another short-block --outta the same damn boneyard!-- and we was on the road in lessen a week. An' I did every goddam nut an' bolt myself!"

To tell the truth, I had a little trouble believing that last part, what with Butch still all busted up the way he was. Oh, the plaster was off his leg and he was getting around a lot better --even using crutches now and then-- but Marlene still had to wheel him around like a damn tea cart if they wanted to make any time at all from Point A to Point B. And for sure Butch's right hand wasn't about to grow any new fingers. Not hardly. So I really didn't see how he could do too awful much in the way of first-person, hands-on mechanical work. And that's when I caught a glimpse of Mean Marlene's knuckles and fingernails, and right away I knew who'd been helping Butch out on that old Ford.

Now you have to understand that Butch's wife was always real particular about her fingernails (you know how some women are) and as far back as anybody could remember, she'd carried around a set of razor-sharp, lipstick-red war claws that any cocktail waitress would've been proud to own. She knew how to *use* those things, too, whether that meant clicking them against a windowpane to show she was bored, waving them back and forth under your nose to get your attention, drumming them impatiently on a tabletop, or creating fresh scar tissue. But not any more. No siree. In fact, Mean Marlene was sporting the hands of an auto mechanic now, right down to raw bruises on all the knuckles and an ugly, purplish-black split nail on her right thumb. And she didn't look particularly happy about it, either. Then again, you'd have a hard time recalling a time when Mean Marlene looked particularly happy about much of anything....

Anyhow, Butch had to grab the doorframe with both hands in order to lever himself up out of the car, and then it was about all he could do to just sort of hang there, wavering, while Marlene brought his crutches around. Why, just getting up out of that car made him breathe heavy. "Hell," he gasped, trying to ignore it, "ol' Marlene an' me drove this sonofabitch all the way back from Tennessee an' she never skipped a friggin' beat. Not *one*. Oh, I may look a little tore up yet, but I still ain't lost my touch around Fords."

"'Course not, Butch," I nodded, "you was always the best around when it came to Fords."

"Sure as hell was. And still *am*, you little jerkoff, still am. And don't you forget it!" He added a limp little elbow dig for emphasis. "An' this job was no goddam picnic, neither. You oughta see what Marlene's brother calls a 'tool set.' *Haw!* Guess it's okay if y'wanna mend a fence or lynch a nigger or something, but it was sure as hell damn crude fr'engine work."

That's when it dawned on me. "Say, Butch," I gulped, my voice going all lame on me, "you're probably gonna want all yer tools back now, arn'cha?"

"Aw, don't worry about it," Butch shrugged, "I'll let'cha know when I need 'em, Buddy. Besides," he added, "I ain't exactly got anything, y'know, *lined up* right at the moment. S'you just keep them tools right here until the time comes I need 'em. Why, maybe that old buzzard Finzio'll even let me drop by an' use 'em now an' then if I got a side job or something t'do."

"*Sure* he would," I agreed, not at all sure that it was true. Truth is, I didn't figure Old Man Finzio would be particularly keen about having somebody in Butch's condition hanging around his gas station. Not unless it was making him some money, anyways. "You know how much the Old Man likes you...."

"Yeah," Butch nodded, pumping out a weak laugh, "about as much as blood blisters and cheap wine hangovers."

"Well, he always liked the way you fixed cars, anyway."

That got Butch to looking down at his hands --the right one like a big, gigantic thumb that'd been smacked once or twice with a five pound sledge-- and he slowly, sadly shook his head. "Fact is," he sighed, "I ain't quite ready t'start up wrenching again. Not fer a damn living, anyways. I just can't get myself around good enough ...."

"Hell, Butch, you're doin' *great,*" I told him, "just great."

"Sure I am," he snorted. "Why, I'll be dancing the friggin' jitterbug in a couple more weeks, won't I?" Then he lifted up his head and just stared out at the cars rolling by on Pine Street. "Truth is," he said in a half-whisper, "I about need a friggin' nursemaid just t'change a God Damn set of sparkplugs. It makes me wanna *puke,* y'know?"

"Yeah," Marlene sneered, "an' listenin' t'ya bellyache about it all the time makes everybody *else* wanna puke, too!"

Butch spun around like he was gonna belt her, but of course he couldn't on account of it would've sent him sprawling across the pavement if he took anything like a decent swing. So there was nothing he could do but just sit there and take it. And then slowly, almost like slow motion, Butch's face softened up into a big, helpless sort of grin and he started to laugh. And a second later I saw that Marlene was laughing, too, and for the life of me I couldn't figure it out. I mean, those two scrapped and spit and clawed at each other like alleycats --all the time!-- but even so, it was obvious Mean Marlene did something pretty special for Butch. Even if she made him pay for it along the way.

Anyhow, Big Ed Baumstein's XK120 was in for a grease and oil that day, and seeing as how it was a swell July afternoon and furthermore seeing as how the Old Man was way across town picking up some Polish bricklayer's dead Studebaker, I figured it wouldn't hurt anything if I took Butch and Marlene out for a little spin. Just a highly professional Test Drive with an Established Mechanical Expert, you understand --not some sort of frivolous, irresponsible joyride in a neat customer car. Right. So I turned the radio way up in the service bay, popped the phone off the hook, locked the john door with the water tap running (like I was in there, you know?), and then the three of us piled into Big Ed's

Jaguar. It was a tight fit, no two ways about it, since Mean Marlene is *way* big in the butt and we had to be kind of careful about Butch's legs. But once we got everybody folded inside and Butch gave me the thumbs-up, I fired up that sweet-running six, eased out the clutch, and we were on our way. I cruised her nice and gentle all the way out to the edge of town, barely idling along in fourth, just enjoying the buttery growl through the Jag's tailpipe and the way everybody stopped dead in their tracks and pointed and waved at us as we oozed gracefully down the street. That sort of thing happened whenever and wherever you drove a Jaguar roadster back in 1952, and it never failed to make you feel pretty damn special and important. Why, it even made Mean Marlene smile, which should've easily qualified that particular July first afternoon for instant National Holiday status.

Once safely clear of the city limits, I blipped her down a couple gears and gave the Jag's gas pedal a heavy bootfull in second and halfway out in third. To tell the truth, Big Ed's 120 felt a little sluggish with three people on board (especially considering that at least one of them owned a butt the size of a prize hog) but Butch seemed to get himself a huge kick out of it anyway. Mean Marlene didn't look nearly so impressed. In fact, she was clutching onto the door and decklid so tight I was afraid she'd leave dents in the damn metal, not to mention yelling for me to slow down so loud and shrill you could hear her over the wind noise and exhaust roar and *everything*. She had herself one hell of a vocabulary, that Marlene did.

When we got back to the station Butch thanked me and Marlene yelled at me some more and then he leaned in real close and said, "Now lemme show *you* something, Buddy." Without another word, Butch hobbled over by the back end of his old Ford sedan, took a long, careful look over both shoulders (like somebody might be watching us, you know?) and pitched me a wink, low and inside. "Check *this* out, Buddy," he grinned, popping the trunklid. Jee-*zus!* Crammed inside the trunk of that old Ford were more damn boxes of fireworks than you have ever seen in your life. Why, there were sky rockets and roman candles and pinwheels and showering fountains and carton after carton of cherry bombs and M-80s and two-inchers and ladyfingers and Lord only knows what else! Truth is, that old Ford wasn't much more than a four-wheeled, self-propelled incendiary bomb.

"Gee whiz, Butch, where'dja get all this stuff?"

"Brought it back up from Tennessee, Buddy. This stuff's cheaper'n pigeon crap down there."

"Jee-*zus*, Butch," I gulped, swallowing a couple times, "wasn't that kind of, you know, *dangerous?*"

"Aw, nothin' to worry over. See what I done here?" Sure enough, Butch had hung an old bus mirror off the passenger-side door pillar so he could look back and tell if anything had caught itself seriously on fire. That Butch thought of everything.

Naturally I had no choice but to buy a whole damn shitload of fireworks out of Butch's trunk (I mean, you never know when that kind of stuff is going to come in handy, do you?) and I even tried to over-pay a little. But no way would Butch let me do it. "Lissen here," he growled, staring me right in the eye, "the only charity this Marine will ever need is a .45 with one bullet in the chamber. You unnerstand me, boy?"

"S-sure, Butch."

"You damn well better had."

After I lifted my new collection of fireworks out of Butch's old Ford and stashed them away under my toolbench, I took him on a little informal cook's tour of the jobs I had going on in the shop. Just one professional car wrench to another, you understand. Along the way, I told him all about the sportscar races out at Bridgehampton, and made sure to mention Tommy Edwards' brutal Cad-Allard and Creighton Pendleton the Third's incredible 4.1-litre Ferrari and Skippy Welcher's ex-everything XK120*M* and even Cal Carrington's broken-down MG TC that was sitting up on pop crates in my Aunt Rosamarina's garage.

"Haw! That sounds like a lotta Goddam fun," Butch mused, rubbing his chin with his bad hand. "I'd sure as hell like t'get in on something like that."

"Hey, no problem," I told him, "no problem at all."

"Oh, *great!*" Marlene snorted through her usual sourpuss sneer, "just what I'd always hoped and prayed for: car shit on the frickin' *weekends*, too...."

Back at my Aunt Rosamarina's garage, Cal's MG project had more or less ground to a halt. The suspension, steering, wheels, and brakes were pretty well squared away, but Cal hadn't rounded up the ready cash for new tires or the radiator repair yet, and we still hadn't so much as laid a damn finger on the engine. Or the bodywork. Which meant things were looking pretty grim, what with that race/hillclimb weekend in Pennsylvania just a scant three weeks away. To tell the truth, I didn't think we had a chance in hell of making it, and now and then even Cal was starting to lose heart. That happens somewhere along the line with *every* major car project. You reach a point where you're ass-deep in stuff that's torn apart and suddenly you just can't see the end of it any more. That's when it always seems like you'll *never* get the damn car back together....

No question we hit our alltime low on the Fourth of July. Cal had been pretty consistently tapped for cash about eight days straight at that point, and when he showed up around noon at my aunt's garage, all he had with him was a little wrinkled-up paper sack that looked way too small to be carrying any of the MG hardware we needed. "So," I asked him, "did'ja do any good on the tires?"

Cal shook his head. "No cash."

"Too bad."

"Yeah. Seems like it's harder and harder to find any loose folding money around the old family homestead. I think they may be getting wise to me."

"It's about time."

"Maybe so," Cal allowed, "maybe so. Then again, it wasn't a total loss."

"Oh?"

I saw an evil little smile flickering up in the corners of Cal's mouth. "Well, I did manage to find *this.*" He reached into the paper sack and slowly withdrew a whole unopened fifth of 15-year-old Pinch whiskey. I'd never seen one before except in magazine ads, what with the fancy gold-leaf label and the bottle all sucked in on the sides like a football with the air gone out of it. No question this was some pretty expensive hooch.

"Geez, Cal, where'dja get it?"

"I *pinched* it."

"You pinched your old man's Pinch?"

"It was the least I could do," Cal nodded, gently breaking the seal and taking a quick pull. Then he passed it over and I took a snort. No question the stuff had a real serious kick to it. And that's how we spent the entire afternoon, standing there around Cal's old TC, sucking up his dad's fancy Pinch whiskey and shooting the breeze about sportscars and racing and life in general. You'd be amazed how much shop time gets used up doing exactly that. Only more often with bottles of beer instead of 15-year-old scotch whiskey. It's safer that way.

As it got on towards dark, we heard the crackle of Fourth Of July firecrackers and the whistle-and-pop of bottle rockets starting up all over the neighborhood, and every once in a while we'd catch a glimpse of a really good one arcing across the evening sky. Which of course gave me an absolutely splendid idea. Or so I thought at the time, anyway. "Say, Cal," I mentioned casually, "I bought me some pretty decent fireworks off Butch...."

Cal's eyes narrowed like an alleycat's. "You *did?*"

"Uh huh. He brought 'em up from Tennessee with Marlene in that old Ford of his. I got all kinds of 'em."

Cal leaned over with one eye closed, sort of Long John Silver style. "Arr, and just where might they be, Jim boy?"

"Upstairs. Under the bed."

Cal took another pull off the bottle (which, to be honest, was better than half-empty by then) and decided to switch movies. He rose unsteadily to his feet, folded his arms firmly across his chest (Indian-fashion, you know?) and scowled. "Um, Kemosabe," he grunted, kind of rocking back and forth on his heels, "fireworks go heap good with firewater."

Sure they do.

Anyhow, I stumbled upstairs and gathered up all the cartons of cherry bombs, skyrockets, pinwheels, showering fountains, ladyfingers, M-80s, and Lord Knows What Else I'd bought out of Butch's trunk, and I'd have to say Cal and me were pretty careful there at first (especially considering all the whiskey we'd consumed), setting them off one at a time on the gravel driveway and watching the old flash-and-bang from a reasonable and secure distance away. But that got kind of dull after awhile. I mean, that's always the problem with fireworks, isn't it? You can't help wanting a little more excitement....

So Cal went rummaging around in the garage and found an old wicker sewing box, and it didn't take long for us to get that sucker loaded up with a whole damn brick of two-inchers. Boy oh boy, that thing hopped and jumped and sputtered and cartwheeled all over the place when Cal torched it off.

"Wow, that was *great!*" Cal whooped as the remains of my Aunt Rosamarina's sewing box fluttered to a halt. "What else you got in there?"

"Looks like maybe a dozen skyrockets. Big ones, too."

"Super!" Cal yelped, rubbing his hands together. "Let's do 'em *all at once!*"

Now, you're probably thinking we'd imbibed perhaps a bit too much whiskey to be messing around with fireworks. And you'd be exactly right, on account of that's precisely when Cal and me damn near burnt down my Aunt Rosamarina's garage. See, Cal found the broken wheelhub off his MG in the garage, and naturally nothing would do but to set it out in the middle of the drive and load every blessed skyrocket we had into the hole in the center. Like a flower vase, you know? Cal rigged us up a common fuse out of an old ball of yarn my aunt's cats played with, but it was kind of damp and dirty and wouldn't burn too good. So my buddy Cal (resourceful fellow that he is) went back in the garage and dipped that yarn in the MG's gas tank once or twice. Just to help it stay lit, you understand....

It worked entirely too well.

As you can imagine, the yarn went up in a sheet of flame the instant Cal touched a match to it, and in a heartbeat we had all dozen fuses fizzing at once. Hmmmm. Well, the first one blasted up out of there exactly as we'd planned --*FOOOOOOOSSSSH!*-- carving a handsome orange-red comet across the sky. But the shockwave was enough to cause our makeshift rocket-launcher to wobble, rotate, teeter up on edge, and finally (in glorious slow motion) fall completely over on its side. OH *SHIT!* I looked at Cal and he looked at me, and instantly we were diving for cover as skyrockets started streaking across my aunt's yard in all directions. Two of them headed into the garage like bazooka rounds --*FOOOOSSH! FOOOOOSSH!*-- scoring direct hits on more varieties of flammable material than you could list in an hour.

"*JESUSCHRISTALMIGHTY!*" Cal screamed.

"*HOLY SHIT!!*" I agreed, and the two of us charged in after them. We grabbed for whatever we could find to beat out the flames (neatly tripping over a pan of mineral spirits in the process and sending it showering into the flames --*KA-WHUMPF!*) and the whole shebang would've gone up for sure if my aunt hadn't come barreling out of her house at that exact moment dragging a huge brass fire extinguisher behind her. She'd been watching through her favorite slit in the curtains (natch) and, fortunately for us, was one of those constantly terrified Civil Defense types who prepare in advance for every sort of household emergency imaginable. Which is why she happened to have a fifty-pound Industrial Size fire bottle hidden right under her basement stairs. And she knew how to use it, too. Why, my aunt charged that fire like Duke Wayne himself, swinging that big brass extinguisher bottle back and forth in front of her like a battle axe. By the time it ran dry, she'd gotten it down to where we could pretty much stomp out the rest. *Whew!*

Once we had the contents of the garage down to merely hissing and smoldering, Cal and me hooked up the garden hose and watered everything down real good. Then we went on a little tour around the yard, putting out some relatively minor skyrocket damage to my aunt's fence, lawn furniture, and rose garden. I was sure my Aunt Rosamarina was going to blow even higher than the skyrockets once we got the last of the fires out, but would you believe it, she didn't say a thing. Not one word. She just *stood* there, wavering a little while alternately blinking and gulping for air like a goldfish on a living room carpet. Then she turned and stalked back into her house, dragging the empty brass fire bottle behind her. But she stopped for just a moment at her back door. "You know, boys," she said without turning around, "I really wish you'd be a little more *careful* with things." And with that, my Aunt Rosamarina disappeared up the stairs to her kitchen and poured herself a water glass full of sherry.

"Jeez," I said after she was gone, "that was *close!"*

"Yeah, it sure *was,"* Cal agreed, shaking his head. But you couldn't miss the happy little smirk bubbling up around the corners of his eyes.

"So," I asked, still feeling pretty shaky, "we got any of that whiskey left?"

"Good question," Cal grinned, and we headed back into the garage to see. But we were kind of creeping along on tiptoes, you know, as if maybe the fire was just sleeping and we didn't want to wake it. Cal found the bottle of Pinch right where he'd left it, standing upright and perfectly untouched on the top of the MG's radiator, as if it was a damn hood ornament or something. It reminded me of the lonely brick chimneys you see pointing up into the sky after a wooden cottage burns down. Anyhow, there wasn't much of Cal's old man's hooch left in the bottom --just one good swig for each of us-- but you'd have to say Cal and me (not to mention my poor old Aunt Rosamarina) got our full measure of excitement out of that particular fifth of scotch.

And then some.

Cal and me came back Sunday morning to survey the damage in the daylight, and to tell the truth, it was pretty damn depressing. Especially considering the way we were both feeling that particular ayem. "Gee whiz, Cal," I told him, "maybe we shoulda just let the damn thing *burn*. I mean, we're *never* gonna get it back together in time for that race in Pennsylvania."

"Sure we are," Cal said, trying to make it sound true.

"But we don't even have *tires,* Cal. And the radiator's gotta be re-cored...."

"No problem," he said, "no problem at all. I'll get the damn money for the tires and radiator. You just wait and see...."

"But what about the *rest* of it," I groaned, "what about the damn *engine?* That thing runs like shit. And the gauge hardly shows any oil pressure at all."

"Maybe it's the gauge?"

I shook my head. "No way we're that lucky. And look at the damn bodywork. *I* can't straighten out those fenders...."

Cal eased himself down on a scorched pop crate, looking as glum as I'd ever seen him. But it wasn't three seconds before his eyes popped open like mousetraps. "I *got* it!" he yelped, "we'll run *modified!!!"*

"We'll *what?"*

"Why, we'll turn this thing into a *real* racecar. You'll see."

By way of explanation, the S.C.M.A. had one class for "stock" MGs (which seldom really were) and another for hopped-up, stripped-down examples, which S.C.M.A.-types referred to as "modifieds." Cal figured it might be easier to rip additional stuff *off* his TC than to try putting it back together the way the folks at the Morris Garages in Abington-on-Thames, England, originally intended. And you'd have to say he was probably right about that. Only problem was Cal's MG never ran particularly strong against the other so-called "stock" TCs and TDs, and some of those modified cars were a whole *bunch* faster. They were all stripped down to the bare bones and had hogged-out, hot-rodded, six-hundred-dollar engines with high-compression pistons and special high-lift camshafts and Lord Only Knew what else. Hell, some of those cars even had superchargers on them. "That's a *terrible* idea," I told Cal.

So of course we did it.

After all, we had a race to make.

And that's how Cal Carrington and me wound up spending that entire Sunday pulling every damn thing that would come loose off his helpless old TC. We took off the bumpers. And the windshield. And the top. And both sides of the hood. I yanked out all the carpeting and door-panel trim. Cal went underneath with a hacksaw and cut off the muffler. Why, by the middle of the afternoon it had turned into a sort of auto-mechanical feeding frenzy, what with both of us clawing and ripping and tearing at that poor car like a pair of sharks on a sickly whale. It didn't help matters any that we were still a little loopy (not to mention bumbling, hung-over, weak-willed, and stupid) from that bottle of Pinch and the garage fire disaster the previous evening, so by nightfall we were tripping and stumbling around my aunt's garage like a couple of the Three Stooges, bumping into things and hitting ourselves in the head with car parts and making goofy Moe-Larry-Curly imitations like *"Wooob-wub-wub-woob"* and *"Nyuck nyuck nyuck"* and that sort of thing. My old friend the Earl of Passaic even dropped in for a visit. "I say, Mr. Carrington," the Earl asked, "won't you be a bit, shall we say, *shy on horsepower?* Especially when compared to the --I believe you Americans call them *hot-rodded?*-- machines competing in the modified division?"

"So *what,* your Dorkship," Cal grunted, tugging desperately on a rear fender that still had one bolt attached. "We're gonna be *light!* You'll see...."

Well, you'd have to say Cal's basic theory was pretty sound. Generally speaking, if you have to choose between *more power* and *less weight,* it's my firm belief you go with lightness every time. Power makes a racecar faster in a straight line, but less weight makes it faster *everywhere.* Unfortunately for Cal, the drivers with the superchargers and six-hundred-dollar racing engines in their "modified" MGs were also stripped to the bare bones on weight. And then some. In fact, some of those guys had special-order, light-alloy body panels and valve covers and even custom-made, machined-aluminum *shiftknobs* to make their cars even lighter yet. Of course Cal and me didn't know all that at the time. But we learned.

Anyhow, by midnight Cal's MG looked like it'd been picked over by vultures. The fenders were gone, the sides of the hood were missing, the top was history, the windshield frame, lights, and bumpers were gone, the muffler was leaning against the wall, the air cleaners had vanished, the heater (or at least what passes for a heater on an MG TC) was laying in a corner, and that's not even mentioning the seat cushions on the passenger side, the carpeting, the inside door panels, the ashtray, and the horn. Truth is, we'd pulled everything off that car you could possibly remove without resorting to a buzzsaw, cutting torch, or explosive charges. And I gotta admit, it looked pretty neat that way, all kind of lean and serious and stripped for action. It also looked a little, aah, *illegal* for general-purpose highway duty, and I started wondering just how the hell Cal was planning to get this --this *thing*-- to that race weekend in Wilkes-Barre, Pee-A. Or anyplace else, for that matter. Not to mention exactly how Cal was going to explain the emaciated skeleton remains of his TC back home at Castle Carrington.

"Oh, I'll just tell my folks it was wrecked or stolen or fell off a cliff or something," he said, waving his hand like it was no big deal at all, "at least I will when they get back from their trip to Europe, anyways...."

Cal Carrington went suddenly flush on me at the very last moment, showing up at my aunt's garage the Thursday before Giant's Despair with a brand new set of Dunlop tires stuffed in the trunk of his mom's Packard and a whole damn shitload of TC parts, including a complete upper and lower gasket set for the engine. Naturally we decided to throw in a last-minute valve job, and of course once we got the head off, we found all the exhaust valves burned --two of them badly-- and a couple busted valve springs to boot. So Cal had to make an emergency parts run over to Westbridge first thing Friday morning while I called in sick at the Sinclair, pinching my fingers around my nose so's the Old Man would think I had pneumonia or something. Not that he believed me for one single, solitary second.

Cal didn't get back from Westbridge till damn near two in the afternoon, and I meanwhile busied myself mounting the new tires and shimming the relief spring to sort of kid the engine into thinking it had some oil pressure. Besides the valves and springs I needed, Cal brought back a fresh set of points and plugs, a new cap, rotor, and condenser for the distributor, a roll of ignition wire and some fancy "racing" plug clips (imported all the way from England, no less), a pair of carb kits and richer needles for the S.U.s, and even a brand new, super-high-voltage Lucas Sports Coil. I told you what happens whenever Cal gets a little money in his pocket.

Working as fast as I could, it still took me the better part of six hours to get the cylinder head reassembled, the carbs rebuilt, and all the ignition stuff put in (which, all things considered, is probably some kind of new world record for MG TCs). While I concentrated on those projects, Cal took the relaced wheels out for balancing, got the radiator fixed at a shop over in Clifton, changed the oil, and generally did what he could so the TC might maybe pass for street legal if anyone should happen to ask. Like a police officer, for example. A little past nine, he asked if he could borrow the keys to Old Man Finzio's gas station. Lord help me, I just handed 'em over. I didn't even want to *know*. When Cal returned about a half-hour later, he was carrying some flexible exhaust pipe and a couple muffler clamps, a roll of electrical wire, and what appeared to be the spotlight off Old Man Finzio's towtruck. For sure the Old Man wasn't going to be particularly pleased about that.

A few minutes later it was time to fire up my quick-and-dirty "rebuilt" MG engine for its first run. I had Cal sit in the car and crank the starter while I flattened my palms over the carb throats to choke the S.U.s the way Sylvester had showed me on that Frazer-Nash over at Westbridge. But the damn thing cranked and cranked and wouldn't fire, and it took me the better part of thirty minutes (checking the fuel pump and plug wires and firing order and Lord Only Knows what else) before I realized I'd left the damn rotor out of the distributor. That kind of thing happens all the time when it's coming up on midnight and you've been slaving away on a racecar project for sixteen or seventeen hours straight and you moreover should've been done and gone long before. It's sort of an occupational hazard.

Anyhow, once I got the distributor rotor back where it belonged, the engine lit off on the very first crank. And jeez, did it ever make a *racket,* boxed there inside my aunt's tiny garage with no mufflers or air cleaners or anything to cut down the noise. It seemed to be popping and surging just a bit, even after it was good and warmed up, so I spent the next half-hour showing Cal everything Sylvester Jones and the Jaguar service manual had taught me about setting up S.U. carburetors. Or what I could remember, anyways. And I'm proud to say that MG sounded pretty damn magnificent by the time I got done, idling with a nice rich lope to it and really snapping to attention when you cracked the throttles. Unfortunately some of my aunt's neighbors turned out to have a tin ear when it came to crisply tuned racing engines. Especially after midnight.

Needless to say, it was well into the wee hours when we finally tiptoed our way out of Passaic, kind of idling along in 3rd and 4th to keep the noise down. Cal had a rusted-out Buick muffler from the trash pile behind the Sinclair sort of half-heartedly wired to the MG's exhaust system, but it didn't really do much good since all the diameters were different and there was a big split along the seam of the casing. He'd also taken the spotlight he gleeped off the Old Man's towtruck and strung it up smack-dab in front of the radiator (Cyclops fashion, you know?) with the feed wire dangling along the side, over the driver's door, around behind the seat cushion, and directly to the battery terminal with no switch or fuse of any kind. But even that was better than what Cal had rigged up in back, where he made do with a couple bicycle reflectors from Woolworth's five-and-dime. You'd have to say Cal Carrington was less than an accomplished expert in the automotive electrical field. Much less.

Without a windshield (or any sort of weather protection, if you want to get really technical about it) things were definitely a tad breezy in Cal's stripped-down TC at anything much over a walking pace, what with the wind whipping our faces until we had tears streaming all the way around our cheeks and puddling up in our ear canals. That's when Cal reached behind the seat and pulled out a couple pair of underwater diving masks he'd picked up at Woolworth's when he was in for the bicycle reflectors. They were bright yellow and about the proper size for a twelve-year-old, and no question we looked goofy as hell when we put them on. But those things came in awful damn handy when it started raining like a sonofabitch in the mountains just outside Allamuchy. In fact, Cal really should've picked us up a couple plastic snorkels while he was at it.

And believe me, that was one *scary* ride, what with the winding mountain roads and heavy rain and those stupid swim masks fogging up all the time and the damn spotlight Cal had hung in front of the radiator vibrating so bad that the beam bounced all over the road (and the trees, and the sky, and everywhere else...). Not to mention that I was sitting on entirely the wrong side of the car as far as I was concerned. Especially when a lone truck came hurtling around a hill out of the blackness and the lugnuts damn near chewed off my elbow. Righthand drive may work real fine over there in England, but it sure leaves the passenger hanging out in the breeze here in the states.

Plus my buddy Cal Carrington only knew one way to drive --*FLAT OUT!*-- no matter if it was daylight or dark, open highway or twisty blacktop, bone dry or glare ice, perfect visibility or so you couldn't see the goddam hand in front of your face. But I must admit, the kid was *good*. Better than good, even. Why, we'd be skittering towards a blind, rainslicked mountain turn with our headlamp beam shattering off a sheer rock face on one side and nothing but a huge, empty black void on the other, and I'd look over at Cal with eyes big as coffee saucers and see he was leaned back all calm and relaxed behind the wheel, nonchalantly chewing gum beneath that ridiculous Woolworth's swim mask as he braked hard, blipped her down a gear, swung the TC hard into the corner, balanced her with the throttle, and powered us up out of that bend in a perfect four-wheel drift. Cal Carrington was some kind of driver, no two ways about it.

But he still wasn't worth dogshit when it came to automobile mechanics, as we discovered rather abruptly when his jury-rigged headlamp wire shorted out in truly spectacular fashion someplace way up in the Pocono mountains, and even the great Cal Carrington had to pull over when he couldn't see the road anymore. At least the rain had stopped and you could even make out a star or two and a frosty little sliver of moon over towards the western horizon. It was kind of pretty, actually. Not that Cal or me much appreciated it, since we were cold and wet as a pair of dead mackerels. And tired. *Real* tired. Naturally we didn't have any electrical wire with us (although we were in excellent shape when it came to the baling variety) and that was perhaps my first-ever glimpse of yet another Great Racing Truism:

If you bring it with, you won't need it.
But if you leave it home, you will need it every time.
Desperately.

Naturally there wasn't a single car passing on the highway (hey, what do you expect in the middle of the Pocono mountains at 4 o'clock in the morning?) and about all we had in the way of illumination was a book of matches that were too soggy to light and a dinky little pen flashlight with half-dead batteries. So we were pretty much stranded, you know? Cal walked up the road a hundred yards or so and located a steep gravel driveway that disappeared up into the forest at about a 45 degree angle. "Hey, Buddy," he hollered, "let's try up here!"

Well, there was a "No Trespassing" sign the size of a small billboard nailed to a tree where you couldn't possibly miss it --not even at night-- and I've always been a trifle funny about wandering up strange private drives in strange backwoods country areas at strange hours like four ayem in the morning. I mean, I know lots of people right here in Passaic who take a real keen interest in their personal property and aren't the least bit bashful about their constitutional right to keep and bear firearms. But Cal just shrugged it off. "Hey, what the hell, huh?" he said, shaking his head at me, "you planning to just sit here by the side of the damn road until the sun comes up?" And with that, he hopped in the TC, fired it up, and wheeled it right up that driveway. Cal Carrington had brass balls, no two ways about it.

Naturally Cal made me walk on ahead with that worthless excuse for a flashlight, trying my best to keep us more or less on the gravel while Cal juddered the TC along behind me, playing the clutch, gas, and brake pedals back and forth like a damn church organist. I couldn't see much of anything, so of course I was tripping over all kinds of ruts and rocks and tree roots and getting myself snagged by sapling branches that'd grown their way clear across the driveway since anybody'd been there last. At least that was somewhat encouraging. About a half-mile up we hit a clearing with the nicest little ski cabin you ever saw set right in the middle. Unfortunately, it was buttoned up tighter than a drum, what with storm shutters padlocked over all the windows and the front door bolted solid. But my buddy Cal didn't even think twice before taking the jackhandle out of his TC and briskly twisting the hasp clear off one of the shutters. Then he used it to break the windowpane so he could reach in, undo the latch, slide the window up, and slither his way inside.

I just stood there, you know, frozen to the spot. "Well, Palumbo," Cal snickered from the other side of the glass, "now you're planning to stay *out there* all night?" You couldn't miss the challenge in Cal's voice, so I took a couple deep breaths, swallowed once or twice, and crawled in there after him. To tell the honest truth, I was starting to suspect Cal Carrington might be one of those Bad Influence types that parents are always warning you about.

At least I hoped so, anyway.

As you can imagine, that ski cabin was real dark and dank and musty inside, and on top of that the batteries in the penlite were just about finished, but Cal managed to find us some firewood piled up by the door and a box of dry stick matches and even a couple moldy old comforters and a can of coffee. So Cal and me sort of "set up camp" --like Boy Scouts, right?-- building a fire in the fireplace and hanging our wet clothes off the mantelpiece to dry and boiling ourselves a pot of water for coffee. Cal wrapped himself up in one of the comforters and dozed right off to sleep, but I was too damn scared to do anything but lay there with my eyes bugged out like Eddie Cantor, listening to every owl hoot, bird chirp, and twig snap like it was the hammer clicking back on a Colt .45.

I rustled Cal awake and shooed us out of there a little before seven, and would you believe it, Cal insisted on taking one of the comforters with us and even leaving a note behind for the people who owned the cabin! It went like this:

Sorry we had to break in to your lovely cabin, but our car died out in a terrible rainstorm while my prize Cocker Spaniel was in labor in the back seat. I'm afraid she delivered on one of your comforters, and I will send it back as soon as I have it properly cleaned. Naturally, I am happy to pay all damages, along with a modest consideration for the use of the hall. Would also offer one of the pups, but unfortunately they were half Labrador Retriever, so we had to drown them in your toilet. Then he signed it with a flourish: *Creighton Pendleton III.*

Chapter 14: Giant's Despair

Tired as we were, Cal and me enjoyed a swell ride down into the Susquehanna River valley that morning. It was a lovely warm July morning with the sun winking down through feathery white clouds and I must say Cal's old TC was running better than it ever had, if I do say so myself. So naturally Cal had a huge smile plastered across his kisser as we cruised down that last hillside into Wilkes-Barre, Pennsylvania. "You know, Buddy," he grinned, "this little beauty feels like a *whole new car.*" I remember glancing at the oil pressure gauge (which was straining hard to reach 25 pounds per square inch) and allowing Cal about one-third of an agreeable nod. "Why, I bet this is the best damn MG I've ever driven," he continued, patting the old girl on the empty screw holes where the little dash mirror would've been if we hadn't ripped it off to make the car a few ounces lighter. "Don't you be surprised if I win the race *and* the hillclimb with this little beauty. She's ready to do it, believe me. I can tell...."

You must admit, my friend Cal didn't have any noticeable deficiencies in the optimism or confidence departments.

I, on the other hand, was going through one of those Grim Reality Inventories that come over you once in a while like stomach flu when you've been up all night, gotten yourself thoroughly cold, wet, frightened, and exhausted, and when moreover every damn muscle in your body aches from bouncing off the floorboards of a stripped-down MG TC that's being driven by some crazy rich kid who thinks he can't die in an automobile wreck like ordinary people. And that's not even mentioning the fact that I hadn't exactly, ahh, *made arrangements* with Old Man Finzio about skipping work again on Saturday. I mean, if I told him The Truth (that I was off to some S.C.M.A. hillclimb and sportycar race someplace in Pennsylvania with Cal Carrington and his derelict MG), well, I just didn't think the Old Man would consider that an acceptable reason for ditching work. In fact, I was sure of it. So when we stopped at a roadside diner for some bacon and eggs, I took a pocketful of change over by the pay phone and put in a call to the gas station back in Passaic to try and smooth things over. I even held my nose, as if I could maybe fool the Old Man into thinking I still had the terrible head cold he never believed I had in the first place. But he must've heard the change drop or picked up all the static on the line, because right away he said, "Saaay, Palumbo, where the hell *are* you?"

"Uh, well, I'm kinda...."

"You're off at th' frickin' *car races* with that runnynose rich kid, aint'cha?"

Gee whiz, it was like the old fart had a crystal ball or something, you know? "Well, geez, Mr. Finzio, I sorta..."

--click!--

So much for that.

In order to cheer myself up, I singlehandedly consumed an entire Triple Play Breakfast Special at that roadside cafe, which consisted of no less than three large eggs (scrambled, natch), three strips of bacon, three pancakes swimming in maple syrup, a huge mound of hash browns, three slices of buttered toast, and three double-mugs of 90-weight coffee. Usually a feast like that will go a long way towards making me feel better, but the truth is it didn't help much at all and I still felt pretty miserable (only *stuffed* and miserable) as we waddled back to the car. That's when Cal surprised the hell out of me by reaching in his pocket and nonchalantly tossing the keys over. "Here," he said calmly, *"you* drive the rest of the way."

And, just like that, the world was once again a wonderful place to be. A sunny morning and a full stomach couldn't do it all by themselves, but suddenly having the keys to a two-seater MG roadster dangling from my fingertips was all it took to bring about a complete and instantaneous recovery.

Cal plunked himself down on the bare floorboards where the TC's passenger seat used to be and pulled a brand-new pair of aviator sunglasses out of his pocket. "Okay, mister Hero Driver," he said, snaking them over his eyes, "let's *hit it!"*

"Saaay," I asked, looking at my reflection in the mirrored lenses, "where'dja get those things?" No question they looked cool as all getout (and certainly a lot more stylish than our yellow Woolworth's swim masks).

"Inside," Cal shrugged, "I gleeped 'em off the counter by the cash register when the guy wasn't looking." Then he reached in his pocket and pulled out yet another pair. "Here," he said, "here's a set for you."

I looked at the sunglasses in his hand and then back at my reflection in the chrome-colored lenses over his eyes. "You know," I told him, sounding exactly like my old man, "you're gonna get us in some *serious* trouble one day...."

"That's what I'm here for!" Cal laughed, grinning from ear to ear like it all made deliciously perfect sense.

I'd never driven any sort of right-hand drive car before, so naturally I had a few little problems getting accustomed to it. Like I jammed the shifter in third instead of first a couple times and as a result stalled the engine pretty regularly at every other stop sign. "Hey, don't worry about it," Cal advised, "just try to get used to how it feels. After all," he added with a strange, inscrutable grin, "you may be *needing* it later." That's when I noticed the fresh, devilish twinkle flickering around the edges of his new aviator sunglasses.

Cal had some sketchy directions scribbled on the back of a rumpled-up envelope, and we did our best to follow them in a series of spiraling, misshapen loops all over the entire city of Wilkes-Barre, crossing and recrossing the Susquehanna River a dozen times while we searched in vain for that S.C.M.A. hillclimb. At least it gave me a little seat time in Cal's TC, and except for the lefthand shift, a snappish clutch, sitting on the wrong side of the car, and steering so ridiculously quick that I occasionally darted clear out into oncoming traffic (!) it seemed like I was slowly-but-surely getting the hang of it. Far as I was concerned, that TC felt skittish as hell (not to mention nervous, jumpy, and jittery) but no question it could carve its way around tight corners better than anything I'd ever driven. And you could really feel the texture of the road through the seat of your pants in that MG. Every bump, crack, and pebble, in fact.

As we passed through one particular intersection for about the fifth or sixth time, we noticed a white XK120 roadster coming towards us from the opposite direction. Or make that an XK120*M*, since it was none other than our old friend Skippy Welcher and faithful squire Milton Fitting, also on their way to the hillclimb at Giant's Despair. For perhaps the first and only time in my life, I was truly happy to see them. "Say," I hollered over, "you got any idea where this S.C.M.A. hillclimb thing is?"

"Follow me!" Skippy whooped, waving his cap in the air like he was Teddy Roosevelt on San Juan Hill. Why, you half-expected his Jag to rear up on its back tires when he jerked out the clutch and squealed away. What a dipshit. But at least he knew where he was going, which was more than you could say for Cal and me. We followed The Skipper's Jag back across the bridge and zig-zagged a few blocks until we suddenly came upon a whole shitload of sportscars parked snoot-to-boot along both sides of a little side street that headed steeply uphill just a few yards past the last building in town.

We had arrived.

The S.C.M.A. armband-types had a registration table set up in front of a white clapboard Real Estate office at the far end of the street, and Cal once again surprised the living shit out of me when he signed us *both* up as drivers. Can you believe it? Of course, I didn't have any I.D. to prove I was twenty-one (which I wasn't) or that I belonged to the S.C.M.A. (which I didn't) but Cal put a quick finger to his lips and calmly introduced me as his 21-year-old cousin Bartholomew from "East Point" (wherever the hell East Point was) and explained as how I belonged to the highly regarded (not to mention highly imaginary) "East Point Sportscar Club" and how I'd quite unfortunately misplaced my wallet on our way over from the far end of Long Island. Boy, was he ever slick at that sort of thing. Never even batted an eye. Not that he could've got that bullshit past a Seasoned Registration Pro like Charlie Priddle. Not hardly. But we lucked into some sweet old lady from Vermont who actually used to collect maple-tree sap with one of Cal's aunts or something every February, and she signed us up without a hitch. It always comes down to who you know and who knows you, doesn't it?

"Gee whiz, Cal," I mumbled as we made our way back to the TC, "why'dja wanna do *that* for?"

"Do what for?"

"You know. Sign me in to drive?"

"Why not?" Cal grinned, waving a carefree hand through the air. "You *worked* on the car, didn't you? One heck of a lot more than I did, actually. Never could've made it without you, right? So why the heck *shouldn't* you drive?" Then he sealed it by giving me an insider wink and one of those quick little shots in the arm like guys do. "You just wait and see," he continued, "why, if things go right, we'll run quick enough to finish first *and second* in our class. You'll see."

"I dunno," I said, staring at the TC's oil pressure gauge and wondering if this was such a good idea, "what if it *breaks?*"

"Well," he shrugged, "then I suppose it would have broken anyway, wouldn't it? Besides, this little beauty is *not* about to let us down. Not a chance. She didn't come all this way just to fall apart on us."

I wasn't so sure. "And what if I, uh, you know, uhh, *hit* something with it? I mean, what if I *wreck* your car?"

Cal raised a finger in the air, flashed me his absolute best rich kid smile, and said simply: *"Don't."*

Hillclimbing was new to me, and it was a lot different from the races Big Ed and me saw out at Bridgehampton. First off, the cars ran one at a time against the clock instead of side-by-side and wheel-to-wheel with each other. That made hillclimbing a lot less risky than *real* racing, but also a lot less interesting and exciting to watch. Especially considering you couldn't see too much from the starting line and also that you had to wait in line a minimum of an hour and a half for each little 90-second squirt up the hill. But that's what made hillclimbing so popular with a lot of rank-and-file S.C.M.A. clubbies who would never even *dream* of getting out there doorhandle-to-doorhandle with other cars at a place like Bridgehampton. Besides, there was more time to stand around jawing with the other rich, trendy sportycar types at a hillclimb (like I said, you spent most of the day waiting in line) not to mention that the steep grade, short straights, and tight corners made hillclimbs mostly all first and second gear, with just a few quick dabs into third for the most daring and aggressive drivers. Which meant there was a lot less opportunity to damage your car, your body, and your precious self-esteem during a hill-climb. Or, as Cal so indelicately put it: "It's a lot easier to be a hero in second gear."

Why, even that scrawny tightass Charlie Priddle ran hill-climbs. And did amazingly well at it, too, seeing as how he always fronted-up some strange, weirdass car that inevitably turned out to be the only one in its class. As you probably guessed, Charlie Priddle was on the S.C.M.A.'s car classification committee. In fact, I think he was chairman. In any case, that clever bit of strategy pretty much guaranteed Charlie a first-place pewter mug every time he entered, no matter how pathetically slow he puttered up the damn hill. Even Skippy Welcher had more class than that.

This particular Saturday morning, Charlie tooled up in a 1922 Rolls Royce Silver Ghost to run in the so-called "Over 2-litre Vintage Touring Class." I swear, that thing was a block long and over five feet high, and looked more or less like a coal-fired steam locomotive compared to the MGs and Jags and such everybody else was running. Why, it was big as a damn parade float! And Charlie drove it like one, too, trundling up the hill on the idle jets while he waved to the crowd and pretended to saw back and forth on the wheel and mugged for all the corner workers like Joe E. Brown. He took slowest time of the day by over a full minute, but, since nobody else was even entered in the "Over 2-litre Vintage Touring Class," that was more than enough to earn him yet another fancy first-place mug for the rose-colored marble mantelpiece back home.

What a dork.

Undoubtedly the worst thing about hillclimbing was the way you had to spend 99 percent of the day waiting in line for your next run up the hill, just so's you could join back up at the tail end of the group less than two minutes later and start your waiting all over again. Plus you couldn't see much of the action once the cars launched themselves around the first curve and disappeared up the mountain. Not that I much minded, since I was really too tired to climb up and join the rubberneckers on the hill, and maybe even a little bit nervous about driving Cal's car, too. Besides, it was a gorgeous, warm, sunny summer day and real pretty country, too. Especially right there by the starting line, where none other than Creighton Pendleton the Third's fabulous girlfriend was waving the green flag to turn the cars loose. She was wearing a crisp white short sleeve shirt with the collar flared up and at least three buttons undone, not to mention one *hell* of a pair of white tennis shorts. In fact, I was sort of glad Julie wasn't there to see how I was looking at her. Or where, for that matter. "Say," I asked Cal, pointing to where his eyes were already focused, "who *is* that?"

"Oh, that's Sally Enderle," he said, sliding his sunglasses down his nose for a better look, "she's a peach, isn't she."

"Boy, *I'll* say."

And no question she knew it, too, because every time a car rolled up to the line, she'd flash that grand, toothpaste-ad smile of hers, ask the driver if he was ready, and wave the green flag with a tiny little shadow of a leap that made her leg muscles draw up like hot elastic. You'd hear the tires chirp and an angry snarl off the exhaust and look up from Sally's rear end just in time to see yet another Jag or MG or whatever disappear up into the trees, engine straining against the incline. Then you could look back at Sally a little more while the noise howled and churned its way up the mountainside, fading like an echo.

I noticed Skippy Welcher's XK120*M* a few spaces ahead of us in line, and no question he got it all wrong when Sally Enderle waved the flag at him, dumping the clutch before he got the revs up and damn near killing the engine. As a result, his famous, super-special, ex-everything XK120*M* bucked and lurched its way off the line in a spastic series of hops and stutters. It was kind of comical, actually. Especially when The Skipper finally got it all gathered up and wailed that poor old Jaguar up to maybe six (or maybe even seven?) grand before slam-shifting into second with a horrifying graunch of gearteeth. I looked at Sally Enderle and she kind of rolled her eyes --*oh, brother!*-- and I smiled back at her and sort of rotated my palms up --*what can you do?*-- and then she laughed me a laugh with sleighbells hung all over it. Boy, did that ever get the old electricity pumping through my system.

And then it was time to roll Cal's fenderless TC up to the line. "Listen," he said casually, nudging me in the ribs, "since I've done this before, why don't *you* take first crack at the hill?"

"M-me?!"

"Why not?"

"Well, er, ahh...." Truth is, I could think of *lots* of reasons. Like fr'instance my only experience with Cal's TC (or *any* right-hand-drive automobile, if you want to get real technical about it) came between my Triple Play Breakfast Special and the Giant's Despair hillclimb that very morning, and I would have to admit that I wasn't fully one-hundred percent comfortable with it yet. Not hardly. Not to mention that I'd never been in any sort of real, *bona fide*, sanctioned-and-observed Contest Of Speed before (not unless you count a few casual stoplight drags in the Old Man's towtruck and one time with my dad's Mercury back when he used to let me drive it). Plus I hadn't the foggiest notion which way the damn road up that hill went once it twisted out of sight around the first turn. And then there was the little matter of the stunningly gorgeous Sally Enderle standing up there at the starting line in her magnificent white shorts. I sure as hell didn't want to do anything lame or stupid in front of *her*. Not on your life. But with all those doubts twisting and swirling around in my head, I still knew I couldn't say "no." That's because I knew the lamest, stupidest, most embarrassing, least forgivable thing of all would be to back down....

So my hands were shaking just a little as I climbed in over the MG's gutted-out door panel and fumbled to get Cal's old polo helmet over my head and the earwires of my fancy new aviator sunglasses snaked in underneath the flaps. Cal tried to calm me down by telling me to "just take it easy" and that I should remember "to *flow* the car through the bends" (which sounded kind of difficult, seeing as how I couldn't hardly flow pee through my bladder at that point) but behind it all you couldn't miss the nasty little smirk of a challenge. Typical. Even though Cal was as good a friend as I ever had back then, time and again he'd push me and prod me right to the limit --and beyond!-- just to see how I'd handle it. Truth is, Calvin Wescott Carrington caused me to scare the living shit out of myself more times than I care to remember. But he also got me to do things I never, *ever* would've done all by myself. Things a guy could feel a little proud and cocky about afterwards. Like going up that hill for the very first time....

I remember it like it happened yesterday:

My heart was pounding so hard I could hear it over the bark of the exhaust as I inched Cal's stripped-down MG up to the line, and I was glad my knees were hidden underneath the dashboard where nobody could see them shaking. I had the taste of fear like dirty pennies in my mouth. But I gritted my teeth, braced myself, nodded over in the general direction of Sally Enderle, and gave it everything I had. And boy oh boy, was it ever *hectic!* First you accelerated flat-out up through first and second gears to a nasty right-left combination they called "The Devil's Elbow," and that was followed by a steeper grade up through a tunnel of trees to a sweeping set of esses that some guys (like Cal, for instance) bragged they could take in third gear, followed by a final uphill banzai charge to the finish line. I guess it sounds pretty simple now, but that's not what it felt like at the time. Not hardly! Trees and bushes and fenceposts and telephone poles came whipping past in a frothy green blur on both sides, and every damn hump, twist, bend, and crest in the road seemed to *JUMP OUT!* at me like those spring-loaded spooks on the Ghost Train ride at Palisades Park. I swear, that was the longest one minute, thirty-eight-point-three seconds I'd ever experienced in my entire life! And I must've done it all on a single breath, too, because I found myself panting and gasping for air the instant I crossed under the finish-line banner. My hands ached from hanging onto the wheel so tight and I could hardly get my feet to work the pedals and slow down once I'd cleared the top. But by God I *made* it! And without spinning, crashing, flipping, or over-revving the engine.

I have to admit, I was pretty damn proud of myself.

At least until my buddy Cal went up a half-hour later and knocked more than ten whole seconds off my time. And the sonofabitch claimed he was going *slow,* too, on account of he wanted to learn the stinking course!

While we waited in line for our next run, Cal struck up a conversation with the owner of a shiny-black MG TD that was lined up a few spaces in front of us. The car was absolutely showroom fresh, right down to a squeaky-clean red leather interior that didn't look like it had ever been sat in --not once!-- and blemish-free chrome hubcaps that glistened like wet mirrors in the sunlight. Personally I always liked the knockoff wire wheels on the old TC better than the perforated-steel baby buggy variety on the newer model, but I guess that's the way it goes sometimes with progress. Standing next to the TD was this thin, pale, somber-faced guy with hollow cheeks, sunken eyes, and a scant few dozen strands of hair plastered down east-west across the top of his head so it would maybe fool people into thinking he wasn't really bald. That never works. Anyhow, his name was Carson Flegley, and it turned out he'd just bought his TD from Colin St. John a few days before and that furthermore the Giant's Despair hillclimb was his first S.C.M.A. event of any kind. So it came as no surprise that he was pretty well rattled (which I, for one, could certainly appreciate!) and his new MG wasn't helping matters any on account of it was running like shit on the hill. Oh, she'd start and idle and highway cruise just fine, but trying to power full-throttle up that steep incline made her stutter and gag something awful. Naturally my friend Cal figured he was now an accomplished expert on the art and science of adjusting S.U. carburetors (I mean, he'd spent the better part of a whole half-hour watching me set up the ones on his engine, right?) so it wasn't five minutes before he had his head wedged under the hood of Carson Flegley's new TD and began fiddling indiscriminately with the various float level, jet height, throttle position, and needle depth settings that make S.U.s work properly. When they feel like it, anyway. You could see Cal was making a real mess of it, but I let him go on for a good twenty minutes or so before casually leaning in over his shoulder and asking, "Uh, Cal, did I ever explain Butch Bohunk's First Rule of Engine Tuning to you?"

He looked up at me over his shiny new aviator sunglasses and shrugged. "Can't say as I recall. What's it about?"

I cleared my throat a couple times and did my best to say it exactly the way Butch would have, right down to the gravelly growl in the voice and spitting on the pavement when I was done for proper punctuation: *"Y'all better make sure you got yer God Damn sparks in order before y'start fuckin' around with th'God Damn carburetion."*

"Oh?" Cal said, mulling it over. Then he reached for the TD's distributor with both hands, and it wasn't long before he had that poor, helpless MG screwed up so bad it wouldn't even run. He'd ask Carson Flegley to tug on the starter knob and she'd just grind and fart, grind and fart, and every now and again blast a two-foot sheet of flame back out through the carburetors. Carson Flegley's face was starting to look like milk going sour, and I got to thinking it was maybe time to reach in and lend a hand. But you can bet your ass I waited for Cal to *ask*.

Once I got Cal out of the way, I carefully step-by-step put all the carb and distributor settings back to where they were in the first place, and only then went searching around for the *real* trouble. And it didn't take more than five minutes to locate a renegade tuft of wire insulation that was jamming the advance plate in the distributor. Ah-*ha!* On top of that, the point gap was down to around six thousandths (if that) and the dashpots of both S.U.s were positively bone-dry. No question the mechanics at Colin St. John's MG dealership performed a truly piss poor Pre-Delivery Inspection. And I decided to do this Carson Flegley fellow a favor and put it all right for him. I mean, there wasn't much of anything else to do while we were waiting in line, was there? So I freed up the advance mechanism and gave it just a tiny squirt of oil, put a dab of red grease on the distributor cam and re-set the point gap, dialed-in the timing with a test light I rigged up out of a single-filament taillight bulb and a couple strands of 12-gauge electrical wire, and finished the job by topping up the dashpot dampers with a little Castrol 30-weight. And I'm proud to say that sucker fired up on the very first pull and settled down to a nice, steady 800-rpm idle. Hey, what do you expect from a *professional?* But she still sounded a little choppy to me, so I bent my head in real close and took the time to set the mixture just right and balance the S.U.s, cocking my ear back and forth from one intake to the other while fiddling with the jet nuts, idle screws, and throttle-rod clamps until those two carburetors were hissing in absolutely perfect unison. "There," I said, tightening up the final clamp, "*that* oughta do it."

And it sure as hell did! On its next run, Carson Flegley's TD pulled clean and strong all the way to the top, and he came down off that hill happy as a guy who'd just gotten his ashes hauled by Rita Heyworth. He even sort-of smiled. "Hey," he said, sticking out a soft, pale, bony hand, "thanks a *lot.*"

"Hey, no problem," I told him.

"Here," he said, reaching for his back pocket, "let me give you a little something...."

"Not a chance," Cal broke in. "You just put that away. Glad we could be of service. Isn't that right, Buddy?"

"Uh, s-sure," I grumbled as I watched Carson Flegley's wallet slide back into his pants.

"Gee whiz," he sighed, "I sure wish I could find somebody like you to work on my MG *all* the time."

That's when I noticed the Jersey plates on his TD and a little chorus of alarm bells went off in my head. "Might not be a problem," I told him. "I see you come from Jersey, right?"

He nodded.

"You live anywheres close to Passaic?"

"Sure *do!*" Carson grinned, his head bobbing up and down. "My family runs a funeral parlor over in East Orange. Why, I'm there almost every day. Passaic's only a few minutes away...."

Now, to tell the honest truth, undertakers have always sort of given me the willies, mostly on account of I can't help thinking about exactly what it is they *do* with the stiffs, you know? Or if they wear gloves while they do it. I swear, it's like I think I smell formaldehyde and used body parts whenever I get close to one. But with Carson Flegley, I had to put my personal feelings on manual override and make an exception, not only because he seemed to be a pretty nice guy and liked low-slung British two-seaters, but also on account of he had the makings of a prime, Grade-A service customer over at Old Man Finzio's gas station. Especially if he kept running his MG in competitive events like the hillclimb at Giant's Despair, which are absolutely certain to wear out English mechanical parts even faster than normal every-day street abuse. I figured a few more solid, cash-money service customers might just change Old Man Finzio's attitude about sportscars. Or at least keep him from firing me, anyways. "You just bring the little rascal over to Finzio's Sinclair in Passaic whenever she needs a little attention," I told Carson Flegley. "I'll keep her runnin' right for ya."

And I did, too.

Once I got done with the job of field-tuning Carson's MG, the three of us hung around by the starting line for awhile, drinking lukewarm bottles of root beer and watching Sally Enderle flirt with all the drivers. She really knew how it was done, no lie. Why, every time a new car rolled up to the line, she'd find some excuse to lean in and check her lipstick in the fender mirror or maybe kick up a heel like there was something stuck to the bottom of her shoe or maybe even bend clear over as if she saw a worrisome cut or split on one of the tire sidewalls. But whatever she did, Sally Enderle made damn sure every red-blooded male person on that hill was paying close attention. I know I was. "Saaay," I wondered out loud, "I thought she was supposed to be Creighton Pendleton's girlfriend?"

"Yeah, I guess so," Cal nodded, taking a swig off his root beer, "when he's *around,* anyway...."

"You mean, not *always?*"

Cal shrugged. "I hear Creighton's over in England this week, checking out some super-special new Jaguar racecar. I don't imagine Sally Enderle's the type to just hang around by the phone, waiting for some guy to call...."

"No, I guess not."

And that's about when Sally decided it was getting a bit too warm for her up by the starting line, so she asked the next driver to wait just a second, parked the green flag between two perfect knees, pulled the shirttails up out of her shorts, and tied them together in front of her, exposing a truly magnificent expanse of smooth, sleek, tanned female midriff. "Oh, Lordy," I moaned, "that's got to be the single most beautiful feminine creature I have *ever* seen."

"Yeah," Cal agreed. "She thinks so, too."

Me and Cal and Carson each got another run in later that afternoon, and although I went nearly six seconds quicker than before (and --ahem-- measurably faster than Carson Flegley and his brand new TD) Cal Carrington beat us both. And by a *bunch*. In fact, his time of One Minute, Twenty-Six-Point-Eight Seconds (1:26.8) stood up for second-fastest MG run of all, just a few tenths behind some well-regarded local hotshoe with a Shorrock supercharger on his TD. You could tell all the S.C.M.A. regulars were mightily impressed with that run, because a lot of them (particularly the guys driving the other fast MGs) started sort of casually wandering by every now and again to run their eyes over Cal's ratty TC and see if they could maybe pick up on some of the many hush-hush MG Speed Secrets we'd developed behind closed doors in my Aunt Rosamarina's garage.

It was actually kind of funny.

Naturally I was real happy for Cal, but I must admit it was gnawing at me something awful how the sonofabitch could be almost *seven whole seconds* quicker than me up a 90-second hill. In the same damn car! I mean, it's not like I didn't know how to drive, you know? And that's why stupid, poisonous thoughts like *"why should some good-looking rich kid be so damn much FASTER than me?"* and *"we both put our pants on one leg at a time, don't we?"* and worst of all *"by God, I'm gonna SHOW 'em!"* were rattling around in my head and making me just a little desperate. More than a little, even.

Which is why my jaw was setting up hard and tight as a chunk of pre-stressed concrete by the time I climbed behind the wheel for my third and final run up the hill. No question I was hell-bent on knocking *at least* five seconds off my time (maybe even more!) and I wasn't too particular about how I got it done, either. Why, I wasn't scared of that damn hill anymore. Not one bit. Nor was I particularly worried about crashing Cal's raggedy old MG. No, I had fallen victim to the biggest single fear a driver can ever have when he climbs into any kind of racecar: *the fear of not going FAST enough.*

So I had the steering wheel locked in something of a Death Grip as I rolled Cal's TC up to the line and prepared for my final assault on the blacktop road that poured down off that mountain like a sneering asphalt waterfall. My eyes narrowed down to a pair of heartless gunslits as Sally Enderle raised her green flag, flashed me her trademark thousand-kilowatt smile, and cooed, "Y'all ready, darlin'?"

I looked Sally Enderle right in her luminous green eyes, stomped down on the clutch, jammed the shifter into first, tightened up my stranglehold on the wheel (in fact, it's amazing the rim didn't just shatter), gunned the engine --*WWAAAHHHHHHH!*-- and nodded....

And, unless I miss my guess, that's exactly when Cal's number four connecting rod decided to break in two and violently fling itself (along with assorted valve pieces, piston bits, and crankcase fragments) clear through the left side of the engine block --*WWAAAAHHHHHHHHHHH--KLANKKK!*-- and I suddenly found myself enveloped in a foul-smelling, deathly-silent cloud of steam and oilsmoke as the green flag fluttered down and everybody --Sally Enderle included-- burst out laughing like a pack of wild hyenas. *Haw-haw-ha-haw-haw-haw!* I could feel a hole melting open in the pit of my stomach and my face started burning like a dead short in a battery cable. "Hey there, Sport," Sally Enderle giggled, damn near gagging on it, "that's one pretty fast MG you got there...."

HAW-HAW-HA-HAW-HAW-HAW!

Right then I remember wishing I could shrink myself down to the size of a fieldmouse so's I could crawl into the TC's oilpan and be alone in there with all the other busted junk. Then Cal came stomping through the coolant mist wearing about the meanest, angriest scowl I had ever seen on him. Why, his fists were clenched so tight that it made all the blood drain out of the knuckles. So naturally I expected the worst. But after standing there for a minute or two, alternately glaring at me and gnashing his teeth and staring in utter disbelief at the puddle of oil spreading itself beneath the TC's engine compartment, it was like some sort of magic safety valve opened and Cal just rolled gently back on his heels and sighed. "Hey, no problem," he said, laying a hand on my shoulder while his mouth stretched out in a thin, tight-lipped smile, "why, it could've happened to *any*body...."

And in my heart of hearts, I knew he was right. After all, I hadn't *murdered* that poor old TC. Not at all. Why, the damn thing had simply decided *to commit suicide* while I happened to be in the driver's seat. Yeah, that was it. I mean, we weren't even *moving,* for gosh sakes. And we knew up front the oil pressure was suspect, didn't we?. But somehow none of that offered much comfort. For reasons I will never completely understand, the simple act of sitting down behind the wheel makes you instantly and irrevocably responsible for everything and anything that may or may not happen to a racecar until the moment you get out of it. And sometimes even longer. And that includes Act-Of-God stuff like being swallowed up in random earthquakes or getting zotzed dead-center by a freak bolt of lightning. The simple rule of thumb is *if YOU'RE in the car, it's YOUR fault.* Regardless of the circumstances. And you always feel guilty as hell about it, too.

Then Cal took his hand off my shoulder, walked slowly around to the front of the TC, removed his fancy new sunglasses, shook his head one last time, and proceeded to haul off and kick that damn MG squarely in the radiator core. Hard as he could. *"You worthless, two-faced pile of SHIT!"* he bellowed, giving it another couple shots, *"We sweated fucking BLOOD over you!"* But the MG just sat there, contemptuously drooling oil off its undercarriage. And then --all by itself!-- the radiator core sprung a tiny leak right where he kicked it and commenced peeing a thin, brackish stream of steaming-hot engine coolant all over Cal's Bass Weejun loafers.

No doubt about it, that car had a sense of humor.

And an ugly one, at that.

But one of the nicer things about sportycar people is how they will always come over to commiserate and even offer to help out any way they can when a fellow racer hits a patch of trouble. Especially if there's a nasty wreck involved or if the mechanical disaster is serious enough so as to be utterly hopeless (which, of course, means that nobody will actually have to *do* anything, just stand around shrugging their shoulders and murmuring condolences and sympathetically shaking their heads). As you can imagine, our new acquaintance Carson Flegley turned out to be amazingly adept at that sort of thing (in spite of this being his first-ever S.C.M.A. event) but then, I guess you'd have to rank Carson as something of a ringer when it came to the condolence business. For sure he had The Look down pat (you know, that prefab combination of sadness, hope, and deep, *deep* understanding that guys in his line of work have to turn on and off like a faucet a dozen times every day). In fact, Carson was a *bona fide* natural talent in that respect, on account of he looked that way all the time. "Gee, that's a damn shame," he said with great-yet-understated emotion, shaking his head at the jagged hole in Cal's engine block. "Is there anything I can *do?*"

"Tell you what," Cal said without skipping a beat, "I'd sure as heck like another crack at that hill...."

Carson looked at Cal, then at the hill, then at his shiny new TD, and back at Cal again. "Er...uh...ahh...," he stammered, swallowing a half-dozen times while Cal flashed his absolute best rich kid smile directly into Carson's face. "S-sure. W-why not," he said at last in a helpless, crumbling voice. "H-help yourself, Cal...." And just like *that,* he handed over the keys to his brand-spanking new MG. Can you believe it?

"Hey, *thanks!"* Cal grinned, pumping Carson's arm till it damn near came loose at the shoulder. Then he took off (before Carson could think twice about it, of course) to have one last look at the hill before his run in Carson's car. But he did remember to take the keys with him, just in case Carson came out from under the ether and had himself a change of heart. That left Carson and me to push the TD forward by hand as each car ahead of us took off on its last, balls-out charge up the hill and we moved ten feet closer to where Sally Enderle was standing in her fabulous white tennis shorts.

Cal didn't come back for damn near 45 minutes, and you could see as how Carson was getting a little nervous as we got closer and closer to the starting line and Cal (not to mention the keys to Carson's MG) was still nowhere to be seen. But Cal had taken himself a pretty thoughtful and serious walk up that hill, and he didn't come down until he had carefully eyeballed every hump, corner, bevel in the road, and pavement change. He also checked out how all the fast guys were taking the corners, and even tried to figure how he might do it a little better. Far as I could tell, Cal was about the only driver who did that all day long, and no question it gave him something of an edge.

Anyhow, we had rolled Carson's TD all the way up to second in line by the time Cal came sprinting down the hill (at the very last instant, natch) and gracefully hopped behind the wheel. "Well," he said, fastening up his helmet strap, "I guess it's *showtime.*" Before Carson could say a word, Cal fired up the engine and nodded over to Sally Enderle. "Okay, gorgeous," he said, patting the TD's dashboard, "let's *do* it!"

And did he ever.

Cal had the revs just right and came off the clutch the instant Sally so much as *twitched,* and that black MG shot away to the sound of a smooth, solid screech off the right rear tire. He snicked it into second precisely at the redline and arced out of sight with his foot buried all the way to the floorboards, and you could hear that little 4-banger wailing Wide Fucking Open all the way up the hill. He even took those fast esses at the top without lifting --in *third*, no less!-- and when his time came down, it was the fastest damn MG run of the day. *1:25 flat!* And in a bone stock, right-off-the-showroom-floor TD that he'd never so much as *sat* in before! Why, my buddy Cal was even quicker than all those "modified" MGs, including that well-regarded local hotshoe with the supercharger on his engine!

It was quite a performance, no two ways about it.

Chapter 15: A Bad Night at Brynfan Tyddyn

They had the usual big trophy party after all the actual hill climbing was done at Giant's Despair, and naturally Charlie Priddle made a big show of collecting the first place hardware he'd won by default in that monstrous Rolls Royce of his. Like I said, it was the only car entered in the "Over 2-litre Vintage Touring" category, but you would've thought Charlie'd won the damn 24 hours of Le Mans the way he strutted up to the podium to get his stinking tin cup. And that after the asshole made such a show of barely *creeping* up that hill --not even *trying* to go fast, you know?-- and then acting afterwards like he could've gone just as quick as anybody (and probably even quicker) if he'd only felt like bringing his supercharged grand prix Maserati single seater (the only one in the states, natch) or his ex-works Aston Martin DB2 Vantage coupe (ditto) and moreover been of a proper mood and mind to really put the spurs to either one. That attitude pissed Cal off to no end. "He's nothing but a fucking glory thief," Cal snarled, spitting on the ground, "and what he does takes away from all the guys who really get out there and *try.* "

Even I could appreciate that, and the sooner Charlie Priddle was off the podium (which, to be honest, wasn't much more than a couple pop crates with some checkered-flag bunting draped over it) the better I liked it. Fortunately, Charlie and some of his Old Money S.C.M.A. pals had a fancy dinner engagement at some restaurant nearby where the appetizers cost more than what you or I would normally feel like spending for a full seven-course meal, and they all took off in his enormous Rolls as soon as he'd collected his first-place hardware. And good riddance, as far as Cal and I and an awful lot of other people were concerned.

What a pill.

But there were still tons of other sportycar *aficionados* to party with at Giant's Despair (including well-known TV and Radio personality Dave Garroway again, now with a twincam XK120 engine stuffed under the hood of his handsome SS-100 Jag) and most of them were a lot of fun. My personal favorites were the MG types, who kept crowding in around Cal and Carson and me, toasting us and congratulating us like Cal was the

great All-American quarterback who'd just won the big home-
coming game and we were, well, the guys who usually got to
carry his shoulder pads and helmet. But it was nice being the
center of attention for a change (or even that close to it) and I
must admit the MG crowd kept us all well-supplied with Dixie
Cups full of cold beer (one right after the other, in fact) throughout the entire awards presentation ceremony. The funny part was
that the S.C.M.A. still had Carson Flegley listed as the driver of
the black TD, and therefore an exceedingly surprised and happy
undertaker from East Orange, New Jersey, wound up swilling his
beer out of a shiny first-place mug at the very first S.C.M.A.
speed event he ever entered! Cal told him to keep it, too, which
was a mighty nice gesture. Especially since Carson didn't look
real likely to be winning a lot of first place hardware on his own.
Not hardly. But Cal never cared too much about the plaques and
medallions and silver-plated mantleware they handed out after the
racing was done. Just about the driving itself. He was exactly the
opposite of guys like Charlie Priddle in that respect. Which of
course made perfect sense if you thought about it.

After entirely too many rounds at the trophy party, a few of
the local MG people helped us find a garage nearby where we
could stash Cal's blown-up TC for the balance of the weekend,
and then a whole bunch of us went out to supposedly eat dinner
at some Chinese restaurant on the other side of the river. But,
what with the party at the starting line and dragging Cal's TC
over to that garage and getting lost once or twice in the process
and having to organize and re-organize our meandering MG
parade every ten blocks or so to pick up stragglers and listen to
the local MG guys argue over whether we were heading in the
right direction, the Chinese place was closed by the time we got
there. So we all got drunk as hooty owls instead. The local MG
types helped with that, too, since Cal and me were both underage
(although, as I suspected, Cal had some pretty first-rate fake IDs)
and they'd sort of sneak us into places in the middle of a whole
stampeding herd of them. I wore my nifty new aviator sunglasses
(which of course meant I was bumping into all sorts of things,
seeing as how it was nighttime and none of the places we went
into were particularly well-lit) and somebody handed me an old
weatherbeaten fedora to put on my head so I would maybe look a
little older. It was the kind of hat you'd imagine Old Man Finzio

might wear to church (if, in fact, he ever went to church) and the MG people kept telling me to keep it down low over my forehead so nobody could tell how old I was. I figured I looked like one of those hot New York jazz musicians, you know? Maybe a saxophone player. And a highly underage saxophone player, at that. With strangely raw knuckles for a musician. Not that the barkeeps and tavern owners around Wilkes-Barre much cared, since the MG crowd represented a real Cash American goldmine every time they walked through the front door of a drinking establishment and took up command positions along the bar. They were good tippers, too. Especially after the fourth or fifth round. Truth is, I don't remember if we ever actually ate a meal that night (or, in fact, much of anything else) but I do recollect the following morning in vivid and hideous detail....

I shuddered awake to the piercing shriek of countless tiny, high-revving racing engines wailing past at full throttle, and opened my eyes to find myself folded-up in the back of somebody-or-other's light blue DeSoto 4-door. I had Cal's stolen comforter kind of half-heartedly wrapped around my shoulders and my face hurt on account of I'd been using a Sears Craftsman toolbox for a pillow. It was not what you could call a particularly comfortable place to sleep (or even pass out) and the truth is I had absolutely no idea where I was, how or when I got there, or for that matter why on earth I was wearing a shoe with no sock on one foot and a sock but no shoe on the other. Not that I really much cared, seeing as how every part of my body ached like I'd been worked over by the entire Gambino crime family the night before. But nothing in all of recorded human history hurt so much as my head. In fact, I remember reaching up gingerly with my fingertips to see if there was perhaps an actual crack in it someplace. Why, if I could've just laid my hands on that missing shoe, I would've thrown it hard as I could at the racecars screaming past less than ten yards away.

With superhuman effort I hoisted my body upright, pulled back on the handle, swung the door open, and gracefully fell out on the ground, whereupon I looked up to find myself sprawled at the feet of Cal Carrington and a bunch of the local MG guys. "I declare," he snickered, "it *lives!*"

"Real funny," I groaned, not the least bit amused. Oh, I'd had a few minor-league hangovers in my time (mostly after family weddings and graduation parties and that sort of thing) but never anything so vicious and wicked as this. Not hardly. One of the MG people tried to help me out with a couple aspirin and another fixed me up with a mug of hot coffee, but I was still feeling pretty rocky as I hunted around for my aviator sunglasses to cut down on the glare. "Say," I asked nobody in particular, "where the hell are we, anyway?"

"Why, Brynfan Tyddyn, of course."

"Brynfan Tyddyn?" I puzzled, turning the name over and over in my head. Why, just saying the words was like trying to talk with your mouth full.

Turns out "Brynfan Tyddyn" was this huge, woodsy country estate that belonged to a real live Pennsylvania state senator, and the name meant "Big Farm by the Hill" or "Big Hill by the Barn" or "Big Barn by the Farm" or something in this strange language used by the people who ran around England in animal skins before vowels were discovered. Now the particular state senator who owned the place was *incredibly* wealthy (the kind of wealthy you can only get by being born into it) and, like a lot of other toney, upper-crust individuals with fancy summer homes, ivy-covered winter mansions, and plenty of time to fill, he loved playing around with fast, expensive, European sportscars. And his estate at Brynfan Tyddyn was a pretty swell place to do it, too, seeing as how it was big as a damn state park and had all these winding blacktop driveways and access roads snaking this way and that through groves of fruit trees and across rolling meadows full of dandelions and wildflowers and thousands of fat, industrious honeybees. It was pretty as all getout, no lie, and I suppose I should've felt real privileged and honored just to be there (I mean, garage mechanics don't generally get invited to many social functions involving either country estates *or* state senators) but my head was pounding something awful and my stomach was doing one of those disgusting ocean-swell corkscrew rolls, and to tell the truth all I wanted at that point was to be back in the apartment over my Aunt Rosamarina's garage, gobbling handfuls of aspirin with Alka-Seltzer chasers and not straying too far from the commode.

That's when Cal suggested that maybe a little "hair of the dog" might help. Now you've probably sussed that I wasn't much of a drinker in those days --not compared to those sportycar guys, anyway-- but Cal assured me that all his old-money relatives and highclass society friends took themselves a little nip first thing in the morning after a rough night out. For medicinal purposes only, you understand. "Helps jumpstart the old batteries," he told me. Naturally Cal just happened to have a half-empty pint of bourbon handy, and, seeing as how there was no way I could feel any worse, I held my nose, clenched my teeth, and took a slug. And then another. And then one more. And, believe it or not, pretty soon I started to feel a little better. Although later it started to occur to me that hanging around with this rich, fashionable, highly distinguished Imported Sportscar crowd was turning me into a fine old specimen of a streetcorner rumpot.

I hung around pretty close to the MG bivouac for the next couple hours, drinking coffee with an occasional shot of bourbon in it and trying to get my eyes to focus properly again. But even with the edges all fuzzy, you'd have to say Brynfan Tyddyn was one of the most beautiful, elegant places I'd ever been in my life, what with the forests and meadows and this huge ivy-covered brick colonial right in the middle of everything. It was also an incredibly swell place to hold a sportscar race, although you'd have to say it was perhaps a little bit *dangerous,* on account of the pavement was barely a single lane wide and you had trees growing right up to the edge of the road in several key spots. A driver sure couldn't make many mistakes at a place like Brynfan Tyddyn. Not unless he wanted to collect himself a brickwork driveway pillar or a couple stout treetrunks. Which is probably why the S.C.M.A. wouldn't allow big cars like Jags or Allards to race at Brynfan Tyddyn. That was kind of nice, actually, since the smallbore guys always raced more or less in the shadows of the Big Iron and never got their fair share of the glory. Plus it was doubly appreciated since my head wasn't at all ready for the blare of Jaguar sixes or the reverberating, ground-throbbing gut-rumble of Allard V8s that particular ayem. Not hardly.

We had a tasty picnic lunch courtesy of the MG guys (which went down okay but didn't sit all that well later on) and afterwards Cal and me went wandering around the senator's estate to admire the cars and watch the races. As you can imagine, Cal spent most of the afternoon pacing up and down like a caged leopard and muttering under his breath about what a shame it was the TC blew up and how he could drive Goddam *rings* around the rest of the guys out there. It just wasn't *fair,* you know? Why should *they* be having all the fun? Not being able to race was eating Cal up pretty bad, no two ways about it.

But we had a good time anyway, and I started to learn more and more about sportscar racing as practiced by the S.C.M.A. regulars. First off we saw a race for these tiny little modified cars (Cal called them "tiddlers") in which this strange, pygmy-sized Italian device called a Bandini (which looked like some kid's pedal toy and probably weighed about the same) streaked off to an absolutely commanding lead, only to drop out a few laps from the checker when its stupid battery strap fell off. And so I picked up on yet another Great Racing Truth: *more races are lost to dumb little mechanical bullshit than to brilliant virtuoso driving or superior equipment.* Anyhow, the Bandini's retirement left the race to a much prettier little Italian roadster called a Siata Spyder. It was painted bright yellow, and although it had a tiny, made-in-America Crosley 4-cylinder under the hood (and supercharged, at that!) you couldn't miss the special Italian grace and flair to the Siata's fenderlines. In fact, it looked like a miniaturized edition of Creighton Pendleton's 4.1-litre Ferrari from a lot of angles. Honest it did. But it sure didn't *sound* like any sort of Ferrari V12 you ever heard. Not hardly. Truth is, that Siata sounded more like a sewing machine in heat....

Next up was a race for these strange little cigar-shaped open wheel racecars from England, which were powered by 500cc Norton and J.A. Prestwich motorcycle engines and built to such a ridiculously tiny scale that they made even the tiddlers seem positively enormous by comparison. I guess open-wheel Formula cars were all the rage among the well-heeled sportycar types overseas, and a few American enthusiasts had brought them back to race here in the states. They looked like big tin waterbugs to me, and you couldn't use them for anything except racing, on account of they didn't have lights or fenders or, in fact, much of *anything* except an engine, a gas tank, a big hole in the middle for the driver, and as few scraps of metal as possible to hold all the pieces together. Personally, I didn't see the attraction. I mean, they had no *style* or *class* or *stature* to them. Not like a

Jaguar XK or a Ferrari. Plus the damn things popped and banged like firecrackers in a tin can and smelled something awful from the doped-up, alcohol-based fuel they were running. But I had to admit they were pretty damn quick --especially around a tight, narrow, twisty little circuit like Brynfan Tyddyn-- and one of them actually cut the fastest single lap anybody ran all day. Really it did. The problem was you couldn't *see* the speed. Not like you could when somebody like Tommy Edwards wheeled his monstrous Cad-Allard around Bridgehampton. But you could tell the owners thought their little English single-seaters were pretty God Damn special. In fact, they were even sort of smug about it, waltzing around the paddock talking about "real, *pure* racing cars" and using uptown words like *"monoposto"* and *"Gran Pree"* all the time. But there were only four of the little boogers on hand (one "Kieft" and three "Coopers," not that you could really tell the difference) and some guy named Dick Irish pretty much ran away and hid from the other three, so it wasn't really too exciting.

But the last race of the day more than made up for the other two, as we had ourselves a real wheel-to-wheel barn burner from the green clear through the checker between this transplanted Englishman by the name of John Gordon Benett in a stripped-down, Nordec-supercharged MG TD (which Cal told me was about the quickest damn MG in the country, bar none) and a brand new, *very* special Porsche roadster in the hands of a guy named Phil Walters. I'd never heard of either one of them, but Cal said they were both topnotch drivers, and proved it by keeping his mouth shut throughout the entire race.

And what a race it was! Why, those two charged around the track like they were tied together --lap after lap!-- the Porsche skating through the turns with its rear end hung out to dry and the front wheels ruddering opposite-lock into the skid, and the MG wailing along barely *inches* astern, sniffing and jerking and pawing for some way --*any* way-- to get by. But the Porsche just had a little too much for the MG, and Walters took a squeaker of a win with John Gordon Benett's supercharged TD right up his tailpipe all the way to the checker. What a race! "Boy," I said afterwards, letting out a breath I must've held for at least the last six or seven laps, "those guys really know how to *drive!*"

"They should," Cal explained. "They're *professionals.*"

That kind of surprised me, since I knew the S.C.M.A. was pretty damn vocal about staying Strictly Amateur and not allowing any kind of prize money or sponsor names painted on the sides of the cars like you saw at the Indy 500. I sort of assumed that Hired Gun drivers fell into the same sort of category, you know? But some guys just want to *win* (even if all they're winning is a tin cup and a piece of honor) and there was nothing in the books to keep the owner of a fast car from putting a "quick friend" behind the wheel. Just to see what he could do with it, you understand. And that's how you wound up with a cool, experienced hand like John Gordon Benett (who'd raced professionally all over Europe) driving a factory-supported MG TD against a guy like Phil Walters (who raced for money on the Triple-A oval circuit under the name Ted Tappet) at the wheel of a highly tweaked Porsche that belonged to a certain "wealthy sportsman" who was real eager to see it win a few races.

I mean, it was all just for fun, right?

Still, it's always great to see drivers who really know how it's done, especially when two of them wind up head-to-head in near-equal cars and you're lucky enough to be perched on the fences watching. Only trouble is, it makes all the rank-and-file duffers, wannabes, hobbyists, and paddock pretenders look pretty damn lame by comparison.

After the races, Cal and me wandered into the paddock and stopped by to congratulate the drivers of that Porsche and MG. They were lounging around beside the cars, wrapped in a scented cloud of hot oil vapor and the smell of crisp metal, shooting the breeze and laughing it up pretty good with this short, solidly built little fellow with sad eyes, a granite jaw, and thick, black hair that swirled up off his forehead like flames off a campfire. Cal naturally waltzed right up like we were all old school chums and slapped an arm around Phil Walters' shoulder. "Hey, that was one hell of a race, Phil," Cal told him, working his hand up and down like a pump handle.

"Oh, uh, thanks," the Porsche driver nodded. "Old John tried to make it tough on me today, didn't he?"

"*I'll* say."

"Made me run her right to the limit."

"We saw."

"Why, every time I looked in the mirror, it was full of this damn MG. I just couldn't seem to get rid of the bastard."

"Oh, we did our best to keep it interesting," the English MG driver grinned, "but I'm afraid that Porsche was just a wee mite too quick for us today."

"Yeah, Mr. Walters," I tossed in, "that Porsche of yours is really *fast!*"

"Oh, thanks," he said, "but it's not *my* car."

"It's not?"

"No."

"Then who does it belong to?"

"Actually," the little guy with the sad eyes and wild hair said, almost like he was apologizing, "it's mine."

"Well, then congratulations to you, too. That was one hell of a swell race."

"Oh, don't congratulate *me,*" he said in the softest, politest American voice you ever heard, "I'm afraid John Gordon would have whipped us pretty soundly if *I'd* been at the wheel."

"Buddy," Cal said grandly, putting an arm over each of our shoulders, "meet Briggs Cunningham."

The name rang a little bit of a bell, you know, but I couldn't say as I really placed it. At least not at the time. "Well," I told him while shaking his hand, "that's an awful nice Porsche you got there anyways, Mr. Cunningham."

"Oh, this is just sort of a toy we play around with. I have a couple big cars, too."

"Big cars?"

He nodded. "I suppose you'll see them sooner or later if you keep coming to the races. We bring them out for a little run every once in a while. Will you be at Elkhart Lake?"

"Elkhart Lake?" Heck, I'd never even *heard* of a place called Elkhart Lake, and I was sort of embarrassed when I had to ask him where it was.

"It's up in Wisconsin," he explained, "no more than an hour north of Milwaukee. Great place. You shouldn't miss it. Wonderful spot. Absolutely wonderful."

"It's the week after Grand Island," Cal tossed in.

"Grand Island?" I said.

"Up by Niagara Falls," Cal nodded, "around the last weekend in August. You guys planning to make that one?"

"No, we'll still be over in Europe," Briggs Cunningham said like it was nothing at all, "racing in France...."

And slowly it was beginning to dawn on me that there were people in this sport who could take off whenever they felt like it and go traipsing all over the whole damn country --all over the whole damn *world,* even!-- just to indulge the urge to race their fancy sportscars. It made you wonder what the hell they did for a living, you know (if anything!) and why the heck *I* couldn't have been a member of The Lucky Sperm Club like them. It just didn't seem fair. On the other hand, simply hanging around there with all their snazzy cars and swell parties was one hell of a lot better than anything I had going on back home in Passaic. And that's when I realized I wanted more out of life than wrenching on tired, rusted-out Plymouths at the Old Man's Sinclair and listening to my dad lecture me about the many wonderful union benefits of his chemical plant job in Newark. Maybe I even wanted something more than getting into Julie Finzio's pants....

Anyhow, the bunch of us chewed the fat back and forth about racing and sportscars and the relative merits of Porsches versus supercharged MGs until the sun was beginning to creep down behind the senator's mansion, and while all that was in progress my friend Cal somehow managed to work himself a deal to have his derelict TC hauled all the way back to New Jersey inside Briggs Cunningham's spiffy enclosed trailer. That was one hell of a nice gesture on Briggs' part, since it meant somebody from the Cunningham crew (of which there were at least a half-dozen) had to *drive* their stripped-down Porsche all the way to New York City, and it had just a little half-moon racing windscreen and not much of anything else in the way of weather protection. Cal and I knew from grim personal experience how ugly an experience *that* can be.

Naturally Cal stayed behind to help out with his TC, and so I hitched a ride back to Jersey with Carson Flegley in his black TD. As you can imagine, it was nice having all the rudimentary automotive amenities like a top and a windshield and a few inches of upholstery under the passenger's butt (which was on the correct *American* side of the interior in Carson's car) not to mention something that actually resembled a heater hidden down under the dash for the trip through the mountains. But it still wasn't what you could call a particularly pleasant trip, on account of I was real exhausted and all the pick-me-up bourbon and trophy-party beer had long since worn off and I generally felt like I'd eaten a dead rat, fallen down a fire escape, and been left in a damp alley to die. Plus it took us absolutely for*ever* to reach Passaic with Carson Flegley at the wheel. Now don't get me wrong, I was plenty happy that Carson didn't try to carve his way through the mountains in World Record Time like my friend Cal (thank goodness!) but he was so worried about getting a damn stone chip or a mud splash on his new TD that he'd pull over to the side of the road and wait for a spell any time another car or truck got anywheres *near* close to us. Plus he'd picked up some dumb notion that you should vary your speed every other minute and never exceed 50 miles per hour when breaking-in the motor on a new English sportscar. I tried to explain to him about the difference between *engine* speed and *road* speed, and also that those flat-out runs up Giant's Despair most likely made complete nonsense out of any sort of normal break-in schedule. But Carson couldn't see it on account of he didn't understand gearing at all and had never even sniffed 40 going up the hill. Not to mention he was dead-set determined to stick *precisely* to the break-in procedure Barry Spline had so carefully outlined when he took delivery of his car.

Even if it made no sense at all.

I mean, who was he going to believe, some punk gas station mechanic from Passaic or a guy who came from a real MG dealership and wore a classy blue shop coat and moreover spoke with a genuine, one-hundred-percent-authentic British accent? And who could blame him?

So it was one long, *loooonnng* ride back to the apartment over my Aunt Rosamarina's garage, and I'd have to say it seemed even longer on account of Carson Flegley wasn't what you could call much of a conversationalist. Then again, I didn't do much to encourage him. After all, who wants to hear an undertaker talk shop?

Chapter 16: Fired and Hired

Believe it or not, I somehow managed to get myself relieved of duty at the Old Man's Sinclair come Monday morning. I guess it all started when I rolled in about two hours late, still bleary and tongue-stupid from the all-night ride back from Wilkes-Barre, Pee-A and the general, numbing after-effects that seem to follow every S.C.M.A. race weekend (or at least every one that *I've* attended, anyway). No sooner had I stumbled through the office door than I found myself on the receiving end of a rasping, hacking, nose-to-nose lecture from Old Man Finzio about the difference between A God Damn Garage Business and A God Damn Nursery School. "We ain't a bunch of nose-in-the-air rich assholes 'round *here,*" he snarled, shaking a bony finger under my nose, "not like all them highhats you been runnin' around with at the races. Nossir. 'Round here folks gotta *work* t'earn a God Damn livin'. An' they sure as hell can't *work* if they don't bother t'God Damn *show up* in the mornin', now can they?" You could see the Old Man was pretty worked up, and it started to remind me of one of my dad's Sunday afternoon post-ballgame speeches. But nastier. And no question Old Man Finzio's breath smelled a lot worse. Especially at close range.

But I stood there and took it, nodding and shaking my head at appropriate intervals as if I was listening to every word, even though most of it was coming in as thunder and static on account of my antennae were down that particular ayem and I was therefore missing out on many important details. I do recall a lot about the evils of two-seat foreign automobiles and the idleness and sloth of rich people (especially the kind who drove those two-seat foreign automobiles) and how all those kinds of wealthy assholes (like the ones I'd met through the S.C.M.A., for example) were corrupting his beloved Republican party from within and turning it to their own idle, slothful, greedy, unpatriotic ends. Which naturally led into the usual stuff about the lack of proper morals or decent work habits among my entire age group in general and me, Buddy Palumbo, in particular. I'm sure the Old Man could've easily gone on all morning, but he broke down in one of his trademark coughing jags about halfway through the well-known "lack of responsibility" part, and so I missed out on the big *"that's why this whole damn country's going to hell!"* payoff that inevitably comes at the end.

But the Old Man most likely would've let it go at that if I hadn't spent the entire rest of that morning bumbling around the shop like one of those dead-eyed zombies you see in the drive-in picture shows, tripping over stuff and bumping into things and generally turning everything I touched into a certified Class-A Disaster. First I knocked over the coffee pot and broke it. Then I snapped three studs in a row trying to get the damn exhaust manifold off some guy's Dodge Wayfarer that was in for a valve job. Next I lost the cutting torch and couldn't find it anywhere (and I had it right in my damn *hand,* you know?) after which I proceeded to set it gently down --in full operational mode-- on the hood of Dr. Angelo Robustelli's brand new Lincoln Capri 4-door, which was in the shop for its very first oil change. As you can imagine, the torch seared a splendid, thumb-sized scorch in the Lincoln's factory-fresh lemon/ivory paintwork, about six inches back from the hood ornament where you couldn't miss it unless you had a laundry bag over your head.

But I think the Old Man still might have let it slide (hey, we all have bad days now and then, don't we?) if only Julie hadn't showed up an hour or so later to clean up the office and pencil some numbers in the books. As you'll no doubt recall, I hadn't been seeing too much of her over the past couple weeks on account of all the time I'd been putting in on Cal's TC over by my Aunt Rosamarina's garage, and to tell the truth, I hadn't been real good about calling her, either. So you could really feel the old frost when she passed by my workbench on her way into the office, and I smelled trouble right away when she motioned for me to join her out behind the shop a few minutes later. No question she had something besides a friendly "longtime-no-see" chit-chat on her mind. Sure enough, we hadn't so much as turned the corner before Julie wheeled around and started in on me full blast. *"Why should I NEED this garbage?"* she screamed, icy fire spitting out of both eyeballs, "Huh? You tell me, Mister Buddy Palumbo! *WHY?!!"*

"But Ju--"

"You think I got nothin' *better* to do? *Huh?* Is that what you think? *Huh? IS IT??!!"*

"A'course not, Julie, I--"

"Think you can just call me up any old time you feel like a little kissy-face at the drive-in? *Huh?* Is *that* the way it is?"

"Aw, Ju--"

"And then let me rot by the stinkin' phone for weeks on end while you go screw around with those frickin' racecars!"

"But Julie --*Honey*-- Cal and me had an awful lot of stuff to do. It gets like that somet--"

"Yeah, *sure* it does! You was so frickin' busy y'couldn't find *FIVE GOD DAMN MINUTES* t'pick up the frickin' phone and call, just to see if I was maybe still alive."

"But *baby--"*

"Don't 'baby' *me*, Mister Buddy Palumbo. You make me *sick*. And I mean *SICK!* Why should I *need* this garbage. *Huh?* You tell me. *WHY??!!"*

Now I desperately wanted to stay on good terms with Julie, because when you got right down to it I really liked her an awful lot. Not just because we did stuff out behind the station in the Old Man's towtruck on Saturday nights (or used to, anyway) but also because she was the only female person besides my mom and sisters that I felt really close to. You know what I mean? So naturally I felt pretty damn scummy for ignoring her the way I did, and for that reason I just stood there and took it like a man, nodding and shrugging and staring at my shoes while she paced back and forth in front of me like one of Butch Bohunk's Marine drill sergeants, letting me have it with both barrels. And it oc-curred to me as I listened to Julie run down her near-endless list of all the thoughtless, mean, nasty, self-centered, and totally inexcusable things I'd done (or hadn't done and should have) that, while racecars and women could both give you a lot of pleasure, companionship, and personal satisfaction, they required completely different sorts of attention. Why, you could work on a racecar around the clock for six days straight in order to make a race weekend, but then leave it buried under a tarp all winter long with no hard feelings whatsoever. Women obviously re-quired a little more consistency of effort. And whenever a mis-treated automobile got really fed up, it most usually went dead silent on you, while women apparently did the exact opposite.

But I was patient and kept my mouth shut and pretty soon I could see she was running out of steam and even starting to cry a little bit, and although I've never claimed to be much of an expert on dealing with the female of the species, I *do* know that's a fellow's one and only chance to turn these deals around. "Aw, baby," I told her softly, kind of easing my way towards her, "I'm *real* sorry. Honest I am. It's just that racing's so, I don't know, so damn *exciting*. Why, it's the most exciting thing I've ever done in my life. Really it is. Sometimes I just get sort of, you know, *involved....*"

"Yeah, I know," she sniffed, "too involved to even so much as bother to pick up the phone...."

"Aw, listen, Julie...," I said, reaching out and wrapping my fingers around her elbows,"...someday you gotta come to the races *with* me. Why, then you'd see for yourself. Honest you would...." I pulled lightly on her arms and felt her glide gently forward into my arms,"...we'd have a *super* time there together. Really we would."

"We would?"

"Suuure we would," I told her, nuzzling into her hair, "no two ways about it. You'd *love* it."

"Hmph. Just like I love hangin' around gas station garages on Saturday nights, I suppose?"

"Aww, baby, it's not like that at all. Sure, sometimes you gotta pay the price. But believe you me, its *worth* it. Why, you should *see* all the fancy cars and rich, highclass people we hang around with at the races. Real live *celebrities,* even."

"Oh yeah?" Julie said, perking up just a little, "like who?"

"Oh, well, ahh, let's see," I mused, racking my brain for names that might impress her. "I've seen that Dave Garroway guy from TV a couple of times already...."

"He's the one with the chimpanzee, isn't he?" she said, not looking particularly stunned.

Hmmm. And that's when I realized **MOVIE STARS!** were what I really needed. "Well," I continued (like I was just getting warmed up, you know?), "how about *Tyrone Power?"*

"Tyrone Power?" Julie asked, her eyebrows sliding up a notch or two, *"he* goes to the sportscar races?"

"Suuure he does. All the time. And *Jackie Cooper*, too. He races a Jaguar like Big Ed's...."

"He *does?"*

"Uh-huh. Why, he even wrote about it in a magazine called *Road & Track."*

"He did?"

"Yup, he sure did. So did Clark Gable."

"CLARK GABLE??!!" she yelped, eyes popping open like mousetraps, *"the* Clark Gable?"

"Um hum," I nodded, casually looking down at my fingernails like I'd just had a ten-dollar manicure.

That's when Julie's eyes narrowed down and she started looking at me kind of sideways. "Say, this isn't just another load of the old Palumbo bullshit, is it?"

"No. Of course not," I told her, acting properly horrified and insulted that she would ever even *think* such a thing.

"Even the part about Clark Gable?"

"Absolutely. Clark Gable goes to the races whenever he's not all wrapped up in some picture."

"You're sure?"

"It's the God's-honest truth. I swear." And it *was* true, too. Or at least that's what I'd heard from a couple of the MG guys that night on the town after Giant's Despair. Of course, I'd never actually *seen* Tyrone Power or Jackie Cooper or Clark Gable at the races, but that was simply because they did most of their own personal sportscar stuff out in California where they lived. But Julie didn't need to know that right away, did she? "And listen," I added, watching the celebrity-sparks flickering up in her eyes, "you should see some of the *places* we go. Why, just yesterday Cal and me were at this huge country estate in Pennsylvania that belongs to a real live state senator."

"You *were??"*

"Um-hmm. And you should've *seen* it, Julie. There were forests and trees and gardens and a great big brick mansion right in the middle of everything. Why, we even *slept* there."

"You're *kidding."*

"No, I'm not. And I can't wait to take *you* to places like that with me." As you can see, I decided it would perhaps be better not to mention that my "accommodations" at the senator's estate amounted to a stolen comforter, a Sears Craftsman toolbox, and the back seat of an old 4-door DeSoto.

"Sounds pretty dreamy," she admitted, her eyes dancing.

"Gee whiz, Julie," I continued softly, pulling her in close again, "I can't help imagining how much nicer it'd be to have somebody, you know, *special* to share it with...."

"You mean like *me?*" Julie whispered while gently rolling her head into my shoulder.

"Sure like you, Julie. Like you and nobody else. Why, you'd be about the prettiest girl there, too."

I felt her stiffen up like a dead mackerel the instant I'd said that. "What do you mean, *about?*" Julie wanted to know, her eyes narrowing dangerously.

Whoops.

"So tell me, Buddy," she asked in a dangerously singsong voice, "they got a *lot* of pretty girls at those races?"

"Oh...well...ahh...umm," I mumbled while visions of Sally Enderle and her incredible white shorts popped in my head like flashbulbs, "certainly none as pretty as *you*, Julie...."

"Honest?" she said, twirling a few strands of hair around her finger like a female spider spinning a web.

"Oh, no question about it, Julie. No question at all."

"That's very nice," she whispered, leaning in close enough so my head filled with the smell of her perfume and I could feel her various female parts pressing in against me.

"It sure is," I whispered back, nuzzling against her cheek.

"Isn't it?" she purred, bringing her lips right up to my ear so the words sent waves of heat pulsing through my system. Boy, did that ever get me *excited!* I wrapped my arms around her and Julie put hers around me and when we started to kiss, she surprised the hell out of me by opening her mouth just a little and more or less inviting my tongue inside.

WOW!

And that, of course, is precisely when Old Man Finzio came stomping around the side of the building to see what his niece and his star employee were up to on company time. Seeing Julie and me all tied up in a love knot like that stopped the Old Man dead in his tracks, and his jaw had to work itself up and down a few times before it could produce any kind of recognizable noise (if you call the sound of a rusty nail getting pulled out of an old oak plank "recognizable," anyway). But it wasn't a split-second before the Old Man was bellowing away at the top of his lungs in perfect New Jersey English.

"YOU!" he shouted at Julie, *"You get the hell INSIDE!"*
Julie jumped off me like I had suddenly become electrified and
scurried off around the corner like a mouse running for its hole.
"And as for YOU, Palumbo," the Old Man growled, turning to
me with a dangerous new edge in his voice, *"you pack up yer shit
up and get outta my gas station. And I mean NOW!!"*

"Aah, geez, Mr. Finzio, if you'd jus--"

"SHUDDUP!" he screamed, running his eyes up and down
me like a rake. *"I'll be damned if I'm gonna let my little niece
play God's Gift t'every damn hard-on west of the Hudson River.
No SIR! 'Specially not with one a'my God Damn EM-PLOY-EES!
And for damn sure not on my God Damn company time. YOU
HEAR ME, PALUMBO?"*

Sure I heard him. Hell, everybody in Passaic heard him.

*"Now you got just ten minutes t'clear yer shit outta my
shop!"* he growled, the loose turkey-skin above his collar turning
all sorts of tropical-sunset colors. *"You understand me, boy? TEN
MINUTES!!!"* And with that he spun on his heel and stalked back
into the building.

For a few minutes all I could do was just stand there, reeling
and blinking and praying deep down inside that I'd wake up and
discover it was only some kind of bad dream. But of course it
wasn't, even though it still didn't seem *real*. Like I was watching
myself in a movie or something, you know? But there was no
getting away from the grim reality of the situation when I tiptoed
back into the service bay and found the Old Man already hard at
work on *my* Dodge valve job. Naturally I wanted to try and talk
to him --to maybe reason with him, you know?-- but I was all
kind of choked up and hollow-feeling inside and afraid my voice
might crack like some little kindergarten kid with a skinned knee.
Not that the Old Man was in any kind of mood to listen, seeing
as how wherever I went around the shop, he'd make sure and
turn his back just enough so I was always looking squarely at his
spine. Julie was nowhere to be seen, either, and finally there was
just nothing left to do but pack up Butch's tools and go. So I
carefully wiped off each wrench, socket, and screwdriver with a
clean shoprag, packed them neatly away, and closed the lid to
Butch's toolbox. "Okay if I leave these here for a few days?" I
heard myself ask.

"You bet'cher damn ass you'll leave them tools here," the Old Man snarled without turning around. *"Why, them is Butch Bohunk's tools, not YERS. And don't you ferget it!"* Then he jammed his head under the hood of that Dodge and pretended like I wasn't even there. So I locked Butch's toolbox, heaved it down off the bench, and set it frontside-backwards on the shelf below. Then I covered it up with a fender blanket and slipped the key into my back pocket. No way would Butch want somebody like Old Man Finzio getting into his tools. Why, in less than a week they'd be scattered all over the shop like bomb fragments.

And after that, there wasn't much to do but hang up my coveralls on the wall over by the space heater and walk on home. Gee whiz, it wasn't even noon.

Back at my apartment I flopped down on the bed and tried my best to sleep, but of course there was no way. My body and mind were both still beat-out exhausted from the weekend at Giant's Despair and Brynfan Tyddyn, but all my nerve ends were jangling like fire-truck alarms and the best I could do was just lay there with my eyes slammed shut while all these, these *things* swirled around my brain like roadside scenery whipping past a car window....Could I really be *finished* at the Sinclair?....John Gordon Benett's MG and that fast Cunningham Porsche skating around a turn like they were tied together at Brynfan Tyddyn.... What was I going to do about Butch's tools?....Making out with Julie out back behind the Sinclair on Saturday nights....No more borrowing the Old Man's towtruck....Rushing to finish Tommy Edwards' brakes in the nick of time at Bridgehampton....Skippy Welcher looping his Jag into the haybales and damn near collecting Creighton Pendleton's Ferrari in the process....Who'd take care of Big Ed's XK120?....The kiss Sally Enderle planted on Creighton Pendleton after his big win at Bridgehampton....Sitting next to Julie on the front seat of Big Ed's Caddy the night she got sick on the ferris wheel at Palisades Park....Charging up the hill at Giant's Despair in Cal's old TC....All the thankless hours we spent slaving away on that worthless piece of shit in my Aunt Rosamarina's garage....The fifth of Pinch and the resulting fire-works disaster on the Fourth of July....Could I really be *fired?*....That job offer from Barry Spline at Westbridge....And most especially the fresh, sweet, hot, lingering sensation of Julie Finzio's mouth opening up under mine....

It must've been well past midnight when I finally dozed off, and I guess I more or less slept my way clear through the day on Tuesday. Or at least I stayed in bed all day. I mean, what did I have to get up for? Truth is I'd never experienced the humiliation of getting fired before, and it made me feel angry, depressed, confused, dirty, guilty, and totally worthless. All at the same time. And that's not even mentioning the possibility that I might eventually wind up broke, hungry, and homeless. All told, I had maybe sixteen dollars wadded up in a sock in my top drawer and maybe another buck or two in loose change scattered around the apartment. Period. Not much to show for a guy who was supposedly earning himself a full-time, adult-type living, was it?

On the brighter side, my Aunt Rosamarina wasn't the type to throw me out in the street just because I was down on my luck, and I could always cadge a meal or two in my mom's kitchen, especially if I broke down and told my folks I'd got *fired* from my swell grease-monkey job at the Sinclair (although telling them sounded worse than starving to death at the time, but then I wasn't real hungry yet, either). I remember that dumb kid's fable kept running through my head (you know, the one about the grasshopper and the ants?) where the ants work hard all summer and put stuff away for the wintertime but the grasshopper goofs off and lives hand-to-mouth while the sun shines and damn near starves to death (or is it freezes to death? or maybe starves *and* freezes to death) when the cold weather rolls in. Anyhow, it occurred to me that I most likely had some grasshopper blood up my family tree somewheres.

But time passed (like it does) and by Wednesday morning I was feeling almost human again, and I even had this crazy notion that I could maybe go over by the Sinclair and somehow patch things up with Old Man Finzio. So I washed and shaved, put on the closest thing to a clean shirt I had on hand, and headed over to the station to see if the Old Man had softened up any. But when I got there I saw he was just pulling a "Help Wanted" sign out of the office window, and some burly-looking stranger in a string T-shirt was in the process of heaving a big red toolbox out of an unfamiliar Chevrolet station wagon and hauling it in through the overhead door.

Well, so much for that.

So I went back to my apartment and sulked for a good two or three hours before deciding to gingerly peel two dollars off the skinny roll wadded up in my sock and head over to Westbridge to see if maybe Barry Spline had any job openings. Believe me, it was tough getting into Manhattan without the Old Man's tow-truck or one of Big Ed's Caddies to drive, and I swear I spent the better part of two whole hours on assorted busses and subway trains, each one smelling slightly worse than the last as I got closer and closer to Westbridge's dirty little corner of Manhattan. I ultimately had to hoof it the last five blocks from what I thought was the nearest bus stop, and it was past noon by the time I walked into the Westbridge shop. Naturally Barry Spline and Colin St. John were both out to lunch, and the only people inside were Hans, Bjorn, and Vito, none of whom spoke any English at all unless they wanted something off you. So I went looking for Sylvester, and of course found him right where I expected, slouched against the brickwork in the alley behind the shop, thoughtfully drinking his lunch. Sylvester figured to be an excellent person to talk to, seeing as how he was unquestionably a seasoned expert on the subject of getting fired.

"*Sheee-it,*" Sylvester growled, taking a long pull off his bottle, "What th'fuck *you* got t'worry about."

"Well," I said, trying my best to make it sound desperate, "I got *fired.*"

"So?"

"So I don't have a *job* anymore."

"So?"

"So I'm *outta work,* Sylvester."

"So what? You still *single,* right?"

"Sure."

"You ain't got no *kids,* right?"

"A'course not."

"You ain't missed a meal yet, has you?"

"No. Not really."

"You still got a lil' money in yo' pocket?"

"Yeah. Some."

"How 'bout yo' rent? Is yo' rent paid?"

"Through August, anyway. But my aunt'd probably let it slide awhile if she knew I was tapped out...."

"Sheeeeeeeee-it!" Sylvester cackled, slapping one of his big, calloused hands on my knee, "you ain't *outta work,* son. You is on fucking *vacation!"*

You must admit, Sylvester Jones had a really unique way of looking at things.

Anyhow, Barry Spline was back behind the parts counter when Sylvester and me walked in from the alley, and he seemed pretty much interested when I told him I might perhaps possibly be looking for employment. "Only trouble," Barry told me, sort of whispering behind his hand, "is we got ourselves a bloody full crew right h'at the moment. More than full, in fact. Really don't see how we could use h'another set of 'ands just now. Fact is, I'd liketer get rid of one of these blokes. Things r'off a bit on the service side just at present. Yer understand."

"Uh, sure."

"But we'll be sure t'keep yer in mind h'if things change...."

"Gee, th-thanks," I said, my insides going all pale on me.

Then Barry looked me up and down with this strange, unusually thoughtful expression on his face. "Then again," he mused, gently stroking the end of his nose, "we could *maybe* put yer on as a race mechanic."

My mouth popped wide open. *"You COULD?"*

Barry nodded, "Why, we can most always find a spot for a decent race mechanic."

"Gee whiz," I gushed, "That'd be *great!"*

"I had a feelin' yer'd like it," Barry grinned.

But then I caught the glimmer of something sneaky in the corner of his eye. "Saay," I asked him, trying to sound real adult and mature and professional about it, "what exactly does a race mechanic *do,* anyways?"

"Why, whatever bleedin' *needs* to be done, of course. 'Round this shop, we recognize Race Mechanicin' as a bloody highly skilled form of h'enployment. Indeed we do. Most of your garden variety nine-to-five grease monkeys can't do the bleedin' job a'tall. Not a'tall. And that's a bleedin' fact."

"Hmmm," I said, pretending to mull it over. I mean, I didn't want Barry Spline to think he was dealing with some dumb, wet-behind-the-ears highschool pushover who didn't know what the score was (although he could probably see my tongue hanging out past my knees at the mere *thought* of working as a real, live, *bona fide* Race Mechanic). But I knew better than to just jump at the opportunity like some punk kid who just fell off a turnip truck (hey, I know how to negotiate a deal as well as the next guy) so I made sure to let Barry see me rolling the idea around in my head for three or four seconds before I told him I'd take it. And I wasn't the least bit shy about staring him right in the eye when I finally got up the nerve to ask, "Ahh, say Barry, d'ya think you could maybe tell me a little something about what this job, er, you know, how much it pays?"

"How's that?"

"This Race Mechanic job, Barry. Whazzit *pay?*"

"Oh, well," Barry shrugged, waving his fingers through the air like he was scattering stardust, "most usually, we start out our Racing Mechanics out at ten dollars a day --that's a *full* day, mind you-- and five dollars the half-day. Complete race weekends are usually twenty-five dollars each. That's expenses included, of course."

"Oh, of course," I said, nodding like I knew what he meant. But I wasn't real sure, so I asked, "You mean I get *extra* money to cover my expenses on race weekends?"

Barry looked at me like I'd just attempted to lop off one of his fingers. "Certainly not!" he snapped. "A Race Mechanic's expense money is always considered to be *h'included* in the twenty-five-dollar weekend fee."

"Oh."

"But it never costs much to stay up at the races. And there's always plenty of free food and drink about."

That I already knew.

"And you'll be doing most of yer bleedin' work 'ere in the shop, so I wouldn't worry much about it."

"And how many days would I be working, exactly?"

"Two, maybe three days a week. More on race weeks. You 'ave to understand, mate, Race Mechanicin' is a bloody part-time position on a strictly as-needed basis."

"Uh-huh," I said, rolling the numbers around in my head like loose marbles. Far as I could tell, the sum total I'd be making as a Race Mechanic at Westbridge figured to be something less than half of what I was earning full-time at the Old Man's gas station in Passaic (at least if you didn't count Big Ed's tips and the cost of daily transportation into Manhattan, anyways) but on the other hand it represented a chance to work on MGs and Jaguars and Allards instead of the Fords and Plymouths and broken-down Chevrolets I got as a steady diet at the Sinclair. Not to mention actually getting *paid* to go to the races. "Well," I said, trying to sound real cool and casual about it, "that sounds pretty interesting, Barry. When exactly would I start?"

"Oh, I suppose we'd be needing yer t'come in some after-noons and evenings each and every race week. Let's 'ave us a look at the schedule" (pronounced schedge-yewll, of course). He rummaged around in the top drawer of Colin's desk until he found a dog-eared copy of the S.C.M.A. calendar. "Ah, 'ere it is. We've got ourselves a race at Grand Island --that's up by Niagara Falls, y'know-- come the end of August. Then h'nother one at Elkhart Lake the following weekend. That's in Wisconsin, y'know. Mark my words, that'll be one busy damn five days in between. I reckon yer'll 'ave t'start comin' in, oh, say, the week before Grand Island: Our Racing Mechanics most usually start in right after lunch, and should always be prepared t'stay as late as necessary t'get the job done...."

"Oh, naturally," I said while my toes quietly jumped up and down inside my shoes. "So tell me, Barry, which cars will I be working on?"

"Why, whichever ones need attention, of course."

"Oh, of course, of course."

"Why, on some of the more 'ectic race weekends, yer'll probably have t'babysit the whole bloody lot."

I could hardly wait. But I had one more question. "Tell me something else, Barry. Which car will I *ride* in? Up to the races, I mean." I was kind of hoping to get some miles in with Tommy Edwards and his wicked Cad-Allard. Why, maybe he'd even let me *drive* it once or twice....

Barry looked at me like I had concrete setting up between my ears. "Actually," he said down his nose, "our Westbridge Race Mechanics don't generally get to ride *anywhere* with the paying customers, mate. That's what bloody wives and girl-friends are for."

"Oh," I said. "But then how the heck am I gonna get all the way up to Grand Island?"

"Why, that's h'entirely up to *you!*" Barry exclaimed, pounding his fist into his palm like it was some sort of exciting Special Bonus you got along with a position as an official Westbridge Motor Car Company (Ltd.) Race Mechanic. "See, yer've got to h'understand, Buddy, there's a lot of *freedom* and *h'independent thought* h'involved in a situation like this. Like I said, not just any bloke can do it."

I could see why. "Ahh...umm...well...y'see, Barry, the truth of it is, I'm not real sure I can find a way up there."

Barry rubbed his chin again and stared off into space like he was planning the invasion of Normandy. "Weeell," he mused, "I reckon yer *might* catch a lift with me in the parts truck...*if* yer pay half on the bleedin' petrol, that is."

I hadn't even started working at Westbridge, and already I was beginning to understand the high turnover of personnel. And that's when something else occurred to me. "Y'know, Barry," I said, "August 30th is almost a whole damn month from now. What am I supposed to do in the meantime?"

"Well, if it was *me,*" Barry grinned, "I believe I'd start looking for a *real* job."

Chapter 17: Carlo's Stallions

Big Ed called me at my Aunt Rosamarina's house a few days after I landed my big new job opportunity at Westbridge, and as you can imagine, he was pretty bent out of shape that I wasn't going to be around the Old Man's Sinclair to work on his Jag or his Caddies any more. "Whaddam I gonna do now?" he groused, chewing the butt end of his stogie directly into the receiver, "my damn Jaguar won't start an' I'll be damned if I'll let that butcher Finzio anywheres near it. Why'dja quit, anyway?"

"*Quit??!* I didn't quit, I got *fired*. Who told you I quit?"

"Old Man Finzio."

"Figures."

"So," Big Ed wanted to know, "what'cha doin' these days."

I told him about my newly acquired part-time race mechanic job at Westbridge.

"Jee-zus, Buddy, why th'hell you wanna work for that cheap shyster sonofabitch Colin St. John for? Why, I bet he'd steal the damn pennies off a dead man's eyes."

"Yeah, maybe so," I allowed, "but its a chance to be around sportscars all the time. I guess I'm kind of addicted, y'know?"

"Ummph," Big Ed grunted, chomping into his cigar at the other end of the line.

"In fact," I mentioned, casually circling like a vulture, "we got a race coming up at Grand Island at the end of August. Not too far from Niagara Falls, I think. Maybe you oughta think about coming up yourself in the Jaguar."

"Hell, that's way across the whole friggin' state," he snorted. "And besides, the damn thing ain't even running."

"Aw, we can fix that. No problem. And I hear they got a really good entry lined up and everything. Ought to be a real swell time." As you can obviously see, I had visions of riding up to Grand Island in Big Ed's XK120 instead of bouncing along in the back of the Westbridge parts truck with prize-winning British Tightwad Barry Spline at the wheel. Not to mention picking up half-shares on the gas.

But Big Ed didn't sound real receptive to the idea --not hardly-- on account of he was having one hell of a time getting his name put up for membership in the S.C.M.A., and he'd be damned if he was going to drive all the way across New York State just to hang on the fences with the rest of the rank-and-file rubberneckers. By God, he owned a God Damn Jaguar XK120 and By God he wanted to *participate*. And who could blame him?

To tell the truth, I didn't reckon that Big Ed Baumstein would make much of a racecar driver, even if he got the chance. I mean, he wasn't exactly deft or arty with a stickshift or effortlessly smooth and silky behind the wheel. In fact, you could feel him tensing up like he was getting strapped into the electric chair whenever he really put the spurs to his Jaguar in order to show it off. But Big Ed figured he could at least drive a damn racing car as good as that Skippy Welcher character, and I had to admit there was a better-than-even chance he might be right.

The problem was getting *in*.

Big Ed had called people, written letters, bought drinks, and even asked a few of the heavyweight S.C.M.A. armband-types to fancy lunches and dinners. In Manhattan, no less. But of course none of them ever made it, on account of they were always "too busy" or because "something came up at the last moment" --no matter how many weeks in advance Big Ed called to invite them. You could tell it was pissing him off no end. And why shouldn't it? A guy like Big Ed didn't much appreciate getting the old Official Brushoff routine from a bunch of ivy-covered Old Money Protestants just because he had a Jewish last name and traded in garbage and scrap machinery for a living. Hell, his money was as green as anybody's, wasn't it? And he was a *lousy* Jew. Why, you could ask *any*body. He never went to temple or fasted on the big hebe holidays or wore one of those little black silk beanies or *anything*. Not to mention that at least three of his several wives (including the reigning Mrs. B) were *shiksas*. But somehow all the resident tightasses on the S.C.M.A.'s membership committee were real damn particular about what church you went to. Even if you never went to church.

And hardly any of them ever did.

Naturally I told Big Ed I'd be happy to take a look at his dead Jaguar, and it wasn't twenty minutes later he pulled up out front in the black Caddy sedan. That seemed kind of odd, you know, since it was the sort of hot, sunny summer day when you'd expect Big Ed to tool up in his white Caddy convert if for any reason his Jag 120 was on the fritz. So I asked Big Ed what happened to the white Caddy, and the blackest, meanest scowl you ever saw rolled down his face like the corrugated steel curtains they pull down over the store windows in Sylvester Jones' neighborhood at closing time. "Oh, I guess you could say I had a little, er, *problem* with one a'my em-ploy-ees over at the new dump we took over in Monmouth County."

"Oh? What happened?"

"Well, I had t'fire the guy, see, because he was showing up drunk alla time. Or not showing up at all."

"And?"

"Aw, he got all pissed off about it. It wasn't ten in the morning and he'd already had himself a snootfull."

"So?"

"So the bastid backed one a'my trucks up into the white Caddy at damn near 40 miles an hour. Smashed the living shit out of that poor car."

"Geez, that's a real shame."

"That's *nothing!* Then the asshole pulled the friggin' lever and dumped the whole goddam load on top of it," Big Ed's voice went down to a mumble. "It was fresh off the farm route, too."

"Really?" I said, kind of starting to laugh. I mean, I just couldn't help it, you know?

"Oh *sure,*" Big Ed snarled, "laugh it up. Real goddam funny...." But then his eyes started to sparkle a little, too, and pretty soon we were both laughing so hard that Big Ed had to pull over to the side of the road because he couldn't see to drive.

"Gee whiz," I told him when I could finally talk again, "that's too bad, isn't it? Whaddaya gonna *do?"*

"Well, one thing I'm damn sure *not* gonna do is go driving around in a pile of pig shit and chicken heads...."

"So?" I asked, starting to laugh again.

"So we made *extra* sure the insurance company'll total the old girl out. I mean, you wouldn't *never* get rid of a smell like that. Not *ever!"*

"So how'dja do it?"

"Aw, we just kinda pushed that Caddy around the yard with a couple a'those big Caterpillar earth movers we got there. Like we was playin' field hockey with it, y'know?" He flipped me one of his patented Big Ed winks (the kind that most usually came with a five-buck tip attached) and unequivocally guaranteed me that his white Caddy convert had indeed done her very last mile. But then a sad, melancholy mist drifted over his eyes. "It's a damn shame though," he said, "I mean, I really *loved* that car. Almost as much as my Jag, y'know?"

"Hey," I told him, "you can always get yourself another one. Heck, the new models'll be coming out in a couple months, and I hear Cadillac's gonna have themselves a brand new convertible model."

"Yeah, I heard about it from the salesman at the Cadillac agency," Big Ed allowed, sadly peeling the cellophane off a fresh dollar cigar, "they call it the Eldorado."

"That's the one. I heard you'll even be able to get it with air conditioning and wire wheels."

"Yeah," he sighed, "I s'pose I can always buy me one a'them. But there was always something, I dunno, something sorta *special* about that white car..."

Boy, I knew *exactly* what he was talking about!

"...the leather always felt, I dunno, sort of *warm* when you touched it. An' Jesus Christ, it had the sweetest, strongest-running engine of any Cadillac I ever owned."

"Yeah, it sure did," I agreed, feeling my own eyes mist over a little as I recalled the night Big Ed let Julie and me borrow it to cruise over by the Doggy Shake and then on to Palisades Park.

"Gee," Big Ed whispered, his voice cracking a little around the edges, "was it ever *fast* and *smooth* for a big, heavy car."

"Yeah, it sure was," I told him. "And gorgeous, too."

"Uh-huh," Big Ed nodded. "Anybody tells you all cars are the same just doesn't know shit from Shinola about automobiles."

You could say what you wanted to about Big Ed Baumstein, but no question he understood how it is with cars. At least how it is if you're the type who tends to get involved with them on a highly personal basis.

Finding the operative glitch on Big Ed's Jag was no problem at all (the electric fuel pump had crapped out, which is hardly front-page news as far as S.U. electric fuel pumps are concerned) but fixing it was something else entirely seeing as how I didn't have any tools handy in the attached garage behind Big Ed's monstrous brick-and-stone house in Teaneck (you remember, the one with the marble columns and concrete lions in front and the little bronze boy peeing into the big round fountain in the drive-way). You'd have to say Big Ed's place didn't have much in the way of a decent toolset, just a claw hammer and a couple pair of pliers and some screwdrivers that looked like they'd been used mostly to stir cans of paint and pry up nails. Then again, Big Ed didn't spend all that much time at home (and virtually none of it puttering around with your typical homeowner-type handyman projects) and all the various Mrs. Big Eds were in the habit of calling local tradesmen when anything around the Baumstein household required mechanical or cosmetic attention.

"Jeez, Big Ed," I told him, "I could really use a socket set to get that thing out of there. Or at the very least a couple open-end wrenches, y'know?"

"This won't help?" he grumbled, passing me a monkey wrench that looked like it went down on the Titanic.

"No, I don't believe it will. See, I really need the proper sort of tools to get this job handled the right way. I mean, you wouldn't want me ripping your Jaguar apart with a claw hammer and a set of garden shears, would you."

Big Ed mulled it over and shook his head. "But you're *sure* that the fuel pump is the trouble?"

"No question about it."

"Well, why don't we run on in to Westbridge and pick us up another one, huh?"

"Oh, I can probably fix this one if I could just get it apart."

"Nah, let's get us a *new* one, Buddy. We can always fix up the old one and keep it for a spare in case the new one ever craps out again." Just that quickly, Big Ed had put his finger on the reason why so many longtime sportscar owners have garages packed to the damn rafters with spare parts that are rarely (if ever) in fully operational condition.

So Big Ed and me rode over to Westbridge in the black
Caddy to pick up his new fuel pump, and all the way there and
back he groused about the passing of his beloved white Caddy
and all the damn trouble he was having trying to get into the
S.C.M.A. But he did stop along the way at a Sears store and
bought himself a complete set of Sears Craftsman tools. Just like
that! Can you believe it? Why, I'd never been shopping with
anybody remotely like Big Ed Baumstein before. Not in my
entire life. He just walked up and down the aisles, pointing to
tool cabinets and socket sets and box-end combination wrenches
and tempered-steel hacksaw blades and double-jointed flex knuck-
lers and Phillips and flat-blade screwdrivers in eight different
sizes and Lord only knows what else. "Y'need one a'*these?*" he'd
ask, poking his finger at a 24-inch set of channel locks or a
rubber-ended mallet or a half-horsepower rotary bench grinder.

"Yeah," I'd say, "it could come in handy some day...."

And just that fast, Big Ed would own it. Why, he even had
to have some of the stuff delivered to his house the next day on
account of we couldn't fit it all in the trunk of the black Caddy
sedan. And a Cadillac Sixty Special 4-door has one whale of a
huge trunk, ask anyone. Fact is, I got Big Ed's Jag running again
in less time than it took us to unload the damn tools! But that's
partly on account of I now had a proper set of wrenches and
sockets and stuff to work with. The Jag seemed to appreciate
that, and ran like an absolute champ on the ride back over to my
aunt's place in Passaic. So I was kind of surprised when Big Ed
rang me up the very next afternoon and asked if I wanted to take
another trip over the bridge into Manhattan. I feared the worst
(could I already be picking up on The Westbridge Method of
Jaguar Repair?) but felt much better when I saw Big Ed tooling
up Buchanan Street in his XK120. "Naw," he said, flashing me
half a grin on either side of his stogie, "she's purrin' like a well-
fed kitten t'day. I got something *else* in mind...."

"Yeah? Like what?"

"You'll see," he told me, and you couldn't miss the way his
grin spread out another inch or so towards his ears.

We crossed over into Manhattan a little after three, and
thank goodness traffic was light because it was a hot summer day
and the needle on the Jag's temp gauge was kind of hovering

over towards the warmish side of the dial. No question a good old New York City traffic jam would've had her boiling for sure. Big Ed drove us down towards the shipping docks, twisting and turning our way through a tangle of bumpy, narrow streets lined with old firebrick warehouse buildings and double-parked delivery trucks and huge stacks of wooden crates and cardboard boxes bringing stuff from all over the world into downtown Manhattan. Finally Big Ed pulled into the driveway of a nondescript cinder-block garage with no sign or anything in front --not even a damn street address!-- and we got out and walked up to a windowless grey steel door that was locked up tighter than a bank vault. Big Ed knocked a couple times, but there was no answer. So he knocked again, only this time a little louder. Still nothing. So he hauled off and beat on that thing so hard it actually shook, sending off vibrations like a big iron church bell. That at last got some shuffling and cursing and undoing of latches going on inside, and finally the door opened just a crack and a large, sort-of familiar Italian nose stuck itself out, kind of sniffing us. "Aay, whaddaya want?" the nose asked. I was sure I'd heard that voice before, but I couldn't quite place it.

"I'm lookin' for Carlo Sebastian," Big Ed told the nose.

"Yeah? An' who is it wants to know?"

"Ed Baumstein."

"Who?"

"Ed Baumstein. From over in Jersey. I'm a friend of Jimmy Lazzarro and Tony Cicci. I wanna see Carlo Sebastian."

"What about?"

I could see the color was starting to creep up Big Ed's neck. "About a goddam *car,* that's what! Now lemme in before I rip this friggin' door right off its God Damn hinges."

The nose looked us up-and-down again, only now backed up by a pair of suspicious, deep-set Sicilian eyes. "Justa minute, ay?" it said as the door closed again and we heard some more shuffling and mumbling in Italian followed by quick footsteps with maybe a set of steel taps on the heels. When the door swung open this time, it revealed a perfectly chiseled little wop with an elegant mane of silvery-white hair, dark, flashing eyes, and a wide, toothy smile that reflected light like a 24-carat gold dessert plate. At least when he wanted it to, anyway. He was wearing a white silk shirt open about three buttons underneath a butter-scotch-colored leather vest, and had an extra-large shop coat draped over his shoulders like it was some kind of opera cape. Real dramatic, you know?

"How may I help you?" the perfectly chisled Italian guy asked, his face cocked sideways like a italicized question mark. He had one of those deep, rich, resonant Continental voices like the guys who sell perfume and stuff on the radio. I thought I'd maybe seen him someplace before, and for sure I'd seen the other guy. He was one of the three mechanics we saw attending to Creighton Pendleton's new Ferrari at Bridgehampton.

"You Carlo Sebastian?" Big Ed asked. The guy nodded and sort-of bowed as he ushered us inside. It was pretty dark in there, what with just a single naked bulb in a little cage over the door-way and a couple dangling trouble lights somewhere in the back where you could hear a ratchet wrench click-click-clicking and the unmistakable sound of a creeper scraping across a concrete floor. I could make out five or six cars scattered around in the shadows, and it took awhile before my eyes got accustomed to the light and I realized *they were all Ferraris! Every single one of them!* My mouth went dry on me and I swear I could hear my heart pounding in my chest. *FERRARIS!! WOW!!!* I stared desperately into the gloom, trying to make them out better.

With a grand flourish, Carlo Sebastian introduced himself as "the ex*clu*sive Ferrari importer and *fact*ory representative to the United States and *all* of North America." Which, back in those days, meant he got his hands on maybe a dozen cars a year. Not much by Ford-and-Chevy standards, perhaps, but these weren't exactly Fords or Chevys by any stretch of the imagination. Why, you could buy yourself a couple each Fords and Chevys for the price of a new Ferrari. *If* you could get one, that is.

There was a lot of pomp and strut to this Carlo Sebastian character, but you had to love the guy because he oozed style and class from every pore and radiated heat like a damn bonfire. And he could turn up that smile of his like a klieg light whenever he felt like it. "My shop is modest," he said, sweeping his hands around like you could have somehow missed how modest it actually was. "Ah, but my *cars...,*" he continued softly, kissing the tips of his fingers, "...there is nothing else like them in the entire world. Not *any*where...."

"We know th--" Big Ed started in, but Carlo Sebastian stopped him short.

"Come!" he said, "let me *show* you!" And with that he flipped a switch on the wall like he was detonating an A-bomb and a row of dim fluorescent lights fizzed on above us. *"Look!"* he cried, leaping out between the cars. "See the kind of automobiles a true *genius* can produce!"

My God, you should've seen those cars! There were three coupes and two roadsters inside the garage, all sleek and deadly and gleaming in the half-light like a silent pack of carnivores sleeping under a jungle moon. Each one had that unmistakable, man-eating eggcrate grille and the signature enameled medallion on the nose with its rampant black stallion reared up against a bright yellow background, but beyond that, you couldn't help noticing that no two of them seemed even remotely alike. Carlo Sebastian was nice enough to take us on a whirlwind tour of his shop, explaining the cars and filling us in on all kinds of stories about Ferrari's brilliant machines and all the many races they'd won and all the brave, brave men who'd driven them to victory. As he spoke, his hands sculptured pictures in the air and his shop coat trailed along on the floor behind him, swirling up little fanfare plumes of dust. That Carlo Sebastian was one hell of a showman, no two ways about it.

The cars were enough to make you wet your pants, anyway.

"This," he said, pointing to one of the coupes, "is a 212 *Export* by *Vignale* [pronounced Vihn-*yah*-laye, by the way] and that roadster is a *Barchetta* [Bar-*ket*-ta] from Superleggera [Soo-per-ledge-*err*-a] Touring [just like it sounds in English]." Naturally I had no idea on earth what he was talking about, but no question I was as impressed as all getout. Turns out the Ferrari factory doesn't actually build all those svelte, sexy bodies you see on Ferrari automobiles. Not at all. The way it works is that Ferrari whips up the chassis and running gear and then ships the whole shebang to one of these body specialist body shop guys they have in Italy to get sheet metal done. Those little panel-beating shops are called *Carrozzeria* (your guess is as good as mine) and Italy must be absolutely lousy with the damn things on account of I heard Carlo Sebastian talk about Ferrari bodies by Vignale, Touring, Ghia, Bertone, Pinin Farina, Boano, Drogo, Scaglietti, Zagato, and Lord only knows how many more. I

suspect some of them aren't much more than little two-by-four, back-alley, father-and-son-type bump shops, but believe it or not, that's where every single one of those svelte, breathtaking Ferrari shapes comes from. One car at a time. And that's why each and every Ferrari is generally a little bit *different* from every other Ferrari. Like a piece of sculpture or something, you know? But somehow, no matter who does the panel-beating, every Ferrari that rolls out of the factory somehow manages to wind up with that special Ferrari *look,* and, like Carlo Sebastian took pains to explain, it's like nothing else in the whole damn world.

But the bodywork is just window-dressing compared to what goes on under the hoods and beneath the fenders of Ferrari automobiles. That's where the *real* magic lives. I mean, there are plenty of smart, handsome, reasonably potent sportscars in this world, but Ferraris are special because they're designed and built --cost no object!-- to do one thing and one thing only: *to go FASTER!* Why, every place you look on a Ferrari, you find design and craftsmanship and incredible detail pointing towards the same, simply understood goal: first across the finish line.

Take the engines, for example: Ferrari V12s are simply the most elegant, symmetrical, and awesomely complex automotive powerplants you'll ever hope to see. The basic idea is very simple: for any given displacement, a large number of smaller cylinders can almost always rev higher, run smoother, and produce more horsepower than a lesser number of large cylinders. But it's the way Ferrari engines are *built* that really sets them apart. Inside they have chain-driven overhead camshafts and hemispherical combustion chambers and countless beautifully machined moving parts, and on the outside they're like fine sculpture, what with cast aluminum cambox covers done up in the sort of crinkly baked-on enamel finish you'd expect to find on an expensive pair of binoculars and no less than *two* distributors --one for each bank!-- driven right off the end of the camshafts and pointing straight forward to keep the hoodline as low as possible. Ferrari V12s use fancy Weber carburetors (sometimes *three* of 'em!) which stand in an orderly row down the center of the vee and probably mix fuel and air together better than anything else on the planet. Why, even the damn *air cleaners* on a Ferrari are handsome enough for centerpiece duty on your dining room table! Two litres not fast enough for you? Then how about two-point-three? Or two-point-six? Or three? Or three-point-three? Or four-point-one? Or four-point-four? Or even *more!* Why, Ferrari tools up whole new engines the way General Motors whips up fresh new color schemes and interior trim.

And at that very moment, wandering around the wondrous cars in Carlo Sebastian's dimly lit garage, I fell helplessly, hopelessly in love with the style and genius Enzo Ferrari breathed into every single one of his cars. Each one was a signed original.

A creature that almost breathed.

But Big Ed Baumstein wasn't particularly interested in crinkle-finish cam covers or Weber carburetors or even Carlo Sebastian's wonderful stories (which were far more entertaining than any opera I've ever seen, and I've seen *two*). What Big Ed wanted --what he desperately *needed*-- was to get his hands on a Ferrari of his own. *Any* Ferrari. That would show those damn tightassed geeks on the S.C.M.A. membership committee that he was in for the long haul and By God meant business. Plus something like a Ferrari might just grease the rails for him all the way to places like Bridgehampton and Brynfan Tyddyn. Which is why he kept edging his way towards the heap of low, hot curves slumbering under a flannel car cover against the far wall of the shop. "So what's that one?" he asked, like he didn't really care.

"Aaahhhh," Carlo Sebastian sighed, his smile brightening up twenty or thirty kilowatts. "That, my friend, is *sculptured fire!*" He swept the cover off like a matador making a pass and underneath was the most dangerous-looking automobile I'd ever laid eyes on: a full-tilt 4.1-litre Ferrari racing car, done up in brilliant yellow with big white number circles on the hood and doors.

"Jee-*zus,*" Big Ed said softly, and Carlo Sebastian nodded.

"How fast'll it go?" I asked like a damn schoolkid.

"Fast enough, my friend, fast enough."

And that's about when Big Ed stepped back and cleared his throat a couple times, and right away I knew what was coming. Big Ed wanted that car --wanted it *bad*-- and it occurred to him that underneath the buttery phrases and continental veneer, Carlo Sebastian was just another smooth-talking automobile salesman. And if there was one type of person Big Ed Baumstein knew exactly how to handle, it was a car salesman. "Saaay, lissen," he said, running his hands down into his pants pockets, "how much would it take --*cash money!*-- to drive this thing out of here?"

Carlo Sebastian looked Big Ed up and down like he didn't comprehend. "To drive it *where?*"

"You know, *outta* here. I'm talkin' *Right Now!* This very minute. *CAAAAASH money!*" As you can see, Big Ed made sure to hit every single Car Salesman Hot Button known to man.

Carlo Sebastian sighed heavily and shook his head, like he was terribly, terribly disappointed. "Oh, my dear friend," he said sadly, "this car is not for *sale,*" he swept his hand around the shop again, "none of my Ferraris are for *sale....*"

"They're *not??*"

"Oh, no-no-no-no! These cars are already *sold*. Ferraris are *always* already sold...."

"They are?"

"Certainly. If you wish to buy a Ferrari, my friend," Carlo explained, holding up a manicured index finger, "you must be prepared to *wait*. As you must assuredly know, nothing of value is ever attained quickly or easily...." For just an instant I thought about Julie and hoped Carlo knew what he was talking about.

I listened to Carlo and Big Ed jaw back and forth for a while, and the gist of it was that you could put down a deposit (a fairly *substantial* deposit!) and Carlo Sebastian would be happy to order a car for you. A "production" model, mind you, not any sort of ex-works racing car. Then it took from eight months to over a year for the car to arrive (and sometimes even longer!) and there was never any guarantee that it would be exactly what you ordered when it finally showed up, on account of the factory was constantly changing, modifying, replacing, and discontinuing model lines, not to mention that Enzo Ferrari always built what he bloody well thought best regardless of what his customers had on order. After all, what did *they* know?

And that was just for the ordinary "production" cars. True ex-works *racing* examples were even more difficult to obtain. Why, *everyone* wanted a Ferrari racing car, did they not? (They didn't, as a matter of fact. Some people were perfectly content driving Kaiser Manhattans and Nash Ramblers. But they were hardly Carlo Sebastian's target audience, were they?) In any case, the Ferrari racing shops produced only a scant handful of full-tilt competition cars every season, and they were *always* spoken for when the factory team was done with them.

Always....

"Get a Ferrari racing car? *Hah!* It is simply not possible, my friend. Not possible at all." Then Carlo reached up his tiny little arm and ran it as far as it would go around Big Ed's massive shoulders. "You must understand," he continued in a fatherly tone, "it is not simply a question of money and patience...."

"It isn't?"

"Certainly not, Mr. Baumstein. Certainly not. For example, *this* car is on it's way to a gentleman from California named Ernesto Julio. You are perhaps familiar with the name?"

Big Ed nodded. Hell, anybody who's ever been in a liquor store knows Ernesto Julio. Why, he did for the California wine business what Henry Ford did for the automobile manufacturing business in Detroit. Exactly, in fact. But I never heard that he raced sportscars. "Say, I didn't know he raced cars," I said.

"Oh, he *doesn't,*" Carlo Sebastian explained, "not himself, anyway. Ernesto Julio is a great *aficionado,* a great *sportsman,* a true *patrone....*"

"A *what?*"

"A *patrone,* my friend. He always buys the very *latest* machinery --the very *best!*-- and searches out the most promising young talents --the *gifted* ones-- to drive for him. That is why we always sell him our most powerful and advanced machines, because...," he looked Big Ed right in the eye, "...because *my* reputation --*Ferrari's* reputation-- is built on one simple thing. *Winning.* We must therefore ensure our racing cars have every possible opportunity to do what they are built and bred for: *to win races!* That is why they are entrusted only to those who have proven themselves to be, shall we say, *capable....*"

Big Ed didn't like that much at all, and you could see the color starting to come up on his face again. Which meant that this was probably an excellent time to mosey off by myself and take a short tour around Carlo Sebastian's shop. I hate scenes, and no question Big Ed had a knack for creating some real beauts.

So I followed the sound of a clicking ratchet wrench into the back of Carlo Sebastian's shop, and located the source when I damn near tripped over a pair of legs sticking out from under one of the 2.6-litre 212 coupes with Touring bodywork. I leaned in over the fender and looked down past the gracefully curved oil filler and the delicate branches of the exhaust header to where a pair of dark, beady black eyes and a large, familiar Italian nose were staring back up at me from directly beneath the finned-aluminum oil pan. "Hi," I said, "wat'cha doin' down there?"

"Whassit lookalike I'm a-doin', ey? Poundin' a-my fuckin' pud?" And that, by and large, was my first formal introduction to Alfredo Muscatelli, who was one of the famous wrench-spinning Muscatelli Brothers from the old neighborhood in Brooklyn. There were three of them all told --Alfredo, Giuseppe, and Sidney-- and they all worked in some capacity or other for Carlo Sebastian. As you probably guessed, Sidney was more or less a half-brother, and therein lies an interesting story.

I first heard the tale of the Muscatelli brothers from one of Big Ed's truck drivers, about how Alfredo and Giuseppe's dad was well-known and highly respected around the old neighbor-hood for the excellent explosive devices he could whip up out of a few simple sticks of dynamite and an ordinary Woolworth's five-and-dime alarm clock. The work wasn't always steady, but it paid well, and Alfredo and Giuseppe's dad was much in demand and made quite a bit of money during the prohibition years.

But it all went terribly wrong one black day in 1926, when the elder Muscatelli fell victim to some terribly shoddy workman-ship on the part of whoever put in the low bid on alarm clocks for the Woolworth chain that year. And so Alfredo and Giu-seppe's father departed to his eternal reward (along with a good half-block of choice Brooklyn real estate) leaving his poor wife and two little *bambinos* to fend for themselves. Needless to say, he didn't leave much in the way of life insurance, as it was rather hard to come by in his particular line of work. But Alfredo and Giuseppe's mother was recommended by friends to a clever young Jewish lawyer named Sid Moskowitz, with the intent of perhaps suing the Woolworth people for leaving her in such a fix. Moskowitz ultimately advised against it, but there was a kind of silver lining in that he took something of a shine to the widow Muscatelli. Especially after he found out about the safe deposit boxes scattered all over New York and New Jersey in the names of assorted obscure characters from Verdi operas. Soon after-wards Lawyer Sid and the widow Muscatelli were married in a civil ceremony, and little Sid Jr. followed right on schedule some seven-and-a-half months later. But during the widow's eighth month, slippery Sid met an elevator operator with exceptional lungs named Loreli Pomerantz, and the two of them mysteriously disappeared just a few days after little Sid Jr. was born --along with most of the safe deposit box goodies. It was the talk of the back porches in the old neighborhood for weeks, and the general consensus was that Something Should-a Be Done. Sure enough, Sid Moskowitz turned up a few months later in Havana, Cuba. All over Havana, in fact, seeing as how the ignition switch on his brand new Packard somehow shorted out against a half-dozen sticks of blasting powder. Rumor has it they put a few Packard parts in the coffin along with the rest of the Moskowitz residue (just to give it a little heft, you understand) because most of Sid Sr. wound up as pigeon food in and around the greater Havana area. It was almost as if Alfredo and Giuseppe's dad had personally reached down from the heavens (or up from Someplace Else) and done the job himself. You gotta hand it to the Sicilians. When it comes to revenge, they have a wonderful sense of style.

Anyhow, young Alfredo and Giuseppe inherited clever fingers and a strong mechanical intuition from their father, and wound up going into the garage business in the old neighborhood in Brooklyn. They were tough, hardworking guys with strong hands, gravelly voices, the right kind of connections (thanks to their father, God rest his soul) and hot loins for anything in a tight skirt, and soon earned an enviable reputation for souping up getaway cars and taking bullet holes out of sheet metal. Business was better than good, and pretty soon the Muscatelli brothers branched out into retail work, fixing carburetors and relining brakes and replacing burnt-out wiper motors for people without violin cases, thick window glass, or long criminal records.

To Alfredo and Giuseppe's everlasting credit, they took little Sid Jr. into the business with them, even though he couldn't so much as change oil without slicing off a knuckle or spilling the contents of the drainpan all over the floor. But little Sid Jr. was quick with numbers and good with the customers and kept the best-organized parts inventory in all of Brooklyn, none of which were exactly strong points with either of his half-brothers. In contrast to the swarthy, barrel-chested Giuseppe and Alfredo, Sid Jr. was a spindly, happy-faced little geek with thinning hair, fading freckles, and a goofy, near-permanent smile. Also unlike the other two, everybody who met Sid Jr. seemed to like him.

Anyhow, the three of them got a reputation around the old neighborhood for fixing mechanical things so they *stayed* fixed and keeping their mouths shut about just who brought what into their shop for service, and as a result (not to mention that people had to hang onto older machinery instead of buying new during the depression and the war years) their business grew and prospered. But a crackdown by some cowboy assistant D.A. with dreams of being a councilman or judge or something brought unwanted attention to their thriving little garage business in 1949, and ultimately caused many of their best customers to take their work elsewhere rather than run the gauntlet of unmarked police cars that were inevitably parked at both ends of the alley. Plus they were getting hassled by the I.R.S. about their books (which amounted to basically two washtubs full of notes and scribbled receipts -mostly in Italian- which had somehow accidentally had a couple loads of laundry done in them. Heavy on the bleach). These were sudden and devastating developments, and just about the time the three Muscatelli brothers needed someplace to turn, Carlo Sebastian rang them up to see if they'd like to go to work in his new Ferrari shop in Manhattan. To sweeten the pot, there was a free trip to the Ferrari factory in Italy for all three of them (at least until the heat blew over, anyway) if they took the jobs.

So Alfredo, Giuseppe, and Sid Jr. went to visit the Ferrari factory at Maranello for "training" in early 1951, and even got to join the official Ferrari Racing Team for the Mille Miglia, which Ferrari won that year. It was one hell of an incredible race, running flat-out from one end of Italy to the other --*a thousand miles!*-- on ordinary, everyday Italian roads that were (at least supposedly) closed to other traffic for the occasion. It took iron men with nerves of steel to drive in a race like that, and both Alfredo and Giuseppe considered stateside racing pretty damn lame by comparison. In fact, if you said much of anything about S.C.M.A. racing to Alfredo, he'd make a face like Benito Mussolini and sneer: *"HAH!* You call-a *dis* racing? *I* tell you *racing:* A Tousan' Miles, up anna down Italy, troo'da mountains, troo'da rain, troo'da fog so fuckin' a-tick you could-a no find-a you own assa-hole. Now *DAT'S* a-racing!" Then he'd generally punctuate with some sort of colorful Sicilian hand gesture or a twelve-inch hip thrust.

I guess Sid Muscatelli enjoyed Italy, too, even if he didn't exactly work out too well as a Ferrari racing mechanic. Not hardly! In fact, I heard he was a total and complete disaster. Worse than Old Man Finzio, even (if you can believe it). Sid Jr. poured oil in radiators, dropped washers down carburetors, and cross-threaded every nut and bolt he got his hands on. Why, during one especially crucial pit stop, Sid supposedly pulled the right-side tires off the leading Ferrari --worn right down to the damn canvas, mind you-- switched them around front-to-back, and put them right back on the car! The poor driver tore off in a cloud of smoke while the fresh tires still sat there, stacked neatly by the curb. Sid Jr. also had a habit of smearing everything he touched with blood (his own, of course) but fortunately it didn't show because the cars were painted bright red anyway. On the other hand, Sid was funny and likable and possessed a unique talent for negotiation. His skill with hotel owners, restaurateurs, and local hookers made him welcome on the team even after they learned not to let him anywhere *near* the damn racecars.

And now all three of the Muscatelli brothers worked for Carlo Sebastian, Alfredo and Giuseppe doing all the hands-on mechanical stuff while Sid Jr. ran the parts, bookkeeping, and Customer Excuses departments. To tell the truth, I envied the hell out of those guys, on account of they got to spend their days working around Carlo Sebastian's garage-full of Ferraris, because those cars were so beautiful and exotic and, well, *hot*.

Chapter 18: The Glamorous Life of a Racing Wrench

By mid-August Barry was finding stuff for me to do pretty regular around the shop at Westbridge, mostly on account of Vito got himself fired for stealing parts to do side jobs on customer cars at home and then threatening to slit Barry's throat with a straight razor when Barry asked him about it. Which meant I started taking the two-hour-plus Public Transportation train-and-bus ride into Manhattan almost every morning so I could arrive at Westbridge just after lunch. Barry absolutely insisted on that, because it meant he only had to pay me for a half day, no matter how late we worked. And some nights we worked *late*.

I didn't have much in the way of proper hand tools, what with Butch's toolset still temporarily stuck underneath the workbench at the Old Man's gas station in Passaic, but Big Ed let me "borrow" a few things out of the collection he had from the afternoon we cleaned out the tool department of the local Sears Roebuck store, and Sylvester would usually let me dip into his battered old 10-gauge steel toolbox whenever I needed something besides the pliers, screwdrivers, hammer, open ends, and adjustable crescent wrench I used on most of my mechanical projects. Fact is, I didn't need too awful much in the way of sophisticated equipment on account of I was the New Guy around Westbridge and therefore got stuck with all the stupid grunt jobs (grease and oil, cleaning dirty parts, tire mounts, wax jobs, rusted-up exhaust pipes, filling shocks, etc.) while Sylvester, Barry, and the regular Westbridge foreign-accent crew handled all the critical assembly work and fine tuning. Every single day I'd find a fresh assortment of Jags and MGs and whatnot lined up against the back wall, and the shit lists stuck under their windshield wipers or taped to their steering wheels would inevitably have *my* initials penciled in next to all the dumb stuff you could train a damn monkey to do. To tell the truth, it was getting me down just a bit. I mean, I figured I was probably at least as good a wrench as anybody else in the shop (except for Sylvester, of course) but Colin and Barry were afraid to trust me with anything really difficult or complicated on account of I was so young and only had a couple months' experience around English cars. Besides, they needed *some*body to work transmission casings over in the parts tank and clean all the gooey, sticky, smelly cosmoline gunk off the new cars that came over on the boats from England and then mount the bumpers and windshields and mirrors and stuff. They'd discovered you could fit a lot more cars in the hold of an ocean-going freighter if they didn't stand any higher than the fenderline, and the Jags and MGs definitely needed that cosmoline coating so's they wouldn't start rusting away to nothing until they were safely in the hands of their new owners. And I was the guy who got to do it. Lucky me. But every car shop needs a resident dirtbag peon to do all the ugly, nasty, filthy, disgusting stuff nobody else wants to do, and the job almost always falls in the lap of the last guy hired, the part-time helper, or the youngest person on the floor. Which meant I was three-for-three in the Westbridge Motor Car Company (Ltd.) Shop Peon sweepstakes.

But at least I got to hang around a lot of nifty sportscars (in fact, I got to hang around, over, inside, and clear underneath them!) and I was learning one hell of a lot about how the English automobile manufacturers put their cars together. Or *almost* put their cars together, as was often the case. But it was a great education, even if I did seem to be putting in an awful lot of hours for a guy earning part-time pay. Most usually I'd work around the shop all afternoon (right through the heat of the day, natch) attending to oil changes and stuff on assorted MGs and Jaguars belonging to Colin and Barry's ordinary rank-and-file "boulevard" customers, and we wouldn't even *start* on the damn racing stuff until well past what most normal people would consider dinnertime.

Barry would usually pack it in around seven-thirty or eight, just as it was turning deep twilight, but some nights he'd let Sylvester and me stay on a little later to finish up this or that after he was gone. That was always kind of fun, on account of we'd talk about stuff while we worked, and I came to appreciate that Sylvester Jones was a pretty darn interesting guy. Bitter as hell, but *interesting*. He knew all sorts of stuff about mechanical gizmos and life in general (just like Butch, you know?) and also just like Butch, he didn't get along with too many people at all. In fact, Sylvester always carried around an extensive mental list of all the people who could bring him boundless joy by simply stepping in front of fast-moving steam locomotives or picking up angry pit vipers by the business end. Right at the top of that list were all the mean cracker sergeants he'd met and endured in the service, the shifty black dice jockeys he shot craps with two or three times a week, a conservative flat 97 percent of the white population in general, damn near all his blood relatives, and always and most especially, Colin St. John. "You look in the fuckin' dictionary," Sylvester told me, "you'll see ol' Colin's picture right next to the word *'asshole.'* Ah ain't lyin'."

Also like Butch, Sylvester invested an awful lot of time and creative energy into imagining particularly terrible and unfortunate things that could happen to all those countless people he didn't like. "Sheeee-*it,* son, they oughta put all them damn cracker sergeants in a big ol' hydraulic press," and he'd illustrate by holding his arms out in front of his chest like the jaws of a giant bench vise, "an' then you jus' pull the damn lever an' let it *ease on down...,*" he'd slowly bring his arms together, "...until you hear all them cracker skulls pop and splatter like a buncha ripe watermelons." Then he'd usually add some really ingenious and disgusting popping noises he'd learned how to make with his mouth and forefinger when he was in the army. "When you all done, alls you got lef' is a bad smell an'a big ol' smear of cracker grease." It was beginning to dawn on me that Sylvester Jones and Butch Bohunk really had an awful lot in common, and that it was too bad they would've gotten into a fistfight if you ever sat them down together for a glass of beer.

Anyhow, Barry Spline wouldn't think of trusting Sylvester or me with a shop key, so he'd button up the office and parts department, lower and padlock the overhead door on both sides, and set the alley door to latch itself automatically when it closed behind him. Then he'd slyly remove the cash drawer (like we didn't know what he was up to, right?) and take off into the night. As a result, Sylvester and me had to be real careful not to get locked out if we went into the alley to grab ourselves a smoke or a little fresh air or something. And believe me, you *needed* a little fresh air every now and then when you were trying to work on a steamy August night with all the damn doors shut and no breeze at all in that shop except a sad little hamster wheeze off the wall fan up by the service counter. Sylvester most usually bought us a cold sixpack down at the corner liquor store (at least once Barry was gone, anyways) and that helped some, but we had to remember to take the empties out and stick 'em in a trash can behind some other building so Barry couldn't tell we'd been drinking in his shop. Not that he didn't know what we were up to, of course, but you don't want to insult a guy by leaving the evidence right out there in the open so you have to deny it. Anyhow, we'd both be pretty well wrung out by the time we finished up around 9:30 or 10. Sometimes even later.

Afterwards, Sylvester'd most usually give me a lift over by the bus terminal on his way to some gin mill or crap game in Harlem or wherever the hell else he might be headed on any particular evening, and it was always kind of neat riding through the late-night summer streets of Manhattan with Sylvester and his rusty old Plymouth. There's a certain brand of invisibility that comes with a car like that, and we could cruise along real slow and eavesdrop on the drunks spilling out on the sidewalks in front of streetcorner taverns or listen in on the rapid-fire chatter and jangle of jewelry from cabloads of night-clubbers and theater-goers stopped next to us at traffic lights or even pick up on the latest hot neighborhood gossip from the ordinary folks clustered on their front porches or simply out walking the dog in the warm evening air. We'd have the windows down and the vents rotated full backwards so as to get a little breeze through the interior, and we'd most usually have at least one warm beer left that we'd pass back and forth between us and that I'd have to hide down below my knees anytime we drove past a police car or saw a cop out walking his beat. There was always something exciting and electric about those rides through midtown Manhattan on warm summer nights, even if I was just on my way over to the damn bus station in a beatup old Plymouth with a surly black grease-monkey from Harlem at the wheel. It made me feel real *mature* and *experienced,* you know?

Pretty damn wise and clever, too.

The bad part about my new race mechanicing job at West-bridge was how every damn minute of my life seemed to be spent either working on cars or getting to and from work, and it was all I could do each day to just flop down on the bed back at my apartment in Passaic and grab a few desperate hours sleep before the alarm rang and it was time to get up and do it all over again.

Why, it was like my old man's stupid chemical plant job! Only it took longer to get there and the pay was worse. Lots worse, in fact. And I was working nights and weekends, too. I suppose the smart thing would've been to find myself some place to stay in Manhattan (in fact I did sleep right there in the shop a couple times when Sylvester and I worked real late or if maybe he bought us two sixpacks that night instead of one) but somehow I knew deep down inside that the deal at Westbridge was just a temporary sort of thing. Not that I really wanted it to be, you understand, but it was one of those things you just sort of *feel*. Besides, the historical turnover of wrenching talent at Colin and Barry's shop gave me some pretty decent reasons for feeling that way. Plus, much as I liked the idea of being a professional Exotic Sportscar Racing Wrench right in the heart of the biggest, most exciting city in the whole world, I also knew in my heart that I was still just a wrench-twisting kid from Jersey who didn't really fit in. When you got right down to it, I suppose I *belonged* back at some ordinary streetcorner gas station on the wilderness side of the George Washington bridge. And preferably Old Man Finzio's place in Passaic, seeing as how that's where Julie Finzio was.

Truth is, I wasn't getting to see Julie at all, and I was surprised by how much I missed her. Of course, I didn't really have the time, money, or any sort of motorized vehicle to take her out on a proper date --not even to the Doggie Shake or the drive-in movies-- and I wasn't so sure she would've been interested anyways. After all, she'd probably got herself a giant, economy-sized load of grief off Old Man Finzio about what he caught us doing out back behind his station, and the way her mother made a point of answering the phone just so she could hang up every time I called left no doubt that Old Man Finzio had filled her in as well, and no question Julie's mom was not real pleased about the situation. Not at all. Gee whiz, it wasn't like Julie and me were really *doing* anything, you know?

Things weren't much better around my folks' house. I'd broken down and told them I got fired over dinner one Sunday evening (right in the middle of some of my mom's fabulous pine-apple-glazed baked ham with candied yams and all the fixin's) and after that, things got pretty tough for me with my old man. Oh, my mom was still great --she always is-- but my dad and me got into one of those deals where we couldn't be in the same room for thirty seconds at a stretch without getting into a big fight about something. Or even nothing. You remember how pissed off he was when I quit that stinking chemical plant job so's I could go work at Old Man Finzio's gas station? Remember how he said that was a stupid, dumb, dirty, lousy, lowlife, shitty-ass excuse for a job? Well, now he was even *madder* on account of I wasn't working there anymore! Can you believe it? Plus he was angry that I'd got myself fired --like it was *my* fault, right?-- and even more pissed off about how Cal and me damn near burned down my Aunt Rosamarina's garage. As you can imagine, that had been a pretty hot news item all over the neighborhood (ranking just behind late results from the Helsinki Olympics and General Motors' surprise announcement that they were going to offer Air Conditioning on selected models for 1953) and even the rank-and-file union guys at the chemical plant had heard about it. So every time I went over by my folks' house to cadge a free meal or get my mom to do my laundry or even just raid the damn refrigerator, my dad would wind up hollering at me. For no reason at all, you know? And that would of course get me mad right back at him, and pretty soon we'd be screeching and howling and snarling and spitting back and forth at each other like a pair of damn alleycats. My mom learned from watching her stupid birds out in the back yard to know there was no earthly sense trying to get between two male members of any species once they've decided not to get along (especially if they happen to be a father and a son) so she'd generally go down to do her ironing or sneak upstairs to fluff up the pillows a couple hundred times to get herself out of the line of fire once the fireworks started. And most often they'd start with something real simple and stupid, like fr'instance if he caught me gnawing on a cold chicken leg or wolfing down the last piece of my mom's Dutch apple pie. *"So,"* he'd snarl, *"you think you can just waltz in here any time you feel like it and take hold of any damn thing that strikes your fancy, don't you?"*

"What?!" I'd snarl right back, making sure he got a real good solid look at whatever I was chewing. *"Y'mean I'm not even allowed to EAT here anymore?"*

"YOU earn a living! Or at least that's what you CLAIM, smartass! Why don't you go out and buy your OWN damn food for a change?"

"I DO buy my own food! All the time! I just come over now and then t'see how you and mom are doing. That's what a son is SUPPOSED to do, isn't it?"

"Yeah. Sure. You really touch my heart. That's why I always catch you with your God Damn nose in my refrigerator!"

"Oh, now it's YOUR refrigerator."

"Sure, it's my refrigerator, you insolent little piece of shit. Who the hell you think PAID for it."

"MOM!" I'd yell upstairs, *"YOU BETTER STAY THE HELL OUT OF YOUR HUSBAND'S REFRIGERATOR."*

"CUT THAT OUT!" he'd bellow even louder.

"YEAH, WHY SHOULD I?"

"BECAUSE I SAID SO!!"

I must admit he had me beat on bass resonance and sheer, windowpane-rattling volume (he'd obviously had a lot of high-level training at his shop steward job) but anytime my old man threatened to shout me down, I knew exactly what to do. I'd simply march over to the refrigerator, take out one of his ice cold beers, lever off the cap, and drink it right in front of him --real slow and deliberate, you know - just so I could watch him sputter and change colors. Sometimes he'd even haul back like he was gonna belt me one, but we both knew I was too quick for him and he'd kind of pretend to think better of it (like he was doing it for *my* benefit, you know?) and say something real disgusted like "You're pretty God Damn cocky for a kid that can't even hold onto a job as a God Damn gas station grease monkey."

That's when I'd wipe the last of his beer off my chin, look my old man right square in the eye, and agree with him. It drove him *nuts*. "You bet your ass I am," I'd sneer, and then walk out real quick before he maybe forgot I was too fast for him and took a swing at me. You've probably gone through shit like that in your own family, right? In fact, I bet it happens to every kid while he's growing up, just as sure as chicken pox and puberty.

My buddy Cal was having family troubles, too. Seems his folks found out about Giant's Despair and Brynfan Tyddyn via the well-known Carrington family grapevine (most likely due to that sweet old sap-collector lady from Vermont who was working registration) and they decided to take away what was left of his MG and also grounded him for the rest of the summer. Not that Cal was about to *stay* grounded, you understand, but no question it was much tougher for him to get around without his old TC or the spare set of keys to his mom's new Packard. Not that the TC was in any shape to drive anyway, since it was at least one engine block, one connecting rod, one piston, two valves, an oil pan, and several dozen billable hours of machine-shop time away from even marginally operational. Not to mention the thing was still lacking several important pieces of routine road equipment such as fenders, headlights, a muffler, windshield wipers, or even a windshield for the wipers it didn't have anymore to wipe. I guess Briggs Cunningham's truck driver dropped Cal's dead MG in front of my aunt's house the Monday morning after Wilkes-Barre weekend (right about the time I was getting fired over at Old Man Finzio's, in fact) but a couple days later a towtruck with New York plates appeared out of nowhere and hauled it off to God-only-knows where.

I talked to Cal on the phone a couple times, and of course he tried to make it sound like everything was rosy and that he didn't really care all that much one way or another. But if you listened close, you couldn't miss the thin, hollow ring to his voice. Like the people you hear in the hallways of intensive care wards and funeral parlors and such. *Everything's gonna be fine, Buddy. This'll blow over. No problem at all. You'll see....*

The screwy part is I *believed* him when he said that stuff, on account of I knew how desperately Cal wanted --Cal *needed*-- to get away and go racing again, and I knew he'd do whatever it took --*anything*-- to get back behind the wheel of something with a loud exhaust and four wheels under it and a racing number painted on the side. But I was also honest and realistic enough to know it wouldn't be anytime soon, no matter what Cal said.

All of which meant I was feeling pretty much alone in the world, what with Cal serving time out at Castle Carrington and Julie Finzio more or less Officially Off Limits and Big Ed sulking all the time about how those assholes on the S.C.M.A. membership committee didn't want anything to do with him (at least when he wasn't busy sulking about how there wasn't anybody around the Old Man's Sinclair who knew how to take care of his cars any more) and my folks' house turning into a damn battle-ground on account of continual flareups and ugly skirmishes between my dad and me. Why, the only thing left in my life was working in the shop at Westbridge and getting myself to and from working in the shop at Westbridge, and that is not what you would exactly call a complete, well-rounded sort of existence.

So I decided to drop by over at Butch's place, just to chew the fat and see how he was doing and maybe ask if he'd like to join me on the trip to Grand Island for the race out there. After all, he had a car to get us there (even if it wasn't much of one) and besides, I thought it was something he might really enjoy. Hell, just getting away from Mean Marlene for a couple days figured to do him a world of good all by itself. And I knew Butch could pick up and go at the drop of a hat because he really didn't have much of anything to do with himself any more. Which was pretty damn sad if you ever sat down and thought about it.

Butch and Marlene lived in an ugly little clapboard house right behind the chemical plant where my dad worked, and it had more or less gone downhill ever since the day Butch got hurt (not that it was anything out of *Better Homes and Gardens* before that). Truth be known, Mean Marlene was not what you could call a real persnickety housekeeper --not hardly!-- and Butch didn't help matters any on account of he could never resist the lure of any sort of abandoned motorized contraption that needed "just a little fixing up" to be "good as new again." So Butch and Marlene's front lawn looked a lot like one of Big Ed's scrap-yards, what with cracked engine blocks, seized-up air compres-sors, rusty hand-crank washing machines, burnt-out space heat-ers, pre-war outboard motors, and even a couple big industrial wall fans scattered all over the place, each and every one of them waiting for Butch to find the time (and parts) to do "just a little fixing up" so they could be "good as new again."

Marlene was gone that particular day (I guess she'd got herself a job waiting tables someplace) and I found old Butch sitting out on his rickety front porch with the guts of a Plymouth carburetor spread out in front of him on this three-legged card table he had propped up against the railing. He seemed real pleased to see me (he even smiled, no lie!) and when I asked him how he'd like to go up to the races at Grand Island with me, Butch damn near jumped clear out of his wheelchair. "Hell, *yes!*"

he whooped, slamming his lump hand down on the card table so hard the little brass carburetor parts jumped every which way. "Why, I been stuck here in this friggin' place s'damn long I'm about t'go stark raving buggy! Marlene drives me nuts. Sittin' on this damn porch drives me nuts. The stink off that friggin' chemical plant drives me nuts. Hell, it's burnt the damn hairs right outta my nostrils. See?" He tilted his head back to show me the inside of his nose.

"So you wanna go?"

"You bet your God Damn *ass* I do!"

"That's great," I told him, "just great. Why, it'll be just like the Old Days, you know?" Not that Butch and me really had much in the way of Old Days. At least not road trips or anything like that. In fact, about the furthest we'd ever gone together was just across Manhattan and the Williamsburg Bridge to pick up some hydraulic jack parts in Brooklyn. But it sounded good.

About then Mean Marlene came clattering up the street in Butch's old Ford, and right away I began having second thoughts. I mean, no way was that heap going to exactly, aah, *blend in* with the polished-up MGs, Jaguars, Ferraris, and so forth you'd expect to find at Grand Island. And besides its obvious cosmetic shortcomings, that old Ford was banging and popping something awful and listing way over towards the left rear like a harbor tugboat taking on water. Looked to me like it might be a couple busted leaves in the spring on that side (or maybe they'd just gone soft and sagged a few inches) but whatever it was, it made that old Ford look pretty damn comical. At least if you weren't planning to take a cross-country road trip in the damn thing. Confidence-inspiring it was not. "Say, Butch," I mumbled, giving his rusty old Ford a serious professional eye-balling, "you think that crate'll *make* it?"

Butch's jaw tightened up and his eyes narrowed down to slits. "Hell *yes!* that car'll make it," he snarled. "Why *wouldn't* it? Y'fergettin' who put that damn thing t'gether? Y'fergettin' who taught you every God Damn thing you *THINK* you know about automobiles?"

"No, Butch, I...."

"Besides," he added, squeezing off a wink, "if the sonofabitch breaks, we'll just up an' *fix* it! After all, we're Goddam car mechanics, ain't we?"

Chapter 19: The Great Grand Island Buffalo Hunt

There was an awful lot of stuff to do around Westbridge come race week, so I was down at the shop every single day --full time, no less!-- and it seemed like the instant I'd get done changing the oil and filter in a Jag 120 or checking the wheel-spoke tension on an MG's spare or packing oil cans and brake fluid and tubes of chassis grease in appropriate-sized cardboard boxes and stacking them in the parts van, Barry'd be right there in front of me with another block-long shit list of things that required my immediate attention. In fact, you had to be impressed with the way Barry kept coming up with stuff for everybody to do, somehow keeping it all straight and organized while his crew was scurrying around in all directions like the last passengers on the Titanic. He might not have been much for clutch jobs or busted rear ends or yanking out engine blocks, but Barry Spline sure knew what had to be done next if you wanted to get a flock of sportscars ready for a race weekend.

But it was an awful lot of work, and I wound up pulling a pair of tandem all-nighters Tuesday and Wednesday nights, and daybreak Thursday found me still hard at it, helping Barry and one of the foreign-born grease monkeys load damn near everything left in the shop into the parts van. Then Barry pulled out in the drive, lowered the overhead door, locked everything up tight, and drove off, leaving me to take the damn hour-and-a-half bus-and-train ride over to Butch's house in Jersey. It didn't even occur to the sonofabitch to offer me a lift. Typical. Then again, maybe this was just another sterling example of the *freedom* and *independent thought* Barry said you got along with a job as a Westbridge racing mechanic.

In any case, it was almost straight-up noon by the time I got to Butch's place, and another hour or so before we got done packing his stuff and dropping by my apartment so's I could grab a quick shower and do the same, and I reckon it was mid-afternoon when we finally hit the road in Butch's ratty old Ford, taking off across most of New Jersey and virtually all of New York State towards Grand Island.

In case you don't know, Grand Island sits in the middle of the Niagara River about seven miles north of Buffalo, and somehow the S.C.M.A. had cooked up a deal with the local city fathers to put on a road race as part of their big blowout Grand Island Centennial Celebration extravaganza. The S.C.M.A. could arrange that kind of thing on account of lots of the S.C.M.A. regulars were the city father type themselves. Or at least their fathers or grandfathers were. Besides, the S.C.M.A. races stood out as by far the most exciting feature attraction of the entire Grand Island Centennial festival weekend. Unless you're partial to highschool marching bands and pie-eating contests, that is.

But it was one whale of a long drive to get there --almost 400 miles-- and I had to do it pretty much solo on account of there was still no way Butch could operate a set of pedals. We tried it where Butch sat behind the wheel and steered while I kind of angled my feet in from the passenger side and worked the clutch, gas, and brakes for him, and I'd have to say he really got a charge out of that. But after we damn near ran up the backside of a gravel truck just outside Paramus, I decided that maybe wasn't such a good idea. At least not until we got way out in the boonies someplace with no other traffic around. So, tired as I was, I wound up doing most all the driving while Butch just sat there in the passenger seat with a road map spread out across his lap, smoking cigarette after cigarette and telling me what road to take and how far we were from the next town and yelling at me to "get the Goddam lead out" every time we got bottled up behind a slow-moving truck or a car with one of those doddering old grey-haired geezers at the controls. You know, the ones you can barely see from behind (just the tops of their heads, right?) who sit all scrunched up against the wheel with their noses about jammed through the horn ring and drive like violin music is playing in their hearing aids and it's a mortal sin to go anything over thirty-five miles an hour.

But every now and then we'd get us a clear stretch of road, and then Butch'd have me run that old Ford as hard and fast as she'd go. And of course I was happy to oblige, mashing down on the gas until it damn near put a dent in the firewall. The damn thing'd wheeze and shake and vibrate like a damn paint-mixer at anything much over 45, but that didn't bother Butch and me. Not one bit. And though I can't say exactly how fast we got that rusty old Ford going (seeing as how the speedometer needle wavered all over the dial like some long-lost relative at a train station) I'd hazard to say we topped eighty a couple times on the downhill slopes. Believe me, that's godawful scary *fast* in a junkheap like Butch's old rattletrap Ford.

Butch routed us up New Jersey 23 through Paterson, Beaver Lake, Hamburg, Sussex, and Colesville to Port Jervis, then northwest on route 97, kind of running alongside the Delaware River for a spell. It was real pretty country, what with the river running all fresh and clean and frothy down below us and lush, forest-covered hills and these big limestone rock formations rising up tall as the Manhattan skyline on either side. It reminded me how much handsome, empty, free-roaming space there is in this country once you get outside the big towns and cities. Living in a place like Passaic, you'd never even know it was there. In fact, I kept wishing Julie was there to share it with me, seeing as how old Butch was not exactly the type to appreciate clean air and fine scenery. Or at least to say anything about it, anyways.

We stopped to eat around 7:30 at a little railroad-car roadside diner near a town called Damascus, and that's where Butch and me had our first major difference of opinion. He didn't want me to haul his wheelchair out of the back and roll him into the restaurant. "Naw," he growled, "gimme them Goddam crutches. I ain't about to be wheeled around ever'where like a Goddam tea cart." I went along with him (against my better judgment) and naturally it took Butch just about forever to hobble and scrape and stumble his way across the parking lot, and he damn near fell flat on his face going up the three little steps by the door. I caught myself looking around real sheepish, you know, as if I was *apologizing* or something, and I'm glad Butch didn't see me do it. I mean, why should I give two shits about what a bunch of damn truck drivers and hash-house waitresses think in some broken-down diner in a backwoods town with a screwy, turban-head name like *Damascus?*

Turns out I must, though, because right after we ordered our hamburgers I swallowed hard a couple times and explained to Butch how I felt about it. "Look, Butch," I said, talking real quiet so none of the coffee-and-doughnut jerks who were staring at us out of the corner of their eyes and craning their necks to listen in on our conversation could hear, "I don't mind pushing you around in that wheelchair, Butch. Honest I don't." I saw his eyes start to squint down angry again, but I kept after it. "We'll cover a *lot* more ground that way. Really we will. You'll see."

Butch wavered for a moment, and about the time I was expecting him to uncork both barrels and let me have it full blast for suggesting such a thing, he just kind of sagged back in his seat and rolled his eyes slowly upwards towards the ceiling fan. "Yeah, I s'pose," he admitted in barely more than a whisper, staring up at the gently-twirling blades, "I'spose you're right. But what a Goddam pain in the ass."

"It sure is," I nodded, and took myself a king-sized bite out of a hamburger that tasted an awful lot like coal tar.

After dinner we gassed up, poured a can of oil in the Ford, tossed another couple quarts in the back seat (just in case, you know) and pulled in at a liquor store a mile or so up the road for a cold sixer of beer. But the jerkoff behind the counter wouldn't sell it to me on account of I wasn't 21, so I had to haul out the wheelchair, load Butch up, and roll him back inside just so he could actually hand over the cash. Like it made a big difference, you know? And naturally Butch got sort of hot about it and decided to call the counter guy a couple names. In several different languages, in fact. Not that there was any real doubt what the translation would have been if you said it all in English. But the weasel at the cash register didn't have any shame at all and yelled right back at Butch, wheelchair and all. "Now lissen here," he screeched in a voice like a rusty leaf spring, "I ain't about t'jep-or-dize *my* state liquor license over a couple broken-down, beer-guzzling stumblebums. No sir."

Well, that did it, and Butch came up out of that wheelchair like a shot to give the guy a well-deserved sock in the nose. But of course he couldn't keep his balance and I had to grab him by the scruff of the neck to keep him from falling right through the big glass cigar case they had next to the front counter. Boy, what a mess *that* would've been! Somehow I managed to wrestle Butch back down into his wheelchair, and then there was nothing to do but snatch our beer, scoop up the change, and hustle our buns the hell out of there before the guy could do anything to retaliate. It was a pretty damn ugly scene (to say the least!) and surprisingly

it made me think about Mean Marlene and what she had to put up
with every single day of the year. No question my friend Butch
Bohunk had himself one *very* short fuse.

I got Butch loaded up and we drove along in silence for a
good hour or so, just sipping our beers and keeping our mouths
shut and listening to all the countless rolling, rasping, grating,
thumping, squeaking, whistling, and gyrating noises that old
Ford made as it rumbled on down the road. It wasn't until we
were a good fifteen miles east of Binghamton that I finally got up
the nerve to throw my two cents in. "Look, Butch," I said,
measuring my words carefully, "you really gotta watch out for
that temper of yours. It's gonna land us in some real serious
trouble one of these days."

"Mmmph," Butch snorted, "how many other little sissygirls
they got back home at the Palumbo household?"

"Hey, I *mean* it, Butch. Nobody's gonna take a sock at *you,*
right? So who stands to catch hell, huh?"

Butch sighed and opened up his pocket knife so he could
lever the caps off our last two bottles of beer. "Y'know," he
said, taking a good long pull, "I ain't been in a decent fistfight
since I got messed up in my accident. Prob'ly never will again. I
reckon I miss that more than fuckin'. Honest I do."

I believe he did, too.

We finished off our beers and Butch smoked himself another
cigarette as we drove into the last of the sunset someplace between Binghamton and Elmira, and it must've been pretty handsome to look at, because neither of us said much of anything until
the final smudges and swirls of purple and raspberry-orange had
faded from the evening sky. Then we stopped and gassed up the
Ford just outside Binghamton (two quarts of oil this time) and I
was so tired that Butch tried another stint behind the wheel with
me working the pedals from the passenger side. We drove for
maybe fifty or sixty miles that way, but it was even tougher than
handling the car solo (in fact, it got me pretty damn frazzled, if
you want to know the truth of it) and I finally got Butch to pull
over at a little roadside grocery to get another pack of cigarettes
and let me take over again. Butch wanted another sixer of beer,
too, but the lady inside said she didn't sell alcoholic beverages of
any kind. Said she didn't believe in them. Not at all. You know
how some people are....

Butch kind of nodded off to sleep after that, and I guess you'd have to say that was one of his greatest natural talents: Butch Bohunk could sleep just about anywhere. In damn near any position. And I'm talking a *real* sleep, too, not one of those phony closed-eye fakes you pull when you're riding the knife-edge between half-asleep and wide awake and trying to kid yourself into dozing off. You could tell it was the McCoy on account of the way Butch'd start snoring like a gentle ocean surf rolling in and every once in awhile you'd hear him snort or see him twitch just a little and then he'd be muttering and mumbling into his shirt collar as his head lolled forward onto his chest and he dreamed dreams of sonofabitch Marine sergeants, broken-down Fords, big, meaty women, and splendid fistfights.

All I could do was keep driving, and that can get pretty damn monotonous after awhile no matter how nice the scenery is. And after dark, you don't even have the scenery to look at, just the endless dotted centerline coming at and at and at you through the jiggling yellow blobs of headlamp light. But I pressed on into the night, heading due west, and I got so damn woozy that I missed a turn or something just after midnight and all of a sudden there weren't any highway signs anymore. Or highway, for that matter. It slowly dawned on me that the white centerline was missing and that somehow the road beneath us had turned from smooth and straight to rough and swervy. But after so many hours of traveling, you get to a point where you hate to stop and turn around --hate to break that droning, hypnotizing sense of *momentum*-- and so you Press On, hoping to find your way back on course without having to admit defeat and double back. And that's how we wound up on this narrow, choppy, high-crowned dirt cowtrail that didn't amount to much more than two muddy wheel ruts with a strip of scraggly weeds growing up the middle. The pitching and bouncing woke Butch up, and right away he wanted to know where the hell we were. "Jesus, Palumbo, where the hell *are* we?"

"Uh, I'm, ah, not exactly sure, Butch...."

"Whaddaya mean, *not exactly?*"

"I mean I, uhh, kind of lost the highway."

"Lost the highway? Whaddaya mean, *lost* the highway?" He was starting to sound a little upset, no doubt about it.

"Well, we're, aah, not *on* it anymore."

"How y'know?"

"Well, uh, first off, they don't generally make state highways outta dirt, do they? Besides," I said, pointing out the windshield, "state highways most usually don't have barns built at the end of them, either."

Sure enough, there was a big old grey wooden barn dead ahead, more or less completely blocking the road. I slowed to a stop, but before I could so much as grab reverse, this Paw Kettle type in a pair of oversize bib coveralls (and not much else) came gimping out of nowhere with a shotgun under his arm. *"What's yer business?"* he screeched, waggling the business end of his shotgun to make sure we recognized exactly what it was. Which we most certainly did.

"Uh, we, ahh, kinda got ourselves lost off the main highway," I tried to explain, but the farmer had apparently formed a pretty solid opinion about us already and raised his shotgun up to shoulder level.

"I'll give ye jest thutty seconts t'get off my proppity!" he shouted, glaring at us down the gunsight.

"Gee whiz, mister, could'ja at least maybe just tell us where the main highway is?"

"Back where ye came from, idjit!" the farmer yelled, clicking back the hammers on both barrels. *"Now GIT!"*

Have you ever tried backing an old Ford with a plywood slab over the rear window down a rutted, curving dirt driveway? In the middle of the night? At high speed? With a shotgun pointed your way? Well, if you have, it should come as no surprise that I managed to get us into a haystack, a ditch, and a decent-sized manure pile in quick succession, then sideswiped the gate clear off the old geezer's fence as I whipped us around backwards onto the public right-of-way. As you can imagine, the farmer didn't appreciate that much at all (especially ripping the gate off his fence) and let loose a blast from his shotgun in order to properly register his displeasure.

"Jee-ZUS!" I yelped, hammering the gas pedal to the floorboards, "the sonofabitch is *shooting* at us!"

But Butch didn't seem too upset about it at all. In fact, he was laughing his ass off. *"Haw Haw Haw Haw!"* he bellowed, eyes wild and happy as a kid on Christmas morning, *"Haw Haw Haw Haw Haw!"* Why, he was whooping it up so raucous and rowdy that he damn near choked on it. Butch slapped me hard on the knee as we sped out of range. "Aw jeez, Buddy," he gasped, dabbing his shirtsleeve at the corner of his eye, "I ain't had this much goddam fun in *ages!*" No question Butch always loved a little raw-boned excitement (especially if there was a good dose of violence and danger mixed up in it) and I guess you just don't get much of that when you're stranded in a damn wheelchair.

But we were still lost. And I mean *LOST.* Best I could reckon, we were on some strange, pitch-black country backroad heading hell-only-knows-where, and the sky was all overcast so's Butch couldn't make out the moon or stars or anything to figure out which way we were heading. Not that it would've done much good, since the pavement swooped uphill, downhill, left, right, through S-curves, Y-intersections, and assorted switchback bends until neither of us had the least notion whether we were pointed North, South, East, West, Up, Down, or Sideways. Every great once in awhile we'd come to some backwoods intersection marked with a little hand-painted wood sign that read "COUNTY ZP ALT" or "APPLESAP SPRING RD" or something like that (none of which were on our map, natch) and it was right about then I noticed the fuel gauge was registering pretty much dead empty. Oh, *great!* Of course, you never really know about fuel gauges until you've done a little personal experimenting and actually run a particular automobile bone dry once or twice, but this one certainly looked like it meant business. For sure the needle was pointing towards the hopeless side of "E." Still, it seemed awful soon for us to be out of gas (after all, we'd filled up right after sunset outside Binghamton) and I wondered if maybe we'd picked up a little hole in the tank someplace. Like about the size of a shotgun pellet, perhaps?

Which is more or less how Butch and me wound up spending that particular Thursday night (or early Friday morning, to be more precise about it) parked on the side of a deserted country backroad someplace in the unfamiliar boondocks of greater New York State, tired, dirty, shitass lost, and on the verge of running out of gas. The Marine Corps always taught Butch that it was important to have a workable backup contingency plan on tap for when emergency situations presented themselves, and I'm proud to say he knew exactly what to do. He had me pull over to the side of the road, shut off the engine, and told me we were going to spend what was left of the night right where we were in his old rattletrap Ford (which, you will no doubt recall, ran through a rather substantial manure pile earlier that same evening and smelled distinctly of cow shit). But Butch couldn't see any sense using up the last fumes in the tank just so's we could stumble around in the dark looking for a damn gas station that wouldn't be open till morning anyway. "I guess we bunk right here," Butch growled, sounding none too happy about it.

"You think we'll be, you know, *safe* out here?" I wondered. As I've explained before, I'm basically a city boy --born and raised around Passaic-- and like most other city boys I always imagined it'd be real quiet and peaceful stuck out on a farm country back road in the middle of a pitch-black farm country night. But believe me, it's nothing of the kind. There's all sorts of hooting and mooing and cackling and rustling in the bushes going on --some godawful *big* stuff, too-- and I swear every single time a twig snapped or an owl hooted or a frog burped anywheres nearby, it made me jump like I'd got a jolt off a live coil wire. I even tried rolling up the windows to muffle the noise, but that just turned up the manure smell a couple hundred percent off the Ford's undercarriage. No question we must've taken a pretty healthy chunk out of that farmer's fertilizer supply. "Jeez, Butch," I said as we tried to settle in for the night, "I'm real sorry about all this...."

"Aah, don't worry a thing about it, Buddy," he said, trying his best to shift into a comfortable position. "Why, I ain't had this much fun since I can't remember when. No sir. Reminds me what *real* life useta be like. Just wish we had us a little bottle of somethin' to keep us company...saaay, wait a minute! Take a look under the seat, willya?"

So I reached under the seat (jeez, there was all *kinds* of stuff down there!) and rummaged around until I located what Butch was after: a half-empty pint of sloe gin in a wrinkled-up paper bag. "Haw! I *knew* it!" Butch beamed, "I knew old Marlene'd have a goddam nip bottle tucked away someplace. Lemme see it." Butch took a pull and I had a sip myself and then we more or less polished it off, passing back and forth without a word while we listened to the frogs and crickets and whatever the hell else was rustling around out there in the darkness.

To tell the honest truth, I didn't sleep very good that night, but old Butch dozed off right after the sloe gin was finished. Like I said, he could sleep damn near anywhere. It was a gift, you know? But like always he snored something awful and mumbled on and on about some butt-kicking jerkoff sergeant he had in the Marines named "Washits" or "Woahshits" or "Werschitz" or something, and the general gist of it was that if he wants to stay healthy and keep all his bone structures intact, that particular Marine sergeant better steer clear of Butch Bohunk for the rest of his life. On the plus side, Butch's snoring and snorting and muttering helped drown out a lot of the creepy animal noises going on in the trees and bushes around us.

It was already coming up light by the time I finally fell asleep, and I swear it couldn't have been fifteen minutes later that some local rooster started crowing his ass off and blasted me wide awake again. But when I looked out through the windshield, it was like staring into a bucket of grey paint. A thick, heavy fog had settled in around us like an enormous rain cloud that was just too damn big and heavy to float, and you couldn't even see the edges of the road beyond the front fenders of Butch's old Ford. And was it ever *quiet*. Fact is, I can't ever remember a morning that ghostly silent and liquid still. Why, you could almost hear the wet dripping off the leaves.

Then old Butch unloaded a Good Morning fart that easily could've blown up a half-dozen party balloons, and that more or less broke the mood. I think it would've topped ten full seconds if you'd had a watch on it. "Hey, asshole," Butch snarled, opening one eye an angry eighth of an inch, "you waitin' for a God Damn *engraved invitation* t'get yer God Damn ass in gear?"

"No, Butch, it's just I...."

"Well I gotta crap, see, so you better start findin' us a place where I can do it." He farted again to show me he meant business, and then began fishing around in his pockets for his breakfast cigarette.

So I fired up the old Ford and we took off, creeping along real slow on account of the fog. We were still disastrously low on gas, and on top of that not at all sure where we were, where we were going, or even what damn direction we were headed. But wouldn't you know it, no more than a mile up the road we came to a crossroad intersection with a nice, wide, smooth asphalt two-lane with a freshly painted white stripe down the middle and even a stopsign on our side to mark the spot. It was a major highway, all right --no doubt about it-- but seeing as how we had no idea which way West might be (or North, or South, or East, for that matter) we decided to flip a coin. It came up "tails," so we turned right, and I made sure to take it real easy and coast on all the downhills in order to stretch whatever fumes and droplets we had in the tank as far as they would go. Not that you could've gone much faster in any case, since the fog was like a wad of grey cotton wrapped in tight all around us and I had to navigate by a scant few feet of centerline and the gravel by the edge of the road. Every now and then we'd break through into a clear area where we could see the sky seemed just a shade or two lighter over to our right, so it was better than even money we were heading North. Which was probably good, as near as we could figure. Then the road'd dip down into a hollow and just like that we'd be back in the soup again. Our gas gauge couldn't have read any emptier, and just about the time I expected the engine to start gagging and sputtering, we broke out of a heavy fog patch in the middle of a tiny, two-bit town called North Java, which consisted mostly of a general store (closed), a pay phone (not working), and a roadside vegetable stand where some oversized local grease monkey was stuffed underneath an ancient Dodge pickup truck, trying to fix a leaky oil pan at 5:30 in the morning.

"Say, buddy," I hollered over, "where's the nearest gas station? We're kinda lost...."

"Lost, eh? Where ye headed for?"

"Grand Island. Near Buffalo."

"Buffalo, eh?" The big guy under the pickup started to snigger, "then I guess ye could say yew boys...," you could see he thought this was awful damn funny, "...that yew boys'r *ON A BUFFALO HUNT!*" and he let go a high, shingle-rattling cackle that made the ground shake all around him.

"Ahh, look here," I tried to explain, "we're also about outta gas, see, and...."

"Outta gas?" he said. "Outta gas? And *lost,* too? Why that's real sad, boys," he was starting to giggle again, "real, real sad."

"Yeah," Butch growled, glaring at him, "an' I gotta find me a can soon. You understand me? *Real* soon."

"Weeeell," the big guy said, scratching thoughtfully at the scraggly reddish-brown beard around his chins, "I figger the nearest gas station is, oh, mebbe thutteen or fourteen miles."

"I ain't gonna make it!" Butch moaned through gritted teeth, a desperate hint of panic rising in his voice. I can't say as I'd ever heard a sound that helpless or pitiful out of Butch Bohunk before, and it was just a little scary.

"Weeeell, I got a one-holer out back there. Ye kin use it if ye like...," he looked us over again real careful and then quickly added, "...fer a dime, anyways."

Butch looked at me and I looked back at Butch and we both understood that this was no time to haggle. So I ran over and handed the big guy under the pickup his lousy dime and then did my best to help Butch up to the outhouse. We couldn't use the wheelchair on account of it was on a hill with bushes and trees and rocks and stuff and just this little beaten-down dirt path up to the door, and I couldn't believe how the mountain-sized local jerk just stayed there under his damn truck like a denim-covered compost heap and let us struggle it out by ourselves. Why, I had to damn near carry Butch a couple times and we had a hell of a time getting his pants down without him falling clear over, and then it was even worse trying to swing the damn door open and lever him into position over the stinking hole. And I do mean stinking. Then naturally there wasn't any toilet paper, so I had to run back down and beg some off the big guy under the pickup.

He wanted an extra nickel for that.

It took a good half-hour to get Butch loaded back up in the Ford, and I must admit it was starting to dawn on me how incredibly, impossibly difficult (*and* humiliating) it was for a guy in Butch's condition to do the simple little everyday things that everybody else just takes for granted. Like taking a damn crap, for example. Made you wonder how people like him keep getting out of bed every morning, you know?

As you can imagine, we'd had it about up to *here* with the money-grubbing lardass under the old Dodge truck, but we were also about out of fuel (not to mention options) at that point, since the needle on the Ford's gas gauge was resting against the peg like a fallen timber. "Say, buddy," Butch asked, trying his best to work up a friendly smile, "y'think you could maybe fix us up with a gallon or two of gas?"

But the big guy under the pickup pretended like he didn't even hear us and kept working away on his oilpan gasket, taking all the bolts out the hard way by flopping an open-end combination wrench over and over in very tight quarters, an eighth of a turn at a time.

"We'd be happy to pay for it," I added sheepishly.

That got the guy's attention. He jiggled his way out from underneath the oilpan, kind of squirming along on his back because he was just too damn wide to roll over and crawl out like a normal person. And that pickup was up on cinderblocks and had a good two feet of ground clearance! But it was easy to see why when the guy grabbed the front bumper and struggled mightily to haul himself upright. Jee-*zus,* what a monster! Why, he had to be at least six-six or six-seven, and easily on the far side of 350 pounds. What a monster! He was wearing the biggest damn pair of coveralls I'd ever seen outside of a Barnum & Bailey sideshow attraction, and one of those goofy hayseed beards like some kind of electrified fur halo around his pumpkin-sized face. But although he may have *looked* like some big, dumb, hulking, back-country hick, he sure as hell understood an open wound of economic opportunity when he saw one, and the guy was all business when it came to selling gasoline. "Suuuure," he smiled, filling up the entire passenger-side window with his head, "I might could provide ye a leetle gas. Ye got enny cash money on you?"

Butch flashed him two wadded-up singles.

"Help ye'self," he grinned, gathering up the money in a melon-sized hand, "take all ye want...up t'two gallons, that is."

"Two gallons!" Butch wailed, but I gave him a quick shot in the ribs to shut him up. After all, the mammoth vegetable-stand bumpkin from North Java had us by the short hairs and knew it. I mean, can you imagine paying a whole damn *dollar* for one lousy gallon of gasoline?

Me, either.

And naturally there wasn't anything like a proper siphon hose handy, so I had to take one of the beer bottles off the floorboards of the Ford, climb under the pickup, undo the fuel line clamp with a screwdriver, separate the hose, fill the bottle, slide the hose back on, crawl out, empty it into the Ford, and then do the whole deal all over again. And again. And again. While I was pouring gas in the Ford, I noticed a little damp spot forming on the gravel underneath. Sure enough, we'd picked up a tiny little pinhole leak in the tank, right next to the brazed-in bung on the bottom. "Shit, Butch," I said, "lookit that."

"Hey, no problem," Butch said, and turned to the guy in the overfilled coveralls again. "Say, you got any hand soap anyplace around here?"

"Hmm. Might have. Cost ye, though."

"How much?" Butch growled, his eyes narrowing.

"Oh, I'd say about twenty cents?"

Butch's nostrils flared. "Howzabout a dime, huh?"

The big guy rolled his eyeballs skyward and pulled on his beard a few dozen times, mulling it over. "Naw," he said at last, "times bein' how they are, I don't see as how I could see my way clear t'sell ye enny soap fer less'n twenty cents. 'Specially seein' as how you're stuck out here at five-ought-thirty in the mornin' an' I got it t'sell. Supply and demand, don't ye know. That's the American Way."

Butch glowered and growled and grumbled, but in the end he wound up digging a dime and two nickels out of his pocket and handing it over. Then the big guy went around behind his pickup and rummaged through all sorts of chicken wire and 2x4s and linoleum tile scraps and stub-end rolls of tarpaper insulation until he came up with a small, dirty chunk of Ivory soap. "I use it fer soapin' wood screws," he explained, "but it's almost brand spankin' new. Bought it just last month. Honest I did."

Butch looked at it real close and wiped it on his shirt a few times to clean it off, then had me crawl under the Ford and rub it over where the fuel was seeping out. I'd never heard of that trick before, but it worked like a damn charm and stopped that leak right before my very eyes. Really it did. Then it was back to crawling under the pickup, filling up the beer bottle, crawling out from under the pickup, pouring it in the Ford, crawling back under...you get the idea. Naturally gas went all over the place (mostly on *me*, natch) and even after a dozen or more trips the needle on the gas gauge hadn't so much as budged.

But the local guy must've figured we'd gotten our two gallons worth, because he stopped me just as I was about to slide under his Dodge for the umpteenth time and asked if he could maybe take a quick look at the bottle. I handed it over without thinking, and he just hauled off and threw it as high and hard as he could. And he had quite an arm on him, no lie. The bottle rainbowed clear up over the telephone lines and came down a good hundred yards away, landing dead-center in the middle of the highway and shattering like ice. "Nice doing business with ye, boys," the big guy cackled, and waddled back over to finish up his oilpan job, taking each and every bolt out with his open-end wrench, one flat at a time.

Boy, were we ever *pissed!* Not only had he screwed us out of two dollars and thirty-five cents for what should have been about forty cents worth of gas, but the big jerk had rubbed our damn noses in it as well. But there was just nothing you could do short of taking a swing at him, and as a general policy I never pick fights with people who outweigh me by more than twice. It's just not worth it, you know? So the asshole *had* us, and there was nothing left for me to do but put my ears down, drop my tail between my legs, and take off.

SHIT!

Naturally old Butch was even madder than I was, and said *he* would've dragged the fat bastard out by the heels, kicked him in the head until blood ran out both ears, and taken our God Damn money back. Then he yanked out another cigarette and started angrily fumbling around for his lighter, but I had to stop him on account of I still reeked something awful from gasoline and the last thing that old Ford needed was a major interior fire.

As we drove on down the road, it occurred to me that stuff like that never happened when I was traveling with Big Ed or one of the many bucks-up Westbridge customers. In fact, just the opposite. Pull in someplace in a gleaming new Jaguar roadster that costs more than what most lunchbucket jerks earn in a year and folks can't do enough for you. *Free for nothing!* But show up lost and out of gas in a broken-down, five-dollar Ford sedan and they'll screw you every time. And act mean as hell while they're at it. Like the enormous vegetable-stand grease monkey from North Java said, it's the American Way.

Chapter 20: Dangerous Day at Grand Island

We stopped in East Aurora for gas later that morning, and even managed to borrow a hose to spray off the Ford's undercarriage so it didn't smell like cow manure anymore. Or at least not as bad, anyway. Afterwards Butch and me got breakfast at a streetcorner coffee shop and got ourselves cleaned up a little (which is about as cleaned up as you can get in a streetcorner coffee shop mensroom) and took off again for Grand Island. The weather had cleared up completely, and we enjoyed a nice drive through West Seneca, Cheektowaga, and Amherst to the Niagara River, but ran into a hellacious mess of a traffic jam once we got near the toll bridge onto Grand Island. Gee whiz, sportscars and family sedans full of racers, fans, centennial celebrants, and general all-purpose curiosity-seekers were backed up bumper-to-bumper for more than a mile, mostly on account of they had the S.C.M.A. registration tent right smack dab on the other side of the bridge, and so naturally it was taking each and every car at least ten minutes to get through the necessary bullshit and red tape before they could either enter the paddock or be on their way. Which of course meant everybody else had to just sit there and wait in line (most of the Jags steaming away merrily under the hot August sun) and since our dear old friend Charlie Priddle was in charge, there was no way you could even *think* about entering the paddock and parking your car before walking back out to the S.C.M.A. tent to register. It was simply out of the question, you know?

So it took us damn near an hour to get across that damn bridge and sign in with the Westbridge crew, and then the armband people at the gate didn't want to let us in on account of we didn't have one of Charlie Priddle's precious little Official Parking Stickers on the windshield (not to mention that they were obviously less than impressed with style, general presentability, and lingering manure odor of Butch's old Ford). But instead of turning around and fighting our way back out to registration, I told them we were from Westbridge, pointed to Butch, his crutches, and the wheelchair in back, and then rolled my palms up in the well-known New York streetcorner shrug. The armband people looked at Butch, looked at the wheelchair, looked at each other, and hurriedly gathered together for a hushed, behind-the-hand conversation about what should be done. After an incredible amount of nodding, finger-pointing, head-shaking, mustache-tugging, and elbow-scratching, they grudgingly agreed to let us through, but only after we *promised* to hide that rusty old Ford behind something large and solid where nobody could see it and it wouldn't be such an eyesore. That was the first time I was ever actually glad we had Butch's wheelchair along with us.

We found Barry Spline and the Westbridge parts truck parked along a stretch of snow fencing on the back row of the paddock, and naturally everything was frantically up for grabs trying to get the cars ready for Friday's practice sessions. To tell the truth, Barry didn't seem too thrilled to see me once he got a load of Butch, the wheelchair, and our ratty old Ford (not to mention that I wasn't looking particularly sharp or chipper myself that morning) but he said hello and had us park more or less out of sight on the back side of the truck, and from that moment on, my Friday at Grand Island turned into a complete and total blur. Why, if I wasn't tapping knockoffs and checking tire pressures on a TC, I was changing oil on an XK120 or chasing a filter out of the parts truck or pulling a windshield off one of the cars or synchronizing carburetors that had somehow found their way out of balance on the road trip up from Manhattan. And I can't tell you how many times I found myself crawling around in the dirt on my hands and knees trying to find some damn bolt or clip or cotter pin or something that'd rolled itself off a fender and dropped in the grass. In fact, I think there must be some Universal Law of Automobile Mechanics that explains the strange, three-way proportional relationship between how tired you are, how much of a hurry you're in, and how many small, irreplaceable parts you drop in the grass.

And of course the more cars we got ready to race, the more came roaring back in off the circuit steaming hot and streaming oil and showing symptoms of all sorts of brand new problems, glitches, suspicious noises, and ugly smells we had to chase down and repair. We weren't just working on the usual Westbridge customer cars, either, since racing was a *bona fide* commercial venture as far as Barry Spline was concerned, and he stood ready and willing --clipboard in hand-- to tackle any damn English sportscar problem in the paddock.

As long as the job paid cash, that is.

So there was just no end to it, one thing after another, and it didn't take long to realize that I was the only honest-to-goodness Westbridge mechanic on hand at Grand Island that weekend. Nobody else even showed up. I guess the other designated crew guys either got lost or got sick or wised up and quit at the last minute sometime early Thursday morning, and seeing as how Barry was still not real comfortable about bringing Sylvester Jones to the races with us, he and I were the only Westbridge representatives in the paddock at Grand Island.

Which meant that my old friend Butch came in real handy, wheeling himself around as best he could to lend a hand putting tape on headlights and painting numbers on doors with shoe polish, not to mention doing us a swell job on bench work like bum electric fuel pumps (we *always* had a few of those) and distributor plates and carb rebuilds. Barry and me set him up in the shade of the parts truck with an old wooden outhouse door laid across two sawhorses and a little tray of hand tools, and I swear Butch was happy as Old King Cole, cursing gaily through his teeth in five or six different languages while he fiddled merrily away with contact points and carburetor packing gaskets and this and that. Wheelchair or not, Butch turned out to be quite a useful asset, because he knew what he was doing and Got Things Done. Sure, he couldn't do the *big* stuff anymore, and he still had an awful tough time making that ugly lump of a right hand do what he wanted, but Butch could take something apart on his little makeshift workbench and tell you in two seconds if it could be lashed up or jury-rigged some way to make it through the weekend. Oh, Barry didn't particularly appreciate how he cursed at everybody and everything and the way you had to keep bringing him this or that all the time, or especially his habit of *fixing* things instead of simply demanding new parts (many of which Barry had readily available in the Westbridge parts truck at his special, 50 percent-over-retail Race Weekend prices). But even Barry Spline had to admit that Butch was a real big help to us that Friday at Grand Island.

While the three of us were simultaneously slaving away on a Jag with a slipping clutch, an MG with a jammed starter motor, an Allard with its entire exhaust system coming adrift, and yet another MG with some bent pushrods due to an over-enthusiastic owner who apparently didn't understand what a tachometer was for, who should pull in next to us but Skippy Welcher and Milton Fitting, accompanied by more damn racing gear than you have *ever* seen piled into a 2-seat automobile. It's a wonder the rear springs didn't just give up the ghost and collapse from sheer exhaustion. While Squire Milton set about unloading Skippy's extensive collection of vital racing stuff and stacking it in a neat, evenly spaced, perfectly aligned row along the snow fencing, The Skipper decided to waltz over and see if he could negotiate a reasonable deal on a new oil filter element for his ex-everything XK120*M*. Naturally Barry was up to his eyeballs in a bewildering array of assorted British Car Problems, but of course that made no difference whatsoever to Skippy Welcher. No sir. It wasn't like The Skipper didn't *care* if you happened to be desperately busy with something else, but that he simply never even seemed to notice. "So, tell me," The Skipper asked, his eyelids flickering ominously, "how much would'ja charge me for an oil filter for my Jag, huh?"

"With or without an oil change?" Barry gasped, straddling the transmission tunnel of the XK120 and pulling desperately with raw, bloody, grease-blackened fingers to get the damn gearbox separated from the engine block. That kind of job always gave Barry fits, and he had sweat beads the size of ball bearings popping all over his forehead and rolling down his cheeks.

"Well," Skippy mused, thoughtfully stroking his chin, "why don't you just give me a price *with* the oil and with*out* the oil. I'm perfectly capable of changing it myself, you know. Or at least my squire," he twitched his head in the general direction of Milton Fitting, "can do it for me. He's really the expert on that sort of thing. Changing oil, I mean. Does it for me all the time. Uses real *vegetable* oil, too. None of that crappy mineral stuff. *Never* use mineral oil in a Jaguar. Gums up the works, you know. We tried it once. *Hah!* Gummed up the works, just like I told you. But, of course, we didn't know any better. Why, you should've seen how that...."

And that's about when I stopped paying attention and went back to installing the starter Butch rebuilt on one of the MGs. I'd learned there was a point at which you could actually stop listening to what The Skipper was saying and let it all turn into a kind of whining, grating, squeaking, gyrating, eccentrically oscillating background noise. The kind a dry speedometer cable makes if it's got a couple bad kinks in it....

But you couldn't ignore Milton Fitting. Not if you tried. Oh, he didn't walk around in his own personal bullshit storm like The Skipper always did, but I kept catching him out of the corner of my eye as he went about the simple, basic, straightforward, everyday race-mechanical task of checking out the wheels and tires on Skippy's Jag. Jee-*zus,* did he ever make a damn ritual out of it. Milton had this special little toolkit all prepared for the job, which consisted of a rolled-up square of sisal floormat, a four-pound brass-head knockoff hammer wrapped up in a clean shop rag, a slender inch-pound torque wrench with a special split box-end to slip over the threaded tensioning nipples on wire wheels, a little spouted squirt can of penetrating oil, a tuning fork --like piano tuners use, you know?-- and the fanciest damn tire gauge you ever saw, which came all the way from Germany in its own velvet-lined leather case.

Anyhow, Milton would lay out this special toolkit next to a particular wheel and then take at least a full minute to carefully unroll his little piece of sisal floormat and get it positioned just *exactly* where he wanted it (which meant dead-nuts centered in front of the knockoff hub and precisely 90 degrees right-angle to the side of the car). Then he'd slide a one-foot by three-foot sheet of plywood under the car, roll a big 2-ton service jack on top of it, and gently raise that corner of the Jag a foot or so off the ground, doing it one slow, tentative stroke at a time. Once he could see a few inches of daylight under the tire, he'd block the frame with never less than five or six jackstands and carefully chock the other three tires --front *and* back-- so that Skippy's XK120 was resting as solid and steady as a poured concrete foundation. But Milton'd walk around it once or twice anyway, peering underneath and pushing gingerly on the fenders with his fingertips, making absolute, positive *sure* that Jaguar wasn't about to suddenly leap off those half-dozen jackstands and run away from him.

After Milton satisfied himself that Skippy's Jag was completely and totally immobilized, he'd kneel down on his little sisal mat and address the wheel in question, giving it several serious shakes, alternating his hands between 3 and 9 o'clock and 12 and 6. Whatever he was feeling for never seemed to please him, and he'd invariably unwrap the brass-head hammer and give the knockoff ears a couple solid whacks. Then he'd shake the wheel again, most usually followed by a couple more heavy licks with the hammer. When he finally got the knockoff as snug as he wanted (which amounted to damn near stripped, far as I could tell) he'd wrap up the hammer and take out his tuning fork. First he'd check it one time, dinging it off the hub and listening real close, savoring the sound like it was the most pure and perfect musical tone he'd ever heard in his life. Then he'd run it around the inside of the wheel, checking the exact, precise key and pitch of each and every spoke. He'd close his eyes and chew his lip while he did it, concentrating so hard you expected to see steam rising out of his ears, and somehow he'd *always* manage to find a few spokes that sounded a half-note flat to him and needed a little tightening. That was pretty amazing, seeing as how Milton went through this drill maybe five or six times every single race weekend. Then out would come the slender little inch-pound torque wrench and the spouted squirt can of penetrating oil to pre-lubricate the threads on the suspect spokes. Milton had a special technique for using his little toy-sized torque wrench, which amounted to holding his breath until he turned a deep, brilliant shade of purple and sticking his tongue so far out of his mouth that it wrapped halfway around to his ear.

Once Milton finished delicately tightening each and every offending spoke nipple, he'd run the tuning fork around the rim one last time for a final pitch check, pack his little torque wrench away, and then unsheath his very favorite tool of all: the fancy German tire gauge in its velvet-lined leather case. Milton was forever dragging this enormous 10-gallon military surplus air tank around to the races with him, and believe me, he needed it, since Milton regularly spent a minimum of five whole minutes at every single tire (including the spare!) putting air in and bleeding it out and putting more air in and bleeding more out and so on and so forth until he got those damn tire pressures just *exactly* where he wanted them for that particular corner of the car on that particular day at that particular altitude, humidity, ambient temperature, barometric reading, and phase of the moon. He'd never tell you what pressures he was running, either (like it was some big, dark Government Secret, you know?) and the jerk would even lean his shoulder over to block the view, just to make *sure* you couldn't see the numbers on his fancy German gauge. As if anybody in their right mind would copy speed secrets off Skippy Welcher's much-crashed Jaguar, you know?

After Milton was satisfied that one corner of the car was absolutely, positively *perfect,* he'd carefully pack his tire gauge away in its velvet-lined case, run the jack up a few painfully slow strokes, hesitantly remove the jackstands and wheel chocks, lower the car like it was the damn cornerstone of the Great Pyramid of Cheops, slide out the jack and the plywood sheet, neatly roll up his little sisal mat, move to another corner of the car, set down his special toolkit, unroll his little sisal mat, and do the whole damn deal all over again. I swear, it took Milton the better part of a whole hour to do four stinking wheels --honest it did!-- and just watching him work was enough to make you want to strangle the sonofabitch.

We had a little extra trouble to deal with on Friday when all the Allard drivers started dropping by at regular intervals to complain about skittish handling, and no question the brutes were a real handful on the narrow, bumpy, high-crowned surface at Grand Island. "Why, the car's simply *uncontrollable,"* one of the slower guys whined, dabbing his forehead with a cologne-scented bandana, "and you know how terribly, terribly serious that can be...*out there....* " He let that last part dangle like a carcass on a meathook while staring off in the general direction of oblivion, and my personal opinion was that people like him really had no business in racing. Especially not in big, hairy-chested machinery like Allards. Hell, if all you wanted was to parade around in goggles and driving gloves and put on airs at parties, you could embarrass yourself just as easily in an MG TD or one of those pretty little Crosley-engined Siatas. Why pick something that scared you half to death?

But since the other Allard guys were singing essentially the same tune (although not whimpering about it near so much) and since they were also mostly Westbridge customers (and *cash* customers, at that) we wound up checking every damn Allard shock, spring, wheel nut, steering knuckle, idler arm, and tire pressure in the whole blessed paddock to see if we could find anything wrong. But of course we couldn't, and the inescapable conclusion was that it was some sort of backbone difficulty or perhaps insufficient stiffness of the upper lip on the part of the drivers. It sure made me wish Tommy Edwards was there to show those crybabies how a *real* racecar driver makes the best of a tough situation and gets on with the job at hand. Like all really savvy race drivers, Tommy understood that the sport often boils down to "horses for courses," and when you found yourself up against a tight, narrow, bumpy circuit that made your heavy, high-powered Allard stomp and snort like a mad bull in a china shop, it just evened things out for all the tracks with steep hills and long straightaways where an Allard driver could take advantage of all that V8 grunt under the hood and simply motor away from the other cars like they were dragging anchor chains behind them. Good drivers accepted that, and no way would Tommy Edwards have carried on like those other guys. Not on your life.

But Tommy and his evil black Allard were nowhere to be seen at Grand Island. Something about trying to stay married, according to the scuttlebutt I overheard from other drivers and crews around the paddock. Truth is, there's always a lot of that sort of thing going on around sportycar racing. I guess you could call it an occupational hazard.

We had to work late into the evening Friday night to get that Jag 120 clutch job buttoned up, and when we were finally done, Barry Spline packed up his gear, bid us a weary good-night, and took off for town in one of the customer MGs (on a strictly professional Road Test Evaluation Drive, you understand) leaving Butch and me behind to pretty much fend for ourselves. The sonofabitch didn't even ask if we needed a couple dollars to take care of dinner or maybe a room with a decent shower or a bed with clean sheets. What a guy. But Barry was a stickler that you never got your race weekend pay --not one red cent of it!-- until the job was fully complete, and naturally that meant back at the Westbridge shop in Manhattan come Monday morning. Or even Tuesday, if he could get away with it.

Then again, you couldn't really blame him, since stories of race mechanics with fresh wads of cash in their pockets invading quaint, smalltown drinking establishments and subsequently calling to get bailed out of quaint, smalltown jails at 3:30 in the morning were not exactly uncommon. And even if your crew managed to avoid unpleasant encounters with the local police or unwanted complications with prematurely developed highschool girls, they still wouldn't be worth dogshit as wrench-twisters come the next day. So no way were you going to get dime number one out of Barry Spline until after the last sparkplug, oil filter, spool of wire, and can of brake fluid were safely restocked in the Westbridge parts department on Monday morning.

Butch and I made the best of things and set up camp in the parts truck, moving the air compressor and all the larger boxes outside and gathering up newspapers and shoprags and stuff to make ourselves a half-assed sort of mattress. Luckily we also gathered up several free beers and a couple hefty swallows of rye whiskey from various mechanically bedeviled racing types still lingering around the Grand Island paddock, and I'd have to say both Butch and me slept like newborn babies that night. Oh, the bugs made a regular seven-course meal out of us, but we were just too damn tired and used up to care.

Come Saturday morning we had more car trouble when one of the MGs decided to start popping out of second gear and another one had the needle-and-seat in the rear carburetor jam wide open and leak fuel all over the exhaust manifold, resulting in a brief but spectacular engine-room fire. Luckily there was no serious damage, but cleaning up after a fire (and, worse yet, a fire extinguisher) can be a pretty messy business, and I can't say as I recommend it. Plus we had the usual pre-race checking and re-checking of fluid levels and tire pressures and beating a final make-sure tap on all the knockoff hubs, not to mention listening to continued complaints from the Allard drivers, who were having trouble keeping up with ordinary Jag 120s and coming in off the track with their eyes popped open like fried eggs. No question the cars were a handful at this track, leaping and pounding from one bump to the next like shallow-hull speedboats in choppy water, and the Allard drivers ultimately decided to have themselves a major sitdown with the S.C.M.A. officials after

Saturday morning's qualifying session. The upshot was that they all volunteered to withdraw their entries and not run in the big Grand Island Centennial Celebration feature race later in the afternoon. *Volunteered,* can you believe it? Boy, no way would Tommy Edwards have gone along with a program like that. No way at all. Of course, Tommy was a *racer,* and none of the Allard drivers on hand at Grand Island were anywheres near in his class. They didn't understand one of the most basic and important race driving lessons of all: *knowing when it's time to simply back off and go SLOW!*

After lunch it was race time, and all of a sudden there was nothing left for Butch and me to do. At every race event I've ever attended, there comes a time when you've either got everything finished up and ready to go or you can pretty much forget about it. I mean, they don't exactly wait around for you to set your timing or finish rebuilding your carburetor (or even tie your damn shoelaces!) when it's time for the green flag to drop. In fact, I think it's that exact sense of *pressure* and *urgency* that makes racing so damn intoxicating. And addictive....

Since there wasn't much of anything going on with the customer cars, I asked Barry if maybe Butch and me could take off to watch the races and he said okay, just so long as we checked in every now and then and were there at the end of the day to help load up. Fact is, old Barry Spline was in a pretty damn cheerful mood that morning, and you could clearly see why every time he bent over and you caught a glimpse of the sizable bulge in the back pocket of his coveralls. That was all folding money in there --damn near an inch thick of it!-- and I doubt more than half those bills had Washington's or Lincoln's picture on them. Yes sir, the Westbridge Motor Car Company, Ltd., had itself one *very* successful race weekend at Grand Island in 1952. And without laying out a lot of unnecessary extra cash for labor or mechanic's expenses, either.

Anyhow, I loaded Butch up and we headed over by trackside to find ourselves a good vantage point, and right away I discovered the second Big Convenience of the weekend about pushing somebody around in a wheelchair: you don't have to shove your way through a crowd to get anyplace. Not hardly. Why, people move aside without even looking at you. In fact, they make a big point of *not* looking at you, sort of aiming their eyeballs up and to the right as if they recognize a famous circus act or a rare species of South American fruit bat just a few feet above and beyond your left earlobe. As a result, you can finesse yourself a pretty darn good spectating spot with a cripple and a wheelchair. The bad part is you can't move around very easily from one place to another, and that is really the *only* proper way to spectate a sportscar race, since it gives you a feel for the rhythm of the track and how it flows from one corner to another.

Far as I could tell from the map in the program, the Grand Island racetrack was a lot like Bridgehampton, what with 3.7 miles of narrow blacktop stitched together in a big, uneven rectangle, with some uphills, some downhills, no less than two bridge crossings over Spicer Creek, a few fast, sweeping curves along East River Road, and four 90-degree righthand turns to sort of string it all together. Butch and me set ourselves up across from the apex of the first righthander, which was really just an ordinary crossroad intersection where Whitehaven Road junctioned into East River Drive. The surface looked awful narrow and ripply to me, and you could see real easy why the Allard drivers were having problems. And it didn't help any that there were a significant number of relatively solid objects close along the roadside, objects an errant sportscar might very easily collect.

Like spectators, for example.

Fact is, they didn't have much at all in the way of crowd control at Grand Island. Not hardly. Oh, they had the usual tire company signs and sparkplug banners and such strung up on twine to keep people back, but those came down early on, and after that the fans pretty much wandered wherever the hell they felt like wandering for the entire rest of the day. Even *right across the damn track* if some ignoramus thought he could make it between racecars! Can you believe it? The S.C.M.A. armband people tried their best to stop those idiots, but about all they could do was wave and holler and jump up and down like kids with busted coaster wagons, and that just didn't do much good. Even the P.A. announcer got into the act, alternately begging, pleading, insisting, and *demanding* that spectators stay the hell off the racing surface. But there were only a half-dozen loudspeakers around, and, what with the echo effect from one to the next and the engine noise off the racecars and everything, it came out all garbled anyway. Sure, if you stood absolutely, precisely smack-dab in front of one particular speaker and listened real close, you could clearly make out: *"KEEP OFF THE COURSE! PLEASE!! CLEAR THE RACECOURSE!!!"* but if you stepped back even a few short paces, it turned into the sound of somebody broadcasting Polish through a window fan and no way could you understand a single word. Not that anybody was much listening anyway, since everybody wanted to get down *close,* you know, so they could *feel* the hot shockwave of exhaust as the racecars thundered past --*Wide Fucking Open!*-- just a few feet in front of them. It was *NUTS!* And I know, because Butch and me were right down there with the rest of the goofballs....

The first race was a 10-lapper for novice drivers, and as you can imagine, it was pretty entertaining, what with lots of flailing elbows and cars weaving and squirreling all over the place. A guy named Bob Ryberg won in a blue XK120M similar to the one Skippy Welcher owned (except I don't believe it was *ex-*anything) and our boy Carson Flegley was in there, too, hustling his black TD along in a highly agitated manner towards the back of the pack. You could see he was one of those white-knuckle types who hang onto the steering wheel like they're dangling off the landing gear of a Sopwith Camel while it's strafing enemy trenches, and I'd picked up enough pointers from Cal Carrington and Tommy Edwards to know that's simply no way to drive a racecar. But you had to hand it to Carson for being so damn determined, even if he was all jerks and edges behind the wheel. Carson had a bad (and typical) rookie habit of turning in real early for the corner, missing his apex by half the width of the roadway, and then trying to compensate by forcibly squaring off the end of the turn to keep from skating off into the dirt. That *never* works. He ultimately dropped both left-side wheels off the pavement and wound up snapping back the other way and mowing down an entire row of rural delivery mailboxes --right in front of us!-- and that caused one of the local cops on hand to go have a serious chat with the S.C.M.A. armband crew and insist that they get us (the spectators) the hell away from that corner. Too dangerous, right? So a couple corner workers ran over and started shouting and waving and jumping up and down at us, and they kept it up until we all sort of inched our way twenty or thirty yards upstream on Whitehaven Road. But now we were smack-dab in the middle of the braking zone, and on the very next lap, some overeager doofus in a pea-green Jaguar coupe locked all four and looped it sideways through a nice plot of staked tomato vines just a few feet from where we were standing. So now the local cop and the S.C.M.A. armband people were a little perplexed as to exactly where the hell they should tell us not to stand. Not that it made much difference, since no matter what they said or where they told us to go, it wouldn't be five minutes before another wave of fans rolled in and filled up the trackside space again. The crazy part was nobody but the cop and the armband crew seemed the least bit worried. Like we were all somehow *in* on it --right along with the drivers!-- and for some idiotic reason trusted them not to do anything so brave or foolish as to put their lives (not to mention *ours*) in serious jeopardy. Which made no sense at all if you'd spent any reasonable amount of time around an S.C.M.A. paddock and met some of those highstrung assholes face to face. I mean, people like Skippy Welcher (and even Carson Flegley) didn't exactly fill you with a sense of cool confidence and calculating self-control. Not hardly.

But in spite of a few spins and Carson Flegley's trip through the mailboxes, there was no serious damage to either flesh or metal and the program moved on to the second race, which was a 10-lapper for smallbore production cars. The field included lots of Porsches and MGs and a couple of those nifty Italian Siatas that looked like little miniature Ferraris (but sounded more like angry lawnmowers). Two of them were running right up front, dicing it out with a couple Porsches and a supercharged MG, when all of a sudden the cars stopped coming around. Right away everything got real quiet --*spooky* quiet-- and I thought maybe the P.A. announcer said something or other about an accident. But of course you couldn't make it out, so now everybody was standing around mumbling and shrugging their shoulders and trying to figure out what the hell was going on. About five minutes later, a white Cadillac ambulance whooshed by --siren wailing, mars lights flashing-- and you could see some poor guy was stretched out in back with a doctor in a white lab coat bent over him. The ambulance disappeared up East River Road, heading towards the bridge, and left behind a silence so deep and empty you could hear water moving in the river a half-mile away....

We waited the better part of an hour for the S.C.M.A. to get things cleaned up and squared away, and then --just like nothing had happened at all!-- the smallbore cars came around again to finish their race. Can you believe it? Somebody called Tom Hoan wound up winning it in a stripped-down, supercharged TC, but he was chased hard the whole way by some guy named Hansgen in one of those pretty Siatas. No question he was getting everything there was (and then some!) out of his car, and I made a mental note that this Hansgen guy might be worth keeping an eye on. All in all, I guess you'd have to say it was a pretty decent contest. But of course nobody was much interested. All the trackside crowd wanted to know about were whispered details of The Big Wreck and whatever happened to the poor guy they carted off in the ambulance.

We got part of the answer between races, when a local gas station towtruck came groaning up East River Drive, dragging what was left of a Porsche coupe behind it. Jee-*zus,* what a mess! The roof was all flattened down on one side with big clumps of turf hanging off of it, the hood and decklid were ripped clear off, both doors dangled open, and every piece of glass on the car was shattered to bits. You could see the left front wheel was missing entirely and the left rear was folded way underneath the back fender, and so the Porsche was kind of skittering and scraping along behind the towtruck, making ugly noises like chalk screeching on a blackboard. The car was a total --no question about it-- and you couldn't help wondering how bad the guy was hurt. Or maybe if he wasn't hurting at all anymore....

Naturally the accident put everything way behind schedule, and the S.C.M.A. had to shorten the big-bore race and cut the mixed big- and small-bore Grand Island Centennial Grand Prix down to an hour in order to finish before dark. Neither was much of a show, since who else but Creighton Pendleton the Third and his 4.1 Ferrari were on hand and waltzed off to easy victories in both heats. Nobody else was even close. What with Tommy Edwards back home trying to patch up his marriage and all the other Allard drivers too chickenshit to even run, nobody could so much as catch a whiff off that Ferrari's tailpipes. Far as I was concerned, watching Creighton Pendleton and the gorgeous, chestnut-haired Sally Enderle take victory laps in that brilliant red Ferrari of his was getting more than a little stale.

After the checker I wheeled Butch back into the paddock to help Barry load up, and we overheard a lot of loose talk about the guy who crashed his Porsche and exactly how it happened. The general gist of it was that he got a little sideways through Ferry Bend (by far the fastest corner on the entire circuit) and compounded the problem by making about the biggest single mistake a racing driver can make when his car starts getting away from him. He *lifted!* Once that happens, it's usually all over, since no driver on earth is quick or subtle enough to catch a car when it snaps back the other way at high speed. Especially a Porsche. In fact, Porsches are more or less famous for it. Anyhow, the car apparently shot off the road backwards, hooked a rut all funny, and went into a series of violent end-for-end flips. The driver damn near came out on the second one, and that's how his left arm got caught between the roof and the pavement when it came back down again. Eyewitnesses told us his arm cracked in the air like a damn bullwhip. It was a real nightmare on wheels....

Late word from the hospital said that the guy had multiple fractures of his left arm and right leg, a couple cracked ribs, all kinds of cuts and bruises, and a severe concussion. Far as I could see from the remains of that Porsche, he was damn lucky just to be alive. Worse yet, they didn't have any sort of accident insurance at Grand Island --not one penny!-- so the S.C.M.A. officials were taking up a collection in the paddock, passing the hat to sort of help the guy out with his hospital bills. Can you believe it?

But by far the luckiest people were the spectators down at Ferry Bend. Somehow that Porsche managed to cartwheel down the track at better than eighty miles an hour, ricocheting off the scenery and shedding jagged chunks of metal every which way, and it *never got into the crowd.* Why, those people were pressed in five- and six-deep along both sides of the road! If you ask me, it was a real, live miracle. Honest to God it was. In fact, the only spectator injury of any kind was a slightly bruised knee some guy got off the front wheel after it tore loose from the car and went bouncing down the road on its own. But imagine what would've happened if that Porsche had flipped into the crowd. Jee-*zus,* arms and legs would've gone flying like bowling pins! It made you sick inside just to think about it.

Chapter 21: Coming Home

We had Saturday night and all day Sunday to make our way back from the races at Grand Island, and Butch and me even pooled our resources (if you can call four dollars and eighty-five cents "resources") and got ourselves a cheap tourist cabin at a worn-down roadside place just east of Binghamton. It was a shabby little room that needed a coat of paint and a few window-panes, but at least the beds were clean and there weren't any bugs. Not that it would've mattered much, since I was so tired I could've slept standing up in a shower stall. Even with the cold water running full blast.

But all night long I kept having these dreams about Julie coming up to the races with me, and what it might be like for the two of us to share a room like the one Butch and me were shar-ing. Or better yet, a little nicer. You know what I mean. But then the scene shifted and Julie and me were at the racetrack together the following day, and that's when everything started to turn all strange and scary on me --like it does sometimes in dreams. I remember I was over by the Westbridge parts truck, trying to simultaneously fix three sick MGs and two busted Jag 120s and the throttle linkage on a Cad-Allard (like some sort of wrench-wielding cartoon octopus, you know?) and all the while Julie is standing there with her arms folded across her chest like she's waiting for a train that's about five hours late. But old Barry Spline is walking up and down in front of us like a drum major in the Rose Bowl parade --clipboard in hand-- lining me up even more Jaguars and MGs and Allards and what-have-you that need mechanical attention in the worst possible way. Then, right out of nowhere, Creighton Pendleton's Ferrari comes screaming in off the track in a shower of gravel that glitters like rhinestones, and he whips it around to a magnificent figure-8 halt directly in front of Julie. Damn near runs her over, you know? So Creighton jumps out like he wants to see if she's okay, and next thing you know, the two of them are sort of smiling at each other and talk-ing in whispers, and I can't do a damn thing about it because I'm stuck in the background like a piece of cardboard stage scenery, fighting desperately to get this frozen-up water pump off one of

Barry's piece-of-shit MGs. But I can't get it loose, because every time I take off a nut or a bolt or undo a hose clamp, it grows another one. And another one after that. And by now Julie and Creighton are starting to nuzzle into each other and even kiss a little bit (and *French* kiss, at that!) but I can't call out to her on account of I'm holding the new water pump gasket for that piece-of-shit MG in my mouth. You know how it goes in bad dreams. And when I try to run over there and make them stop, I discover I can't even move on account of my wrists are shackled to the exhaust manifold of that blasted MG, and I come to realize that I can't go *anywhere* until the damn job is finished. So naturally I try working faster. And faster. And pretty soon I'm spinning wrenches so fast my hands are nothing but a raw-knuckled, ten-fingered blur. But of course it's no use, and in the end all I can do is stand there, hunched over the engine compartment of that stinking MG with my guts turning to jelly while Creighton Pendleton The Third roars off into the sunset with *my* girl next to him in that bright red Ferrari of his....

What a nightmare!

So although I slept clear through till nine ayem Sunday morning, I didn't wake up feeling particularly rested or re-freshed. Not hardly. I told Butch about my dream over a couple scrambled eggs and coffee, and he thought it was colossally stupid. After all, why would a handsome, well-bred, bucks-up asshole like Creighton Pendleton (the Third) want anything to do with some blue-collar carhop dolly from the Doggy Shake on Fremont Avenue? Especially when he already had himself a lean, sharp, rich, classy girl like Sally Enderle? Why, a guy like him wouldn't even give somebody like Julie Finzio a second look. And that got me even more upset. I mean, who the hell did this Creighton Pendleton character think he was, anyway? Too good for my girl, huh? Well, we'd just see about *that!*

Not that I was getting to see all that much of Julie myself ever since the day I got fired from her uncle's gas station. In fact, I wasn't getting to see her at all any more, what with my endless work-and-travel schedule as a high-line (if highly under-paid) "race mechanic" at Westbridge. And it occurred to me, as we drove Butch's old Ford eastward across New York State towards home that quiet Sunday morning, that I really, *really* missed seeing Julie. Why, I even missed working at her uncle's lousy gas station, in spite of the fact Old Man Finzio was about the meanest, orneriest old fart I'd ever met in my life. But at least I was on my own hook at the Sinclair, running my own jobs and figuring out what to do next for myself instead of playing the position of third-string, bottom-of-the-totem-pole Grease Flunky at Westbridge. So by the time we reached the Jersey line a little past noon, I'd decided what I really wanted to do was quit my fancy-ass "race mechanic" job across the bridge in Manhattan and move back into my old life.

The problem was I still wanted to go to the races and be a part of all the action and work on all those interesting cars. Desperately, in fact. Seems I'd come down with a pretty bad case of the racing disease myself, and once you get a dose of it, there's just no getting rid of it. Real life is just so damn dull and tame and predictable by comparison. But I had this hot little kernel of an idea budding in my head that there might be some way --what with Big Ed Baumstein and Carson Flegley both hot to trot and living real convenient to the Old Man's gas station in Passaic-- that some way, somehow, I could maybe find a way to make it happen back at the Sinclair.

I dropped Butch and his rusted-out Ford off in Newark late that Sunday afternoon and then took the bus ride back to my aunt's place in Passaic. But before heading up to my apartment, I stopped at the corner grocery store to put my very last dime in the pay phone and call Julie. Sure, I could've done it for free at my aunt's house, but that phone always came with an extra set of ears and at least three or four snoopy, arrogant alleycats strutting around like they owned the place and staring directly in your face while you were trying to carry on a private conversation. Plus there were usually another half-dozen of their bastard alleycat kittens playing tetherball with the receiver cord, and that could also get very annoying. So the pay phone at the corner grocery had become sort of my personal communications center ever since I'd moved into the space over my Aunt Rosamarina's garage. I mean, there was no way a guy earning part-time racing mechanic's wages at Westbridge could afford such a frivolous luxury as his own private phone line. And what good would it do anyway, since I was never home to answer it?

I remember dialing up Julie's number and waiting through the long silence before it rang, kind of shuffling back and forth from one foot to the other while I desperately tried to figure out just what the hell I was going to say. Especially if her mom answered. But I lucked out and Julie picked up the phone herself, and when I heard her say, "Hello?" it sent a wave of cold, tiny shivers through my system.

"Uh, hi, Julie..."

"Buddy?"

"Uh, yeah, ahh...."

"Where *are* you?"

"Uh, at the grocery store over by my apartment, actually. Right between the rye bread and the mustard, ketchup, mayonnaise, and picalilli."

"What on earth are you doing there?"

"Well, uh, I guess I'm sort of calling *you,* aren't I?"

There was a long pause, and I got this feeling like maybe her mother had just waltzed through the room. "Listen, Buddy," Julie finally whispered, her mouth right up close against the receiver, "you stay right there at your place. You hear me? I'll be over in a little bit," and she hung up before I could say another word. *Click!*

Well, *that* was sure a surprise. In fact, I had to grab onto the bread rack to keep myself from keeling clear over into the condiment shelf. Julie Finzio was actually coming over to my apartment...*COMING OVER TO MY APARTMENT?!!* And suddenly I realized I'd better get my butt back there pronto to see what I could do about tidying things up so Julie wouldn't think I was some kind of major-league, prize-winning Slop Hog who lived in a walkup garbage dump.

So I ran all the way back to my aunt's house and bounded up the garage stairs three at a time, but when I finally threw open the door, it was even worse than I remembered it. What a *pigsty!* Then again, I hadn't been using the place for much except to flop out for a few hours every couple nights, and I can't say as I was ever considered a particularly persnickety housekeeper. Ask anybody in my family. Especially my mom or sisters. Which is probably why my apartment reeked from a badly decomposed pepper-and-egg sandwich and some well-aged carry-out coleslaw I'd somehow neglected to throw out a week or two before. Not to mention that the floor and most of what I laughingly referred to as "my furniture" were covered with mildewy layers of well-used mechanic's overalls and yellowed underwear, while orphan socks were scattered all over like they'd been having some sort of Walt Disney toe-and-ankle dance party while I was gone. And a quick glance in the mirror confirmed that I was not looking (or smelling) particularly presentable myself. Fact is, the closest I'd been to a bar of soap the entire weekend was when I stopped up that leak in the gas tank of Butch's old Ford.

Fortunately it took Julie the better part of an hour to get herself ready and sneak out of her mom's house (I guess she told her she was going to a movie or out bowling or something with one of her girlfriends) and that gave me plenty of time to rush around my apartment like an electrified crazy person, throwing both windows open and chucking the old garbage and the worst of the coveralls, socks, and underwear in the trash out back. I mean, I could always go back for the clothing later, right? I even snuck in through the side door of my aunt's house and gleeped the fan out of her kitchen window and a couple of those *potpourri* things out of her top linen drawer to maybe make my apartment smell a little nicer. Lord knows *any*thing would've helped....

Now my Aunt Rosamarina normally didn't approve of me coming into her house unless I knocked at the front door and waited for her to open it a chain-locked quarter-inch or so in order to verify that I was indeed her nephew Buddy Palumbo and not some escaped mental patient cleverly disguised to look and sound exactly like me. But it was Sunday evening, so my aunt was in the midst of one of her traditional sherry-soaked Sunday night bubblebaths, which essentially consisted of one bottle of lilac-scented bubble bath, one bottle of cream sherry (inside my Aunt Rosamarina, natch), and about twenty-five or thirty gallons of extremely hot water. She'd lay there in her tub for hours on end, surrounded by a few dozen of her favorite cats while listening to classical violin music on the radio, reading assorted poems and essays out of thick library books, and sipping sherry out of a converted peanut butter jar (which held a lot more in the way of sheer liquid volume than the proper longstemmed crystal wine glasses she kept in the breakfront in her dining room). Every once in a while she'd reach her toe up and open the hot tap for a minute or so to keep the water around her nice and steamy, and, as you can well imagine, my aunt could get *very* relaxed in there on a typical Sunday evening. In fact, I don't believe she even realized I was in her house that night.

Anyhow, I got my Aunt Rosamarina's fan blowing in my window with those *potpourri* things dangling in front of it on an old shoelace, and I must admit my apartment was finally starting to look and smell as good as your average non-condemmed tenement slum. The only problem left was the bed. I mean, it looked so damn *obvious,* you know, sitting there smack-dab in the middle of the floor on the far side of the room (not that my apartment was really large enough to have what most people would consider a "far side"). Why, it was like that bed had somehow inflated itself --like a blow-up beach toy!-- until it filled up half the damn room. And it didn't help that the bedclothes had apparently been dragged through a mud swamp and subsequently run over by a bulldozer. It goes without saying that I didn't have any fresh sheets or pillowcases on hand at my apartment, and, since time was growing desperately short, I finally just grabbed the whole mess with both hands and flopped it over --mattress, sheets, magazines, half-eaten doughnuts, and all!-- and covered it up with that olive drab wool army blanket my mom gave me for cold winter nights.

With the apartment more or less squared away, it was time to rip off my well-used traveling clothes, wad them up and stash them under the sink, and take a lightning-quick shower in the tiny 18x18 all-metal Sears shower stall my dad and I put in when we were fixing the place up so my Aunt Rosamarina could rent it. I banged the shit out of my knees and elbows in there on account of the water temperature would fluctuate like a bad electrical short from Just Right to Ice Cold to Full Scalding Hot and back whenever my aunt reached her toe up to run a fresh stream of water into her bath, and there is just no place you can jump inside an 18x18 all-metal Sears shower stall without bouncing off the damn walls. The neighbors must've thought I'd given up sportscars and taken up the kettledrum, you know? And of course I didn't have a bar of real, honest-to-goodness bath-and-shower soap in my apartment (no surprise there!) so I had to resort to an old bottle of dish soap I had under the sink. At least it figured to make me smell nice, even if it was a tad on the slimy side.

I was just drying myself off when I heard a gentle knock on the door. Jee-*zus!* It was *Julie!* I scrambled to wrap a towel around me as the door swung open, and I damn near dropped it when I saw her standing there in the doorway with the soft, gauzy-purple summer evening sunlight flowing in around her like a 5-watt halo. She was wearing that sleeveless yellow sweater I liked so much (you remember, the one that stuck to her like some kind of fuzzy Angora paint) and her hair was all done up in fresh, springy black curls. Boy, did she ever look *great.*

"Jeez, Buddy," she smiled, looking down at my towel, "you didn't have to *dress up* or anything...."

"Uhh, sorry, Julie. It's just I was, uh, sorta trying to get the place cleaned up a little, see, and I, uhh...."

"You call *this* cleaned up?" she laughed, her eyes sweeping around the room. "Jesus Christ, Palumbo, you've been trying to get me up here for over a year now, and now I can't for the life of me imagine why."

"W-well," I stammered, "I just got back from a race weekend at Grand Island, see, and I...."

"Don't worry about it," Julie grinned, and walked herself right inside. Just like *that.* With me standing there in a towel and everything! In fact, she came straight up to me, put her hands on my shoulders, and gave me a hot little peck on the cheek. It surprised the living shit out of me, you know? "So," she said, "how've you been?"

"Oh, I dunno," I said, gulping once or twice, "I guess I been okay. How'bout you?"

"Okay, I guess," she sighed. "I've kinda missed you, though. Sort of, anyway."

"I've kinda missed you, too."

"Oh, *really?"* Julie snorted. "That's news to me, Palumbo."

"Look," I tried to explain, "I been real busy with my job and the traveling and all...."

"I guess *so,"* she snapped with a mean little edge to her voice. "You been so busy you can't find the time to even call me once or ask me out on a frickin' date, haven't you?"

"Aw gee, Julie, your mom always answers the phone and hangs up on me...."

"Oh? And how would *you* know? You haven't so much as *tried* to call for at least three weeks."

"Aw, it hasn't been *that* long...."

"Like hell it hasn't. The last time my mom hung up on you was three weeks ago Friday. August 8th, to be exact."

"Are you *sure?*"

Julie nodded, and I knew better than to argue. Hard experience had taught me that women possess an uncanny memory for precise dates, times, places, and circumstances whenever they require such information to make a particular male of the species feel guilty and/or apologetic.

"Well, y'gotta understand," I explained lamely while a slow burn worked its way up my cheeks, "I been real sorta, you know, *busy,* see, and...."

"So, I guess that means I'm just not *important* to you anymore? Is that it?"

"No, Julie, it's just...."

"Or maybe it's just I'm not real good company, huh? I guess I must *bore* you." She wasn't really scolding me, you understand, but sort of teasing me the way girls do when they want to see you squirm a little. "Gee, Buddy," she continued airily, "it's too bad this just doesn't *mean* anything to you anymore..." and she leaned in real close so her lips were right up against my ear and whispered "...*isn't* it?"

Jee-*zus,* her breath rushed through my system like a hot gush of air blasting through a subway tunnel on a warm summer night. I put my arms awkwardly around her and prayed she wasn't paying much attention to the hard, hungry lump rising up underneath my towel. "G-gosh, Julie," I mumbled into the top of her head, "I've really missed you. Honest I have."

"You have? Really?"

"Uh-huh," I nodded, nuzzling my cheek gently against her curls. "Fact is, I can't tell you how good it is to see you again. Honest, Julie. Why, it makes me feel...."

"I can *see* how it makes you feel," she laughed, staring down at the lump in my towel and shooting me one of those dirty-girl winks she'd picked up out of the movie magazines.

As you can imagine, that instantly turned me the color and temperature of a freshly baked beefsteak tomato. I embarrass real easy, no two ways about it. In fact, I can get embarrassed just thinking about getting embarrassed, if you know what I mean.

"So," Julie continued, kind of wandering away from me and sitting herself down oh-so-casually on the edge of my mom's army blanket, "how've you been, Palumbo?"

"Aw, okay, I guess."

"Really?"

And that's when I felt this godawful big sigh come out of me, like the last bit of air leaking out of a bad tire valve. "No," I finally admitted, looking down at the floor, "not really. I've been working my goddam ass off at Westbridge --for *nothing!*-- and I've just about *had* it with that piece-of-shit Race Mechanic job over in Manhattan."

"You have?"

"Uh-huh. Why, it's got to where it just isn't worth it any more, you know?"

"I sure do," Julie nodded wearily, leaning forward on the edge of the bed and resting her chin on her hands.

And suddenly I realized I didn't have the slightest notion what to do or say next, and in the flutter of a heartbeat the room got very, *very* quiet. So quiet it was like the loudest noise you ever heard. "Uh, gee," I finally asked her, "can I, er, ahh, *get* you anything, Julie?"

"Well, what've you got?"

My eyeballs took a quick rotational inventory of the apartment and came up empty. "Well, umm, when you get right down to it...," I rolled my palms helplessly upwards, *"...nothing."*

We got a pretty good laugh off that.

"So," I asked her for about the five-hundredth time, "how're things going over at the Sinclair?" I was still standing in the middle of the room with my towel wrapped around me, trying to figure out how to get myself over to the bed where Julie was sitting without having it look like I was actually trying to get over there next to her. "How's that new mechanic working out?"

"Which one?" Julie laughed.

"Whaddaya mean, *which one?"*

"Well, we've had at least three since you left...."

"You *have?"*

"Uh-huh."

"But, gee whiz, I've only been gone a couple weeks...."

"Well, you know what they say about good help being hard to find. Too bad you left, Palumbo."

"If you remember right, I didn't so much *leave* as got my butt *fired,"* I reminded her.

"Yeah," she smiled, "and it was a pretty nice butt to have around the place, too."

All by themselves, my legs carried me over to the edge of the bed and sat me down beside her. And Julie didn't seem to mind one bit, either. In fact, it almost seemed a little *too* easy, you know? "So," I said again, my voice cracking around the edges, "your uncle's been having some wrench trouble?"

"And *how!"* Julie laughed, tossing her curls back. "The guy who came right after you wasn't too bad, but my uncle caught him stealing parts out of the store room to do side jobs at home and fired him on the spot."

"That must've been a pretty ugly scene."

"Oh, it was. And then we had this big fat guy from Clifton who didn't show up half the time."

"That's nice."

"Uh-huh. And the last one was even worse."

"What could possibly be worse than stealing parts and not showing up for work?"

"Well, how about dropping a customer's car off the lift?"

"Yeah," I had to agree, "that would probably be worse."

"It was actually pretty funny. Honest it was. He was trying to fix the exhaust on Mrs. Muccianti's Pontiac, and he kind of had it hanging off the side of the lift...."

"So he could get at the pipe, right?"

"Right, so he could get at the pipe. But then one of the bolts was stuck or rusted or something, so he went in his toolbox and got this big, long, uh...."

"This big, long, breaker bar."

"Right. This big, long, breaker bar. And he hooked it up on the bolt and started yanking and pulling...."

"And pulling and yanking...." I could almost *see* it, you know? Just like watching Old Man Finzio.

"Anyhow, just as he's leaning into it for all he's worth, something under there snaps and he goes sprawling flat on his face in one direction while Mrs. Muccianti's Pontiac topples off the lift the opposite way." Why, I could see it like I was there! In fact, I even imagined myself a little cartoon soundtrack of shattering glass and trash cans falling down flights of stairs....

"So what happened then?"

"Well," Julie giggled, "the car sort of landed between the lift and the wall. Kind of standing on its side, you know? They couldn't even get the lift down because the car was stuck under it, and my uncle wound up having to get the towtruck and drag it out of there before they could flop it back down on its wheels again. It was one hell of a mess."

"I bet he was real happy about *that.*"

"Oh, he was downright *thrilled.*"

"What did he do?"

"Well, for starters he chased that poor mechanic all the way down the block with a monkey wrench. Wouldn't even let him back inside to get his tools. The guy had to go find himself a traffic cop to make my uncle let him in to get his toolbox. It was pretty funny, honest it was. At least if you weren't my uncle or Mrs. Muccianti...."

"Did it do a lot of damage to the Pontiac?"

"Oh, not too bad, considering. It wrinkled up the door and the side moldings and put a little pavement rash on the paint. And of course most of the windows got broken and a bunch of oil and gas spilled all over the place. My uncle couldn't even light himself a cigarette for the rest of the day."

"Now *that's* serious."

"Yeah. It was the guy's first job, too."

"His *first* car?" I asked incredulously, my eyes flickering up like a pair of birthday candles. "I'd say that wasn't exactly real professional of him, was it?"

"No, I guess not," Julie laughed. "I think maybe he was a little stiff, too. You could smell it on him."

"You'd be surprised how much of that goes on in the wrenching business."

"No, I don't think I would, Buddy."

"No, I guess not."

And then all of a sudden we were just sitting there looking at each other again, so I kind of leaned in and kissed her. Not one of those wet, steamy Hollywood kisses, but just a nice, soft kiss that was all warm around the edges. The kind of kiss that makes your toes curl. "You know, Buddy," Julie sighed dreamily, "I bet you could get your old job back if you really wanted it."

"You think?"

"Yeah, I do. Big Ed comes around asking for you all the time, and he won't let anybody else so much as *touch* any of his cars. Not even the Cadillacs. I think he's taking the Jaguar to some English guy over in Englewood, but you can tell he's not real happy about it. Not at all. And this skinny guy in a black suit keeps dropping by with one of those MG things...."

"That's gotta be Carson Flegley."

"Yeah, that's him. He looks kind of like, I don't know...."

"Like an undertaker?"

"Yeah, that's him all right. Anyhow, he asks about you all the time, too. And that rich guy with the other MG...."

"Cal Carrington?"

"Right. The handsome one. He's been by once or twice himself. Even gave my uncle a couple dollars for some spotlight you guys stole off his towtruck."

Good for him, I thought.

"Anyhow, you really oughtta drop by and see how things are. My uncle hasn't been feeling too good lately, and...."

"Hasn't been feeling good?" I asked, surprised I cared much about it one way or the other. "Why, that old fart never acted like he felt good a single day in his life. How the hell can he tell the difference?"

"Well, he's been going to the doctor a lot."

"He has?"

"Yeah. Twice last week."

"You know what's wrong?"

Julie shook her head. "But you know my uncle. He wouldn't go *near* a doctor's office unless he thought he was pretty damn sick. That's why he needs a really good, solid mechanic to help out around the station now. Somebody he can *trust*, you know?"

"Oh, sure. And he's really gonna trust *me*, right? Gee whiz, Julie, you were there when he fired me. Hell, you were the damn *reason* he fired me...."

"I wouldn't be surprised if that's all blown over by now, Buddy. Especially now that he really *needs* somebody. Besides," Julie added, looking at me sideways out of the corners of her eyes, "I don't think he gives two shits about what I do or who I do it with. Not really. He just doesn't want to have to *look* at it."

"Or have it happen on company time."

"That either."

"Which reminds me," I said, unleashing a little of the old hairy eyeball myself, "what *have* you been up to lately?"

"And what business is it of *yours?*" Julie snarled, arching up her eyebrows. "You think I should just wait by the stinking phone all night and day so I can be there whenever the great Buddy Palumbo gets an urge to call? Is *that* the way you think it's supposed to be?"

No question she was yanking my chain --hell, she had every right to!-- but you couldn't miss how the gleam in her eye was saying something completely different from the angry words bristling out of her mouth. "Aw, Julie," I whimpered, "you know it's not like that. Not at all."

"So *you* say."

"Aw, c'mon, Julie. Let's make up."

"Yeah? What for?"

"What for? Why, so we can start hanging around together again, that's what for."

"Oh? Hanging around together? And just what exactly does that mean?"

"You know. Going out together and stuff. You haven't been going out with anybody else, have you?"

All of a sudden the temperature in that room dropped about twenty degrees. "A lot you care," Julie sniffed, but you could tell she was avoiding my eyes.

"But I *do* care," I told her, "I care a *lot*. So c'mon Julie, *tell* me. Have you been going out with anybody else or what?"

"Why should I tell *you?* You don't tell *me* about all the girls you've been running around with at those races. Not that I really want to know...."

"There's nobody, Julie. Honest. Nobody at all."

"Really?"

I looked her right in the eyes and nodded. "Hell, Julie, I don't have time to sit down and take a decent crap on a race weekend, let alone chase after girls."

"Honest?"

"Absolutely. And believe me, the girls they have at those sportscar races wouldn't be interested in some lowlife, greaseball automobile mechanic from Passaic. Not hardly."

"So you haven't been seeing *any*body?"

I shook my head. "How 'bout you?"

"Oh," Julie sighed, looking down at where her legs poked out from underneath her skirt, "I went out a couple times with that David Sweeney guy who used to manage the kitchen at the Doggy Shake on weekends...."

"You *did?*" I gasped, my insides going all hollow on me.

"Yeah, *sure* I did," Julie growled, sticking out her lower jaw, "why the hell shouldn't I?"

She had me there. "B-but," I protested, "if he's the one I'm thinking of, he's gotta be *at least* thirty years old...."

"He's twenty-eight," Julie said flatly.

"And he's half-*bald,* for chrissakes."

"No, he isn't."

"Sure he is."

"Well, maybe just a little bit. On top."

"So," I asked, trying to act real casual and continental about it, "did'ja have a good time with this David Sweeney guy or what?" Have you ever noticed how men tend to press women for steamy, intimate details of all the things those women have done with other men, details which they (the original men) would really be much better off not knowing?

"Oh, we had a *swell* time," Julie mumbled into the shoulder of her sweater, "the jerk turned out to be half octopus."

"Half octopus?" I asked, pretending like I had no idea at all what she meant.

"You know. The way he was trying to get his hands into everything all the time. Our last date he invited me to the damn wrestling matches, and *we* turned out to be the main event...."

The *bastard,* I thought, my guts flopping over like a ten-pound carp on a fishing pier, and I had to stifle the sudden urge to rush over to the Doggy Shake, grab this David Sweeney character by the Adam's apple, and punch the dirty, scheming sonofabitch right in the nose. I mean, what right did *he* have trying to get away with the same kind of stuff *I* was trying to do with Julie? I mean, she was *my* girl, wasn't she?

Well, wasn't she?

"So, uhh, how many times did you go out with this David Sweeney guy, anyway?"

"Jeez, Buddy, does it matter? I mean, the guy turned out to be a fourteen-carat jerk, okay?" She looked down at her knees again and added softly, "Besides, I'm not seeing him any more."

"But you see him at work, don't you?"

"Nah, he's not there anymore. I guess he took a job as night manager at some sit-down dinner place on the New York side. Up near Scarsdale someplace. I don't even think the jerk lives around here anymore."

I could tell by the tone of her voice that this David Sweeney character hadn't exactly worked it out with Julie ahead of time that he was planning to pull up stakes and leave town, and it got me more than a little curious as to what went on between them. On the other hand, here was Julie Finzio, right where I'd always dreamed and wished and hoped and imagined her, right here in the apartment over my Aunt Rosamarina's garage --right next to me on the damn *bed,* for gosh sakes!-- and it seemed a better time to concentrate on the here and now rather than hashing over the sickening details of some phantom boyfriend who was (hopefully) past tense now anyway.

"So," I said, sliding my arm around her, "you been seeing anybody else lately?"

"Well, I'd like to see more of *you,* Buddy...," she looked down at my towel, "that is, I'd like to see you *more often.* "

"I'd like that, too," I agreed, and moved in for another kiss. It was a hot one this time (for both of us --I could tell!) and pretty soon we were all wrapped up with one another and even stretched out fully parallel-to-the-ground horizontal on my bed. Why, she even let me run my hand up underneath her sweater and unhook her bra strap! And she knew exactly what I was doing, too. I'm *sure* of it.

But just as I was getting to the point of Full Frothing Hormone Alert, Julie stopped me again like she always did (what else?) and said that she really had to be getting along before her mother started missing her. But the truth is I didn't feel too bad about it (at least once I got over the usual whimpering, pleading, teeth-gnashing, and nervous-system aftershocks) seeing as how I'd been ignoring Julie and treating her like dogshit ever since the day I got fired from the Sinclair, and I couldn't believe how incredibly, unbelievably *nice* it felt to have her back again. And maybe someday her front, too....

For the very first time, that sort of thing actually seemed like it might be in the cards for us, and it had my internal juices rolling at full boil. After all, we'd gone further that Sunday evening than we'd ever gone before, and that meant I could probably go back and get that again. Anytime I wanted. That's the way it worked back in the Fifties. It was like your hands were behind-the-lines commando squadrons trying to occupy hostile territory --fingers creeping along a stealthy, tentative quarter-inch at a time, constantly on the lookout for enemy opposition-- but once you'd managed to conquer a particular plain, peak, hilltop, or valley, you could always go back and occupy that spot again. Every time you made out. It was kind of an unwritten law, you know? Of course, you had to always follow the same slow, tedious, careful maneuvers and remember not to skip any of the right words or necessary preliminaries, but so long as you played by the rules and kept your girl happy and content the rest of the time, you could maybe even go for a little more.

Chapter 22: Coventry's Secret Weapon

There's no doubt I had quitting on my mind when I rolled into Westbridge just precisely past noon the Monday after Grand Island, since all during the bus-and-train ride into Manhattan I'd been planning and rehearsing just exactly what I was going to say and how I was going to go about it. By far the most satisfying approach would've been the old, time-honored *"screw you, I QUIT!!"* outburst, followed by a few choice Italian hand gestures along with a quick, pithy recap of how much *fun* Butch and me had sleeping in the damn parts truck and how much I appreciated the opportunity to work full time (and even *over*time!) for part-time pay, not to mention how tremendously rewarding it was to finish every race weekend with less money than I started, and moreover how much I enjoyed being treated like a third-class, piece-of-dogmeat, bottom-of-the-totem-pole member of the human race in general.

But that really wouldn't have been fair, and I knew it. After all, I'd taken this lousy job with my eyes wide open (bugged out, in fact) and besides, I was still desperately sick with the racing disease, and no question Colin St. John and Barry Spline were right in the eye of the storm where that sort of activity was concerned. So I figured it was important to stay nice and friendly with them, no matter what. Like I said once before, you never want to burn your Westbridges.

I thought a lot about trying the old *"better deal somewheres else"* gimmick, but the truth is you usually pull that one out of the air when you're trying to get a quick pay raise or some kind of increased benefit package at the place you're already working. Not that you ever had to worry too much about employee benefits at Westbridge Motor Car Company, Ltd., on account of there weren't any. It was a matter of company policy.

The last and by far most diplomatic option (which I chose) was the old *"personal reasons"* routine, which is always the favored line of bullshit when you're trying to stay on reasonably good terms with the people you simply can't stand to work for anymore. My plan was to trot out yet another bogus horror story about my poor old sick maiden Aunt Rosamarina back in Passaic

--maybe give her a lingering incurable disease or something this time-- and explain as how, although I really *wanted* to stay on as a part-time foreign car race mechanic at Westbridge, my many vital, pressing, and important family responsibilities at home and blah, blah, blah, blah, blah.

You get the idea.

But the entire speech kind of slipped my mind as soon as I walked in through the overhead door and saw my old friend Tommy Edwards all huddled up in a corner with Barry Spline and Colin St. John. No question something really BIG was brewing on the racing front, and right away I could feel this ratlike gnawing start up in my gut because my insides *knew* how much I wanted to be a part of it. "Hey, sport," Tommy called out as soon as he saw me, "how's the young master mechanic doing these days?"

"Oh, pretty good," I allowed, walking right over to him, "still a little tired from the weekend, though."

"Grand Island?"

I nodded.

"Damn. Sure wished I could've made it. Had some, ahh, *personal* business to attend to...."

"I heard."

"Oh *really?*" Tommy said through tightly clenched teeth. "And pray tell *what* exactly did you hear?"

Barry and Colin were glaring at me like a couple pair of Lucas P200s on high beam, and it didn't take a college graduate to realize I'd really put my foot in it this time. "Well, er, aahh," I stammered, trying like hell to figure out what to say next, "I just sorta heard, well, what I mean is, I heard...."

"Oh, what the bloody hell," Tommy sighed, shaking his head, "it's probably all true enough, whatever it was."

"It, uhh, it wasn't really anything," I mumbled into my shirt while my face changed color like a traffic light.

"Oh, that's all right, sport," Tommy told me, mustering up a hard-fought smile, "race paddocks are worse than the bloody military when it comes to gossip and rumors. Might as well put your personal business on a bloody full-page ad in the Sunday Times." Then he let out another long, weary sigh. *"Women,"* he observed to no one in particular, "sometimes I wonder why the good Lord ever saw fit to make them with heads...."

"Amen to that, brother," Sylvester sang out from the back of the shop, and everybody broke out laughing.

Then Tommy asked me how things went at Grand Island (even though he'd surely already gotten the inside dope from Barry Spline) and it was a pretty nice feeling that he thought enough of my opinion to ask. "It was okay, I guess," I told him. "Some guy flipped a Porsche coupe and got hurt pretty bad."

"I heard."

"And all those other Allard guys chickened out and wouldn't run in the big feature race on Saturday afternoon."

"I heard that, too," Tommy said through a grim smile, his nostrils flaring just a bit over his salt-and-pepper mustache.

"They complained the track was too rough and narrow and that their cars were bouncing and jumping all over the place...."

"Hmpff," Tommy snorted, "some of those blokes couldn't pee a hole in the snow."

"Think *you* would've run?"

Tommy leaned back against the parts counter and thought it over for a moment. "Well, I reckon it's not entirely fair of me to pass judgment, is it? After all, I wasn't actually *there...* "

"True enough, true enough," Colin agreed diplomatically.

"...but on the other hand," Tommy continued, a nasty little spit-and-polish edge coming into his voice, "I can't imagine why anyone would drive a bloody racing car all the way across the entire length and breadth of New York State and then not *race* the silly thing. I mean, what on earth *for?*"

"Bloody hell *right!*" Barry growled, and spit in the waste can behind the parts counter for emphasis.

Then we stood there for a while, just listening to the clicking of ratchet wrenches and the gurgling sound of oil draining out of an MG crankcase somewhere along the back wall of the shop, and finally I got up the nerve to ask, "So, what are you guys up to, anyway?"

Tommy looked at Barry and Colin and then back at me. "Oh," he said with a mysterious little swirl to his voice, "I suppose you could say we're scheming up a little surprise...."

"For Creighton Pendleton?" I asked.

"For him as much as anybody, I reckon."

"Mind letting me in on it?"

"Letting you in on it? Why, my clever young mechanical genius, you're *part* of it."

"I *am?*"

Tommy nodded and snaked his arm around my shoulder. "Indeed you are, sport, indeed you are. Why, you and I are going to take a little trip together."

"We *are?*"

"Right-o," Colin nodded with just the faintest flicker of a smile, "first thing tomorrow morning, in fact."

"Jeez," I asked breathlessly, "what's it all about, huh? And where the heck are we going?"

"All in good time, mate," Barry advised dryly, "all in good time. We'll be taking a little run over ter the warehouse later this afternoon. You'll see for yerself...."

"I will?"

"Right-o," Colin nodded, "indeed you shall. Let's just say I need you and Tommy to transport a couple of rather, shall we say, *special* Jaguars to a small town in Wisconsin and let it go at that. Assuming you can afford the time, that is."

And just that quick, I forgot all about the notion to quit my part-time race mechanic job at Westbridge, and instead of giving Colin the speech I'd rehearsed on my way in that morning (you know, the one about my poor old sickly Aunt Rosamarina back in Passaic) I stumbled all over my tongue telling him I'd be only too happy to oblige.

"You'll need a jacket, a raincoat, a change of clothes or two, and a toothbrush," Tommy told me, "and I'd recommend a pair of sunglasses and a hat with a decent brim."

"And be sure that bloody hat fits *tight,*" Barry added with a quicksilver grin, "or yer'll lose it for sure."

I was on a creeper underneath a much-abused secondhand MG TC a few hours later when Colin St. John walked over to have another word with me. Truth is, I was only too happy for the interruption, seeing as how the owner of this particular MG apparently thought his car was an XK120 Jaguar in disguise and insisted on trying to make the poor thing perform accordingly. Especially away from stoplights. With predictable results to the engine, clutch, and driveline. You always hate working on cars like that (even though they're a guaranteed mechanical goldmine) because you know the jerk who owns it is only going to beat the living shit out of it all over again when you give it back to him. I mean, what's the point? And it's never long before the ham-fisted asshole comes rolling back into the shop again (for the umpty-umpth time) to complain about yet some other weary mechanical component that has finally (and *rightfully*) given up the ghost and burst, bent, broke, burned, shattered, snapped, melted, cracked, kinked, crumbled, ruptured, fractured, exploded, or some ugly multiple combination thereof. Worse yet, the jerkoff will almost always throw in a little nasty, off-the-cuff lecture about what a horribly designed, poorly engineered, indifferently assembled, and totally unreliable piece of crap his car is, and moreover how the damn valve float is preventing him from revving it all the way to the last numeral on the dial so he can blow it properly sky high the way God and Nature intended.

People like that don't deserve neat cars.

Anyhow, I was lying on my back underneath that sad, exhausted MG, fighting to get its corduroy-ripple-finish flywheel separated from the crankshaft flange, and naturally the damn thing just didn't want to cooperate. Which made perfect sense if you thought about it, since as soon as this particular MG allowed me to fix it, the poor thing would be right back in the brutal, pitiless hands of the meathead who owned it, and you couldn't hardly blame that car for not wanting to go. In fact, that flywheel was hanging onto that crankshaft flange like Grim Death, and I was trying to gently finesse it off without resorting to a violent, Old Man Finzio-style fit of beating, heating, prying, and cursing. So there I was, lying on my creeper under that sadly abused MG, busily levering and tapping and tapping and levering away at the problem, when I caught sight of Colin St. John's neatly pressed pants cuffs, polished wingtip oxfords, and rubber-tipped walking stick making their way across the concrete towards me like John Wayne's P.T. boat in the movie *They Were Expendable,* and I knew right away something was up. "I say," Colin's voice echoed down from the rafters, "it's about time for that run to the warehouse we spoke about earlier. Let's be quick about it."

"Sure," I grunted, trying my best to gently *pop!* the flywheel loose with a prybar and a long screwdriver coming in from either side, "be right with you."

I heard Colin's lighter click open and the usual wet, sucking sounds as he fired up that fancy curlycue pipe of his. "I believe my intention was *now*, Mr. Palumbo," he puffed with a hard snap to his voice. You always knew Colin was getting impatient when he started calling you by your last name, military-fashion, and that meant you'd best get your ass in gear or be prepared to have it reamed out to an entirely new diameter. So I had no choice but to lay down my tools and slide myself out from under that TC, leaving the flywheel hanging halfway off and wedged all catty-wumpus on the crankshaft flange. A good mechanic just absolutely *hates* to leave a job dangling like that. It's just not a natural place to stop, you know?

But Colin had decreed it was time to go, and so Barry had me clamber into the minuscule back seat of Colin's personal Daily Driver (which was a light blue Morris Minor that particular week) and believe me, the back seat of a Morris Minor was never designed to hold anything so large and bulky as a full-grown human being. Unless it was maybe a midget or pygmy or some poor guy who got his legs blown off in the war. And Barry made me twist and bend and contort myself around back there to put at least three layers of newspaper and a fender blanket under me so's I wouldn't soil the upholstery. That was real important, on account of Colin always had the speedo cables disconnected on all his Daily Drivers so they could be sold as brand-spanking new automobiles when he was done with them, and while it was nice to have hardly any miles on the clock, there was really no way you could cover up wear and tear on the interior....

Once they had me packed in the back of that Morris like a canned ham, Colin and Barry got in the front seat and we headed across Manhattan to the meat truck garage where Colin stashed his shipments of new Jaguars so that every single one on his showroom floor could be *"absolutely, positively the LAST ONE in the country."* Along the way, the Morris developed itself a bit of a carburetor stumble and a serious gas smell, and when it got so bad the engine started to sputter and choke and make ugly gargling noises at every stoplight, Colin pulled over to the curb and had Barry and me take a quick gander under the hood to see if we could maybe figure it out. I mean, we *were* supposed to be a couple of the best damn British car mechanics in New York, weren't we? Why, one of us even had a proper English accent. At any rate, the stream of raw fuel pouring out the float bowl overflow vent looked to be a pretty good indication that the needle and seat valve on the carburetor was stuck wide open, but of course we didn't have any tools --not even a damn adjustable crescent wrench!-- to undo the lid and fix it. So Barry took the tire iron out of the trunk and gave Colin's Morris a good, solid *whap!* to the top of the floatbowl lid, and that cured it! Honest to God it did! I always considered that one of the most endearing features of those early English cars. Sure, they had more than their fair share of nasty little mechanical gremlins (and Lord knows a Morris Minor wouldn't climb much over a ten percent grade with two or more people on board) but, like so many of those other early-fifties British cars, Morris Minors had so much damn *character* and *personality* going for them. And they could be wondrously easy to fix. Why, sometimes all it took was a good, hard rap on the knuckles....

With the carburetor problem sorted out, we continued on across town to the meat truck garage where Colin kept his new Jaguars, and along the way I kept trying to find out what was going on and how in the world *I* fit into the picture. "So," I said, "could'ja maybe tell me exactly where it is that me and Tommy Edwards are going, huh?"

"As I said before, you and Tommy are going to transport a pair of rather, aah, *special* XK120 Jaguars across country for me," Colin answered, looking at his nails.

"Oh? And what's so *special* about them, huh? Are they like the one Skippy Welcher owns?"

Colin looked at Barry and Barry looked back at Colin. "Oh, I should think they're a bit more special than that," Colin said, eyeballing me in the rearview mirror. "Wouldn't you say so, Mister Spline?"

Barry grinned at me over the seatback like the cat who just ate the canary, and I've got to admit my curiosity glands were pumping at full volume by the time we pulled up in front of Colin's meat truck warehouse.

"I reckon this is one cross-country trip you'll remember for a rather long time," Colin remarked as Barry got out to unlock the overhead door, "for a rather long time indeed...."

We drove inside the garage and Barry pulled the steel door down behind us, and it was pitch black in there after the bright sunlight outside. Colin flipped on the Morris' headlamps and we followed the two dancing blobs of yellow light down a narrow alleyway between two towering rows of sleeping meat trucks, made a tight U-turn with a faint, rubbery screech off the tires, and headed up a naked concrete ramp towards the second floor. "The cars you and Tommy are taking to Wisconsin are up here," Colin explained, lighting up his pipe again.

"Wisconsin?"

"Right-o. Elkhart Lake, to be precise. Ever heard of it?"

"Yeah," I said, "sort of."

"I thought you might. As I said, they're a rather *special* pair of XK120s...."

Barry Spline was grinning so damn hard I thought his teeth would shatter.

But before anybody could say another word, we came up over the top of the ramp and right directly in front of us, lit up in our headlights, were two low, sleek, liquid-smooth puddles of aluminum alloy with short, graceful racing windscreens and knockoff wire wheels. One was painted a green so deep and dark it was almost black, and the other was a soft, gleaming silver-grey, and you could tell right off they were Jaguars on account of the rounded, upright grilles with thin, curved, vertical bars and the bronze cat's-head medallions just above them. But right there any resemblance between those two cars and any Jaguar automobile *I'd* ever seen came to a sudden, startling halt. Why, those two were *racing* cars --no two ways about it!-- single-minded, pure-blooded, and purpose-built to be lower and lighter and tighter to the ground than any road-going Jag 120 you ever saw. They were both righthand drive (what else?) and had riveted woodrim steering wheels and sleek, faired-in plexiglass covers over the headlamps to try and cheat the wind at high speed. A pair of naked exhaust pipes ran along the rocker panels on the passenger side, and the mufflers didn't amount to much more than a couple empty tin cans stuck on as an afterthought. Like you were really going to drive something like this on the damn *highway*, right? "Jee-*zus,* Barry," I gasped, "what the hell *are* those things?"

"This," Barry said, stepping out of the Morris and patting the dark green one on its smooth, softly-rounded hood, "is a Jagyewhar XK120 C-type, Buddy, and I reckon it's about the best bloody long-distance racing car ever built."

"Indeed it is," Colin chimed in, "no doubt about it. Why, a C-type like this won first overall at the Twenty-Four Hours of Le Mans last year," he paused to suck a little more fire through his pipe, "and on its maiden attempt, as well."

"That really got the attention of the bloody Germans and h'Italians, I reckon," Barry beamed, "and they would've made it two in a row this year except the bleedin' new h'erodynamic bodywork wouldn't let enough bloody air into the radiators. Put the whole bleedin' team out with over'eating before nightfall. But they were bloody *fast* enough to get the job done, make no mistake about it."

"Wow!" I said, looking the cars up and down. The only place I'd seen curves like that before was inside Julie Finzio's yellow Angora sweater.

"Now, you must understand," Colin continued, looking me squarely in the eye, "these are the first and only Jaguar XK120-C competition models in the entire country, and our aim is to have them racing at Elkhart Lake this coming weekend. Tommy will be driving the green one for us, and *you,"* he stared at me so hard my joints went solid, "are to deliver the silver one into the hands of Mr. Ernesto Julio of California. He'll be bringing his own driver. Do you understand?"

I nodded, not really sure that I did.

"We need ter get a little break-in mileage on the drivelines, mate," Barry explained, "and besides, h'its always a good idea ter log a few miles and make certain nothing's about to fall off before yer actually *race* the bloody thing...."

That made a lot of sense. Not to mention putting a fizzy little Top Secret Test Pilot buzz in the pit of my stomach.

"Now, Tommy Edwards *personally* selected you for this trip --Lord only knows why-- and I want you to be *extremely* careful with these automobiles," Colin warned, poking me in the chest with his pipe stem. "I'm sure I need not mention that these cars are not only very, very, *very* expensive, but they are also *totally irreplaceable*. Do you understand me, Mr. Palumbo?"

That I understood.

"Right, then. Take the Morris back to the shop and we'll meet you there in a bit. And, while you're away to Wisconsin, I want you to do absolutely *every*thing and *any*thing Tommy Edwards tells you. Is that clear?"

"Uh-huh."

"And should you, in any possible way or for any possible reason, find some way to harm one of these automobiles, I want you to remember one simple thing."

"What's that?"

"Make bloody well sure you die in the wreck. It'll be easier on you that way...."

Chapter 23: Cross Country by C-Type

I showed up at Westbridge early the next morning with a spare pair of jeans, three or four T-shirts, and a few changes of socks and underwear that I'd picked up over by my mom's house (she always seemed to have a little clean stuff waiting around for me on a kind of haphazard, stock-rotational basis) along with my toothbrush, a big Turkish towel she insisted I take along with me, my grey windbreaker, and the only hat I could find, which was a Brooklyn Dodgers baseball cap I'd picked up at Woolworth's just to aggravate my dad. Like I've said before, he was a *big* Yankees fan. I had all the stuff packed in a white cloth laundry bag with a drawstring at the top on account of the only proper suitcases we had at my folks' house were some of those big old straw-colored jobs you see down by the bus depot, and I sure didn't want all the highclass racing types to see me with one of those things. Not hardly. Plus they would absolutely *never* fit into the available luggage space of a C-type Jaguar (of which there isn't really any as you or I might normally recognize it). My oldest sister had an overnight case that was about the right size and volume, but it didn't even merit consideration since it was bright pink leatherette and had a full-color cartoon picture of Cinderella on the lid.

When I got back to Westbridge, Barry told me to not to even bother starting in on that MG project again, seeing as how I'd be leaving the shop just as soon as Tommy showed up, and we'd most likely be gone until at least the following Tuesday. So I made myself a cup of coffee and kind of sneaked back to straighten things up a little around that poor old abused TC. I knew they'd have to hand the job off to one of the other mechanics --probably Sylvester-- and there isn't a wrench in the world who likes jumping into a car project after some other knucklehead has taken it apart. I mean, you never know what's been done and what hasn't been done, or where to find all the pieces or the coffee can of nuts-and-bolts hardware you need to screw it all back together. And I especially hated the idea of Sylvester sliding under that car and finding out I couldn't even remove a damn flywheel! So I kind of eased myself under there to maybe give it one more try, and wouldn't you know it, I didn't so much as touch the teeth along the edge of the ring gear and that stubborn old flywheel simply fell off in my hands. Just like *that!* Stuff like that happens every now and then in the world of auto mechanics, but nobody except a well-seasoned grease monkey can appreciate what an awesome and mysterious experience it is. Like the stories you heard back in grammar school about that King Arthur guy pulling his famous sword out of a stone.

I knew right away this was going to be one *very* special day.

Tommy Edwards showed up about fifteen minutes later, carrying a small army duffel with his helmet and trackside clothes in it and a well-worn leather bag with fancy tooled-in initials holding the rest of his gear. He had me put together a tool kit and a bunch of likely emergency spares to carry along with us, and it was a tough job figuring out exactly what we ought to bring along with us and what we could leave behind. I mean, there isn't what you could call an actual "trunk" on a C-type Jaguar racing car. Not hardly. I mean, you hardly need your toothbrush, your shaving kit, or an extra pair of socks when you're rocketing towards the Mulsanne hairpin at 150 or so in the middle of the night at LeMans! So all the Jaguar designers provided is a little nook-and-cranny space around the spare tire and a kind of makeshift shelf along the rocker panel next to the seats and whatever you feel like stuffing down into the left-side footwell if you're not planning on taking any passengers along with you. At least not for any distance, anyway.

As a result, I settled on a spare wheel and tire for each car, a set of cold racing plugs screwed into the neat little machined aluminum block the Jaguar racing shops made exactly for that purpose and bolted down to the doorsill up where it met the dash panel. I also packed another set of warmup plugs, some richer jets and needles for the carbs (not that I really knew when, how, or why I should put them in), a case of straight 40-weight Castrol down in the footwell on the passenger side of both cars, a small scissors jack, a couple blocks of wood, a flashlight, a clipboard, a stopwatch, a spare point set, condenser, distributor cap and rotor, two cans of brake fluid, two oil filter elements, a knockoff hammer, a basic 3/8ths-drive socket assortment, a set of British Standard combination wrenches, two tins of gear oil, a tub of wheel-bearing grease, a small, bullet-shaped grease gun, three flat blade screwdrivers (a regular, a stubby, and a monster), two

Phillips head screwdrivers (regular and stubby only), three sets of pliers (a regular, a needlenose, and a Channel-Lock model), one set of all-purpose Vise Grips, a feeler gauge, a hacksaw, a rat-tail file, and enough bailing wire, rope, twine, and electrical tape to bind and gag King Kong. Barry threw in a set of brake shoes --just in case, you know?-- and some other miscellaneous valve shims and odds-n'-ends spare parts that came in the trunk of the green car, for what reason I couldn't possibly imagine. I mean, what on earth was I going to do with a set of crankshaft end-play shims at the damn racetrack?

As Tommy Edwards always said, there's a point at which you just flat *forget about* fixing the bloody racecar and start in on the bloody beer....

I guess it seems crazy today that Tommy Edwards and I took off from the heart of Manhattan on the morning of Tuesday, September 2nd, year of Our Lord nineteen hundred and fifty two, heading for the sleepy little town of Elkhart Lake, Wisconsin, in a pair of the very latest, fastest, and certainly most overloaded Jaguar automobiles in the entire Western Hemisphere. The trip figured to be over a thousand miles each way, and those C-types didn't have much in the way of mufflers, tops, windshields, or heaters on them. Not that you exactly *needed* a heater in a Jaguar racing car. Just the opposite, in fact. And there wasn't any such thing as a cross-country Interstate system in those days. Not hardly! Or fast food restaurant franchises or popular, nationally advertised motel chains along the way. Sure, it took a lot longer to get from place to place back then, but at least you got the down-home flavor of the countryside you were passing through and met a few of the local street-corner characters that made each little whistlestop town somehow different and special. I guess travel was more of an adventure back then. Especially if you were driving something as wild and raw and outlandish as the only two C-type Jaguar racing cars in the entire country!

But I have to admit I was pretty damn nervous as Tommy and me wheeled out of the shop into west-side Manhattan street traffic. The growling, liquid-silver C-type felt so taut and eager and hemmed-in that it seemed ready to scoot right out from under me if I didn't keep a real tight rein on it. And the racing clutch didn't help matters any, on account of it was hair-trigger quick and had exactly two operational positions: totally disengaged and Full Squirt Forward. I swear, it worked more like a damn toggle switch than a clutch pedal, and you had to be sure there was a little room ahead before you lifted your left foot up towards the Point Of No Return. On top of that, the C-type's engine was a bit cammy and high-strung for Manhattan traffic (to say the least!) and it would go all soft and fluffy at the bottom end if you lugged it or let it idle at stoplights. So you had to do a little judicious foot-juggling to keep the C-type rolling along in harmony with the taxicabs and city busses and the delivery trucks that could suddenly whip into or out of an alleyway when you least expected it or stop right smack-dab in the middle of the damn street to unload a couple thousand pounds of honeydew melons or a few hundred secondhand typewriters or sixty or seventy dozen gross of ladies' straw hats and matching handbags just in from the sweat shops in the garment district. Right in the middle of the damn street! Then again, that's the way they've *always* done things in Manhattan, and probably always will. The best I could do was just follow along behind Tommy and the green C-type, trying my best to keep pace and make everything mesh smoothly together, but not really doing too good a job of it.

We crossed the George Washington bridge in heavy midday traffic, and I pulled up next to Tommy at a stoplight on the Jersey side and asked if we could maybe make a little side trip over by the Doggy Shake in Passaic so I could see Julie and tell her where I was going and when I'd be back (and incidentally make all the rank-and-file lunch customers at the Doggy Shake choke on their malteds when me and Tommy cruised up in our matching pair of Jaguar C-types). I'd tried to call Julie the night before to explain as how I hadn't exactly quit my job at West-bridge, but she was working and there was just no way I could get over to see her on account of I had to go over to my mom's house to get clothes and stuff. Okay, so maybe I *could* have got my butt over there if I'd really wanted to, but the fact is I thought she might be a little upset about my not quitting at West-bridge so I could come back to work at her uncle's gas station, and even more disgusted about my sudden, drop-everything trip to Wisconsin. The good news was her mother didn't hang up on me (for the first time in ages) although she wasn't exactly what you would call real friendly, either.

"Yooda gas station boy, right?" she rasped into the receiver (as if she hadn't been personally and repeatedly responsible for hanging up on me every blessed time I'd called for the past five weeks, right?).

I allowed as how I was, and asked very kindly if perhaps Julie might be at home.

"She's a-notta home. She's a-work."

"Well then, I wondered if I might perhaps leave her a short message. Just a few words...."

"Lissen, gas-station boy," she hissed through her teeth, "you gotta anything to say to my Joolie, you tell her youself, okay?"

Then she hung up the phone.

Click!

Still, you'd have to say that brief conversation represented a major breakthrough in my relationship with Julie's mom. I mean, we were at least *talking* again, you know?

In any case, I figured Julie might be a little more understanding if she saw me in person with Tommy Edwards and those two irresistible Jaguar racing cars. Even girls understand the way certain cars are so sleek and hot and sexy that they turn you all to pudding inside. In fact, I think sometimes females may understand that even better than guys, on account of women generally have a keener appreciation of style and class and high fashion than male types normally do (or at least than normal male types normally do). Plus they don't get all bogged down in the mechanical innards and wrist-pin personality of an automobile like men tend to. It's just that women tend to be more interested in stuff like the perfect color nail polish and their best friend's bridal dress and how exactly the white birch or knotty pine kitchen cabinets are going to go with the flower-print wallpaper. All of which I'm sure are worthy, vital, interesting topics for discussion if there's simply no way to sneak out the back door and meet your buddies again down at the racing garage.

Anyhow, Tommy and me cruised up past Palisades Park and the Teterboro Airport towards Passaic, and arrived at the Doggy Shake just as the stragglers from the local lunch crowd were finishing off the last of their French fries, and most of them just about fell off their stools when we growled up the drive and parked right in front in those two brand-new Jaguar racecars. Unfortunately Julie wasn't there to see it, but Tommy and me fortified ourselves with a couple cheese-and-mushroom burgers and afterwards toasted our trip with a quick root beer float apiece (which we had to hold in our hands on account of there's simply no place to hook a window tray on a C-type Jaguar) and Tommy absolutely insisted on treating. He left the girl a whole dollar tip, too, just to make sure word would get back to Julie. And *how!*

After lunch we retraced our steps and picked up the New Jersey Turnpike right near Palisades Amusement Park. Tommy motioned me over to the side just before the toll booth and asked how I was doing. He had to yell a little over the lumpy idle coming out the side pipes. "Everything shipshape, sport?" he wanted to know.

"Yeah. I guess so. I'm having a little trouble with the clutch in traffic."

"You'll get used to it," he laughed. "Here, take this," and he tossed me a wadded-up cigarette pack with a twenty-dollar bill folded up inside. "That's for tolls and anything else you might need along the way."

"Gee whiz, *thanks!*"

"Right, then," Tommy grinned. *"TALLY HO!"*

And with that, he revved the green Jag's engine up to about four thousand or so and deftly unloaded the clutch, rocketing away with the back wheels spinning and rubbersmoke churning off the tires.

"All right," I said to the shell-shocked kid in my rearview mirror, "just like the man said: *tally ho!*" and left my own two dollars worth of Dunlop's best on the New Jersey concrete. We were on our way!

Out on the turnpike, the C-type really came into her own, running along at an effortless 75 or 80 miles an hour without so much as breaking a sweat. Why, you could even take your hands off the wheel at that speed and it would just track along like it was on rails! I'd never been in anything like that before in my entire life! Comparing it to a standard-issue XK120 was like comparing a regular XK120 to a Nash Rambler or a Henry J. It was that much faster and lower and tighter and lighter on its feet. And the New Jersey Turnpike was an absolutely fantastic stretch of road for a car like that. It was four lanes wide with a divider in the middle, and although the posted speed limit was just 55, you could see pretty far ahead and back behind you in the rear-view mirror, so there wasn't too much worry about cops as long as you kept your eyes peeled. Plus everybody we passed --and we were passing *everybody!*-- looked at those two Jaguars like they were a couple flying saucers just swooped down to that Turnpike from outer space! Kids plastered themselves against the back windows of Pontiac hardtops and bullet-nosed Studebakers, and the puffy women in flower-print sundresses occupying the passenger sides of the front seats of those cars would crane their eyeballs around their husbands' profiles to get a better look at us, and sometimes even hazard a sneaky little wave. And the husbands never noticed, on account of they were too busy gaping at us themselves. Why, some of them got mesmerized to the point of veering off the edge of the pavement or swerving dangerously close to the divider median. To tell the truth, it was downright intoxicating, and it got even worse when Tommy decided to "blow the carbon out" a few miles south of Elizabeth. I heard him downshift to third at about 75 or so and watched the rear end squat and squirt away from me as he buried the gas pedal and the green Jag quickly began disappearing into the distance. Naturally there was nothing I could do except drop down to third myself and bury the throttle. I mean, what choice did I have? A few seconds later we were weaving through light traffic at well over a hundred, and I'd be a damned liar if I didn't admit that we were up over 120 --*two miles every minute!*-- before we hit the redline in third and snapped a quick upshift into top! Why, I was hanging on for all I was worth, my fingers wrapped around the woodrim steering wheel in a white-knuckled death grip, praying on one hand that Tommy'd ease off and hoping in another devilish little corner of my brain that he'd keep his foot hard in it all the way up to Wisconsin! I finally chickened out at something around a hundred and thirty or so, and no question that was as fast as I'd ever gone in an automobile in my life. But old Tommy kept the pedal down clear through 5500 in top, which worked out to roughly 144 miles an hour. Give or take a few. On the God Damn New Jersey Turnpike, for gosh sakes! In the middle of an ordinary lunchbucket Wednesday afternoon....

Wow!

Well, so much for "taking it easy on the cars."

The 1952 edition of the Rand-McNally road atlas will tell you it's precisely 88 miles from New York City to Philadelphia, and that it should take you about three hours at a reasonable and proper rate on account of traffic and all, but Tommy Edwards and me were hauling into the northern outskirts of Philly almost a full hour in front of the advertised Rand-McNally numbers, and that's only because Tommy had to ease off and wait for me a bunch of times because I got nervous as hell at anything much over 95 or 100. Especially in traffic! But Tommy didn't think a thing of it. "Bloody great road, isn't it?" he hollered over the exhaust rumble as I pulled up next to him at a stoplight in Elkins Park, "but the one coming up is even better. You'll see."

Sure enough, after we finessed our way through the small towns and villages on the north end of Philadelphia, we picked up the Pennsylvania Turnpike at Conshohocken, and that turned out to be the most fantastic stretch of highway I'd ever seen in my life. Of course, it helped some that I was wheeling a C-type Jaguar racing car. It started off a lot like the turnpike in Jersey, except that the *legal* speed limit was seventy miles an hour. SEVENTY MILES AN HOUR! I couldn't believe it. And of course Tommy automatically added another 40 or 50 on top of that whenever he thought we could get away with it. But he was always careful to slow down a couple notches whenever we came up on traffic. "No need to frighten the populace, sport," he told me later, "it's impolite, don't you know?"

We passed by King of Prussia and New Centerville and Valley Forge in quick succession, and that last one got me to thinking about how we once fought a bunch of Englishmen like Tommy for the right to run this country --and beat them out of it, too-- and now here I was, an ordinary wiseass gas station kid from Passaic, New Jersey, following an actual British fighter pilot on some brand new kind of Commando Raid on these United States, ripping through the historic gut of our country in a brand new English sportscar that made the size, power, weight, speed, and handling capabilities of your average American Road Barge seem laughable by comparison.

The Pennsylvania Turnpike stretched a full 105 miles from Philadelphia to Harrisburg, and Tommy and me covered it in well under two hours (instead of the 2:45 Rand-McNally suggested) and that included a lot of creeping along town-to-town stuff north of Philly before we ever hit the turnpike. I couldn't believe we didn't get ourselves shagged by the cops, but Tommy was real sharp at spotting the black State Trooper Fords with their gumball machine mars lights stuck on top, and he always got us hauled down to something approaching a reasonable pace before we came swooping past them like a couple ground-hugging Sabre jets. Even so, one of them pulled us over anyway on the outskirts of Harrisburg, but it turned out he just wanted a closer look at the cars. Tommy motioned for me to stay put in the silver car while he undid the hood on the green one and showed the cop what was underneath, and the guy was so impressed (probably as much with Tommy's accent as the hardware under the Jaguar's hood) that nothing would do but that he fired up his siren and mars light and led us on an exclusive little three-car parade into the town of New Cumberland for dinner. He turned out to be a pretty neat guy (for a cop, anyway) and you could tell he really liked those two Jaguar racecars and couldn't hardly get enough of Tommy's racing stories. Neither could I, come to think of it, since they were always real funny the way Tommy told them. I mean, most guys tell racing stories just to impress you (and everybody else within earshot) and sometimes the more they try to impress you, the more you wish they would maybe go find somebody else to try to impress. But Tommy always made it seem like he never did anything especially brave or daring or skillful in a racing car, but rather that he just happened to be in the right car at the right time when he won. Which naturally got you thinking and imagining that maybe *you* could've done the same things *he* did --no problem at all!-- if you'd just happened to be there in that right car at the right time at Bridgehampton or Watkins Glen or even at the Twenty-Four Hours of Le Mans....

It was a little past six when we finally rolled out of Harrisburg, full up with a good fried chicken dinner, two tankfuls of the best gas we could find, and ready to take on the most magnificent 196 miles of highway I'd ever seen in my life: the run across the Appalachian Mountains between Harrisburg and Pittsburgh on the Pennsylvania Turnpike. The big, wide, four-lane roadway climbed and dove and swooped its way up long, steep inclines and even steeper, scarier, bobsled-run descents, and the view out over the edge was absolutely spectacular, what with the sun arcing down towards its late-summer rest ahead of us, painting the forests on the western hillsides with a rich, golden-orange light and filling the valleys below with deep, purple-tinged shadows. I'd never seen anything so huge and handsome and breathtaking in my life. Not that I could really pay much attention, since Tommy had the bit between his teeth and was hustling us along at well over a hundred most of the time and slicing clear across both lanes through the corners (at least when there wasn't too much traffic!) to make them wider and smoother so we could maintain the pace. I had to drive my ass off to keep up, but at least I wasn't clutching the steering wheel in a death grip anymore. In fact, me and that silver C-type had gotten more or less used to one another by then, and I'd even grown accustomed to Tommy Edwards' hellish rate of progress. Why, a hundred miles an hour seemed almost normal, you know?

We arrived at the Breezewood toll plaza just after dark, and I was really astounded by the sight of Breezewood itself off to our right. I'd never seen a town anything like it. In fact, from a distance, it looked like a huge, ultra-modern gas station that stretched for three or four city blocks rather than any kind of ordinary live-in, go-to-work, church-on-Sunday town I'd ever seen. Why, it was nothing but a long, narrow concrete shelf set deep down in a valley --right next to the highway-- and from one end to the other it was nothing but filling stations and overnight motels and drive-ins and glass-and-linoleum sitdown restaurants, one right after the other, with all of it bathed in a pool of eerie, lavender-tinted fluorescent light. Nestled there in the bottom of that valley, you could see the town of Breezewood from miles away as you descended down the Pennsylvania Turnpike from either direction, and all those cafes and drive-ins and gas stations and motels did a cracking business on account of Breezewood was the perfect (and only!) convenient place to stop for quite a distance. It was also located about an average motorist's one-day trip out of New York City, so the greater majority of your rank-and-file truckers and vacation travelers stopped there. I'd never seen anyplace like it before, and of course had no idea that I was looking The Ugly Future squarely in the face....

But we had plenty of gas left in the LeMans-sized fuel tanks on the C-types, so we cruised right on by Breezewood, heading for Pittsburgh. Now, the so-called "travel experts" at Rand and

McNally figured it should take your average lunchbucket jerk in his Ford, Plymouth, Oldsmobile, Pontiac, or DeSoto about five full hours to cover the distance between Harrisburg and Pittsburgh --including the normal pee, gas, and dinner stop in Breezewood-- but, like I said, Tommy Edwards and me and those two Jaguars were beating the living hell out of Mr. Rand and Mr. McNally's ideas about how long it should take to drive from one place to another. So we just set our sights on Pittsburgh, a good hundred miles away, and Tommy seemed hell-bent on making it in less than an hour. But he did ease off to a safe, sane, and relatively sedate 75 or 80 as we passed by Breezewood and whenever we came up on slow-moving clots of traffic. After dark, those Highway Patrol cruisers start looking like every other pair of headlights and taillights until you're too damn close to do anything about it, you know?

Outside of that, the darkness didn't seem to make any difference to Tommy at all. But it sure as hell bothered *me,* burrowing into this endless, churning, yellowish hole burning itself into the blackness at something around a hundred-plus and trying like hell not to lose the taillights of Tommy's green Jaguar up ahead (which sometimes got so far away they turned into two little red pinpoints that stared at me like rat's eyes and threatened to vanish completely if I didn't keep my foot in it). Every now and again we'd come to one of those amazing tunnels that the Pennsylvania Turnpike highway engineers carved clear *through* some of the mountainsides, and all of a sudden the exhaust noise off those two big, throaty Jaguar sixes would quadruple in volume, echoing in on us off the walls, and the yellowish, death-ray glow through the plexiglass headlamp covers would rake through that tunnel like a pair of streaking electrified halos, damn near showering sparks off the concrete. Then we'd burst out on the other side and all the noise and light would blast off into space again like a balloon exploding. I have to admit that charging through those tunnels gave me a serious case of the willies (not to mention swooping around blind curves at better than 90 miles an hour with nothing but a tender little strip of guardrail between me and the yawning black emptiness on the other side) and I remember wishing I maybe had Cal Carrington along to take over the wheel, on account of I was getting tired and sloppy and not incidentally starting to scare myself silly.

As you can imagine, I was wrung out like a used dishrag by the time we pulled off for the night at McKeesport, just a little southeast of Pittsburgh. It was a little after ten, and as we rolled down the exit ramp off the turnpike, I noticed I was soaking wet from perspiration and that my bottom half was damn near melted off from all the heat coming in through the Jag's firewall, while my top half felt just as damn near frozen. But of course I didn't notice any of that while we were driving --no time to think about it, you know?-- and it seemed like we were hardly crawling along when we slowed down to a meager 35 or so and headed into town. Why, I swear I could've gotten out and walked alongside, it felt so blessed slow.

Tommy found us a little tourist motel less than a mile off the Turnpike, and although the so-called "Deluxe Cabin Accommodations" advertised on the sign out front turned out to be seven or eight tiny, white-clapboard sheds not much bigger than your average outhouse, at least they were neat and clean and even had a few geraniums planted in the window boxes out front to make them look sort of homey. Plus the pimple-faced young attendant came barreling out of the office like his shirttails were on fire once he got a load of Tommy and me tooling up in those two C-types. *"Jimminy!"* he gulped. "What the heck *are* those things?" So I explained to him as how they were the very latest and fastest long-distance racing cars in the whole damn world, built by Jaguar all the way over in Coventry, England, and how we were on our way to this big sportscar race in Wisconsin --just breaking them in with a little cross-country run, you understand-- and furthermore how the guy in the green car was none other than Tommy Edwards, one of the top racing drivers in the whole blessed universe. I have to admit I was kind of pleased at the way the guy's jaw dropped open a little further with each new tidbit of information, as if it was a hydraulic jack and I was working the handle. But Tommy got a little flustered when I went into the part about what a super duper, Internationally Renowned Hotshoe Driver he was, and I could tell from the expression on his face that it was maybe about time for me to shut up.

"Look here, sport," he told the pimple-faced motel guy with his mouth hanging open in front of us like a dead carp, "you think you might have a place for us to sleep tonight?"

"Huh?" the guy said, looking back and forth from Tommy to me to the two sleek Jaguar racecars and back to Tommy like the whole bunch of us had just beamed down from outer space.

"A room," Tommy explained. "You know, like those over there. We'd ever so much appreciate a place to clean up and get a good night's sleep."

The guy sputtered there for a moment, trying to get his thoughts together and his jaw jacked back up into a normal speaking position, but then he exploded in all directions like a busted radiator hose. *"S-sure!"* he gushed. "Y-you bet. Why, y'can have *my* room if you wannit. It's a little bigger than the others, see. Even has a kitchen on it. I got food in the icebox, too," he looked around over both shoulders and added in a whisper, "an' I even got a couple beers in there...."

That sounded pretty good to me, but Tommy wouldn't hear of it. "No need for that," he told the kid, "but thanks anyway. Ever so much. One of your regular cabins will do quite nicely." Then Tommy turned to me and asked, "You don't mind bunking together, do you, sport?"

"Suits me," I said, feeling pretty special that Tommy didn't mind bunking with me, either.

"Tell me," he said to the motel guy, "you think there might be a spot handy where we could park the cars overnight. Someplace secure, you understand. They're quite valuable."

"They're the only XK120C Jaguar racecars in the entire country," I explained (as if the motel kid had any idea on earth what that meant).

"You just leave them right there, sir," he told Tommy, kind of snapping to attention while simultaneously fussing to get his shirttails tucked into his pants *"I'll* keep an eye on 'em for you. Glad to help out."

"Why, thank you."

"I even think I've got some towels out back in the linen box. They're not dirty or anything. I can put a couple over the seats for you if you'd like. For the dew...."

"You sure it's not too much trouble?"

"No, *sir!"* the kid said, grinning like an idiot. "No trouble a'tall. Heck, I'm stuck here in the office all night anyway. It'll give me something to do."

And so Tommy and me left the two rarest, fastest, most valuable Jaguars in the whole blessed country parked there on the gravel drive outside that little cabin motel in McKeesport, Pennsylvania, and headed off to bed down for the night. As Tommy unlocked the door to our cabin, I glanced back and saw the motel guy pull a rocking chair out of the office and set it down on the gravel right next to the two Jags, and I wouldn't be surprised if he spent the whole damn night there. In fact, I bet once he saw our light go out and waited an hour or so to make sure we were asleep, he probably even climbed over the door panel of one of those cars (no way you could find the latch-pull on a Jaguar if you didn't know where to look for it) and sat himself down behind the wheel. It's hard to resist an opportunity like that --especially for some teenage motel-clerk kid from McKeesport, Pennsylvania-- and I imagine as he peered out through that low-cut plexiglass racing windscreen, he even made believe he was passing a couple of Allards and Ferraris on the midnight straight-away at someplace like LeMans (doing at least a hundred-and-fifty, natch) and he was probably even making a bunch of those phony racing-engine noises with his mouth. Like he was giving somebody the raspberries, you know, only with downshifts....

Lord knows that's what *I* would've done.

One of the things you have to get used to if you're going to pursue a career as a Full-Fledged Professional Racing Mechanic (even a Part-Time Full-Fledged Professional Racing Mechanic, in fact) is that you wind up sharing a lot of strange, unfamiliar rooms --not to mention other, less formal sleeping quarters-- with a bunch of strange, unfamiliar people you don't really know all that well. Truth is, it can make you pretty uncomfortable now and then. Particularly if the other guy makes a lot of weird, disgusting noises when he sleeps or grinds his teeth all night or has nauseating personal hygiene habits like picking his feet and smelling it. And sometimes, even if the guy is neat and clean and quiet as a churchmouse, you still can't get to sleep on account of there's this strange, unfamiliar person in the bed just a few feet away from you, and you can feel from the tingle in the air that he's not asleep --not *really*-- and there's just no way in hell you can relax and doze off until you're absolutely, positively *sure* that he's asleep first. Don't ask me why. So lots of times the two of you just lie there perfectly still all night, *pretending* to be asleep but keeping each other awake by doing exactly that. Sure, it sounds crazy, but the worst part is how you both generally drop off into a deep, heavy slumber just as the sky's getting light, and of course fifteen minutes later the alarm is ringing and it's time for all good Professional Racing Mechanics to roll out of the sack. Don't ask me why it always seems to work that way, but lots of times it does. And that's one reason why Professional Race Mechanics tend to look so haggard and worn out in the morning. Of course, you can usually get around that edgy, hard-time-getting-to-sleep routine with a few generously administered overdoses of beer, scotch, vodka, rye, or bourbon (and surely there's nothing like sharing a fifth with somebody to make you both sleep as deeply as a pair of hibernating ground squirrels) only that tends to be the *other* thing that makes Professional Race Mechanics look so damn haggard and worn out in the morning.

But bunking in with Tommy Edwards was no problem at all. He insisted I go in and wash up first, and when I came out of the john with a terrycloth towel wrapped around me, he had this little silver flask set out on the nightstand with two small silver shot glasses beside it. "Have a quick snort of brandy?" he asked, pouring both of them right up to the top. "Cheers," he grinned, and clinked the shotglasses together. "You did a pretty fair job out there today, sport."

"Aww," I said, looking down at the carpet.

"No, really," he said, tossing back his shot of brandy. "Nicely done."

"Thanks," I told him, sitting myself down on the edge of the bed and taking a slow sip off the rim of the other shotglass. The liquor tasted all crackly hot like a good wood fire, and it must've been some pretty expensive brandy, on account of it didn't burn my gut too much once it got down there.

"Now finish up and let's see if we can get ourselves some sleep," Tommy said. So I drank what I had left and then Tommy picked up the two shotglasses and screwed them back on top of that nifty silver flask and headed into the bathroom. I waited until after the door shut to take my towel off and find myself a pair of underwear to sleep in, but I guess that's only normal, you know? And it occurred to me, as I eased myself between the sheets, that Tommy was about the only racer I'd ever met who could take just one short drink out of a bottle and then pack it away --with plenty left in it!-- instead of continuing to knock 'em back and knock 'em back until the whole damn bottle was gone. By the time Tommy came out of the shower, I was fast asleep.

Tommy roused me out of bed about six-thirty the next morning on account of there was a heavy overcast and Tommy wanted to get some miles in quick because it looked like rain up ahead. "I reckon we'll have breakfast in Ohio," he told me as we gathered up our stuff and carried it out to the cars. The motel guy had kept towels over the interiors all night --changing them every now and then like dressings on a wounded soldier-- and it looked like he'd spent quite some time wiping the cars down as well. Maybe even polishing them a little, since you could smell fresh wax and there wasn't a single, solitary bug splat on either one. Tommy wanted to give him a little something for his trouble, but the guy wouldn't take it. In fact, he wound up giving us a couple free cups of coffee and half of his morning sweet roll instead.

"Say, sport," Tommy asked as we were about to pile into the cars, "feel like swapping mounts for a spell?"

"Huh?"

"You know. You take this one for awhile and I'll try the silver one."

"Sure. Why not."

So I hopped into the dark green C-type and Tommy sat down behind the wheel of "my" car and we took off, and it was easy to fall into that 85- to 110-mile-per-hour rhythm again once we got back on the turnpike. I was amazed all over again at how confident and stable and solidly planted the C-type felt at that speed --just loafing along with a fingertip touch on the wheel, you know?-- and the only way you could tell how fast we were traveling was when we zoomed past some off-to-work local citizen in a Ford sedan and scared the poor bastard halfway off the road. In the distance ahead of us I could see thick grey smoke rising like an ascending shadow off the Pittsburgh steel mills and filtering up into the lighter grey overcast of the sky. That of course got me thinking about my old man and his union job at the chemical plant. Only this was steel country, and somewheres out there beyond the guardrails, a million grey-faced union guys just like him were punching time clocks at foundries and mills and casting factories and rolling plants and getting down to work. It sent a cold shiver through me, and I pushed the gas pedal all the way to the floorboards as if I could somehow accelerate away from that feeling and leave it behind. It was guilt, I suppose. I mean, here were all these worn-down guys in worn-out coveralls, shuffling into work every morning like a legion of zombies, what with their tin lunchboxes and morning-edition newspapers and thermos bottles of thick, black coffee dangling from their arms. And here *I* was, streaking across the Pennsylvania countryside at two miles a minute in one of the fastest, sexiest, most valuable racing automobiles in all of North America. Fact is, I felt like I'd *escaped* from something, you know?

The Pennsylvania Turnpike ended abruptly at the Ohio border near a little town called Petersburg, just a mile or so past the last toll gate. There were a lot of big, dusty-orange road graders and construction equipment all over the place, and you could see how someday they intended to make that road into one long, skinny concrete stripe running right across the belly of America like a piece of kite string tied around its waist. But it ended a little bit southeast of Youngstown back in 1952, and it was a lot tougher making decent time once you got off the turnpike and back on the two-lane. Not to mention that the country gets ironed down flatter and flatter as you leave the Appalachians and head west towards the great plains. Don't get me wrong, it's still nice to look at --especially the little white-clapboard towns you pass through along the way, what with their village squares and county courthouses and proud church spires-- but you can't help noticing how the countryside gets kind of dull and monotonous compared to the mountains in Pennsylvania.

Still, you get to do a lot more with a car on a town-to-town blacktop two-lane than you can out on the turnpike, where it's usually just Foot Down In Fourth all the way and never having to shift or steer hard or grab for the brakes unless you see a toll-booth or a lurking Highway Patrol cruiser up ahead. On the two-lane, you had to work harder and concentrate a little more, what with slowing for towns and accelerating out of them, braking and downshifting for the occasional tight switchback, and --best of all-- pulling out to pass slower cars and overloaded produce trucks. As you can imagine, that was a lot of fun in a brand new

C-type Jaguar! A quick blip down to third (or even second some-times) and a hard punch on the throttle were all it took to leave the local yokels, out-of-state vacation travelers, and cross-country truckers gaping in your wake. And what a sound that barely muffled Jaguar six made when you pulled the cork on it! Why, Tommy and me were passing three, four, even five at a time, slicing in and out and around them like a pair of highspeed fight-er planes buzzing a slow-moving convoy.

Truth is, I'd never felt so big or strong or quick or wise or devilishly clever in my whole entire life.

But I did notice a few subtle differences between the green car and the silver one. Not anything you could actually reach out and put your finger on, mind you, but a sort of hard-to-pin-down difference in the *feel* of two cars. That's one of those mysterious things that every sympathetic mechanic understands, even though he knows it makes no reasonable sense whatsoever. But the fact remains that no two cars are ever *exactly* alike --even if they're built side-by-side at the factory by the same few pairs of hands out of supposedly identical parts lifted one-right-after-the-other out of the same damn parts bins. And that's especially true of racing cars, which tend to be a little more hand-fitted and are certainly more susceptible to the "luck of the draw" as far as combustion chamber shape and cam profile and valve seat finish and friction losses in the bearings and perfectly meshing gears and dead-nuts wheel alignment and a million kazillion other tiny little details are concerned. Far as I could tell, the green car was just that little infinitesimal bit *quicker* and *tighter* than the silver one. Not that anything was particularly *wrong* with the silver C-type. Far from it, in fact. It's just that the green car, for whatev-er collection of minute, hidden, unfathomable, and unmeasurable reasons, wound up feeling the more agile, spirited, and athletic of the two. And so it made perfect sense that Colin St. John was selling the silver car to Ernesto Julio to take back and race in California and keeping the green one for himself at Westbridge.

What else would you expect?

We stopped for breakfast a little after eight, and over eggs, toast, and bacon, Tommy and me compared notes on the two cars. I was real pleased to discover he'd felt the same things I did about those cars and figured "his" Jaguar was definitely the better of the two (albeit not by much). Then Tommy pulled out a bunch

of folded-up highway maps and worked us out a route for the rest
of the trip. Tommy figured we had a choice of heading north and
picking up 224 south of Youngstown or taking a jog south to
U.S. 30 near Lisbon. We decided 224 looked like our best bet,
because it cut straight across the state all the way to Tiffin, which
was pretty close to the Indiana border. I felt really proud that
Tommy wanted my opinion on the best route, seeing as how I
was the only real Native American between the two of us, and I
made sure to study everything very carefully before opening my
mouth. Not that I had the slightest idea what I was talking about,
you understand, on account of I'd never been out that way before
(or much west of Trenton, if you want the bitter truth of it). But
when you spread a roadmap out between a couple cups of morning coffee, some of those little red and blue lines just seem to call
out to you. Of course, there's no way of knowing what a road is
really going to be like until you're actually on it, but the general
rule of thumb goes something like this: when you've got plenty
of time and the countryside's pretty, you want to find yourself
the little squiggly lines that meander alongside rivers or maybe
twist their way up and down a mountain range --you know,
sportscar roads-- but when you've got to be someplace for a race
and it's still three or four states away, you want to find the short-
est, straightest distance possible, avoid as many towns as you
can, and hope to God you picked a route with not too many
Highway Patrol cruisers and mostly the soft, slow, lazy brand of
smalltown policemen who spend the bulk of their on-duty hours
hanging around the local barber shop.

Route 224 turned out to be about as good a way as any to
get ourselves across Ohio, but it was painfully slow going after
the high-speed freedom of the turnpike. The official speed limit
was only 50, and although Tommy was never exactly real concerned about official stateside speed limits, it did slow down the
cars we were trying to pass, and of course you have to be a little
more careful on two-lane highway so's you don't pull out to pass
a local egg truck and catch 20 tons of interstate Peterbilt right in
your face. Still, the C-types made a pretty easy job of it. You
could pop down into third and lay into the throttle and be around
your average John Doe road obstacle in no time at all. On the
other hand, you had to be a little patient, on account of sometimes the road was blind up ahead or maybe you were stuck

behind a gravel hauler or a tanker truck and couldn't see at all. Plus our Jags were righthand drive, and that made pulling out from behind any sort of decent-sized truck into something of a religious experience. I noticed Tommy would always take a quick glance in the mirror, just to make sure I was there and knew enough to floor it and follow him around. We had a few close calls, but I guess that goes without saying. Every once in a while, we'd hit an empty stretch and Tommy'd run us up to about 120 or so, but that was as much as he'd dare push it on Route 224 across Ohio, on account of you had a lot of little towns and roadside businesses and whatnot to worry about, and the last thing the local population expected was a couple of righthand drive Jaguar racecars streaking across the countryside at damn near the speed of sound. Plus Route 224 ran right smack through the center of a bunch of little towns like Western Star, Leroy, Homerville, Ruggles, and Delphi, and there was no choice but to slow right down to 40 or so and grumble along on the idle jets in third. But they were pretty little towns (most of 'em, anyways) and it was kind of neat how everybody looked at us with their jaws dropped open and eyes bugged out on stalks. Especially the highschool girls, who were mostly hanging out along Main Street, enjoying a little window shopping or maybe an ice cream soda during those last few precious summer weekdays before school started up again after Labor Day. I saw some boys in muddy green sweatshirts and cleated shoes coming home from football practice, carrying their helmets loosely at their sides while they bragged and cracked wise about what they'd done (or were planning to do!) with those same highschool girls we saw up on Main. But those smalltown football heroes all stopped dead in their tracks when they got a load of Tommy and me heading their way, and they stared at us --shell shocked and reeling!-- like a bunch of cartoon characters who'd just been hit with an iron frypan. It occurred to me, as I smiled serenely back at them, how much older, wiser, smarter, cooler, and infinitely more mature I was than those poor hicks, and I slyly wondered if *they'd* ever witnessed the kind of melting-hot smiles and yearning stares like Tommy and I got from those girls up on Main Street....

It took us over five and a half hours to cross Ohio, and to tell the truth it got pretty blessed dull there on Route 224, what with the towns popping up one after the other and the truck traffic and all. So Tommy decided to re-route us kind of Free Form Northwest just past Tiffin, taking off the numbered highway and trying out all the tiny, unnumbered county roads on the map just for a little variety. They turned out to be wonderful farm-country backroads with high crowns, shady valleys, roadside barns, rural mailboxes, surprising curves and switchbacks, and the inevitable car-chasing farm-country dogs you find all over rural America. Of course, none of those mutts had much of a chance against a C-type Jaguar racing car, but I've got to give credit to one particular Golden Retriever, who took a shortcut across an alfalfa field and made a real race of it for damn near half a mile. I suppose taking those backroads cost us a little time, seeing as how you had to be careful and back off at regular intervals since every hidden bend or rise in the road might be hiding a stray cow or a slow-moving hay wagon on the opposite side. And some of them surely did. But they were neat places to drive, and you could feel that the Jags were enjoying it every bit as much as Tommy and me were. Of course, we had a hard time keeping ourselves headed in the right direction, what with all the swoops and turns and intersections, but every time we came barreling up to one, Tommy'd glance right and left and make a snap decision as to which way he wanted to go, and in less than a heartbeat he'd have the clutch out and smoke spinning off the tires. Why, it was all I could do to hang on and try to keep up. Sometimes, when Tommy'd wait until the last instant before deciding which way to turn, I'd have to lock up the damn brakes to keep from sliding right into the back of him! Boy, old Colin St. John would've gotten himself pretty worked up if he'd been there to see it, you know? But Tommy seemed to always know exactly where I was, and he'd roar out of the way as I skittered up behind him with the car all up on tiptoes, snatched down to second, fishtailed around after him, and charged up through the gears --right on his butt-- like we were maybe racing each other at someplace like Bridgehampton! I got scared once or twice that I was going to fishtail that silver Jag right into a ditch or a fence-post, but I was starting to get a little confidence, too. Like maybe I could really get the hang of this stuff after all.

We ran into a light rain just as we crossed over into Indiana, and at first it was kind of fun and refreshing, even though we had to slow down quite a bit. But then it got a lot worse and hard to see (those short little racing windscreens weren't much good in the wet) not to mention that water was streaming over the dash cowling and in through the doors and even up from someplace down in the footwells, and on top of that my Dodgers hat was of the exact proper aerodynamic shape to send a stream of cold, dirty rainwater right down the back of my shirt collar. Pretty soon the sky got so blessed dark we had to put the headlights on --not that it helped much-- and I must admit I felt pretty relieved when we came to a stopsign and found ourselves face to face with a major numbered highway again. It was Route 8, heading into the town of Auburn, which is where they used to build those big, stylish, super-expensive Auburn cars before the depression set in during the thirties and more or less dried up the market. Those were some pretty magnificent automobiles --especially the super-charged, boat-tailed Speedster models-- and not even Ferrari or Rolls Royce ever built cars with more class, grace, and elegance. They were about the last American cars you could really be proud of, you know, those Auburns, Cords, Duesenbergs, and V12 Packards. But then times got tough and the war came and I guess there just wasn't much need for cars like that any more. Or maybe there simply weren't any people left who were up to the scale and standard of those cars....

Anyhow, Tommy found us a gas station with a good-sized garage attached (a Sinclair, natch) and he made a deal to park the Jags inside and get us a couple oil changes while we waited for the worst of the storm to pass. The owner was pretty impressed with our cars, and he seemed only too happy to let us freshen up and put some dry clothes on in his john. He even made me a deal on a pair of clean coveralls and a pretty decent rain slicker after I looked down into the passenger-side footwell of the silver C-type and saw my mom's laundry bag more or less floating in a pool of water at the bottom, so of course all my clothes were thoroughly drenched. Then the guy lent us an umbrella and directed Tommy and me across the street to a little corner place called (naturally enough) The Auburn Grill, where we each had ourselves a bowl of homemade beef stew and a slice apiece of some very decent Dutch Apple pie. A la mode, natch. It wasn't as good as my mom's, of course, but I'd have to say it was amazingly close for some little two-bit coffee shop smack-dab in the middle of nowhere. Anyhow, it took the better part of two hours for the rain to slack off, and during that time Tommy and I had quite a conversation about how he got started in racing and what it took to do something like that properly. "Oh, I don't think a bloke's got to be particularly *brave* to be a racing driver," he told me while thoughtfully stirring his tea, "not really. Foolhardy will often do just as well."

"Aw," I said, "you're just saying that."

"Oh, I suppose you're right. But it's really nothing like you'd imagine from reading all the tabloid stories or watching those dreadful Hollywood movies about racing. Not at all."

"It isn't?"

"Oh, good heavens *no!* Why, they paint it up all blood and guts and Devil-take-the-hindmost. 'A fair fight and may the best man win' and all that sort of rubbish. Utter nonsense."

"Really?"

"Why of course. It's the bloody *cars* that win races when you get right down to it. The drivers can only *lose* them...."

"I don't get it."

"Well, the bloody truth of the matter is that a racing driver is always limited by what his machine is capable of doing on any given day or over any given stretch of road. His job is simply to bring it up as close as he can to that level of performance and keep it there for the whole bloody race," Tommy took a long, thoughtful sip of tea, "but of course you never can."

"You *can't?*"

"Oh, of course not. Why, you're constantly making little mistakes with the car and screwing things up here and there. It can't be helped."

I couldn't believe what I was hearing, you know? Why, I'd seen Tommy Edwards drive, and as far as I was concerned, he was about the most perfect damn racecar driver in the galaxy.

"Trust me, Buddy. There's simply no such thing as a perfect race. Or even a perfect single lap. Why, I don't believe there's even such a thing as an absolutely dead-nuts perfect corner. You're always seeing all these little things that you could've done just that small bit *better....*"

"Wow," I said, letting out a low whistle.

"In fact, I reckon the better you are at it, the more you see each race as a pretty bloody grim collection of errors, miscues, fumbles, mistakes, and missed opportunities."

"Even when you *win?*"

Tommy nodded. "Of course. Sometimes even moreso."

I shook my head, trying to make sense out of it.

"The saving grace is that you're up against other blokes who put their pants on one leg at a time, and they tend to be just as stupid, pig-headed, and ham-fisted as yourself. So at least you've got a sporting chance. It's a little like fighter piloting that way."

"You did that in the war, didn't you?"

"Oh, a little here and there."

"What was it like?"

"A bit scary, actually," Tommy laughed, "but also quite exciting. Moreso than anything I've ever done, when you get right down to it. Here's you in your machine and there's the other fellow in his, and it all comes down to who has the best machine, the most nerve, and the better mixture of skill, instinct, shrewdness, and patience. You need the ability to concentrate and stay cool when the other bloke is getting hot under the collar."

"And you gotta be *quick*, too," I added.

"Oh, I suppose," Tommy agreed reluctantly, "but the grave-yards are full of chaps who tried to get by on bravery and fast reactions. It's a deadly combination."

"It is?"

"Absolutely. Experience is probably the most important thing --seat time, don't you know-- because you can't *think* about what you're going to do in the heat of battle. You've simply got to *know*. By the time you've thought your way through and taken the time to evaluate a situation, it's generally over...."

"Wow...."

"In fact, I reckon that's what I love so much about motor racing. It's exactly the same --you and your machine against the other bloke in his-- except that you're on the ground instead of up in the sky and none of the participants necessarily have to get themselves killed in a motor race. But the feeling of speed, concentration, and competition is quite similar."

"So that's how you got started?"

"I suppose it is...."

"Right after the war?"

Tommy nodded. "I reckon I simply needed something to replace the war, you know? It sounds rather silly, but there just isn't much out there to compare with what I did in the service. Not just the air battles, but simply being a *part* of it, too. Being, you know, a 'member of the club,' so to speak. That's what I found again in motor racing."

"Well, you're sure plenty good at it."

"Oh, please," Tommy laughed, turning a little pink around the ears, "I'm just a bloody journeyman, really. Lots of brute muscle and experience but not too awfully much talent."

"Why, you're absolutely *great!*" I told him.

"It's nice of you to say so, but I think 'reasonably good' might be a bit more accurate."

"What's the difference?" I asked.

"Well, let's just say that a 'good' driver is one who can win with the best car. After all, that's what he's *supposed* to do."

"And a *great* driver?"

"That's easy. He's the fellow who can win when some other bloke has the best car...."

Chapter 24: Elkhart Lake

The village of Elkhart Lake sits on the edge of a beautiful, spring-fed lake about an hour north of Milwaukee, where the water is so darn clear you can see bottom when it's twenty feet deep. It was left behind when one of those ice-age glaciers moved through the area a couple million years ago, along with a bunch of steep hills and deep valleys and dramatic, bowl-shaped hollows and mounds of rocks called Kettles and Moraines, which is how the region got its name. These days the ice is gone and the countryside is all rolling farmland and thick, green forests and bright, sunshiny meadows full of honeybees and wildflowers and stuff like that. All of which makes for some really fine sportscar roads, complete with ups and downs and lefts and rights and whoop-de-do pavement dips and long, *long* straightaways where you can really let a big, powerful automobile stretch its legs. And that's exactly what a pair of bucks-up midwestern S.C.M.A. types thought when they flew over Elkhart in light plane sometime back in the fall of 1949, searching for just such a place to play with each other and their expensive four-wheeled toys.

And when those S.C.M.A. guys drove in for a closer look a few weeks later, they discovered a faded, struggling little resort town that was not only ready-made for hosting races, but eager as hell to have them. Besides the beautiful lake and the swoopy, sinewy blacktop roads around it, Elkhart also had plenty of vacant hotel rooms and empty tourist cabins and nearby supper clubs and even golf courses and boat rentals and, of course, enough friendly local taverns to keep everyone properly occupied before the racing began and long after it was over. Needless to say, the local businessmen, bankers, innkeepers, and bartenders were only too happy to entertain all the dollar-heavy sportycar racers and their crews (not to mention any Fred Average-types who might show up to spectate) so they greeted the S.C.M.A. with open arms. It was a perfect match, you know? And that's how Elkhart Lake came to host its first-ever S.C.M.A. road race in July of 1950, using about three and a half miles of country backroads just west of town and God only knows how many kegs of local Wisconsin beer. It wasn't real big or well-publicized, but everybody had a great time and so word spread and naturally the event got a lot bigger the next year. The powers that be altered the circuit so it was over six miles long and ran right through the middle of town, and once again everybody enjoyed the hell out of themselves and made plans to come back again next year. And bring their friends along, too. All of them.

And I could see why, as Tommy Edwards and me pulled up to the intersection of Wisconsin Highway 67 and Sheboygan County A and turned left, following the little overhanging painted arrow that pointed the way into the town of Elkhart Lake. It was late Thursday afternoon, and the place was already filling up with MGs and Jaguars and OSCAs and Allards and Lord-only-knows what else, most of them piled high with suitcases and duffel bags and picnic baskets, and some even had add-on chrome-tube luggage racks on the back with full-sized, ocean-going steamer trunks lashed on top. Seeing as how most of the heavy-duty sportscar activity back then was happening on either the East Coast or the West Coast, Elkhart Lake made a dead-nuts perfect middle ground for everybody to meet and hash out once and for all (or at least until next year) who had the fastest cars and quickest hotshoe drivers and best-looking girlfriends. In fact, the S.C.M.A. organized a so-called "Rallye to Elkhart Lake" from starting points all over the whole United States to bring sportscar *aficionados* from every corner of the country to the event, and it was truly amazing to see MGs and Jags and such sporting license plates from Texas and Florida and Utah and California and Washington and Maine and, well, damn near every other state in the union. It was amazing they all made it there, too.

Anyhow, Tommy and me followed County A two blocks into town, crossing the railroad tracks across from Schuler's Bar and turning left onto Lake Street, past the IGA grocery store and Gessert's Soda Shop on the right and the train station across the street where all the rich meat-packing families from Chicago and brewery families from Milwaukee used to get off for their summer vacations and get-away weekends back around the turn of the century. Why, if you squinted your eyes just right, you could almost see them --gruff, tired-looking men with walrus mustaches and watch chains and bowler hats carrying the suitcases of chatterbox wives in frilly dresses with matching parasols, while squealing, laughing little boys in short pants chased frantic circles around them-- and no question the town of Elkhart Lake hadn't changed an awful lot since then. It was still a quiet, peaceful, handsome, and down-home friendly place to go to get away from it all. Or at least it was until the racers got there....

I liked the look of it right away.

A couple blocks down from the train station, Lake Street curved hard left to run along the shoreline of about the prettiest little fishing and swimming and sailboating lake you have ever seen, and that's where Tommy waved for me to make a big U-turn and pull our Jags up to the curb smack-dab in front of the green-and-white awning that marked the main office building of Siebken's Resort Hotel. It was right next door to the Osthoff Resort Hotel and directly across the street from the entrance drive to Schwartz's Resort Hotel, and those were the places where most of the racers stayed. And it was difficult to tell exactly where one Lake Street resort ended and the next one began, since all three were made up of neat, clean-looking white clapboard buildings with rolling green lawns and matching green shutters on the windows, and so it was hard not to think of them as a sort of matched set. But you couldn't miss that there was a little friendly rivalry and neighborly competition going on between them. Schwartz's had the bigger beach and a nice, elevated front porch with shuffleboard courts and a beautiful view out over the lake, while Siebken's had that green-and-white canvas awning in front and an outdoor bandstand and rooms done up with genuine old-fashioned antiques. The Osthoff was the "official" S.C.M.A. headquarters, but a lot of the racers liked the food at Siebken's better. Not to mention that Siebken's had unquestionably the best damn racing bar I had ever seen in my life. Not that I'd been in all that many bars at the time. But it always seemed to be chock-full of racing people and racing talk and clinking glassware and occasional rolling peals of laughter, and you could feel the instant you got anywheres near the place that everybody inside was really happy to be there.

Naturally Tommy steered us over there for a quick one before we checked into our room, and sure enough it seemed like everybody we'd ever met at the races was in there, crowded around the tables and packed three-deep at the bar, drinking Milwaukee beers like Schlitz and Blatz and Pabst Blue Ribbon and swapping racing stories and speed tips and tall tales about their heroic drives up to Elkhart Lake from cities and towns all over the whole damn country. I saw Creighton Pendleton the Third and two of the Muscatelli brothers shooting the breeze over by the far door, and directly behind them was the beautiful, chestnut-haired Sally Enderle, getting ignored the way gorgeous women often do in a racing bar. So Sally had herself draped over the top of the big Wurlitzer jukebox, checking out her reflection in the mirror-finish chromework as she halfheartedly punched in "Come On A-My House" by Rosemary Clooney, "It Takes Two to Tango," "Kiss of Fire," "I Get Ideas," and "Your Cheatin' Heart," the brand new song by Hank Williams. That seemed like a pretty good reason to mosey on over to the jukebox myself and check out the music, kind of casually leaning in over Sally's shoulder like I didn't particularly recognize who she was (as if you could mistake Sally Enderle for any other female human being on the planet --especially when she was wearing a halter-type midriff top and one of her snug-fitting pairs of shorts). I've noticed that only well-built, well-toned, and evenly tanned women can wear stuff like that properly, and I must admit Sally Enderle qualified with honors on all three counts. Anyhow, there I was, leaning in over Sally's shoulder, pretending to check out the songs on the juke (and incidentally getting a pretty spectacular peek down the front of her halter top) when she all of a sudden rotated around and put the two of us nose to nose and eyeball to eyeball, so close I could smell the clean, delicate scent of her perfume and feel a little tingle of heat across my cheek every time she breathed. "Uhh, hi there," I smiled, my voice cracking just a little, "remember me?"

"Hello?" she said, looking at me like I was a closet door.

"You're Sally Enderle, aren't you?"

She gave me an almost invisible nod, and it was about then I realized I was standing there in the same damn clothes that had been lying in a laundry bag in pool of dirty water at the bottom of the silver C-type's footwell all Wednesday afternoon and evening (and that's even before I put them on and wore them all morning in the hot sun through downtown Chicago traffic and then on the road another two and a half hours up to Milwaukee and another hour-plus up to Elkhart Lake) not to mention that I hadn't had a shower or combed my hair or brushed my teeth or anything since around 10 PM the night before. Then again, here was the gorgeous, chestnut-haired Sally Enderle --standing right smack-dab in front of me!-- and there was no turning back now. "Uhh, w-well," I stammered, kind of stumbling every which way over my tongue, "don'cha remember? I'm the guy who blew up that TC in front of you at Giant's Despair."

I noticed a grim little two-watt flicker of recognition come up in her eyes. "Oh?" she said, dropping it down to a watt and a half. "So you're the one who blew his TC up at the starting line."

"Uh, not quite."

"You didn't blow it up?"

"Oh, I blew it up all right. Sky high, in fact. But it wasn't exactly, uhh, *my* MG."

"Oh?"

"Nah. It was Cal Carrington's car. You know Cal?"

You could see that Cal's name rated about twenty-five watts with Sally Enderle. "So," she wanted to know, "if it was Cal Carrington's car, why on earth were *you* driving it?"

"Well, see, Cal's sort of my, uhh, *friend,* you know? Besides, I work on it a little for him every now and then...."

"Oh, that's right," she said, looking past my left earlobe to see if there was maybe anyone else along the bar to talk to, "you're that *mechanic,* aren't you?"

"Uh, yeah. You could say...."

"Excuse me," Sally interrupted, "but I think I see somebody I know," and before I could say another word, she'd taken a quick, dainty step to the side and slipped right around me. "Bye now," she called over her shoulder without looking back, "see you again some time...."

Yeah. Sure.

Which of course left me standing there all by my lonesome in front of that big Wurlitzer jukebox, staring into the turntable display like I was looking over the edge of the Grand Canyon, my ears glowing about the same shade of red as the illuminated plexiglass panels on either side. Of course I pretended like I was going over all the songs real carefully so everybody would think that's what I really came up there for (as if anybody was even looking, you know?). Anyhow, I wound up playing a couple syrupy Nat King Cole tunes (which always seemed to get Julie in the mood) and a repeat spin of Hank Williams' "Your Cheatin' Heart," although I didn't exactly know why.

As I said, just about everybody I'd ever met or seen at the races seemed to be in the bar at Siebken's that particular late Thursday afternoon, and I even noticed my old asshole-buddy Charlie Priddle over in the corner with a couple of the other armband types, having a *very* serious discussion about the scoring procedures for the so-called "Monte Carlo Rallye to Elkhart Lake." It was already obvious that the thing hadn't been very well organized (what with whole metropolitan cities as some of the checkpoints and much of the scoring done on the honor system) and most of the teams drifting in from every point on the compass had no idea where to even turn in their score sheets. Which was okay with the Rallye Committee, since they really had no idea how to evaluate the sheets and rank the winners anyway. Fact is, the whole idea of the Monte Carlo Rallye to Elkhart Lake was to get sportycar enthusiasts from all over North America to come together in one place at one time for a few friendly drinks and a bunch of sportscar conversation. Most of them didn't expect anything more than the phony Monte Carlo Rallye license plates and smaller matching dash plaques they got for entering. But Charlie Priddle had his eye on the big, silver-plated loving cup they had for the winner, and he was doing his level best to make damn sure it wound up on his mantelpiece back home --right next to that fine first-place mug he "won" so convincingly at Giant's Despair. By God, he'd read the rules for that damn rallye, and they plain-as-day specified a substantial handicap percentage based on the age of the automobile. And now, seeing as how the scoring was unquestionably a hopeless shambles, and furthermore seeing as how he had arrived in Elkhart Lake at the wheel of unquestionably the oldest automobile entered (supposedly the same exact 1914 Stutz that Barney Oldfield used to win the Los Angeles-to-Phoenix Cactus Derby that year), there wasn't a single, solitary shred of doubt in Charlie Priddle's conniving little mind that *he* should be declared the winner --even though one of the Porsche guys from Oklahoma claimed he saw Charlie and a couple of East Coast piano movers unloading the Stutz from a flatbed trailer in Fon du Lac, no more than thirty-five miles away. Anyhow, Charlie and the other official types looked to be taking the matter very, *very* seriously. Why, you would've thought they were planning the blessed invasion of Normandy or something.

I recognized a few of the MG guys from Giant's Despair and Brynfan Tyddyn shooting the breeze and guzzling beers up along the bar, and so I leaned in and joined them for a round. They were mostly talking about how some brilliant idiot had stuffed a Ford V8-60 flathead into a TC, and moreover how the short wheelbase, narrow track, skinny tires, nose-heavy weight distribution, and little pie-plate brake drums made it something of a handful around a road circuit. "Whoever winds up driving that blasted contraption better stock up on his supply of Brave Pills," one of them advised, and the rest of the MG guys clinked their beer mugs in solemn agreement.

Even old Skippy Welcher came trolling through Siebken's bar a couple times, Milton Fitting in tow, looking desperately around for any free pair of ears that would have him. I made sure to keep the back of my head pointed towards him, and headed for the john pronto when I thought The Skipper recognized me and started muscling his way through the crowd in my direction. And who should I run into coming out of the mens' room but my old English-accented, Jaguar-driving travelling companion, Tommy Edwards. "Hey, Tommy," I said, "where've you been?"

"In there," he told me, "shaking hands with the Prime Minister." Anyhow, we'd no sooner walked up the two steps to the main bar room than some guy in a bright red polo shirt hailed us over and bought Tommy a drink. "What took you guys so damn long to get here?" he asked. "Why, we've damn near used up all the booze in this place without you."

"Took us three bloody hours to get through that blasted hometown of yours," Tommy grumbled as the bartender poured him a gin and tonic, "and let me assure you those new C-types don't much fancy city traffic."

"I expect not," the guy grinned, "but are they *fast?*"

"We'll find out later this weekend, won't we?" Tommy grinned right back. "Buddy," he said to me, "I want you to meet Eddie Dearborn, the fastest damn Cad-Allard driver in the whole bloody country," he shot me a wink, "or that's what he *tells* people, anyway...."

"At least that's what I tell people when *you're* not around, you stinking, no-good, crumpet-eating piece of dogmeat. Say, is this kid old enough to drink?"

"Sure he is. But I'm not quite so sure about *you....*"

"Hell, I was *born* old enough to drink. Everybody knows that. *HEY, DOUG!"* the guy in the polo shirt yelled down the bar, *"GET US ANOTHER ONE!"* And in no time at all I had a tall, frosty mug of beer in front of me --the first of many I would enjoy over the years at Siebken's Bar.

"So," Tommy asked, "who figures to be quick here?"

"Well, there's you and there's me, of course. But that goes without saying, doesn't it?"

"Right," Tommy agreed, clicking their glasses together. "Why, perhaps we ought to just flip a coin for it right now and save everybody a lot of needless wear and tear on the motorcars."

"Good idea, Edwards. Brilliant, in fact. Did you think that up all by yourself?"

"No, I most likely had some help."

"Figures. Anyhow, I don't think it'll work."

"Oh? And why not?"

"Don't think we'll be able to talk Cunningham into it. He brought the whole blasted LeMans team with him this time. Two roadsters and a coupe. And just wait till you take a gander under the damn hoods...."

"Oh? What're they running?"

"I'm not gonna tell you. I mean, why spoil the surprise? You'll see for yourself soon enough. But he's got Johnny Fitch in one of the roadsters and Phil Walters in the coupe, and Briggs is gonna handle the other car himself."

"Fitch won up here last year, didn't he?"

"Sure as hell did. Going away."

"And what happened to you?"

"Me? I broke a wheel bearing. You know that."

"Well, that's not exactly the way *I* heard the story," Tommy grinned, slipping me a wink.

"Well, you've obviously been misinformed, Edwards. But then, we've all come to expect that sort of thing from you. *--HEY, DOUG! THREE MORE DOWN HERE!--* Why, I'm constantly amazed that we won the damn war with people like you as our allies. Probably would've made out a hell of a lot better with the damn Germans...."

"No doubt," Tommy agreed, giving me a quick little elbow-nudge in the ribs.

"Damn lucky, that's what we were. Just damn lucky."

"I'm sure. But no matter how you try to change the subject, Mr. Eddie Dearborn, my friend Buddy and I are not leaving this spot until we hear all about last year's race and the famous Eddie Dearborn wheel bearing failure."

"Aw, it just broke. Why, you can ask *any*body."

"I have asked," Tommy grinned, "and they all claim you ran clear off the bloody road and collected yourself a haybale."

"Of course I did!" Eddie howled, banging his palm on the bar, *"how'dja think I broke the damn wheel bearing??!!"*

Needless to say we got a pretty good rise off that, and as I recall, Tommy Edwards and me never exactly got around to getting cleaned up or going out to dinner that particular evening. We just stayed there at Siebken's, drinking beer and wolfing down a couple fat roast beef sandwiches right there at the bar. They were served on thick slices of black bread with lettuce and tomato and horseradish mustard and about a quarter-pound slab of the excellent local Wisconsin Swiss cheese on top, and did they ever taste great after our long day on the road. Besides the time I spent chewing that sandwich, I don't think I stopped laughing except to breathe or take another swallow of beer until we left Siebken's bar some five hours later to see about a room.

I reckon it must've been eleven or so, and while Tommy went up into the office to check us in, I took myself a little unsteady stroll down the sidewalk to get our stuff out of the two Jaguars. There were sportscars of every type imaginable parked nose-to-tail up and down both sides of the street, but even so the two C-types had collected themselves a sizable crowd. Not hard to fathom, since they were sitting right under a streetlamp and looked low and mean and evil as a pair of oiled-down panthers glistening there in the half-light. As anybody who knows anything about sportscars can tell you, there's a very special feeling when you see a bunch of gawkers gathered around some really exotic car --talking in hushed tones and peering in under the wheelwells and staring at the dashboard over the red-tipped glow of cigarettes-- and you're lucky enough to be that special, one-of-a-kind guy who waltzes right on through the crowd, pops the door, and hauls his own personal luggage out of footwell on the passenger side. Even if that "luggage" is just a soggy old laundry bag. "Say," one of the cigarette glows asks, "this is one of those new Jag competition jobs, isn't it?"

"Yup."

"Boy, I never seen one before."

"Nobody has," I said like it didn't mean anything at all to me. "These are the only two in the country."

"Wow! Are you one of the drivers?"

"Well, aah, *sort* of. I mean, I drove it *here....* "

"But are you gonna *race* it?"

"Nah," I told him, pretending like it didn't makc any difference (but knowing that it made all the damn difference in the world), "Tommy Edwards is driving the green one for, uhh, *our* shop, and some West Coast hotshoe is gonna be in this one."

"Oh? Y'know who he is?"

"I dunno. He drives for some big, important wine guy from California. They're taking the silver car back there after the races are over. Gonna race it out there in California."

"That's gotta be Ernesto Julio."

"Yeah. That's him."

"Then the driver must be Phil Hill."

"Who?" I said, like I'd never even heard of him (although the name sounded awful familiar, and I was sure I'd heard it mentioned once or twice before).

"I saw Phil Hill drive out at Torrey Pines back in July. Lapped the whole blessed field in a two-point-six Ferrari. Believe me, Tommy Edwards' gonna have his hands full with that guy."

"Oh, *really,* " I said down my nose. I mean, this West Coast jerk had obviously never seen Tommy Edwards *drive*. But there wasn't much else to say --I mean, the gauntlet was down, you know?-- so I gathered up our stuff out of the two C-types and headed up the steps to the office. On the way, who should I notice huddled in the shadows by the side entrance to the bar but my old buddy Creighton Pendleton the Third, standing real close and talking in whispers with one of the young hometown cocktail waitresses I'd seen serving drinks and food inside. Or at least that's who I thought she was, but I couldn't really be sure on account of it was so dark and everything. But no question it was definitely *not* Sally Enderle. At least, not unless she'd suddenly grown a couple bra-cup sizes and sprouted a blond ponytail. I even glanced into the bar to make doubly sure, and there was Sally Enderle over by the jukebox again, smiling and laughing and knocking back shots of peppermint schnapps with a bunch of prep-school types as if she didn't care much one way or the other where the hell Creighton Pendleton might be. Or maybe she just didn't know....

Made you wonder what the hell Creighton Pendleton could be thinking, you know? I mean, to have a sleek, spirited, high-class girl like Sally Enderle on a string and then take a chance fooling around with some underage local nobody, well, it just didn't make any sense to me. Especially seeing as how Sally was right there on the other side of the tavern wall, no more than ten feet away. Then again, maybe old Creighton The Third was trying to make some kind of point with her. Or maybe he was just one of those Compulsive Chaser types who simply can't resist going after a little fresh meat whenever and wherever they come across it --just so they can get a quick taste of something new and rack up another kill. I always thought I wanted to be one of those guys myself (I mean, doesn't everybody?) but now, all of a sudden, I wasn't so damn sure anymore.

After that I went looking for Tommy again, and finally caught up with him in yet another bar, a quiet little wood-paneled nook they had hidden down under the stairs in Siebken's main office building, right behind the restaurant. It was more of a brandy-snifter kind of place than the big, noisy tavern across the yard, and that's exactly what Tommy was sharing with this incredibly tan older guy who had flowing, silver-white hair and the kind of billowy, wide-open white silk shirt you'd expect to see Errol Flynn wearing in one of those Hollywood pirate movies. I'd never seen a male person dressed like that except maybe once at a Halloween costume party, so I knew right away this guy had to be from California. I mean, nobody from Jersey dresses like that. At least not in public. "Hey, sport," Tommy called over, "pull up a bit of rail and have a nightcap with us."

I stepped up to the end of the bar and Tommy's elegant-looking friend lit himself a long, pencil-thin black cigar and nodded for the bartender to pour me a brandy. He was about fifty or so, and I must admit he looked pretty damn tough and leathery in spite of the longish hair and puffy silk pirate shirt. But he didn't seem to talk much. In fact, he hardly said anything at all. "So," Tommy wanted to know, "how are things out by the cars?"

"Aw, some wiseass said you were gonna have your hands full with that California Hotshoe in the other Jag."

"Oh *really?*" Tommy said, arching his eyebrows up like Eddie Cantor, "and did he mention who the blazes this fellow might be?"

"I dunno. Some guy named Hill, I think."

"Hmmm. I don't suppose that would be Phil Hill, would it?"

"Yeah. I think that's him."

"I see," he said, and turned back to the guy in the white silk shirt, "you ever heard of him?"

The guy with the skinny black cigar shook his head and even added an elaborate, New York-style shrug. But you could tell he was fighting real hard not to laugh.

"Well," I continued, wondering what the hell was so damn funny, "the guy outside said this Hill character's won a bunch of races out on the West Coast. Says he lapped the field at some-place called Torrey Pines back in July."

"Do tell," Tommy said like it didn't mean anything, and the guy in the pirate shirt nodded.

I drained the last of my brandy and the guy next to Tommy pointed for the bartender to bring us all another one. "So," I asked Tommy, "you ever run against him?"

"No," Tommy said evenly, "not wheel-to-wheel, anyway. But I understand the bloke's been building himself quite a reputation out west." He turned to the guy with the silver hair again. "You know anything about this Hill fellow?"

The pirate shirt raised itself up in another New York shrug.

"Ahh, don't worry about it," I told him, "Tommy'll show 'em *all* the quick way 'round come Sunday. Won'cha, Tommy?"

"Well, I'll certainly give it my best," he allowed through a narrow grin, "and I hope that will be sufficient."

The guy with the pirate shirt couldn't contain himself any longer and burst out laughing like the lid blowing off a pressure cooker. I saw Tommy was laughing right along with him, and somehow I knew I was the butt of the joke, even though I had no idea what it could possibly be about.

"Buddy," Tommy grinned, clapping his hand on my shoulder, "I'd like you to meet the chap whose car you've been abusing so thoughtlessly for the past three days." He stepped back so I was face to face with the silver-haired guy with the thin black cigar. "Buddy," Tommy said with a grand sort of flourish, "shake hands with Ernesto Julio."

The guy stuck out a tanned, muscular hand with two fat gold rings on the last finger. "So," he growled in a deep, threatening voice, "Tommy says you beat the living crap outta my car on the way up here...."

"N-No sir," I stammered, "I never did. Not even once. I took it real nice and easy the whole way."

"Bullshit! You kept up with this guy, didn't you?"

"Uhh, sure I did. Of course. I just followed along behind Tommy and did whatever he did the whole way here."

"Then I *know* you beat the shit out of that car! Why, I bet you wound it clear past the goddam redline every goddam chance you got!"

"No sir, Mr. Julio, I never did. Not even once."

He leaned in so our noses were almost touching. "Oh, yeah?" he snarled. "Not even *once??"*

I looked down at the empty brandy snifter in my hand and kind of shuffled my feet around a few times on the floor. "Well," I admitted, "maybe just once or twice...."

"GOOD!" Ernesto Julio bellowed, slapping me on the back, "that's exactly what the damn things are for! Right, Tommy?"

"Right!" Tommy agreed, tossing off the last of his brandy.

Ernesto Julio insisted on buying us one last round and spent the entire time beating me up about how bad I'd messed up his damn car --boy, did he ever know how to put the needle in!-- and afterwards Tommy and me staggered off to bed. And I do mean staggered. Along the way, I asked if he really thought he'd have any trouble with that Phil Hill guy from California. "Well, he's won quite a few races now, hasn't he?" Tommy acknowledged with steely little edge to his voice. "Then again," he added through a crocodile grin, "we didn't come all this bloody way to run second, now did we?"

"Hell *NO!"* I yelped, leaping up the stairs three at a time and damn near falling through the railing, "we came here to beat the living crap out of *everybody!"*

And that's what it's usually like the night before a big race weekend begins. You're always bubbling over with excitement and enthusiasm (not to mention more than your rightful share of hooch) and you're always thinking deep inside that this time, this time it's gonna be *your* weekend. Maybe not your weekend to *win* (I mean, there are only so many cars with a realistic chance of winning any particular race, and everybody except terminal lamebrains like Skippy Welcher knows it) but maybe your weekend to do a little better than you ever have before. Your weekend to drive faster and smoother and cooler under pressure than you ever have before. Your car's weekend to run a little stronger and sweeter and longer than it ever has before. Both your weekend to perhaps creep up slowly-but-surely from behind and *pass* that rat-bastard sonofabitch you've been chasing all season long. And maybe even the faster-yet rat bastard sonofabitch ahead of him! Every racer sleeps soundly on Thursday night, because on Thursday night everybody's a winner in their dreams. And they stay that way until the rest of the weekend proves them wrong....

I awoke Friday morning to the dull, scratchy thump of haybales being unloaded from a flatbed truck and piled around a lamp post just outside my window, and the sound shuffled and scratched and skittered around inside my head like a three-pound rat trying to claw its way out of a bowling ball. No question it was your typical race-weekend Friday morning, and so naturally my head hurt something awful and my body felt like several huge lumps of putty held together with rusty cabinet hinges. I pulled myself unsteadily out of bed and felt my way along the wall towards the john to get myself one of Butch Bohunk's infamous Morning After Cocktails (two Bayer aspirin with a Bromo Seltzer chaser) and I was fortunate to find the necessary ingredients right there on the sink. Obviously somebody was looking out for me. Then I crawled back to bed, eased myself down into the soft, squishy featherbed mattress, covered myself with the puffy down comforter, and waited for the medicine to do its work.

Fact is, I was surprised I didn't feel a hell of a lot worse. After all, we'd damn near closed the bar the night before (while putting a sizable dent in Siebken's brandy supply) and all that after a long, hot day's drive up from Chicago and not much in the way of dinner. But at least Tommy made me take a quick shower before I flopped into bed, and so for a change I didn't wake up feeling like I'd been rolled in a mixture of oatmeal and road salt the night before.

I'd also slept better than I could ever remember, and it wasn't just the brandy. There was something about the clean, cool, fresh country air wafting in off the lake and the gently oscillating rotational hum of the old brass ceiling fan that made that little room at Siebken's the absolute perfect place for summertime sleeping. And the smell of sweet, freshly baked blueberry muffins and hotcakes on the griddle made it the perfect place to wake up in the morning, too. Even with a hangover.

I saw that Tommy was already up and gone, and as I looked around, I couldn't help but notice what a bright, cheery sort of place this was. Morning sunlight was streaming in softly through gauzy, flower-print curtains, and there were old fashioned Irish lace doilies on the chairbacks, dresser, and bedstand. The wallpaper matched up perfectly with the curtains and the pillow covers on the bed, and there were old-time paintings of gardens and corner parks and Gibson girls with parasols on the walls. Fact is, it seemed more like a guest room in somebody's house than a hotel room, and I kept thinking that it was the exact kind of room I wanted to share with Julie Finzio some day. And someday soon, if possible.

I finally rolled out and headed downstairs a little before eleven, still feeling a tad rocky but not nearly so bad as that ugly morning I'd endured at Brynfan Tyddyn. A quick pants-check revealed I still had most of that crumpled-up twenty Tommy tossed me at the entrance to the New Jersey Turnpike four days before. Hell, he hadn't let me pay for so much as a hamburger or a glass of beer or even a damn stick of gum since we'd left Westbridge. Quite a change from a race weekend with Barry Spline! So I went into the dining room and ordered myself a man-sized plate of scrambled eggs, toast, hash browns, and a side of corned beef hash and drank two tall glasses of orange juice and about a half gallon of coffee to clear my head and settle my stomach a little. It was a big, airy, happy-looking room with windows opened up all around like a sun porch, and you couldn't miss the smell of homemade cakes and fresh-baked bread drifting in from Siebken's little basement-level bakery room across the way. No question it was going to be a gorgeous day, what with bright sun filtering down through tree branches that were just starting to get their first tinges of autumn color and a nice, soft breeze blowing in off the lake. I saw about a dozen other racing people in the dining room --some on breakfast, some already into lunch-- and I couldn't believe how quiet and relaxed it felt to be there. But out on the street, you could hear voices and the bustle of activity as S.C.M.A. workers and a bunch of local volunteers continued putting up haybales and lengths of snow fencing to contain the racecars on one side and the expected crowd of spectators on the other. It looked like there was going to be a hell of a turnout, since an endless caravan of fans and rubberneckers were already flooding up Highway 67 from Plymouth. Why, it wasn't even noon on Friday, and already they had more people milling around town than they'd had all weekend the year before. There was just no way to stop it....

After breakfast I took a little stroll up Lake Street towards the train station and Schuler's Tavern, and I swear you could hardly move what with all the cars and people and tootling horns and all-purpose confusion going on. The State Police sent a couple patrol cars over to help out the local cops, but those guys looked as baffled as everybody else. I mean, there was really no place to *send* anybody, you know? So a couple local Chamber-of-Commerce types made a quick deal with some nearby farmers to turn their fields into parking lots, and by mid-afternoon, nobody except *bona fide* S.C.M.A. racers and rallyists were getting into town except on foot. But they kept on coming anyway, and you couldn't miss the prickly tingle of excitement and anticipation that gathers on a big crowd, like static on a thick wool blanket.

From the curbside in front of the train station, you could see how the Elkhart Lake "race circuit" came rolling into town on County J and sweeping right around Schuler's Tavern and headed right through town on Lake Street, past the barber shop and the IGA store and the start/finish line right in front of Gessert's soda shop. Then it continued on down a few blocks underneath the trees and lamp posts until it made a hard, second-gear left between the entrances to Siebken's and Schwartz's and swept past the front lawn of the Osthoff resort. After that came a long, gradual, dropping-away righthand curve along the shoreline. I decided to take a little hike down that way and maybe see where the circuit went after that. I mean, both the C-types were gone someplace, and there wasn't much else to do except check out the racetrack or go into the bar again, and I figured that was about the last thing I needed at the time.

A couple random MGs and Jags and such passed me as I walked along the edge of the pavement, and it was obvious these guys were out trying to learn the course a little while dodging spectators and other cars and all the armband people piling up haybales and stringing up snow fencing and hanging oil company banners (not to mention the local townfolks who were busily setting up lemonade stands and bratwurst grills and nickel-a-cup beer tappers in their front yards). It was kind of neat to walk along there with all that feverish pre-race activity going on, and yet be able to turn my head just an inch or two and be looking out at sailboats gliding effortlessly across the water and listening to the putt-putt echo of a little fishing boat trolling along the edge of a weedbed across the way. The noonday sun made Elkhart Lake shimmer and glisten like a hammered silver platter, and no question this was one hell of a beautiful location for a sportycar road race. No two ways about it.

Then I heard a flesh-shredding howl coming up behind me, and next thing I knew Creighton Pendleton's 4.1 Ferrari whipped past with bare inches to spare, doing maybe sixty-five or seventy miles an hour. Needless to say, that about blew me right out of my shoes, and I shook my fist at the back of that Ferrari as it wailed out of sight. I saw Sally Enderle's chestnut hair whipping in the wind in the passenger seat next to him, and she even flipped me a little backhand wave as they disappeared around to the right past Fireman's Park. Or maybe it wasn't a wave after all. Anyhow, I'm sure they were both laughing like hell....

I followed the road down another couple hundred yards, curving gently and endlessly to the right past the Fireman's Park public beach (where all the locals without fancy beachfront property went to enjoy the lake) and while I was busily squinting my eyes to get a better look at the many promising young lady dairy-farmer types sunning themselves on the beach, who should pull silently up behind me but a familiar black MG TD with none other than Cal Carrington and Carson Flegley in the cockpit. Cal was at the wheel, so it should come as no surprise that he crept right up behind me and then let fly with the air horns (Carson'd bought himself a set like the ones on Big Ed's XK120) and the two of them had to about peel me out of the trees afterwards.

"How y'doin', Buddy?" Cal said through a wicked smile.

"I'll be fine after I take a couple of your teeth out."

"Aw, c'mon. We were just having a little fun."

"Yeah, just a little fun," Carson added, like some kind of pasty-faced parrot.

Fact is, Carson looked even a bit pastier-faced than normal, and you couldn't miss how he had himself rigidly wedged into the passenger seat with his arms pressed forward for all he was worth against the dashboard cowling. Obviously Cal had been showing him around the circuit, and the experience hadn't done much at all for Carson's complexion. "Hey, asshole," Cal grinned, "you lookin' for lost parts or something?"

"Nah. Just thought I'd take myself a little walk after breakfast and see what's going on around here."

"Breakfast? Hell, it's past noon, Buddy. And on a weekday, no less. Why, I always thought you were a damn blue-collar working stiff."

"Didn't you hear? A rich uncle of mine died and left me his whole blessed estate."

"You mean *you* have inherited the world-famous Palumbo family fortune?"

"That's the one."

"Gee whiz, Buddy," Carson asked, serious as could be, "what're y'gonna *do* with it?"

"Well," I said, looking just as serious right back at him, "I reckon I spent about half of it in the bar last night...."

"Yeah," Cal cackled, "and he's gonna buy himself another beer with the other half tonight!"

We got a pretty good laugh off that. Even Carson Flegley. Once he got the gist of it, anyway.

"So," Cal wanted to know, "who you with this time?"

"Tommy Edwards," I explained. "We brought those two C-type Jaguar one-twenties out from Westbridge."

"You rat-bastard son-of-a-bitch! You mean you actually got to *drive* one of them?"

"Sure did," I nodded, modestly digging my toe in the grass. "Tommy and me took off from New York on Tuesday. Just the two of us and those Jaguars. And believe me, those things are *fast!* Why, we were hardly ever under The Ton from one end of Pennsylvania to the other."

"You lucky bastard," Cal growled. "Why, I'd give my left nut to drive one of those things. My right one, too, come to think of it."

"Hey," I shrugged, "it's all part of the job...."

"Up yours."

"You're just jealous."

"You bet your sweet ass I am."

"M-me, too," Carson sputtered, head bobbing up and down.

"So," I asked Cal, "you got any racing plans this weekend?"

"You know me. I *always* got plans...."

"Dreams is more like it," Carson sniggered behind his hand.

"Wet dreams is more like it," I added for amplification.

"Ahh, screw you both."

Now it was my turn to laugh. "No, really," I said when I was about finished, "you got anything lined up?"

"Maybe. One of the MG guys brought a TC with a Ford V8-60 in it, and he's having trouble making it go."

"I heard about it in the bar last night."

"Yeah, that's the one. Seems it doesn't especially want to go around corners. Or slow down, for that matter. But I think the guy is maybe just a little frightened of it. Maybe even more than a little."

"It's scaring the living crap out of him!" Carson nodded enthusiastically.

"Anyhow," Cal continued, "a couple of the MG guys from Giant's Despair recommended he ought to let me give her a try. Just to see if I can do any better."

"I'm sure you would."

"So am I."

Like I explained before, Cal Carrington didn't have any noticeable deficiencies in the balls or confidence departments.

"So," Cal asked, "you planning to walk your way around the whole damn circuit?"

"Can't say as I've really thought about it."

"Well, don't. Hell, it's six-and-a-half miles, for gosh sakes! Your dogs'll be dead tired before you get halfway around."

"If I make it that far."

"Why don'cha just hop in with Carson and me? We can all take a couple laps together. C'mon...."

I looked at the big Cheshire Cat grin spread across Cal's face and the chalky color on Carson's cheeks and I can't really say it sounded like such a great idea. Even though I trusted Cal Carrington completely when it came to racecar driving, that didn't necessarily mean I wanted to be a firsthand witness when he was showing off his stuff. Especially as the third fullsize adult human being in a two-passenger MG sportscar. "I dunno," I said hesitantly, "doesn't look like there'll be enough room in there for all three of us."

"Aw, c'mon. We'll make room. And I'll take it nice and slow. Honest I will."

"Honest?"

"Cross my heart," Cal said, crossing his heart. So I climbed in over the door and Carson did his best to make his skinny little body even skinnier and we took off. "You know what's great about this?" Cal asked.

"No. What?"

"If I slide off the road and get us both killed, we got our own undertaker on board to take care of things."

"That's a comforting thought."

"Isn't it."

"I guess that's why I like hanging out with you."

"Why's that?"

"You always think of everything ahead of time."

"Well," Cal shrugged as he wound the MG out in second, "somebody's gotta look after things...."

Thanks to all the sportycar types out "learning the circuit" plus normal local traffic and the dozens of armband people out piling up haybales, Cal could never really get up a good head of steam in Carson's MG. And I must admit I was thankful for that. But it was a beautiful bunch of roads anyway, and I could only imagine what they might be like under flat-out, balls-to-the-wall racing conditions, when you could use both lanes to widen and smooth out the curves and corners (and not have to back off and jab the brakes because you were about to eat the two-story back end of a hay wagon). From where they picked me up in front of Fireman's Park, the circuit continued to gently bend around to the right, kind of easing and then tightening again as it passed under the trees in front of the Quit-Qui-Oc golf course on the left and the entrance to Pine Point resort on the other side. They called the whole section "The Wacker Wend" after a wealthy Chicago-based racer and enthusiast named Freddy Wacker, who was one of the guys who originally flew over Elkhart in a light plane and played a huge part in bringing sportscar racing to the area in the first place back in 1950. According to Tommy

Edwards, Freddy Wacker was also one hell of a decent racecar driver, and Tommy wasn't the kind of guy to throw compliments like that around lightly.

At any rate, the road curved slightly left out of the Wacker Wend and climbed an easy hill past the entrance drive to Sharp's Cottages, and then it was hard on the brakes for a T-intersection right-hander into what I considered the neatest and prettiest part of the whole track, a diving, climbing, left-right-right corkscrew combination through Hammil's Hollow, followed by a mile-plus straightaway run past the old country schoolhouse, where even little tiddler cars could get up a mighty impressive head of steam. There was a downslope at the end that got the cars going even faster, and then another hard 90-degree T-intersection right (called Kimberly's Korner after an avid S.C.M.A. racer named Gentleman Jim Kimberly, who was the passenger in that light plane with Freddy Wacker when the racers "discovered" Elkhart Lake --not to mention sole heir to yet another obscenely large S.C.M.A. family fortune). Anyhow, Kimberly's Korner led onto another mile-plus straightaway where the more powerful modi-fied cars could tickle an honest hundred-and-fifty miles an hour as they whizzed past the Hayssen farm and a big electrical power station. At that point, the road made itself a lazy, downhill swoop to the right followed immediately by a tighter uphill sweep to the left, and Cal allowed as how he thought a good driver in a small car could maybe take the whole section flat-out in top without lifting, but that it would be a real white-knuckler for anybody in a Jag or an Allard. "It's places like this," he explained matter-of-factly, "that separate the *real* racers from the bullshitters and ribbon clerks. You gotta be able to keep your foot in it and thread the needle --lap after lap-- and that's where you see the difference between the duffers and the Real McCoy."

"You do?"

"Absolutely. Hell, it's *easy* to be a hero in second gear. But take yourself a really *fast* bend --where you gotta stay cool and be smooth and hold the line when your hands feel like strangling up on the wheel. *That's* where you see what a driver's made of. Y'know what I mean?"

Yeah, I knew exactly what he meant. Only knowing it and actually being able to *do* it in an automobile were two entirely different things. And they always will be.

Following that hair-raising, high speed right-left combination came a little more upgrade and then another long, downhill straightaway through rolling acres of farmland. There was a little righthand kink near the bottom and another hard, T-intersection right by the entranceway to the Broughton Marsh. Ahead was yet another long straightaway, but it was pretty steep uphill so cars couldn't muster up the kind of speed they did on the other two. But maybe the toughest part of the track was coming up at the far end. You were climbing towards this peaked hilltop in top gear --totally blind!-- and all you could see on the other side was the top of this huge pine tree, sticking up like it was planted smack-dab in the middle of the highway! Cal said you had to just aim straight for that tree and keep your right foot hard on the loud pedal, but I knew I could never do it without making a quick security stab for the brakes! When you came barreling over the top, the road dropped away sharply in a sweeping right-left-right bobsled run through some forest and on into town. I flat couldn't imagine what that stretch of pavement might look like at racing speeds. Especially seeing as how there were trees and fenceposts and powerline poles and mailboxes and gravel-filled ditches and all sorts of other ugly stuff just a few scant feet off the roadway. It looked scary as hell to me, and it seemed impossible that the faster cars could *average* over a hundred miles an hour on the 6.5-mile run around Elkhart Lake.

Wow!

Chapter 25: The Politics of Speed

I met up with Tommy Edwards, Ernesto Julio, and the two C-types again later that same afternoon in the back parking lot of the Osthoff Hotel, where they were waiting in line with just about everybody else for their turn through the S.C.M.A.'s "technical inspection," which was required for all automobiles entered at every single S.C.M.A. event. That hotshoe Phil Hill guy was nowhere to be seen, but Ernesto had his mechanic along with him to push the car and open up the hood and stuff so he wouldn't get one of his all-white pirate shirts dirty. Not that he was a sissy or anything, but just somebody with a lot of style who understood that nothing looks worse on an all-white getup than a big, black grease smear or a palm-smudge of gritty dust off an exhaust pipe. The mechanic was a smooth-cheeked young Californian named Chuck Day, who wore his hair in a short blond crewcut, chewed big wads of bubble gum, and stood in sort of a perpetual concave slouch all the time. He didn't say too much, and I wasn't real impressed when I heard he was one of those West Coast Hot Rodder types who run hopped-up old Fords and stuff on the dry lakes out in the California deserts. I mean, what was the point in *that?* Especially compared to racing Ferraris and Jaguars around corners and all through the night at exotic places over in Europe. But Tommy seemed to get on with him real well, and I began to understand when I found out that he was also Ernesto Julio's personal airplane mechanic. I couldn't believe it, you know? I mean, this guy didn't look a day over seventeen! But he was, and apparently he'd even done a tour over in Korea, taking care of Sabre jets for Uncle Sam. No question you had to be impressed with stuff like that.

Anyhow, we got to know each other pretty well while we were waiting there in line while a few white-clad armband types crawled over, under, and around each and every car like it was the first damn Jag 120 or MG TC they'd ever seen in their lives. Not that what they were doing wasn't important, you know, since they were checking stuff like tire wear and spoke tension on wire wheels and making sure nobody had any serious oil leaks underneath the car or loose parts that might inadvertently fall off and wind up squarely in the lap of the next poor fish to happen by. In other words, the tech crew was just going over stuff that any self-respecting wrench would've checked and double-checked himself before ever rolling a racecar out of his home garage. But I'd learned already that you could never take that sort of thing for granted. I mean, I'd worked on Cal's ratty old TC, you know?

The S.C.M.A. tech crew was also making sure that every single car had a set of seatbelts on the driver's side, and that those belts were furthermore absolutely, positively anchored to the frame rails. Tommy Edwards thought technical inspection was more or less a bunch of bullshit --I mean, he figured it was *your* bloody responsibility to make sure your machine was raceworthy-- and he especially didn't like the part about the seatbelts. "If I'm about to go tumbling ass-over-teakettle down the bloody road, the last thing I need is a ton-plus chunk of iron strapped to my backside." A lot of drivers felt the same way Tommy did back then --that you were probably better off getting thrown out of the car in an accident and taking your chances on your own-- and many never bothered to fasten up their seatbelts when they got in to drive, even though the S.C.M.A. regulations were pretty specific about requiring it. In fact, one well-to-do and apparently fearless young fellow from Kansas City gained quite a reputation for bailing out of out-of-control racecars just moments before they hurtled into assorted trackside barriers. His name was Masten Gregory, and he somehow managed to walk away from every single accident! He even went on to make a sort of professional career out of it over in Europe.

Anyhow, the S.C.M.A. tech people also checked out your driver's gear --making sure you had a proper helmet and goggles and leather-palmed driving gloves and such-- and finished up with a ritual dipping of all driving suits in a big washtub filled with a special borax solution that made them all splotchy but supposedly rendered them flameproof. Or at least more flameproof than they were beforehand. As you can imagine, there was a lot of cheap, grisly humor about fiery crashes and impromptu spectator barbecues around the ceremonial S.C.M.A. borax tub.

But tech was going exceptionally slowly at Elkhart Lake on account of we had the standard-issue S.C.M.A. Major Flap About Something going on to gum up the proceedings. In fact, we had several of them (which was hardly surprising, since this

was *the* big East-West S.C.M.A. shootout, which naturally meant
that we had Charlie Priddle types from all over the whole damn
country gathered together to make mountains out of every available molehill and set any lurking Straw Men on fire). The first
major controversy was about the newly required Magnafluxing
Certificates. Now Magnafluxing is a testing procedure used by
engineers and machinists in the aircraft industry and the like to
find cracks and/or flaws in ferrous metal parts, including cracks
and/or flaws that may not be visible to the human eye. Anyhow,
some well-meaning but misguided people on the S.C.M.A.
competition committee decided it would be a grand idea for all
the hubs and spindles and steering knuckles and such that make
up every racecar's suspension to be Magnafluxed on a regular
basis. Just to make sure there weren't any hidden cracks that
might cause a wheel assembly to suddenly part company with the
car (like the one on Cal Carrington's ratshit TC did at Bridgehampton). Now this was actually a pretty good idea, but it didn't
exactly take into account that you had to dismantle everything
and hot-tank the parts all squeaky clean before you could send
them out for Magnafluxing. Not to mention that you had to wait
a few days (or sometimes even longer) before you got them back.
Plus you still had to reassemble everything and run fluid back
through the brakes and re-set the alignment and whatnot before
you were done with the project. Which was no problem for the
big-buck guys with lots of spare cars to drive and a few paid
mechanics to help get the work done. But Magnafluxing amounted to something of a problem for the rank-and-file S.C.M.A.
racers who used their Jags and Porsches and MGs and such for
everyday transportation. Which made you wonder why in hell the
S.C.M.A. competition committee suddenly decided to *require*
suspension component Magnafluxing certificates for every single
racecar entered at Elkhart Lake that year. They spelled it out
right there in the supplementary regulations listed on the back of
the entry forms. Problem was, a good two-thirds of the cars
showed up without the necessary paperwork.

So now what do you do?

Should you send the people home who don't have their
proper Magnafluxing certificate? Even when "home" may well be
San Luis Obispo or Montreal or Asheville or Lake Charles,
Louisiana? Or do you simply smile and wink and look the other

way when the same exact set of Magnafluxing papers begins to magically reappear again and again with eight or nine or ten different MGs. And what about all the bullshit stories from drivers who *swear* they left their certificates back home in the bureau drawer --even when it's obvious their cars have never been apart since the day they left the damn factory? Or do you (as Charlie Priddle strongly favored) come down on every single one of them like the Wrath Of God, just so's they'd learn their lesson once and for all and never dare do it ever again. And Charlie had a surprising amount of support from some of the guys who *had* their certificates (like that asshole Skippy Welcher, natch) who thought anybody without proper paperwork ought to be barred from racing and sent home. Or maybe just to bed without supper.

Fortunately we managed to squeak the C-types through easily on account of they were brand new and awesome and everybody wanted to see them run. So when Tommy explained as how "Jaguar always Magnafluxes *everything* on their racecars. Even the bloody wood rims on the steering wheels," the tech people just nodded and clucked their tongues in agreement and signed off our tech sheets and gave us our sticker. But it was a lot tougher for some of the other guys, and by the time hard-liners like Charlie Priddle relented and reluctantly agreed to let everybody run (just this *once,* you understand) they'd made sure to change their minds and reverse directions enough times to piss off everybody in the paddock. At least once. Then again, that's what you have to do now and again to earn your fair share of the limelight. Anyhow, it was a fine (and typical) example of the kind of mess you get when a big college fraternity starts thinking like it's a damn state government.

Now, please don't get me wrong about race officials. I mean, there wouldn't even *be* any damn races without all the hundreds of volunteer workers who put up the haybales and fill in the forms at registration and slave over lap-charts in timing and scoring and stand out on the corners with flags all day long no matter if it's broiling sun or torrents of rain or so blessed cold their assholes freeze shut. Why, those folks amount to the very muscle and backbone of the sport. And most all of them do it simply because they flat love the sport --the cars, the competition, the people-- and want to be a part of it. Remember, they're volunteers and do it all for *nothing*.

But then you've got the Charlie Priddle types, who most usually can't drive a lick and are just about boiling over with envy and hunger and insolent contempt for the people who actually can. I don't know why people like that are so attracted to the sport, but there always seem to be a few lurking in the shadows at every racing event I've ever attended. And they usually wind up with a lot of power, too, because they're willing to put in more time and effort and energy than anybody else in return for that power. I mean, you can't get that kind of commitment out of any of the drivers or crews, because they're always too damn busy fussing around with their own personal racecars. So guys like Charlie Priddle tend to weasel their way to the top in clubs like the S.C.M.A. Sure, they don't get a red cent for all their efforts or the countless hours they spend organizing and presiding over race events. But they get paid off in a different sort of coin --seeing real race drivers *crawl....*

In any case, no sooner had the Great Magnafluxing Certificate Debate reached an uneasy resolution (in spite of the tireless efforts of guys like Charlie Priddle and Skippy Welcher, who appeared ready and willing to drone on about it all weekend) than we had yet another Major Flap about scheduling. See, the official weekend schedule (which was of course listed in the official program, and had of course been printed already --at *great* expense-- by the official S.C.M.A. committee in charge) called for a hundred-mile race for smallbore cars on Saturday afternoon (the Kimberly Cup, open to both novice and senior license holders) and two races for bigbore cars on Sunday. The first was another hundred-miler (97.5, actually) called The Sheldon Cup, which was again for both novice and senior license holders and limited to cars between 1950cc and 4 litres, and the big 200-mile Sunday afternoon feature was for senior license holders only and any cars over 1950cc that wished to compete. Naturally there were a lot of guys who wanted to run both events (like fr'instance Tommy Edwards and that Phil Hill guy who drove for Ernesto Julio) and they suggested very politely that maybe the organizers could switch the Sheldon Cup to Saturday, run the smallbore heat Sunday morning, and leave the feature where it was. It made a lot of sense, since that meant the Saturday spectators would get to see some of the bigger, faster, noisier cars, the smallbore guys would get to appear in front of the bigger crowd on Sunday, and both the drivers and crews of some of the Jags and such would get to rest up overnight and have a chance to give the cars a decent once-over instead of running back-to-back races on Sunday. This of course made too damn much sense for the organizing committee to accept without a monumental argument, and it was only after extensive lobbying, taking of sides, countless little meetings inside the hotel, and even a few strongly worded petitions circulating around the paddock that they finally gave in and agreed to change the schedule.

"Makes it clear why so bloody many of us drink, doesn't it?" Tommy laughed as he headed off to the bar with Ernesto Julio to celebrate their victory. "Look after the car then, will you sport?" Tommy called back over his shoulder.

"Sure thing."

"And pop by for a quick one yourself when everything's squared away."

"You know I will."

"Knew I could count on you. Especially whenever there's a stein or two of cold beer involved."

He'd really gotten to know me pretty well.

That left Chuck Day and me standing there with the two C-types, and I was just folding Tommy's helmet and driving suit up into the passenger seat when this big Fruehauf semi-trailer with Florida plates on the back wheeled itself into the Osthoff parking lot. It was painted stark refrigerator white with just tasteful little waving checkered-flag logos on the doors. Underneath, the name "CUNNINGHAM" was spelled out in simple, understated block letters. The big rig lumbered slowly around to the back of the lot, and you could see that everybody in the tech line had stopped whatever they were doing so they could stare at it, slack-jawed, like it was a live brontosaurus out for a stroll. In fact, it got so quiet that the only sound was the faint, distant putt-putt echo of that fishing boat trolling around the weedbeds on the other side of the lake. Then the big semi eased to a halt with a shuddering sigh off the air brakes, and all of a sudden everybody was talking in agitated whispers and rushing over to get their first glimpse of the fabulous Cunningham sportscars, just returned from their campaign at the 24 Hours of Le Mans and the 12 Hours of Rheims over in France. They were the only American-built sportscars competing against the factory teams from Ferrari and Jaguar and Allard and the rest over in Europe, and although they hadn't actually won anything yet, they'd surely done a lot more than just show the flag. In fact, there was no question that they could run head-to-head with the best of them. Most of the resident *aficionados* at Elkhart Lake figured the Cunninghams to be the only American cars worthy to be called "sportscars." And most likely they were dead-on accurate. Why, I couldn't believe it when the doors on that big white trailer swung open and a passle of crewmen in neat white Cunningham coveralls unloaded the cars. There were two mean-looking, broad-shouldered C4R roadsters and an incredibly evil C4RK coupe. All three were painted up in the international American racing colors (a creamy refrigerator white with wide blue racing stripes down the middle) and they had bulging fenders and aggressive, mouth-breathing grille openings and finned, cast-alloy knockoff wheels that looked modern as a flying saucer. They were somewhere about halfway between the anvil-heavy bulk of an Allard and the sleek, low-slung grace of our Jaguar C-types, and had the wide, squatted-down sort of stance you might expect from an All-American fullback. And when a mechanic fired one up, you couldn't miss the deep, guttural bass rumble of a big-inch Detroit V8. No question that was the best thing about those cars: they looked and felt and sounded 100 percent American.

Chuck Day and me wandered over for a closer look, and by God you had to be impressed with what a nice, sanitary job they'd done on those cars. Then they popped the hood on one of them, and my eyes just about popped out on stalks. Stuffed underneath was the biggest, baddest Vee-8 ever to roar off a production line in Detroit: a Chrysler FirePower, the undisputed King Kong of American engines back in 1952. The 331 cubic-inch Chrysler FirePower was brand new in '51, and most gas station pump jockeys figured it was about the most powerful American V8 ever. That's because it had huge valves and hemispherical combustion chambers --like a Jaguar, you know?-- so it naturally breathed a lot better than your average, garden-variety Detroit V8. But it was a *BIG* sucker, what with huge chrome valve covers and cylinder heads about the size and weight of solid granite tombstones. And the particular Chrysler FirePower V8s underneath the bulged-out hoods of those Cunningham C4Rs had all the latest go-faster equipment, including special manifolds with four individual Zenith carburetors and special tubular-steel exhaust plumbing and bright blue Scintilla Vertex magnetos sticking up off the back of the block.

Wow!

The most incredible thing of all was that a single individual human being could afford to bankroll this entire operation. I mean, Briggs Swift Cunningham had actually managed to find and gather up all the clever brains and skillful hands necessary for designing and building real world-class racecars, brought them down to West Palm Beach, Florida, opened up a shop, and went on from there. It took more than just an obscene amount of money to do something like that. You had to have a certain, special *spirit* and *patriotism* and *sense of commitment*. Which is why everybody was always pulling for Briggs and his team. Sure, it would've been easy to carp and feel jealous about anybody with the immense, colossal wherewithal to launch his own personal racing team and take it over to compete even-up with the best in Europe. But instead most stateside racers felt proud that somebody was taking a little homegrown American Iron across the Atlantic to keep the Brits and Italians and French and Germans honest. Even thought it meant Briggs' team could pretty much steamroller the opposition at most every stateside event.

Which is precisely why Creighton Pendleton's crew of Muscatelli brothers were trying to get his bright red 4.1-litre Ferrari dropped quietly down into the Sheldon Cup race on Saturday afternoon to run against the 3.4-litre Jaguar C-types. Sure, he'd still run the Sunday afternoon feature (and why not, since odds were he'd be in the running to win his class) but he really wanted a shot at an overall win (I mean, who wouldn't?) and there really wasn't much of a chance of that happening on Sunday afternoon unless John Fitch, Phil Walters, and Briggs himself took a wrong turn someplace and drove all three of the Cunningham C4Rs down the boat ramp at Fireman's Park.

Problem was, the rules were pretty specific that the Sheldon Cup was for cars up to 4000 cc's displacement --*period!*-- and Creighton's Ferrari was known far and wide to be a four-point-one. But somehow he and his crew thought there might perhaps be some way around that little detail (after all, the rules had proven themselves to be engraved in putty two or three times already that particular Friday afternoon) and so you had a smiling, freckle-faced Sid Muscatelli explaining in a soft, reasonable voice to anybody that would listen about how that extra 100cc was only a lousy two-and-one-half percent differential --just eight-point-three measly cubic centimeters per cylinder!-- and how if you took the measurement of the actual Ferrari *piston* (instead of the obviously larger bore of the engine block), well, why they'd be right there, wouldn't they? Of course, what Sid didn't bother to mention was that our C-type Jaguars (which everybody figured to be the cars to beat in the Sheldon Cup) had a helluva lot less at 3442 cc's total displacement.

To the complete amazement of many ignorant and politically naive persons like myself, the Powers That Be (led by --you guessed it!-- Charlie Priddle) decided it was in the best interests of everyone concerned to let Creighton The Third and his oversize Ferrari run in the Sheldon Cup on Saturday afternoon! They came to this conclusion on the grounds that, well, who the hell needed grounds, you know? The truth of it was that Charlie and his cohorts had lost two big ones already that Friday, and everybody concerned felt it was time to let them win something, just in order to keep all the racers properly off balance (not to mention keeping a little peace and political balance in the greater S.C.M.A. operating family). Truth is, it often seemed like you could never get a group of S.C.M.A. official-types to agree on *any*thing. On the other hand, you could probably get instant and unanimous support for the proposition that no self-respecting S.C.M.A. committee member could *ever* allow themselves the luxury of thinking they were right simply because all the facts and evidence supported their position.

You could say it was a matter of club policy.

Chapter 26: Tough Day For The Home Team

The official finish for the S.C.M.A.'s "Monte Carlo Rallye to Elkhart Lake" was listed in the race weekend program for six o'clock on Friday evening, and the rallye organizing committee's Grand Plan was to have all the rallye entrants from all over the whole blessed country parade their MGs and Jags and Porsches and what-have-you down the middle of Lake Street while the local highschool band played a bunch of John Phillips Sousa marches and a huge crowd of onlookers waved and whooped and threw handfuls of confetti like they were watching a bunch of Shriners and American Legionnaires on the Fourth of July. But seeing as how most all the contestants had long since rolled into town, and furthermore seeing as how the rules and scoring had already been abandoned as an impossible mess, most everybody who counted was over at the Quit-Qui-Oc Golf Course, where the Cunningham team was hosting a quiet little barbecue next to the clubhouse for a couple hundred of Mr. Briggs Swift Cunningham's close personal friends. It wasn't any kind of *official* gathering, you understand, but even so it was pretty hard not to get an invite if you had anything whatsoever to do with the races.

Heck, *I* even got one.

As you can imagine, it was quite a spread, what with four 55-gallon oil drums flopped over on their sides, propped up on angle-iron legs, slit lengthwise, fitted with a couple hardware store door hinges and some iron sidewalk grating, and pressed into service as charcoal grills. They had a squadron of guys in white aprons and chef's hats doling out barbecued chickens by the half or quarter and slabs of barbecued spareribs, and next to the grills were big buckets of baked beans with molasses, three kinds of potato salad, two kinds of cole slaw, plus stacked-up loaves of fresh-baked bread from a bakery in Sheboygan and a whole tableful of apple, cherry, peach, and blueberry pies still piping hot from the ovens over at Siebken's. It was quite a spread, honest it was, and naturally there were trash barrels filled to the top with crushed ice and bottles of soda pop, plus no less than five or six beer tappers scattered around at strategic locations. It was quite a deal, no question about it, but also very comfortable and informal, even for guys like me who weren't used to spur-of-the-minute parties that cost more than I made in a year. But at least there was an occasion to celebrate, since this was the first time anybody had seen the Cunninghams since the team got back from Europe. So they had all three cars lined up right there in the middle of the eighteenth putting green, the roadsters on either side and the coupe hunkered down between them, with an American flag planted in the eighteenth hole in front of them an a couple floodlights shining down from someplace up in the trees. Looking at them made you feel proud, you know, like when they play the Star Spangled Banner just before they throw out the first pitch for the World Series. It made you feel proud, you know, like something big and important was swelling up inside your chest.

Briggs Cunningham was there, too, walking quietly around from one person to the next, making sure each and every one of them had enough to eat and drink. And in return, each and every one of them would thank Briggs Cunningham personally --not just for the party-- but also for building those tough-looking Cunningham racecars and taking them over to Europe to show the world that Americans could build something besides fat, chrome-encrusted four-door sedans with automatic transmissions and mushy steering.

As I said, just about everybody who counted wound up at the Team Cunningham party. Even Charlie Priddle. But not until after he dropped by the empty meeting room at the Osthoff Hotel and awarded himself first place in the rallye. Then he went out to the parking lot, fired up his ancient Stutz Bearcat, and proceeded to drive down the middle of Lake Street (as per the original Official Plan) with the big silver-plated first place rallye trophy in the seat beside him. From what I understand there wasn't much of a turnout, just a few of the locals hanging around Schuler's Bar and the soda shop on a warm, pleasant Friday evening, but at least Charlie got the highschool band. Well, *part* of the highschool band, anyway, since there was a late-season Little League game just wrapping up over at the ballfield, and, seeing as how Elkhart was such a small town, most of the brass and percussion sections were busy playing catcher, 2nd base, and two of the outfield positions. That left two flutes, a clarinet, and a xylophone, plus a big marching-band bass drum that still had "BUY LIBERTY BONDS" painted on the sides, which the little brother of one of the flute players (aged about eight) was beating upon unmercifully.

At least they all wore uniforms.

Back at the party, I ran into Cal and Carson Flegley in one of the beer lines, and you could see that Carson was starting to get a little edgy on account of practice was scheduled to start in the morning and his laps around the circuit with Cal had pretty much convinced him that he was in *waaaay* over his head. It's one thing to trundle around on the idle jets, scare yourself silly, and figure it's simply the best anybody could do, but it's quite another when you hitch a ride with someone who really knows how to get on with the program. There's nothing that slams your brain and ego up against the bump stops like being a firsthand witness to what your car can do in capable hands. Take it from me, it gets all sorts of little gears and springs and monkey-motion bellcranks spinning and sproinging and ratcheting around in your head. And naturally Cal was doing his level best to stoke up the fire, since the S.C.M.A. was getting a little nervous about how everybody was stripping down and hopping up their cars for racing, and had therefore decided to award a special trophy to the top-finishing unmodified MG in Sunday morning's rescheduled smallbore race, and naturally Cal was pretty damn certain he could win it if only Carson would let him drive. So he was doing his level best (in a kind of sneaky, underhanded sort of way) to scare the living shit out of Carson Flegley. Not that it took all that much doing. "Sure," Cal said offhandedly, "that blind hill coming into town looks a little scary at first. Can't see a damn thing over the top. Heck, there might be a car stalled or sideways or even flipped clear over, sitting there smack-dab in the middle of the road on the other side. But you gotta take it flat out in top anyways. Only way to get a decent lap time. 'Course, you *could* lift off --even tap the brakes, just to settle the car a little-- but the fast guys'll leave you so far behind it won't even be funny. Pretty embarrassing, actually...."

Carson nodded and swallowed hard a couple times, his Adam's apple bobbing up and down.

"And then there's that swoopy section just past the electric power station," Cal added with a cavalier wave of his hand, "you can't afford to lift off there, either...."

"Y-you *can't?*"

"Hell, *no!* Not in a bone-stock MG, anyways. Not if you wanna be, you know, *competitive....* "

That's about when I decided I maybe ought to wander off on account of I didn't want to accidentally start sniggering and gum up Cal's game. I mean, I wanted to see Cal drive that TD almost as much as he wanted to do it. After all, Cal was sort of *my* driver, and it seemed like some little fractional bit of the glory somehow reflected back on me whenever he did well. And I knew he felt the same way about it, too.

Or at least I hoped he did.

I saw Tommy Edwards over talking with Ernesto Julio and Chuck Day, and with them was a short, thin, quiet young fellow with hollow cheeks, wiry hair, and quick, darty eyes. "Hey, sport," Tommy called out, "step over here and meet Phil Hill."

I walked over and shook hands. "So," I said with just a hint of an edge in my voice, "you're the guy who's supposed to beat my friend Tommy here, right?"

Phil Hill shrugged and didn't say anything.

"Well," I continued, with maybe a few too many beers for inspiration, "I think you're gonna find that's a pretty tall order. Especially in equal cars...."

"Equal cars??" Ernesto Julio howled, rolling his eyes. "Are you trying to get me to believe that Colin St. John didn't keep the best one for himself? Hell, that's what *I'd* do."

"Sure, we kept the best car," Tommy grinned through a crocodile smile, "but from what I've heard, we'll bloody well need it. I mean, old Phil here's been building himself quite an intimidating reputation out on the coast. Haven't you, Phil?"

Phil Hill looked down at the ground like he'd maybe dropped something and shrugged again.

Of course this was all part of the game, working the other guy around a little before you actually got out on the track to run wheel-to-wheel with him. The whole idea was that it didn't matter all that much what you actually said, but rather the way you said it. Just like what Cal Carrington was trying to do to Carson Flegley over on the other side of the lawn.

After that I wandered over to take a somewhat closer look at the Cunningham cars, and they of course had them all polished up and gleaming like huge china figurines. But if you looked close at all, you could see the little telltale dings and chips and metal scrapes left over from their campaign in Europe. I remember reaching out and touching my fingers to the nose emblem of that evil-looking C4RK coupe, and for just an instant an electrified shiver went through me, as if I could hear the rumbling war cry of that huge Chrysler V8, smell the hot metal and oil and soaked-in perspiration in the cockpit, and feel the rolling thunder of the tires as it hammered down the undulating, pitch-black straightaway towards the Mulsanne hairpin at a hundred and fifty miles an hour while tiny French insects splattered themselves against the windshield like miniature fireworks....

No question it took more than just huge piles of money to do something like this.

About then a band started up over by the clubhouse, and they were pretty decent to listen to, even if they mostly played older, slower songs like "The Tennessee Waltz" and "Goodnight, Irene" and that sort of thing. Out of the corner of my eye I saw Sally Enderle standing over by one of the beer tappers, all by her lonesome, and I decided to kind of wander over to maybe say hello and see how long it would take her to shoo me away. But she actually seemed sort of glad to see me. "So," she said through a slightly wavering smile, "how's the mechanic that blows up MGs doing?"

"Me?" I said, looking around like there was maybe somebody behind me. "Oh, I'm OK, I guess."

"Yeah? Me, too," she said. "In fact, I feel *great!*" She rolled her head back so she was looking straight up at the sky, and I noticed she had to sort of hang onto the beer tapper to keep from toppling right over. "Take a look up there. You ever seen so many stars?"

I had to admit I really hadn't, and then it turned sort of heavy and quiet between us, like cement setting up.

"So," I asked her, just trying to make conversation, "y'think Creighton's Ferrari is all set for tomorrow? That's really quite a machine he's got there, yes siree. And where the heck is he, anyways? Haven't seen him around all night...."

Sally lowered her eyes from the Milky Way and looked me up and down like she was trying to figure out where some bad smell was coming from. "Maybe he just decided to turn in early," she snapped, glaring at me so hard her eyeballs seemed to vibrate. "Do I look like his damn keeper to you?"

"Oh, n-no, Sally," I mumbled, "a'course not. I just sorta wondered if, you know, if...."

"Lissen, Bub," Sally growled, pointing her chin up at my face like an automatic pistol, "you don't need to wonder anything about *me*, understand?"

Boy, I could feel my ears burning.

"And as for Creighton's car, why don't you try getting your information from one of the mechanics. You all speak the same language, don't you?"

Geez, I couldn't figure out what I'd done, you know?

So I left Sally Enderle standing there all by her lonesome next to the beer tapper --steam rising from both ears-- and wandered around until I found my buddy Cal all tangled up in a big discussion with a bunch of the MG guys about getting himself a few laps in that Ford V8-powered TC on Saturday. Preferably during the race. Boy, he should've been a salesman or a politician or something, you know? Cal could work somebody over so smooth and polite and friendly and most especially *reasonable* that the poor sap never knew his pocket was being picked, his barn was being burned, or his family was being sold off into slavery until a day or two later. In fact, some of them never felt it at all. Not ever. So I decided not to butt in and maybe spoil the flow of Cal's pitch. Boy, he could be a persistent sonofabitch when there was a ride at stake. Even if it was some dangerous, musclebound morphedite like that MG/Ford V8 hotrod.

Truth is, I was feeling pretty tired by then (I mean, I'd really tied one on the night before, and it didn't make much sense to do it all over again when all the real weekend activity was due to start early the next morning) and so I decided to do something I rarely ever get around to on a race weekend. I left the party early and headed back to Siebken's to get some sleep. But first I wandered out on the eighteenth green for one last look at those magnificent, All-American Cunningham racecars. Boy, they were something, all right. And that's why I made my way around the food tables to give my own personal "thanks so much" to Briggs

Cunningham before I left. And for more than just the swell party, you know? After all, there were plenty of guys around racing who had piles of money to spend, but I'd never seen anybody spend it with nearly the style, smarts, moxie, or spirit that Briggs Swift Cunningham did.

Most guys *bought* stuff with their money, but Briggs Cunningham *made* things. You had to respect something like that.

Just as I turned to leave, the guy who fronted up the band leaned into the microphone and said, "We've got a request from a very pretty lady out there," and they rolled right into a pretty decent piano-and-guitar version of "Your Cheatin' Heart." And when I looked back over my shoulder, I saw it was none other than Miss Sally Enderle making her way unsteadily back from the open-air bandstand....

> you'll walk the floors
> the way I do
> your cheatin' heart
> will tell on you....

The music trailed softly off behind me as I headed up the darkened road towards the Osthoff, Siebken's, and Schwartz's, and it was an absolutely perfect sort of late-summer Friday night, with just a hint of fall chill in the breeze blowing in off the lake and a shadowy wash of cool, silvery-blue light beaming down from a fat silver-dollar harvest moon and more damn stars than I had ever seen in my life. For a change I wasn't too awfully drunk after a racing party, and I could even walk a pretty straight line along the edge of the haybales they had lining the highway on both sides like runs of fat, furry-looking curbings. It made the road look like a long, narrow, flat-bottomed chute sweeping down out of the hard left in front of Siebken's. And was it ever *quiet*. So damn quiet you could hear the water lapping against the wooden docks down by the lake and the faint echoes of laughter and Hank Williams music from the Cunningham party back at the golf course. The only other sound was the soft shuffle of my shoe leather against the asphalt. It was hard to believe that, in less than twelve short hours, this same silent stretch of road was going to be lined with spectators ten and twenty deep along the snow fencing on both sides and the pavement was going to shudder and squirm and pound underneath the fastest goddamn collection of sportscars in the whole blessed country. I could hardly wait....

For me, morning came while it was still purple-grey dark outside, barking through the flower-print curtains with the sound of a tweaked-up MG TD popping and banging and backfiring through the carburetors just below my window. Obviously someone with a little mechanical knowhow had switched some plugwires around --just for the fun of it, you know?-- and now the intended victim was busy waking everybody and his brother up at four-goddam-thirty in the morning on account of he was done with whatever he'd been up to all night and wanted to sneak away for a few winks or so before the raceday dawned in earnest. And I got the distinct impression that this person was not especially, you know, *mechanically sympathetic,* seeing as how he kept shutting the damn thing off, waiting a few seconds, and then cranking it up all over again. As if the stupid motor was magically going to stand up, clear its throat, and suddenly start to run properly again. I looked over at Tommy's bed and he was still out cold, so I decided maybe I'd have a quick run downstairs and see what I could do to fix the situation before this jerk woke all the racers up.

It turned out to be a nice red TD from Detroit, Michigan, and the guy who owned it (who looked more or less like he'd been to bed already, but not to sleep) thanked me a bunch after I deftly lifted the hood and switched the number 2, 3, and 4 sparkplug wires back around to their proper holes in the distributor cap. "Hey," the guy said, kind of wavering back and forth like one of those blow-up PUNCH-ME clowns, "thangsannawfullot."

"No problem," I told him. "Now go get some sleep."

"Saay," he continued, damn near toppling over, "dinneye meetchoo at Gianssdesspair?"

"Yeah," I said, "most likely. I was there with that ratty old TC of Cal Carrington's. He wound up in...."

"I *remember,*" the guy said, drawing back in inebriated awe, "he drove that undertaker guy's TD, dinn'he."

"That's right. Carson Flegley. He's trying to work a deal to drive it again in the race Sunday morning."

"Boy, I sure hope he gettsa shot," the MG guy said, pulling himself up more or less straight, "but he'll sureashell blow me in th'stinkin' weeds iffy does."

"Yeah," I agreed, "he most likely will."

The MG guy blew out a long, wheezy breath that smelled of old hard liquor. "Still, I kinna hope he getsa shot, y'know?"

"Yeah," I said again, wondering just what exactly was holding the MG guy upright.

"Yup, that Cal Carrington guy's really somethin' *special* behind a steering wheel anna gas pedal, y'know?"

"Yeah, he sure is," I agreed for the third time. "He said he's trying t'get a run in that V8-powered TC later today...."

"Y'mean *Robby's* car?"

"Who?"

"Robby. Robby Bernard. He built that damn thing over in Grosse Pointe Shores. Not more'n five miles from my house."

"Really?"

"Sure! But jus' between youanme, he didden so much *build* it as have the guy at the corner gas station do it for him. I think he jus' mostly bought th'parts, y'know?"

"I sure do."

"Anyhow, I think we might real easy fix it so's your friend Cal gets a drive. I mean, Bobby's scared hisself about ghost-white already, an' nobody's even got a full-tilt run at the course yet. I'll put in a good word fr'you. It's the least I can do."

"Hey, thanks," I told him as he plopped unsteadily behind the wheel, "that'd really be swell of you."

"Oh, no," he said, sticking the lever in first, "thank *you!"*

And, believe it or not, on just such random early-morning meetings are many important high-speed deals and spur-of-the-moment racing partnerships born!

There was no way I could go back to sleep --especially since the local volunteers and S.C.M.A. armband types were already drifting out of the early morning half-light to direct traffic and finish up the haybales and string the last of the snow fencing and sparkplug banners. It made me wonder what the hell they got out of it, you know? But I went over and talked to a few of them --even helped them put up a couple lengths of fencing and secure the big PURE OIL banner over the start/finish line in front of Gessert's soda shop-- and you could see that, even though they were over-worked and under-recognized and making nasty, wisecracking fun all the time about how lousy they had it like a bunch of factory union men, underneath it all they were happy as hell to be there --thrilled to be doing a job that really *meant* something. And there's a lot to that. I mean, even though all the carping and grousing sounded a lot like my old man's chemical plant buddies, everybody had a special sort of shine and sparkle in their eyes, not that standard-issue dead-fish look you normally get out of factory workers. Especially the guys with seniority.

I wandered up the front steps into the Osthoff and grabbed myself a free cup of coffee and one of the sweet rolls they had set out for the S.C.M.A. workers, and then I decided to take a little stroll around town and watch this very special Saturday morning begin. The sun was just starting to peek in all bright yellow-orange through the trees, and all along the shoreline, local church groups and privateer townspeople were setting up their sandwich, snack, and lemonade stands, and a few early spectators were already straggling in from the parking areas. They had two or three big fields set aside on the outskirts of town, and additional parking down by Hammil's Hollow, Kimberly's Korner, and the hairpin at Dicken's Ditch out on the backside of the racecourse. I had a crazy notion to take a walk all the way around the circuit. Backwards, in fact, seeing as how I was already pretty familiar with the section between Schuler's Bar and the golf course at Wacker Wend. So I started off, northwards through town, past the start/finish line and Gessert's soda shop and the IGA store and the railroad station and on up the hill out of town that the faster racecars would be descending at three-digit speeds only a few hours later that morning. You never realize how long and steep a hill is until you try to walk it on foot, and believe me, I was about out of breath by the time I reached the top, and more than ready to give up on the notion of walking all the way around the whole damn 6.5 miles. But I went on a little further, just so's I could get out of the shadow of the trees and see the sun coming up clear and fine across a bunch of handsome, rolling acres of prime Wisconsin farmland. Boy, this was sure one beautiful place to hold an automobile race!

When I turned around to head back into town, the sight of that blind hilltop just ahead stopped me dead in my tracks. This was the view the drivers would have as they rocketed up out of the hairpin at Dicken's Ditch, winding out in second, third, and fourth as the road curved gently around to the right and strained uphill. The faster cars would be up close to a hundred miles an hour here, and it looked like that damn pine tree was growing right up out of the center of the road on the other side. How a guy could ever gather up the moxie to flat-foot it over the top of that hill was simply beyond me. You had to be a pretty special sort of person to do something like that. Or maybe just a little short on imagination, you know?

By the time I got back into town, the place was filling up with spectators and most all the racers were up and about and busy monkeying around with their cars. Every now and then you'd hear one start and settle into a cold, lumpy idle, and most often it wouldn't be thirty seconds before some idiot was snapping the throttles open and winging that poor lump of iron clear up to the redline --with no load!-- before the damn oil was even warm. Some people just have no mechanical sympathy whatever, you know? And it's amazing how many of them wind up in the sport of automobile racing....

I found Tommy, Chuck Day, Phil Hill, and Ernesto Julio having themselves a big country-style breakfast over in Siebken's dining hall, and what with the place being mobbed with racers and S.C.M.A. officials and Skippy Welcher making a complete pest of himself by corralling every single waitress so he could complain about how slow the service was and how his melon wasn't ripe enough and how they'd only cooked his whole-wheat toast on *one* side, well, it took us damn near forever to finish up our meal. I had a thick blueberry waffle that was about the best I ever had outside of my mom's kitchen (who knows, maybe even better) and some swell corned beef hash with a fried egg on top. Boy, did that ever hit the spot! There's something about the morning air up in that particular corner of Wisconsin that makes you want a monstrous, heaping, Sunday-sort of breakfast every single day of the week.

There was a drivers' meeting behind the Osthoff at eight ayem, and naturally it started late and you couldn't hear real good, what with several guys doing a little last-minute engine tuning in the parking lot and several hundred little private conversations going on all over the place. The gist of it was that the S.C.M.A. was real glad and pleased to have everybody there, and that --above all-- they wanted a *safe* race weekend. Everybody knew the event was under a microscope after the crowd control problems and near-disasterous crash at Grand Island.

Practice started about a half-hour late at ten-thirty, and we had Tommy and Phil right up towards the front of the herd in the two C-types, so's they wouldn't be all bogged down in a bunch of MG T-series traffic. And I gotta admit, those two Jaguars looked pretty damn swell as they pulled out onto Lake Street and roared away, their race-tuned sixes blaring in perfect unison like the sweetest, mellowest horn section you ever heard in your life. The stream of cars behind them just went on and on and on, charging one-after-the-other out of the Osthoff parking lot like cattle through a chute. If you knew your sportscars, you could even close your eyes and pick 'em out by the sound. An MG. Another MG. A Jag 120. A Crosley-powered Siata. Another MG. Another Jag. Creighton Pendleton's growling Ferrari. The lumpy, inboard-motorboat gurgle of Eddie Dearborn's Caddy-powered Allard. But I noticed something was missing. So I looked around, and sure enough, those three Chrysler-powered Cunninghams were sitting patiently off to the side, ticking over at a deep, grumbly idle, obviously in no hurry to join the last of the cars trickling out of the parking lot. It took me awhile to catch on, but then I understood. They were waiting for the howl of the first couple cars to come echoing downhill towards Schuler's Bar at the other end of Lake Street about four-and-a-half minutes later. Only then did the three Cunninghams clunk their heavy-duty Siata truck transmissions into first gear and swoop out onto the circuit in close formation, with five whole miles of open track in front of them instead of bogged down in a bunch of slow tiddler traffic. Made a lot of sense, you know? Then again, these guys had the legs on everybody when it came to organization, car preparation, race experience, and teamwork. In the long run, that can often turn out to be more important than how fast a car you have or who happens to be sitting behind the steering wheel. After all, far more races are *lost* than *won*.

Think about it.

Anyhow, after the first lap or two I kind of moseyed my way up to the inside of the hard left in front of Siebken's for a closer looksee, and it was pretty interesting to watch all the different cars and driving styles coming through there. I was happy to see that Tommy and Phil Hill were running in close company, well out front of the main pack in our two new C-types, and at first it looked like they were actually even closing the gap to the

Cunninghams about a half-minute or so ahead. But although both the C-types were obviously fast as the dickens, it looked to me that Tommy was trying the harder of the two, getting it full-lock sideways and damn near nicking the haybales on the exit every time through. But damn if Phil Hill wasn't hanging right there on his exhaust, lap after lap, looking so smooth and unruffled that you wondered if maybe they'd somehow swapped paintjobs. I mean, we *knew* the green car was faster, you know?

Too bad that Phil Hill character didn't seem to know it....

Creighton Pendleton was his usual neat, controlled, casual self behind the wheel, and you got the impression that maybe his 4.1-litre Ferrari V12 had a little something in hand for the C-types at this long, fast racetrack. In fact, he seemed to be gaining on them a little once he got through the smallbore traffic. I saw that Eddie Dearborn character was pretty damn exuberant with his big Caddy-powered Allard, and that MG with the Ford V8 under the hood looked all at once darty, nose-heavy, and erratic as all getout when he put the spurs to it. In fact, that Robby Bernard guy pulled in after less than a half-dozen laps with the brakes about gone. That's what happens when you lean on 'em too much or use 'em for a footrest like some guys do.

But by far the most impressive cars out there were the Cunninghams. They looked fast, solid, powerful, and strangely effortless as they rumbled around the circuit in neat formation, carving through slower traffic with ease and leaving everybody behind exiting the corners and at the end of the long straightaways. Somebody said they were topping a hundred-and-fifty miles an hour on the downhill slopes into Kimberly's Korner and Dicken's Ditch. Eventually Johnny Fitch and Phil Walters eased away from Briggs himself in the second roadster, but not by much. Then again, you could tell they were nowheres near flat-out yet. Those guys were simply out learning the circuit and dialing in the cars, saving the last few rpm's, inches of pavement, driving tricks, and tenths-of-a-second for Sunday afternoon, when it counted.

After a while the starter waved a checkered flag and everybody came in for a twenty-minute breather so the course workers could gather up a few dead cars and shoo the crowd away from some of the more dangerous positions they'd occupied around the circuit. By and large, I'd have to say the spectators were pretty damn co-operative and paid attention to the rules. Which, by the way, were spelled out in the official S.C.M.A. race program on a two-page spread boldly titled **THE TEN COMMANDMENTS FOR MOTOR RACING SPECTATORS**.

It went something like this:

I: THOU SHALL NOT STAND ON THE OUTSIDE OF ANY CURVE: When a race driver loses control of his car on a curve, centrifugal force pushes the car toward the outside of the turn.

II: THOU SHALL NOT CROSS THE RACE COURSE DURING AN EVENT OR DURING PRACTICE: The speed of a race car coming toward you is hard to judge. You can't outrun a Ferrari, or even a Crosley! What's more, the lad at the wheel may have to swerve to avoid you and in so doing risk a crash. Don't be responsible for hurting a driver or endangering your own life.

III: THOU SHALL NOT STAND, SIT, OR LEAN ON HAY BALES: Those hay bales around the course have been placed there by an official, who after studying the circuit, has found out just where a speeding car is most likely to go into a spin, skid, or drift off the course. Respect them for your own safety.

IV: THOU SHALL NOT STAND IN ESCAPE AREAS OR ROADS: At the end of a straight there is almost always an escape road or area, which is sort of a safety valve for the lead-foot who lets up just a little too late and finds himself going a little too fast to negotiate the turn or curve, or who finds himself confronted with "fading brakes." Keep out of escape areas--they are reserved for speeding cars and their occupants only.

V: THOU SHALL NOT ENTER UPON ANY DIS-PUTE, INTERFERE, OR TALK WITH RACE OFFICIALS, FLAGMEN, OR GUARDS: Hampering the efforts of officials in the performance of their duty may endanger the lives of the drivers and the spectators. The officials' attention *must* be on the race at all times. Remember, these men are working for your enjoyment and safety. The same can be said for the men and photographers of the working press. They are working to bring this race to the many who can not attend.

VI: THOU SHALL NOT STEP WITHIN 25 FEET OF THE INSIDE OF ANY CURVE: This area, sometimes not marked with haybales, is no place for spectators. The drivers pass close to the inside making this a hazardous spot. Further, drivers may swerve to avoid a car ahead.

VII: THOU SHALL NOT RUN TOWARD AN ACCIDENT: Running to see a crash will only result in mass confusion and hazard to all concerned. Keep off the course! If the flagmen can't see, or have their attention diverted, the race can get out of control.

VIII:THOU SHALL NOT PERMIT A CHILD OR DOG TO WANDER UNATTENDED NEAR THE COURSE: Both children and dogs present a genuine problem at race meets. Keep them in sight and away from the course. Drivers are human --they will swerve to avoid a dog. The dog may be unscratched --the driver? Well --keep every thing off the road!

IX: THOU SHALL NOT APPROACH AN OVER-TURNED CAR WITH A LIGHTED CIGARET: A wrecked or turned car, with leaking or spilled fuel can easily start a blaze resulting in bodily injury to nearby spectators.

X: THOU SHALL NOT CARELESSLY DROP NEWSPAPERS OR ANY OTHER OBJECT ON THE CIRCUIT: Racing cars traveling at high speeds create sufficient turbulence to lift papers that may eventually fall across the windshield of a racing car. Stones, thrown on the course, may be snapped back into the crowd by a tire. Keep all foreign objects off the road!

DO YOUR PART TO MAKE THE RACES SAFE!
SAFE RACES ARE THE FASTEST!

General opinion around the paddock was that the so-called **TEN COMMANDMENTS FOR MOTOR RACING SPEC-TATORS** amounted to some pretty sound advice. But there was still a lot of good-natured needling and ribbing about the notion that cars only went off the outside of curves. Anybody with any experience at all knew it was just as likely --sometimes even moreso-- for a racecar to snap back the other way or get into one of those pendulum-swing, tank-slapper deals and wind up skating off the inside of a corner. Oftentimes backwards.

But, like I said, it was mostly good advice and the huge crowd that was gathering and growing with every passing minute seemed more than willing to listen and abide. Which was a nice change after all the chaos at Grand Island.

And it sounded like most all the drivers were real impressed --or maybe awestruck might be a better word-- by the circuit at Elkhart Lake. It was big and fast and scenic, and about the only complaints you heard were about how narrow it was for passing and how little room for error there was in some of the really fast spots. But that's exactly why drivers like Tommy Edwards and Phil Hill and John Fitch and Phil Walters and Cal Carrington liked the place so much. It separated the men from the boys....

In fact, that's exactly why that Robby Bernard guy decided to step the hell out of his Ford V8-powered MG and let Cal have a try. Hell, that poor guy looked like he'd aged about two whole years for every single lap he was out in that contraption! Cal found me under the flip-up front-end of the Westbridge C-type, doing a between-sessions fluid check and a routine nut-and-bolt inspection. A decent mechanic does that every time a car comes in off the track (and if he doesn't find anything wrong, that just means he did his job properly the last time the car was in). Anyhow, Cal wanted me to drop over and take a look at that V8-powered MG before he went out in it, just to make sure nothing was getting ready to snap, fracture, burst into flame, or blow itself into a million tiny pieces. I was flattered of course, but also a little nervous about it. See, it's one thing when you put a car together yourself, because you know where you've maybe cut a corner or two or done something you really aren't one hundred percent confident about. That doesn't mean you're a lousy mechanic --just the opposite, in fact-- seeing as how it means you *know* what you want to be looking at once you arrive at track-side. But looking at a car somebody else put together (especially a hybrid morphedite homebuilt like that MG/Ford combination) was something else entirely. You don't know what you should be looking at (except for the obvious stuff like fluid levels, knockoff hubs, wheelspoke tension, and loose ball joints and axle bearings) but you really haven't got a clue about the routing of the fuel line or the welds where they shortened and changed the yoke on the driveshaft or even whether the damn radiator has enough capacity for the engine.

Fortunately this job looked reasonably sanitary, and I figured if Cal could drive that ratty old TC of his without worrying too much about it, this thing should be a real piece of cake. The gas station guy who built it made some pretty nice motor mounts and transmission mount adaptors out of mild steel channel, and the weld beads looked like something old Butch Bohunk might've done. They were that nice. Why, that Ford engine fit inside like it almost belonged, except for the fact that he had to run without the side cowlings on the engine compartment in order to make room for the cylinder heads and exhaust plumbing. But most of the quicker MGs were running without the side panels anyway, so it really didn't make much difference.

The engine had been modified and assembled by some speed equipment outfit in Detroit, and it had finned aluminum cylinder heads and a specially cast three-carburetor intake manifold from some hot rod place in California named Edelbrock. They were beautifully made, but I wondered if this particular MG really needed anything much in the way of extra power....

"How's it look to you?" Cal asked me.

"I dunno," I said, giving him about half of an O.K. shrug, "looks like they did their homework."

"That's good enough for me," Cal grinned, and jumped into the driver's seat. He really didn't need much in the way of encouragement.

The officials split up the next practice sessions into "slow" cars and "fast" cars, and they stuck Cal in the same group with the Cunninghams and Allards and Creighton Pendleton's Ferrari (and, of course, our two C-types) and I'd have to admit that not even Cal Carrington could make that MG shine against such powerful opposition. But he did pretty good, running about the same pace as some of the quicker "stock" XK120s while having to pump the brakes three or four times before every sharp corner, and then all of a sudden he didn't come around. I feared the worst, but was tremendously relieved when Cal and the Ford-powered MG reappeared at the other end of Lake Street, trundling along at about twenty-five miles an hour with the right front wheel kind of crabbed in at a pretty severe angle. He pulled into the lot behind the Osthoff and sailed right on by where me and some of the MG guys (including the car's owner) were standing.

"HELP!HELP!HELP!" Cal laughed as he steered around for another slow lap of the parking lot, *"this damn thing doesn't have any brakes left AT ALL...."*

Sure enough, the guy who built the thing ran the left-side exhaust pipe too damn close to the master cylinder, and after getting the fluid so hot it boiled a couple times (so *that's* why Cal had to pump the brakes!) the seal finally gave up the ghost and allowed the brake pedal to flop clear to the floor with no measurable effect on the car whatsoever. "Except," Cal explained wryly, "for maybe that fresh little dimple mark in the seat upholstery on the driver's side...."

It happened in about the worst possible place on the racecourse --at the end of the long, downhill schoolhouse straightaway into Kimberly's Korner-- where the track was coming up the stem of a T-intersection and there really wasn't much of anyplace to go. Fortunately Cal was already lifting off early in order to pump up the brake pedal, and he had the presence of mind to grab a big handful of emergency brake and swing the wheel from one side to the other to slew off some speed before purposely yanking it hard left and spinning the car around to use up the momentum. Truth is, he was damn lucky to keep it from launching right through a ditch and flipping over. And he knew it, too. But somehow he got away with it, and managed to bring the car home with no more than a dead brake pedal and a bent tie-rod from where he bumped into a haybale right at the end of the spin. He was pretty unhappy about that. "Boy, if I'da had two more stinking feet of asphalt, I wouldn'ta hit *anything!*"

Now, you'd think a hair-raising experience like that would dampen a guy's enthusiasm a little bit. But not Cal Carrington. No sir. The first thing he wanted to know was if we could get the brakes fixed and the wheels pointed more-or-less the right way in time for the race at two that afternoon. "Gee whiz," I asked him, "aren't you a little, you know, *scared?* I mean, that coulda been a pretty damn serious wreck."

"Yeah," he shrugged, "I 'spose it could at that."

"That car coulda flipped right over on top of you...."

Cal's face lit up in one of his patented rich-kid grins. "But it didn't, did it?" And that seemed to settle everything as far as Cal Carrington was concerned.

We figured we had about an hour and a half before the Sheldon Cup race later that afternoon, and, seeing as how Tommy and the C-type were running just fine, me and some of the MG guys decided to see if we could maybe fix up Robby Bernard's V8-powered TC so Cal could run it. They liked seeing an MG running faster than most of the rank-and-file Jaguar 120s. And who could blame them? Still, the MG/Ford hybrid was actually running in the same class with our pair of C-Types and Creighton Pendleton's Ferrari, where it really didn't have a prayer of picking up a trophy. Not even with Tazio Nuvolari himself at the wheel. "What's the point?" I asked Cal as I leaned my head in under the fender to have a look at that bent tie rod.

"Hey," he grinned, patting the MG gently on its radiator cap, "it's a ride...."

As you can imagine, it was no simple walk in the park to fix the damn thing, because you couldn't really get at the master cylinder without pulling off the exhaust manifold and piping on that side, and naturally everything was still hotter than a damn barbecue grill down where we needed to be working. So we soaked down a couple shop rags and carefully applied them a little at a time to the exhaust piping so as to cool things off without causing all the castings to crack and shatter like a bunch of heavy-duty Christmas ornaments. Once that was done, it was just your usual, standard-issue, impossible-to-get-at, no-time-left, frantic-panicked raceday knuckle-skinner.

Fortunately somebody from the local MG distributorship had a rebuild kit for the master cylinder on hand, and one of the MG guys scrounged me up a couple empty stewed tomato cans out of the trash, and I turned those into a sort of a cheesy, jury-rigged pair of heat shields for the master cylinder and the exhaust pipe. No question they wouldn't have won me any engineering awards or honorable mentions for fine craftsmanship, but they looked like they might get the job done and they were finished in plenty of time for the race, and those are always the two most important mechanical criteria in a racing paddock. As for the bent tie rod, the best we could do was to heat it up with a torch we borrowed from the guys at the Cunningham trailer --right there on the damn car!-- and kind of pull and pry and hammer it more-or-less straight again. I did the fine adjusting with some kite string and a yardstick we borrowed off the maintenance man who worked at the Osthoff, and if I do say so myself, those wheels looked pretty damn straight when I was finished. Especially if you held your thumb out in front of you and squinted your eyes real good.

Come race time they had all the cars drive around to the train station parking lot and wait while a bunch of S.C.M.A. grid marshals fussed and fidgeted and fought with the crews and drivers about who belonged where. The way it worked at Elkhart was the cars were grouped by class first, and after that the starting positions were pretty much pulled out of a hat. Some guy in a painfully slow Nash-Healey was on the pole, but right next to him (thanks, I think, to a little persuasive lobbying) was our old buddy Creighton Pendleton the Third and his slightly oversize Ferrari. I think maybe the guy in the Nash Healey knew somebody on the starter's crew, and probably just wanted a photograph of his car on the front row to hang up in his den or something. The second row consisted of Cal and the Ford/MG (up where they really didn't belong) and a guy from Cincinnati in a J2 Allard with an Ardun conversion overhead-valve Mercury V8 under the hood. Phil Hill's C-type was back on the third row, right next to Tommy, and I must admit, those two C-types looked mighty low and sleek and modern compared to most of the other iron on the grid.

Soon enough they got everybody more or less lined up (although some of the quicker guys towards the back were upset about being gridded behind moving obstacles like Skippy Welcher's ex-everything XK120*M*, and bitched about it to the officials right up until the engines fired) and then the field rumbled off for a slow pace lap to get everybody settled in and all the mechanical bits up to proper operating temperature. After the field arced out of sight around the hard left in front of Siebken's and growled off into the countryside, I had my first real chance to take a look at the enormous crowd that had descended on Elkhart Lake for the races. Why, there were people five and six deep all the way down Lake Street on both sides, and damn near as many up the hill from Schuler's Bar towards that dangerous blind crest and Dicken's Ditch, another mile and a half away. I have no idea how many people were actually on hand that day (somebody said it was over a hundred thousand!) but wherever you went, you had heads and torsos and elbows coming in at you from all sides.

The field came around and re-formed itself down the middle of Lake Street, and then the starter (it was that same doofus in the Great White Hunter getup I remembered from my very first race at Bridgehampton) climbed up on a little podium off to the side, looked everybody over like a highschool math teacher right before a big exam, and gave 'em the green. Engines roared and tires squealed and you could see there was quite a bit of jockeying for position going on as the field thundered down towards the hard left and all the fast guys struggled to find a way around that slow Nash-Healey. But you could see they were being pretty cautious, on account of all the spectators close by the side of the road and the fact that there really wasn't anything in the way of an escape road at that first corner. As the last of the stragglers disappeared from sight, you could hear the unmistakable wild-animal howl of Creighton Pendleton's Ferrari leading the pack through the Wacker Wend, climbing the gentle hill, and then braking and downshifting for the sharp right into Hammil's Hollow. After that it got pretty quiet for a minute or so, and then you could pick up the echo of the cars from the other side of the lake as they passed the public boat launch just past the electric power station. Sounded to me like Creighton's Ferrari, the two C-types a couple seconds behind and running in close company, another gap, and then a whole passel of cars all in a bunch. I kind of figured Cal and the Ford-powered MG to be somewheres in that bunch. After all the cars streamed through it got quiet again, and then you could just make out the faint yowl of the Ferrari and the two C-types climbing the long, steep hill towards the blind crest with the pine tree growing up the middle of it. No question Creighton and at least one of the C-types gave it a big lift just before the hilltop --maybe even a dab on the brakes-- but the other C-type went over flat stick. You could hear it.

When they roared down into town, it was Creighton in front with Phil Hill in the silver Jaguar all over him, then about a two second gap back to Tommy Edwards in the Westbridge C-type. And then there was just a huge, empty space with nobody in it. On the very first lap! When the rest of the field poured downhill into town, it was an Allard and two of the quicker XK120 Jaguars and some guy named Kulok's Frazer-Nash and our boy Cal

Carrington in that overpowered MG all in a clot, followed by more Jag 120s and a few more Allards and then a whole bunch of cars bottled up behind the pole-sitting Nash-Healey.

"Pretty good race," a familiar voice next to me said, and I turned around to find Chuck Day standing there, casually chewing gum and shielding his eyes from the afternoon sun.

"Yeah," I agreed, "that Phil Hill is really doing a hell of a job in the silver car."

"He doesn't exactly poke around, does he?"

"Not hardly. And we figured that was pretty much the slower of the two cars."

"It was."

"How's that?"

"I said it *was.*"

"Oh?"

Then the cars came by again, and Phil Hill was still right on the Ferrari's rear deck, but the gap back to Tommy Edwards had grown by another second or two. And Tommy looked like he was *trying,* getting it all hung-out-to-dry sideways through the right-hander in front of Schuler's Bar. "Jeez," I said, "he's really pushing it, isn't he?"

"Yeah. Maybe even a little too much."

There was something to that. "So," I asked him, "what did you mean when you said the silver car *used to be* the slow one?"

"Aw, it was nothin', really. Phil complained after first practice that the green car had more suds...."

"And?"

"And so we sorta hunted and poked around until we found the problem."

"Oh? Mind letting me in on it?"

"Sure thing," he shrugged. "It was no big deal. They just made a little mistake at the factory."

"A mistake at the Jaguar factory racing shop?" I asked incredulously, my eyes going all wide-open on me. "Exactly what kind of mistake?"

"Aw, they had the timing mark on the flywheel two teeth off, so everything was running about five degrees retarded. Cams and ignition both. No big deal...."

Well, *he* could say "no big deal," but believe me, it took one hell of a sharp mechanic to figure that out and put it right. I mean, he'd never even *seen* a damn Jaguar C-type before!

Anyhow, the race between Creighton Pendleton and Phil Hill turned out to be a real barn-burner. Phil's Jag was all over that Ferrari like a wet laundry bag, but the Ferrari had just that little bit extra in the horsepower department so Creighton could pull away just enough on the straights to keep the Jag from ducking underneath him on braking into the tight corners. And he made it a little extra tough by driving more or less down the middle of the road, so there really wasn't much room for overtaking. Meanwhile Tommy was slipping further and further back, losing about a second or two every lap no matter how hard he tried. And it must've been double tough on him since he still thought he had the faster of the two Jags. Maybe that's why he was trying so damn hard and slowing himself down.

Cal was putting up a pretty good effort in the Ford-powered MG, hanging on to seventh or eighth place, right behind the quickest of the Jag 120s but slowly losing contact. And then he stopped coming around. I was worried, of course, but figured everything was okay on account of they didn't stop the race or send out an ambulance or anything. Apparently he was just parked somewhere by the side of the road with mechanical problems again. Or at least that's what I hoped.

When the leaders thundered by with about four laps to go, you could see that Phil Hill had dropped back about five or six carlengths instead of hanging all over the back of that bright red Ferrari. "You watch," Chuck grinned, "Phil's been setting him up. This is the lap he gets past." And, sure enough, the silver C-type was solidly in front the next time around. He stayed there all the way to the checker, too.

After the race, they towed Cal in with the right-front end of the Ford-powered MG somewhat rearranged. "What happened?" I asked him as they dropped the car off the hook.

"Aw, th'damn brakes went out again."

"They *did?*"

"Yeah. Pedal went right down to the floor heading into the hairpin at Dicken's Ditch."

"Wow."

"Lucky for me there's an escape road there."

"Sure is," I agreed. "But then why'dja crash it?"

"Aw, there was some damn idiot photographer from The Milwaukee Journal squatted down right in the middle of the damn escape road! Taking God Damn pictures! Can you believe it? I had to damn near drive up a tree to keep from hitting him."

It turned out that Cal had probably saved that photographer's life, on account of he went charging down the escape road at about a hundred miles an hour with no brakes, and when he saw the guy crouched down there with his cameras, Cal had the presence of mind to wait and see which way the guy was gonna jump before yanking the wheel and swerving the other way. It would've been real easy to make a snap decision and turn the car one way or the other, and if the poor lensman happened to jump the same direction, he would've found himself pretty much *wearing* a Ford-powered MG TC.

I looked underneath to see what happened to the brakes, and I was relieved to discover it had nothing whatever to do with the work we'd done before the race. No, this time the brake pipe on the back axle had busted, and it didn't take a Sherlock Holmes to figure out why. Somebody'd left off the little nut that holds the brass T-fitting securely to its bracket on the axle, and so the metal brake line was banging around and getting a nasty little twist thrown into it whenever the axle moved up and down over bumps or around corners. It was only a matter of time. And that's exactly why no self-respecting race mechanic wants to take responsibility for the thousands of little potentially lethal mechanical details of a car he didn't personally nut-and-bolt together.

One of the MG guys brought us over a couple cold bottles of Pabst Blue Ribbon beer (which, I must admit, was pretty damn good) and Cal was all bubbling over with what a super-duper passing move Phil Hill pulled on old Creighton Pendleton. "Creighton was kinda hogging the middle of the road so there was really no safe way around --I mean, the pavement's pretty damn narrow and you're going awful damn fast-- and so Phil just kinda stayed there in his mirrors and worked him over for about ten laps, darting out of his shadow under braking and feinting around in his mirrors, and then, after he had Creighton good and worried, he dropped back a few car-lengths and took a run on him down the backside between Kimberly's Korner and where I was stranded at the Dicken's Ditch hairpin. He had it timed just perfectly, got himself a nice little boost coming up in the Ferrari's slipstream, made like he was gonna pass on the outside, and dipped around to the inside at the little kink going into the braking zone. Without ever lifting his foot off the damn floorboards! Boy, what a pass!"

That was a pretty enthusiastic endorsement from a driver like Cal Carrington. Then again, this Phil Hill character surely seemed to deserve it.

After helping a few of the MG guys get Robby Bernard's Ford-powered TC loaded up on a flatbed so they could haul it down to a garage in Cedarburg run by some guy named Kovacs who could fix just about anything --even on a Sunday afternoon-- I went wandering around the lot in search of Tommy Edwards. But he was nowhere to be found. I located the green C-type easy enough (it was parked right next to the silver one, exactly where it belonged) and Phil Hill and Chuck Day and Ernesto Julio were standing around with the usual crowd of leech-like hangers-on that inevitably gathers around race winners like flies on fresh dogshit. Ernesto Julio had brought out a case of his very special private-stock California wine (it didn't taste too awful much like vinegar) and he even had a carton of real, honest-to-goodness long stemmed wine glasses and some guy dressed up in a formal tux and tails to do the opening and pouring. Some guys are just real handy with money, you know?

"Anybody seen Tommy?" I asked.

Everybody shook their heads and kind of looked off the other way, and it didn't take a genius to pick up on the message. But before I took off to go looking for Tommy in the bar, I had a glass of red and a glass of white (in different glasses, too --the guy in the tux insisted!) and made sure to congratulate that Phil Hill fellow on a hell of a drive and a really nice win. He looked down at the ground and shrugged and thanked me in a quiet, almost apologetic voice, and right then was when I knew this guy was going to go places in the world of motor racing. I mean, there's always plenty of quick guys and eager young talent around, but the right attitude is simply something you've got to be born with. And it's attitude, moreso than skill or guts or even raw, terrifying bravery, that gets the job done on a racetrack.

I located Tommy over in Siebken's bar right around dusk, and he'd obviously already had himself a couple stiff drinks. But they weren't exactly cheering him up. Not hardly. In one single afternoon, Tommy had somehow changed from a guy who could drink all night and never show a bit of it to a guy who could get himself righteously tongue-tied stiff on four or five watered-down scotches. He had a grim, ugly look on his face, and it didn't even help when I tried to explain about the timing marks on the silver Jag's flywheel and how Chuck Day had made that car at least as good as the green one. But Tommy just wasn't interested. Far as he could see, he'd been beaten by another driver in a lesser car, and that had never really happened to him before. It had never even happened in an *equal* car. And that's why it didn't help when I told him the silver Jag was running better come race time.

See, most of the time sportycar drivers are up against guys with different types of cars. Or at least different kinds of tires or different camshafts or different shock absorber fluids or different carburetor needles --you get the idea-- and so there's always some sort of mechanical *reason* to hang your explanations and excuses on. And that's a lot of the magic of the sport, and also why a lot of midfield runners and backmarkers keep hanging around, race after race, enjoying the hell out of themselves even though they're running in mid-pack or worse. There's simply no way to really separate the performance of the machine from the skills and balls and coolness under pressure of the guy behind the wheel, and so an awful lot of middling-decent racers can go home every weekend saying, *"why, if I only had..."* and sleep the sleep of silent winners.

It's one of the great saving graces of the sport.

But the drivers at the top all know who they are and always acknowledge each other. Even if it's just by shrugging or sneering or smiling or spitting on the damn pavement. And every one of them is smart enough and honest enough to know that he's just a simple, stupid, imperfect human being, and the better a driver he is, the more he sees every single race, every single lap, and every single corner as a mountain of tiny mistakes and infinitesimal errors and fractions of a second where he has somehow failed to fulfill the performance envelope of the car. But he also knows the other saving grace of automobile racing: That he's up against a bunch of other stupid, cloddish, bumbling, imperfect, mortal human beings like himself, and while he will never in his life drive that perfect race, that perfect lap, or even that perfect single corner, he can count on the fact that none of the jokers he races against can find a way to do it, either.

The big problem is when a guy who has never been beat (at least not without an excuse he can believe in) gets flat out-run by somebody in the exact identical kind of car. Or, worse yet, by a teammate in the *same* car. Then there's no place to hide. And that's what happened to Tommy Edwards that particular Saturday afternoon at Elkhart Lake. Like all top drivers, Tommy was never so pig-headed and arrogant as to think he could out-drive every other human being on the planet. That would be crazy. On the other hand, the idea that some other chap who put his pants on one leg at a time could out-drive *him* in equal cars, well, that seemed equally impossible. So you didn't have to necessarily believe you were The Best to be a topnotch racing driver. Not at all. You merely had to believe --down in the deepest, darkest reaches of your soul-- that it was bloody damn unlikely that anybody could possibly be *better*. And it was a rough sort of deal when you found out you were wrong. Like Tommy Edwards did that Saturday afternoon at Elkhart Lake. But it happens to *all* racing drivers eventually if they stick to it and hang around the sport long enough.

At least if they live....

Chapter 27: Your Cheatin' Heart

The official Sports Car Motoring Association race weekend program listed a "Concours d'Elegance and Motoring Fashion Show" for 7:30 PM on Saturday evening, and that gave me just enough time for a couple or three commiseratory drinks with Tommy Edwards and then a quick run upstairs to take a shower and put on some fresh clothes. Only I didn't exactly *have* any fresh shirts or pants or anything, on account of I'd put the best stuff I had left on that morning, and then spent most of the day crawling around on the ground under that Robby Bernard guy's overstimulated MG TC. But Ernesto Julio overheard me moaning about it at the bar (he'd come over to buy Tommy a couple more drinks, which he really didn't need at that point) and nothing would do but that I take his key and go up to his room and take whatever the hell I wanted out of his closet. "No problem," he told me, "take any damn thing you want."

"Wow. Even one of those pirate shirts?"

"Pirate shirts?"

"You know. Like the white one you were wearing in the bar the other night?"

"Why not?" he shrugged, turning his palms up. But then he leaned forward and stared at me real hard, eyeball-to-eyeball. "That is," he growled menacingly, "if you really think you're man enough to pull it off. It's real easy to look like a damn sissy in an outfit like that. Especially if you don't have the balls to wear it properly. *Capiche?*"

I told him it was a risk I was willing to take, you know?

So I went up to Ernesto Julio's room and got myself a puffy silk shirt and a pair of neatly pressed tan slacks that were only about two sizes too big for me around the waist and headed back to my room for a major cleanup job before I dared to put that stuff on. Fact is, I spent better than twenty minutes in the damn shower, just trying to get most of the grease out from underneath my fingernails. When I came out of the bathroom, I saw Tommy was there, stretched out on the bed in his driving suit, staring up at the ceiling. "How're y'feeling?" I asked, like he'd been sick or in an accident or something.

Tommy waved one of his hands halfheartedly through the air. "I'll be fine after a hot bath and some dinner," he sighed, his voice all thick and heavy with liquor. "You run along. I'll be down in awhile."

So I got dressed in Ernesto Julio's shirt and pants and headed downstairs to see just what a "Concours d'Elegance and Motoring Fashion Show" could possibly be about. Tommy was still lying on the bed when I left, staring up at the slowly rotating ceiling fan.

"Concours d'Elegance" is a French phrase that means prettying up a car so much that it's too damn nice to drive, and you would simply not believe the variety and condition of the cars they had displayed in neat, angled rows along Lake Street underneath a string of party lanterns. There were the MGs and Jaguars and Porsches and such you naturally expected, all polished up and sparkling in the soft yellow lantern light, but there were other cars, too. Huge, formal, magnificent-looking monsters like Rolls Royces and Bentleys and even a V12 Lincoln Continental. There was a beautiful metallic blue Alfa Romeo 6C 2500 Super Sport coupe that some designer guy from Milwaukee had just brought back from Italy, plus a couple hard-looking pre-war Mercedes-Benz racing cars and one of their flamboyant 540K convertibles that were such a hit with all the Nazi bigwigs during the war. There was a really nice old Model T (you could have any color you wanted, as long as it was black) and a sleek, slippery, and elegant boat-tailed Auburn Speedster, and next to them was an old Overland, an even older Mercer, and of course Charlie Priddle's antique Stutz. There was a Riley and a BMW 328 (which looked pretty damn modern for a pre-war sportscar) and even a marvelous Murphy-bodied Duesenberg parked right next to a block-long, liquid-smooth French thing called a Delahaye. It was definitely one of those Hollywood-type sportscars that are meant more for pulling up in front of fancy restaurants than going around corners, but it was sure as hell pretty to look at. I must've spent the better part of an hour there, just walking up and down that row of cars, trying to take it all in. A lot of people --and especially a lot of women-- simply don't understand the magic of automobiles. But there it was, for all to see, spread out down the middle of Lake Street like a damn smorgasbord.

About nine-thirty they started firing up the concours entrants and wheeling them away, and you could see the clot of official S.C.M.A. concours judges huddled together over by the starter's podium, trying to figure out who should go home with the first-place trophies. Personally, I couldn't see how you could judge any one of those cars as being especially *better* or *nicer* than any of the others. I mean, they were *all* beautiful. Every single one. And the owners had preened them and polished them and even gone over the damn engine compartments with solvents and scouring pads and toothbrushes and Welcher Waxout cotton swabs to make them just as neat and clean and perfect as they could be. In fact, the lengths a few of them went to seemed almost, you know, *silly.* But you could see that some of those concours-types took it awful bloody serious, and you could tell by the steely look in their eyes and the granite-hard thrust of their jaws that they wanted to *win,* just as surely as any of the racing drivers entered in any of the actual races. Maybe even moreso....

I grabbed myself another beer and one of the excellent local bratwurst sandwiches (complete with hot mustard and sauerkraut, natch) from one of the church-group refreshment stands, and then moseyed on down the street to where they were setting up a bandstand for a twelve-piece group from Chicago who played for a lot of high class debutante parties and stuff. But first they announced the concours winners, and suddenly everything made sense on account of they passed out trophies to just about *every-body.* In fact, they had almost as many classes as they had cars in the show! So naturally Charlie Priddle got himself yet another big first-place mug (plus a special award for oldest car in the show) and so naturally he looked happy as a vulture on a fresh kill. Tommy Edwards always called Charlie Priddle "a bloody pot collector," and I was sure beginning to see why.

The official program listed, and I quote, "Dancing In The Streets" as the main activity taking place at ten PM on Saturday evening, and I must admit that the band fired up right on sched-ule. There was quite a crowd left from the Concours --racers and spectators alike-- and it didn't take very long before we had foxtrots and waltzes and jitterbugs and even polkas and free-form square dances going on from one end of Lake Street to the other.

I'd never seen anything like it.

I dropped into Schuler's Bar down on the corner for a quick beer refill, and I noticed Creighton Pendleton over in the back corner with that blond ponytail dolly from across the street, and I wondered what old Sally Enderle would have to say about it if she got wind of what was going on. And it suddenly seemed like an awfully good idea to maybe see if I could find her and sort of casually try to angle her in through the front door of Schuler's Tap. Just to see what would happen, you know?

But I couldn't seem to find her --at least not anywhere close by the bandstand-- so I made my way down towards the resorts, working through bunches of dancers and thick clots of sportycar enthusiasts engaged in terribly intense conversations about oil viscosities and spark plug heat ranges and the proper inflation pressures for racing on various brands and sizes of tires. And all the while that twelve-piece band was filling the air with party music and the string of lanterns overhead was swaying gently in the breeze and there was whooping and laughing and shouting going off all up and down Lake Street like fireworks.

I finally found Sally hanging onto the end of the bar at Siebken's, working on about her sixth or seventh sloe gin fizz. "Say," she said, looking strangely surprised and happy to see me, "you clean up pretty good for a grease monkey."

You know, I'd completely forgotten about Ernesto Julio's tan pants and silk pirate shirt. "Hey, thanks," I told her, kind of pulling my shoulders back, "d'ya think I can buy you a drink?"

"Sure. It's a free country."

So I bought Sally Enderle a drink --another sloe gin fizz-- and we shot the bull for a couple minutes about the Concours display and the "Motoring Fashion Show" she (and most of the other wives and girlfriends) attended over on the back steps of the Osthoff Hotel.

"It was okay," she said, not sounding particularly impressed, "but they didn't have much that *I* liked."

You got the impression that Sally Enderle was pretty damn picky about where she got her clothes.

"Say," I said, thinking about Creighton Pendleton and the blond ponytail sitting in the back of Schuler's Bar at the other end of Lake Street, "you maybe wanna go outside?"

"What the hell for?" Sally asked, sounding bored already. She was pretty drunk, no question about it.

"I dunno. Maybe we could, you know, maybe, uhh, *dance* or something...."

"You know how to dance?" she asked down her nose.

"Sure," I told her. And I actually did. I mean, you don't grow up in a household with three older sisters without learning how to lead.

Sally sucked the last of her sloe gin fizz up through her cocktail straw and thought it over. "Nah," she said at last, "I really don't feel too much like dancing."

"Oh," I said, looking down at where my dirty tennis shoes were poking out from the perfectly creased bottoms of Ernesto Julio's tan slacks.

"Say," she said, jabbing me in the arm, "y'know what *I'd* like to do?"

"What's that?"

"Go for a swim."

"Go for a swim?"

"Uh huh."

"You mean *now?*"

"I mean *right* now!" she said, slapping her hand down hard against the bar.

"B-but," I stammered, fumbling for words, "I haven't got a bathing suit...."

"So?" she snapped. "Neither do I. At least not with me. And I'll be damned if I'm gonna run back up t'the goddam room just t'get one. Not just t'go take a l'il dip. I mean, who the hell needs it, right?" Sally Enderle was drunk, no two ways about it, but there was something else, too. Something dark and mean and premeditated that I couldn't quite put my finger on. "Lissen," she said, "don't be a damn party pooper. C'mon. It'll be *fun!"*

Well, my guts were churning around all pasty-white inside of me, and I felt these little alarm bells I didn't even know I had going off in my head. But I heard myself say, "Sure. Why not?" and the next thing I knew, Sally Enderle had me by the hand and was dragging me out the door and into the night. She ushered us down the darkened far side of Lake Street past the Osthoff, and I guess it should've felt like some kind of dream come true --out there all alone with the beautiful, rich, and incredibly sexy Sally Enderle-- except that instead I felt nervous as hell and also kind of dirty-sneaky rotten at the same time. Like I was, you know, *cheating* in some way on Julie Finzio --even though Julie and me weren't engaged or going steady or even exactly dating each other at the time.

Anyhow, we went down the road a ways and then through a little gate in a chain-link fence and down a steep, narrow flight of wooden steps towards the beach. You could hear the sounds of the big street party and a loud bunch of sportycar drunks on the front steps of the Osthoff fading in the background behind us, and down below, you could see the reflection of that fat harvest moon floating in the water like a bucket of quicksilver spilled across Lake Elkhart all the way to the opposite shore. We were having a little trouble with the steps on account of it was so dark and we were both pretty bombed, but we finally made it safely down to the little ten-foot-wide strip of sand beach at the bottom. Sally leaned her head in next to mine and whispered "Last one in's a monkey's uncle!" directly into my ear, then ran her tongue up and down the lobe for emphasis.

Geez, where do women learn stuff like that, anyway?

But there was no time to think about it, because Sally was already unbuttoning her blouse and shimmying out of her shorts. I yanked Ernesto Julio's silk shirt up over my head (I even think I maybe heard a little *rrriiipppp* when I did it) and fumbled to get out of my shoes and pants. There was a splash behind me as Sally took two steps and dove head-first into the water. And I stood there for just a second, you know, with my thumbs hooked into the elastic waistband on my Jockey shorts, wondering if I really wanted to take them off.

"C'mon," Sally said with just a little hint of a taunt to her voice, "don't be chicken."

"H-how's the water?" I asked while my fingers fought each other back and forth for control.

"Just dreamy. C'mon. Jump in."

"Sure I will," I heard myself say.

"Right. Sometime before Christmas. Haw!" She rolled over in the water and took a couple slow strokes towards the swimming raft they had out about fifty yards from shore. "C'mon, chicken. What've you got to lose? *Bock-ba-bok-bok-bok!*" Sally Enderle could do a particularly humiliating chicken cackle.

So I stripped off my shorts and dived in after her. I mean, why the hell not, you know? The water was icy cold and black as midnight and it occurred to me, as I followed her out towards the floating raft, that I had never been an especially good or experienced swimmer, and that this was moreover just exactly the kind of situation your parents and teachers and camp counselors and church clergymen always warn you about while you're growing up. I mean, all I needed was to drown out here in this cold, black water while skinnydipping naked and drunk with somebody else's rich girlfriend. Why, if Julie or my dad ever found out about it, they'd *kill* me. In fact, they'd take turns....

I was about full up with lake water and gasping for air by the time I got out to the raft, but at least I didn't feel cold anymore. In fact, the water felt all warm and smooth and velvety around me. Sally was hanging off the corner of the raft, and I kind of hand-over-handed my way along the edge until I was right there in the water next to her. "So," she said, turning around so I could feel her up against me, "you made it."

"Yeah," I gasped, trying to move in a little closer.

"Not so fast, Bub," she said, pushing me away.

"Huh?"

"I said 'not so fast.' You understand English, don't you?"

"Uhh, sure I do, Sally. I just don't, y'know, don't exactly *understand,* see...."

"It's simple," she said through a wicked, teasing smile, "I'll let you do anything you want to me --anything at all-- if you can just do one simple thing."

"What's that?"

"Beat me back to shore!" she hollered, and took off full steam towards the beach.

Well, there was no way I could catch her --no way at all-- but I must admit I gave it about the best damn try I ever gave anything in my life. Truth is, I was about two or three heartbeats away from full cardiac arrest when I crawled my way out of the water and lay back gasping on the sand. "Aww, poor baby," Sally cooed, and knelt down to kiss me teasingly on the forehead. She was still stark naked, and as I looked up at her body and felt the droplets of water falling down off of it, I felt something hot and strong and just a little desperate rising up inside me, like the

heave of a huge wave rolling in towards the beach. I reached up
and put my arms around her neck and drew her down into a kiss.
She let me do it, too. In fact, she even helped a little, you know?

But then she stopped me. "Not here," she whispered, "we
don't have a towel or a blanket or anything, and I don't wanna
get sand in my thing."

"Huh?"

"C'mon," she said, "follow me."

And so I did. We put on about half of our clothes and she
took me back up the steep wooden staircase to the street and
around through the shadows to the far side door of the Osthoff
Hotel, then up the stairs to the second floor and down the hall to
her room. Or Creighton Pendleton's room, to be more precise.

It was a hell of a nice room --nicer by far than the one
Tommy and I had-- and even with the lights off, I could see it
pretty well and check it over while Sally went into the can for a
few minutes to do whatever it is girls like Sally do before they
plan to have sex. Then she came out, pulled her blouse up over
the top of her head, shimmied out of her shorts, and jumped
under the covers. "So," she said, looking at me standing there in
the middle of the room like a damn cigar store Indian, "you
planning to come to bed or what?"

"S-sure," I told her. "But I think I maybe gotta use the can
first. You think it's okay?"

"Boy," Sally laughed, "you really know how to sweet talk a
girl, don't you?"

"Uh, well, geez, I...."

"Go ahead," she said, shaking her head under the covers,
"and put a hustle on, willya? I'm cold."

So I went in the bathroom and closed the door behind me,
and I damn near jumped out of my skin when I saw Creighton
Pendleton standing there in the mirror --right behind me!-- but
when I spun around it was only his blue Dunlop driving suit,
hanging on a wooden hanger off the hook on the backside of the
bathroom door.

Boy, did that ever scare the shit out of me!

Naturally it took me forever to get my body to cooperate and
let some of the excess beer out, and when I finally flipped off the
light and went back into the bedroom, it was like the temperature
had changed or something. But Sally knew exactly what to do

about that once I got into bed with her. No question she'd had a lot of experience at this sort of thing. But for some reason, it was all so *unreal*, you know? Like I was looking at a movie or something and not actually there in person, staring down at Sally Enderle and her beautiful chestnut-colored hair plastered down all wet and stringy over the pillowcase, listening to the sounds of the party winding down a few blocks away and wondering if I was going to hear the telltale thump of Creighton Pendleton's footsteps coming down the hall and the icy-fingered click of a key sliding into the lock. Here I was, exactly where I'd always dreamed and fantasized I'd be one day --never for one single second believing that it could ever actually happen-- looking at the illuminated alarm clock dial on the bedstand while I humped away at her like a bored cocker spaniel, wondering why I didn't feel like the luckiest guy in the world....

I left that room just about as soon as it was over. Maybe even a little before. I mean, you know how everybody says you're supposed to feel all melty-soft and dreamy afterwards, and maybe just lie there and smoke a couple cigarettes, watching little phantom neon lights flickering on the insides of your eyelids and listening to the sounds of the street-dance party filtering in from two blocks away. But I didn't feel that way at all. In fact, I felt kind of sick to my stomach and clammy all over, not to mention just a little worried that Creighton Pendleton the Third might just pop through the door at any moment. In fact, maybe that's what Sally had in mind all along --maybe I was just the sacrificial lamb in this deal. Or maybe it was enough that I simply helped her muss up the sheets and left a few telltale wet spots behind. Hell, there was no telling what that girl had in mind. Worst of all, I couldn't stop thinking about Julie. I mean, that made no sense at all! But, wouldn't you know it, the band down the street swung into a heavily orchestrated version of "Your Cheatin' Heart," --complete with a long, mournful saxophone solo-- and before the song was done, I'd put Ernesto Julio's shirt and pants back on and beat it out the door. Sally Enderle didn't even roll over in the bed to say good-night.

> *your cheatin' heart*
> > *will pine one day*
> *and crave the love*
> > *you threw away....*

I crept my way down the side staircase --kind of sneaking along in the shadows, you know?-- and headed straight over to Siebken's bar. But the place was so loud and boisterous it made my head pound, and the truth of it was I didn't much feel like talking to anybody anyway. So I left half a beer on the bar and headed down the street towards the bandstand. The crowd had dwindled down quite a bit --like towards the end of a big wedding, you know?-- and they were doing mostly slow dances to sappy old big-band tunes from the forties and stuff. I went into Schuler's Bar, just to see if maybe Creighton and the ponytail were still there in the back, but of course they were gone. So I ordered myself a snifter of brandy --just like Tommy Edwards would have-- but the bartender wanted to see some I.D. before he'd pour a drop, and of course I didn't have any in the pockets of Ernesto Julio's pants. Fact is, I didn't have any that said I was exactly twenty-one in the pockets of my pants, either, but I'd gotten so used to being served when I was in the company of all the racing people that I got just a little indignant about it.

So the guy threw me out, you know?

There was nothing left to do except head back to the quiet little bar under the steps at Siebken's. But I stopped between songs at the bandstand and asked the guy to play "Your Cheatin' Heart" one more time. "We just played it five minutes ago," he said with a forced smile.

"Yeah, I know. But it's for someone, you know, *special...*"

He didn't look too convinced.

"...and I just *gotta* hear that sax solo again."

Well, that of course got the alto sax player looking at the bandleader all sad and eager and whimpery like a little Beagle puppy, and he caved in. "Okay, we'll play it. Right after the next song. It was a request, too." And he tapped the music stand with his baton and the band took off into "Some Enchanted Evening" from the musical *South Pacific*. They played it really lush, you know, and as I walked slowly down Lake Street, looking at all the people chattering and dancing and enjoying themselves under the warm, yellow lantern light and the sportscars from all over the whole damn country parked nose-to-tail and side-by-side in every available driveway and sidestreet, I realized it really was an enchanted sort of evening, even if I was personally feeling a little bit lost, confused, soiled, and melancholy.

Your cheatin' heart
>*will make you weep*
you'll cry and cry
>*and try to sleep.*
But sleep won't come
>*the whole night through*
your cheatin' heart
>*will tell on you....*

And that's the last I heard of that new Hank Williams song as I headed through the door that led through Siebken's dining room and into the little quiet bar under the stairs. It was packed full of people, but I didn't really know any of them. But that was okay, because somehow the walls of that place always seemed to sort of absorb all the gab and chatter, and you could really be alone in there with your thoughts, even when there seemed to be a lot of people around. I had myself a couple snifters of brandy, but they didn't seem to do very much, and then I decided to take a little walk down the road, past the Osthoff and that steep wooden stairway Sally Enderle and me had taken down to the beach only a few hours earlier. It felt like it was all some kind of dream --like it never happened, you know?-- but I could tell from the hollow, empty feeling inside me and the smell of her coming up from beneath Ernesto Julio's shirt collar that it was real, even if it didn't seem like it. The band had stopped playing over in front of Schuler's bar and you could tell the party was finally breaking up, and now it was getting all black-velvety quiet again, like it always does at Elkhart Lake when things taper off at the end of the evening.

But I wasn't tired, you know? So I walked on up to the Wacker Wend past the Quit-Qui-Oc Golf Course where Briggs Cunningham had thrown that super barbecue party the night before, and then further on up the road to the sharp right into Hammil's Hollow, and, honest to God, I just kept walking and walking all the way around the whole damn six-and-a-half miles of racecourse that night! Took me more than two hours. But I hardly even felt it, because I had things to think about. Only I couldn't, you know? It was like trying to wrap my fingers around something made out of the pre-dawn mist.

I finally got back to downtown Elkhart Lake about 3:30 in the morning, and everything was dead quiet except for a little breeze rustling through the trees and a faint, threadlike squeaking noise off the party lanterns still swaying gently to and fro over Lake Street. I still didn't feel sleepy, but there was nothing else to do but go back to Tommy and my room. I was pretty damp from my long walk out in the countryside and all the other things that had happened, so I hopped in the shower and turned the hot water up until I could hardly stand it and went over my body again and again and again until my fingers were wrinkled up like prunes and the bar of soap was worn down to next to nothing. But no matter how much I tried to wash and clean myself, I still felt scummy all over.

I guess it was coming up light by the time I dozed off a little bit, and then it didn't seem like I was asleep for more than two or three minutes before I heard engines starting up and Charlie Priddle's irritating voice booming over the loudspeakers out in the parking lot behind the Osthoff, calling for all drivers in the Kimberly Cup race for smallbore cars to get themselves and their automobiles up to the grid. Gee whiz, it was almost ten o'clock! I hopped in the shower again --just to wake myself up a little-- put on my dirty jeans and T-shirt, and carefully folded up Ernesto Julio's pants and shirts and set them over on the windowsill. They looked pretty messed up, if you want to know the truth of it, and I made a mental note that I really ought to have them cleaned and pressed (and maybe have that little rip in the silk shirt mended) before I gave them back to him.

At least I felt a little like myself again in my old wrenching clothes. Anyhow, I went downstairs and grabbed a cup of coffee from the back door of Siebken's kitchen, and then I wandered out front on the Osthoff side to watch the smallbore race. There were even more spectators than the day before, leaned up elbow-to-elbow along the snow fencing and spread out on the lawn in front of the hotel on picnic blankets and sitting in fold-up lawnchairs eating sandwiches and apples and stuff out of wicker baskets. It was a perfect day for that kind of thing.

Then the smallbore cars came around on their pace lap, and it looked to me that the race would boil down to a scrap between a bright red O.S.C.A. driven by a fellow named Bill Spear, one of the two quicker Porsches (which were both stripped-down, hopped-up versions like that one Phil Walters ran for Briggs Cunningham at Brynfan Tyddyn), a couple heavily modified MGs, and some highly regarded and beautifully constructed little homebuilt from the West Coast based on components from a small French sedan called a "Simca." To tell the truth, I wasn't really too interested. But then I saw Cal Carrington's familiar old polo helmet sticking up out of Carson Flegley's shiny black MG TD about halfway down the pack, and all of a sudden I was right up on the fences, shouting and waving my arms and yelling for Cal to give 'em hell.

And did he ever. He made a fabulous start and charged right down the very inside into that first hard left to pick up about three or four positions, and by the time they completed lap two, he was up to about tenth place or so and easily leading all the other stock MGs. In fact, he was having a hell of a scrap with one of the highly modified TCs that should've been a hell of a lot faster than any stock TD. Only Cal more than made up the difference, and you could see he was really enjoying getting under this guy and passing him going into the corners every lap, only to have him scream past again on the straightaways out on the backside of the circuit. Only the guy in the hopped-up MG didn't seem to be enjoying it one bit, and he was getting more and more ragged and more and more desperate each lap as he tried to hang onto Cal through the twisty bits. And then he lost it in a big way --right in front of us!-- getting into one of those ugly left-right-left-right tank-slappers and then snapping into a spin when he simply couldn't steer fast enough to keep up with it anymore. And, just like all the drivers and crews worried about when they read *The Ten Commandments For Motor Racing Spectators* in the program, that MG wound up plowing into the snow fencing on the inside of the track, about fifty yards down from the corner and right in front of the Osthoff Hotel. The car wasn't really going very fast by the time it hit the fencing, and all it did was knock some people over. But there were some cuts and bruises and one lady from Des Plaines, Illinois, got a broken leg when somebody fell on her. So they waved a bunch of yellow flags and ambulances came in from all over the place --no question they were prepared for the worst at Elkhart Lake that year-- and most people said they'd seen worse at highschool football games.

Anyhow, that Spear guy's O.S.C.A. won the race, and my buddy Cal won the special award for best finish in a truly stock MG --with ease, natch!-- and afterwards he acted like it was no big surprise and nothing special at all. I was coming to understand that about really good racing drivers: given any sort of a decent racecar, they *expect* to win. And why shouldn't they?

Fortunately they got the mess in front of the Osthoff mopped up quickly, and everything was back in place and ready to go in plenty of time for the big 31-lap, 201.5-mile Elkhart Lake Cup feature race at 12:30 PM. But it was kind of a letdown after all the close battles we'd seen in the other races. Nobody could keep up with the Cunninghams. Why, Creighton Pendleton didn't even show up on the grid with his Ferrari. Somebody said they'd heard he had some valve spring problems, but I was right there when they loaded that thing on the trailer, and it sounded healthy as all getout to me. There were a couple nifty, nicely finished local specials called Excaliburs on hand that looked an awful lot like fighter jets, but underneath the sheetmetal they were really just a couple cut-down Henry Js in lowslung bodywork, so they really weren't up to the competitive challenge. But they looked potent as hell, and somebody told me the guy who built them --a professional automobile designer out of Milwaukee named Brooks Stevens-- wanted to go into mass production as a sort of All-American answer to the MGs and Jaguars from over in England. And they looked plenty sharp enough to get the job done, too, but I guess nothing ever came of it.

Tommy and Phil Hill rolled out to the grid with the two C-types, and, along with maybe that local hero Eddie Dearborn's rambunctious Cad-Allard, they looked to be the only real competition for the Cunninghams. And I must admit that Tommy wasn't looking himself that particular Sunday noontime. His face was all pale and drawn and he had a look in his eye like somebody with a bad case of stomach flu. He'd had himself a pretty rough weekend, no two ways about it. So, when the race finally started, it was the three Cunninghams thundering away from everybody at the green flag and roaring off in close formation again. Johnny Fitch in the number three roadster and Phil Walters in the evil-looking C4RK coupe soon began to pull away from Briggs himself in the other roadster, and you could see those two ace drivers were just sort of playing with each other at that stage of the race, mindful that 200 miles is a long, long way, and that it's all too easy to use up a hundred miles worth of racecar in a few short laps if you really start flogging it to death. Phil Hill drew a fourth row starting position and had to do a little fancy footwork to slice through the traffic, but then he reeled in the third-place Cunningham and even managed a pass after Briggs bottled him up for a few laps. Then he took off after the leading duo, and you could see that he was really dialed in and had the bit between his teeth. But the Cunningham team signaled their drivers that the C-type was after them, and right away Walters picked up the pace and passed Fitch, and then Fitch turned up the wick and repassed Walters, and now the gap back to Phil Hill and Ernesto Julio's silver C-type stabilized, and then it began to grow....

But it wasn't really Phil Hill's fault, on account of the tin-can muffler on the sidepipe of his Jaguar had burned right through on the inside where you couldn't see it, and the way the air came down the side of the car and up over the door and across the interior was putting all the exhaust fumes right directly into Phil Hill's face. At first he didn't realize what was happening or why the track seemed to be wobbling and staggering away from him all the time. But he figured it out after Briggs Cunningham repassed him for third place, and he spent the last hundred-odd miles with his head hanging out over the driver's-side door, trying to get a little fresh air and clear out the cobwebs. Tommy had worked his way through to a lonely, boring, solitary fifth place overall after a brief skirmish with Eddie Dearborn (who wasn't really in Tommy's class, no matter his condition) and his brutal-looking J2X Allard.

So it turned into a pretty boring procession, with Fitch running a few seconds ahead of Walters at the front (but neither one of them really pushing it to the absolute limit), then a long gap to Briggs Cunningham, another long gap to the woozy-but-recovering Phil Hill, and yet another twenty or thirty seconds back to Tommy Edwards. Fact is, the only race worth watching was between a few of the standard-issue Jag 120s back in the pack, but I didn't know any of the drivers, so it really didn't mean anything to me. That's the way it is in car races: if you don't know somebody out there well enough to slap him on the back afterwards and offer him a beer, it can get pretty damn dull.

On the other hand, it was a real thrill to see those Cunninghams run like they did, and everybody there felt pretty special about how Briggs and his team represented all of us when they went overseas to take on the best drivers in the world and the latest, fastest racing machinery from Maranello, Italy and Coventry, England, and everyplace else in between....

Those cars didn't have to make excuses to *anybody*.

After the races I helped Tommy load up our spares and stuff into the green Jaguar and said our good-byes to Ernesto Julio and Phil Hill and that hot-rod genius Chuck Day. There was a big awards banquet scheduled for 6:30 PM that evening, but a lot of folks who had twenty- and thirty- and forty- and fifty-hour drives home were packing up their stuff and heading out just as quickly as they could get the job done. The spectators had already pretty much leaked off down Route 57 towards Milwaukee, and it looked like the big S.C.M.A. victory bash was going to look more like a wake for a poor relation than anything else. At least compared to the parties we'd seen on Friday and Saturday night.

Tommy Edwards hadn't really said too much to me all day. Or anybody else, for that matter. I knew he was having some problems coming to terms with the way Phil Hill had smoked him, and all the hooch he'd packed away while wrestling with it hadn't helped matters any. But he went off with a couple of guys from Briggs Cunningham's team after checking us out of our room, and when he came back an hour or so later, he had a little of the sparkle back in his eye and some portion of the usual military snap to his step. "I say, sport," he grinned, "I need you to do me a bit of a favor."

"Sure thing," I told him, "just name it."

"I have to go someplace right after dinner."

"No problem. I'll give you a lift. Or go along for the ride. Either way. Doesn't matter to me...."

"No, you don't understand, sport. I need to go somewhere with one of my friends from, well, nevermind from where. But the point is I need you to take Creighton's car back to New York for me."

"*Creighton's* car??"

"Of course. He owns the green C-type. Didn't you know?"

"I don't get it. I thought that car belonged to Colin St.John."

"Well," Tommy explained, drawing his head in close to my ear, "it's all supposed to be terribly hush-hush, you understand, but Creighton owns the green car. Bought it sight unseen, the way I heard it. But the bloke wanted to know if it was faster than his Ferrari before he took a chance with it. Smart move, that. Didn't want to burn his bloody bridges with Carlo Sebastian and the Muscatelli brothers. So he asked Colin to keep things quiet and find somebody decent to drive it for him, and Colin rang me up to see if I'd be interested."

"Wow."

"Yes sir, he's a pretty shrewd customer, that Creighton Pendleton is. But he didn't bloody figure on the second car. Didn't bloody figure on it a'tall. And I'm sure old Colin quite forgot to mention it during the transaction."

"That sounds like him."

"Indeed it does."

"So now what happens?"

"Well, *I* go take a blooming hot shower, get myself some dinner, and head for the airport. As for the rest of it, I suppose Creighton'll have Colin St. John sell the Jag before anybody else finds out he's owned it. Then he'll most likely write Carlo Sebastian a rather huge check and buy himself whatever the next hot Ferrari turns out to be."

"You don't think he'll keep the C-type."

Tommy shook his head. "I expect not. Oh, it's a wonderful driving car, and possibly the best in the whole damn world over distance, but it's just not powerful enough for our kind of racing. At least, not on tracks like this one, where torque and top-end horsepower are at such a bloody premium. You need yourself a real brute of a car with a godawful monstrous sort of engine if you want to have a chance of running with the Cunninghams...."

"But aren't they in a different class?"

"So what? Classes aren't what's important. At least not to somebody like Creighton Pendleton. Or myself either, come to that. People like us need to be *in there,* you know?"

"In there?"

"Right. You know, scrapping it out at the front of the pack and all that sort of thing. That's why I'm going back to my Allard first bloody chance I get."

"You think your Allard is faster than one of these C-types?" I mean, that just didn't sound right to me. Why, the Jaguar XK120 C-type looked a whole generation lower and lighter and smoother and sleeker and, well, *more refined* than any blessed Allard I'd ever seen.

"Oh, maybe not *now,*" Tommy allowed, waving his fingers mysteriously through the air, "but mark my words, my young mechanical friend, it *will* be...."

"I don't get it."

"Nor should you, Buddy. Nor should you," Tommy grinned. "Just remember what your fine president Mr. Roosevelt once said."

"You mean about there being nothing to fear but fear itself?"

"No, the other one."

"What other one?"

"The other Mr. Roosevelt. Theodore. Do you recall?"

I shook my head. I mean, all I knew about Teddy Roosevelt was that he had buck teeth and wore spectacles and led some charge up San Juan Hill, and I got most of that information from the movie *Arsenic and Old Lace* with Cary Grant.

"Well," Tommy whispered with an exaggerated wink, "Mr. Theodore Roosevelt advised that one should speak softly and carry a big stick, and I believe I've discovered where exactly such a bigger stick can be found."

"I'm still lost."

"No matter. This is still the time for speaking softly, my young friend. Just get that Jaguar of Mr. Pendleton's back to New York without a scratch, don't let on to anyone that it's his car, and be ready to put some bloody long hours in the next few weeks before Watkins Glen." And with that he handed me a neatly folded wad of five --*five!*-- twenty dollar bills.

"Geez, Tommy, what's *this* for?"

"Road emergencies. You know. But I'd actually appreciate a bit of change back when I see you again in Manhattan," he shot me a little wink, "but not too awfully much."

And without another word, Tommy Edwards lifted his leather overnight bag out of the passenger-side footwell and headed back into the Osthoff Hotel. "And by the way, sport," he called back over his shoulder, "do try not to get arrested...."

Chapter 28: Some Other Sides of Racing

I didn't hang around for the big victory banquet on Sunday night up at Elkhart Lake. I mean, once I got everything loaded up and Tommy Edwards made his mysterious exit, I just flat couldn't wait to get on the road again and back home to Jersey. I wanted to see Julie, you know? More than I'd ever wanted to see her before. In fact, I took off from Elkhart with every intention of driving straight through from the middle of Wisconsin to the Doggy Shake on Fremont Avenue without stopping for food or gas or even to take a damn leak. But that notion faded out pretty quick a little south of Milwaukee, when I started to realize that I was tired as hell and desperately in need of some sleep. Driving solo in the green car was a lot different from chasing after it in the silver one, and without Tommy Edwards out there in front of me at 70, 80, 90, and 100 or more miles an hour like a carrot on a stick was just not all that much fun. Sure, people still stared at me and the C-type goggle-eyed out of their Nashes and Fords and Plymouth Belvederes, but I was past getting excited about it by then. And it was hot and cramped and uncomfortable in that damn thing, and I couldn't believe that I'd never noticed it on the way out from Jersey. Of course, we'd been traveling damn near the speed of sound when Tommy Edwards was leading the way, and I was afraid to go much more than ten or twelve miles-per-hour over the posted speed limits on my own. I mean, what was I going to tell a cop, you know?

I was well past dead tired by the time I reached the suburb of Winnetka on the north side of Chicago. It was full dark by then, and you should have seen some of the houses they had there along the lakefront on Sheridan Road, all lit up with columns and archways and stuff at the end of long, gated driveways. Looking at places like that always made me feel like a little kid with no pennies in his pocket staring in through a bakery shop window. Why, you could almost *smell* the oriental carpets and wall safes behind the oil paintings and straight teeth on all the kids.

It was a world you could never dream of breaking into from the outside, you know?

And I knew it.

But I could maybe sneak a little peek into that life every now and then through racing. And that's why I decided to put myself up for the night at one of the big, fancy downtown hotels off Michigan Avenue in Chicago. I told myself it was just so I'd be sure and have a safe place to park the Jaguar, and I figured that old Tommy Edwards would be more than happy to go along with a story like that. So I followed the ghostly sweep of the Palmolive beacon southward down the Outer Drive into downtown Chicago, and stopped just about smack-dab in front of it at the Drake Hotel. The doorman was all dressed up in gold braid and brass buttons, and once he got a look at that Jag, he didn't need any excuses for my grubby T-shirt or ragged windbreaker or dirty tennis shoes. "Will you be spending the night, sir?" was all he said, and when I told him to be extra careful with the car, he bristled just a bit and said, "of *course*, sir," with a little touch of frost in his voice. So I tipped him a whole dollar, just to melt that ice. And it worked like a charm.

Believe it or not, my room at the Drake Hotel cost the same as a whole weekend's pay as a race mechanic for Barry Spline and Colin St. John, but I didn't care. The bed had real silk ruffles and the walls were an elegant beige with gold-painted moldings, and you could look out the window and see the Outer Drive arcing gracefully northward towards the suburbs and the searchlight sweep of the Palmolive beacon as it rotated through the low-lying clouds at regular intervals, like some kind of illuminated heartbeat reaching out from the center of downtown Chicago. It was past 10:30, which meant it was damn near midnight back in Passaic, but I decided to take a big chance and call Julie anyways. She answered the phone herself, thank goodness, and I can't tell you how great it felt to talk to her again.

She seemed pretty happy to hear from me, too.

"So, how've y'been?" I asked her.

"Same as always. How'bout you?"

"Yeah. I guess."

"I haven't heard from you in quite a while, Buddy."

"Yeah. I know. I been real busy...."

"That's what I figured. The girls told me about you stopping by the Doggy Shake with that English guy."

"Tommy Edwards."

"They said he's pretty cute."

"Cute?"

"Yeah."

Somehow "cute" was not exactly the sort of word I would have ever used to describe Tommy Edwards. But then, girls have their own private language when it comes to stuff like that.

"So where are you?"

"In Chicago. At the Drake Hotel." And I told her a little about my room and the swell view out my window.

"Sounds awful nice," she whispered into the receiver. "I almost wish I could be there with you...."

"So do I, Julie, so do I," I heard myself whisper back into the phone while all sorts of new feelings swirled around inside me. Or maybe they were just urges. Sometimes it's hard for a guy to tell the difference. Anyhow, we kind of hung there on the phone line for the longest time --not saying a thing-- just sort of running up my long distance bill while we listened to each other breathing and maybe even pretended a little like we were actually alone together in that wonderful and perfect hotel room overlooking Lake Shore Drive in Chicago.

After we hung up I didn't feel much like sleeping, so I took the elevator downstairs and went for a little stroll up Michigan Avenue towards the Chicago River. It was chilly that evening, and I had to zip up my windbreaker and pop the collar up around the back of my neck. But it was a nice walk, past all the fancy shops where those rich people from the North Shore bought their clothes. I went up past the Tribune Tower, where the night-shift editors and typesetters and printing press operators were probably hard at work on the Monday morning first edition of that famous Chicago newspaper. But you'd never know it from the outside, where it looked just like every other big, empty stone skyscraper. Across the street was the Wrigley building, all lit up and glowing like carved ivory, and every minute or so the Palmolive beacon would sweep across the sky above it. Fact is, I'd always thought Manhattan was about the prettiest city in the world. Especially the view across the Hudson from the Jersey side around Englewood Cliffs. But as I walked across the Michigan Avenue bridge to the other side of the Chicago River and watched one of the late-night party tour boats pulling in at the dock down below, I had to admit it didn't have all that much over this town. Then I noticed the big, wide street on the other side of the river was named Wacker Drive, after the same Wacker family that the S.C.M.A. driver Freddy Wacker came from --you know, the guy who helped bring the races to Elkhart Lake in the first place-- and I wondered just what it might feel like to look up at a street-sign on a big, wide concrete boulevard with a row of tall, hand-some skyscrapers standing at attention along one side and a series of crowded drawbridges over a busy river on the other and see your own personal family name up there. Heck, I bet people like that don't even notice, you know?

There was a bustle of taxicab activity and people in dressy evening clothes going in and out a big glass revolving door just up the street, and the sign right above it said *"The London House,"* and as I walked up that way, I could hear some swell jazz music pumping out of there every time the revolving door went around. So I thought maybe I'd duck inside and have a listen, you know? But the doorman took one look at me and nodded for me to just keep moving along. Didn't even want to check my I.D.s or anything. Not that I had any to show him.

And that was always the problem coming back from an S.C.M.A. race weekend. I'd somehow forget that I was just a dumb, underage, blue-collar grease monkey from Passaic, and it'd always take me a couple rude awakenings and long looks in the mirror before I remembered who I was again.

But I slept real well that night in the Drake Hotel, and I even left my clothes hanging inside the hollow door to my room so's the butler service would have 'em cleaned for me. And you know what? They were back inside that door, cleaner than they'd ever been and smelling fresh as hospital sheets by the time I got up at around 8:30 the next morning! I bet the rich people who stay in places like that all the time miss the magic in that sort of thing, you know?

So I ordered breakfast from room service and ate my first-ever serving of Eggs Benedict at the antique-white carved wood table over by the window looking out over Lake Shore Drive. It was pretty good, too. And they brought a morning edition of the Chicago Tribune along with my breakfast tray, so naturally I thumbed through it to see what one of the most respected news-papers in the country had to say about that fantastic S.C.M.A.

race weekend up at Elkhart Lake. And eventually I found it, buried on about the last damn page of the sports section (following about four solid pages of earth-shattering stick-and-ball news) and it was just a little half-column story in the middle of the page, right next to a piece about how some golfer named Jim Ferrier won the Empire State Open up in Albany and another story about some stupid polo game in Oak Brook, Illinois. And this was without question the biggest damn sportscar race *ever* in the whole entire midwestern United States --maybe even the whole damn country!-- and the first time anybody in those parts ever got a chance to see the Cunningham team that was carrying the American colors overseas to do battle with the all the big-time European teams on their home turf. Why, Sheriff Kroll of the Elkhart Lake police department figured the spectator turnout at a hundred and thirty-five *thousand* people! That was probably more than any other sporting event in the whole damn country that weekend. But I guess that just didn't mean too much to the editors of the Chicago Tribune. Or maybe it was just that they didn't *know* anything about automobile racing (except for the Indy 500 on Memorial Day, of course) and I guess newspaper reporters don't feel comfortable unless they're writing about something they know and understand and maybe even used to do themselves back when they were little kids and hadn't yet discovered that they weren't really any good at it. Which is probably why that Tribune sports section was chock-full of dumbass stories about the Chicago Cubs and the Chicago White Sox --neither of whom were worth a damn that year-- and pages and pages of boring batting statistics and Earned-Run Averages and reams of copy about how the pennant race was shaping up in both leagues and how some key pitcher's stupid hangnail might keep him off the mound for a couple days. I mean, you'd think baseball was the only blessed sport worth watching in the whole damn country, you know? Then again, guys like my old man laid out in their hammocks every single Sunday afternoon and every single day off work just so's they could drink their damn six-packs of beer and listen to the play-by-play from the old ballpark. At least until they dozed off, anyways....

But the worst of it was how that tiny little story on the back page of the Chicago Tribune sports section was written. The headline went something like this:

RACER CRASHES FENCE; 8 INJURED

So thank you, Hal Foust, Chicago Tribune sports writer, for picking out the most telling and important part of the entire weekend, and then going on to write three full paragraphs about the few skinned knees and bruised elbows and the one broken leg before getting into anything at all about the damn races. But I was to discover this was pretty damn typical when it came to racing coverage in national magazines and major metropolitan newspapers. I mean, if you couldn't slather a bunch of blood and gore over the pages, why bother to cover automobile racing at all? Which is probably why poor old Hal Foust's story was buried way at the back of the Tribune sports section. After all, nobody got killed. And a couple bumps and scrapes just didn't rate any kind of major headline coverage. Especially after what happened at the Farnborough Air Show in England that same weekend, when a brand-new DeHavilland jet fighter dove down eight miles out of the sky --breaking the sound barrier *three* times in the process!-- then shot across the field on a low-level, high-speed run at over 700 miles per hour, eased off, banked up into a lazy turn in order to take a slow appreciation pass over the crowd, and blew apart like a gigantic fragmentation bomb. One of the jet engines landed in a tightly bunched group of spectators on a little hillside, killing twenty-five and injuring sixty-three more, and *that* was the sort of thing you needed to make *bona fide* front-page news. Especially if you had some really gruesome photographs to go along with the story. Why, a few minor-league injuries at some car race up in Wisconsin simply couldn't compare. At least some of the victims at Elkhart were women, or there might not have been any newspaper coverage at all....

No question that dumbass Chicago Tribune story was doing its best to upset my digestion, so I put the paper down, poured myself another cup of coffee from the big china pot room service brought up with my breakfast tray, and just sort of looked out the window at the last of the Monday-morning Outer Drive traffic jam and all the swarms of suits and ties shouldering their way along the sidewalks as the 9-to-5 baseball fan-types made their way in to work. In a strange way, it reminded me of all the union stiffs filing in through the front gate at my old man's chemical plant when first shift started at seven ayem. Only the clothes and the shaves and the haircuts were different. And so I took a little moment to just sort of say "thanks" to nobody in particular for being able to go to the sportscar races and work on racecars at all hours of the night and then sit up here on a damn Monday morning looking down on all those poor slobs who were heading off to do the same damn thing they did last Monday morning and the Monday morning before that and all the other Monday mornings as far back as they could remember....

I didn't check out of the Drake Hotel until after the traffic cleared around 9:30, and I must say I was a little flabbergasted by how much it cost to get your damn shirt cleaned, pants pressed, and eggs Benedicted when you had them hand-delivered to a fancy-ass hotel room overlooking Lake Shore Drive. Sure put a hefty dent in that folded-up wad of twenties Tommy gave me for the trip home. Then again, he said he didn't expect much change back, didn't he? And the last thing I wanted to do was disappoint my good friend and part-time hero Tommy Edwards.

Truth is, I was in something of a hurry to get back home to Passaic and see Julie again, and so I pushed it along pretty good from Chicago down to Fort Wayne, Indiana, and on across the rest of Indiana and Ohio towards Pittsburgh and the beginning of the Turnpike at the Pennsylvania line. But it was a long, *long* drive, and not nearly so much fun as the trip out from Jersey. The novelty of driving the latest and fastest Jaguar racing car in the whole U.S. of A. had more or less worn off by then, and I've got to admit that even my old man's Mercury (or even Butch Bohunk's rattletrap Ford) was a little more comfortable than a racing Jaguar for any kind of long-distance highway travel. There was an incredible amount of heat coming in through the firewall and a cold wind whipping in over the top of the windscreen and I'd lost my Brooklyn Dodgers cap someplace so I got my face sunburned all morning and the back of my neck sunburned even worse all afternoon. And no matter how fast I dared to drive, it seemed to take absolutely *forever* to get from each little two-bit farm town to the next, even though I never stopped at all except to fill up the tank a couple times and do a quick kidney tap in the gas station rest rooms. Even so, it was getting on towards eleven o'clock Eastern Time by the time I saw the purple and orange flames of the Pittsburgh steel smelters licking the sky off to the south and east of me.

No question I was getting pretty tired. But I wanted to get *home,* you know? And when you've been traveling like that for ten or eleven or twelve hours straight, you get sort of lost in the droning, pounding, rolling, rumbling rhythm of it. Sometimes to the point that it's damn near *impossible* to actually slow down and head up an exit ramp to stop. So you keep telling yourself "one more exit...one more exit...one more exit" and, before you know it, you're back out in the boondocks again, climbing up through the pitch-black swoops and curves of the Appalachian mountain range, where there's no towns or exit ramps or even a wide enough shoulder to pull over and grab a few winks. Not that you could ever get your right foot to lift off the gas pedal and move over to the brake so you could do such a thing....

Then I came up over the top of this one hill a little after midnight and there was the town of Breezewood again, sitting down there in the bottom of the valley like a tin platter full of fluorescent light. It was built to be a convenient overnight stop about halfway between Chicago and New York, and it suited me just fine to use it for exactly that purpose. I found an all-night gas station right next to a little blond-brick strip motel, and the highschool kid inside agreed to keep the Jag in the service bay overnite for fifty cents. In fact, he probably would've done it for nothing. In fact, I thought he looked a little *too* eager, so I lifted up that hinged nose section and pretended to check the oil and water levels, but actually removed the distributor rotor and slipped it into my pocket. It didn't figure that you could find much in the way of spare ignition parts for a racing Jaguar in the middle of the blessed Appalachian mountain range at one o'clock in the morning. Not hardly.

Tired as I was, it took me an awfully long time to doze off to sleep, on account of I still had the rolling buzz of the highway pumping through me and the no-longer-mellow growl of that big, barely muffled Jaguar six vibrating in my ears. But I must've fallen asleep eventually, because I remember waking up early the next morning when some dumb tourist in a Buick Roadmaster made a sudden, last-second decision to cut across both westbound lanes of the Pennsylvania Turnpike in order to catch a quick fill-up and a hot cakes and sausage breakfast in Breezewood. Unfortunately, he failed to notice the big eighteen-wheel Diamond-T tanker truck just off his right rear taillight, and the poor truck driver had to throw out all the anchors in a wild, screeching, shuddering attempt to avoid wearing that particular Buick Roadmaster as a hood ornament. Fortunately the trucker managed to gather it up without collecting the idiot in the Buick (after a couple asshole-tightening tanker swings, anyway) and then he let that guy in the Roadmaster know exactly what he thought of that maneuver by leaning on a collection of at least half a dozen high-powered, chrome-plated air horns.

It was not the sort of noise you could sleep through.

Not hardly.

And there was no drifting back off for a few more winks after that, seeing as how once I was awake, I wanted to be off and on my way again. I guess you could say I was maybe a little bit homesick, you know? Which sounded pretty nuts on account of I was hardly ever home even when I was home (if that makes any sense) but somehow it was nice just knowing it was there in case I ever took a sudden notion to drop by. Plus I really wanted to see Julie. And the sooner the better....

So I checked out of the little blond-brick motel and walked across the lot to the gas station where I'd left the C-type, figuring I'd maybe drive an hour or two before stopping for breakfast. But right about then I noticed a 3/4-ton Ford pickup with trailer behind it coming up the westbound ramp off the turnpike, and hitched behind it was a flatbed trailer with a dirt-track sprint car on top. You could tell they'd been driving all night, on account of it was already well past sunup but the Ford's headlamps were still on, and when the rig made a big, wide turn through the lot and pulled up in front of the Cozy Cup Coffee Shop next door, I decided maybe I'd go over and have a slug or two of java myself and maybe even a chocolate-covered doughnut before I started heading east again. So I pulled the C-type out of the service bay, thanked the guy again, and then whipped it around in a fast, screechy arc and brought it up to a halt right next to the tow rig with the dirt-track sprint car on the back.

I always thought those oval-track cars were pretty neat, and no question I had more in common with the dirty-fingernail types who hung around that kind of racing than all the rich heirs, playboys, and black sheep of wealthy families you found on the sportycar circuit. Sure, the sportscars had a lot more *class* and *style* and hightoned pedigree going for them, but there was still something tough and straightforward and homegrown-American about racing these bolt-upright, solid-axle open-wheelers around rough dirt ovals all over the country.

I got out of the C-type and took a little walk around that trailer. It had a Texas plate on the back, and the car on top was painted bright red and metallic blue with gold-leaf lettering and white pinstripe trim. Kind of sharp, actually, but it didn't take too close an inspection to see that it had a lot of rough miles on it. It wore a big, gold-leaf number "77" on the tail section, and the words "WIN-SOME SPECIAL" spelled out along the hood in matching letters. There was still some fresh brown clay and oil spatters all over the nose and the tall plexiglass windscreen, and when I looked inside the narrow, tight, low-cut cockpit opening, I couldn't help but notice how the driveshaft ran right under the driver's seat --directly beneath the family jewels, if you catch my drift-- and that they had to put the shifter on the outside because there simply wasn't enough room for it in there with the driver. The steering wheel was enormous, and mounted close and upright so the driver could really lean his shoulders into it. Then again, I guess that's what you have to do when you're hung out broadside and three-abreast through the middle of a long corner and fighting heavy, bouncing solid axles every which way over ruts and humps or leaning up against the hardpacked berms on the outside groove. No question it took a guy with a lot of balls and moxie to climb onto a thing like that and ride it around the dirt like a damn rodeo rider on a mean Brahma bull. So I took special notice of the name spelled out in smaller gold-leaf letters below the windscreen: "Sammy Speed." What a name for a racecar driver!

I saw two guys in jeans looking at me and the C-type out the front window of the Cozy Cup, so I went inside and sat myself down next to them at the counter and ordered a cup of coffee and some French toast. One of them was short and wiry, with brown, leathery skin, close-cropped hair, and those special fighter-pilot eyes with plenty of crow's feet at the corners. The other guy was kind of pale and soft and pudgy-looking. Right away I figured him to be the mechanic, but you couldn't really tell from their hands. I mean, they'd both obviously been up to their elbows in blackened oil and busted metal sometime recently. Very recently, in fact. "That's a pretty nice rig you got out there," I told them, just trying to make a little conversation.

"You think so?" the pudgy guy grinned. "Tellya what. We'll swap it fr'that sweet little foreign job you just drove up in right here and now. Whaddaya say?" He'd already figured out I was just another grease-monkey wrench-twister, you know?

"Well, if it was up to me, I might be tempted," I told him with an offhand shrug, "but to tell the truth, it's not my car."

"Do tell."

"Yep. I'm just taking it back to New York for a friend of mine. An Englishman, actually."

"That an English car?"

"Sure is," I told him. "It's a C-type Jaguar."

"I've heard of 'em. Won that big twenty-four hour race over in France last year, didn't they?"

"That's right," I said, really impressed.

"I never actually seen one before. At least not in the flesh. How'bout you, Sammy?"

The little guy with the leathery skin shook his head. "Can't say as I have."

"Well," I explained, "they're really *something*. I'm just bringing this one back from the races up at Elkhart Lake."

"Where?"

"Elkhart Lake. Up in Wisconsin."

"I never heard of that track," the pudgy guy said, pulling the last half of a used five-cent cigar out of his shirt pocket and lighting up. "You ever heard of that track, Sammy?"

"Can't say as I have."

"How long is it?" the guy with the cigar wanted to know.

"Six and a half miles," I told him, "up hills and down through valleys and all over the whole blessed countryside."

"Isn't that something!" the guy said, shaking his head. "You ever run on a track like that, Sammy?"

Sammy Speed shook his head. "Nope. Can't say I've ever had the opportunity." Then I saw that special little race-driver spark light up in the corner of his eye. "But I'd do it. Do it in a minute. All's I'd need is a chance."

"He would, too," the pudgy guy grinned. "And I bet he'd do real good at it, too."

"A car's a car and a road's a road," Sammy Speed allowed. "All's a decent race driver needs is an opportunity."

"Amen to that, brother," his mechanic agreed.

I caught myself thinking about Cal Carrington, you know?

"By the way," the pudgy guy said, "I'm Spud Webster and this here's Sammy Speed. You prob'ly ain't heard of him too much yet. But you will."

"That your real name?" I asked. "I mean, that's a pretty darn good name for a racecar driver."

Sammy Speed looked down into his coffee cup and didn't say anything. "Aw, don't mind him," Spud grinned, "he's a little embarrassed about that. Aren'tcha, Sammy?"

"Ahh, g'wan," Sammy growled, "leave it alone."

"His real name is Sammy Slowinski," Spud whispered, leaning in real close like it was some big major government secret, "but he tells people he went and had it legally changed."

"Aw, I do not," Sammy snorted, pretending like he was getting real angry, "I just do it for my work, see." You couldn't miss the little twitch of a smile threatening to break out at the corners of his mouth. "I mean, who's gonna hire themselves a driver named *SLOW*-inski, huh?"

"Yeah," Spud agreed. "It's like all those Hollywood stars, you know? They make up names for themselves all the time."

"Yup," I nodded, "they sure do."

"No reason why a racecar driver can't do the same damn thing, right?"

"No reason at all."

"Glad we agree on that. How'bout you, Sammy?"

"Can't say as it makes much difference t'me one way or the other," he yawned, "just so long as I get t'drive decent cars."

"So," Spud asked, "how'd you guys do up at that road race in Wisconsin?"

"Well," I said, kind of back-pedaling my way around the truth, *"my* driver had a few little problems --you know how that goes-- but our teammate from California won the race on Saturday and finished fourth overall and first in class on Sunday."

"Really?" Spud said, obviously impressed. "What's one of those races pay to win, anyway?"

"Ahh, well," I said, trying to figure out a way to explain it to them, "they don't pay *anything,* see. In fact, the S.C.M.A. specifically *forbids* any kind of prize money at their races."

Sammy Speed and Spud Webster looked back and forth at each other like something had just gone wrong with their ears.

"Then how can y'make a damn living at it?" Spud asked.

"Well, *I* make a living preparing the cars and hustling 'em back and forth to the races and fixing 'em when they break."

"But how 'bout the *drivers?*"

"Well, see, *they're* generally the ones who wind up paying me t'do it. Or actually they pay my boss, see, and then he takes something like eighty-five or ninety percent of the money and gives me what's left."

Spud took a long drag off the stub end of his cigar and shook his head. "But how do the drivers earn a damn *living?*" he wanted to know.

"Well," I tried to explain, "most of these sportycar guys already *have* money. Lots of it, in fact."

"So they actually *pay* to race?"

"And they can't win *anything?*"

"Yep," I nodded, "that's it exactly."

Sammy Speed shook his head and laughed. "I guess it takes all kinds to make a world, doesn't it?"

"Well, Sammy," Spud grinned, "y'gotta understand. It's one a'them sit-down-to-pee *European* sports, see?"

"I guess...."

The waitress brought us over another round of coffee, and I decided to ask a few things about their car and the kind of racing they did. "Well," Spud allowed, "it's an old Diedt chassis with a Meyer-Drake Offy on twin Riley carburetors, and we run about the whole damn Triple-A championship circuit. Or we will this year, anyway. Next May we really want to qualify for the 500 at Indianapolis, but we probably need a little better car for that. Maybe a year-old Kurtis or something if we can afford it...."

Sammy Speed rolled his eyes, and I got the idea that things were just a little tight money-wise on the Triple-A circuit.

"So," I asked, "where're you guys coming from?"

"Aw, we just got done with a race on the big one-mile track up by Syracuse. Jack McGrath won that one. Sammy here finished sixth, I think...."

"Seventh," Sammy corrected him.

"Okay. Maybe it was seventh. But we don't really have the best setup for those long tracks. Not enough power. And we were gettin' a little low on tire money, too...."

"Yeah," Sammy Speed sighed, "you could say we've hit a sort of dry patch the last couple races."

"That's too bad."

"Hey, it happens to everybody now and then."

"Yeah," Spud agreed. "I always figured that was one of the big differences between car racing and most other sports."

"How's that?" I asked.

"The odds stink." He took a final drag off the last three-quarter-inch fragment of his cigar and explained. "Now, you take a look at most of your popular stick-and-ball sports, and half the people who play get to go home winners after every single game. *Half* of them! But you go to a car race --especially a bigtime event like the Indianapolis 500-- and the odds start out at 33-to-1 and get worse from there depending on how your equipment stacks up against everybody else."

"So why do it?" I asked without thinking.

Sammy Speed looked at me like I didn't have a brain in my head. "Y'do it because someday you're gonna catch a break and get a ride in a really competitive car, and that's when you're gonna show 'em all that you *belong.*"

"Then you're *in,*" Spud added, gingerly grinding his cigar stub out on the edge of his saucer.

"So," I asked, "where'd you guys race before Syracuse?"

"Hmm. Lessee," Spud mused, thinking it over, "we ran the week before Syracuse at DuQuoin, Illinois. I think it was Chuck Stevenson won that race. Sammy was up to fourth, but we lost a cylinder. Plug wire shorted out. Insulation melted, y'know? Anyhow, that would've been Sunday, I think. The day before we were up by Detroit for a hundred-miler. Sammy did good up there and finished third...."

"It was fourth."

"Okay, *fourth.* Billy Vukovich won it for J.C. Agajanian up there. Drove his ass off, too."

"He's a wild one," Sammy Speed agreed with a mixture of awe and defiance. "Someday I'm gonna have *me* a car that good. Then we'll see what's what...."

"Your time'll come, Sammy. No doubt about that."

"Nope. No doubt a'tall." You couldn't miss the fierce look in Sammy Speed's eyes.

"Where was I?" Spud asked. "Oh yeah. Detroit, Michigan. Anyhow, the week before was West Allis for the Milwaukee State Fair, and two weeks before that was Springfield, Illinois, and, aw geez, I can't remember it all straight without my notebook, and I left it out in the truck...."

"So that's all you guys do? Just go around to the races?"

"Yup. We're on our way out to Denver for a race on the 28th, and I'm hoping we can stop home in Fort Worth for a week or so t'give the old crate a little rebuild and a few fresh parts. She's pretty wore out right now --the racecar and the tow wagon both-- and it wouldn't hurt fr'me t'check in on my wife an' see if I'm still married anymore. After that, we'll haul on up towards Denver on the 25th or 26th for the race at Centennial Park, then head south again when that one's over for the race in Phoenix on November 11th. If the money holds out, anyways. But at least that's the last one on the schedule fr'this year. And, like Sammy says, we got some irons in the fire for a little better sponsorship deal and maybe even a new chassis for next year...."

"Yeah," Sammy nodded, rubbing his eyes, "that'd sure go a long way towards putting a few more beans on the table."

"Might even get us in the first couple rows at Indianapolis come next May. That's where the *real* money is...."

"Wow!" I said, giving the two of them a low, respectful whistle. "I can't believe you guys actually make a full-time living off of this, you know?"

"Neither can we!" Spud laughed.

"Well," Sammy allowed with a tough, hard edge to his voice, "we been at it three whole seasons now, and somehow we're still at it."

"Yeah," Spud grinned, shooting me a wink, "just *puh-leez* don't ask us how...."

Chapter 29: Ten Crazy Days

I had a lot to think about during the rest of that all-day drive home across Pennsylvania and New Jersey on Tuesday. It was a beautiful early-fall day, and the green C-type was running sweet and smooth and turning heads as always everywhere it went. But I couldn't really just lean back and enjoy it, on account of I was coming to understand --more than ever-- that I was never going to amount to anything more than a grunt-level hired hand around Westbridge, and the fact it offered me a chance to rub shoulders with a bunch of rich, stylish, good-looking people with entirely too much money in their pockets and time on their hands didn't mean any of it was going to magically rub itself off on me. Sure, I loved the exotic cars and the excitement of the racing, and no question it was rewarding to put in your time and effort on a machine and then have some topflight driver like Cal Carrington or Phil Hill or even Tommy Edwards (in spite of his problems at Elkhart Lake) really put the spurs to it and finish up front.

But after meeting a couple guys like Sammy Speed and Spud Webster --guys who were out there on the highways, rolling from one dirt-bullring money race to the next on their last couple nickels, trying like hell to break into the bigtime and make an actual *living* out of automobile racing-- well, all of a sudden all those rich sportycar guys started looking like a bunch of lah-de-dah Play Racers to me. It was all about *money,* see, and I was coming to understand that poor, dull, blue-collar grunts like me generally wound up working for the Colin St. Johns and Barry Splines of this world, or wound up living hand-to-mouth on the road like Spud Webster and Sammy Speed, or --worse yet-- wound up with a permanent lifetime position as some rich dork's Personal Racing Squire like that tight-assed geek Milton Fitting was for Skippy Welcher. And here I was, heading back across the Appalachian mountains in one of the two rarest, fastest, sleekest, and most valuable Jaguar sportscars in the whole damn country, thinking on and off about Julie Finzio and how this really wasn't what I wanted to do with the rest of my life. Sure, I wanted to stay around the cars and the racing --desperately, in fact-- but I wanted a way to earn a damn living at it, too!

It was a shame my old man wasn't around to hear all the stuff that was going through my head. I mean, it sounded almost, you know, sort of *adult* and *responsible* and all that kind of crap. Exactly the sort of junk he used to lecture me about after the ninth inning was over and there was no more beer in the damn refrigerator. Then again, who wanted to give him the blessed satisfaction? Made me wonder just what the hell was going on inside of me. Why, if you'd asked me just a couple months before (especially after that first-ever race at Bridgehampton) how I'd fancy spending the rest of my life as a *bona fide* road-gypsy racecar mechanic --traveling around all the time from one damn corner of the country to another, doing nothing but tending to racecars and making 'em run as fast and far as they could--well, I most likely would've asked where I could sign up. Hell, I'dve even offered to do the job for free....

Only now I'd Been There and Done That for most of a summer, and I had to admit that some of the glamour and glory had scraped off and faded away during the long road trips and longer garage nights and way too many rocky mornings-after and especially after seeing the look in the eyes of Sammy Speed and Spud Webster when they talked about tire money and how far they were from Texas and all the nights they'd slept in the back of their truck so's they'd have enough gas and coffee money to make the next race. And that's really how I came to realize that I was coming down with a terminal case of the Racing Mechanic Disease myself, where all the days start running together like a muddy stream and you never find yourself thinking any further ahead than the next damn race weekend and all the thousands of little details that somehow have to get themselves handled before the green flag waves to turn the cars loose again. And all of a sudden I saw in my mind how a bright, eager, enthusiastic young guy could turn himself into a haggard, bleary-eyed, weak-willed chunk of meat stuck on the end of all the ratchets and sockets and box-end wrenches and pairs of pliers that actually got the job done. Sure, it was exciting...otherwise who would do it? On the other hand, who the hell wanted to earn their living doing dumbass mufflers and shocks and tuneups and brake jobs on the endless stream of Fords, Chevys, Plymouths, and Henry Js that all the eight-hour-a-day working stiffs drove to their jobs every weekday morning and out to Grandma's house for dinner every

Sunday afternoon. But where was the damn *future* in being a racecar mechanic, you know? Never any further ahead than the next damn race, far as I could tell....

As you can imagine, I did myself a lot of deep thinking (not to mention more than a little plotting and planning) as the C-type and I tooled our way eastward across New Jersey. The one thing I hardly thought about at all was my night with Sally Enderle up at Elkhart Lake. In fact, you couldn't really call it a whole night, since the entire episode took less than an hour, and I doubt more than five or ten minutes of that were actual sack time. Believe it or not, I kind of wished it never happened, and I wondered if maybe Sally felt the same. And of course that's when it dawned on me that Sally obviously didn't much give a care one way or the other, and *that* --more than anything else-- was the reason why I wished it'd never happened. I felt so, you know, *cheap*....

So my strange experience with Sally was sitting there in the back of my head like a black door with an ugly secret behind it or maybe one of those licorice candy tins eight-year-old boys keep under their mattresses for their mothers to find, which usually contain month-old nightcrawlers or collections of mouse feet gathered from old traps in the basement or a few large-sized garden spiders or the remains of recently dissected frogs. At any rate, every time I caught myself starting to think and wonder and worry over Sally Enderle, it was no problem at all to start myself thinking and wondering and worrying about something else. And by the time I finally rolled into Passaic around 6:30 PM, I knew just exactly where I wanted to go. I headed straight over to the Doggy Shake to see if maybe Julie was on duty. And for a change I was in luck. From almost a block away, I could see she was standing with a couple of the other girls outside the curb-service window, shooting the breeze about movie stars and nail-polish colors and such and waiting for the next tray of burger baskets and root beer floats to come out of the kitchen. So I pulled over real quick and did my best to kind of straighten my collar and pat down my hair in the little rearview mirror they have mounted on top of the C-type's dashboard. Then I gave the Jag a modest bootfull and came swooping into the Doggy Shake parking lot in a near-reasonable facsimile of a full-tilt powerslide, neatly balancing the Jag's rear tires precisely on the edge of a hellacious squeal. Boy, you should've seen the way everybody jumped up from their tables and jammed their noses against the window! That's a thrill you never seem to outgrow with a really sexy sportscar, no matter how long you've been driving it or how many thousands of miles you've covered.

But of course Julie Finzio wasn't about to let herself get snowed by any God Damn automobile --not even a low, sleek, obscenely expensive racing car like that C-type Jaguar! So she naturally took her own sweet time meandering over to say hello. "So," she said like I was driving a damn Nash Rambler or something, "what'll it be tonight, stranger?"

But you could see in her eyes that she was pretty damn impressed with the Jaguar --not to mention excited to see me!-- and there wasn't any doubt that I felt exactly the same about her. Maybe even moreso. But no way would a girl like Julie Finzio allow herself to get all soft and mushy with all the other Doggy Shake girls watching through the front window. Especially when I'd been off someplace without her for the past couple days. Or at least not without busting my hump for a few minutes first. Just to show me how things were, you know? "So," Julie asked again, pretending like it was all she could do to keep from yawning right in my face, "you planning to eat tonight, or did'ja just drive up here to show off your damn car?"

"I came to show off the car, of course," I told her like it should've been obvious to anybody with a brain. "After all, guys who can afford to drive around in cars like this don't generally eat their dinners at dinky little roadside drive-ins."

"I'm sure they don't," Julie snorted, "and maybe you could see your way clear someday to introduce me to one of them. I've always been real partial to dumb guys with lots of money."

"Howwzat?"

"Well, whoever owns this thing obviously has a few loose dimes and quarters rolling around in his pockets." She looked the Jag up and down, "not to mention a few loose screws rolling around in his head. What does one of these things *cost,* anyway?"

"I'm not sure exactly," I told her, casually inspecting my nails, "but I heard someone say it's around six or seven times as much as your average, run-of-the-mill Ford or Chevrolet." That was really a little bit of an exaggeration, since it was actually more like four or maybe five times as much. But guys always tend to pump stuff up bigger than normal when they're talking to girls as a matter of routine procedure. They can't help it any more than breathing. I think it must have something to do with glands or hormones or something.

Julie let out a low whistle. "Wow," she said in little more than a whisper, "then I guess the guy really *is* rich, isn't he?"

"Most of those sportycar people are."

"And dumb, too."

"How can you tell?"

"That's easy. He's lettin' a bozo like *you* drive it!"

"Well, maybe he inherited the money and doesn't care."

"Must be."

And that's when I realized I was staring so deep into Julie's eyes that it was like running into one of those dark tunnels Tommy and I raced through on the Pennsylvania Turnpike at ninety-five and a hundred miles an hour.

"So," Julie asked without moving her eyes one thousandth of an inch, "you actually know how to drive this thing or what?"

"Sure thing!" I grinned. "Why, I can drive any damn thing with four wheels and an internal combustion engine."

"So I guess I should be pretty impressed, huh?"

"No question about it."

"Oh, of course!" she laughed, rolling her eyes.

"Hey, don't take *my* word for it. Hop in an' see for yourself. Lemme take you for a quick little spin around the block...."

Julie broke her eyes away and glanced over her shoulder at the crowd inside the Doggy Shake. "I dunno, Buddy," she said, backpedaling a little. "I'd love to. Honest I would. But I'm not so sure Marvin'd go for it...."

"Marvin?! Who the hell is Marvin?"

"He's the new night manager. I think he's the owner's cousin or nephew or something. Anyhow, I'm not so sure he'd like me taking off in the middle of my shift."

The little hairs on the back of my neck sprang to attention. I mean, who the hell was this *Marvin* character, anyway. Why, I still got PO'd every time I thought about that David Sweeney guy who used to manage the kitchen at the Doggy Shake on weekends and had the nerve to take Julie out a couple times when I was all tied up with my race mechanic job over at Westbridge. Not that I had any business feeling that way, you understand. Especially not after what happened with Sally Enderle and me up at Elkhart Lake just a few short days before. And of course the instant I started thinking about that, I found myself staring down into the driver's-side footwell with my ears burning a bright cherry red. But Julie didn't seem to notice --thank goodness!-- and I can only assume it was on account of I was so blessed sunburned and windburned from riding cross-country in an open car that she couldn't tell the difference.

Anyhow, Julie went back inside to see if she could maybe go for a quick spin around the block with me, and I felt real relieved when I saw this character Marvin The Night Manager waddle out from behind the counter. Why, he didn't stand an inch over five feet tall and must've weighed in at about two-thirty or so --a real little bowling ball with legs-- and so I didn't figure him as much of a threat with Julie. But he was obviously putty in her hands, since it didn't take her more than thirty seconds (with the help of a few of the other girls, anyways) to convince fat little Marvin to let her go for a ride. Just once around the block, you understand. And I must admit my heart skipped a beat when I saw Julie take off her yellow-trimmed Doggy Shake apron and matching Doggy Shake cap and head out the door towards where I was parked in the C-type. Jeez, you really should've seen the smile spread out across her kisser and the sparkle glittering in her eyes!

At least until she tried getting herself into the C-type, anyways. I still had all the racing gear and my laundry bag and stuff piled on the shelf next to the passenger seat and packed into the footwell, and that made Julie assume a sort of deeply reclined Hammock Slouch with her legs arched up over my laundry bag and Tommy's track gear and all the assorted boxes of spare parts we'd brought along from Westbridge. "You comfy?" I asked her.

"Oh, sure, Palumbo. Like I'm about to give birth."

"Great!" I said, patting her on the knee, "now just hang on!" And with that, I punched the starter button and watched Julie jerk damn near bolt upright as the exhaust pipes exploded into action just below her left ear. She struggled to keep herself up as I reversed out of the parking slot, but flopped right down again when I snicked the lever into first, gave her about 4000 rpm, dumped the clutch, and left two smoldering black stripes of Dunlop's finest all the way out onto Fremont Street. I took the big twincam clear up to redline in first, snapped the shifter back

hard into second, and gave it one more short blast before backing
out at around fifty-five or sixty or so and dropping her gently
down into fourth. I looked over at Julie, and her eyes were
bugged out like a goldfish on a living-room floor.

"Jee-*zus*, Palumbo," she gasped, borrowing one of my own
personal favorite exclamations, "is this thing ever *fast!*"

"I'd say so!" I nodded enthusiastically. "And you know what
else it can do?"

Julie shook her head.

"It can *STOP!*" And I proceeded to throw out the anchors,
double-clutch down to second, whip around a corner onto a sidestreet, yank her *slap!-slap!* left-right the other way up an alleyway between two buildings, and jammed on the brakes so hard
that the car damn near stood on its nose! We were behind the
loading dock of Martino's Appliance Store, and before the Jag
even rocked back level again, I reached over and grabbed Julie
with both hands and planted the Kiss Of The Century right smack
on the center of her lips. And she kissed me back, too! "Jesus,
Buddy," she gasped when we finally came up for air, "what the
hell was *that* all about?"

"I dunno," I told her, my face starting to turn red again, "I
guess I just kinda, you know, *missed* you or something...."

And I guess I really did, too.

I kept the Jag overnight in my Aunt Rosamarina's garage,
and drove it down to Westbridge early the next morning with
every intention of quitting. Julie'd told me how her uncle was
still having a few health problems and all, and that she'd already
kind of greased the way for me to come back to work at the Old
Man's Sinclair if that's what I wanted to do. And as a sort of
Assistant Management Trainee, no less. I guess the Old Man had
been through yet another couple so-called "professional automobile mechanics" since the last time I'd talked to Julie (the latest
one spent most of his time trying to steal the station's customers
so he could work on them as side jobs at home) and Old Man
Finzio was well past ready for somebody he could actually trust.
So I made a point of dropping in on him bright and early that
morning before I headed across the bridge into Manhattan. And
believe it or not, the Old Man seemed almost happy to see me.
Why, for a crazy moment I thought I detected the faintest wee

flicker of a smile twitching up around the corners of his mouth. Although you could never be sure about that kind of thing. Anyhow, he ran his eyes up and down the dark green C-type and gave it a grudging nod of approval. "Well, well, would'ja just look at this here," he rasped in a voice like a rusty scouring pad, "I think it's one a'them famous international racing mechanics I heerd so much about."

"Aw, geez, Mr. Finzio, it's just me. Buddy Palumbo."

"Well, so it is. So it is. Didn't hardly recognize you."

"Must be the car."

"Yeah, that must be it all right." He pulled a wrinkled-up Camel out of the flattened-down pack in his back pocket and lit it up. "So," he wheezed, trying hard not to break down in one of his coughing jags, "what brings an important guy like you around to a little old streetcorner gas station?"

"Well," I told him, sticking out my hand, "I came t'see if maybe I could get my old job back." Now, the truth of it was that I didn't so much want my *old* job back as to maybe put myself a deal together for a much *better* job. One where I fixed and maintained a lot of fancy European sportscars right there at the Sinclair. One where I could wind up *running* the shop one day, and running it the way *I* thought a really highclass foreign car repair shop ought to be run. I had this idea in the back of my head that I could bring in enough high-dollar imported sportscar work to really make a decent living there at the Sinclair, you know? I mean, there wasn't anybody else in the area doing it, and every day you were seeing more and more MGs and Jags and stuff all over the Jersey side of the Hudson. And you could charge plenty on those cars, too --lots more than you ever could for Dodges and DeSotos and Buicks and such-- and most of those sportycar customers were only too happy to pay it if you could just do the damn work properly and get it finished in a reasonable amount of time. Why, I might even be able to get a few racing customers going so I could keep heading off to places like Bridgehampton and Grand Island and Elkhart Lake, Wisconsin, every now and then when the mood struck me. Only this time I'*d* be the one who finished up the weekend with a pocketful of tens and twenties (and maybe even a few fifties!) instead of Barry Spline and Colin St. John, you know? And, judging by the ashen-yellow tinge to Old Man Finzio's complexion and the ugly grating/gurgling noises going on inside his chest, he was gonna *need* somebody to run that place for him. And soon, too.

But I knew you had to be careful about what you said and how you acted around the Old Man. I mean, he'd kicked the shit out of enough poor, sick, crippled-up old mongrel dogs in his lifetime to know that the last thing you wanted was to be was old and sick and crippled-up and helpless. In fact, I'd have to say that particular morning was the first time I ever saw cold-blooded *fear* drifting around like a silent grey mist in Old Man Finzio's eyes. It wasn't fear of being sick or even fear of dying, but that Worst Of All Fear of winding up helpless and having to rely on other people. The thought of it had turned Old Man Finzio all dried-up and trembly inside, right below the surface where you could see it plain as day if you knew him well enough.

And I couldn't say as I blamed him, you know?

Anyhow, the Old Man and me shot the bull back and forth for a couple minutes, and he even allowed as how he'd maybe *think it over* about letting me come back to work there at the Sinclair. Maybe. If I asked him real nice.

So I did.

Needless to say, Barry Spline didn't take too kindly to my notion to just pack up and leave the job at Westbridge later that same morning. "Where's yer bloody sense of *loyalty?*" he wailed, his nostrils flaring angrily. "Why, we've one bloody race ter go yet h'at Watkins Glen *--the biggest bloody race of our whole bleedin' season!--* and that's th'time yer bloody well decide yer wanter run home t'yer bleedin' momma!"

"Gee whiz, Barry," I told him, "it's not like *that.*"

"Oh? And just 'ow is it then? We got ourselves the biggest bloody last-minute project of the whole bleedin' year t'finish up fer Tommy Edwards, and yer not gonna be around t'do yer bleedin' share...."

"How's that?" I asked, just a little curious about what that project could possibly be.

Barry curled his lip at me. "Can't bloody tell *you,* mate. Why, h'its top bloody secret!" He spit on the floor behind the parts counter for emphasis.

"Really?! What *is* it?" I asked, kind of sucking in my breath. In spite of all my thinking and planning and plotting and considering on the long drive back from Wisconsin, I was still a sitting-duck sucker for an interesting racecar project.

"Can't give any bleedin' information h'out ter somebody like yerself 'oo won't even be around t'lend a hand...."

"I don't get it."

"Well, why not just take yerself a bloody look 'round the back of the shop, eh?" Barry growled, and walked into the office.

So I did, and it didn't take long to find Sylvester Jones bent over a huge, gaping hole smack dab in the middle of Tommy Edwards' Allard. "What's goin' on?" I asked him.

"How th'hell should *I* know?" Sylvester snorted, fiddling with the fuel and oil pressure lines on the Allard's firewall. "They tells me t'pull out a damn engine and I *pulls* out a damn engine. Even if th'damn thing is running jus' fine as it can be. *Sheeeee-IT!* It don't make no differents t'me...."

Sure enough, the hot-rodded Caddy V8 out of Tommy's Allard was sitting on a hand truck parked against the back wall, still trickling a little blackened oil and brackish water out onto the concrete floor. It made me wonder what was up, you know? I mean, no question that was one *fast* Cadillac engine sitting back there against the wall.

About then that Colin St. John came out of his office like a launched torpedo, and I swear I almost saw a wake behind him as he headed across the floor in my direction. *"So!"* he snapped in a high, shrill, icy voice, "I understand you're planning to leave us today. Is that the case?"

"Well, er, uhh," I mumbled into my shirt collar, feeling like a rat abandoning a sinking ship, "it's just I, uhh, I...."

"Don't mumble, young man," Colin growled with ill-concealed disgust, "spit it out."

"Well, see, it's like this," I told him, hunting around for words like a guy pretending to look for change in his pockets when he knows he doesn't have a cent to his name. "I been doing a lot of thinking, see...."

"And?"

"And, well, Manhattan is just so far away from *home,* you know...." I said it like that seedy little apartment over my Aunt Rosamarina's garage was someplace off a Hallmark greeting card, what with maybe a roast turkey on the table and a warm fire crackling and the whole blessed family gathered around to watch my father sleep off his customary holiday drunk.

"So that's why you're *quitting?*" Colin demanded, drawing himself up like he had a wire pulling on the top of his head.

"Well, I kinda got a girlfriend, too, and she's been tellin' me she's plain sick and tired of never seeing me anymore and never going out to movies together and stuff...."

"But you've had this girlfriend all summer long, have you not?" Colin asked with a prosecuting attorney's edge to his voice.

"Well, yeah. Sorta." I could see he wasn't buying it. Not hardly. "And, well, I also got this opportunity to run my own shop back at the gas station in Passaic, see...."

"Oh, I *see* all right," Colin snorted contemptuously, "in fact, I see *perfectly*. You have an opportunity to take the skills and knowledge you have learned right here --in this very shop!-- and using them to leave us in our time of greatest need so that you can go into business against us." Colin looked down his nose at me like I was a smear of road slime. "I do have that all proper and correct, don't I?"

"Well, uhh, geez, Mr. St. John, if you put it *that* way...."

"Oh?! And could you perhaps explain some *other* way that I should put it? My understanding as of ten minutes ago is that you plan to simply take your leave --on a moment's notice!-- and leave us in a lurch with the biggest, most important event of our entire summer season at hand, not caring in the least that we have undertaken a *major* engine project on your supposed 'friend' Mr. Edwards' Allard..."

"Ahh, gee whiz, Mr. St. John...."

"...a project that will undoubtedly *not* be completed in time for Mr. Edwards to race at Watkins Glen because of your sudden and capricious departure." He fixed me with a look of withering disgust and then sadly shook his head. "You are planning to leave us," he asked me point-blank, "aren't you?"

"Uhh, well, gee whiz, a'*course* not, Mr. St. John," I heard myself say, "I mean, you'd have to be a real heel or something to do a thing like that...."

"Indeed," Colin agreed softly, and just like that I realized old Colin St. John had somehow maneuvered things around and turned the tables on me.

Again.

"But I'm still planning to leave after Watkins Glen," I threw in lamely, trying to salvage myself some small, tiny fragment of self respect.

"That will be fine with us," Colin agreed coolly. "As a matter of fact, we usually terminate the majority of our race mechanic positions after the last event of the season anyway." He said it like they had maybe two or three dozen race-weekend grease monkeys working there at Westbridge instead of just me.

So without really thinking about it, I'd somehow agreed to stay on at Westbridge two more weeks until after Watkins Glen was over. And that in spite of discovering that I was most likely about to get fired anyway once the damn racing season was over! Not that it was anything personal, you understand. Just the normal, seasonally adjusted economics of the racing business....

I went across the street to the sandwich shop where I could at least be a little bit alone and called Julie's mom's house. But there was no answer --thank goodness, really-- so I called the Sinclair and told Old Man Finzio that I'd given my two weeks notice at Westbridge (like that's what I'd planned to do all along, you know?) and would be ready to come back to work at the Sinclair on Monday the 22nd. He didn't much more than grunt and snarl once or twice into the other end of the line, and it was actually nice to hear him sounding a little more like his nasty old self again. "Say, lissen," he said before hanging up on me, "y'oughter call Big Ed sometime. He's been droppin' by with that fancy-ass English sportscar of his, lookin' fer you...."

"Oh?"

"Yeah. Couple times at least. Y'oughter give him a call over to the scrapyard."

"Okay. Sure I will. Thanks."

The Old Man hung up on me, which was more or less his way of saying goodbye.

So I got the number from information and rang up Big Ed at his scrapyard over by the Jersey shore, and he right away dropped whatever he was doing and picked up the phone as soon as he heard it was me on the line. "Hey, long time no see," he said around his cigar, "whaddaya been up to?"

"Aw, not too awful much. Just workin' my ass off down at Westbridge. But I been goin' to a lotta those sportscar races and stuff all summer."

"So I heard. I see a couple of those friends of yours over at the meetings every now and then, see."

"Meetings?"

"The S.C.M.A. meetings over in Manhattan."

"You mean you got *in?*" I couldn't believe it, you know? I mean, the last I heard Charlie Priddle was still Head Man on the S.C.M.A.'s membership committee (not to mention just about every other S.C.M.A. committee you could think of) and he'd made it pretty obvious he'd sooner take his liver out with a pair of needlenose pliers than let Big Ed Baumstein join the club.

"Naw," Big Ed groused at the other end of the line, "I didn't get in. But I started showing up at the damn meetings anyway. Just to piss that Charlie Priddle asshole off, y'know?"

"What a swell idea."

"Yeah, wasn't it though. Anyhow, I'd just sort of hang around the bar and buy a few rounds for some of the guys before the actual meeting started in a private room upstairs. Charlie even put a guard at the door just t'make sure I couldn't come in. But I didn't even try, see. Didn't want to give the little prick the satisfaction of having me thrown out, you know? But I got t'know some of the other members pretty good. It even turns out we do a little scrap machincry business here and there with some of 'em."

"Oh?"

"Yeah. Some of 'em actually hold down jobs and *work* for a living. Really they do."

"But you still can't get in?"

"Nah. Not unless I have that Priddle asshole fitted for a building foundation or a concrete dock piling someplace first."

"That's too bad."

"Nah it isn't."

"It isn't?"

"Nah." And then it got real quiet on the other end, and I could almost see Big Ed's cigar making its usual Wild Idea rolls and twirls and figure-eight spiral loops right above the receiver. "I figgered a way so's I can race my Jaguar anyway, see."

"You *did?*"

"Uh-huh. And believe me, it's gonna piss off that Charlie Priddle jerk something awful. But there ain't a damn thing he can do about it."

"Why, that's, that's, that's..." I was stumbling for a word, you know? "...that's just *terrific!*"

"Yeah, ain't it. Anyhow, that's where you come in."

"I do?"

"Yeah. I need for you t'come up to Watkins Glen with me this next weekend. T'help me get the car squared away and all."

"Sure, Big Ed. Glad to. I got a lot of experience at that sort of stuff now. Honest I do."

"So I heard. Everybody says you do a good job."

Big Ed couldn't have made me feel any better if he'd given me a two hundred dollar tip. But then I remembered the deal I'd just made with Colin St. John. "Say, listen," I told him, "I got one little problem though," and I explained to Big Ed about my two weeks notice at Westbridge and the big mystery project I had to help with on Tommy Edwards' Allard.

"No sweat," Big Ed said without skipping a beat, "I run a business, an' I unnerstan' how stuff like that goes. Just see you find time t'go through my Jaguar before we hafta leave for the races. The guy I got workin' on it now's got it screwed up something awful. It runs like shit, no lie."

"Shouldn't be a problem," I told him, all the while taking a certain perverse pride in knowing the Jag was running poorly without my attention. "By the way, how'dja ever manage to swing a deal so's you could race with those tight-assed S.C.M.A. types, anyway?"

"I ain't saying nothin'. Not to you or anybody else. But you'll see soon enough up at Watkins Glen. You and Charlie Priddle and all those other two-bit Ivy League assholes whose families came over on the damn Mayflower," Big Ed took a long, slow drag on his cigar. "I got a nice little surprise worked up for those nose-in-the-air S.C.M.A. guys...."

It sounded like another one of Big Ed's world-class ideas, and no question I wanted to be a part of it. "So what can I do to help?" I asked.

"Just get the damn car ready. I can leave it over by Old Man Finzio's if you want," he took a quick pull off his cigar, "the grapevine sez you're comin' back t'work there anyway."

"Gee whiz," I damn near gasped, "how'dja know *that?*"

"That niece of his with th'big knockers told me. You know, that Julie you like so much."

"Oh, really?" I sort of choked, "and exactly when was that?"

"Last week, I think. Or maybe the week before...."

And that's when I started wondering all over again about who the hell was actually in control of my life. I mean, just when I was starting to get this notion that I was really Taking Charge Of Things for a change and turning into the captain of my own ship, I come to discover that I'm most likely just another dumb below-decks slob with an oar in the water.

You ever wonder like that?

Back inside the garage at Westbridge, I asked Barry what the Big Deal was with Tommy Edwards' Allard. "Yer'll see in h'about an 'our or so, mate," he said with a mysterious wink. "Let's just say we need yer t'go on a quiet little cross-town parts h'excursion with Colin and me, eh?" And sure enough, Barry came around an hour or so later and pulled me off the post-race nut-and-bolt inspection and lube-and-oil job I was doing on the green C-type. The rumor around the shop was that the C-type had been sold again, and we had to get it all spiffed up, prepped, and pretty for its new owner before Watkins Glen. Anyhow, I only had a little more to do --just the brake adjusters and a spoke-and-knockoff check-- and I really would've just as soon finished it up. But Colin was in a big damn hurry on account of "we had to meet something someplace," and I must admit that sounded a little strange to me. It also seemed odd that we needed three whole people to go on a damn run in the parts truck, you know?

But it was never my business to ask questions around the shop at Westbridge (not that I would've got much in the way of answers even if I did) and so I packed up my tools and clambered into the back of the parts truck while Colin and Barry climbed in front (what else?) and then did my best to stay more-or-less seated on the hard steel wheelwell while we bounced, shimmied, hopped, and juddered our way across Manhattan towards the Williamsburg bridge. I still had no idea where in hell we might be going, and naturally Colin and Barry were deep into their usual, highly private, Lord Of The Manor/Faithful Manservant smalltalk, and I might as well have been a junkyard engine block or a sack of oil-dry or even a damn potted date palm sitting there in the back of the truck. It made me think about how nice and courteous and *friendly* both of them used to be back when I was a Paying Customer instead of a lowly, piece-of-dogmeat Grunt Peon employee. I especially remembered how Colin himself used to ease me slyly aside for "a swifty" out of those Niagara Falls glasses of his every time I stopped by to drop a large wad of Big Ed's folding money behind the Westbridge parts counter. But everything changed the instant I went to work for him. Why, you'dve thought I instantly lost fifteen or twenty I.Q. points --like maybe I'd tilted my head a little too far and they'd rolled out of my ear or something.

Then again, I've noticed that the English have always been a little, you know, *stuffy* about social pecking orders and such. Everybody in their proper place, don't you know? Like the deal at Westbridge was that the paying customers always spoke direct-ly to Colin St. John (when he was around, anyway) and then Colin talked to Barry, and then Barry came around to tell all of us dumb, lumbering working stiffs out back in the shop what to do with the damn cars. It was actually amazing how those two could make up an entire multi-tiered and military-style Chain Of Command out of barely enough people to fill your average clothes closet. Here in the states, blue-collar types are generally pretty vocal about being equal to their bosses (and then some!) in every way but take-home pay. Especially the union guys. But the English all seem to believe in this time-honored secret-handshake Human Grading System based on social position, family blood-line, and coin of the realm (usually in that precise order) and most of them are pretty devout about it. Even the guys at the lumpy end of the stick. But, like Colin always said, "If you don't keep minding your *sirs* and *madams* on a regular, twenty-four-hour-per-day, seven-day-per-week basis, the whole damn thing just collapses like a bloody house of cards. Why, just look at what's happened here in America...."

At any rate, we crossed over the Williamsburg bridge into Brooklyn, took Grand Street east to Bushwick, jogged south a few blocks, and then headed east again on Atlantic, and it wasn't until we picked up the Sunrise Highway that I realized we were on our way to Idlewild airport. But I still couldn't figure why on

earth we were going there, or what Colin St. John could possibly
have in mind that required three whole people and a parts truck
to accomplish. So my curiosity glands were pumping overtime by
the time Barry wheeled us up the entrance road into Idlewild, and
they accelerated to Maximum Flow as we passed right on by the
passenger terminal and headed up a little side access road that
curved around behind the building and dumped us right out on
the flight line. Jeez, I'd never been out on an airport flight apron
before, and I've got to admit it was a little overwhelming. All
around us, big four-motor DC6s and twin-engined, tail-dragger
DC3 gooneybirds were getting between-flight service and loading
up with passengers and luggage. We even passed by one of those
long, incredibly graceful Lockheed Constellations (you know, the
ones with the three tailfins) done up in Pan American Clipper
Service colors, and apparently just returned from someplace
warm and tropical, judging from the flower-print shirts and straw
hats on the departing passengers. Like I said, I'd never been out
on an airport flight line before, and it put a little hollow buzz in
my gut being so close to the airplanes. They were just so damn
big and *noisy*, you know? And then one of those monstrous
double-decker Boeing B377 Stratocruisers passed right over us on
its landing approach --engines howling!-- and it seemed like an
entire Manhattan skyscraper was toppling over in our direction.
Which is probably the reason I tried to dive for cover (of which
there wasn't any in the back of the Westbridge parts truck) and
banged my head on the opposite-side wheelwell. "I say," Barry
called back, "did'jer have yerself a wee fright there, mate?" And
Colin and Barry proceeded to enjoy themselves a nasty little
chuckle at my expense. Real funny, you know?

Anyhow, we followed along the perimeter of the flight
apron towards a faded grey hangar with some ex-military freight
planes and a few beatup forklift trucks parked around it. "Wait
here," Colin told me, and he and Barry disappeared into the
building. So I sat there with the back door open and watched that
huge Boeing Stratocruiser as it taxied past, and it was hard to
believe that anything so heavy and enormous could possibly get
itself off the ground. I mean, any schoolkid can tell you that your
average chunk of metal won't fly any farther than you can throw
it (a fact you can demonstrate yourself with any garden-variety
coffee can, claw hammer, monkey wrench, or anvil) and those

things certainly weighed in a lot lighter than a Boeing B377 Stratocruiser. Why, it was scary just thinking about it. Plus I'd had enough ugly mechanical experiences with automobiles not to have the greatest trust or faith in the designers and engineers who spend their workdays poring over drafting tables (not to mention the clock-punching production-line workers who screw stuff together in manufacturing plants) and you must admit that the sky is a little short on places to pull over and have a quick looksee if any serious problems crop up. So it was kind of scary being so close and watching those huge, rivet-winged monsters rolling down the runway --engines roaring against the throttle stops and the whole thing kind of vibrating-- gaining speed and gaining speed as they strained upwards. I swear, my heart stopped cold every time I saw one of them lift its wheels up off the concrete and climb into the sky....

"Ahh, Mr. Palumbo? Excuse me?"

I wheeled around and Colin St. John was staring at me over the seatback. "Huh?"

"Everything's set. Come give us a hand now."

So I followed him into the hangar, wondering just what the hell was up, and we stopped in the middle of the floor next to a wooden crate the size of a Frigidaire icebox. I cocked my head so I could read the label on the side, and sure enough it was addressed to Tommy Edwards c/o Westbridge Motor Car Company, Ltd, Manhattan. I noticed the return address was someplace in Detroit. Hmmm. Well, the three of us could hardly budge the thing --not even with two of the air-freight attendants helping-- and Barry had to back the parts truck right into the building so they could load it in with one of the forklifts. With a lot of grunting and shoving and cussing and sweating, we eventually managed to get the crate more or less levered into the back of the truck, and the sheer weight of it compressed the springs so much that I expected the front wheels to pick right up off the ground! It didn't look real safe or stable to me --not hardly!-- so we took a bunch of rope and a piece of chain and kind of lashed it down as best we could, and then all three of us squeezed into the front seat to try and balance the load. On our way out of the airport, a strange, thunderous whooshing sound passed over us --like the noise Niagara Falls makes, only coming from the sky-- and I looked up to see one of those brand new British Overseas Airways Comets coming in from someplace in Europe. That was the first-ever passenger jetliner, and it was brand-spanking new back in 1952. I remember thinking how incredible it was that ordinary people (well, ordinary *rich* people, anyway) could just walk up to a ticket counter and book passage on a jet flight across the Atlantic ocean. All it took was money. And were they ever beautiful airplanes, too. I even thought so after two of them suddenly fell out of the sky shortly after takeoff during the spring of '53. Turned out much later that the square side windows were the culprit, and unseen cracks were developing at the corners. The company fixed that by changing to round windows, but of course by then the Comet had a terrible reputation and nobody in their right mind wanted to fly on one. Truth is, I didn't much fancy the notion of climbing inside *any* of those damn airborne cigar tubes, piston-engined, jet, turboprop, or otherwise. Airplanes fascinated me, but the idea of actually riding in one way up there in the sky scared the living shit out of me.

Anyhow, it took us damn near two hours to get back to the shop on account of Barry wouldn't go much over 20 miles-per-hour with that monstrous big crate in back, and even so the three of us wound up wincing in perfect unison every time we went over a bad bump or dropped a wheel through a pothole and felt that thing lurch and rattle and bang against the floorboards behind us. But we made it, and then it took damn near everybody in the shop (and even one or two passers-by off the street) to get that huge box out of the truck and down on the shop floor. "So," I said, wiping off my brow while I walked around the thing a couple times, "what the hell's *in* there, anyways?"

"Well, it's this way, sport," Tommy Edwards chuckled as he came in through the overhead door, "let's just say it's that *bigger stick* I was telling you about at Elkhart Lake." Boy, it sure felt good to see Tommy again, and I was happy to observe that he had a little of the old Tommy Edwards spring in his step and some of the old Tommy Edwards glint back in the corner of his eye. No question he hadn't been himself throughout that whole business with Phil Hill and Ernesto Julio and the two C-types up at Elkhart Lake, and sometimes you worry that stuff like that is going to be permanent. But you could see Tommy had his confidence and enthusiasm back again, and it was like he could hardly wait for Barry to grab a crowbar off the workbench in back and open that crate. The lid came off with a nasty, grating, chalk-on-a-blackboard scraping sound as the nails pulled up out of the wood, and that's when I found myself staring down at the biggest, widest, meatiest damn automobile engine ever to come stomping out of Detroit. It was a hemi-head Chrysler Firepower, of course --just like the ones I'd seen in the Cunninghams up at Elkhart Lake! Why, it even had the same kind of four-carburetor intake manifold (only with Carter carburetors this time) and a smoothly swept-back set of exhaust pipes that looked like something off a church organ.

Wow!

"Its got 'igh compression pistons and oversize valves and a special, h'experimental racing camshaft," Barry said proudly, "and the lads in Detroit who built it figure a bit over *three hundred and ten* bloody horsepower at the flywheel," he nudged me in the ribs, "give or take a few...."

"So," I asked him, "what exactly are you planning to *do* with this thing?"

"Why, you and me and old Sylvester over there are going to shove the bloody thing under the bonnet of Tommy's bleedin' Allard, of course."

I stared into the big wooden crate, noting the way the huge cylinder heads filled it completely from one side to the other, and how the smooth, streamlined banks of exhaust tubing fanned out underneath, and it occurred to me that this was one *hell* of a large motor to try and shoehorn into a 2-seater English sportscar. Even a great, hulking 2-seater English sportscar like an Allard.

"You sure this thing will fit?" I asked Barry.

"Well, me and Sylvester did a little preliminary measuring before Tommy ordered the bloody thing," Barry grinned, "and, far as we can tell, it's going to be pretty bleedin' close all the way. Pretty bleedin' close indeed...."

"Boy, *I'll* say."

"Sheeeeeeee-*it!*" Sylvester sighed, shaking his head. "This gonna be one hell of a fuckin' deal. You jus' wait an' see...."

And of course it was.

But Tommy Edwards was about as excited as I'd ever seen him. "You just wait till we get this little beauty buttoned in the car," he gushed, patting the big Chrysler on one of its massive valve covers, "then we'll see about those bloody C-types and Cunninghams and Ferraris." Why, he was just like a kid on Christmas morning, you know?

But I couldn't see it. Much as I liked and respected Tommy Edwards, it seemed to me that his big, chunky Allard was starting to look like a bit of a dinosaur compared to newer cars like the C-type Jaguars and Cunningham C4Rs. Sure, you could always find some way to cram more horsepower under the hood, but you couldn't make an Allard any smaller or lower or lighter --in fact, that big hulking Chrysler engine was going to make it even heavier than it was before!-- and, far as I could see, lighter weight and better brakes and niftier handling were the things a driver was going to need if he really wanted to run even-up against the new generation of racecars from England and Italy and West Palm Beach, Florida. But Tommy Edwards didn't see it that way. After all, he'd always been the fastest guy in an Allard --and he'd won himself an awful lot of races, too-- and no question he hadn't done quite so well in other cars. So he was developing into sort of a hardcase Allard nut, and it was maybe blinding him a little bit to what else was out there. It happens all the time in automobile racing, where a really decent race driver develops himself an unhealthy loyalty for a particular make or model, until over time he changes from "a good racecar driver" to "a good Alfa driver" or "a good Jaguar driver" or "a good Allard driver" or "a good Porsche driver" or whatever, and that's usually the most they ever amount to after that. The best drivers --the guys at the very top of the game-- may have themselves a few pet cars or personal prejudices, but they seldom have any particular brand loyalty to speak of. The car is just a damn tool to get the job done, and your really *serious* racing driver doesn't give a damn if the car's painted bright pink or shaped like an ocean-going tugboat, just so long as it's new enough and fast enough to run up front and strong enough to go the distance.

And, in a nice way, I tried to tell Tommy as much. But he didn't see it that way. "Oh, I don't know," he answered quietly, smiling down at his new Chrysler V8, "I reckon the C-type Jaguar is a better car on overall balance. And Creighton Pendleton's Ferrari is certainly a formidable device. But I think with this new bit of iron between the frame rails, there's one race my old Allard will *always* win."

"What race is that?" I asked him.

"Why, the race to the next bloody corner, of course!"

Right or wrong, it seemed like Tommy'd decided that if the car could just do that for him, he was enough of a driver that he could pretty much take care of the rest....

Needless to say, Julie Finzio was less than thrilled when I called her up that afternoon to tell her I was staying on at West-bridge for another two weeks. "Yeah, *sure!*" she hissed into the phone. "It'll be two more weeks, and two more weeks after that, and then another two weeks and another two weeks and on and on until you're old as my uncle. You'll see. Those nose-in-the-air English jerks are playing you like a damn violin!"

"No they aren't," I tried to tell her, "it's just we got a whole bunch of work t'get done on one of the cars before that race up at Watkins Glen on the 19th and 20th. I can't just ditch out on them, honey. It's just not right. Besides, it's only two more weeks. Honest it is."

"Hmpff," Julie grunted into the receiver. "And you expect me to believe that? Do I honestly look that stupid to you?"

"It's the truth, Honey," I pleaded, "really it is."

But Julie wasn't exactly listening to what I had to say. You know how females can get when they're angry. Especially tough, streetwise Italian types like Julie. *"So,"* she snorted into the receiver, *"this* is the thanks I get for kissing up to my asshole uncle so's he'd hire you back on at the Sinclair...."

"But I *am* coming back to work at the Sinclair. Really I am. If you'd jus--"

"Well, thanks a lot, Buddy Palumbo. Thanks an awful lot."

"B-but, Julie...."

"Don't you 'b-but, Julie' *me,* you lowlife, bullshitting jerk. Oh, *sure.* You just couldn't *wait* t'get back here to Passaic so you could come to work at my uncle's gas station and we could start spending a little time together...."

"Julie. *Please!* Listen to me! I SWEAR TO GOD I WILL BE BACK AT YOUR UNCLE'S GOD DAMN GAS STATION ON MONDAY MORNING, SEPTEMBER 22ND --BRIGHT AND EARLY-- AND IF I'M NOT, MAY GOD ALMIGHTY STRIKE ME DEAD WITH A LIGHTNING BOLT!"

"Just remember this, Palumbo," Julie snarled into the phone, "if *He* doesn't, *I* will!"

It was probably a good idea to take Julie literally when she said stuff like that. For your own safety, you know?

So now all Sylvester and Barry and me had to do was try to wrestle that monstrous Chrysler V8 into Tommy Edwards' Allard and have it fired up and ready to roll in seven days so Tommy could drive it up to Watkins Glen on Wednesday morning. And if that doesn't sound like an absolutely monumental sort of task, then you have obviously never attempted to change anything on an automobile from the way the manufacturer-of-record originally intended. Suffice it to say that Sylvester and Barry and me spent almost every minute of that week buried elbow-deep in Allard Innards and doing our best to take care of all the assorted mechanical mismatches and "clearance problems" that come with every engine swap. Although the general oilpan profile of Tommy's new engine would more or less fit between the Allard's frame rails, certain of its other protrusions and dimensions were trying to occupy space already filled with rather solid chunks of automobile. And of course none of the motor mounts were in the right place and the linkages didn't match up right and the water pump outlet was on the wrong side and pointed the wrong direction and, well, you get the idea. Fact is, we never could've got the job done if it wasn't for a Polish-born machinist from someplace over in Brooklyn named Roman Syzmanski.

Roman Syzmanski was already becoming a little bit of a legend around East coast racing garages back in the late summer of 1952. He was a pale, tubby-cheeked sort of guy with thinning hair and a quiet voice and thick, wire-rimmed bifocals. He was difficult to understand because he spoke so softly, and also on account of he'd only mastered a few hard-object nouns and some of your more basic present-tense verbs in English. I guess he left Poland in 1938 with little more than the clothes on his back, and worked his way up to owning a tiny little back-alley machine shop over in Brooklyn, where for years he made parts for all kinds of industrial machinery and manufacturing equipment. But then he got "discovered" by some local repair garages (including the Muscatelli brothers) who found out he could do valve jobs and bore cylinder blocks and regrind crankshafts and weld up cracked water jackets and straighten bent cams and re-thread stripped stud holes quicker and cheaper and better than anybody in New York. Then somebody from Frick-Tappet Motors got him to help figure out motor mounts and plumbing and bell housing adaptors and such for a few weirdass engine installations, and all of a sudden Roman Syzmanski found himself in the automobile racing business. I guess he enjoyed it (although you couldn't really tell, since Roman never seemed to smile or frown or show much emotion in general) and no question he didn't have to hunt around to find himself machine work customers from then on.

I was over at his shop several times that week while we fought with the engine swap on Tommy's Allard, and it was amazing how he could look at something you were trying to do --like fr'instance mate up that Chrysler V8 with the three-speed Cad/LaSalle transmission in the Allard-- and pull at his eyebrows for a couple minutes, take a few measurements, and in a day or two come up with *exactly* what you needed to get the job done. His lathes and drill presses and such were all pretty old and mostly all German (in spite of the fact that he didn't care much for the Germans --not hardly!) but he kept all of it neat and clean and in good running order, and the simple fact was that Roman Syzmanski could take those machines of his and make you damn near *anything* out of metal. He didn't act like it was anything special, but every racer on the Eastern seaboard knew that machinists like Roman Syzmanski were rare as good, clean, low-mileage used cars.

But, even with Roman's help, Barry and Sylvester and me kept running into problems. Like getting the exhaust piping to clear the steering gear and getting the throttle linkage up where it needed to be and so that it opened all four carburetors evenly and cutting a hole in the hood so it'd close over those huge cylinder heads and let the four little chrome-pot air cleaners stick up in the breeze. I don't think the three of us got more than a couple hours sleep a night during that crazy week before Watkins Glen --and none at all the last frantic two days-- and we were also busy getting a bunch of other customer cars ready and getting the green C-type all squared away for its new owner (whoever it was) and I was meanwhile running back and forth to Jersey so I could spin a few wrenches on Big Ed's Jaguar in the middle of the night and all day Sunday over at the Sinclair. He'd got the

Old Man to give me a key, and I had to work my ass off to straighten out all the idiotic stuff that other mechanic had done to Big Ed's car. The main problem was the thermostatic actuator for the cold start valve again, but the guy obviously didn't know about that and tried to compensate by leaning out the carburetors. He even changed the damn jets! But I tracked it all down and fixed it, and even re-set the valve clearances (which is one hell of a big job on a twincam Jaguar) and adjusted the timing chain and then finished it off with new plugs and points and a razor-sharp tuneup. Then I test-drove it into Manhattan on Monday morning, and spent the next forty hours straight putting all the final little finishing touches on Tommy Edwards' engine swap, stuff I figured would take a half-hour or so --at the most!-- to complete.

But, like Barry Spline said as Tommy Edwards punched the starter button and fired up that big, honking Chrysler Hemi at nine-thirty ayem on Wednesday morning: "h'its always the first ninety percent of a job like this that takes the first ninety percent of the time..." we watched Tommy's Allard charge off down the street towards Watkins Glen in a thundering cloud of tiresmoke "...but h'it's that last ten percent of the job that always takes the *other* ninety percent of the time..."

Chapter 30: The Glen

I left Westbridge about ten-thirty and drove Big Ed's Jaguar back across the George Washington Bridge to pick him up over by his scrapyard on the Jersey shore. It was a big place spread out over a couple of acres with a few rusty tin buildings and a high, ugly wood fence around it. But there must've been some good money in buying and selling used industrial machinery and metal scrap, because otherwise Big Ed could never have afforded that monstrous house of his with the circular entrance drive and the two stone lions out front, not to mention his Cadillacs and the Jaguar I was driving and the current Mrs. Big Ed's showroom-cherry Chrysler Town and Country convertible and most especially all the ex-Mrs. Baumsteins he had to take care of on the side. And yet his place of business hardly looked like a goldmine, you know? In fact, it was exactly the kind of broken-down roadside eyesore that civic-minded types would rather see turned into an empty lot. And I must admit, that would've been a huge improvement from the standpoint of scenic eye appeal.

The Jag was running like a charm (natch) and Big Ed had his travel bag packed and ready by the door so we were out of there in minutes. But we still had to stop by my folks' house so's I could grab a quick thirty-second shower and snatch some clean clothes off the card table next to the ironing board in the basement. My mom was home and it was really nice to see her again --even if it was just for five minutes-- and of course she fussed a lot about how nobody in the family ever got to see me anymore. Right in front of Big Ed, too, so it was kind of embarrassing. But then she insisted that he have a late-morning cup of coffee with her and try some of her famous Dutch Apple pie (a la mode, of course) while I was in the can getting ready. There was really no way Big Ed could refuse, and so he had to sit there and listen to my mom ramble on and on about how the darn bluejays were picking on the wrens and chickadees around the six or seven bird feeders she had set up around the back yard, and also about how terribly worried she was about her favorite downy woodpecker on account of she hadn't heard him drilling holes in all the trees and telephone poles like a miniature jackhammer for several days. There was really no stopping my mom once she got started, but what with all her kids more or less gone (or just in-and-out for a few minutes at a time) and my old man being kind of a five-star grump and not much of a conversationalist, my mom was almost like Skippy Welcher when she got to sit down with a fresh pair of ears. But she was bright and pleasant to be around, and no question her Dutch Apple pie a la mode made listening to her unquestionably worthwhile. Why, I even took a slice along for the road. But without the a la mode, of course.

Big Ed took over the driving after that, and I'm forced to admit that he was pretty damn impressed with how well his XK120 was running. "Boy, you got this thing runnin' like brand spankin' new," Big Ed grinned, unwrapping yet another one of his seventy-five-cent Havana cigars. "What was the problem with it, anyway?"

So I tried to explain to him about the starting carburetor and the thermostatic actuator and what the other mechanic had done wrong, but you could see I'd lost him before the end of the first sentence. That happens all the time when grease monkey automobile mechanics try to explain stuff to rank-and-file citizens. All of a sudden you look in their eyes and realize you might as well be talking Greek or Hindu or Swahili or something. But that was okay, on account of I was pretty tired and really didn't feel much like talking. So I just laid back against that soft red leather and pulled my old army blanket up over me and listened to the rolling purr of that smooth-running Jaguar six.

We followed the same route up through Jersey and into New York state that Butch Bohunk and I took back in August on our way to Grand Island, and like always, it didn't seem as long or far the second time through. Not to mention I'd done a lot more long-haul road traveling than ever before that summer, and that tends to give you some pretty long legs over distance. Besides, it was a beautiful early-fall sort of day, and it was real nice just leaning into the seatback with the afternoon sun on my face and that green wool army blanket pulled up around my chin, kind of pretending to sleep, but with my eyes open just a sliver right at the bottom of the lids so I could take in some of the light and color and all without really looking at anything. I thought a little about Julie and going back to work at the Sinclair every now and then, but mostly I remembered how it was on that Saturday morning back in May, sitting there in this exact same seat in this exact same XK120 Jaguar while Big Ed and me headed out towards Bridgehampton and the first sportycar race either one of us had ever seen. Jeez, that seemed like a long time ago --ages, in fact-- only at the same time it seemed like maybe only yesterday or the day before. The big difference was that now the yellow-orange colors and the smell of harvested fields were in the air instead of the fresh wet green of springtime. But then I thought about all the things that had happened and people I'd met and places I'd been and most especially all the things I'd learned about sportscars and racing and life in general. Stuff you pick up without thinking about it and don't even realize you're learning at the time. But it all stays with you, you know?

We stopped for an early bite of dinner at that same little railroad-car roadside hashhouse near Damascus where Butch and me stopped on our way out to Grand Island (you remember, the one where he wouldn't let me wheel him in and insisted on using his stupid crutches) and I really can't say why I told Big Ed it was a good place to eat, since the burgers tasted a lot like coal tar. But it was the only place I knew around there, and sometimes you wind up going back to the same lousy local joints time after time just on account of they're familiar. And that's probably how whole regions of the country get reputations for bad food. Anyhow, Big Ed asked the waitress what was the best piece of meat they had and she recommended the butt steak, and I decided to take my chances with the chicken-fried steak. While we waited for the guy in the kitchen to do his worst, I kept bugging Big Ed to tell me how he was gonna convince Charlie Priddle and the rest of the S.C.M.A. armband-types to let him race. But he wouldn't tell me a thing. "It's kind of a surprise," he grinned, his cigar rolling gently and evenly from one side of his mouth to the other, "an' I don't want to take a chance and maybe jinx it. You'll find out soon enough." And then he oozed out a mean little whisper of a chuckle that made all my nerve endings tingle with anticipation. I couldn't wait, you know?

My chicken-fried steak was dry and tough and covered with a muddy-brown gravy that was about the same consistency as rear-axle gearlube and didn't taste or smell an awful lot better.

Big Ed's butt steak wasn't much better, and he claimed he was surprised that they didn't serve it with a buzzsaw (or at least a pair of bolt cutters) to help whittle it down into bite-size pieces. On the way over to the counter to pay the bill, Big Ed let me know in no uncertain terms that *he* was going to pick out the restaurants from there on in. And I couldn't say as I blamed him, you know? But even so it was kind of neat going back into that place again, just so's I could think back a little more about all the stuff that had happened to me during that summer and how much everything seemed to have changed. In fact, when I went inside the mens' room to wash up and comb my hair after dinner, I couldn't help noticing how much *older* and *wiser* and maybe even a tiny bit *tougher* the guy staring back at me out of the mirror looked than the one I'd seen in that same exact mirror only a few short months before.

Anyhow, who should come powering up in front of the diner in a shower of gravel just as Big Ed was paying the bill but Skippy Welcher and his faithful squire Milton Fitting. But the truly amazing thing was the car they were driving. Believe it or not, they were in the green C-type from Westbridge --*my* C-type, for gosh sakes!-- and no matter how many times I blinked my eyes or rubbed them with my fingers, I couldn't get rid of the frightening, ridiculous, nauseating sight of Reginald "Skippy" Welcher himself at the controls of the ex-Creighton Pendleton the Third (even though he'd never actually driven it) C-type that I'd personally driven back and forth across half the whole damn country just two weeks before. To make matters worse, Skippy was wearing a set of those split-panel fighter-pilot racing goggles and a Union Jack silk scarf tied around his neck like some kind of dandified cowboy from Liverpool or Cornwall or someplace like that, and naturally he had about a two-ounce Monarch butter-fly squashed all over the top of his goggles and forehead up on the lefthand side. I swear, the sight of it made my chicken-fried steak want to start backing up on me. And I'm not talking about the squashed bug, either.

"What ho!" Skippy Welcher shouted, waving his fist grandly through the air.

"What ho, yourself," Big Ed answered, staring at the C-type with eyes full of envy. He'd never seen an XK120 C-type before. "Say, what th'hell *is* this thing, anyway?"

"The very latest and best out of Coventry, my good man!" Skippy shouted through a maniacal grin. "A work of high art. An instrument of destruction. A *singing sword!*" The Skipper's face was starting to melt and pop all over like hot lava.

Well, as interested as Big Ed was in Skippy's new car, he'd also been involved in enough meandering, unending, one-sided conversations with Skippy Welcher to realize that no automobile on earth was worth going through that again. "Well, see you at the races," he told Skippy, fumbling for the Jaguar keys in his right-front pocket.

"Indeed we will!" Skippy replied, snapping off a smart two-fingered military salute and one of his patented gold-tooth smiles. *"TALLY HO!"* he hollered into the sky, popping the clutch and tearing off into the sunset with the wheels showering off rooster-tails of gravel and the engine right on the verge of valve float. I swear, the bastard didn't upshift into second until he was damn near out of sight. And that's when I realized that he never even got out of the car to eat or gas up or take a pee or anything. He'd only stopped on account of he saw Big Ed's XK120 out front, and wanted to make sure that whoever owned it had a decent opportunity to fawn and gape and drool all over his brand new toy. Truth is, it made me physically sick to see a ham-fisted asshole like Skippy in that car --*my* car-- but one of the things every sportscar mechanic has to learn is that neat cars never have much of a choice about who winds up owning them. That's why you inevitably find some of the most achingly beautiful, right-eously handsome, and awesomely fastest machines in the hands of rich handjob jerks like Skippy Welcher. The hard part is real-izing that it's not the car's fault....

Big Ed had me take over for the last hour-and-a-half push up to Watkins Glen, heading north on Highway 96 out of Owego, then following it east out of the little town of Candor, and pick-ing up 234 at Van Etten for the last spurt up through Swartwood, Cayuta, Alpine, and Odessa to the junction with Route 14 at Montour Falls. It was beautiful country, with hills and forests and flat-bottomed valleys and towering rock faces with little trickling waterfalls peeking through the leaves and foliage all over the place. Traffic was heavy on Highway 14 heading north out of Montour Falls, and there were more MGs and Jags and such than you could shake a stick at. We needed gas anyway, and Big Ed decided we'd had about enough of chugging along in bumper-to-bumper traffic, so he had me turn off the highway and take Main Street down into the town of Montour Falls. It was just your average little smalltown street, you know, with a drug store and a food market and a hardware store and a hamburger joint or two and a couple hotels for the tourists who came up there in the summertime to fish for trout in Catherine Creek and play miniature golf and buy phony Indian souvenirs and look at the scenery. And there was some pretty spectacular scenery to look at, too. Like right down at the far end of Main Street there was a sheer rock wall the height of a New York skyscraper with a frothy-white waterfall pouring down it like the water was tumbling right out of the sky. And just across the street from that steep, majestic waterfall was a little one-story, reddish-brown brick building with columns in front that looked like small factory smokestacks. Inside were the law offices of a guy named Cameron Argetsinger, a local lawyer and sportscar enthusiast who more or less put the whole deal together for the S.C.M.A. to start racing on the roads around Watkins Glen back in 1948. I guess that was about the first place they ever raced --at least right out there in front of the public instead of up and down the driveways and access roads of all their fancy East Coast mansions and estates-- and just like Bridgehampton and Elkhart Lake, the local innkeepers and shop owners and bartenders were only too happy to have all those racer-types coming around. Why, it was only Wednesday night, and the roads into Watkins Glen itself were clogged damn near solid with racers and crews and S.C.M.A. armband types and the usual collection of general curiosity seekers. And it was only Wednesday night! A lot of them were camping out, too --people from New York and Pennsylvania and New England and Jersey and even a whole bunch down from Canada!-- so the night air was filled with sparks leaping off crackling wood fires and the smell of grilled meat.

Big Ed had booked us a cabin at the Seneca Lodge outside Watkins Glen on the advice of a couple S.C.M.A. regulars he'd bought drinks for before the club meetings that he couldn't attend on account of he wasn't a member. "It's a little rustic compared to some of the other spots around town," they advised him, "but the food is good and a lot of people stay there because it's the only place where you can find a place to sleep that's walking distance from the Seneca Bar." The obvious conclusion was that the best of the racing parties happened around the Seneca Bar, and only those who stayed on the premises could stagger home to bed on foot afterwards.

The gas station pump-jockey in Montour Falls told us how we could take a shortcut and avoid most of the traffic by heading uphill past the falls out of town instead of going back to highway 14, and we tried following his directions over a couple other roads and highways and a set of railroad tracks and then taking a right on a dirt road next to a faded red barn and following that down to a T intersection and then turning right and...well, suffice it to say we got plenty lost and managed to see a lot of the night-time countryside north and west of Watkins Glen before we ever located ourselves a place to park in front of the Seneca Lodge. And finding the damn parking slot once we got there was almost as tough as finding the place itself, since the lot was jammed full of MGs and Jags and Porsches and Siatas and Aston Martins and BMWs and Ferraris and Maseratis and just about every other kind of low slung, short-wheelbase, two-seater automobile built anywhere you could think of in Europe. The lodge itself was a big, raw wood, log-cabin sort of place made up of a large, open dining hall that was jam-packed to the rafters with laughing, jabbering racers and a little lean-to bar off the back that was jam-packed even tighter.

Big Ed checked us in and we dropped our stuff off in the cabin (which, as promised, was about as basic and rustic as you could get and still call it an actual man-made housing enclosure). But the air smelled of pine needles and wood fires and freshly harvested crops, and you could hear owls hooting here and there up in the trees and little furry things rustling around in the bushes which made the Seneca Lodge a very pleasant and serene sort of place to be.

At least until you ventured in the bar, anyway....

I guess every great racetrack has its own legendary tavern located someplace close by, and for one reason or another the little add-on drinking room at the back of the Seneca Lodge dining room was the chosen spot at Watkins Glen. And you couldn't say it was on account of the beer was any colder or the drinks were any fuller or the furniture and decor particularly appealed to racing types. No, the racers came there because they'd come the year before, and the year before that, and each time they found good food and friendly faces behind the bar and a room they could pretty much fill up with whatever sort of bullshit and nonsense they wanted to. A racing party never took too much in the way of planning, just plenty of drinks and a place to happen. And a little loud jukebox music in the background helped, too.

And it was a nice feeling, now that I'd been around for a whole summer, that people from the races nodded my way or flashed me a quick little half-smile of recognition. Everybody except Sally Enderle, that is, who made a real point of looking right through me as if I had been rendered suddenly and completely invisible. Then again, I wasn't really surprised. Besides which I had no idea on earth what I would've said to her if she'd done me the courtesy of acknowledging that I was indeed another English-speaking human being whom she might have once had some brief, passing acquaintance with some time in the far distant past. Like say fr'instance eleven days ago at Elkhart Lake. But like I said, I was just as happy that she was hanging on Creighton Pendleton's arm again and ignoring me the way people of my cultural background and social class deserved to be ignored. At least when you were done with them, anyway....

Big Ed bullied us up to the bar right next to Creighton Pendleton, and that made it even tougher for Sally to look right through me, so she resorted to letting her eyes take a quick detour around me every time she scanned the room for somebody important that she desperately needed to talk to. And naturally it didn't take her long to spot a likely prospect, pop up on her tiptoes, wave gaily, and take off for some other corner of the barroom with a less obstructed view. It was hard to believe I used to think she was such hot stuff, you know? Although she still filled out a midriff shirt and a tight pair of shorts better than just about any female I'd ever seen that wasn't on a movie screen.

But, like old Butch always said about Mean Marlene, "I'd druther have a woman ugly clear through than pretty on the surface and ugly underneath. It ain't so disappointing that way."

With Sally Enderle gone off Creighton's arm, Big Ed saw an opportunity to strike up a conversation with him, and he did it the usual Big Ed Baumstein way by offering to buy him a drink.

"Say, I'm Ed Baumstein," Big Ed said, sticking out his hand and even removing his cigar for the occasion. "Me an' Buddy here saw you win that race up at Bridgehampton in May."

"How nice for you," Creighton Pendleton allowed, kind of looking down his nose at Big Ed.

"Yeah. And I'd sure like t'buy you a drink. That was some pretty damn fancy driving you did up there."

"Was it?" He said it like neither me or Big Ed would know fancy driving if we saw it. Then again, I guess guys like him have people pestering them and fawning all over them all the time and I suppose it must get a little tiring after awhile. Or at least that's the excuse they use for treating the rest of the world like pus boils on a gnat's ass.

But Creighton Pendleton wasn't above taking a free drink when one was offered. Just so long as it didn't come with any strings on it and he only had to hang around until it was served. "Yes sir," Big Ed continued, not about to be brushed aside, "you did one hell of a job with that Ferrari."

"Hm."

"And that's one hell of a car, too."

"Isn't it."

"I'd like to get myself a car like that someday. One just like that, in fact."

A nasty little smile was beginning to curl up around the edges of Creighton Pendleton's mouth. "Well," he said into the swizzle stick of his last tall gin-and-tonic, "why don't you just buy yourself one, hmm?"

"Aw, I tried. But it's tough to do." Big Ed knew he was getting hosed around, but he was after something and not about to ruin things by getting mad or giving up. "I tried buying one off that Carlo Sebastian guy, but he didn't have a car for me."

"Oh really?"

"Nah. He said maybe I could get one someday --one of the *street* models, you know-- but there was no way I could land one of the real racing models like you've got."

"And why is that?" Creighton was really jerking him around just to see him squirm, but Big Ed was a pretty shrewd customer underneath, even if he didn't look it at all.

"Well, I figure there's only so many of those cars to go around, right?"

Creighton Pendleton nodded as the bartender placed his new tall gin-and-tonic on the edge of the bar.

"So guys like you --guys who've raced Ferraris before and proved what they can do with 'em-- get all the latest hot cars just as soon as they get them across the Atlantic."

Creighton nodded absently, his eyes starting to look around for some other people to stand and enjoy his drink with.

"So anyway, see, I was thinking maybe I could buy that car of yours off you when you get your new one from the factory over in Italy, y'know?" Creighton Pendleton the Third slowly rotated his head in Big Ed's direction and looked him up and down as if seeing him for the very first time. "I'd give ya a good price for it, see, and you wouldn't need it anymore on account of you'd have your new one, right?"

Creighton took a long, slow pull on his drink. "Well, Mr. Baumstein--"

"Call me Big Ed, okay?"

"Well, Mister, umm, 'Big Ed,' I'm sure that's a very intriguing proposal. Very intriguing indeed. But I'm afraid it's just simply not possible."

"Oh? And why's that?"

"Well, let's just say I've always had a little sort of, um, *arrangement* with Reggie Welcher, and he always gets first crack at all my racecars when I'm done with them." Creighton Pendleton was the first guy I'd ever heard call Skippy Welcher "Reggie," but it sounded just right when he said it. Like ivy climbing up old masonry walls.

But Big Ed was not about to give up. "Well, that's a pretty sweet deal for both of you I guess. But what if somebody like me offered you a little more money...."

"A *little* more money?" Creighton asked, arching up one eyebrow. "And what exactly might *that* mean?"

"Oh, I dunno," Big Ed shrugged while cash register bells rang in his head like fire alarms, "let's just say enough to make it worth your while...."

Creighton Pendleton stirred the ice in the bottom of his glass and sighed as if he was thinking it over. "Well, Mr. Baumstein, I'm afraid I'm still a little unclear as to how much that might be. In dollars, that is."

I could see that Creighton was just jerking him around, you know, trying to get Big Ed to name a figure just so's he could look down his nose at it. But Big Ed had been in enough deals in his life --automotive and otherwise-- to know that the first guy to utter a figure *always* loses. So he tried the old Colin St. John turn-the-tables-on-'em maneuver, which is inevitably in every used car trader's bag of tricks, and generally starts off with playing dumb as a fencepost and pretending that the fish you're dealing with is obviously ever so much smarter, wiser, shrewder, more knowledgeable, and probably even better looking than you are. "Tellya what, Creighton," Big Ed told him while ordering up another round of drinks, "I'm new to all this sportscar stuff and really have no idea at all what a car like that Ferrari of yours might be worth --new or used-- so why don't you just tell me how much it would take to get in line ahead of everybody else whenever you're done with it and ready for a new one, huh?"

Creighton Pendleton rubbed his perfectly chisled chin and thought it over, searching for the exact appropriate combination of words that would chop Big Ed off at the ankles like a stalk of celery. "Well, that's really a tremendous offer, Ed," he said with what sounded like genuine reluctance and gratitude, "but I'm afraid I'll have to pass it by."

"You will?"

Creighton nodded, picking up the second tall gin-and-tonic Big Ed had ordered for him. "You see, it's not just a question of money between Reggie and myself."

"It isn't?"

Creighton shook his head. "No, I'm afraid it isn't. We've always had this, well, this *understanding* about my cars, you see. Reggie always gets them when I'm done with them. Simple as that. Price has never been an issue."

"It hasn't?"

"Absolutely not." Creighton took a quick sip off the top of his drink. "I simply tell Reggie what I think the car is worth and he writes me a check. We never dicker over price."

Big Ed had never heard of such a thing. And neither had I, come to think of it. In fact, I got the impression that it was most likely an enormous load of bullshit laid out for the purpose of fertilizing the notion that Big Ed and me were nothing but a couple of Johnny-come-lately goofball outsiders. Especially after

I caught the teasing glimmer of laughter flickering up in the corners of Creighton Pendleton's dark, penetrating eyes. "Well," Big Ed grumbled, realizing he was headed up a one-way, dead-end street with no place to turn around or double back, "you just keep it in mind, okay."

"Oh, I surely will," Creighton assured him, "after all, it's a really *generous* proposition." He said "generous" like it was some kind of incurable medical condition, you know? "Then again," he added as he polished off the last of his second free drink, "I've never had much of a head for business." He pushed his stool out away from the bar, obviously preparing to leave. "But then I guess I've just never actually *needed* one...."

And next thing we knew, Big Ed and me were all alone.

Come Thursday morning we had registration and technical inspection over by the courthouse in downtown Watkins Glen, and that's when I finally got to see Big Ed's Top Secret plan to race his Jaguar with the S.C.M.A. He'd gotten one of the other members to enter his car (I'm not sure, but I think it might have been Tommy Edwards) and he presented himself at registration as simply the driver. Now there was always a lot of that sort of thing going on, with guys like Colin St. John and Ernesto Julio and even Briggs Cunningham entering cars for other people to drive, so no way could any of the hardline S.C.M.A. clubbies say anything about it. But then there was the little problem of what made Mr. Big Ed Baumstein think he could safely and wisely operate an automobile at racing speed. Just *who,* the S.C.M.A. wanted to know, had ever told Big Ed that he had the qualifications to be a racecar driver, anyway?

And that's when he pulled out a little leathergrain folder like lawyers and life insurance salesmen carry around and produced a *bona fide* racing license from the American Automobile Association and a bunch of ironclad paperwork and documentation to go with it. Now the Triple-A sanctioned almost all of the bigtime oval track racing in the U.S. of A. back in 1952 (including the Indianapolis 500) and Big Ed knew that they had co-sanctioned the first couple races at Watkins Glen along with the S.C.M.A. So it was already a matter of record that the S.C.M.A. accepted A.A.A. racing licenses. In fact that Phil Walters guy who drove for Briggs Cunningham had raced the triple-A circuit for years under the name of Ted Tappet, and so Charlie Priddle and the rest of the S.C.M.A. tight-asses had themselves a real serious problem with Big Ed Baumstein, on account of there was no way they could keep him from racing without creating a hell of a red tape procedural mess. And those guys knew full well what they were up against, too, on account of they absolutely lived and breathed red tape and procedural messes every single day of the week. In fact, sometimes you got the notion it was their whole reason for being, you know? At any rate, they couldn't refuse his entry without refusing the other entry (or entries) from the guy who made it for him (whoever that was) and they couldn't keep Big Ed from driving unless they also shut out one of the star drivers on the Cunningham team. And that of course wouldn't do at all. So Charlie Priddle and his armband-buddies were out-maneuvered and out-flanked, and they knew it. The only loop-hole left was to try and find something wrong with the car, but I knew my stuff and had Big Ed's Jag race-prepared in absolutely perfect working order, and she was as ready to run as the best cars there that weekend. Not to mention that we had quite a few drivers and mechanics and such on our side by then. The truth of it was that Charlie Priddle and his marauding wolfpack of ama-teur racing officials were only a very small percentage of the rank-and-file S.C.M.A. membership. The problem was that they wound up *running* the show on account of all everybody else wanted was an opportunity to fire up their cars and *race*....

Tommy Edwards came over to congratulate us after we cleared tech, and then he kind of eased Big Ed aside and told him to watch himself and be careful and not do anything stupid on account of Charlie Priddle and his armband buddies would be watching him like a bunch of hungry vultures, just waiting for an excuse to take away his rather dubious ticket and send him pack-ing. "Keep your eyes on mirrors, sport," he advised Big Ed, "but don't *ever*," he wagged his forefinger playfully under Big Ed's nose, "don't ever even *think* about moving over to make room for an overtaking car."

Big Ed looked confused. "How's that?" he asked.

"When a faster car comes up behind you," Tommy ex-plained, holding his hands out palms-down in front of him to illustrate like racers always do, "the poor bloke has no idea if you've seen him or what on earth you're about to do."

"So?"

"So the safest thing for everyone involved is for you to just drive along on your proper line and let *him* worry about how to get around you."

"It is?"

"Absolutely. It's the only way a faster driver can be sure of where you'll be. If you take a notion to be a good sport and pull over to make room, he may well have already committed to passing you on that side. Do you see what I mean?"

You could see the gears spinning behind Big Ed's eyes while he imagined what Tommy was talking about. "Yeah," he said, "I see. You wind up in his lap."

"That's it exactly," Tommy smiled, and patted Big Ed on the shoulder. "Outside of that, just have fun, glance in your mirrors every now and again, and don't do anything stupid."

"Hey, thanks," Big Ed told him.

"Oh, and try to get a little slow practice in around the circuit today and tomorrow. There won't be any on race day."

"There won't?" I asked, wondering what guys were supposed to do if they'd never raced there before.

"No, I'm afraid not, Buddy. They can't close down the roads until early Saturday morning, and, what with three races on the schedule, there simply isn't time."

"But how'rya supposed to know which way the damn road goes, huh?" Big Ed wondered.

"Well, they *do* give the cars two or three warmup laps just before each race on Saturday, but I don't suppose that's really any decent way to familiarize oneself with the circuit."

"Oh?" Big Ed said, looking just a little bewildered.

"Look," Tommy said, "I've got an idea. Let's you and I take a quick lap or two right now."

"Right now?"

"Absolutely. I can show you around a bit. Then you and the mechanical Boy Genius go out for a few more laps this afternoon --not at speed, you understand, just to more or less get the *feel* of things-- and then I'll take you out again tomorrow morning for a little fine tuning. How's that?"

Naturally Big Ed couldn't thank Tommy enough, and by then I was pretty sure that he was indeed the guy who'd entered the white XK120 for Big Ed. Not that he was saying anything about it, on account of there were more than a few S.C.M.A. bigwigs with their oh-so-blue noses pretty well out of joint over a guy named Big Ed Baumstein running around loose in their private little playpen. But you could see Tommy was getting something out of the deal, too, on account of he seemed to be gaining a lot more of his old confidence and *Dawn Patrol* swagger back by acting as a sort of tutor and big brother to Big Ed. And I was enjoying the hell out of it, since every now and then Charlie Priddle would stalk past us with a look in his eye like he was having serious liver trouble. I mean, it couldn't have happened to a nicer guy, you know?

While Big Ed and Tommy were out touring the course, I ran into Cal Carrington and a few of the MG guys from Giant's Despair over at a little grey clapboard coffee shop on Franklin Street, which was the main drag down through the little resort town of Watkins Glen and also served as the start/finish straightaway of the Watkins Glen race circuit that weekend. Turns out Cal rode up in the black TD with Carson Flegley again, but this time Carson was bound and determined to drive in the Queen Catherine Cup race for smallbore cars himself (by God, it was *his* damn car, wasn't it?) and so Cal was out shopping for a ride again. And he wasn't having much luck, either. The guy with the Ford V8 in his MG was a no-show after putting the evil device into a spin, a ditch, and a tree in quick succession during a "test run" after the repairs were completed from Elkhart Lake, and although he wasn't hurt personally, the car was going to need the entire winter to get back in decent shape again. Not that it was ever in particularly decent shape to begin with.

"How're things goin' with you guys?" Cal asked while he sopped up a few quarts of Vermont maple syrup with the last of his French toast.

So I told him about Big Ed's Triple-A racing license and the look it'd put on Charlie Priddle's face and all about shoveling that huge, fire-breathing Chrysler Hemi into Tommy Edwards' Allard and how I suspected that Tommy was the guy who entered Big Ed's 120 for him. I was happy to see that Cal got almost as big a kick out of it as I did. "So," I asked him, "you got any fish on the line this weekend?"

"Well, the prospecting hasn't gone too awfully well," he sighed, swirling the last of the coffee around in his cup, "but then, we didn't roll in until about two ayem and I've only had this morning to work on it."

"Something'll turn up."

"It sure as hell better. I'm supposed to be standing up at my sister's wedding back home this weekend, and all bloody hell's gonna break loose at Castle Carrington when I get back. It'd be a damn shame to catch all that flack for *nothing....* "

I could see his point.

"Well," Cal grinned, snaking on his aviator sunglasses and flashing me all those straight, brilliantly white rich-kid teeth, "time t'go to work. Wish me luck."

"Good luck," I told him. And I meant it.

"And say," he added as he eased himself out of the booth, "you think you could maybe pick up the tab for breakfast. I'm a little, er, *financially embarrassed* right now."

"You're *always* flat deadass broke," I told him, "every damn time I see you."

"I'm *never* broke," he corrected me with a wicked rich-kid grin, "it's just that my resources are almost always tied up in high-yield but generally non-liquid assets, and as a result I from time to time find myself temporarily between money. Anyhow, can you pay for breakfast?"

"Yeah, why not," I agreed with a helpless laugh, "after all, why the heck should a high-line, well-to-do person like yourself be expected to carry any loose change around in his pocket?"

"That's right! After all, it might very well soil the lining...."

There was nothing I could do but shake my head, you know?

"Thanks, pal," Cal said over his shoulder as he headed towards the door, "you saved me having to crawl out the damn men's room window again...."

Same old Cal, no two ways about it.

After breakfast I walked up and down Franklin Street and looked into the barber shop and the bakery and a bunch of little tourist shops that sold ice cream cones and Indian curios and stuff. It was amazing how much the same and all at once how much different Watkins Glen was from Elkhart Lake, Wisconsin. Especially when you got down to the far north end of Franklin

Street and found yourself looking out at Lake Seneca, which was absolutely huge and grey and serious compared to the warm, friendly-looking little lake at Elkhart. Lake Seneca was over twenty miles long and disappeared far into the distance to the north, and was wide enough east-to-west so that the opposing shoreline seemed small and hazy and you had to squint your eyes to make things out. And even then you couldn't. It was like a small ocean, you know? The kind of lake you could never even think about swimming across because it would swallow you up without a trace.

Down through town at the other end of Franklin Street was the entrance to the other big tourist attraction in Watkins Glen, the state park, which was built around a scenic, woodsy glen full of steep rock faces with tall, spindly waterfalls spilling down them and plenty of trees and dense, leafy foliage. It was a really nice spot, you know, and they had this stone stairway up to the very top that took more than an hour to climb. I know, because I did it. I mean, there wasn't much of anything else to do, right?

When I got back down to street level, I wandered around some more looking at all the cars and people that were flowing into the town of Watkins Glen from all directions and filling it up to overflowing. Why, Big Ed could hardly drive his bone-stock XK120 down the middle of Franklin Street without overheating the damn thing, and it wasn't even all that warm out. But traffic was tied up in a damn knot with armband people unloading banners and haybales and rolls of snow fencing off the back of trucks and Porsche and MG-types double- and triple-parked while they jawed back and forth about where to eat and where to drink and where they all were staying, not to mention all the rank-and-file tourists making the rounds of the restaurants and arcades and curio shops and snack peddlers, and often as not wandering right across the damn street whenever and wherever they felt like it. Big Ed said it took him every bit of fifteen minutes to make it the five lousy blocks or so from the other end of Franklin Street to where I was waiting to meet him in front of the courthouse, and the gurgling noises coming from under the Jag's hood left no doubt he was telling the truth. "Think I better shut it off?" he asked me, staring bug-eyed at the temp gauge.

"Well, it might be better for us to maybe go around again if you can get a little clear running once you're out of town. You shut her off when she's real hot and she'll get even hotter."

"She will?"

"Sure," I said, reaching down to yank the door pull and hopping inside, "once you shut an engine off, the water stops circulating and she climbs up even higher. It's okay if you're just gonna leave it cool off, but if you're planning to fire it up again real soon, you're probably better off to see if we can find a place to give her a short run up to forty miles an hour or so and push a little wind through the radiator."

That made sense to Big Ed, so he eased out into traffic and chugged us down towards the south end of Franklin Street, past the Atlantic gas station and the Glen View souvenir shop and the Knotty Pine restaurant to the all-important first corner, where the racecourse swept hard right and then almost immediately curved around to the left again as it climbed up the long, steep grade of Old Corning Hill. And all of a sudden we were free, out of all the bumper-to-bumper traffic and herds of rubbernecking pedestrians, charging up that hill that curved around gently to the right and then just kept climbing and climbing and *climbing!* Big Ed wound the Jag all the way out in second and upshifted into third --foot to the floor-- and you could feel the way that hill was sucking the guts out of the Jag's engine. Made you wonder what driving a TC or a TD would be like. Or worse yet one of those dinky little Crosley Hotshots. Why, you'd be lucky not to *lose* rpms in one of those things, even with the throttle mashed clear to the stops. And then I started thinking about the big, hot-rodded Chrysler engine we'd crammed into Tommy Edwards' Allard, and how maybe he really knew what kind of "bigger stick" he needed for Watkins Glen after all....

The road flattened out and then dropped down into a shallow, tree-covered gully just past the turnoff for the Seneca Lodge, and then it headed up into some narrow, sweeping esses coming up out of the trees and a pretty decent straight section with a deep, gut-hollowing dip right in the middle where the road dived abruptly down and up under a railroad bridge. We were doing maybe sixty-five or so in the Jag, and you could really feel the car coming down hard on the springs in the hollow at the bottom and then getting all queasy-light and floaty as it rocketed up off the hump on the other side. And it didn't help much to look over and see that Big Ed's knuckles were a bloodless white, his eyes were wide as coffee saucers, and he'd bitten off the business end of his cigar and apparently swallowed the rest. And I could see why when I looked up and saw the flat, gentle sweep to the right and curl back to the left ahead of us. Tommy Edwards told me later that this was the spot where Sam Collier got himself killed in Briggs Cunningham's Ferrari during the second lap of the 1950 Watkins Glen Grand Prix, and it was all too easy to see how such a thing could happen. Like all the really dangerous spots at Elkhart Lake (and everyplace else, if you want to really get technical about it) this was simply a nondescript little bend in a narrow road. But it was approached at very high speed in top gear and the fast guys took it without lifting. Or at least they *talked* about taking it without lifting, anyways. What made it doubly dangerous was the penalty: there was simply no place to go if you misjudged it. A stout, solemn grove of trees stood up ahead and off to the drivers' left like a legion of green-cloaked monks with their heads bowed in prayer, quietly *waiting*....

So I was naturally a little relieved when we came up on a bunch of S.C.M.A. smallbore racers out to learn the course themselves --most of them in MG TCs and TDs and stuff like that-- and Big Ed had no choice but to back out of it and fall in line at the end of the queue. Especially after I saw what was coming up next. We'd climbed I don't know how far uphill ever since we'd turned right off Franklin Street in downtown Watkins Glen, but as we braked for the right at School House Corner, the track suddenly decided to lose all that elevation in a big, *big* hurry. The roadway plummeted downhill through a wrenching series of tight, bobsled-run switchbacks with trees close in on all sides, pounded across a humpbacked old stone bridge right at the bottom, and started climbing again through another dense forest until it broke through right at the top and the oiled gravel paving turned to hard-packed dirt. There was a dramatic, broadsliding right called Archy Smith's corner (which reminded me just a little of an oval dirt track, the way a good driver could toss the car kind of sideways and steer it with the throttle) and then hard on the gas down Railroad Straight --still on hardpacked dirt-- and over a rough railroad crossing that tossed the cars in the air so's you could see a foot or more of daylight under all four wheels.

Or at least you could if the driver didn't worry all that much about his car and had the moxie to keep his foot in it. Then came another pavement change --to cement this time-- right as you passed the upper entrance to the Glen State Park, and then you found yourself cresting the top of a gentle rise to one of the most spectacular and daunting sights in all of racing. There you are, way up at the top of a steep, massive hillside, looking out over Lake Seneca all wide and deep and somber down below and the tops of the trees climbing up the grade from the outskirts of Watkins Glen. You're entering Big Bend, which is a fast, endless, downhill sweep to the right taken in top gear with no guardrail on the outside and tumbling oblivion hanging under your left elbow like an armrest. It was undoubtedly another one of those spots that separated the men from the boys, and I didn't need Cal Carrington or Tommy Edwards to point it out or explain it to me. Not hardly. The pavement changed again as the road descended into Watkins Glen like a hawk swooping down out of the sky, and at the bottom there was a sharp left at Milliken's Corner followed immediately by a ninety-degree right onto Franklin Street again just across from the Jefferson Hotel. It was 6.6 miles all the way around, and I'd have to say that I thought the circuit around Elkhart Lake was scary right up until I took that ride around Watkins Glen with Big Ed. The Glen maybe wasn't as fast on lap average as Elkhart because of the steep climbs and the fact that there weren't so many long, flat-out straight sections, but it was narrower, had steeper ascents and descents (*especially* the descents!), ran over four different kinds of paving, and was generally reckoned to be more difficult and demanding by most of the drivers. Besides, people had died there....

Chapter 31: The Blackest Day

We partied it up at the Seneca Lodge that night with Cal Carrington and Tommy Edwards and Barry Spline and a bunch of the MG guys, and Cal was in pretty good spirits even though he hadn't found anything to drive. Then again, staying in good spirits and keeping his confidence up were never problems for Cal --especially when he had a minor-league snootfull-- and you had to keep that sort of outlook and appearance up if you ever expected people to take a chance on you and hand over the keys to their expensive imported racecars. I caught myself thinking what a swell deal it would be if Cal could meet up with that Ernesto Julio guy from California and maybe get a chance to drive one or two of his cars. Not that Ernesto Julio didn't already have himself a super-duper driver in Phil Hill, you understand, but Cal was my friend. In fact, you could say we were sort of blood brothers ever since the nights we spent cutting our fingers, splitting our nails, and gashing our knuckles on that worthless piece-of-shit TC of his in my Aunt Rosamarina's garage. Oh, we hadn't exactly jabbed ourselves with a Bowie knife and stood there solemnly thumb-to-thumb like the Cowboy Hero and Honorable Indian Brave in the western movies, but we'd both left plenty of late-night and early-morning blood samples all over that jagged, cantankerous MG --and we'd done it *together*-- and as far as I was concerned, it amounted to the same thing. So whatever good things happened to Cal on a racetrack and whatever success he achieved somehow seemed to reflect back on me. I don't know why that should be, but I could feel it in my gut.

Friday the Cunningham team arrived with their big semi-trailer car transporter and their freshly cleaned-and-pressed white coveralls and set up an impressive bivouac in a roped-off corner of the parking lot across from the Jefferson Hotel, right there on Franklin Street. They had all three cars again and the same three drivers, and you could see everything had been painstakingly hosed off and hammered out and touch-up painted and polished down to a smooth, gleaming finish again during the two short weeks since Elkhart Lake. Then again, you could *do* that sort of thing when you had a good organization and a lot of willing hands available (and moreover enough ready cash in the bank to put paychecks in those same hands come the end of each and every week). The idea that one single man could make all that happen out of the bulge in his hip pocket was a constant source of awe, bewilderment, and amazement, even among the rich guys from Long Island and White Plains and Connecticut who owned multiple Jags and Ferraris and chauffeured Series 75 Cadillac limousines for going to shows and nightclubbing and suit-and-tie dinner trips into Manhattan. Briggs did it all with a style and scale and sense of commitment that put everybody else in the shade, and it says a lot about the guy that everybody seemed to like him anyway. They also respected the heck out of him for what he'd done. Which was quite an accomplishment, since money has a way of making people look ugly (especially to blue-collar lunchbucket knuckle-busters like myself) but somehow Briggs Cunningham wore his like a shining suit of armor. And with the Home Team colors on the damn shield, too....

Phil Hill and Chuck Day showed up a half-hour later with Ernesto Julio's silver C-type, which I understand they left parked in S.H. Arnolt's big warehouse garage on Ohio Street in Chicago after the race weekend at Elkhart Lake, flew home to California, and then flew back again just ten days later to pick it up and drive it out east for Watkins Glen. Seems there was some special deal cooked up for Johnny Fitch to drive it in the Seneca Cup warmup race for unrestricted cars Saturday morning before Phil Hill took it over for the big Watkins Glen Grand Prix feature event later on Saturday afternoon (while Fitch meanwhile planned to hop back into one of the Cunninghams). I guess Briggs' team wanted themselves a firsthand reading on the C-type from one of their own drivers, and Ernesto Julio was only too happy to oblige (with, of course, the unspoken understanding that Briggs would be the car's new owner if the damn thing got fetched up against a tree someplace). Phil Hill didn't seem too put out about it, and Chuck Day reckoned he'd have no trouble landing himself something else to drive in the Seneca Cup. I wished him luck, you know, but the fact is I was a little depressed about it, seeing as how the presence of a Known Commodity like Phil Hill on the open market cut down the odds of a Seneca Cup ride for my buddy Cal Carrington even further.

And all the while, streams of cars and people kept pushing and flowing and oozing their way into Watkins Glen from every direction, stuffing that little resort town until it was ready to burst at the seams. The race drivers could hardly get anything at all out of "practice" by noon on Friday, on account of all the roads were clogged with people looking to get into town or looking to get out of town or looking for friends they were supposed to meet or trying to find a place to stay. And there were more people coming all the time! In fact, that was one of the hottest topics of discussion Friday night long around the Seneca bar:

"I heard there's over *fifty thousand* spectators here!"

"I heard it's more like a *hundred* thousand!"

"That's what I heard, too! And you can't get a damn room anyplace for a hundred miles!"

"Really?!"

"Absolutely!"

"That's not true! I heard someone from the sheriff's office said it was over a hundred and *fifty* thousand people, and you can't get a room anyplace around for a hundred and *fifty* miles!"

It went on and on like that all night long. By closing time, it was up to roughly a half-a-million people and no hotel rooms were available in the entire upstate section of New York....

Ernesto Julio arrived at the Seneca bar later on that evening after a long drive down from Syracuse in a brand-spanking new 1953-model Packard Caribbean convertible (in kind of a deep plum color with creamy grey leather) and it was unquestionably the first one of those things that anybody had ever seen. The rumor going around was that he'd flown in from someplace in California that afternoon, taken a cab over to a Packard dealership in Syracuse, and supposedly *bought* that car off the showroom floor --just so's he'd have something nice to drive around in for the weekend (although I overheard somebody else speculate that it was really just a *rental*, you know, and that he hadn't paid much more than twice or three times what I earned in a month to use that brand-new Packard for three or four days at Watkins Glen). Truth is, the grueling ten-day Garage Thrash I'd endured with Tommy's Allard at Westbridge and Big Ed's XK120 back in Passaic had put me a little out of touch with the staggering flash and style and wide-open money tap you found around S.C.M.A. sportycar racing. But --as always-- it only took a day or two back in the field to get accustomed to it all over again. Why, these people talked about flying back and forth across the country to pick up cars and buying brand-new Packard convertibles just to use them for the weekend and taking off for Europe or Palm Beach or Bermuda or someplace for a vacation (whenever their busy racing schedules allowed, anyway) like it was *nothing*. And it was all too easy for a guy like me to get himself intoxicated with the smell and taste and feel of it and start thinking like he was really an integral part of that life instead of just one of the damn supports holding it up.

On the other hand, it was impossible not to enjoy it, and even nose-in-the-air stiffs like Creighton Pendleton could be pretty damn amusing when they decided to let their guard down to have some fun. Like fr'instance that particular Friday night in the Seneca bar. I guess a few people who knew the whole story on the green C-type had come up to Creighton on the side and given him a rough time for selling such a rare and magnificent racing car to a major-league doofus like Skippy Welcher. Especially seeing as how the cars were always grouped by class on the grid for every race, so that C-type was going to put Skippy right up at the front of the pack in a potentially *very* fast automobile. Which is another way of saying it was going to put him in an ideal position to cut people off, hold up faster drivers, and generally wreak havoc on the natural order of things. But Creighton Pendleton the Third stuck to his guns and explained as how he had a longstanding Gentlemen's Agreement with The Skipper about getting first crack at his racecars whenever he was ready to sell one, and Gentlemen's Agreements always carried a lot of weight with the S.C.M.A. clubby types, even though few of them actually were. And you couldn't miss the dose of sheer, shrewd genius to the plan, on account of it simultaneously guaranteed Creighton Pendleton whatever ridiculous price he asked for his used-up racecars and also kept at least one more fast, potent, and highly competitive automobile out of competent hands. That was worth something to a guy who liked to run at the front like Creighton Pendleton.

Still, it was obvious Creighton realized he had to at least do *something* --make some sort of token gesture or other-- that would all at once show he shared everybody's concern about Skippy and the C-type, offer The Skipper a little constructive advice (not that he was ever much likely to follow it), have a bit of fun at Skippy's expense, and most of all put a little distance between himself and the potentially dangerous combination of Reginald "Skippy" Welcher and one of the two latest, fastest damn Jaguar racing cars in the country. And I must admit, Creighton Pendleton figured himself out a pretty slick way to do it, too. About ten o'clock Friday night, with the Seneca bar and the restaurant behind it packed wall-to-wall and all the way up to the rafters with racing people, Creighton clambered right up on top of the bar --so he was towering over *everybody,* you know?-- and started ringing this old-fashioned school bell as hard as he could, clanging it back and forth over his head until the whole place went quiet around him like somebody'd thrown a big wool blanket over all the noise. For just an instant all you could hear was the ringing of that bell, and when it stopped the place was quiet as a Protestant funeral. Creighton looked slowly around the room at all the silent, wondering faces --every one of them staring right back up at him-- and gently lowered the bell from over his head. Then he fed them one of his famous, knowing smiles. "Well," he said in an after-dinner-speech sort of voice, "it's good to see all of us here again at Watkins Glen, isn't it?"

The crowd responded with a smattering of applause and some randomly mumbled nods of approval.

"And it's even better to see us all having such a wonderfully good time, right?"

That turned the rheostat up on the crowd a few notches and some of them even raised their glasses and tipped them up in the general direction of the bar. But mostly everybody was waiting to see just what the heck was going to happen. I mean, Creighton Pendleton wasn't normally the type to stand up and address a whole bunch of strangers like some hack political nominee. More usually people came around and tried to talk to *him,* you know? I mean, who needs to make speeches and press the flesh and suck up to John Q. Public in general when they've already nailed down the position of Crown Prince For Life....

"Now, as some of you already know," Creighton continued, pausing just long enough so he could see everybody try to lean in a little closer over their tables, "I was fortunate to come into ownership of the green Jaguar XK120C that my good friend Tommy Edwards drove so valiantly for me at Elkhart Lake..."

The crowd responded with rumbles of hushed surprise and a quick, half-hearted flutter of applause for Tommy.

"...and I had designs on racing that car myself when the opportunity presented itself." Creighton paused again to take a slow, weighty sip of beer. He sure knew how to play a crowd, no lie. "But," he continued, "it has subsequently become obvious that not even yours truly can ride two separate horses with the selfsame ass."

That brought a round of polite laughter.

"So I have decided to stick with my Ferrari --even though it's the older of the two cars-- because that car has come to own an enormous piece of my heart, and the two of us have traveled so many wonderful racing miles together..."

You could hear the muted grunts of sympathy and under-standing coming from everywhere around the room (although I personally noticed Creighton somehow forgot to mention that the Ferrari was by far the more powerful of the two racecars....)

"...and yet it seemed unfair to keep a wonderful car such as the Jaguar from its obvious destiny. And so, with the greatest possible reluctance, I was forced to sell it to someone who could take it out on a racing circuit --where it *belongs!*-- and give it some proper high-speed exercise...."

More nods and grunts of approval from the bar.

"And, as with all my cars, I gave my good friend Reggie Welcher first shot at the C-type, and my family banker will be only too happy to tell you that he snapped it up without hesita-tion..." More laughter, mixed in with some hushed, angry mut-tering on the part of regular-issue XK120 drivers who were now going to have to start every damn race from grid positions behind Skippy's new C-type, "...but it seems to me," Creighton contin-ued, raising his voice up over the rumble of the crowd, "it seems to me we left one *very* important piece of equipment off the car when we handed it over to Reggie...." He let the mystery dangle there for a minute or two while everybody in the room blinked and swallowed and looked back and forth at each other, trying like hell to figure out what was coming next.

"And so, fellow racers," Creighton said at last, "I'd like to ask my dear friend Reggie Welcher to step up here for a moment so I can give it to him. And," he added in a stage whisper, "I do indeed mean *give it to him!*"

The Skipper stood up at the back of the room and marched himself up proudly between the uneven rows of tables --gold tooth glittering like a beacon in the middle of his best Village Idiot smile-- like he was on his way to receiving the blessed Congressional Medal of Honor or something. And when he got up to the bar, the Muscatelli brothers were there waiting and boosted him up so he was standing on top of it, right next to Creighton Pendleton, the two of them towering over everybody like Ike and Dick Nixon at the Republican Convention that year. "Reggie," Creighton said gently, snaking an arm around The Skipper's shoulders, "you've always known what I think of you, and even more importantly what I think of your driving..."

The Skipper's smile spread out even broader (which just goes to show you how much old Skippy Welcher had on the ball, since everybody else in the room knew *exactly* what Creighton Pendleton was talking about).

"...so my friends the Muscatelli brothers and I have come up with a very special, one of a kind, and absolutely Top Secret piece of speed equipment that we think you most certainly need to have on your new racecar." He looked down behind the bar. "May I have it, please?"

The bartender handed Creighton a good-sized cardboard box that was all wrapped up with brightly-colored paper and ribbon like some eight-year-old's birthday present. "Here," Creighton said, handing it over to Skippy, "and make sure you use it the way it was properly intended."

Skippy ripped off the paper like a kid on Christmas morning, tore the box apart, and suddenly found himself holding one of those great big outside mirrors like they mount on the windshield posts of semi trucks and city busses. It was painted the same deep British Racing Green as his new Jaguar, and there was a head-on photograph of twenty or thirty standard-issue XK120s (most likely taken on the grid at Elkhart Lake or Bridgehampton or someplace) pasted down on the reflecting side.

Needless to say, the place went nuts. Why, even Skippy Welcher seemed to be enjoying it. But you couldn't miss thinking that he maybe didn't get it at all, and was just happy to have all the pomp and circumstance and attention that went along with Creighton's presentation. Then the Muscatelli brothers took that enormous mirror outside and mounted it dead-center on the dash cowling of Skippy's C-type (which somebody had moved so it was parked just outside the front door) and you had to admit, they'd put some thought into figuring out a quick, practical, and secure way to do it. Then again, you never expected anything less from those guys. Naturally a good two-thirds of the crowd came out into the parking lot to watch the big mirror installation ceremony, pronounce toasts to its future use, and not-too-quietly laugh their asses off at Skippy Welcher. And The Skipper seemed to take it all with a sort of spastic good grace, waving and smiling and laughing right along with everybody else, his ridiculous little --*heh heh, heh heh*-- cackle clattering up over the rest of the crowd noise like a pile of shingles falling off a roof.

But then The Skipper noticed *me,* standing there right behind the Muscatelli brothers, and he stepped up in front of my face and stared at me full blast with those flinty little eyes of his. "They think they're having a little joke at my expense," he whispered through clenched teeth while still smiling and waving grandly to the crowd. "But they'll see. They'll all see. And you'll see, too, young man. You'll see, too...."

I didn't like the look in his eye one bit.

The party around Skippy's Jag more or less ran out of steam after a while and everybody either drifted back into the bar or wandered off to bed. Except for me, that is. I just kind of hung around there by myself in the parking lot, wandering up and down among the haphazard rows and clusters of sportscars. The sky above me was filled with thousands upon thousands of tiny, twinkling stars and a thin silver crescent of a moon was just climbing its way up over the tree line, and together they were pouring a strange, dim, icy-blue light down over all the MGs and Jaguars and Aston Martins and Ferraris and Bugattis and BMWs and Porsches and Allards and OSCAs and Siatas and Frazer Nashes and Crosley Hotshots and even Ernesto Julio's brand-spanking new Packard convertible, gleaming off fenderlines that were smooth or sleek or proud or jaunty and reflecting here and there off chrome-plated grilles and windshield frames. They were all so wonderfully *different,* you know? And that made me think about all the clever, brave, bold, and frivolous things you could do with a little iron and steel and creative human imagination if you just had somebody on the other end willing to pay the price.

As you can imagine, that got me thinking back over all the things I'd done and people I'd met and places I'd gone and most especially all the damn cars I'd worked my ass off on that summer. And it occurred to me how comfortable and at ease I'd become with every single one of those exotic, expensive, mysterious two-seaters parked there in the Seneca lot. Why, they were just *cars,* you know? *Special* cars, to be sure. And *beautiful* cars, it went without saying. And no doubt exciting to be around. But I knew I wouldn't hesitate a second before taking a wrench to any one of them if it needed a little fixing or fine tuning, you know? Not that I knew everything there was to know about European sportscars, you understand. Why, a good mechanic *never* thinks he knows everything there is to know about *any* automobile --not even a Nash Rambler or a two-door Ford-- and any time you start thinking you do is precisely when you start getting yourself into some hot, *hot* water. But at least now I had the confidence that what I *didn't* know I could maybe figure out. Or at least know who to ask, anyway. And in wrenching --as in racing and just about everything else in life-- confidence is half the battle....

I noticed it was getting pretty cold out there, but each time I passed by the lodge building and listened to all the muffled whoops and hollers coming from inside, the less I felt like climbing up the steps and going in again. What I really wanted was to call Julie, you know? But it figured to be pretty late and no way would her mom be real pleased if I did. Especially if she happened to answer the phone. But damn if they didn't have a pay phone screwed into the outside wall of the Seneca Lodge, right there on the porch next to the entrance-way to the main dining room. And, wouldn't you know it, I had a bunch of loose change jangling around in my pocket, too....

Naturally it rang and rang and rang, and just about the time I started to panic and went to hang up before anybody could answer, someone picked up the receiver. "Whoozis?" an angry voice hissed at the other end of the line. It was Julie's mom all right (what else?) and, as you can imagine, she didn't sound exactly pleasant.

"Uhh, hi there, Mrs. Finzio," I said like I was handing her a dozen roses, "is Julie at home?"

"Whaddaya mean, izza my Joolie home? Of course a'my Joolie's home. Why, it's past a'middanight, fer'Godda sake."

"Jeez, is it *that* late?"

"A'sure it is. Whattsamatta wit'you, anyways?"

"Uh, gee whiz, Mrs. Finzio, I...."

Then I heard a big commotion going on at the other end of the line, and next thing I knew, Julie was on the phone with me. And the funny part is I knew it was her before she even said anything. It was like I could just *feel* it, you know?

"Buddy?" Julie said, sounding half asleep, "is that you?"

"Yeah," I admitted, feeling pretty stupid since I didn't really have much of anything to say, "it's me."

"Is anything wrong?" She sounded a little worried, you know? Really she did.

"Uhh, n-nothing, honey," I told her. "Nothing at all."

"Then why the heck are you calling so late?"

"I dunno," I mumbled, kind of shuffling back and forth on my heels, "I just wanted to, you know, *talk* to you...."

"At twelve-fifteen in the morning?"

"Gee whiz, is it *that* late?"

"Yeah, it sure is." Now she sounded sort of angry. But just a little bit, you know? "Say, have you been drinking?" she wanted to know.

Of course it was a race weekend, so that pretty much went without saying. "Jeez, I'm sorry I got you up," I apologized, sounding particularly lame, "hope you're not real sore about it."

"It's my mom who looks sore about it," Julie said with just the faintest flicker of a laugh. And I could see her mom, too, standing there in her bathrobe with her hair up in curlers, her arms folded angrily across her chest, and sparks shooting out of both eyes. Why, it wasn't hard to imagine at all.

"Well, I guess maybe I better hang up then and let you guys go back to sleep."

"I guess you'd better."

"Well, g'bye then."

"G'bye." She went to hang up, but then I could feel her stop and wait for a second at the other end. "Buddy?" she said softly, her mouth right down next to the receiver.

"Yeah?"

"Thanks for calling."

....*click!*

That little talk with Julie sent a nice, soft, warm sort of ache rolling through my system, and when I hung up and looked around at where I was again, it reminded me about how damn *perfect* it would've been to have Julie up there with me that very weekend. That very *minute,* in fact, standing there in the parking lot of the Seneca Lodge with the stars and the pine trees and that little crescent sliver of a moon overhead and muffled echoes of laughter filtering out from the party that was still going on at the bar. There was just enough chill in the air to make us want to snuggle up together as we headed off to bed in our own little log cabin. It sounded pretty damn good to me, you know?

So I made my way back towards the cabin, all wrapped up in hot, steamy little fantasies about me and Miss Julie Finzio. But they disappeared like smoke the instant I opened the door to our room. Big Ed was in there already, curled up like a sleeping hippopotamus and snoring up a storm. Jee-*zus,* I'd never heard a noise like that in my life! At least not out of a human being, anyway. It was like thunder rumbling up through wet gravel all mixed up with the sound a rickety old railroad bridge makes when a slow freight passes over. Anyhow, it took me a long, *long* time to drift off to sleep that night, and not one single minute of it was that real deep, pure, warm black hole of a sleep that leaves you feeling rested and refreshed in the morning. Sometimes you just need to be alone....

But raceday always brings its own special buzz of excitement to perk you up, and as-per-usual I was up at the crack of dawn with my eyes popped open like a couple of fried eggs --even though I was about eighty-five percent exhausted and really could've used a few hours' sleep. At least I didn't have much in the way of a hangover, and that was always a pleasant surprise on a race weekend morning. It was overcast, grey, and damp outside, and a chilly dew had settled itself down over the trees and grass and all the brightly colored cars in the parking lot. You could smell hot coffee and frypans full of sizzling bacon and scrambled eggs and hash brown potatoes starting up over in the kitchen, and I decided it would be a great idea to go over and have myself a real honest-to-goodness, major league breakfast feast, since this was probably going to turn into a long, *long* day before it was over.

Along the way I passed Big Ed's cream-colored XK120, and there was no way you could miss how it wasn't sitting exactly right. Why, the front bumper was right down on the grass and the dash cowling wasn't any higher than the one on the MG TC parked next to it. Something was very definitely wrong. So I walked over and took a look, and it didn't take a whole lot of investigating to come to the conclusion that all four tires were flat. It would've actually been sort of funny --at least after the initial spurt of anger wore off-- and certainly in line with the kind of pranks and hazing that get dished out to rookie racing drivers as a matter of general policy. Only the sonofabitch who pulled *this* stunt was downright malicious. Instead of just pushing down on the button and letting the air out (or maybe even unscrewing the entire valve out of the stems and walking off with them) this rat bastard had snipped the damn valve stems clear off the inner tubes with a pair of side-cutters or something, and so I'd have to somehow get Big Ed's car up off the ground, pull all four wheels, find some way to truck them into town, locate a new set of inner tubes someplace that would fit our 6.00 x 16-inch Dunlops, dismount and remount all the tires, get the wheels balanced, bring everything back up to the Seneca, put them on the damn car, and get it back down to the pits before they closed the roads for the first race and made getting around anyplace in Watkins Glen pretty much impossible.

So much for my major league breakfast.

But I got it handled, thanks to people like Tommy Edwards and Carson Flegley and especially Ernesto Julio, who didn't even think twice about lending me that brand new Packard Caribbean of his so I could carry the tires down into town for repairs. In fact, he damn near *insisted* on it, and actually seemed kind of happy about the idea --as if the opportunity to do outlandish things didn't come around often enough in his life. "But what if I get it *dirty?*" I asked him, eyeballing the creamy grey leather interior on that plum-colored Packard convertible.

"Oh, what the hell," he grinned, "that's what soap and water and guys like you are for!"

And I had to admit, he was right.

Anyhow, I had everything loaded up in the Packard by the time Big Ed rolled out for breakfast, and I told him to just stay put and take it easy for an hour or so and that I'd take care of everything. I mean, the last thing I needed was a loud, angry, highly pissed-off Big Ed Baumstein all over me while I was trying to get a large job done in a very short amount of time. Besides, I'd discovered long before that there's a special sort of Professional Courtesy that exists between streetcorner gas station employees (or ex-employees) and if you kind of casually let one of them know you're also a member of the brotherhood, you can get yourself an awful lot in the way of favors and cooperation. Especially when time is short and there's a racecar involved.

And that's exactly the way it worked that early Saturday morning in Watkins Glen. I got three of the inner tubes I needed off Barry Spline (who was none too happy about getting hauled out of bed at the Jefferson Hotel before 6:30 ayem) and the fourth one out of the spare in Big Ed's trunk. I couldn't just use it the way it was on account of he'd hit a pothole someplace a pretty solid lick and bent the rim (not to mention a few spokes) and there was no way you could use that spare on a racecar. Then I found an Atlantic gas station with a tire-mounting stand and a couple tire irons handy and a compressor to supply the air, and I talked the pump jockey into letting me use the stuff even though neither the owner or the night manager or the resident smalltown grease monkey were on hand. After all, it was race day in Watkins Glen, and the village shut down for the occasion like it was the Fourth of July. "Y'know, I'll get my ass fired if th'boss ever finds out," the gas station kid told me while I worried one of Big Ed's tires off with a couple irons. "Jiminy, I'm not s'posed t'let *any*body come in the shop. Not ever. And if...."

"Look," I told him, "this is an *emergency*, understand?"

"Yeah," he said, not sounding real sure about it in the least, "I *guess* so...."

After I got done and the kid helped me load everything back into the Packard, I reached in my back pocket and handed the kid a folded-up dollar tip, slipping it to him under my palm just the way Big Ed used to do when I worked on his Caddies back at the Old Man's Sinclair. "Jeez, *thanks,* mister," the kid gasped, holding the bill out in front of him like it was a damn sawbuck or something. Truth is, I couldn't remember anybody ever calling me "mister" before, you know?

Of course I had Big Ed's Jag squared away in plenty of time to make it down to the pit area across from the Jefferson Hotel before they closed the roads and the races started, and a quick check-in with Tommy Edwards indicated that everything was shipshape with Tommy's Chrysler-powered Allard as well. So there really wasn't much of anything to do except grab myself a spot along the snow fencing someplace and watch the races, you know? Along the way, I ran into a sad-looking Cal Carrington, who was wandering around the pit area with an uncharacteristic scowl plastered across his face and his hands thrust down deep into his pants pockets with the thumbs hooked through the belt loops. I guess Carson Flegley had sort of timidly held his ground about trying to drive the MG himself that weekend, and since the only real practice sessions were the three quick warmup laps before each race, there'd be no opportunity for Carson to change his mind and hand the car over to Cal even if he wanted to. Cal did manage to finagle himself a deal to drive some older guy's XK120 right around closing time at the Seneca bar on Friday night, and he was really looking forward to having a crack at something as big and powerful as a Jag 120. Only now that morning had arrived and the illuminating effects of the liquor had worn off, the older guy who owned the Jag was having a few serious second thoughts. And then some. But of course there was no way he could just come right out and *tell* Cal that he was backing out of the deal. After all, that wouldn't be *gentlemanly,* you know? So he'd come up with some phony-baloney cock-and-bull story about the needle on the oil pressure gauge fluctuating up and down unpredictably during the short drive down the hill to Franklin Street that morning, and while it would be perfectly okay for him --the owner-- to blow the damn engine sky high, he surely didn't want to put an earnest, innocent, intelligent, and obviously very honorable young fellow like Cal Carrington in the singularly uncomfortable position of finding himself responsible for a devastatingly expensive repair bill. And those are the exact words he used, too: "a *devastatingly* expensive repair bill," just so Cal would be sure and understand that he was doing it for Cal's own good. "Aah, don't worry about it," I told him, "you'll get plenty more chances to drive racecars in this lifetime."

"Yeah, sure," Cal snorted, turning the corners of his frown down even further.

"No, *really,*" I told him. "I mean, everybody knows what a super driver you are. You'll get your shot...."

"That's easy for *you* to say," Cal groused, nudging a few bits of gravel around with the toe of his Bass Weejuns. *"You're* not missing your sister's damn wedding back home just to be up here for the races. Jesus Christ, Buddy, my life may not *go* much past Monday morning...." And then, without any sort of warning, that mischievous old Cal Carrington rich kid smile spread out across his face like sunlight peeking out from behind a cloud bank. "Aah, what the hell," he sighed, "let's go watch the damn races and see if any of these dumb jerkoffs can drive."

So I checked in one more time with Big Ed and Tommy Edwards, and everything was fine. Tommy even told me he'd keep an eye on Big Ed and whisper soothing words into his ear every now and then. Which sounded like a pretty good idea, on account of you could tell by the way his eyes were starting to bug out and how his stogie was hesitantly wobbling its way from one side of his mouth to the other that Big Ed was getting a serious case of the pre-race jitters. Truth is, *all* race drivers get that from time to time (like before every single race, if you want to know the truth of it) but it's more obvious with rookies simply because they're too damn preoccupied to try and hide it....

The first race of the day was the Seneca Cup for so-called "unrestricted" cars, and Cal and me worked our way through the crowd towards corner one at the south end of Franklin Street while the race cars assembled on the grid for their three warmup laps. Most of the heavy runners like the Cunninghams and Tommy Edwards' Chrysler/Allard and Creighton Pendleton's 4.1 Ferrari and all the standard-issue XK120s and such were saving themselves for the big feature Watkins Glen Grand Prix later that afternoon, so you had a field made up of mostly those dinky little open-wheel Formula III cars from England and some strange hybrids like a Chrysler-powered Lea-Francis special and even a few stripped-down TCs running on alcohol fuel and breathing through Rootes-type superchargers. The pre-race favorite was a very accomplished (in fact, more-or-less notorious) S.C.M.A. regular named George Weaver, who drove a somewhat scruffy but blazingly-fast 4.5-litre Maserati open-wheel Grand Prix car called Poison Lil. It was an older car --from before the war, even-- but that thing was a real thoroughbred, and the super-charged V8 was about as monstrous and handsome an automotive powerplant as you'd ever hope to see. Then again, the Maserati brothers were master machinists by trade back in Italy, and everything they made out of metal was absolutely beautiful to look at. Except maybe for some of the frame welds. At least the ones in non-critical areas, anyway. And those didn't count, you know? Anyhow, the Maserati ran on some exotic fuel blend that made your eyes tear and your nose run like my old man's chemical plant job, and that engine made a noise like a squadron of dive bombers wailing down on some hapless European town whenever George Weaver cracked it open all the way to the throttle stops. Like I said before, that car was a genuine, thorough-bred racing machine, and sprang from the same exact hands, minds, shop, and family tree as the Boyle Special Maserati that Wilbur Shaw drove to victory at the Indianapolis Motor Speedway in 1939 and 1940 and damn near all over again in '41. But Weaver's Maserati was an older car by 1952, and there figured to be some *very* serious competition from the silver C-type Jaguar that Ernesto Julio had so generously lent out to Cunningham team driver Johnny Fitch for, umm, "evaluation."

And that's exactly how the race played out, too. After the three warmup laps the cars gathered up on the grid in the middle of Franklin Street again, and when the Great White Hunter guy (yeah, it was him again!) brandished the green, George Weaver lit the fuse on that supercharged Vee-eight and his Grand Prix Maserati took off like a scalded cat, leaving two steaming streaks of melted rubber almost all the way down to the first corner! That Maserati open-wheeler was one *fast* automobile, no lie! Mean-while, Johnny Fitch was maybe just being a little more careful and conservative at the start (always a good idea when trying out somebody else's expensive racecar, and even more especially when that somebody intends to run it in another race later on that same afternoon!) but he started picking up the pace after the first lap or two and was right on the tail of Weaver's supercharged 4.5-litre Maserati by the end of the third lap. Next time around, the C-type was in front by at least a couple hundred yards, and you could see the Maserati was losing ground and the hard edge had come off its engine note. The Weaver Maserati went out a lap later with clouds of very expensive-looking bluish-white smoke coming out of the tailpipes (head gasket was my guess) and it really wasn't much of a contest after that, as John Fitch and the silver C-type continued to stretch it out easily the rest of the way home. But it was really something to watch that John Fitch fellow drive, and even Cal Carrington had nothing but respect and admiration for the way he handled that car and hit the exact same line --down to the damn *inch,* you know?-- lap after lap after lap. Fact is, it made you wish Skippy Welcher would've put that Phil Hill guy in the green one, just so's you could've seen those two duke it out head-to-head around Watkins Glen in identical cars. Jeez, I would've paid cash money to see *that* race!

Next up was the so-called Queen Catherine Cup for small-bore cars (which made you wonder who the heck comes up with those names, anyway) and although it was a big field and there was the usual cut-and-thrust dicing between the stock MGs down in the middle of the pack, the race for the overall win was again a real snore. Bill Spear won going away in one of those incredibly handsome little OSCA MT4s, and Jim Kimberly (yeah, the same one Kimberly's Korner at Elkhart Lake was named after) finished a distant second in one just like it. They were beautiful little cars, those OSCAs, and I heard from Cal and Barry Spline that they were actually built by the Maserati brothers in Bologna, Italy --the very same guys who dreamed up that awesome, 4.5-litre supercharged single-seater Grand Prix car we saw in the first race-- after they quit working for a big industrialist guy named Omer Orsi who bought them out when they were going bankrupt for the fourth or fifth time and moved them up the road a ways to a town called Modena. I guess the brothers didn't like Modena very much, and they certainly didn't like working for some big, high-powered industrialist guy. It wasn't their style, you know? So the very same day their contract with Orsi ran out, they packed up their shop rags and machine tools and moved back to Bologna, where they could live the way they wanted to live and build the cars they wanted to build and go bankrupt again every now and then whenever the mood struck them. Only problem was they couldn't use their own name on account of that Omer Orsi guy owned the rights to it. At least so far as it had to do with fast automobiles, anyway. So they called their cars OSCAs (which I guess stood for Officiallizzone Specialliazzone Constructiazzzone Automobillinni or something like that in Bologonese Italian) and no question they hadn't lost their talent for building some of the fastest, slickest, most beautifully proportioned Italian racecars you ever saw in your life. Only they couldn't afford the hardware (or tires, for that matter) to build BIG racecars anymore, so they built little ones instead. And were they ever *neat!*

"Ba fangu, Signore Orsi, eh?"

Anyhow, third place in the Catherine Cup race went to that West Coast guy Roger Barlow in his pretty blue Simca special, but he was way back and more or less cruising around on his lonesome. Fact is, except for a little MG dogfight going on halfway down the pack, the only interesting thing was watching our buddy Carson Flegley flog his black TD around. He was well towards the rear end of the field, of course, and that got Cal to mumbling and muttering about how *he* should've been out there instead of Carson. But I pointed out that at least Carson wasn't dead last (in fact, I think he may have had as many as five or six cars behind him at one point, and at least three of those were running on all four cylinders) and besides, he'd managed to keep it on the road and out of the local scenery, and you'd have to say that was a real major improvement in his driving style. Better yet, he *finished* the damn race --his first ever, I think-- and even managed to pass another car right there towards the end. As you can imagine, Carson was floating about two feet off the pavement when he clambered out of his steaming TD, and I don't think I ever saw a guy looking as happy and proud and satisfied with himself as Carson Flegley did the moment he lifted up his goggles and pulled off his helmet. Why, he could hardly talk, and there was even a timid little swagger in his step as we headed over by one of the souvenir stands to get ourselves some ice cream. And old lint-in-the-pockets Cal Carrington *bought* (can you believe it?) and that really put the icing on the cake. Carson had a grin hung across his face like it was hooked onto both ears, and you could tell that --at least for those precious few moments of his life-- Carson Flegley had indeed become the strong, brave knight who slew the ferocious, fire-breathing dragon, the courageous lone private who saved the whole damn platoon, and Rita Hayworth's favorite leading man...all rolled into one!

Why, if you could just find a way to bottle up that sensation and sell it, you'd make yourself a million kazillion dollars....

As per usual, things were running more than an hour behind by the time the cars started pulling out of the pits onto Franklin Street for the big Watkins Glen Grand Prix feature race. It was after 3 o'clock, and, what with all the people milling around the racecars and the general confusion getting them lined up properly and the reports I overheard coming in from the corners that there were spectators wandering across the racetrack, I kind of wondered just how they were going to get everything back together for the race. The three Cunninghams pulled smartly out into the first three grid positions, and I was thrilled to see my boy Tommy Edwards chuffing out to take the fourth slot on the outside of the second row with that jet black Allard we'd slaved over all week long before the race. You really don't mind putting in the effort when you see your car right there up front with the *fast* guys. But the joker in the deck was two rows behind him, as none other than our favorite lunatic jerkoff Skippy Welcher pulled up in his newly acquired C-type Jaguar, waving to the crowd on both sides of Franklin Street and flashing them his gold-tooth smile and revving the Jag's engine like there was a first-prize trophy for bending the most valves on the starting grid. Directly ahead of The Skipper (and looking plenty concerned about it!) was Creighton Pendleton in his blood-red 4.1 Ferrari, and next to him was Phil Hill in the other C-type, staring straight ahead with no expression on his face at all. He almost looked mean, you know, but it was really just concentration. Phil Hill knew that the Cunninghams and Tommy's Chrysler/Allard and even Creighton Pendleton's 4.1 Ferrari had a lot more sheer grunt than his "little" 3.4-litre Jaguar, and, what with the steep grade up Old Corning Hill after the first corner, there was no question he'd be lucky to just hold position for the first half-lap or so. And you could see the wheels turning and gears meshing under his pudding-bowl racing helmet as he went over the track in his mind, trying to figure out exactly where and when and how he might try to sneak past one of those guys up ahead. I can't recall ever seeing a guy think that hard before, and you knew right away that Phil Hill was destined to drive some pretty important racing cars in some very important races....

It was a good ten minutes before they got the rest of the field out and lined up on Franklin Street, and my guy Big Ed Baumstein was one of the very last. He actually should've been six or seven rows up from the back based on class and engine displacement, but Charlie Priddle and his armband brigade decided that it might be better to start Big Ed at the tail end of the field where he couldn't do much damage, and for once I had to agree with the wisdom of their decision. In fact, it was a pity they couldn't do the same damn thing with Skippy Welcher. At any rate, I went over by Big Ed to see if he needed anything, but he was pretty much past talking to by that point. He had on this brand-new, gleaming white racing helmet without a scratch on it (always the sure sign of a rookie) and he'd even had it painted the exact creamy-ivory shade as his car. That's about as far as I ever saw Big Ed attempt to go in terms of color-coordinating his wardrobe. He also had a pair of split-lens aviator goggles pulled down over his eyes, and through the glass you could see the look in his eyes was both fearsome and desperate, all at the same time. This figured to be a pretty rough afternoon for that poor old XK120 of his....

It took another fifteen minutes before they got all the crews and wives and girlfriends and news photographers and meandering hangers-on cleared out of the way, and then the Great White Hunter guy circled the green flag over his head and the engines fired all up and down the grid, the sound fluttering all the flags and banners and reverberating off the glass shop windows down the entire length of Franklin Street. Then the starter jerked his arms skyward and pointed them off, and the field snaked away with a roar for their three allotted practice laps. We heard them trundle through the right-hander at corner one and echo like thunder up Old Corning Hill, and then the sound drifted off into the countryside and all of a sudden it was very quiet, even with all the thousands of spectators lining the street seven- and eight- and ten-deep along both sides of the roadway. Why, you could hear the rustle of a slight breeze through the leaves and bushes and the gentle flap of the red, white, and blue cloth pennants they had strung up between the telephone poles that ran through downtown Watkins Glen. I even heard birds chattering back and forth to one another up in the trees....

It seemed to take forever for the cars to come around, and when they did, it was no surprise to see the three Cunninghams all together in a knot, accelerating brutally out of the last corner and rocketing down Franklin Street at what looked like better than a hundred miles an hour. Briggs himself was on the point, and you got the notion that neither Phil Walters or Johnny Fitch were about to take a quick dive to the inside and try to out-brake the boss. At least not during the practice laps, anyway. A little ways back was Tommy in the Allard, working hard on finding himself an empty bit of pavement so he could try out his new engine combination alone instead of mixing it up with other cars. Creighton Pendleton was right behind him, probably trying to find out what the Allard had and where it was weak, and you could see Phil Hill was doing exactly the same as Tommy, working on an open piece of track where he could really come to terms with what the C-type could do for him on a power circuit like Watkins Glen. The really good drivers are always thinking and plotting and planning about exactly what they're going to do come race time. The other guys just *go!*

Like Big Ed, for example, who was still way back at the tail end of the field, but obviously giving it everything he had. He was winding that poor old engine right up to 6500 --or more!-- and shifting like he was trying to rip the lever out by the roots. And so it was no big surprise to me when he failed to come around at the end of the second practice lap. I just hoped the damage wasn't too serious, seeing as how that Jag of his was supposed to be my ticket back home when the racing was over.

"You think he blew it up?" I asked Cal.

"Well, if he didn't," Cal allowed with a wry smile, "it sure wasn't for lack of trying...."

The field came around at the end of the last practice lap and formed up on the grid, and I ran out real quick to see if everything was okay on Tommy's car and find out if he knew what happened to Big Ed.

"She's running like a bloody rocket," Tommy grinned, "but I didn't want to show my hand to those blokes in the white cars up ahead. But we'll have a little something on tap for them when the bloody green drops. You'll see...."

"Did'ja see Big Ed?" I asked him.

"Oh, he's all right."

"You sure?"

"Absolutely," Tommy nodded, "but I don't know if I can say the same for his car...."

"Oh?"

"He's got it parked over to the side on the downhill before the stone bridge. Looked like there was an awful lot of smoke and oil. Think he might've dropped it down into first instead of third there for a moment. That's all it takes, you know...."

"Yeah," I said, "I know."

Shit.

Then one of the armband people rushed up and shooed me away, so I grabbed Cal's arm and we started bulling ourselves a path down towards corner one. We really could've used Big Ed right then, and I had to think that he probably would've been better off if he'd been there with us, too, instead of out there on the circuit with a busted Jaguar.

We only got about halfway down to the corner before the green dropped, and you couldn't really see much of anything as the pack thundered past in a confusion of splattering exhaust and swirling dust and cars streaking by like a rocket-powered freight train. Brake lights flashed desperately as they slowed hard and downshifted for corner one, and then the noise wailed up Old Corning Hill --louder and more desperately than before-- and faded off into the distance until it was deathly quiet all over again. And then a huge, flat grey cloud moved itself stubbornly in front of the sun and the temperature seemed to drop eight or ten degrees in an instant. There was nothing you could do but look back and forth at all the people hanging tightly along the snow fencing and wait....

It was the three Cunninghams again, all in a line and roaring out of the last turn onto Franklin Street, but Tommy's Allard was right on them like a shadow, and there was no mistaking the move when he pulled out of line and passed the last of them --right in front of us!-- and made it stick all the way down into the first turn. "He's *got* 'em!" I whooped, clutching Cal's arm.

"He sure does!" Cal whooped right back, "and I bet he's not done yet!"

"Not hardly!" I hollered, jumping up and down inside my skin. "Not hardly *at all!*"

There was a good couple hundred yards before the next cars came by, and sure enough it was Phil Hill with Creighton Pendleton's Ferrari glued right to his decklid. You could see the Ferrari was faster in a straight line and trying to line up for a pass, but

Phil kind of clogged up the middle lane so there really wasn't room for a decent move on the inside, and Creighton had no choice but to ease off and think better of it. By the next time around, Phil had enough distance on him that it really wasn't much of an issue anymore.

After Hill and Creighton's Ferrari came a whole bunch of other Allards and XK120s and right away Cal and me looked back and forth at each other with the same question in our minds: where was Skippy Welcher and the green C-type? But no sooner had we thought of it than The Skipper appeared, stumbling and stuttering his way up the start/finish straightaway at a brisk walking pace until the engine finally cut out completely and left him coasting to a halt right in front of us with no music at all coming out of the exhaust pipes.

"Oh Lordy," I thought, "what's he *done* to that poor car?"

He'd come to rest in a pretty bad position --right on the line Tommy'd taken to pass that third-place Cunningham-- and of course he was grinding the starter like he was ringing the door-bell to an empty house, trying to get it to fire up and go again. It obviously hadn't occurred to him that there must be a reason why the fire had gone out. Milton Fitting was nowhere to be seen (maybe he was off someplace checking tire pressures, you know?) so Cal and me hopped over the fence to see if we could maybe help out. Or at least get him out of the way before the cars came around again. We had a little better than four minutes as best as I could figure, so Cal and me flopped the latches and lifted up the pivoting one-piece alloy hood --The Skipper still grinding away relentlessly on the starter-- and it didn't take any kind of mechanical genius to figure out what the problem was. Skippy Welcher's brand-new C-type Jaguar was out of gas! It happened that we were just a few yards up the road from that Atlantic station where I'd gotten Big Ed's tire problem handled that morning, so I vaulted over the fence and ran up to the pumps, and believe it or not, the kid who'd helped me was al-ready out there with a jerry can, filling it up for us. I looked down at my watch and figured we had maybe a couple minutes left at best, so as soon as he had a few gallons inside I grabbed the can and kind of crashed my way through the snow fencing and did a high-speed waddle back to where the green C-type was sitting, dead in the water, with The Skipper still hard at it with the starter button. You could hear it was already starting to turn real slow and making that occasional, disappointing *click-click-click-click* noise that starter solenoids start to make when the battery has had quite enough of them, thank you.

We fueled her up and slammed down the hood, and by then there was no way that poor old car would start itself, so Cal and me and some armband people who'd been screaming at us to get out of the God Damn way gave the Jag a hefty push (putting, I might add, several nice-sized palm dents in the alloy rear deck) and the C-type caught after about fifteen feet or so and stuttered away, gasping for the float bowls to fill up and feed the suction. Me and Cal gave each other a quick appreciation nod, and then the armband types were shoving us back behind the fencing because the leaders were due to land in our laps any second....

And this time Tommy was up to second! And he was really bearing down on the lead Cunningham, too! But I couldn't help noticing that it was Briggs himself in the lead, and I wondered if maybe the other two Cunningham drivers were maybe holding back just a bit to see if Briggs could hang on and stay ahead of Tommy's Allard. Surely if he got passed, the other two would be completely within their rights to run a little harder (if they could) so one of the Cunninghams could still win the race.

Phil Hill was about halfway between those guys and Creighton's Ferrari, and you got the idea that he might be a factor for the overall before this thing was over. The C-type may not have had the legs on the field for power, but you could see how smooth and fast and nicely balanced it was running by itself, and Phil Hill was getting the most out of it and yet still saving plenty of car for the last half of the contest. A hundred miles is a long, *long* way around a track like Watkins Glen, and the really gifted drivers have a knack for seeing all the way to the checkered flag from the instant the green flag goes down.

We strained our eyes up Franklin Street towards the last corner, and the first car to appear was --Omigod, it was Skippy Welcher!-- sailing out of the turn in a jagged, unkempt broadslide and blaring that sweet Jag six right up to the redline (and then some) as he charged down towards us. But not a fifty yards behind him was Tommy's roaring black Allard --in the lead!-- with three Cunninghams gathered up in a vicious clot right behind him. You could see that Tommy was going to catch The

Skipper right as they hit the braking point for turn one, and I could feel the hairs rise up to attention on the back of my neck. But then I saw the corner workers waving the blue overtaking flag at Skippy, and he must've seen them, because he looked down in that big bus mirror the Muscatelli brothers had fastened to his dash cowling and nodded like the situation was well in hand. Tommy pulled out to pass on the inside, and that's when The Skipper did the one thing a slower driver should never, *ever* do when being overtaken. He pointed his finger off to the outside and pulled right across the Allard's nose to leave room for Tommy to pass on the proper racing line. He was just trying to be courteous, actually. Only Tommy was already committed, and he had no choice but to yank Hard Left on the Allard's wheel while the car was already starting to load up on tiptoes under heavy braking. The Allard slewed out to the left, tail swinging wide, then caught traction for an instant and swung back the other way, teetered for a heart-stopping moment --up on two wheels!-- and then made that final, uncontrollable, inescapable snap back to the left. It would have spun all the way around --if only there'd been *room!*-- but instead it sideswiped the snow fencing on the far side of the track, sending fence slats and cardboard boxes and race programs and half-eaten hotdogs flying like an explosion. Then the outside wheels bit *hard* into the pavement and the Allard went into a tumbling, flailing barrel-roll, shedding fender panels and headlight buckets and trim rings and --I can see it now-- Tommy Edwards himself.

The car skated across the track and smashed itself hard into a light pole --upside down-- while Tommy skidded and bounced and rolled up the racetrack and came to rest in a tightly curled lump right in the middle of the track-out line for corner one. *And the whole damn field was bearing down on that corner at a hundred-plus miles an hour!* Corner workers grabbed every flag they could lay their hands on and brandished them wildly through the air, and I saw Tommy's form curl itself up even tighter as racecars thundered around him on all sides, some missing him by inches --or even fractions of inches!-- time and time and time again. It seemed to take forever before the last one passed....

But --somehow-- not one of them hit him, and as soon as the last car cleared I was up over the snow fencing and running as fast as I ever had towards where Tommy's body was laying, still curled up like baby sleeping in its crib. Only he was shaking. I got there before anybody else, but then I didn't know what to do. I was afraid to reach out and touch him --like I might make things worse, you know?-- and a wretched feeling of helplessness came over me like I was drowning in it. Then Cal got there and some of the armband people, and it was Cal who reached down and tapped Tommy gently on the shoulder and asked, "You okay down there, Tommy? Can you hear me? Are you okay?"

"Believe it or not," Tommy's voice came up from what sounded like very far away, "I think I am." His helmet slowly raised up from between his broad shoulderblades and he gingerly leaned it back and forth from left to right and nodded it up and down. "Bloody hell," he said in an soft, amazed whisper, "I do believe I'm all right...."

"You *sure?*" one of the corner workers asked.

"Don't move!" one of the others cautioned.

"Oh, piss off," Tommy groaned, and pushed himself unsteadily up to his feet. You could see he had a bad cut on his left forearm and an absolutely huge pavement raspberry all up and down his right thigh, but he gently shook himself here and there and here and there all over again and found nothing else terribly amiss. "No broken bones apparently," he said with a half-hearted smile, "but I reckon I'll be pretty bloody sore tomorrow."

"Thank God!" I said, not really believing that *anybody* could possibly be that lucky.

"But I suppose I've just about used up my bloody Allard." He turned around to take a look, and that's when we saw all the anguish and confusion going on down at the entrance to the corner where Tommy's Allard had sideswiped the fence. There were people scattered all around on the sidewalk and grass like fallen bowling pins and other people crouched over them and corner workers and officials and the first medics on the scene running madly around from victim to victim, trying to assess the damage and take care of those who needed help the most. And, right in the middle of everything, crumpled up next to the curbing like a heap of soiled laundry, was the crushed, battered, and inescapably lifeless body of a seven-year-old boy.

"Oh my bloody God," Tommy gasped, sagging to his knees, *"Oh my bloody God in heaven...."*

Chapter 32: Aftermath

It took forever to get things sorted out that afternoon at Watkins Glen. A bunch of ambulances came with medics and stuff to take care of all the people who were hurt, and it turned out that most of the injuries were broken legs and wrists and shinbones and such from when Tommy's Allard banged against the fence and sent people flying. Except for that one poor little dead boy, who was pressed right up against the fence slats and must've froze right to the spot when he saw that car careening towards him instead of running for cover --right *over* people if he had to!-- like a more mature human being would have done. Tommy's left-rear fender caught him full blast and dead center at about seventy or so miles an hour, and that's all there was to it.

I'd have to admit that the S.C.M.A. and the police and the local volunteers did a pretty good job of cleaning everything up --especially given the circumstances-- and in about ninety minutes there was a brief discussion about whether the race should be restarted. A few of the S.C.M.A. clubbies who'd towed in from all over the whole damn country to race wanted to do it, and the truth is that there was a certain heartless merit to their argument. I mean, nothing on God's green earth was going to mend those broken bones or close those open wounds or bring that poor little seven-year-old boy back to life, and the idea of *quitting* just because some people got hurt didn't sit right with many of the racers. And the fans, too. But the State Police had other ideas, and the discussion about whether the race should be restarted or not was over in a hurry once those guys put their collective feet down. The party was *over,* and it was time for everybody to pack up and go home.

There's nothing more to see here, folks....

And Tommy Edwards was in pretty rough shape, too. He tried walking back towards the pits with us, but he didn't make it more than a few sobbing, choking, unsteady steps before the exhilarating *I got away with it* rush leaked out of his body and he realized that he was hurt a lot worse than he thought. Turned out he had a broken wrist and five cracked ribs and a dislocated shoulder in addition to the cut and the pavement rash you could see on first glance, and he had to sit himself down kind of sideways on the asphalt and wait for an ambulance to come and take him away to the hospital. Cal and me tried talking to him, but he was like off in a different world, just staring straight ahead without seeing or hearing anything and shuddering faintly every now and then like he was cold. "Do look after the car now," he said without looking at us as they loaded him into the ambulance.

Big Ed's car needed looking after, too. He and the Jag came down Franklin Street on a hook about an hour after the accident, and things didn't look good at all when I popped the hood and took a quick peek underneath. There was oil all over the place and a jagged hole about the size of a league hardball in the side of the engine block. Obviously he'd wound it up until a damn rod broke, and no question this was going to be one of those "devastatingly expensive repair bills" that the other XK120 owner warned Cal Carrington about. "I was right next to this guy, see," Big Ed explained ruefully, "and it was like I couldn't hear my own motor because his was makin' so much racket," he looked down at the oily mess in his engine compartment, "or I dunno, maybe I just forgot to shift...."

You had to hand it to Big Ed for not coming up with a bunch of bullshit excuses. That only makes it worse. Although it seemed kind of coarse at first that he didn't seem too distraught about the accident. Or at least not as much as the rest of us. But then I realized that Big Ed was out on the other side of the circuit when it happened, standing by the side of the road and staring down at the steaming pool of oil and water forming under his XK120, and, what with all the heartache and confusion down at the south end of Franklin Street, it took damn near an hour for the wrecker to come and get him. So Big Ed had plenty of time to think about how stupidly he'd messed up his car and how much money it was going to cost him to fix it, and he really wasn't too receptive when he got the news about the accident. Besides, he hadn't actually *seen* it like Cal and me had, and it was pretty much cleared up by the time they hauled him down off the mountain. So it was like something that happened in some other place far away to Big Ed --like something you read about in the newspapers, you know?

We had a hell of a time making arrangements to take care of Big Ed's broken Jaguar and Tommy Edwards' wrecked-and-rolled Allard. There just weren't any trailers around to get the job done, and it would've cost Big Ed an arm and a leg to have the local towtruck operator haul his Jag all the way back to Jersey. And Tommy's Allard was well past towing in any case. Big Ed finally managed to get a hold of one of the trucking firms that hauled scrap steel and used machinery and equipment for him, and they dispatched a big semi with a bunch of rope tie-downs inside from someplace in northern Pennsylvania to pick the cars up. Without even thinking about it, I told him to have them both hauled back to Old Man Finzio's Sinclair station in Passaic.

And of course there was a big official flap going on with Charlie Priddle and his armband posse. This was a major opportunity for them to flex their muscles and *do* something. And, by God, they were not about to miss out on something as delicious and irresistible as that, regardless of the sadness and seriousness of the occasion. In fact, so much the better, since it enhanced the majesty and importance of their actions even more.

Anyhow, they huddled together in a private room in the Jefferson Hotel for hours, listening to eyewitness reports and jabbering back and forth and interviewing anybody they could lay their hands on like a damn Congressional House of Un-American Activities Committee meeting. They were still at it after we got the remains of the Allard dragged back to the Atlantic station where we had the Jag stashed (and Big Ed slipped the gas station kid a fiver, so that particular Saturday was really a step up into a new tax bracket for him) and nobody heard the results or anything until a week later back in New York.

They pulled Tommy Edwards' racing license for a year --can you *believe* it?-- and hit Skippy Welcher with a dinky little one-race suspension. I mean, he *pointed,* you know? Far as I was concerned, it was the most flagrant miscarriage of justice since Sacco and Vanzetti. But it sure got everybody's attention, and that was really the whole idea.

Big Ed and me wound up riding back to Jersey in the rear end of Barry Spline's parts truck, sitting on cases of 40-weight Castrol and kind of wedged in sideways between the fan belts and spark plugs and gasket sets and fuel pumps and brake shoes and spare wheels and tires. Truth is I don't remember much of anything about that drive except that it was uncomfortable as hell and seemed to take forever and nobody talked much. Oh, and that Barry charged us *each* for half the gas (but I guess that went without saying, you know?). Anyhow, it was well past one o'clock in the morning by the time we got to Big Ed's house, and he lent me the black Caddy sedan so's I could follow Barry down to Westbridge and pick up my tools and stuff to take over to the Old Man's Sinclair come Monday morning. And it was amazing how right and proper and natural that seemed, even after everything that happened to me and all the things I'd done and learned those few months down at Westbridge. It was like from the very beginning I'd known that my situation at Westbridge was only temporary, and that I somehow really *belonged* back home in Jersey, working at the Old Man's filling station and sleeping in my own bed every night and being closer to Julie. Or maybe it's just I was too damn tired and used up to care....

For sure I'd miss Sylvester, but then I knew I'd see him again and again when I came over to Westbridge on parts runs to pick up stuff for Big Ed's Jag and any other British sportscar owners I could pick up as customers over at the Sinclair. And somehow I knew without even thinking about it that there'd be quite a few. So I didn't feel anything particularly earth-shaking, sad, or momentous as I loaded Butch Bohunk's tool chest into the cavernous trunk of Big Ed's Caddy Sixty Special. Except maybe that it was a lot heavier than I remembered it, what with all the British Standard sockets and wrenches I'd added to his collection. Why, it was a pretty damn fine and complete set of English Sportscar Mechanic tools now, and that's exactly what I intended to use it for over at the Old Man's gas station.

And so I found myself driving back across the George Washington bridge into Jersey again at about three-thirty in the morning, and it was all dark and quiet outside and I was about the only damn car on the road. I could see the lights of downtown Manhattan twinkling in my rearview mirror like the stars I'd seen up in the sky over Watkins Glen less than thirty hours before. Only now that seemed like years ago, as if the world had gone through at least a dozen or more winters since then....

I think I might have been crying a little, too.

I pulled into the driveway by my Aunt Rosamarina's house just as the first purplish-black silhouettes of the trees and houses along Buchanan Street started to stand out against the darkened predawn sky. I made sure to lock up Big Ed's Cadillac before heading up the creaky wood stairs to the apartment over my aunt's garage. And did I ever have a surprise in store for me when I opened the door and gave the light-cord a half-hearted yank. Why, somebody'd been *in* that place while I was gone --and cleaned everything up for me! Jeez, the floor was swept and there were no loose socks or underwear scattered around anywhere and all the dishes were done and neatly stacked away under the sink and all my clothes were washed and ironed and folded away all neat and proper in the little broken-down chest of drawers I had over by the window. Why, the damn bed was even made! And with fresh sheets and pillowcases, too....

At first I thought maybe my mom did it, but that didn't make any sense. I mean, she had enough to do cleaning up after my dad, you know? And it sure wouldn't be like my Aunt Rosamarina to go snooping around somebody else's apartment, even if she did own the building. And no way would any of my sisters make my bed unless it was to short-sheet it for me. No, it had to be Julie. And, sure enough, hidden under the pillow was one of those sappy Hallmark cards with pink flowers all over it, and inside was a short little note from Julie. "Welcome home, Buddy," it said in Julie's smooth, rounded script, "Love, Julie." And then, down at the bottom she added, "and I threw away those horrible magazines you had hidden under your mattress. They're disgusting!!" And I knew right away she'd probably looked through every page of every single one.

I felt my ears starting to burn, you know, but at least it made me smile. That was the first smile I could remember crossing my face in what seemed like days. Ages, in fact. And I felt a little better as I stretched myself out on my nice, clean, perfectly made bed and started thinking about what I was going to do next. There was no way I could sleep. Or at least no way I could *let* myself sleep, anyway, since I kept seeing my own personal newsreel footage of Tommy's horrible wreck up at Watkins Glen over and over on the inside of my eyelids every time I closed my eyes. I had this crazy feeling like it was maybe just some kind of awful nightmare, you know, and if I could just Stay Awake, the day somehow still wouldn't be over and there was some crazy chance that things might turn out differently. But if I allowed myself to drift off to sleep, that day would be sealed forever and turn into a piece of history that could never, ever change....

And that's when I opened my eyes and found brilliant midday sunlight streaming in through the window and heard some of my mom's stupid birds chirping back and forth to one another up in the tree branches. I looked over at my alarm clock and saw that it was past twelve-thirty, and I'd already jumped halfway up out of bed before I realized it was Sunday and all I had to do all day was get Butch's tools unloaded over at the Sinclair and return Big Ed's Cadillac. It felt so strange and unnatural not to have something that desperately needed fixing or some damn car to get ready for the races or some busted Limey shitbox or other that needed my attention down at Westbridge. Why, I even felt a little *guilty* about it while I made myself a cup of coffee and laid back down in bed. But I couldn't go back to sleep, and as I laid there, staring a hole through that cramped little 18x18 tin shower stall my dad and I had put up at the far end of the room, everything that happened over the weekend started seeping back into my head like a slow water leak, and I knew I had to get up and get out of there if I ever wanted to be able to sleep there again.

I took myself a shower and put on some of those nice, clean clothes Julie'd washed and ironed for me and packed away in my dresser drawers. Then I went outside and it was an absolutely gorgeous late-September day, what with a real summertime sort of sun hanging up in the sky and the trees all turning color and the smoky smell of burning piles of leaves along the curbsides on every street. I saw families walking home from twelve o'clock Mass, and it reminded me how far away I'd drifted from that kind of life. Why, I used to go to Mass with my mom and sisters every single Sunday when I was little. Or my dad'd crack me one, you know? Sometimes he'd even come with. I couldn't remember exactly when I stopped going, except that I knew it was when my dad and me started not getting along, and I think I did it as much to piss him off as anything else. Not that I liked going to church all that much (I mean, who does?) but I could take it for an hour a week no problem --just to keep the peace.

I got in Big Ed's Caddy (on a hot day, there's simply nothing worse than climbing into a black car that's been parked out in the sun with the windows rolled up!) and decided to sort of tool over by the Doggy Shake and see if maybe Julie was on duty. And sure enough she was. But the place was pretty busy what with the after-church crowd and all, and Julie kind of brushed me off when I waltzed up, planted a sweet little peck on her cheek, and thanked her for cleaning my place up. "Hey, no problem," she said, eyeballing a family of nine --from an ancient, craggy old grandmother with her hair up in a bun right down through a bawling baby wrapped up in a fuzzy pink blanket-- who had just sat themselves down at the last available table in her section. And all her parking stalls outside were full, too. So she had to go to work (I guess that fat little drip Marvin was really keeping an eye on her, you know?) so I sat myself down at the counter on one of those rotating stools and ordered myself an oliveburger, some french fries, and a root beer float from one of the other girls (which I can't really recommend for breakfast, but that combination is sort of The Specialty of the House over by the Doggy Shake). While I waited for my food to come up (which it usually does at the Doggy Shake, sooner if not later) I kept trying to get Julie to come over and sit down with me. But she was real busy with all the people --especially the family at the big table, who wanted everything from warm milk for the baby to something like oatmeal or applesauce or creamed corn for the old grandmother, who'd apparently left her teeth at home on the bedstand and couldn't chew-- and more or less ignored me. Even when I gave her my absolute best imitation of a Clark Gable "c'mon over here, baby" sly-wink-and-nod combination.

So there was nothing to do but just sort of hang around and wait for the crowd to thin out over on Julie's side. I noticed that somebody'd left a newspaper on one of the chairs across from me, so naturally I picked it up and went looking to see if there was any news about the accident up at Watkins Glen. And, sure enough, there was. It was the New York Times, though, and so it was just a sedate little one-column blurb back on page 54, right next to an ad for a new recording of Giuseppe Verdi's opera *Don Carlo* that was now available at Liberty music shops. No question a story like that would've made the damn front page of the Daily News. Especially if they had some really gruesome pictures.

Anyhow, the story in the Times read like this:

SPORTS CAR RAMS CROWD, KILLS BOY

Watkins Glen, N.Y., Sept. 20 -- A 7-year-old boy was killed and at least twelve other persons were injured today as a sports car participating in the fifth annual running of the Grand Prix race veered into spectators on Franklin Street, the main street of the village.

The accident occurred shortly after 5:35 P.M., as forty cars of foreign make swung into....

"Foreign make?" I muttered out loud. Jeez, hadn't this guy ever heard of the Cunninghams?

"You down to talking to yourself now?" I looked up and it was Julie, of course, standing over me with her eyes all bright and sparkly under her red-and-yellow Doggy Shake cap and that fabulous movie-magazine-cover smile of hers gleaming. Why, I couldn't remember her ever looking that good, you know?

"Nah," I said, kind of folding up the paper so she maybe wouldn't see the story about that poor seven-year-old kid up at Watkins Glen, "I just saw something dumb in the Times is all."

"I saw it too," she told me, nodding down at the newspaper as a slow, dark cloud passed over her face. "Did you see it?" she asked quietly. "I mean, did you see it happen?"

"No, I didn't," I lied, "I was way over on the other side of the track." I really didn't feel much like talking about it, you know? Especially with somebody on the outside of the sport like Julie. Fact is, it made me somehow feel all dirty and guilty and uncomfortable inside, like maybe *I'd* had something to do with it, just on account of I'd been there when it happened and had personally helped put together the damn car that killed that poor gradeschool kid and injured all those spectators and almost did in my friend and hero Tommy Edwards in the bargain.

"It must've been awful...," Julie said softly, her voice trailing off at the end.

"Yeah," I told her, "it was."

Then we just kind of sat there for awhile, looking around the place at everything else but each other's eyes.

"Hey," I finally said, trying to make a little conversation, "thanks again for cleaning my place up."

"Somebody had to do it."

"No, really. That was an awful nice surprise."

"No big deal," she shrugged, "I just didn't want to maybe pick up some kinda disease or bugs or something off you from living in that dump."

"Yeah," I admitted, "I suppose I could use a few lessons about housekeeping."

"Hmpf," Julie sniffed, "men are pigs. They never know *any*thing about keeping a nice place to live..."

"I guess not."

"...it's 'cause their mothers spoil them..."

I had to agree. I mean, she was right.

"...they cook for them and clean for them and wash dishes for them and pick up after them...."

It sounded like a pretty good deal to me.

"...and then they expect you to be around all pert and pretty and ready to go whenever the heck they feel like it..."

I could hear her mom's voice coming through loud and clear, and I was starting to wonder what exactly had gotten into her, you know? But she was really rolling now, and there was nothing to do but sit back and shut up and wait for her to more or less run out of gas. If you just sat there and kept nodding every ten seconds or so, that usually took about two and a half minutes. You could time it on a watch.

Sure enough, Julie ran out of steam right on schedule, and then I thanked her again for cleaning up my place.

"Like I said," she shrugged again, "no problem."

"Well, it was an awful nice surprise when I got home from the races last night. Or actually more like this morning."

"So," she said, kind of letting the word hang there in the air, "you think you're about through with going to those races?"

"Oh, I don't know. It's kinda hard to say. See, I'm goin' back to work at your uncle's gas station tomorrow morning...."

"I know," she said through a big, happy smile, and you couldn't miss the bright little flicker of a spark coming up in her eyes, and I must admit it made me feel all warm and safe and cozy inside. Then again, I knew in my heart that I was hooked on the excitement of racing and hanging around with all those fabulous cars and rich, crazy characters. I mean, Real Life was just too damn dull and predictable and, well, *unimportant* by comparison. But there was no way you could explain that to somebody on the outside like Julie.

Especially when the body of that poor little seven-year-old kid wasn't even in the damn ground yet....

"I dunno, Julie," I said, giving it my very best Detached Professional voice, "I been working on an awful lot of those cars lately, you know?"

"I sure as hell do!" she said with a nasty, unfunny little laugh. "That's why the hell we never get to see each other any-more. You're always down at that damn dealership in Manhattan at all hours of the night --*supposedly* working on cars-- and I can't even get taken out for a damn Coke or a movie on the weekends 'cause you're always off to hell-and-gone someplace at the races." I could see she wasn't really *mad* at me, you know, but then it wouldn't be like Julie Finzio to miss a chance to give me some shit if the opportunity presented itself. I guess it's one of those Involuntary Reaction things like they teach you about in Science class.

"Well, I wouldn't worry about it too much anymore," I told her, kind of circling my way around the subject. "Racing sea-son's about over with until next spring, and I'm planning to plant myself smack dab in the middle of your uncle's service bay and go to *work*. Hell, it'd be nice to have some damn folding money of my own for a change."

"It sure *would,*" Julie agreed, visions of sit-down restaurants with linen tablecloths and tuxedoed *maitre d's* dancing behind her eyes. "There's a lot of stuff we could do on two incomes...."

That one flew right by me. But that's on account of I was busy picking my spot to zoom in for the kill. "Anyhow, that's why I think I should keep working on sportscars when I move in again at the Sinclair. I figure we could make a pisspot fulla money off them. Butch thinks so, too..." --not that I had actually *asked* Butch what he thought (or even spoken to him in quite a long while) but I was sure that's what he would've thought if I'd thought to call him up and ask.

"But no more racing?"

"Well, that depends," I answered, kind of back-pedaling. And then I told her about the fat wad of tens, twenties, and even fifties Barry Spline habitually folded up in the side pocket of his blue shop coat by the end of each and every race weekend. You could see as how Julie looked pretty interested in the money, but she was still more than a little suspicious about racing.

Like it was another woman or something, you know?

"But that means you'll be *away* all the time," she said in a perfect, off-key New Jersey whine, "and what's the point of making yourself a lot of damn money if you're not gonna be around to *spend* it?"

I had to admit, there was a certain stupid-yet-undeniable logic to her argument. And that was my opening to close the trap. "Well, seeing as how you work at the station part-time yourself, I was thinking you could maybe start going up to the races *with* me. As my sort of, you know, *assistant.*"

"Oh, *sure!*" she snorted, "my mom'd really go for *that,* wouldn't she."

"But it's *business....*"

"Look, Buddy, both you and me and my uncle and my mom know *exactly* what kind of business that is. Monkey business. Do I look stupid to you or something?"

"Well, no...," I told her,"...a'course not, Julie. It's just...."

"Listen to me, Buddy Palumbo. And listen real good." She leaned forward and stared me right in the eyes, and I've got to say it froze me to the spot. "I like you, Buddy. I like you a lot. And I'm really looking forward to having you around the station again and maybe goin' out on dates and stuff on the weekends," she inhaled a long, slow breath, "but I'll be damned if I'm gonna wind up five or ten years from now all by myself in a stinking little apartment in Greenwich Village like your sister Mary Frances, with some damn beautician or secretary or dental assistant for a roommate and nobody to go out with but a bunch of jerks and leftover creeps while my friends have big fancy church weddings and move into decent houses and start raising families for themselves. You understand me, Buddy Palumbo?"

Obviously Julie had done herself a lot of thinking on the subject while I had been busy with racing. "Gee whiz, Julie," I told her, "we're just talking about a couple lousy race weekends here, you know...."

"Forget about it, Buddy. Just *forget* about it. I like you an awful lot, but I'll be damned if I'm gonna let myself turn into one of those tramps who go around passing out free samples. Not Julie Finzio. Not in *this* lifetime. I wanna be able to look Father Dominico right in the eye when I come out of confession...."

"But that's supposed to be, you know, *confidential,* isn't it?"

"They recognize your voice. Everybody knows that."

"And anyways, you hardly ever go to church. At least not that I've seen."

"Yeah? Well, maybe I oughta start. In fact, I'll be there next month for my friend Serafina Massucci's wedding..." --all of a sudden everything made sense!-- "...and it wouldn't hurt you one bit to be there with me, Buddy Palumbo."

"Oh, s-sure," I stammered, "I'd, uhh, *love* to go."

"In a pig's eye."

"No, honest. *Really* I would...."

And that's how I wound up going to a big Italian church wedding in Passaic, New Jersey, on Sunday, October 26th, instead of being where I wanted to be, down in Albany, Georgia, with all my racing buddies for the big S.C.M.A. SOWEGA race event at Turner Air Force base.

Truth is, the S.C.M.A. was damn lucky to be able to hold another racing event of *any* kind after the well-publicized disaster at Watkins Glen. Naturally the papers made a big deal out of it --there was even a grisly two-page spread in *Life* magazine-- and, seeing as how it was an election year and all, everybody with headlines to pursue and a soapbox to stand on was coming out against road racing in a big way. After all, it was an easy target. The state legislature in Wisconsin decided to enforce a law they already had on the books that banned racing on public highways, and that was pretty much that as far as the Elkhart Lake road races were concerned, and there was a big public outcry around Watkins Glen that threatened to shut down that event as well (although they did manage to run there for a few more years, but at a new circuit set up way out in the countryside, far from downtown Franklin Street, where they convinced everybody that they could control things a little better). In fact, there probably wouldn't have been much in the way of road racing at all anymore if it hadn'tve been for a big, tough, cigar-chomping Air Force general named Curtis LeMay, who was head of the Strategic Air Command and a real sportscar buff as well. He hated commies, owned an Allard himself, and traveled in the kind of high-powered social circles where he rubbed elbows with a lot of the kind of rich, famous, and influential people that you also found cluttering up the paddocks at S.C.M.A. race events.

Anyhow, General LeMay liked fast, powerful sportscars and the one-on-one, man-and-machine competitive challenge of racing. I guess he saw the same similarities to air combat that Tommy Edwards told me about while we waited out that rainstorm in the Auburn Grill on our way to Elkhart Lake. In fact, General LeMay had a pet theory (which he even managed to test out a few times, mostly with negative results) that you could stick any of his ace S.A.C.-trained Air Force pilots into a decent car and beat the living crap out of those lah-de-dah S.C.M.A. club racers and their subversive foreign cars.

But, regardless of his opinions or politics, General Curtis LeMay turned out to be the guy who single-handedly saved road racing here in the United States from almost sure extinction. And the way he pulled it off was nothing short of amazing. See, the Strategic Air Command had all these big bomber bases scattered all over the countryside --mostly out in the boondocks someplace where they were at least a little more secure from prying commie eyes-- and he somehow convinced all his buddies at the Pentagon that it would be a really swell idea to hold road races on some temporary circuits laid out on the runways of those S.A.C. bases as motivation and entertainment for his men in the field.

And, believe it or not, they went for it!

Now running races on airfields was nothing new. Most of the popular tracks over in England at the time were actually old leftover airfields where B17s and B24s and Arvo Lancasters and such used to take off for bombing raids on Germany towards the end of World War II. That included places like Silverstone and Ibsley and Snetterton and Castle Coombe that Tommy Edwards and Colin St. John had told me about. And, here in the states, they'd run airport races on the runways and taxiways of the Convair airfield in Allentown, Pennsylvania, and another one in a driving rainstorm up in Janesville, Wisconsin, and a couple more out on the West Coast someplace. Not to mention that big twelve-hour endurance contest down in Sebring, Florida, back in March. But it was a difficult job, what with having to shut down a whole entire airport for a day or two and rerouting all the air traffic and such in order to make it happen. At least, it was difficult for anybody except a guy like General Curtis LeMay, who could get it handled with a couple quick phone calls as long as he had the rest of the brass hats in the Pentagon behind him.

And that's exactly what he did.

In fact, General LeMay managed to work a deal with the rest of the brass that "his" airmen ought to do most of the actual work when it came to setting up the circuits and manning the corner stations and keeping an eye on the crowds as part of their normal Air Force duty, and that caused a few raised eyebrows here and there on Capitol Hill when letters started pouring in from Concerned Citizens (in other words, people with entirely too much time on their hands) who lived in places like Podunk and Dogpatch and Bumjump, Idaho, and wanted to know why Their Tax Dollars were being used to put on races for a bunch of spoiled rich kids and wealthy racing bums. Or why their sons in the armed services of the United States of America were spending their duty hours flagging a damn car race instead of keeping their eyes peeled full time for the advancing Commie Menace. General LeMay countered all that flack by funneling the money they made off spectator admissions and such into what he called "hobby rooms" on all the bases, which were basically shops and garages where his favored servicemen could pursue a little fun and recreation during off-duty hours. Like fr'instance wrenching on a few fast, powerful automobiles so his ace pilots could show those lah-de-dah sportycar guys a thing or two the next time they rolled into town.

At any rate, the SOWEGA event (which, by the way, stood for SOuthWEstern GeorgiA, and was not a hog call) at Turner Air Force Base was the very first of what eventually wound up being called "the SAC races," and they became pretty much the meat-and-potatoes of the S.C.M.A. racing schedule for the next few years. Now some of the drivers --especially the really *good* drivers-- complained that the flat, featureless SAC airport tracks were sort of Mickey Mouse compared to the daunting hills and swoops and beautiful (if occasionally scary and entirely too close to the roadside) scenery at places like Bridgehampton and Elkhart Lake and Watkins Glen. But the airports were *safe,* and that was an enormous difference between them and the real open road circuits. Why, if you went off course, about the worst that happened was you plowed through a bunch of pylons or hit a stack of haybales. Or just kept going, since the runways were generally four, five, and sometimes even six lanes wide instead of the scant lane-and-a-half or two lanes you had on the country roads around Long Island, East-Central Wisconsin, and upstate New York. Plus the airport circuits were pretty much flat (if sometimes a little bumpy from the tar expansion strips where the concrete slabs butted together) and didn't have all the humps and jumps and ripples and high crowns you found on the natural open road circuits.

But by far the most important difference was that you could control the spectators at an airport circuit and keep them a safe distance from the racecars. Sure, they couldn't get down close to trackside any more, where they could actually *feel* the howl of a twelve-cylinder Ferrari or the thunder of a big V8 Allard when they came hurtling by with the throttles wide open. And, though they could see pretty much the entire circuit at an airport track (at least if there were grandstands or something so they could get up high enough) spectators generally had a hard time appreciating the speed and cornering action of the cars on those wide, flat, empty-looking airport runways....

Chapter 33: Missing SOWEGA

As promised, I showed up at the Old Man's Sinclair bright and early on Monday morning, September 22, wearing a nice clean pair of coveralls (thanks to Julie, of course) and a pretty good attitude, too. That didn't last too long, of course, since the Old Man was as mean and cantankerous as ever, and wanted me to start right in on a nasty-looking muffler job on some out-of-work meat cutter's '49 Nash. He was about the third owner of that old heap, and you could tell that neither he nor either of the previous owners owned a garden-variety rubber hose or a scrub bucket in decent operating condition. Or at least they never used them on that car, anyway. In fact, one look at the filthy interior of that car was enough to make you want to stop buying meat at your local corner grocery store.

It made me realize how much I'd taken for granted all the little hidden benefits of working on sportscars in general and ones that were raced in particular. Except for the odd shitbox like Cal Carrington's raggedy old TC, they were almost invariably neat and clean and free of moldy, rusted-up bolts and thick, black, smelly layers of sludge on the oilpan and undercarriage. Yup, most racecars were regularly kept in the kind of condition that Big Ed Baumstein insisted on for all his cars, and working on them made you forget for a while about all the greasy, corroded, ill-maintained, and generally broken-down crud wagons that John Q. Public and his wife drove to work or down to the drugstore to buy a newspaper every day. At least until you had to pick up a socket set and a cutting torch and try to put a new muffler on one, anyway. And it didn't help matters any when that semi-trailer showed up from Watkins Glen with Tommy's wrecked Allard and Big Ed's blown-up Jaguar inside. I wanted to drop what I was doing under that shitty Nash and start tearing into the Jag right away. But Old Man Finzio wouldn't hear of it. "Yew jest finish that job yew got already," he rasped, tugging out yet another bent-up Camel, "them damn furrin' contraptions of yers kin damn well wait."

And I wasn't about to start arguing with him. At least not on my very first day back. And especially seeing as how I wanted to talk to him later about how I saw things shaping up at the Sinclair and what my plans for the station's future might be. Still, it didn't make much sense to me. I mean, we could charge good money --and I mean *real* good money-- for an engine overhaul on Big Ed's Jaguar, and you had to wonder if the out-of-work meat cutter who owned that broken-down Nash could even afford to pay his bill. He was one of those down-and-out types who want you to do a Basic Butcher patch job (even if you *know* it won't hold up) and, if you absolutely insist that they pay the price of a brand new muffler from the auto parts store, they always want you to connect it up to the rusty old pipes that are already there, just so they can put off paying another five or ten bucks that they're obviously going to wind up paying you anyway --and then some!-- just a few short paychecks down the road. I used to sympathize with people like that, but that's just something you have to outgrow if you're ever going to make anything of yourself in the world of automobile mechanics. "I'm afraid poor people make poor customers," was the way Colin St. John phrased it, and he even had a couple pet names for them down at the Westbridge dealership. He called them "mooches" and "LOFs" (for Lack Of Funds) and generally made very ugly fun of them behind their backs once he'd given them the quick-and-dirty brushoff and shooed them out of the shop.

But I came to realize that Colin was right, because people like that didn't want to pay for anything except the barest possible spit-and-baling-wire repair that would get their wheezing old heaps clattering down the road again --egg-shaped wheels wobbling and oscillating in four different directions-- under some semblance of their own power. And they often showed up carrying their own parts (so you couldn't make a fair and reasonable markup off the discount you got from the parts store) and often they were wrong or used or cut out of some wreck in a junkyard someplace that was maybe not even the same exact year or model. And then it was *your* fault that the damn things didn't fit. People like that were just never satisfied --*never!*-- and usually wound up going around from one gas station and repair shop to another for each new disaster, because they'd decided that whoever the last guy was who worked on their car was a thief and a crook who was trying to pick their pockets and simultaneously pull the well-known wool over their eyes. The sad truth of the matter was that, if you allowed yourself (out of decent human kindness and charity) to do business with LOFs and mooches, you inevitably wound up trying to figure your way through a car that fifteen or twenty of the cheapest, dirtiest, worst Butcher Mechanics in town had already worked on. And not one of them more than once. And so you always lost money. Sometimes you even got threatened with a baseball bat.

None of that bothered Old Man Finzio. He *loved* doing business with poor folks who were down on their luck every now and then, on account of it guaranteed him an opportunity to be mean and belligerent above and beyond the call of normal duty. It would always come to a head when the car was done and the poor mooches came to pick it up and the Old Man presented them the bill. And it was *always* more than the original estimate. That went without saying on almost every job, but it was a lock when you worked on one of those raggedy old mooch heaps because it always took longer and got you madder and dirtier and more frustrated than working on a car in a more normal condition of upkeep. And of course the poor LOF who owned the car would argue like hell on account of he probably didn't have the extra five or ten bucks floating around in his bank account to cover the difference. And that's when Old Man Finzio would come out from behind his service counter and stick his grizzled, bony chin with its four-day growth of stubble right up into their faces --usually with the glowing tip of his latest bent-up Camel leading the way as a sort of Advance Guard-- and inform the poor slob in no uncertain terms that he was holding their damn car hostage (or at least that's what it amounted to) until the damn ransom was paid. If you remember, it's the same damn thing he pulled on Cal Carrington when we brought his bent '47 TC back after the wreck at Bridgehampton back in May. And, just like Cal, those people'd fume and fuss and argue and threaten to sue and even cuss him out until they were blue in the face. But Old Man Finzio would just stand there and take it with his eyes flashing and the end of his cigarette trembling dangerously. Why, he almost seemed to bask in their anger, you know, like someone sunbathing out on the beach, rolling ever-so-slightly from side to side every now and again to make sure they got a nice even tan.

But eventually, after all the screaming and yelling and cussing and pleading, the deadbeat people who owned that poor old deadbeat car would have to go home and break their kid's piggy bank or put the touch on their relatives --again-- or maybe go in for an eight-hour shift of cheap day labor or sell themselves a pint of blood, but whatever it was, they always wound up coming back to the gas station with a furious, humiliated look in their eyes and their tails dragging down between their legs and paid the damn bill. And that's when Old Man Finzio would give them their keys and throw them off the property. *"And don't come back!"* he'd yell after them, his eyes dancing.

"You don't hafta worry about *that,* asshole!" they'd yell right back as they drove off down the street with their middle fingers extended skyward like flagpoles. "You don't hafta worry about that at *all!"*

Then Old Man Finzio would smile a thin, bright smile and light himself up another bent-up Camel and just kind of stand there by the cash register for awhile, swaying ever-so-gently and dreamily from side to side, savoring the moment.

But, regardless of the pleasure he took from it, doing work for people like that wasn't really good for business. And it was one of the things I wanted to talk to him about changing at the Sinclair. Especially after I saw that he wasn't taking his usual full measure of joy out of Presenting The Bill or throwing that out-of-work meat cutter off the property when he came back a few hours later --eyes properly furious and humiliated, tail dangling down humbly between his legs-- to pay the damn money and pick up his stinking lousy piece-of-shit Nash.

Fact is, the Old Man wasn't looking like his old self much at all any more. He could still get mad as hell at the drop of a hat and yell and screech until the turkey-neck skin above his collar turned damn near purple. But he couldn't *sustain* it anymore. At least not for more than a few minutes, anyway. And he wasn't moving right, either, kind of shuffling around the office and service bay and out to the pumps like a wind-up toy with the spring running down. But the biggest change was that he really didn't seem to care too much anymore. Not about anything. So when I went up to him later that afternoon and told him about my ideas for the station, he just sort of nodded and shrugged and looked out the front window like he was staring out at the ocean.

And then he sighed and said,"Sure. Why not. You do it any damn way you want. Any way at all." And with that he got up, went out through the overhead door, climbed into his towtruck, and drove off down Pine Street. Just like that. And he was gone all afternoon.

So I was in business!

My first big sportscar job at the Old Man's Sinclair was Big Ed's blown-up Jag, and I had to grab a few passers-by off the street to help me roll it into the service bay for a little post-mortem diagnosis. But then the phone rang and it was some tax accountant guy about the starter motor on his Hudson. So I set him up an appointment for service and made a note that some-body had to go pick up his car when the towtruck came back. Then I went back to do some more work on the Jag, but right away a lady in a DeSoto pulled in for a fillup and oil check, and I noticed one of her back tires was almost flat on account of it'd picked up a nail, so I had to take that off and fix it before I could do anything else. Except run the pumps for two more cars that came in off the street and answer the phone a couple more times when it rang. One of the calls was from Carson Flegley, about maybe doing a little Speed Tuning on his MG. He'd read some article in *Road & Track* magazine about hopping up MG motors, and he was all hot to trot about doing it to his car so he could go down to that race in Georgia and maybe finish all the way up in mid-pack for a change. Personally, I thought he was crazy for even thinking about it. I mean, the biggest problem with that car and racing --as Cal had proved beyond any shadow of a doubt-- was the loose nut behind the steering wheel, and it didn't make much sense to start hot-rodding the engine and making the car too nervous and high-strung for normal street duty when you couldn't even get all the potential out of it when it was bone stock. But Carson had fallen victim to what I call "The Bumper Syndrome," which happens when a racing driver (or would-be racing driver) sees a rear bumper sitting out in front of him all during a race --like a tasty carrot dangling off the end of a string in front of a donkey's nose-- and he can't manage to do anything about it except follow it around. Nine times out of ten, that race driver will daydream all day and stay awake nights trying to figure out how to turn that rear bumper ahead of him into a front bumper in his rearview mirror. And he will go to some pretty damn stupid and ridiculous lengths to make it happen. He will also invariably spend a *lot* of money, and that's why I told Carson Flegley that I thought it was a swell idea and I'd be more than happy to do it for him. But he'd have to give me a deposit for parts and leave the car for a couple weeks, though....

"How much do you want?" he asked without skipping a beat. Like it was *nothing*, you know?

"Oh, I dunno," I told him, trying to figure out some kind of plausible number, "maybe seventy dollars or so...."

"How about a hundred. I'll drop it off tomorrow."

"Uhh, sure. That'll be fine."

So now I had two major sportscar projects lined up and some guy in a pickup out by the pumps waiting for gas and that DeSoto lady's tire to finish (not to mention a speedo cable job on a Mercury that had to be ready by five o'clock) and somebody in an Oldsmobile with Ohio plates pulling in to ask directions. And then who should swoop in off the streets but Big Ed Baumstein. And you should've seen what he was driving! He'd made a deal with the local Cadillac agency to get the very first 1953 model Cadillac Eldorado convertible in New Jersey --white with a red leather interior like his Jaguar this time, so they'd make a sort of matched set in his garage. It had wire wheels and that new panoramic wraparound windshield that was exclusive to Eldorados in the Cadillac line that year, and I'd have to say it was about the most beautiful hunk of homegrown Detroit Iron I'd ever seen in my entire life. "Hey, howya doin'?" Big Ed grinned around his cigar, "good t'have ya back in Jersey."

"Hey, thanks," I said, running my eyeballs down his new Caddy. "Nice car. When d'ja pick it up?"

"Just this morning. It's still in the wrapper."

"Yeah, I can smell it." There's always that special smell to new cars, you know? And a certain feel, too.

"Yep," Big Ed grinned, "she's cherry all right. But I'll fix that soon enough. Get a few miles on 'er. Let her hump the road a little and develop herself a little personality...."

I knew exactly what Big Ed was talking about. "So," I asked him, "how does she drive?"

"Aw, nothin' like my Jaguar. That's my *baby*. But y'cant beat a Caddy convert when it comes to cruisin' around town."

"Especially a brand spanking new one," I agreed.

"Yeah. And a special edition like this one, too. They ain't gonna make very many of these."

I could see the DeSoto lady was starting to walk up and down like people do when they're trying to politely let you know that you're being incredibly rude, wasting their time, and ruining their entire day. "Look," I told Big Ed, "I'd love to sit down and chew the fat, but I got a lotta stuff to take care of and I'm here all by myself."

"Where's that rat-bastard Old Man Finzio?"

"Dunno. He took off in the towtruck a couple hours ago."

"Well, you tell the sonofabitch I said hello."

"He won't care."

"I know he won't care. That's not the point. I'm tryin' t'be *nice*, see?" Big Ed pulled the cigar out of his face and showed me a big fake grin. "It's *important* t'be nice in this life."

"I wouldn't know," I told him, and we both had a good laugh off it.

"Say listen," he said before he pulled away, "what's the late word on my Jag, anyway?"

"I just started looking at it a couple minutes ago," I told him, "and I really won't know what all's involved until I get it torn all the way down. But I do know this," I added, looking him right in the eye.

"What?"

"It's gonna be pretty damn expensive. You got a rod right through the side of the block."

"Hey," he said with a helpless little laugh, "anything worth doing is worth doing all the way, right?"

"Yeah, I guess so. By the way, what'd you rev that poor thing to, anyway?"

"I dunno," Big Ed shrugged, "I wasn't exactly looking at the damn tach, you know?"

"I'd say that's pretty obvious, judging from the hole in the crankcase, anyway...."

"Say, you need any money for parts or anything?"

"Oh, I probably will down the line a ways when I get some idea of what we're up against."

"Nah," Big Ed told me, "you take something now. That way you can get rolling and get the damn thing fixed."

"Don't you want an estimate first?"

Big Ed looked at me like I'd said something to hurt his feelings. "I don't need me an estimate. Not from *you*, Buddy. You just take a little down payment here," he reached into his pocket and pulled out a fat, raggedy wad of bills in a silver money clip, "and let me know if and when y'need any more." And right there and then he peeled off two hundred dollars --*two hundred dollars!*-- and handed it over to me. Just like it was *nothing!*

"S-say," I gulped, "you need a receipt or anything?"

"Take that receipt and wipe yer ass with it," Big Ed laughed, and he stuck his new white Caddy Eldorado in Drive and wheeled it around the pump islands and back out onto the street with its brand new whitewall tires squealing. And that's when I noticed that the phone was ringing again and that the lady with the flat tire wasn't looking nearly so polite and Quietly Desperate any more. In fact, she was starting to look very genuinely pissed off.

So I answered the phone and made an appointment for a tuneup and oil change on some guy's Ford and got the lady with the damn tire squared away and took another quick look under the hood of Big Ed's Jag and filled up a Buick wagon out at the pumps and then decided I'd better get busy on that Mercury speedometer cable before the owner showed up to get his car and found it sitting right where he'd left it without ever having the hood popped. People *hate* that.

The Old Man finally rolled back in around four-thirty, and he had an even more far-off look in his eyes than when he left. I told him about the Hudson with the bad starter motor that needed to be brought in on a hook and explained to him that I really couldn't get much of anything done in the service bay with all the damn interruptions I'd had throughout the day. "Where'dja go, anyway?" I asked him.

"I hadda go see my damn stupid quack of a doctor," he snorted, and spit on the ground. "Gotta go see the jerk sonofabitch again next Monday." That sounded like trouble, on account of Julie was only coming in on Tuesdays and Thursdays by then, and there was just no way I could get anything useful done in the service bay if I had to shag phone calls and tend the pumps and take care of every asshole who dropped in off the street.

"Look," I told the Old Man, "I'm gonna need some help in here if I'm gonna make us any money on the repair side."

Old Man Finzio looked at me like I was threatening him with a straight razor. "Look here, sonnyboy," he started in (and I always knew it meant trouble when he started out with that "sonnyboy" stuff), "I can't hardly earn enough off the damn pumps to make ends meet as it is, and now you wanna go out and *hire* somebody?" He shook his head like I was some kind of prize-winning idiot.

"Listen," I tried to explain, "the *real* money is in fixing those English sportscars, see. We can raise up our labor rates another dollar an hour on those things. Maybe even a dollar-fifty. The guys who own 'em will be happy to pay it, just so long as we do good work and get the cars finished on time...."

"Finished on time?" he sneered incredulously, like I had uttered the unspeakable. And, indeed, failing to meet promised delivery dates was something of a sacred canon in the repair shop business. Not just down at Westbridge Motor Car Company, Ltd., but just about everywhere else, too. Although you had to admit that Barry Spline and Colin St. John had raised it up to the level of an art form.

But then I showed him Big Ed's two hundred dollars --cash money!-- and all of a sudden the Old Man's face kind of softened, like wax melting down off a candle. "Ahh, what the hell," he grumbled, "y'run it any damn way you see fit. I just don't much care any more." And he headed out the door and down the street towards the liquor store at the corner of Pine and Madison.

He didn't even take the two hundred bucks.

So I started spreading the word around that I was officially in the foreign sportscar repair business at the Old Man's gas station, and it didn't take long before I had more damn work than I could handle from the S.C.M.A. racer types and all their lah-de-dah sportycar friends (not to mention all the people who'd sworn they'd never go back to Westbridge again, not even on a bet) who had all discovered that it took a little special skill and experience to do things properly on those cars, and it was not the sort of talent you normally ran into at your average, rank-and-file corner filling station or back-alley repair shop. But I couldn't count on the Old Man being around all that much on account of he was always running off to see the damn doctor (and even when he was there, he wasn't much good for anything except pumping gas and pissing off customers) so I asked Julie if maybe she could come in a little more often to take care of the phones and the office. But she was making pretty good money over at the Doggy Shake, what with tips and everything, and there was just no way I could offer her that sort of deal at the Sinclair.

And that's when I had a brilliant idea. I called up old Butch Bohunk to see if he'd like to get his ass into the gas station business again. *"ME?"* he damn near gasped into the receiver. "You want *me* to come back to work at the station?"

You could tell he was pretty interested. To say the least.

So I explained to him about how weird the Old Man was acting and how I couldn't get the damn cars fixed --and I had 'em lined up, for gosh sakes!-- on account of all the other piddly bullshit I had to take care of, and old Butch was about as excited as I'd heard him since the day I asked if he wanted to go to the races at Grand Island. "Hell, *yes!*" he shouted into my ear, "I'm about gone buggy from just sittin' around this friggin' house with my damn dick in my hand."

"Can you get yourself over here tomorrow morning?"

"Sure as hell can, Buddy. I'll have Marlene to drop me off."

"That'll be great," I told him. And then something else occurred to me. "Uh, Butch?"

"Yeah?"

"We, ahh, see, the fact is, we can't afford to, umm, to *pay* you very much. At least not right away."

"Aw, that's okay," he said, not the least bit upset, "I ain't worth very much these days, either...."

And that was the beginning of my stint as Chief Operating Officer and part-time Floor Sweeper at the Old Man's Sinclair station. Hiring Butch on turned out to be a real stroke of genius, because he knew how to order parts and get the right thing first shot out of the box and he could even get around good enough to handle the pumps now and then once I made a little ramp to get his wheelchair down the little concrete step out of the office. He'd pretty much given up on those crutches of his once he realized that his legs were just not about to get any better and that it was too much for him to try and haul himself around on the strength of his shoulders and forearms. But he'd made some real improvements in what he could do with his decent left hand and that fingerless lump on the other side. Why, he could do Bench Work like carb rebuilds and distributors and such right there in the office, and he'd gotten to where he could wield a welding torch left-handed and still lay down about the prettiest damn bead you ever saw in your life.

So life was good. I had help so I could concentrate on fixing the cars we had lined up behind the shop and all along the edge of the lot. And I could even show up in the morning at seven to write up the new repair business coming in and then walk across the street to the little sandwich shop and have myself a jelly doughnut and a couple cups of coffee while I leisurely read the morning paper. And there was a lot of interesting stuff in it, too. Stuff about a great big world out there that I'd forgotten about completely all summer long while I was working my ass off as a racing wrench for Colin St. John and Barry Spline. Rocky Marciano won the heavyweight championship off 38-year-old Jersey Joe Walcott, and even though Walcott was from Jersey, I had to go with Marciano because he was white. Not to mention Italian. I mean, that went without saying, you know? And that snakey-eyed little weasel Dick Nixon that Ike had for a running mate was all over the news because of some slush fund he had kicking around that the Democrats who run the newspapers found out about, and he gave this big speech on T.V. about his little dog and his wife's cloth coat and his fight against communism and how he wasn't a quitter and, well, not too awfully much about that money everybody was originally wondering about. I still liked Eisenhower, though, and picked the Republicans as most likely a better deal than that egghead Adlai Stevenson with the hole in his shoe.

It was rough going running my own show for the very first time, on account of you always wind up biting off more than you can chew and the normal surge of natural human greed makes you take in work you should maybe turn away on account of you simply can't resist the lure of the old Long Green. And that's why I was starting to work the same kind of crazy hours at the Sinclair as I did down at Westbridge, staying until ten or eleven o'clock at night --or even later sometimes!-- and always there bright and early at seven ayem in the morning so's I wouldn't miss any of the new service prospects I had lined up. But at least I was making some decent money for a change, since I'd force-fed a deal to Old Man Finzio where I was making a hefty percentage off the hourly service rate --especially on the sportscars-- on top of my Regular Pittance gas station grease monkey wages. Plus I was getting a chunk of the markup on all the car parts we were moving through the shop, and on top of that I didn't have to take that damn two-hour train-and-bus ride into Manhattan every day to get to work or come back home again. Truth is, it felt pretty strange and wonderful to have several fat stacks of currency piled up in the worn little wooden drawers of the Old Man's cash register every evening by closing time, and it was nice to have a wad of them in my own pocket come Friday night.

It was plenty enough money to take Julie out for a sit-down dinner and a show, and I could always have my pick of the customer cars around the shop for transportation, since it was always real important for a skilled mechanic to test drive all the cars that passed through his hands so he could alert owners about impending service needs, developing mechanical problems, and timely routine maintenance requirements. Especially when those cars included a few sleek, sexy Jag 120s and jaunty little MGs. One night I picked Julie up in Carson Flegley's shiny black TD and whisked her off for an evening of high-class entertainment that included antipasto, minestrone soup, spaghetti and meatballs, and cappuccino at Bachigalupo's up on Center Street in the suit-and-tie part of town, and then a trip across the bridge into Manhattan to see that new wraparound CINERAMA picture show on Broadway. Geez, it was like you were really *on* that roller coaster, you know? Other nights we'd maybe take in a regular movie on the Jersey side or roll a few lines over at the bowling alley or play miniature golf or even shoot a few rounds of pool together or a skate around at the roller rink, and then afterwards I'd drive us down along the Jersey shore and we'd park over by the Coast Guard station and watch the submarine races. Truth is, it was starting to get a little cold for that sort of activity --especially in an English sportscar that didn't have much in the way of what a person raised on Fords and Chevys would consider a proper heater-- and those cars were never exactly cut out for that sort of duty anyway, since you had to be something of a contortionist to even share a little random body heat in something as tight and cramped as an MG TD. And it was even worse in cold weather with the top up and side curtains in place. Besides, all that was somehow starting to change between Julie and me. Oh, I still wanted to get into her pants as bad as ever, but now all of a sudden I wasn't in such a mad, desperate damn *rush* about it. Sure, we still made out in parked cars at the end of all our dates, and one night Julie even asked if we could get the borrow of one of Big Ed's Caddies on account of she wanted to go to the drive-in to see Betty Hutton and Cornel Wilde in *The Greatest Show on Earth*. But I felt funny about asking, you know? Even though I was sure he'd be more than happy to do it.

Speaking of Big Ed, I had his Jag engine pulled out and stripped down and scattered all over the shop in crates and boxes, and, if you want to know the truth of it, I was feeling pretty nervous about ever getting it back together again. I mean, for all the work I'd done on Jags down at Westbridge, I'd never had one of those excellent twincam sixes stripped right down to the bare block before, and, as I looked around the service bay at all the boxes of bolts and fittings and castings and miscellaneous hardware, I started to have doubts about my ability to actually reassemble it into a living, breathing, internal combustion automobile engine. Luckily I had Butch Bohunk around to give me support and encouragement, which generally came in the form of weary, disgusted head-shaking combined with uplifting advice such as "what're ya worried about, asshole?" and "y'*call* yerself a God Damn automobile mechanic, Palumbo, but far's I can see, yer nothin' but a crybaby little sissygirl with a damn toolbox," and "Jesus Christ, didn't I teach you *ANYthing?*" In spite of all his years in the service, you couldn't say Butch had learned a whole hell of a lot about morale or motivation. But that was just his way, and once you understood that, he could be an enormous help on a deep and serious car project. And no matter how upset he got with my rank stupidity or lack of confidence, he'd always wind up leaning his head in to show me what I was missing or what I had to do next so I wouldn't have to put things together and then take them apart again two or three dozen times before I got everything properly back together.

Roman Syzmanski the machinist turned out to be a real big help, too. Oh, it was a long haul to get stuff to him all the way over on the other side of the city, but he could look at parts (like that engine block with the hole in it, for example) and rub his chin and move his eyes in real close with his set of magnifying lenses flipped down over his eyes and go over it again with a set of micrometers and then tell me that he could maybe fix it up every bit as good as a new one. And believe me, Jaguar six cylinder engine blocks weren't exactly easy to come by back in 1952. Or cheap, either. Roman saved the block and the crank and pressed in a new liner for the cylinder where the rod had blown out, but he insisted we put new connecting rods in all six cylinders and not just the bad one. He inspected and re-balanced the pistons to match them up with the new one, and did a balance job on the clutch-and-flywheel assembly as well. "Zo tell me, how does thiz perzon drive?" he asked in a thick accent while eyeballing the clutch unit.

"Like an animal."

"Might az well put in new clutch az long az is apart."

So, as you can see, I had a lot of good help and advice and people I could go to for a little secondhand wisdom in my new sportscar repair business at the Sinclair. But even so it was a little worrisome and nerve-wracking to have engines torn all the way down like I did on Big Ed's Jaguar. I bet surgeons feel that same little spastic demon of panic when they suddenly look down and realize they've got somebody split wide open right in front of them and that it's their damn responsibility to put them back together and close them up again.

Which is exactly what was bothering Old Man Finzio, too. Turns out they wanted him to go into the hospital the second week in October so the doctors could open him up and take a look inside. I couldn't imagine what you might find inside a guy like the Old Man except for maybe lizards and scorpions and cornered rats with their eyes flashing, but I guess the doctors figured they might find something even worse. And Old Man Finzio thought so, too.

He didn't say much about it, of course. Fact is, he didn't even tell me he was going in until two or three days beforehand, when I was already trying to figure out some way that I could finesse myself out of taking Julie to that Serafina Massucci's wedding so I could sneak off down to Georgia for the SOWEGA races. I guess the shock and horror of Watkins Glen sort of faded after awhile (even though it was always there in the background someplace, like the lingering shadow of something you can't quite see anymore) and I was surprised to find that I simply couldn't wait to get back to the sly, desperate fun of racing again. Like I explained before, it's sort of a disease, you know?

Besides, I had cars to take care of down there. Well, one car, anyway. I'd finished going through Carson Flegley's engine according to that *Road & Track* article, milling damn near an eighth of an inch off the cylinder head and fitting bigger valves and stronger valve springs and having Roman open up the ports with a die grinder and polish everything in there and around the combustion chambers to an absolutely chromelike mirror finish. Then I put everything back together and fitted richer carb needles and Champion LA-11 sparkplugs and a high output Lucas BR-12 ignition coil. When it was all done, I took it for a spin over by Carson's family's funeral parlor so he could check it out and take it for a little test drive. I left the air cleaners off, too, and although I couldn't be sure how much of it was actually more power and how much was just the mighty rush of air getting sucked into the carburetors, the car certainly *felt* faster. Carson thought so, too, although he had to kind of shoo me around the side of the building and sneak off to take a quick ride --somber black suit and all-- on account of they had a big funeral going on for some heavyweight local politician and he had to drive the hearse once the chapel service was over. It simply wouldn't do for one of the funeral directors to come tootling up in an MG TD with an unusually crisp exhaust note just as they were carrying the casket out. Not even a black one.

Big Ed wanted to go to the SOWEGA races, too. But there was just no way I was going to have his car done, you know? I had parts over at Roman's shop and pieces coming in from England and I could see from two weeks away that it simply wasn't going to happen, no matter what I did. But naturally Big Ed was not about to give up, on account of this was the last race of the year (at least east of the Rockies, anyway) and he really felt he maybe had to do something to make up for his dismal performance at Watkins Glen. Like perhaps actually start a damn race, you know? And when I told him the engine for the white car couldn't be finished, he started asking if maybe there was someplace we could find another whole engine --like out of a wreck or something?-- but I called down to Westbridge and even out to the Jaguar distributor in California, and there was simply nothing around that we could pick up on a moment's notice. "That's okay," Big Ed told me, "I got an idea...."

And I didn't much like the way his stogie was rolling around in his mouth.

Sure enough, he drove up the very next day in --you guessed it-- Skippy Welcher's ex-everything XK120*M*. What with his new C-type and all, The Skipper didn't much need his old 120, and Big Ed was able to cut himself a pretty slick deal for it, too (at least to hear him tell it), especially considering it was a last-minute thing and Big Ed was in a mighty big hurry to own that car. But Big Ed could be a pretty shrewd customer when it came to buying cars (Lord knows he'd done it enough times in his life!) and he was fortunate to catch The Skipper in an unusually good mood following a regular weekly visit by his 19-year-old oriental masseuse.

Personally, I was a little gunshy about getting close to any automobile that Skippy Welcher had anything to do with --like I might catch some kind of creeping mental disorder off it or something, you know?-- plus I wasn't real big on trusting Milton Fitting's wrench work without checking it over real carefully first. So I spent three or four long nights in the garage going over every damn nut and bolt on that car until I'd convinced myself that everything was in working order and nothing looked likely to fall off. At least nothing I could find, anyway. And I didn't charge Big Ed a penny for it, either. "Nah," I told him as he hopped aboard to start that long, long drive down to Georgia, "this one's on the house."

"Aw, I can't let'cha do *that,* Buddy."

"No, really. This one's on me."

"You *sure?*"

"Absolutely."

"Well, geez, *thanks*. I'll try t'bring it back in one piece fer you this time."

"You do that."

Just then Carson Flegley and Cal Carrington came wheeling into the lot in Carson's TD. They waved and tootled the horn at us. "Well, s'long," I told Big Ed.

"Yeah. S'long. Sure wish you was goin' with us...."

"Yeah. So do I. But what with the Old Man in the hospital and everything, there's just no way I can do it. Besides, if I miss that damn wedding next Sunday, Julie'll absolutely *kill* me. And it'll be a slow, painful death, too. She promised."

"I bet she did," Big Ed laughed, and stuck the gear lever into first. I felt part of me go with them as those two cars rumbled off down Pine Street, the MG looking all upright and jaunty and the Jag as smooth and sleek as a circus seal.

God, I wanted to be going with them!

Chapter 34: The Halloween Party

I guess everybody had themselves a pretty good time at those races down in Georgia. Big Ed actually got to run a few practice sessions and even started the race before he got a little too excited and clouted a stack of haybales with the right-front corner of his ex-Skippy Welcher, ex-everything else XK120*M*, and it wasn't even much of a dent, either. Especially considering that Jag had been crunched just about everywhere at one time or another, so it wasn't like he was breaking its cherry or anything. But it pushed the fender lip down into the tire and so Big Ed had to drop out of the race after it happened. Which was, I believe, on the very first corner of the very first lap. Oh well, at least it was an improvement.

My buddy Cal got himself a drive in that Ford V8-powered MG TC again, and from what I heard, the beast was very much improved from Elkhart Lake. Like this time the brakes held up for a whole six laps before the pedal started sinking towards the floor with every hard application --and Cal didn't know any other way to use brakes except by way of hard application-- and so he sank back through the field to finish just outside the top ten. But he ran right up towards the front for those first six laps, briefly harassing Creighton Pendleton's Ferrari for third overall and holding off the best of the standard-issue XK120s until the car wouldn't slow down anymore. It was one of those incredible nickel-rocket driving performances that impressed everybody who saw it at the time, but was quickly forgotten as the race droned on and left no lasting memory afterwards, except among Cal's friends and fans (who were pretty much one and the same, if you got right down to the truth of it). Johnny Fitch won again in one of the C4R Cunninghams --nobody else could stay with him-- and both Fitch and Creighton Pendleton's Ferrari were clocked at over 168 miles-per-hour on the long straightaway that ran down the main bomber takeoff and landing runway on the Turner base. Skippy Welcher went down in spite of the one-race suspension he got for causing the terrible accident at Watkins Glen (they should have banned him for life!) and after all attempts at getting his suspension lifted fell on deaf ears, he handed the green C-type over to another longtime S.C.M.A. racer named George Huntoon of West Palm Beach, Florida, for the 4-litre and under contest. Which he won going away, proving beyond any doubt that the C-type was a car to be reckoned with anywhere.

But the big news was how well the event was run and how incredibly *safe* it was. General LeMay himself drove all the way down from his headquarters in Omaha, Nebraska, in his Allard (along with his wife, who must've been one tough, durable sort of lady) in order to keep a personal eye on things, and his boys did a job that made the regular all-volunteer S.C.M.A. armband crew look pretty damn lame by comparison. All the races started exactly on time (except for one that began some thirty seconds late, and you can bet the poor enlisted man responsible heard about it afterwards) and everybody except the actual drivers and crewmembers was kept so far back from the action that a fellow named Ned Dearborn from the National Safety Council (who was on hand as an invited guest) said: "I have never seen anything comparable to the safety measures taken by this meet to ensure safe crowd control and I want to compliment everyone who had a part in it."

That was pretty darn impressive, no two ways about it.

Of course the bad part was that none of the estimated 60,000 people who turned out to watch the races could see much of anything, since it was like watching a bunch of loud, brightly colored little toys running up and down the runways, way off in the distance. But I guess smaller doses of red-blooded excitement will always be the price of guaranteed security, in racing and everything else in life....

By far the highlight of the entire weekend (at least for those of us on the immediate Jersey side of the George Washington bridge) was the performance of Carson Flegley and his newly hotted-up MG TD, which, thanks to the undeniable engine-tuning genius of one Buddy Palumbo, Esq., finished all the way up in the middle of the MG herd that was duking it out somewheres about halfway between Jim Simpson's leading OSCA and the last-place Crosley Hotshot. Better yet, Carson finished at least seven or eight sets of front-and-rear bumpers ahead of where he'd run at Watkins Glen. And, as you can well imagine, he was *ecstatic*. In fact, nothing would do but that Carson decided to host a big season-ending racing party at his place of business just as soon as he got back home to New Jersey. And that was a really perfect fit (considering Carson Flegley's line of work, anyways) since the very next available Friday night after the SOWEGA races in Georgia was...*Halloween!*

It was decided by general consensus that the Friday night Halloween gathering at Flegley Memorial Chapels in East Orange should properly be a costume party (what else?) and so I had a beard done up on my face with greasepaint and a tooth blocked out to go along with the rest of my half-hearted pirate outfit (a bandanna tied up over my head, an eyepatch, and a little plastic cutlass from Woolworth's Five-and-Dime) when I went to pick Julie up over by her mom's place in the Old Man's towtruck. There just weren't any decent cars running over by the Sinclair that night. Julie was all done up as a Gypsy, with her hair all frizzed out and these big brass hoop earrings and a lot of bright crimson red lipstick and cheek rouge. She was wearing I think a white men's shirt with about three buttons undone (and four once we got in the truck and safely out of eyeshot from her mother) and a flared red skirt with a wide black patent leather belt and matching shoes. She actually looked an awful lot more like a hot streetwalker than a gypsy (if you want my opinion, anyway) and no question it was hard to keep my eyes off of her. Or my hands for that matter, either. *"Hey!"* she squealed, "knock it off. You'll mess up my costume."

"It's gonna happen sooner or later anyway, baby. So why not sooner?"

"Just keep yer frickin' hands to yourself, Palumbo," she laughed, her eyes dancing, "like I told you before, don't let the look fool you. I'm not one a'those girls who goes around handing out free samples...."

And she wasn't, either.

Anyhow, we got to Carson Flegley's Funeral Parlor about nine, and you could tell the party was already going full blast on account of all the MGs and Jags and Rileys and stuff parked out in the lot. But the building itself looked just as somber and dreary as mortuaries always look, what with big, thick, heavy velvet drapes drawn fully closed over all the windows and just a faint little golden-yellowish glow coming through the crack in the middle. There were a matching set of little coach lights with the same deathly yellow glow to them set into the brickwork on either side of the entrance, and, all things considered, it was the kind of place that made you feel like talking in whispers before you ever even knocked on the door.

At least until that door swung open with Carson Flegley himself behind it, all done up as Count Dracula with a satin-lined cape, major-league fangs, and about a half gallon of fake stage blood running down his chin. "Gooot eeeveningggg," he said in a surprisingly decent imitation of Bela Lugosi, "and vellcommm to my castle...." This was a side of Carson Flegley I'd never seen before. Then again, he had all the working credentials for the part, didn't he?

We came inside and Carson quickly closed the door behind us. He really didn't want any past, current, or potential future customers to get a whiff of what was going on inside Flegley Memorial Chapels this particular Halloween night. After all, it wasn't very dignified, and families trying to find a proper and delicate way to get rid of their corpses are always real big on dignity. Although I personally don't think it helps much one way or the other, you know? Anyhow, Carson had all the racing people jammed into a long, sad-looking chapel room at the far end of the hall, and you should've seen some of the getups those people were wearing. Of course a lot of them were pretty rich --in fact some of them were *very* rich-- and rich people just love to show off by taking frivolous stuff like costume parties to absolutely ridiculous extremes. It's part of the basic responsibility package that goes along with being obscene stinking rich. Charlie Priddle had on this incredible Dead Aristocrat outfit from the time of the French Revolution, complete with silk stockings and patent leather shoes and a satin vest and a three-cornered velvet hat and a powdered silvery-white wig and this nifty fake guillotine blade embedded squarely into the back of his neck. If they had been giving out a prize for the best costume at Carson's party, no doubt Charlie Priddle would've won it. In fact, that's probably exactly what he had in mind.

Big Ed came as a gorilla, which was another perfect fit, but the head part was real hot and he couldn't smoke his cigar, so most of the evening he walked around without it, and it was amazing how natural and right he looked with his real head sitting up on top of that huge, hairy gorilla suit. And he was with some girl in a German milkmaid outfit --complete with waist-length blond braids-- and she kept one of those little white satin eye masks over the top half of her face all night long. Fact is, I don't believe she was the then-current Mrs. Big Ed Baumstein (if you catch my drift). Barry Spline just turned his white Parts Counter shop coat around backwards so it looked sort of like a strait jacket, and wore one of those goofy eyeballs-out-on-springs eyeglasses you can pick up at a trick store (or maybe even at Woolworth's around Halloween time) and topped it off with some equally goofy plastic buck teeth. "Say, you supposed t'be an escaped lunatic or something?" Big Ed asked.

"Certainly bloody not," Barry told him, trying his best to talk around those stupid buck teeth, "I'm supposed ter be Milton Fitting!" But he had to sort of whisper it, on account of Milton and Skippy (or was it Skippy and Milton?) were standing right behind him, dressed up in a rented horse outfit. As you can well imagine, everybody was snickering behind their backs all night long about the fight they must've had over who got the back end.

Tommy Edwards showed up a bit later wearing his old fighter pilot uniform from World War Two, and you could see he was working hard on keeping a stiff upper lip and putting together a major hangover all at the same time. Truth is, things were going pretty lousy for Tommy at the time. He still hadn't fully recovered from the accident at Watkins Glen (either physically or mentally) and, although he knew in his head and heart that it wasn't really his fault, he was having a hard time getting his gut to feel the same way. Plus he was having what looked like possibly the very end of his troubles with his wife Ronnie, since the rumors that circulated quickly around the room as soon as he showed his face indicated that she had already seen a lawyer about a divorce. Not to mention that the S.C.M.A. wasn't looking real likely to reverse itself about his one year suspension, even though everybody you talked to privately (including that tightass rat-bastard Charlie Priddle) thought it was a crock of shit. The problem, it seems, had nothing to do with making the just and proper decision in the case, but rather with the difficulty of reversing a decision that had already been made and admitting that you'd made a stupid damn mistake in the first place. That was an extremely hard thing for a group like the S.C.M.A. armband squad to do. And it always would be.

So Tommy Edwards had sort of changed on everybody, turning from a quick, sly, tough, devil-may-care ex-Fighter Pilot who could drink all night long and never show a drop of it into a sad, melancholy loner who could drink all night and get stinking, falldown drunk. It just went to show you how much attitude and confidence have to do with the way people carry themselves. He was standing over in a corner by himself, sucking up a water glass full of some absolutely lethal Halloween punch, and I decided to bring Julie over and introduce her and see if I could maybe snap him out of it a little.

"Bloody pleased to meet you," he nodded towards Julie, raising the fingers of his right hand unsteadily over his eyebrow and clumsily flopping his heels together. "I say, Buddy," he grinned at me, "she's a bit of all right, isn't she?"

"Yeah," I told him, snaking my arm protectively around Julie's waist, "she sure is that, all right."

"You're a bloody lucky man," he said, raising his glass to me, "a bloody lucky damn man indeed. If she's faithful and any bloody good in the sack at all, you ought to marry that girl."

I felt the color coming up on my face, and right away Tommy knew he was stinking drunk and out of line and started to get all fumbly and apologetic about it. "I say," he said to Julie, his eyes looking down at the floor, "I'm awfully bloody sorry. Awfully sorry indeed," he stifled a belch, "I'm afraid I've had a bit too bloody much to drink."

I looked over at Julie and saw everything was okay, so I decided the best thing was to change the subject. "Hey, don't worry about it," I told him, "we've all been hittin' the sauce pretty hard. Haven't we, Julie?"

"Yeah, sure," Julie said. You could hear a nice, soft, understanding quality to her voice, kind of like the echo of the ocean you can hear in a seashell....

"So," I said, "I heard somebody say you went down to that race in Georgia."

"So I did," he took another swallow of punch, "but not to race. Can't bloody race for another year, according to those bloody twits on the competition committee. They don't understand the quirky little ironies of this sport, the most basic of which is that you can very easily have another chap's accident *for* him. Happens all the time. In fact, if any of the lot of them had any reasonable amount of seat time, they'd bloody understand. But instead *I'm* the one who's bloody responsible," you could see he was getting pretty worked up about it. "Those idiots on the competition committee need to look up their bloody assholes to see if their hats are on straight." Then he remembered Julie was standing right there next to us. "Oh, um, pardon me, Miss Finzio," Tommy said quietly, looking down at the floor, "what I meant to say is that I question their judgment. In fact, I question their bloody ancestry as well."

"So it's no soap with those guys, huh?"

Tommy shook his head. "But I'm thinking of going back to England anyways. Things have fallen apart a bit for me here, and at least I can still bloody race over in England. Besides, who wants to hang around here in the states and race on a bunch of bloody airfields?"

"You don't like the airport races?"

"Bloody hell *no!*"

"But why? Everybody says how safe they are...."

"Well just *look* at them! They're just one bloody drag strip after another," he shook his head disgustedly and drained the rest of his punch, "and then it's hard on the brakes for another flat, fiddly little second-gear corner, and then another bloody dragstrip after that. I mean, where's the bloody *penalty?!* If you go off the bloody road at Elkhart Lake, you're in some deep, *deep* trouble. And that's as it *should* be!" And then Tommy Edwards excused himself to get a refill that he hardly needed at all.

It was sad to see Tommy like that, and it made me think about how racing could hurt your spirit just as surely as it could batter and bruise your body. But then, that's exactly what Tommy was talking about when he mentioned "the penalty" just seconds before. And I came to realize it was that very penalty --which could rise up at any moment with swift, sudden, ugly finality-- that made racing so consuming, compelling, delicious, and addictive. The good part was it didn't happen very often (if it did, then everybody in the sport would have to be classified as a complete and total idiot) and the odds had proven that you could race your whole damn life and walk away without a scratch. And many racers did. But the fact that the danger was *out there,* lurking in the shadows of the fast curves and the high-speed esses, made everything that happened on a racetrack somehow more Real and Valuable and Noble and Important than all the things that went on from day to day in everyday life. No question Tommy Edwards understood all that, too. Fact is, he probably knew in his heart of hearts that this was simply his turn to play the victim. And most likely not his last turn, either....

Creighton Pendleton and Sally Enderle were the very last to show up --fashionably late, of course-- and Creighton was wearing his usual powder-blue driving suit with "Creighton Pendleton III" embroidered above the breast pocket in silvery-blue thread and carrying his racing helmet loosely at his side with his string-backed racing gloves and aviator goggles dangling oh-so-casually over the visor. He took pains to explain as how "a costume party is where you get the chance to dress up as what you'd really *like* to be, and I guess there's just no one I'd rather be than who I am, you know?" Far as I was concerned, it was amazing he could get that head of his into the damn helmet. Naturally Sally Enderle went the whole nine yards on her costume, arriving in a truly dazzling Harem Girl outfit with these sheer, puffy, shimmering pink silk pants that you could pretty much see through, plenty of smooth, tan midriff showing, and about six pounds of glistening golden necklaces, waist chains, and earrings. I got kind of embarrassed about being in the same room with her and Julie, both at the same time, and I could feel my ears starting to burn when she headed over in our direction. But she swept right past us like were a couple of uncomfortable folding chairs on her way to the punchbowl, so it came out all right after all.

Julie and me had another round of punch ourselves, and then Carson Flegley came around to take anyone who wanted to go on a Halloween tour of his mortuary. Truth is, I felt a little nervous about it in the pit of my stomach. I mean, this wasn't some spook train ride at Palisades Park. No sir, this was the real McCoy. And Julie didn't look real excited about the idea, either. But it would've been even worse to just stand around there by the punchbowl and listen to all the catcalls and *bok-ba-bok-bok* chicken cackles when everybody else filed out of the room. So we got in line and followed Carson Flegley down the hall and up a flight of stairs to the second floor. I'd never thought about it before that, but almost every funeral parlor I'd ever seen had either a second floor on it or a separate wing with no chapels in it and a door that was always closed in front of it, and up those stairs and behind those closed doors is where the actual business part of the funeral parlor business happens. Not the bodies or anything, mind you. Those are usually down in the Cool Room in the basement. But rather the place where the money transactions that buy things like new Cadillac hearses and hopped-up MG TDs take place. There were a couple quiet offices with big, round, heavy wooden conference tables off to one side and thick, sound-deadening wallpaper on the walls (so you could handle more than one set of sobbing, red-eyed relatives at a time when business was really good) and, across the hall, was...The *Showroom!*

"The *what?*" somebody asked.

"The showroom," Carson said, dragging it out and rolling his rr's in his best Bela Lugosi impersonation. But everybody was looking at him like they didn't understand, so he switched back to his normal, everyday little pipsqueak voice and explained. "You know," he said simply, "for the *caskets....* " And with that, he opened up the heavy, leather-covered door so we could follow Carson's sweeping black cape into this big, low, dimly lit room with bare walls covered in a sedate orangish-tan print wallpaper. About a dozen caskets of various sizes, colors, materials, trim, hardware, and most of all price ranges were arranged neatly around the floor on raised, carpet-covered stands. Sure enough, it looked like Count Dracula's New Car Showroom. And I guess that's exactly what it turned into on that particular October 31st Halloween night of 1952.

"This place gives me the creeps," Julie whispered in my ear.

"Yeah," I told her, "me, too."

But some of the other guests seemed to be enjoying the hell out of it, laughing and sniggering and making sick jokes and even lying down in some of the merchandise to try them on for size. "Hey, be careful now," Carson Flegley warned in his normal, highly excited voice, "those things are *expensive!*"

"Hey, what's this one over here?" somebody asked.

We wandered over along with everybody else, and there on one of the carpet-covered stands was the biggest damn coffin you ever saw in your life. Why, it was wide across as a damn grand piano. And it was painted up a glossy, creamy ivory white with gilt trim and what looked like real gold-plated handles. Jeez, was it ever huge.

"Oh," Carson said sheepishly, "that's what we call our, umm, well, our Lardass Model. Every funeral parlor carries one. After all, you gotta have something on hand and ready to go if a really, ahh, *large* Loved One passes away...."

I looked all around the crowd and about the only guy anywheres near big enough for that thing was Big Ed. And even he would've had plenty of room to spare. Even in his gorilla suit. With the head part on, too.

"Jeez," Big Ed said, eyeballing the workmanship, "it looks pretty damn fancy, don't it?"

"Well, uhh, see, it's sort of like this," Carson mumbled, even more sheepish than before, "when somebody that size passes away, the family doesn't really have very much to choose from, you know? So we sort of, umm, put only the very top of the line model on display."

"What a splendid idea," Colin St. John called out from the back of the room. He was dressed up as a damn pilgrim. Can you believe it?

"Boy, that thing looks big enough for two people!" Charlie Priddle said.

"It bloody well does," British Air Force pilot Tommy Edwards agreed, leaning unsteadily up against a nice polished mahogany model. "I say, Buddy, why don't you and your lovely date try it on for size?"

"Geez, no, Tommy. I *couldn't....* "

And of course that was all I had to say to get the catcalls and chicken cackles started up all around us, and they kept on growing and growing until there was nothing left for Julie and me to do but either slink out and never see any of those people ever again for as long as any of us lived or lie down in that creamy white casket together and let them lower the lid on us. Just for a second, you know?

And so there we were, Julie and me, lying side-by-side in the pitch black darkness inside that huge white coffin with all those racing people gathered around us, laughing and drinking and carrying on. But they might as well have been a million miles away, on account of all you could hear was a faint shuffle of feet and a few muffled, indistinguishable voices. It was darker than anyplace I'd ever been in there, and I could feel Julie all warm and soft and cozy next to me and smell the heavy reek of her gypsy costume perfume working its way up my nostrils, and without thinking, I let my hand sneak over to where it wanted to go. *"Hey!"* she whispered, not mad at all, "whaddaya think you're doing, Palumbo?"

"Nothing," I whispered right back, leaving my hand exactly where it was. And she let me, too.

And that's when I heard myself propose marriage to Miss Julie Finzio, there in a quiet whisper inside that big, wide white coffin large enough for two, laid out in the casket showroom of Carson Flegley's funeral home with all those costumed racing people gathered around us but somehow a million miles away....

When they opened the lid, everybody saw that Julie was crying just a little out of the corners of her eyes, and they all thought it was on account of she was scared or something, you know? Which just goes to show you that none of them knew too awful much about my Julie or what kind of a tough, gutsy girl she was. But they'd find out soon enough. They'd find out.

Anyhow, some of the people followed Carson downstairs after that to take a look into the Cool Room where they kept the stiffs that were waiting to get dressed up and planted, but that sounded a little too grim for either Julie or me, so we just kind of hung back and let all the mainline ghouls file downstairs ahead of us. Then we went into the parlor that was serving as the central party room and grabbed ourselves another couple glasses of punch and headed out into the parking lot. It was real dark and cold and peaceful out there, with a chilly wind rattling through the few withered brown leaves left on the tree branches and a crumpled-up piece of newspaper scraping its way across Sherman Boulevard like a crab scuttling for its hole. You could feel winter coming in the air, and so Julie and I climbed up into Old Man Finzio's towtruck and started it up to get the heater going. But we didn't drive off just yet. We just sat there in the cab with the engine running, not turning the lights on or putting it in gear or even saying much of anything, and then Julie leaned over and gave me the best kiss she'd ever given me in her life. Not the hottest, maybe, but unquestionably the absolute *best*.

And so we just sat there, leaning the tops of our heads together against the back cushion, watching all the other party goers coming one by one out between the little pale yellowish-gold carriage lights that flanked the main entrance of Carson

Flegley's funeral parlor. And, as I watched them climb into their Jags and MGs and what-have-yous and heard them pull out on the choke cables and grind the starters and stutter off into the night, I knew deep down in my heart that I'd be seeing a lot of them again. Especially if they insisted on trying to drive those things through the winter. And I knew I'd be going to the races with some of them again, too. Maybe not all the races. But at least some of them. Because I'd been bitten by the racing bug myself, and, no matter what else happens, that's a disease you can never really get rid of. Not hardly.

The very next day, November 1st, 1952, scientists from the Atomic Energy Commission set off a hydrogen bomb blast in the Marshall Islands that blew a little atoll named Eniwetok clear off the face of the earth. Of course nobody knew about it back then on account of it was all very Top Secret hush-hush at the time, and just a few days later, General Dwight David Eisenhower got himself elected president of these United States in an absolute landslide. And I would've voted for him, too. Only I couldn't.

After all, I was only nineteen....